VARANGIAN

The Wanderer' Part 3: The East 988 -1000

By R. Hyslop

First published in Great Britain 2008
Cuthan Books
(cuthanbooks@btinternet.com)

Copyright © Robert Hyslop

The right of Robert Hyslop to be identified as the author of this work has been asserted by him in accordance with the Copyright, Designs and Patents Act 1988

ISBN 978-0-9558718-2-5

All rights reserved. No part of this publication may be reproduced, stored in a retrieval system, or transmitted, in any form or by any means, without prior written permission of the publisher, nor be otherwise circulated in any form of binding or cover other than that which it is published and without a similar condition including this condition being imposed on the subsequent purchaser

Cover design by RPM Print & Design
Printed and bound in Great Britain by
RPM Print & Design
2-3 Spur Road, Quarry Lane, Chichester,
West Sussex PO19 8PR

To medieval heroes and tellers of tales

as well all those in the modern world

who study and love them

Cover Illustration: Reverse side of a rune inscription near Stockholm of a returning Vara

It says: *"runa rista . lit . rahnualtr .huar a . kriklanti . uas . lis . forunki "*

Or: *"The runes be cut let Ragnvaldr. He was in Greece, was the host's leader."*

With acknowledgement to Peter@birkatraders.com

As elsewhere in 'The Wanderer' the introductory passages are mainly drawn from the rich vein of Anglo-Saxon poetry. Biblical quotations are based on a translation of the Latin Vulgate version of St. Jerome. Obviously, Greek versions would have been used within the Byzantine Empire.

Throughout this work 'Gadarike' is used the areas now covered by Russia & the Ukraine etc..

'Varangian' - Contents

Foreword — Page 5

'The Wanderer' 7: Gadarike 988-990 A.D.

7:1	The Great Bell	Page	7
7:2	Hunt for a Princess	Page	37
7:3	Spreading the Gospel	Page	81
7:4	Among the Khazars	Page	119
7.5	Escape from Gadarike	Page	153

Russia Afterword — Page 190

'The Wanderer' 8: Miklagard 990-998 A.D.

8:1	Imperial Favour	Page	191
8:2	Crete	Page	221
8:3	The Paper Chase	Page	253
8:4	Revelation	Page	289
8:5	The Whore's Murder	Page	319
8:6	The Bulgar Hoard	Page	345
8:7	The Turkish Horsemen	Page	383

Miklagard Afterword — Page 414

'The Wanderer' 9: Palestine 998-1000 A.D.

9:1	Awaiting Eternity	Page	415
9:2	The Centre of the World	Page	443
9:3	Journey's End	Page	479

Palestine Afterword — Page 533

Maps showing places featured in the novel:

Gadarike	Page	534
Byzantium	Page	535
Palestine	Page	536

Ethelwulf's Family Tree — Page 537

Endnotes for 'Varangian' — Page 538

Foreword

This volume is the last of the Trilogy entitled 'The Wanderer' set in the northern world of the late 10th century. Here is the story so far.

Ethelwulf, Thane of Arne in Dorset, was a restless youth whose life was transformed when he witnessed the murder of King Edward at Corfe in March 979 by agents of his royal stepmother. He became an outlaw, helped by his cousins, Edwine and Morkere. They fled into exile across the Channel. However, involvement in the plots and rivalry on the Norman island of Jersey forced them to leave for Ireland in 981. The move proved disastrous as they tumbled into the struggles between Gael and Viking which were reaching their climax. The exiles clashed with a treacherous native King, found a firm friend in the axe-wielding Gunnar and were expelled from the island. This ends Volume 1 of the Trilogy.

Arriving in Iceland (984) they immediately became embroiled in a blood-feud following a duel and appeared to make more enemies than friends before being expelled from the island after a riotous meeting of the Althing (985). They sailed to the court of Harald Bluetooth in Denmark and helped savage Wends destroy brigands before themselves being almost destroyed by the pagans. They were forced to join Styrbjorn in his disastrous attempt to seize the Swedish throne (986) before slipping eastwards to Gotland and Finland. Here they aroused the enmity of Viking groups exploiting the natives, first in the far north and then on the shores of Lake Ladoga. Again they sought safety in flight (988), this time towards the Viking powers of Holmgard (Novgorod) and Kenugard.(Kiev), dominating the area called Gadarike (Russia). So ends Volume 2 of the Trilogy.

The Wanderer 7:1

'A man deprived for long
Of lord's advice knows this,
That when sorrow and sleep
Together grasp the weary traveller
He thinks he holds and kisses
His lord, laying hands and head
Upon his lord's knee as he had done
In sharing gifts in earlier days.'
('The Wanderer')

The Great Bell

"In the name of Our Holy Father, have mercy!" screeched the old woman lying in the snow dampened by the dull red of her blood.

Edwine turned, stared and then lurched his skis into a furious halt. His twin, so close behind, was shaken out of the exhausted half-dream which had entwined his body through the past three hours by the suddenly-halted shape of Edwine. He cursed and slid sideways, bumping up over the snow-gripped roots of a pine and just avoiding collision by a flurry of his mittened hands.

By now Edwine was on one knee trying to force some nabid[1] between the woman's cracked lips. At first she resisted, her eyes, tortured by the biting cold and dazzled by the vicious glint of snow, remained firmly shut; then some instinct forced the lips apart and the bitter moisture started trickling through her parched throat. Her fingers, blackened by frostbite, reached to force even more liquid between her lips; Edwine firmly pushed them aside, guzzling anything into a parched throat under such conditions could only mean death. What did it matter? This creature was dead anyway; life had been ripped away from her by the sharp blow of a club which had cracked open the left side of her head. To lie, untended and unwarmed, for even an hour in the sudden wintry conditions gave no hope; better to have died instantly than to sprawl there, steadily freezing and waiting for oblivion.

Yet something had clung to life. Somehow she'd heard the swish of their skis as they made their way south from Ladoga. By now Ethelwulf and the advance party would have set up some form of camp in this hell. For that was what this all was - hell without the everlasting fires but peopled by the demons remembered from the walls of Wareham[2] in another lifetime, in another world.

His thoughts were broken by the dull ache of the frightened grey eyes which clamoured for some hope in HIS dulled, aching features. No creature deserved to die like this. He forced a smile from somewhere, hugging the memory of sunlight England, and the woman relaxed. Her lips quivered in a soundless litany of thanks or else a toneless plea for mercy; it was impossible to identify her intentions because fear still hung in her eyes when she died.

"Well, brother, Father Aidan[3] would be pleased with you," mocked Morkere, as the side more suited to the harshness for survival in this wilderness asserted itself over the gentler side nourished at Stokeford.[4] Edwine glared resentfully at his brother but realised the taunt was well deserved. Why should he risk the lives of the dozen warriors travelling with him to give a few moments of comfort to a dying Slav peasant? Whoever had killed her could still be out there, lurking among the snow-cloaked dark woods on all sides, masked by the gathering threat of yet another blizzard. He let the peasant's head slump back down on to the reddened snow and looked around. It had been a stupid action, one that would have invoked the fury of Gunnar; fortunately, the Gall-Gael[5] wasn't there. He saw the look of urgency in the eyes of his brother and remembered their cousin had entrusted him with the safety of the rearguard.

There was no pursuit from the friends of Erik Barelegs[6] who must long ago have given up the chase. Warriors of Aldeigjuborg[7] claimed to be lords of the dense woods of Karelia but they'd no role fin the more generously-spread expanses of these forests. The waters of the Volkhov were jealously guarded by the warriors of Holmgard.[8] Furs and hides could be traded at Ladoga freely but no armed force dared venture further south into the territories of their overlord.[9] Because Holmgard itself lay on the western bank of the Volkhov, the Vikings had kept to the western bank to avoid its treacherous ice-caked currents in the depth of winter. Even so, they knew such a journey also had its unnatural hazards; the forests hid bands of refugees, dispossessed by squabbles over furs or victims of the expansion of Vladimir, the ruthless son of Svjatoslav of Holmgard.[10] Vladimir[11] had expelled his brother, Jaropolk, from Kenugard [12] nine years previously. Naturally, most brigands terrorising the forests south of Ladoga would claim they also were lawful heirs cruelly expelled by upstarts; their victims knew different. Certainly the country was not living up to its name of Gardarike.[13]

There was not even time to conceal the corpse from the wolves hovering just out of bowshot, waiting to feast on any stragglers or those who gave up their struggle against nature. Without a word the twins resumed their journey, anxious to meet up with the main party before what passed for sun finally gave up its feeble attempt to light that savage world.

*

"So a war party must have crossed our trail," mused Ethelwulf when his cousins reported the incident. He was concerned; although no war-band would casually try its luck against a body of well-armed Vikings. His eyes scanned the dark trees hugging what dim light lay to the left of the party. If Morkere had read the signs correctly, out there, somewhere, could be trouble. It would be impossible to place any warriors to shield his left flank; a trail had been scraped through the forests by generations of traders, hunters and brigands but it was a mere scar on the pine landscape. There was no hope of getting back to their ships that day. He regretted the need to plunge into the hostile forests in search of supplies and trading furs.

"We must find shelter before light gives out, cousin," muttered Morkere, as he sidled up next to his leader. Ethelwulf smiled; it was strange how one cousin so easily slipped into his thoughts, while Edwine remained a world away. An intended brief foray in search of pelts and meat for the expedition had drawn him southwards.

He glared across at Gunnar, contemptuously sniffing the woods to their left. The Gall-Gael's fury had robbed them of any guide for this miserable country; perhaps Einar had made a mistake and directed them into Odin's Eye[14] instead of the waters of Volkhov. Only a sudden fog had concealed them from pursuit; the next day they discovered the water-road to Holmgard and, in desperation, had plunged into the unknown.

At first, the journey was easy. 'Alsvid'[15] edged its way through the reeds shielding the Volkhov from the chilled waters of Ladoga. Ethelwulf's vessel contained a band of forty warriors - enough to discourage the hostile while tempting those with silver to hire such a force. All the Vikings wanted was to escape the vengeance of the Ladogan Varangians - and then find fresh employment for their weapon-skills in the south. From now on the northern seas were barred to them, to the south lay the realms of Holmgard and Kenugard and beyond those the half-mythical world of Miklagard.[16] The journey became more difficult as the current quickened making it exhausting to row their vessels upstream into the unknown. They'd failed to come across any villages where trade (or warfare) could secure them supplies. Not enough food had been taken on board as they'd scurried south from their enemies.

So, reluctantly, their longship had been halted and placed under a small guard while the bulk of the force set out on a hunting expedition. That had been three days ago, as the hunt had proved far more difficult than foreseen. Not only did the region lack settlements, there was also a shortage of deer, moose or even rabbits. Late autumn should be an excellent season to try out nature's bounty, but Ethelwulf was alarmed at the scarcity of suitable game. For years the forests on the northern bounds of Holmgard had sheltered armed bands with the attempts of first the Ladogans to set up bases in the area and then Varangi from the south to exact tribute from its peoples. Warfare had destroyed villages, slaughtered much of the local population and generally over-exploited local resources as warriors travelled and fought their way across the grim forests of the Ilmen Slavs.

Yesterday a small herd of reindeer had been surrounded, slaughtered, skinned and their meat cut up into manageable packs. Apart from that there'd been little profit in the expedition and they were returning to their ships, determined to make their way somehow towards Holmgard at the northern end of Lake Ilmen.

As the Vikings settled down for the night, in pairs snuggling for warmth beneath skins and furs, Pekka sniffed the air. The old man frowned and whistled softly to himself, gazing up at the moon before embarking on a virtual monologue..

"Luckily the Helmets of Secrets obscure the Whirling Wheel[17] on this night of nights." He paused and turned towards Ethelwulf. "There's trouble in the air," he confided," the night winds warn me of strangers coming this way with death in their hearts."

Nobody questioned the Karelian's judgement; he possessed enough instinct in the dark forests of the north to prove Gunnar's jibe that the old man was half-troll, conceived during the darkest night of the year. The surly features of Pekka allowed a smirk to slip across his mouth at the comment, although his grey eyes remained cold. Small lines of concern formed around his lips as he stared into the darkness, willing his eyes to burn a path into the gloom.

"Can we hide?" asked Edwine. He saw a doubt rising in Gunnar's eyes and laughingly added, "Because an ambush is always the best way to greet unwelcome visitors."

"Perhaps if we moved more into the forest....." offered Morkere and was interrupted by his cousin.

"Making sure we removed whatever traces might remain of us - "

"Assuming we really are about to be attacked!" snarled Gunnar, not keen to abandon a spot which just fitted his long back. There was a dry rattle from Pekka which passed for a chuckle. They all knew he'd never been wrong in sensing danger in the forests of Karelia, so why should it be any different in the region south of Ladoga?

Even as he raised the question, Gunnar began to roll up his fur cape. Whatever part of him might doubt, his brain told him not to ignore any warning. He made sure 'Angrboda'[18] rested in the midst of the furs; one had to take care of one's friends.

Quickly the Vikings retired deeper into the darkness to the east, away from the trail. Behind them glided Pekka, carefully removing any traces left in the snow. To the west of the trail the river Volkhov mockingly slid along, licking at the occasional piece of bark or ice which had found its way into its ice-cold waters. The remains of their fire had been scraped up by Thorkel and Halfdan and then removed away from the trail. Pekka lightly brushed snow over the bare-patch, fortunately helped by the steady fall of snow which added a natural crispness to his handiwork.

Safely enshrouded by snow-laden trees, resistant to the cold, by the feeble light of the moon, the Vikings again tried to get some kind of rest. Ethelwulf himself was unable to sleep; every time he closed his eyes, Pekka's reference to the Helmets of Secrets conjured up the vision of Thorkalata[19] screaming out his doom:

> "No soil nor sea will succour you.
> As Skoll[20] my shade will harass you,
> As Gjall, my gore will swallow you ,
> As Greip[21] my hands will grapple you,
> Down to the portals of Hel itself!"

Next to him Edwine slept the sleep of the dead, for once possessing the ability to shut out cold, darkness and fear to recoup energies which amazed his twin; Morkere lay awake remembering the death of Erik Bare-legs and all that had provoked it.

Pekka remained on guard, along with Turgeis Silver-Tooth, the quarrelsome Ostman, and Magnus Osvifsson; both tucked in between two pines. Pekka almost allowed amusement to flicker in his eyes, and then remembered how, even in such a dark and hostile night, Turgeis could sense ridicule. What was wrong with the man? At one time or other over the last five years he'd quarrelled with eight out of every ten of his comrades, sometimes with blood being spilled and compensation being exacted. Yet he was a sure-footed fighter, a trusty man to have at your back and one on whom battle had the strange effect of making calm. Pekka remembered the first time he'd seen a change worthy of the Sly One[22] himself; Turgeis had accused Antti Hyva of stealing his purse (a ridiculous notion), screaming abuse so that the good-natured Finn had no choice but fight to uphold the honour of his clan. As soon as knives had been drawn, the Ostman's rage had dropped like a mask and with a frightening coldness he'd brushed aside the Finn's guard and stuck his blade into the other's throat. It was almost as if he had a demon within him that could only scramble out through battle. Then, with the purse found, Turgeis had flamboyantly offered a blood-price, knowing Hyva had no kin to avenge him. Pekka didn't like the man.

Somewhere to the south, Pekka's ears heard a soft sound, just the crack of a fallen twig being trod on by a quickly-moving warrior. No animal would make such a noise because only man lacked the sense to stay hidden from the cold unless forced to do otherwise. Was it necessity which drove warriors at such a pace along the trail? Pekka thanked his father, whoever he'd been, for giving him ears to detect any disturber of the silence of darkness. Without a word he stretched out his spear and lightly prodded the nodding Turgeis; he was rewarded by a menacing hiss and then the Ostman heard the flurry of sound coming from the south. Without a sound all three men drifted even more into the darkness; there was no time to warn the sleeping warriors. Pekka was sure distance from the trail would prevent any stranger tripping over them - but what if any of them made a sound? So what! Pekka was sure these madmen from the West could give a good account of themselves - and he wouldn't stay to find out if the odds looked uninviting.

Time passed and the flurries of sound among the snow became the steady swish of a sledge being dragged and the dull trudge of accompanying feet. Pekka waited, nestling his cheek against the flat-side of his spear-blade. He could hear no voices so the party had a sense of discipline, but he could also detect a sense of panic; not only was the time wrong for any journeying through the forests of Ladoga but the pace was too hurried. The party might be hurrying towards some destination but far more likely they were fleeing from danger. Pekka had learned the feeling well-enough since throwing in his lot with the Westerners.

Suddenly his memory recovered the image of Martta and his two boys gathering wild fruits and berries before the raiders had come. On that occasion his ears had failed them and he'd heard their approach too late to be of any use. His family hadn't been able to hide before the attack burst in upon them and destroyed his world.

A wicked blow from an axe had sent him into darkness and it had been hours before his eyes could again detect the stars. By then his family had vanished, any tracks masked by a recent hour's fall of snow. For a whole year he'd sought them and then drifted towards Ladoga in despair; he'd never seen his family again.

Now Pekka could hear the subtle clink of harness and the grunt of whoever was dragging the sledge; even more suspicious as any proper sledge would come fully equipped with dogs and not rely on the labour of men. By now the travellers had almost reached that part of the trail watched over by the three sentinels. Pekka strained his ears and was pleased to detect no sound from his companions; in his turn breathing became the only controlled exercise which might betray life.

At last he could see the travellers, if only by the half-hearted moonlight which betrayed the trail through the forests. They were led by a tall, silver-haired man, who was one of the strangers possessing skis and so made little noise as he passed along the trail with the minimum of effort. For a brief moment his eyes seemed to meet those of Pekka, and the Finn recoiled from the cold malice in the stare. His fingers tightened their grip on his spear as he expected discovery but then realised no human sight could penetrate the darkness of the trees flanking the moonlit path. Even so he felt the stranger was searching him out, had detected him and dismissed him as being of no importance. Some strange kind of pride was infuriated by the curtness of such a rejection; then reason warmed his self-confidence with the impossibility of such contact. Even as his fingers relaxed the stranger swung on, followed by about twenty warriors dressed like the Varangians of Lake Ladoga although Pekka guessed their homes lay to the west, perhaps even beyond the Dvina among the hinterland of Grobin[23] or Apoula. Then came the sledge, dragged by six men sweating to the point of exhaustion even on so frozen a night; these wretches were flanked by four ski-borne warriors carrying whips. However, it was the cargo of the sledge which almost made Pekka betray himself with an uncontrolled gasp; perched firmly in the centre of the sledge was the largest bell he'd ever seen. He'd only seen three bells before in his life and they'd been far to the south in Kenugard; yet they couldn't match this brute which towered above all the surrounding activity. It had the dull colour of bronze and couldn't match the beauty of the silver bell he'd seen in Kenugard itself, but for sheer size it put any other bell he could imagine into the shade. Even as he gasped the sledge passed along the trail with the soft swish of its blades and the despairing grunts of its slaves. Then came another twenty warriors, trotting with a precision which showed familiarity with the snow-heavy tracks of Ladoga.

Gradually, the sounds disappeared into the silence of the forest and Pekka slid out from his shelter and made his way across to where Magnus Osvifsson should have been but he wasn't there. Turgeis displayed his silver tooth in a malicious grin.

"Magnus slipped away to warn our warriors," he paused and a gleam of contempt flickered in his eyes. "Don't tell me those Finnish ears of yours missed all that!"

Pekka said nothing, but seethed inside. Was he getting old or just merely over-absorbed in the bell? Magnus was a very quiet mover, but he still should have heard him creep off towards their camp; as for the waking men, the noise should have been clearly heard in the forest. Then he thought again. No, Ethelwulf and his men had demonstrated their ability to slip into action with remarkable quietness already in his own land. Perhaps it was not such a terrible mistake. He attempted an air of arrogance.

"It was indeed quietly done, so the Suomen[24] did manage to teach Westerners something!" was the somewhat surly reply, but Turgeis could see the Finn was somewhat disappointed at being caught out. This put him in an even more goading humour.

"And what treasures of troll-craft can be garnered from a Finnish wood?" he sneered. Fortunately he was interrupted at this point by the arrival of Magnus followed by Edwine and two other Ostmen.

"More than you could fix in your head to save your life," laughed Edwine, quietly, adding as he could see a dark look appearing on the face of Turgeis," which could be said of all of us."

At this point Eric Snubnose intruded himself between Turgeis and Edwine, as if by chance, while addressing Pekka. "We're anxious to hear details of the party which precedes us on the trail." He paused and fixed his cold blue eyes of his fellow-Ostman. "We may have full need of every sword and war-axe we possess if they come across our vessels before we can catch them."

"Yes," agreed Pekka, a shrewd look appearing as he added, "for what they carried would fit far more snugly on the deck of a dragon-head[25] than being dragged through the snow by slaves."

Turgeis agreed. The war-party which had rushed by offered little booty, but did pose a threat to their ever escaping from this ice-filled wilderness. Without another word the six warriors quietly made their way deeper into the forest towards the main party.

*

Ethelwulf was not pleased by the news. Whatever was the purpose of the war-party which had passed ahead of them, it was certain they were brigands. To let such creatures seize their vessel would be disastrous. He was sure 'Alsvid' was skilfully concealed, but it was protected only by five warriors under the command of Thorstein. If he and over thirty warriors could catch up with the brigands there remained hope. Before what passed for dawn was beginning the Vikings had grouped themselves on the main trail. Quickly, and with a practice gained by up to ten years of fighting, they formed a column three deep. This had the advantage of readily turning into a defensive line if attacked from the flank; an additional gain was everybody could be forced into a fast pace for fear of jibes such as 'earme meowle.'[26]

As mile followed mile Ethelwulf tried to work out the destination of the brigands. Clearly they'd not be heading for Ladoga itself, which meant a limited use for any vessel based on the Volkhov. As soon as that hope arose it was dashed by the thought the brigands could seize his ship, use it to transport the bell on to the lake itself and then probably head westwards. A safe sale could be made at Visby on Gotland, and safer further south, on the shores of the Christian Emperor himself - provided they could get that far. Unlikely, as the Swedish Sea was always a dangerous region, especially after the death of Styrbjorn[27] had failed to settle the enmity between the Swedes and their neighbours. Again hope arose when he reasoned their pace must be better than that of slaves dragging a bell! Then he thought of the sledge and the snow and how this slowed down most of the company who lacked skis. He'd sent ahead Morkere and a few men, equipped with skis, to harass the brigands if required, but had small hope it would prove of any use.

Soon after dusk had settled across the forest they neared the shallows where 'Alsvid' had been concealed. Here he found Morkere with a confident smile on his lips. Apparently the precautions to mask the presence of warship had proved successful. Natural foliage had been deepened by tree branches yanked across to provide higher screening and behind the camouflage lurked sentinels, armed with bows and spears to resist any assault. The brigands had noticed nothing because they'd passed by the concealed vessel as dusk was blotting out any significant details. In fact, Thorstein had actually sent off Jussi Sure-foot in pursuit, to keep track of the brigands and report back their destination. He'd been intrigued by the bell, such awkward plunder; for some reason they'd missed the main Viking party so, Thorstein correctly deduced, Ethelwulf would be in pursuit.

Ethelwulf was delighted by the Viking's initiative but had no incentive to attack the brigands. Their crime was a matter to be settled by others. He'd secured few supplies but it was clearly time to move on southwards. The Wanderer didn't wish to be caught up in any recovery operation by the owners of the bell so next morning they should cautiously make their way southwards. Now, however, was the time to rest. Even so, Ethelwulf detached a dozen warriors under the command of Gunnar to prepare a suitable ambush if any approaching force should prove hostile. Pekka was given the task of removing any traces of their presence, a matter performed with surprising speed despite the growing darkness.

*

At dawn Ubbe the Stout reported the approach of a large war-party from the south. As they were travelling quickly they'd possibly pass by the concealed vessel without noticing the Vikings. Ethelwulf was pleased he'd not removed any of the camouflage, although he was concerned Gunnar's force might not be ready for the newcomers. He'd scarcely time to check this before the strangers were upon them. In front skied four slim bearded-figures, scouring the snow for any traces of their quarry. Halfdan Straight-eye whispered he'd already targeted the closest scout, confident the other three were equally marked down by bowmen. Ethelwulf, however, with a curt shake of the head, refused to launch any attack, hoping the pursuers would pass by their defences.

Suddenly one of the scouts stopped and let out the howl of a wolf. Still Ethelwulf held his hand; to attack now would give advantage to the strangers as only some had yet appeared.

With surprising speed the main party arrived and Ethelwulf noted they easily matched his own force in numbers, although he retained the distinct advantage of surprise which, under such conditions, might prove crucial. Suddenly a huge, red-bearded warrior, clothed in sable-furs and gripping in his left hand a wolf-spear, stepped forward. Carefully he examined the forest to the side of the trail and a strange smile appeared on his lips. He shouted in some alien tongue, at the same time throwing down the wolf spear. Ethelwulf had been about to order the attack when he realised the stranger was offering some form of parley; he'd no idea of the language being spoken but the gesture was obvious, the stranger had no desire to fight. Before anybody could stop him he yelled out a response in broken Swedish, "We strangers no want fight!"

The warrior paused and then replied, "We Rus...we talk.. no fight!"

"This should be an interesting conversation," muttered Morkere but was silenced by a glare from his cousin, who stepped forward, throwing aside his spear as a gesture of peace.

"We go Holmgard.. no fight - "

"You see..." there was a long pause as the stranger searched for a word in his limited vocabulary. Finally a scrawny, black-bearded companion yelled out, "thieves with ....with iron - "Again there was a pause until the first speaker intruded. "...thing!"

"So they're after the bell," stated Morkere; only such a bell as they'd seen would be large enough to warrant the term 'iron thing'. He turned to Ethelwulf and spoke rapidly in their native West Saxon, to avoid newer recruits understanding what he said. "This is good news, cousin." He was rewarded by a frown but continued. "I'm uneasy about a large body of cut-throats in our rear, ready to join with Oleg's ruffians." He paused before dropping his voice. "Let's join these strangers and wipe out such a threat before it has a chance to strike."

Edwine added his support and Ethelwulf recognised the sense of the suggestion. They'd been seen by these strangers; any report would add speed to the pursuit, if not additional warriors. On the other hand, together they might run into a force sent by Oleg Gunnarsson, Lord of Aldeigjuborg; if so, he might persuade his new companions they were another war-band seeking plunder and provoke a successful attack on the Ladogans. Of course, he realised everything depended on efficient communication. So he called forward Lars Estridsson who'd spent three years trading along the Volkhov and professed to have a good knowledge of the barbaric form of Swedish which passed as the language of Holmgard. He could see the red-bearded leader had the same idea, selecting a warrior to act as an interpreter. This was a good sign: two interpreters would prevent any distrust during negotiations. With Lars at his side Ethelwulf stepped forward to meet the leader of the Holmgard war-band.

The conversation proved most successful. Both leaders used interpreters who checked each other, commenting on a particular phrase but both intent on securing effective dialogue. The Holmgard war-leader was Oleg Askoldsson; later his story was to show he'd been born in Pskov and had travelled the whole lengths of the Volkhov, Dneiper and Donets rivers over the last ten years, blending the roles of trader, raider and mercenary with great success. The interpreter was Vladimir Vagnsson, the offspring of a Swedish father and a Khazar whose facility for learning languages quickly made him a close companion of Morkere.

After some other minor pleasantries, such as Ethelwulf introducing himself and adding the half-truth they were journeying south to fight as mercenaries, both sides got down to business. It appeared raiders had stolen the Great Bell of St. Basil, cast at Kursk of the purest iron and then passed northwards to Smolensk before being offered in tribute to Holmgard after defeat in war. It had been planned to erect the bell within the walls of the Kremlin itself, as a thanksgiving to the Almighty for the recent conversion of the Rus to Christianity. However, raiders had seized the offering on its way north, obviously with the aim of converting the bell into weapons.

Soon it was agreed Ethelwulf and his warriors would join the hunt for the raiders, recover the bell and then go south and enter the service of Holmgard. Oleg added prospects for mercenaries there were improving with every drive to the east against the Viatchians and Cheremesians. The great river Volga could carry the daring right down into the midst of Moslem territories. Ethelwulf remarked that, if he did choose to go on further, it would be to visit the city of Miklagard of which he'd heard great tales in his youth, rather than grow old surrounded by unbelievers. Oleg laughed at this, insisting a visit to Miklagard might suggest little difference between the Greeks and the Moslems when it came to unbelief.

"But we can't discuss the future when immediate duty calls," said Ethelwulf and Oleg agreed. They had to assemble forces and set off to recover the bell and Ethelwulf was ready to contribute thirty men, although ensuring there were changes among the ranks. So, Thorstein was replaced in charge of 'Alsvid' by its former helmsman, Edwy Osbertsson, and a few other men swapped roles.

All this took up two hours and it was approaching midday before the enlarged war-party was again on the trail of the raiders. They knew their quarry must have been slowed down by the bell and Ethelwulf was confident they'd catch up with the raiders before the following dawn. As he skied along the path he wondered why he was risking the lives of his men in another's quarrel. Although he possessed little space for manoeuvre, he could try to keep out of the fight as much as possible, while still being among the triumphant victors. Of course, he was slightly outnumbered by the Holmgard war-band

and had no wish to perish on some forgotten trail in these woods. What strategy would let him share in victory at minimal cost?

As Oleg followed in the tracks of his new recruits he too was considering the situation. He preferred having such warriors in front of him, just in case the westerners were tempted to join the raiders. Ethelwulf was concealing why they were journeying southwards; clearly they were hunted men. Would the Ladogans pay for their heads? Although his force outnumbered the westerners, they handled their weapons with obvious experience and skill – and he hadn't liked the way the axe-wielding giant had greeted him when they'd been introduced; Oleg gathered the stranger's name was Gunnar and that he came from the far west, but he'd been mostly fascinated by the long-handled axe which the westerner strapped to his back after tying his skis to his feet. Such men could prove be very dangerous - and he wasn't the only stranger openly hostile. Perhaps at Holmgard, when the strangers were surrounded by greater odds, they could question their presence among the Rus.

Soon two Slovenes, Tarq and Sigr, returned to report the raiders were resting not far ahead. The bell had toppled half-over at a bend in the trail, lodging itself firmly between two trees. It had taken several hours, and considerable strain on their patience, for the raiders to chop down one of the trees and yank free their prize. Together with Krel they'd watched from the other side of the river the efforts of the raiders, especially as the leader was adamant no damage should be allowed. First several skins had been wedged between the bell and the tree due for demolition, limiting the effect of axe-blows on the bell; almost too late the leader had realised the impact of the axe blows would cause tree and bell to be driven against the second tree, causing damage from the other side. Quickly skins had been slid on that side before the work began. It had taken some time for the first tree to be severed just below the bell and then for its trunk to be manoeuvred away from the prize. Before the trunk had been prised away the leader had ordered ropes to be tied around the bell to prevent it toppling backwards. All this had proved necessary as the bell was gradually shoved into an upright position on the sledge. Then the leader had ordered the raiders to rest before continuing their retreat northwards. This allowed Tarq and Sigr to retire back along their path to Oleg and the war-band, leaving Krel to maintain a watch on their quarry.

As their tale unfolded Ethelwulf, frantically mastering the gist of the account, realised the scouts had used the opposite bank to avoid running into the raiders unexpectedly. That route would allow a force to bypass the raiders and put themselves into a perfect ambush position; also that force should suffer fewer casualties in any fight with the raiders.

It took great effort not blurting out his scheme as Oleg rapidly explained the import of what the scouts had reported. There were still two hours of daylight, the raiders were tired and their morale must be low, and the close pursuit of the war-band hadn't been detected or else the raiders wouldn't be resting. For a few moments there was silence; then Ethelwulf suggested his force should advance along the path followed by the scouts and set up a pincer attack on the raiders. Oleg's eyes narrowed as his doubts about his allies were re-awoken; would these Vikings join the raiders to share the plunder after fighting off the Holmgard war-band? He could see no such planned treachery in the grey eyes of the westerner, but he could detect a nervousness which showed something was being held back. Should he insist on retaining some of the westerners among his own war-band - or would that appear too readily as a reliance on hostages? Should the men of Holmgard themselves ambush the raiders? These westerners might then join up with the raiders and fight off his attack. Oleg decided he'd have to trust his new ally, making sure to grab the bell as quickly as possible, because its theft might be tempting to the westerners.

So Ethelwulf's warriors were guided across the Volkhov using some the rocks which periodically broke up its northward flow. Once across the river he knew his men would feel happier, being no longer surrounded by warriors who might resort to treachery at any time to rid themselves of strangers. Sigr was handed over to him as his guide but the Slovene showed little love for the task. Only the greater authority of Tarq prevented complaint, although the grey-bearded tracker's features readily revealed what he felt about the matter. Of course, nobody among the westerners could communicate easily with the Slovene, even Lars Estridsson's vocabulary was limited to perhaps two dozen words. However, Gunnar whispered to Ethelwulf that when it came to persuasion he'd never known his war-axe to be lacking in argument. Ethelwulf grimly nodded, remembering the times the Gall-Gael's violence had nearly brought about disaster. Anyway, after an exchange of what sounded like whines and which passed as the Slovene tongue, Sigr turned his back on Tarq and silently made his way northwards.

The path proved much better than Ethelwulf had expected and clearly only custom had made the right bank of the Volkhov the more popular trail, although he remembered that closer to Ladoga there was no such ease of choice. The pace was steady and the Vikings could easily keep up with the tracker. Sigr was immediately followed by Lars, then Edwine, although only reluctantly did Gunnar allow the tracker get beyond the easy reach of his axe. With unusual modesty Gunnar took up the rear position, although the Vikings kept loose order as they advanced with little attempt at silence northwards.

At last Sigr suddenly came to a halt and turned with a savage look in his eyes. By sign language he demanded silence and embarrassment forced the Vikings to stop and look at each other as if their fellow was the cause of all the noise. With silence secured, Sigr turned and carefully made his way northward once again; this time his companions made every effort to be quiet, even Gunnar putting in that extra control over his stride to reduce the noise. After about fifty yards Krel emerged from the shadows, apparently taking in the situation with no attempt at questioning. He was smaller than Sigr but his body was equally muscled and he seemed almost oblivious of their unusual companions. Sigr in whispers initiated the rattle of words which provided an update on the situation. Once he'd considered the situation Sigr approached Ethelwulf and silently beckoned him to follow. The two stepped into the shadows and the warriors took the opportunity to rest, enjoying possibly the last few moments of silence they'd experience in life.

On his return Ethelwulf quickly outlined the position to Gunnar and the twins. The raiders were preparing to move on, realising more secure shelter would be needed before they stopped for the night. They'd have to move quickly if they were to cross the river and position themselves in ambush before Oleg attacked. Of course, there were only isolated crossing points and it'd be impossible to stay in contact with Oleg. He'd no idea when the attack would come and, if fortune turned her back, he might find his blocking force attacked by the raiders before Oleg made an appearance. Might Oleg deliberately delay the attack to let the raiders wear themselves out destroying the westerners? No. To do so Oleg would risk the pact between the two groups and he was sure the Holmgard mercenary feared that above everything.

After arranging his force into four units under his three leading companions and himself, Ethelwulf signalled Sigr to continue northwards; he noted Krel returned to the shadows, doubtless to inform Oleg of what had happened. After almost three hundred yards Sigr halted and pointed to the river, clearly indicating a suitable place to cross and set up an ambush. However, Ethelwulf shook his head and waved the Slovene onwards; the sneering response made it clear the tracker felt the westerners had little intention of risking danger. In a way he was right; Ethelwulf didn't want to be crossing the river when any scouts from the raiders could come upon him; also, to position his force so close to the enemy would increase the prospect of suffering attack before Oleg could intervene.

It was another three hundred yards before a suitable grouping of rocks in the river revealed another ford. This time Ethelwulf led his men down to the water's edge, carefully placing Oswald Strutter in a position from where the Sussex man had a clear view of the track on the opposite bank. Then Morkere led his men into the waters; Thorstein initially baulked at the iciness of the Volkhov, then smiled awkwardly and pushed after his leader; the other five warriors in the group plunged in without hesitation.

Gunnar waited with unusual patience until the last man had crossed the water. Shrewdly he calculated it wouldn't be useful if half of the force were caught mid-stream by the advancing raiders; besides he was watching out for any points of difficulty in crossing experienced by the first group. The river, if cold, appeared somewhat sluggish and, apart from a slip from Ricsige of York which provoked smiles all around, there was no incident. So Gunnar led his seven men across the river and was immediately followed by Edwine, confident his twin could slow down any advance by the enemy before his seven men could get could across. Ethelwulf was less trusting; only at the last minute did he recall Oswald Strutter from his post and give the leading position to Pekka. Before he stepped into the water the Karelian cast a quick glance upriver, almost expecting to hear a yell as the raiders charged; once assured, however, of a peaceful crossing Pekka proved the fastest to make the other bank, leaving behind the second man, Asgrim Blue-Jowls, and the rest of the group. Soon the entire force had crossed the river Volkhov and taken up position, masked by woods at the side of the main track.

Ethelwulf's strategy was quite simple. His warriors were positioned to drive the raiders into the river – if the war-band got that far. Of course, he hoped Oleg would launch his attack before the raiders reached this position, and was confident sounds of battle would warn him it was time to join in. At the last moment he decided to play doubly safe and summoned Sigr to his side. Bending down he started using his sword to draw in the soft snow a crude drawing of a bell with a snaky river next to it. Then he drew a cross and pointed to himself; then pointed vigorously to the bell and back down the trail. The tracker nodded and Ethelwulf, sweeping his sword to the other side of the river, prodded the earth as if striding along until he was opposite 'the bell'. Again the tracker nodded so Ethelwulf drew another cross further back down the 'track' and pointed to Gunnar on his skis. There was a look of bewilderment on the face of Sigr so Ethelwulf strode stiffly around, imitating the posture of Oleg and repeating that leader's name. A knowing smile appeared and he nodded so Ethelwulf prodded his sword into the ground as if advancing on the 'bell'. When he reached it he furiously swung his sword several times through the air. The tracker nodded so Ethelwulf pointed to him and with his sword-point 'hopped' back along the river until opposite the first cross before miming calling across the river. Sigr laughed and set off back across the river.

"If only our old neighbours could have seen that!" chuckled Morkere and his brother joined in.

"Yes. That would have lightened the mood after mass on Good Friday." There was a soft cackle of laughter among the band but for some it was tinged with sadness as they remembered that never again would they be able to walk the woods and heaths of Dorset.

Ethelwulf turned abruptly away and marched deeper into the forest to prevent anyone seeing the tear which threatened to moisten his eye. How often had he prayed history could be reversed and he'd no longer travel to Corfe on that fateful morning and thus ruin the lives of so many?

"But then, cousin, 'if only's' never did make a tasty pie," spoke a soft voice behind him. Ethelwulf turned to see Morkere a half dozen paces behind him and was once again astonished at how easily the twin managed to pick up his moods.

*

From his position across the river Sigr noticed that, all too soon, the raiders had re-assembled their column and were setting off for a more secure base. For a while he didn't move, being torn between following them, slipping back down-stream to warn the strangers, or trying to get the Holmgard contingent to hurry into the attack. Of course, there was a fourth option, to leave these savages to slaughter each other in their own way, but his cousins were with them and family loyalty meant he shouldn't desert his post. He tried to imagine how his father would have reasoned. If he followed them he'd be doing nobody any good as the strangers would surely hear the approach of the bell without any help from him; it would be pointless to simply scurry off to warn the strangers of the obvious. So he should advance upstream to encourage the Holmgard force to attack immediately.

He set off rapidly away from the raiders and soon came to a suitable ford across which he plunged. As he emerged he suddenly encountered a hostile warrior. Sigr recognised him as the one called Ragnar One-Ear and also recognised the look of suspicion in the eyes. For a horrible moment Sigr realised Ragnar thought he was a deserter, caught with no chance of defending himself.

Then the voice of Vladimir Vagnsson halted the thrust of the Ragnar's spear. "Think, Ragnar. If our scout had decided to run off, he certainly wouldn't slip over to OUR side of the river."

Tarq and Krell now appeared and Sigr managed to blurt out the threat to the strangers. Vladimir picked up the gist of the outburst and turned towards Oleg, attracted to the hubbub on the river-bank.

"The raiders are advancing rapidly towards the Westerners," he said and Oleg frowned. If he delayed either the raiders would smash their way through his new allies or he'd find those same allies had changed sides. Better not give Urd[28] the chance to ruin his mission so easily. He ordered his war-party to advance with all possible speed, regardless of the noise, and set off at a furious pace along the track.

*

Pekka was the first to hear the approach of the raiders. It appeared as a change in the silence but was really the soft squelch of the heavy bell being dragged across the snow. Only then did he become aware of the faint sounds of shouting as the raiders drove their slaves into even greater efforts - not that they could have known two war-bands were threatening their passage. The leader knew defence across a narrow trail might prove difficult, whereas ahead lay a stretch of more open country where a more decent camp could be constructed.

Soon the rest of Ethelwulf's warriors could hear the sounds of the approaching enemy and some began nervously to check their weapons, almost as if to assure themselves it was an axe or spear around which their fingers tightened. Gunnar carefully lay aside his fur cape and rested casually on his axe. There was a distant look in his eye as he quietly waited for what now appeared to be his sole aim in life – kill or be killed.

Several men notched arrows to their bows so that, at the given signal, they'd be among the first to strike against the enemy. However, Ethelwulf well knew timing was all-important; striking too soon might well block an effective attack by the bodies of their victims, in effect forming a stronghold for the living. On the other hand, a well-performed arrow attack on both front and rear of the passing column might make escape impossible and help drive the survivors into the river. He'd not expected – hoped – to be the first to strike at the enemy and hadn't given the required orders. Now, before it was too late, he passed the word along to the closest bowmen to strike at the rear of the column when he gave the order.

Even as the sounds indicated the raiders were about to burst into view they suddenly stopped. Ethelwulf and Edwine exchanged glances. There was an unpleasant silence among the trees as if Nature was awaiting an outburst of uproar. As the silence continued some of the men began to show increasing signs of nerves. What was happening back there on the track? Had the raiders somehow detected the waiting ambush? Ethelwulf wished he still had Sigr to send back across the river to check on the situation, but then reasoned that might have been detected by the raiders. He'd have to wait and trust something else had stopped the advance.

Almost immediately the answer came with sounds of a rapidly advancing band of warriors. That couldn't be the raiders as it sounded further away. It must be Oleg's force. Ethelwulf hesitated: should he attack immediately, in case Oleg himself were to run into an ambush or simply wait until he heard the sounds of battle?

He chose neither but by a series of hand-signals assembled his force into a compact group which straddled the track. Now out in the open, their best defence must be attack so he quietly led his men, at walking pace, in the direction of the raiders. Soon he stopped and listened. The advancing column was extremely close.

Suddenly he heard shouts of surprise, anger and frustration as men realised a battle which they hadn't expected was upon them. He waited another moment as the shouts became stronger and then ordered a rapid advance, passing the word along that he didn't want their silent approach ruined when they first saw the enemy.

His men hadn't trotted a hundred yards before they came upon the struggle. The raiders had drawn themselves up in a tight formation in front of the bell, behind which their slaves cowered under the watchful eye of two warriors. It was the slaves who betrayed their approach; one let out a tremendous yell, uncertain whether these new warriors were coming to help their oppressors or join in the attack. At that the two sentinels shouted a warning and several of the raiders turned to face the new threat. A few, however, deciding the gods had definitely turned against them, fled into the forest.

As Ethelwulf reached the raiders one cut at him with a strange-looking sword. Ethelwulf parried but, as he thrust at the warrior, one of the slaves grabbed at the man's legs, launching him off his feet. Before Ethelwulf could do anything, the slave had been joined by a fellow slave in scrabbling over the raider punching, biting and clawing at any part of the body open to attack. The warrior slashed out in defence and there was a scream from one slave as his arm was severed at the elbow. Ethelwulf put an end to the battle by stepping up and cutting down at the exposed face of the raider. He noticed a dark face, filled with hatred as his sword cut deep into the forehead. A slave tried to cling to the legs of his deliverer and he had to kick him viciously in the face to free himself from this burden.

The raiders had been almost overthrown by the initial rush. The six warriors facing the westerners were cut down and the remainder firmly placed their backs against the bell, preventing a direct attack by the Westerners. It was then the silver-haired leader was felled by an axe wielded by a scrawny leather-jerkined Rus and this caused a collapse of the resistance. About six of the raiders managed to cut their way through their attackers and plunge into the Volkhov. Here a couple found their swimming skills didn't prevent them being swept away to their deaths; the rest, however, made it to the opposite bank and safety. By now the Westerners had manoeuvred around the bell and their assault encouraged an even fiercer attack by the Rus. Fifteen of the brigands were killed on the spot and the remaining half-a-dozen, casting aside their weapons, threw themselves to their knees to receive the execution which custom promised would follow.

Oleg, however, had other ideas. First he ordered the release of the three slaves who'd survived the battle, despite the murmurings of his followers who could see a fine profit among the slave-traders of Ladoga disappearing. Oleg insisted he was obeying the instructions of Prince Yaroslav[29] himself that the captured Rus should be restored to liberty - complaints that suited more the ravings of a Christ-god lover than a decree of their dreaded master.

But their mood changed when Oleg declared the captured raiders should be enslaved on the spot and made to drag the bell back to Holmgard. He didn't need to add that there, doubtless, they could be sold in markets to the profit of every single member of his band. Naturally the freed captives were delighted, snatching up the weapons discarded by their tormentors and threatening to butcher the raiders there and then. At this there was a roar of anger from the Rus in general, the weapons were recovered and the freed captives were threatened with a recovery of harness. It took some time before order could be restored, the bested raiders yoked to the bell and the whole expedition able to set off for Holmgard.

*

"Lars says those raiders who got away have joined up with Jaropolk," whispered Ricsige of York, always the first to spread bad news. Of course, Jaropolk, expelled by his brother, Prince Vladimir, from Kenugard nine years before, was still a subject of rumour. Nobody knew what had happened to him for certain but some said he was slowly collecting together an army to recover his inheritance – nobody dared add the truth that such would be welcomed by many subjects of Kenugard. Others insisted the exiled prince had died years before, deserted by almost everyone and only rumour kept his name alive. Ethelwulf wondered what Jaropolk, if he'd survived to welcome the fugitive raiders, would gain by attacking an expedition transporting the bell back to Holmgard. Certainly a force of over seventy warriors should discourage anyone except the most determined – or insane. Yet he had to admit the seizure of the bell would be a great humiliation for Prince Yaroslav of Holmgard; perhaps Jaropolk could even use it to secure the backing of the clique who'd supported him after the death of his father, Svjatoslav, sixteen years before, and with it power in Kenugard. At the very least the iron contained within the bell might fetch a welcome price in any of the markets along the shores of the Swedish Sea.

When he discussed the rumour with Oleg, the red-bearded Varangian roared with laughter until tears dimmed his eyes.

"Stranger to the Rus you are," he sneered. "When man falls no man helps."

Ethelwulf would have loved to answer he'd known several men who'd survived disaster, returning to triumph over their enemies. Language, however, prevented any such retort but he made sure HIS warriors were on the alert for any counter-attack from the woods. He hadn't liked abandoning 'Alsvid' with but a small guard as his main force marched south. His apprehension was not helped by noticing that, for all his bluster, Oleg made sure guards at night were doubled and Krell was ordered to drop back with two Rus to keep an eye open for any threat from the rear.

So the party made their way to Holmgard without incident – except for the escape of one of the raiders. He was considered of little loss, except by the released captives governed by a mixture of hatred, revenge-lust and a frantic need to recover some wealth. Oleg gave them permission to depart – but without any of the weapons they'd acquired and lacking assistance. This immediately quelled their protests, although dark looks followed the chieftain for the next two days and Ethelwulf was certain Oleg had made himself at least two more enemies.

As they grew nearer the city the efforts of the enslaved raiders became increasingly reluctant. Everyone knew that, out in the wilderness, escape (if not survival) was always possible. Once within the grasp of the Prince of Holmgard death or, at the very least, miserable enslavement was inevitable. It needed all the persuasion of whips, spear-points and kicks, to help them drag the recovered bell up to the gates of the city.

*

Ethelwulf had never before enjoyed that heightened wave of emotion brought on by a triumphal entry into a city. He'd read all about Roman generals being constantly reminded of their mortality as they enjoyed a triumphal entry into the imperial city. But that had all been in Dorset long ago - simply one dream among others which visited his sleep. Now actually involved in such an event he could appreciate the feelings of a Caesar or a Marius – and would have admitted he relished the emotion. The muscles in his legs seemed to lengthen as he tried to add to his height, wishing that, for once, he possessed the elaborate helm he'd seen displayed in far-off Dublin by Sigtrygg Silkenbeard or the lofty headgear favoured by some of the Icelandic leaders. Beside him the other Westerners felt a similar emotion tearing at their over-awed minds as they briefly enjoyed their triumph.

Not that the bell's escort had any of the discipline of ancient Roman legions, nor did they bring that immense plunder which had transformed a minor Italian township into the capital of myth and legend. All they were bringing was a bell, albeit somewhat large, drawn by slaves, over the snowy approach to the gates of the capital of a half-savage outpost on the edge of the world. Even so, it was enough for the people of Holmgard to throw open the gates, swing down from the wooden ramparts, shout hosannas and cheer the victory of their forces over darkness. Only a week before they'd been in despair, realising a gift from their suzerain, Vladimir, had been lost and he'd demand full payment for this insult to his authority. Now it was all different; honour had been restored.

At last the procession halted in front of the small building which claimed the title of being Holmgard's cathedral. With no place strong enough to hold the bell, a special dais was erected in front of the wooden building. There the bell would be struck from the outside and not sounded by clappers as in the West. The slaves manoeuvred the bell into position and then were ushered to the side, grateful that completing their journey hadn't culminated in their slaughter. Of course, these days Christianity was supposed to have abolished blood sacrifice but that was only a thin veneer concealing a barbaric heart; a truth today might not survive tomorrow, even if the ruler assumed the style of servant of Christ. In fact, among the population only a minority had taken to the new faith enough to let it seriously affect their lives. Possibly about the same proportion remained loyal to older gods - whether of the Norse pantheon or Slavic origin - while the majority remained indifferent to the competing faiths. Indeed, not far from the site dedicated to the bell men could still detect the base of the image of Perun, the thunder-god, carrying a thunder-stone in his hand.[30] Offerings were left there - whether to Perun or the newly-installed Christ-God was uncertain.

*

"Our Lord of Kenugard will have heard of these new warriors from the north," stated Oleg to Prince Yaroslav. Both knew that, despite occasionally indulging his oldest surviving son, there were doubts about the lad's legitimacy since Vladimir's sudden conversion to Christianity. Anyway, Vladimir always distrusted anyone with power to grow independent of himself; a feeling heightened by recalling how he'd severed the legitimate heir from his inheritance

Vladimir, after subordinating the genesis of their race at Holmgard to a subordinate position, had installed Svyatoslav, bastard off-spring of his father, as "Advisor" to the young prince. In fact, the skinny, anaemic-looking creature was nothing but a spy for the Lord of Kenugard, knowing that everything he possessed was merely his at the whim of their master. The Advisor sported the shaven head adorned with a single war-lock and the drooping moustache favoured by his father. But there the resemblance ended because the younger Svyatoslav lacked the acumen or drive of the great conqueror, being content to be the servile ears for his half-brother, the Lord of Kenugard.

For once, Yaroslav was free of the ever-present agent of his father for the "Advisor" had injured his leg one week before and was constantly summoning priests to his bedside in the belief prayers counted more by their weight than sincerity in ensuring the healing powers of the Christ-God. The young prince, although not twelve, had demonstrated a shrewdness beyond his years, if only in having selected as his real advisor Oleg Askoldsson. Even so, the prince, lacking any desire to conspire against his father, hadn't yet learned that others could conspire against himself.

Svyatoslav had secured the somewhat unwilling acquiescence of Yaroslav to Olga, sister of Igor, lord of Pskov, being dispatched to Kenugard as a suitable concubine for Vladimir. Although the Lord of Kenugard had sealed his conversion to Christianity by his betrothal to the sister of the Emperor of Miklagard, he didn't abandon his ancestors' custom of surrounding himself with as many concubines as possible.[31] It had been a bold move to try and stem the threat from the Greeks of the south. For well over one hundred years the Varangians, styled by their subjects as Rus, had lorded it over the Slavs, secure in both their paganism and in their links to their homelands around the Swedish Sea. In the last ten years, mainly due to the decisions of Vladimir of Kenugard, this two-fold base had been undermined by growing links to the south, with its pernicious practices and religion. Men like Svyatoslav wished to weaken such links, either by corrupting Vladimir so that he turned his back on Miklagard or fostering trouble between his state and that to the south. They saw the successful penetration of the Volga, and its access to the Black Sea, as the ruin of their state. They'd been devastated when Vladimir had helped the ruler of the Greeks earlier that year,[32] instead of using the turmoil in the Empire to succeed where his father had failed a generation before.[33]

Oleg had at first opposed the surrender of the princess to the Lord of Kenugard, but not for reasons of state policy; he'd been attracted by Olga and his feelings had been returned. However, the pair, aware how Olga was merely an article to be promised or sold in the cause of diplomacy, had managed to keep their passion hidden. Oleg found himself going along with the proposals of the hated Advisor partly out of loyalty but increasingly for reasons of his own ambition. Having become the slave to his passion for the princess he was prepared to arrange for her disappearance, along with his own, in the fond hope they could escape the vengeance of Vladimir of Kenugard. He reasoned that Vladimir would become so immersed in dealings with the Greeks he'd forget a bride he'd never seen. Oleg sketched out the plan in his head; somewhere on the way to Kenugard he'd carry off the princess and cover his treachery by arranging for one of the war-bands - Khazars, Pechenegs or Krivichians, it made no matter - to massacre the escort. Officially the whole episode would be put down to yet another attack on the Rus by one of their many enemies. Perhaps Olga and himself could return to Pskov one day, perhaps not; Oleg was confident they could avoid the attentions of Vladimir of Kenugard.

With all his plotting Oleg was reluctant to sacrifice men with whom he'd served for so long. These newcomers from the north offered the answer. He could willingly see them sent to destruction and sleep with a good conscience. So he suggested to the Prince of Holmgard he should personally escort the princess, but with the escort made up of the new Varangians from the north. He was pleased the incapacitated Advisor supported the suggestion.

Yaroslav thought his father would be delighted to receive a new contingent of troops from the northern lands. Although the shrewd prince wondered why they'd suddenly appeared in his realm he was quick enough to pass along a potential source of mischief. He summoned the leader of the newcomers, together with his principal lieutenants, officially to give the expedition his blessing.

A slave ushered the newcomers in and Yaroslav examined the four men standing before him with great care. All of them were tall, although one easily over-topped the others. Their leader, whom Oleg whispered was called Ethelwulf, had fair hair and grey eyes. His shirt of mail had an air of over-use about it and his manner was one of command. Yaroslav had been told he'd come from the land of the Saxons on the edge of the world to the west; he'd wanted to satisfy his curiosity about such a realm but didn't think that suited his dignity so chose to stay silent. The giant, with dark hair and a fierce beard, possessed the manner of a berserk and, for a brief moment, even with his guards present, the young prince felt a sense of awe. He saw how the stranger's fingers lightly played upon the haft of the great axe grounded in front of him. He wondered why such a man should to accept orders from this 'Ethelwulf'; but then he looked more closely at their eyes and saw the Saxon's held a calmness which came with quickness of decision and a history of success, whereas the green eyes of the giant seemed haunted by past horrors and were a prey to tension and insecurity.

The last two warriors Yaroslav had been prepared to dismiss until he realised how alike they were and yet how different. Both stood before him with a passivity given to those who, while content to follow orders, had a certainty they could handle any problems life might hurl in their way. One was left-handed, with black hair and an insolent look in his brown eyes; the other had brown hair, with brown eyes possessing an honesty not present in those of his companion. Both men carried spears as well as swords. Yaroslav wanted to know if the two men were brothers, but again decided the dignity of the House of Rurik[34] didn't permit himself to ask such questions. Of course, he could always ask the strangers to tell him how and why they'd entered Holmgard, but he sensed Oleg was anxious to be away, probably before his uncle was fully recovered. Yaroslav merely nodded his head at the greeting from the strangers and waited for Oleg to explain what would be required.

Oleg set about the task quickly and efficiently. He began by pointing out that, if their aim was to serve as mercenaries, they'd find greater opportunity in Kenugard. He added Vladimir Svyatoslavich, Lord of Kenugard, was a master of war and had expanded his dominions in all directions since he'd begun his reign over ten years before. He'd been tempted to mention the recent seizure of Cherson[35] by Kenugard but decided he didn't want to alarm the newcomers if they had doubts about serving so far south.

Ethelwulf intruded, merely to show willingness to go along with the implied suggestion that, even as far west as the land of the Danes they'd heard of Vladimir, marvelling how his successes in wars provoked the envy of the great and powerful. He didn't add those feelings had really been aroused by the hundreds of slaves from the neighbouring peoples flooding the slave markets of Gotland and Bornholm for several years. The supply appeared inexhaustible and, as Ethelwulf knew from sharing with mixed fortunes in such enterprises,[36] simply aroused the envy of the northern world

"Our lord but recently sent detachments which kept the ruler of the Greeks on his throne,"[37] smiled Oleg who, with no love for the ambitions of Miklagard, hadn't really approved of the recent campaign. He added their opportunity at Holmgard itself for armed intervention was somewhat limited. He didn't add this was because of the almost insane fear Vladimir of Kenugard had of rebellion.

Before any of the strangers could intervene Oleg explained it had been agreed to send to their lord a princess-bride. He wasn't sure how far the newcomers had picked up news of all the developments in the south. They must have heard about the conversion of Vladimir but they must also have been told of an earlier attempt to drive adherents of the Christ-god from his lands. Personally Oleg doubted whether the Lord of Kenugard would really persist in a religion which restricted the traditional pleasures of kings.[38] He stressed this would ease their acceptance and was pleased to note Morkere smiled at this - not, as Oleg supposed because he approved of the plan, but as he was convinced Oleg wanted to get their men either away from Holmgard or inside Kenugard.

Yaroslav intervened at that point, indicating speed was essential He'd heard his father had recently married a Greek princess - this provoked a dark look from Oleg which all but Ethelwulf missed - and so it was essential their gift should arrive before his father's taste for brides from the north had lessened.

Gunnar smiled at that as he thought few rulers with genuine Viking blood would ever tire of such maidens in preference to the soft, fragile blooms from southern climes.

Ethelwulf asked when they'd be expected to depart and was somewhat shocked when Oleg said that they'd be off within two days. The Saxon wanted to know what they'd be supposed to do with 'Alsvid' – being now resigned to abandoning the longship in effect on the borders of the Holmgard realm. He'd been assured by several members of the entourage of Yaroslav that he'd receive a fair price for it as there was always a need for longships to further the growing trade between the Rus and the Swedish Sea. Although he doubted the price would be fair, he could see there'd be little choice - and if they must leave within two days his options had narrowed even more!

*

Ethelwulf was amazed how, within the space of two days, they secured a good price for 'Alsvid'. He'd been sorry to see her go, but the price was judged fair and Ethelwulf managed to convert most of the silver gained into four small jewels which he divided among himself and his three chief companions; the balance of the silver was cut into small strips so that, in the end, the whole company was able to set out with silver in their belts.

The newcomers found two days passed remarkably quickly. They were lodged together in three huge log cabins, everyone equipped with furs to keep out the cold, if not with one or other of the remarkably co-operative women from the population. In the marketplace Morkere was most surprised by the amount of coloured glass, beads and silk betraying alien origins. He discovered they'd come, mostly by way of the Volga river, from Islamic lands to the east. He was shown some very peculiar coinage, being assured it came from far to the east, from a land called 'Sin'; however, he was unwilling to believe such a land existed because of the many obvious lies told by the Arabic trader.[39]

Some of Ethelwulf's men took to wearing the elaborate and colourful costume worn by many of the traders they met in the town. He tried to point out that bright scarlet caps and baggy trousers made of green-dyed wool were not only in bad taste but distinctly impractical. However, he quickly abandoned his criticisms when he saw a dangerous look appearing their eyes. Let them either be forced to leave behind all their finery or discover how little could survive the rigours of a journey south.

Many of the men remained for most of the period of inactivity in some form of alcoholic stupor. They found their new silver easily went on the fine ale brewed in Holmgard and that, strangely enough, the more they drank, the more quickly their silver evaporated. Two enjoyed the pleasures of a Rus funeral, returning to tell, to whoever was willing to listen, of standing in line so they might enjoy the body of the dead man's concubine, Finally, after the girl had been offered to fourteen men, all claiming to be close friends with the deceased, an old hag had been summoned to strangle the wretched girl, worn out with her efforts to satisfy such friends all afternoon. Thereupon the dead trader and concubine had been placed in a small boat which had been dragged over to the far shore and set on fire. While it burned a group had chanted prayers to Odin, from whom all success in this ice-filled land had come.[40] Both admitted that at this point in the proceedings they'd both slipped into sleep, worn out by ale and sex. Even so they insisted it was the best funeral either of them had ever attended, and hoped they might enjoy another in the near future.

Meanwhile Ethelwulf set about learning as much as he could about the surrounding peoples.[41] To the south-east were the Viatchians and the Krivichians; to the south-west were the Polochanes and the Derevlians. Far to the south were the Pechenegs[42] and the faded force of the Khazars.[43] In sum, this country was not the happiest place to find oneself - unless there was need for employment as mercenaries. The Kenugardan state was in a condition of almost siege by various Slavic groups. The previous ruler, Svyatoslav, after expanding his domains in all directions, had fallen a victim to the Pechenegs[44] - and not before Kenugard itself had successfully resisted a Pecheneg attack.[45] And yet Pechenegs were sometimes used as mercenaries by both Greeks and Rus, and Kenugard had extensive agreements with these troublesome neighbours.[46]

The Rus seemed less in awe of their other Slav neighbours who supplied the simple boats used on the rivers of the state, with the addition of more traditional elements. Even so, these peoples sometimes launched war-bands to harass travellers, perhaps in imitation of the Pechenegs, necessitating expeditions to exterminate threats to decent trade.

*

On the appointed day Ethelwulf was ready, along with the fifty warriors who'd elected to seek employment in Kenugard – his own force had been supplemented, as in the past, by locals who had urgent need to leave the vicinity. One or two of his original crew chose to stay in the Holmgard area, hoping to earn a living as trappers and traders. Others had either drunk too much or been waylaid by the robbers or whores who relieved traders of their hard-earned silver. Anyway, they hadn't assembled in time in the main square in front of the log-house of the ruler of Holmgard.

Edwine drew his cousin's attention to the absence of any other troops. Ethelwulf was surprised but his questions were quickly answered by Oleg who arrived with half-a-dozen men. He asserted that only a month before eighty men had gone south in answer to the summons by the Lord of Kenugard; serious warfare had broken out with the Pechenegs whose attempts to exact heavy payment from the Rus was starting to have a strangling effect on the growing trade with the Greeks of Cherson.

Further discussion was avoided by the appearance of Prince Yaroslav, accompanied by one of the most shifty individuals Ethelwulf had ever seen. Oleg whispered he was Svyatoslav Svyatoslavich, the Advisor to the young prince. Ethelwulf considered that neither the large pearl ring in the left ear nor the shaven scalp helped to distract attention from the narrow eyes, apparently smarting under the bright sunlight, which flickered from left to right as if in constant fear of assassination.

The impression was not improved when the Advisor decided to speak, going over the ground explained to Ethelwulf two days before. As he mentioned the Princess Olga a slim figure, enveloped in furs as protection against the biting cold, made her appearance. Ethelwulf presumed that was the Princess, mainly because she was followed by two other female figures less elaborately protected against the weather. She was tall and slim, but whatever charms were planned to distract Vladimir of Kenugard were safely hidden from envious eyes. Neither Ethelwulf nor his cousins detected the change in manner which took over Oleg; Gunnar saw him stiffen, as if ushered into the presence of someone with the power of life and death, and was puzzled. He recalled how some, mainly slaves, tensed when about to approach old Bluetooth but recalled that was because an outbreak of the king's rage could mean instant death. But then those creatures had seemed to lose colour whereas Olaf appeared to grow red with the effects of the cold. Whatever Gunnar thought he kept to himself.

Initially, they'd travel in four of the adapted canoes supplied by Krivichians across Lake Ilmen and then down the river Lovat. At some point they'd have to portage their craft cross-country until they could exploit the river Dneiper to carry them on to Kenugard.

Ethelwulf noticed how quickly Oleg shuffled the Princess and her slaves on to the smallest of the vessels. He made it very clear that none of Ethelwulf's force would be welcome on the vessel manned only by the few men he'd brought with him. The other three vessels were soon filled with the escort force. Ethelwulf commanded the leading craft, Gunnar followed him, then the vessel commandeered by Oleg. The twin sons of Aelfhere brought up the rear.

With scant attention from Prince Yaroslav and his entourage the expedition set off for Lake Ilmen.

*

The Wanderer 8:2

"My lord asked me to dwell here with him;
Few loved ones had I, loyal friends
In this land; that is cause enough for grief.
('The Wife's Lament')

Hunt for a Princess

The journey across Lake Ilmen and entry into the River Lovat had been uneventful, and distinctly frustrating. Ethelwulf considered insulting how Oleg shielded the Princess from the eyes of any of the newcomers. In fact, Morkere maliciously suggested that perhaps she wasn't a princess at all but merely an ancient crone Oleg was planning to trade as old bones with some of the savages to the south. Gunnar kept his mouth shut at this comment, recalling the Rus leader's reaction to the arrival of the three women was certainly not how anyone would have greeted an old crone!

They'd made camp immediately after entering the River Lovat and Oleg made sure that he, his men and the princess were bivouacked some distance from the main party. Edwine had merely shrugged off his twin's malicious comment but Ethelwulf was intrigued by the identity of exactly whom they were escorting. He'd abandoned any attempt at straight questions because Oleg made it very clear they were most unwelcome. So he had to resort to guile.

The first day had proved much easier travelling than the more experienced Rus had expected. Oleg had warned they might have to portage their vessels over some stretches of the river because of the low level of water. However, autumnal rains had sufficiently supplied the river with enough water to carry the four vessels safely to their first overnight stop. Having tied up the boats securely to the river banks they set about making camp. Eventually the last story-teller had finished for the night and they'd all settled down.

Suddenly Olaf at one end of their camp and Edwy, the former helmsman of 'Alsvid' raised the alarm. Both claimed to have seen strange shapes circling the encampment and heard the unwelcome crack of twigs which revealed the presence of man. Immediately Ethelwulf and about six men rushed to protect their charges, managing to reach the tents housing the Princess and her slaves slightly before Oleg, who'd been fast-asleep until kicked awake by a couple of his men. Rather rudely Ethelwulf tore aside the tent-flap and revealed a very startled, and very beautiful, dark-haired girl.

She proved incapable of responding to Ethelwulf's urgent demands that everyone should head for the boats before their means of escape were destroyed by the enemy. Oleg stepped up and roughly pushed Ethelwulf aside. In what Ethelwulf presumed was the native tongue of the inhabitants of Pskov, but which had the attraction of a banshee howl to his ears, Oleg must have explained to the princess the camp was under attack. Her two slaves by that time were hastily packing the possessions of the princess despite the protestations of Morkere who insisted speed was essential if they hoped to save their lives.

Almost as soon as it had begun the panic was over. Edwine quickly ordered four men, under the command of Pekka, to advance carefully into the forest to check out the danger. Soon they returned without encountering any trace of the enemy, although they'd come across the half-eaten carcass of a small moose which showed wolves were probably active in the area. At that there was general laughter and the slaves began to restore the princess's property to its normal place. Olaf was teased by his friends, especially Pekka, for over-reacting to what was clearly the normal activity of the forest. With his woodcraft he should have read more successfully the chances of attack. He admitted he'd assumed that whatever guard had been set had been overcome. The guards were actually Edwy and another of the original followers of Ethelwulf, Egbert of Slepe. Each blamed the other for first raising the alarm and both were laughed at.

As they all settled down, Ethelwulf whispered to Morkere. "So now we know, cousin. She's certainly not an old crone."

"Indeed, that makes me wonder why Oleg is so protective."

"I'd be protective," interrupted Edwine, "if my charge were as beautiful."

"But then we know, brother," chuckled Morkere," how prone you are to let Cupid usurp your reason." He gave a knowing smile to Ethelwulf who felt inwardly delighted his little ruse had worked. Tomorrow he must pass on the silver penny he'd offered the two guards and Olaf for so successfully crying wolf. He looked across at where Oleg was restoring himself to the furs which shut out the cold of the late autumn night. For a brief moment their eyes locked and he sensed his trickery hadn't deceived Oleg. Ethelwulf closed his eyes and turned his mind to consider that possibility. He was sure Oleg would consider it simply a sign of nosiness, an unwelcome interest in the affairs of others, and act accordingly; he expected the Varangian to be more distant over the next couple of days. That he could handle easily, especially if it meant the princess abandoned the shroud of security which had irritated many of the newcomers, including himself. However, what did worry him was why Oleg had been so secretive. Had he been ordered by prince Yaroslav, or even the Advisor, to make sure the newcomers should have no knowledge of their charge? No, because the princess from the very beginning had taken every means to conceal herself from the newcomers; in this she'd been actively assisted by Oleg. That was the problem. Experience had taught the Wanderer no warrior like Oleg would risk arousing the enmity of others, and the only reason suggesting itself didn't bode well for the future married bliss of Vladimir of Kenugard.

*

Soon what had started out as flowing waters in the river dropped to a level which endangered their craft, despite the narrow draught of vessels especially constructed for transport on the rivers of this country. Accordingly, Oleg sent on ahead a couple of scouts to the settlement of Gnezdovo where he said they could find experts in the necessary portage. He added such aid would have been necessary anyway before they were able to employ their boats on the more generous waters of the Dneiper to carry them down to Kenugard. He'd hoped that, considering the amount of water in the lower reaches of the Lovat, they could have got much closer to Gnezdovo by water but the Norns[47] had decided otherwise.

Morkere sidled up to Ethelwulf as Oleg walked off and whispered in his ear. "Now we'll see whether Oleg has made any special arrangements for our charges." When his cousin raised a questioning eyebrow he added. "Unless he makes special provision the princess will have to trudge along the bank like the rest of us!"

Ethelwulf smiled at what his cousin had surmised. No woman should hesitate about a stiff walk along such tracks, especially when protected by a strong force. In such surroundings horses had limited use so men, women and children were forced to rely on either their feet or sledges when water proved inhospitable.

Meanwhile the expedition was forced to address the problem of preparing the vessels for portage. This meant they had to be emptied and become as light as possible. Food, camp equipment and weapons were removed from the vessels and carefully stacked in anticipation of the wagons which had been promised.

*

Gnezdovo made a good living from assisting the portage of vessels across the country between the rivers Lovat and Dneiper. Over the previous century trade had expanded between the barbaric North and the civilised South, namely the realms of the Byzantines and the Caliphate. Both areas needed to ensure an easy passage for trade and so Gnezdovo blessed its ideal position in this economy.

This expedition offered an extra opportunity for profit from the townsfolk and they hastened to gain by it. Apparently the Prince of Holmgard was most anxious for the expedition to reach his overlord at Kenugard but nature had decreed otherwise with insufficient water in the Lovat to row or sail down to the normal halting-point. This, in itself, meant more silver for the local population and Oleg seemed willing to pay out more just to ease the progress of the expedition. Morkere looked at Ethelwulf when the Varangian dipped into the pouch containing a good supply of silver pennies. Ethelwulf knew what was passing through his cousin's mind; why would a Varangian be so willing to accept the exorbitant demands of these townsfolk? Probably a mere hint of violence from such a well-armed group would have cut down the demand as the locals wouldn't have wished to lose either valuable men or the goodwill of powerful neighbours if it came to a fight. Oleg, however, paid up with a smile as if telling the world the great didn't bother with such petty measures. Of course, there were extra demands because of the number of vessels but, despite their slight build, Oleg failed to get a cut in the original price.

With the tedious matter of payment settled, the locals could take over and allow their experience to mastermind the transporting the vessels to the easier waters of the Dneiper. Ethelwulf was glad it wasn't his responsibility to pay these scavengers; he could see the furious glint in the eyes of Gunnar and shared some of the rage. Obviously the locals possessed the necessary skill and experience. However, Ethelwulf wondered why such a mighty prince as Vladimir of Kenugard allowed trade to be so exploited. Perhaps he'd already turned his eyes so much to the south and Miklagard he was unable to see the exactions of the townsfolk. More probably the locals sensed the urgency in Oleg and determined to profit by it. In which case Ethelwulf was back to Oleg's motivation and completely lost.

He was dragged back to reality by screams from one of the locals unloading large logs from the wagons they'd brought. Due to the haste with which Oleg had infected their leaders, a pile of logs were released too soon and instead of tumbling on to the ground swept aside one of the men, crushing his leg in the process. This provoked high-pitched jabbering from his companions, but little sympathy. He was hustled aside, propped up against a tree while his companions returned to earning the promised bonus.

On one wagon a litter was speedily assembled to the fascination of the Vikings who'd never seen such a conveyance before. No sooner had the uprights been put in place than the princess, still carefully shrouded like the most precious object in a harem, climbed into the litter. The job of accompanying the precious cargo was given either to Oleg's trusted Varangians or to the locals; Oleg clearly wanted to keep the Vikings as far as possible away from the princess, as if too-close contact would besmirch her. Morkere whispered to Ethelwulf that clearly they had short memories in Holmgard for many had seen what the princess looked like and such a beauty couldn't easily be forgotten. Ethelwulf replied he didn't see it as a deliberate insult to his men, but was intrigued by the possible purpose of such a charade.

The two slaves had to walk behind the litter. One or two of the more daring Vikings tried to fall in alongside the two women, to get into conversation and possibly acquire more pleasure before the trek was completed. At that Oleg would approach with obvious irritation, appealing to Ethelwulf to keep his men in order, insisting that, in Holmgard, even slave-women demanded some degree of privacy. Edwine once spluttered at this too-obvious lie; no warrior would accord any slave - certainly no female slave - any privacy at any time. His twin nudged him in an attempt to avoid upsetting a man with influence in this land. However, he was too late and Edwine saw a look of malevolence pass across the features of Oleg before Ethelwulf could impose himself between the two men, loudly assuring the Varangian that no man would intrude on such customs of Gardarike. At the same time Morkere roughly ordered the men to return to the main mass of the party and was grudgingly obeyed. So the two slave-women were left to follow their mistress in isolation.

"Apparently," muttered Ethelwulf to Morkere, again in the front rank of their men, "Oleg fears the slave women might reveal secrets."

"True, cousin," replied Morkere. "I fear he'll need watching long before we reach our destination."

"But not now," answered Ethelwulf. "with his boat on dry land and surrounded by people who'd strip him of his very clothes if they saw a profit!"

Although Morkere was moved to agree he felt his cousin was being too harsh with the townsfolk of Gnezdovo. They were dedicating considerable effort in providing a service to traders, realising they commanded a crucial stage in the operation, so naturally they were after as large a profit as possible. If the service was good then it'd be worth the silver, if not, their swords might seek compensation.

The source of profit to the townsfolk of Gnezdovo had become obvious. The logs were used as rollers. Over the years the townsfolk of Gnezdovo had assembled a large collection of logs of similar size; the progress of transported vessels was aided by the continuous clearing caused by the passage of heavily-laden wagons. In addition, years of practice made the operation run with remarkable efficiency.

The piles of weapons, food and other supplies were quickly loaded into two wagons each pulled by two oxen; with the goods loaded the wagons set off, accompanied by two of the men brought by Oleg. Then the real work began. It wasn't easy to lift each of the boats out of the river but soon they were all placed on a pathway of logs. Before the haul began there was a period for rest, despite the irritation of Oleg.

This time was used by some locals to attach each of the vessels to two oxen they'd brought with them. At last they all set off; as soon as the last vessel had been dragged over the logs a team of locals rushed to carry the logs to be laid in front of the leading vessel. At first it was hard work because, having been forced to abandon the river earlier than customary, the track was not as well-shaped as the later stages promised to be. Even so, a small group of locals walked ahead of the main party, clearing any undergrowth which might impede progress and the more uneven ground was, as far as possible, smoothed out by two men armed with the long spades common to the region, filling in hollows and cutting down ridges. Although the locals, with their oxen, took the key role in the actual haulage of the vessels, teams of Varangians and Vikings were expected to apply their muscles over some of the more difficult stretches. Leaders weren't spared, nor wished to lose prestige by refusing to share in the hardships of their men, but Ethelwulf hated the sweat and ache which marked his spell.

Once they'd reached the actual gap between the waters of the Lovat and the Dneiper the work became much easier. Indeed, the path was so well-used the oxen could take on the sole task of haulage, with guidance and support from the locals. Behind the vessels strode the expedition, seizing the opportunity of playing lords following a procession of slaves. So they made their way for over two days until they came to the first navigable points of the Dneiper. Here the oxen were unattached and, as if by magic, simply blended into the forest. The two wagons already stood there, awaiting the removal of the vessels from the log path to the waters of the river. This was accomplished, not without some grumbles from men growing used to an easier path through life. The equipment was returned to the vessels and the expedition recovered their accustomed places.

As it was the time to say farewell to the townsfolk of Gnezdovo, Ethelwulf would have expected some form of feast to mark the occasion, for he had to admit the townsfolk had performed an excellent service and the whole stage known as the great portage had proved easier than he'd expected. Oleg, however, had other ideas. He dismissed Igor, the leader of the townsfolk, with what almost verged on rudeness. There were no extra presents, no invitation to share in some of the casks of ale carried by the expedition, and even smiles seemed at a premium. Certainly the leader was not taken to the princess - although none of the Vikings realised she'd never even been introduced to Igor who'd merely seen a heavily-cloaked figure climb into the litter. Perhaps some of his men helping to carry the princess might have picked up some clues as to her identity; if so, Igor was well-enough disciplined to withhold any questioning till after the expedition and the townsfolk had parted.

So, just as evening drew on, the expedition set sail on the generous waters of the Dneiper.

*

The next day saw an easy day's sailing. A stiff breeze from the north meant, for once, there was no need even to place the oars in the rowlocks and the expedition's members were able to settle back and relax. Of course, idle hands gave way to idle thoughts.

"They do say the Pechenegs, or whatever you call them, take people off their boats and eat them alive," stated Egbert with the authority of an experienced traveller. His companions exchanged grins as they realised he'd obviously taken to heart the lies peddled in the backstreets of Holmgard. One or two winked at each other to indicate they'd been present when he'd swallowed such a ridiculous story.

Of course, it was true the Pechenegs took great delight in taking people's heads, but that was merely so they could measure their prowess against that of others. They were a warlike people, mounted on short-legged, tough ponies and principally armed with spears and, sometimes, bows. They loved presents which their khans accumulated as signs of status.

Yet, Ethelwulf knew it would be long before they encountered that people, who were almost confined to lands south of Kenugard.

Even so, in the area to the north of the principal city of the Rus there was good cause to be on one's guard. The name for the country, Gardarike, was well deserved as there were many Slavic tribes alternating between policies of peaceful trade, open warfare and brigandage with whoever travelled along the extensive river system. Now they were entering territory peopled by the Krivichians so he ordered careful watch to be kept by his men.

"I've heard," began Edwy, "the khan of the Pechenegs uses the skull of Svyatoslav, once Prince of Kenugard as a drinking vessel."

Before he could stop himself Ethelwulf was forced to add ,"That's undoubtedly true because writers have reported the Bulgar Khan used the skull of a Greek emperor hundreds of years ago in a similar fashion."

"How do you know this?" growled Thorkel Snub-Nose, always suspicious when anyone mentioned writers whom he regarded as the biggest peddlers of lies since the world began.

"I can't remember exactly," confessed Ethelwulf, embarrassed he'd been drawn into such a discussion, "but I think it was in the life of Charles the Great, Emperor of the Franks, by Einhard the Monk."[48]

Here the discussion ended as Sven the Far-Sighted spotted two riders some distance to the west of the river, who immediately turned and disappeared over the horizon. Perhaps if he'd had one of the Varangians from Holmgard in his boat Ethelwulf might have asked him to identify the riders. However, Oleg had made sure every one of his men was isolated from the Vikings as if unwilling to supply any information or comfort in a hostile land. Ethelwulf tried to remember to ask Oleg himself about the riders later at camp that evening. As it was he was content to gaze at the banks as they drifted past, with an occasional backward glance at the boats commanded by Gunnar and his twin cousins, fearing to go further into Gardarike without the comfort of knowing they were with him.

*

By the time they'd pitched camp in the evening and some of the men had caught enough fish to supplement the meagre rations supplied by Svyatoslav Svyatoslavich, Ethelwulf had forgotten all about the two riders, but Thorkel Snub-Nose, ever-ready to question authority hadn't.

"Who were the two riders watching us from a safe-distance this afternoon?"

With scant respect Thorkel hadn't directed his question but, as his sharp eyes settled on Oleg, clearly an answer was expected from the expedition leader.

After a slight hesitation the Varangian denied seeing any such riders. This, however, merely aroused murmurs from the men who, between themselves confirming such riders had appeared, had watched them for some time. Oleg realised that, as the appointed leader of the expedition, he couldn't deny keeping a good lookout; so he said the two riders must have been Mazovians probably put off from approaching the river by the strength of the expedition. Ethelwulf said nothing but couldn't recall the name of such a tribe as living anywhere near the river. He was sure he'd paid close attention to the traders who spent their lives travelling up and down the river -system. In his head he rehearsed the tribes they'd mentioned: to the south-east were the Viatchians and the Krivichians; alongside the Dneiper were the Polochanes and the Derevlians; between Kenugard and the great sea to the south were the Pechenegs. If the Mazovians existed they didn't live in this part of Gardarike.[49] Yet another mystery - was Oleg simply lying or was he mistaken? The Varangian leader had seen the two scouts, and if he couldn't recognise their tribe by the trappings they exhibited, Ethelwulf was certain others on the boat would have identified them.

Oleg retired to his accustomed position to the left of the tent in which the princess slept. In front of it lay the Varangians from Holmgard. They were on one side of the large fire; on the other, grouped around in a monstrous half-circle were the fifty Vikings who'd elected to come south. There were three guards on watch where the Vikings slept and one more - a Varangian at Oleg's insistence - to the north of the princess. These sentries would all be relieved halfway through the night. Ethelwulf was not happy at how the expedition had become two clearly demarcated groups; he was puzzled by Oleg's apparent suspicions of the Vikings but assumed there was a history of defections by similar war-bands and Oleg didn't want to fall a victim to such treachery. It had been too late to enquire about such matters once they'd left Holmgard, but he was determined to ask questions when they'd safely delivered the princess at Kenugard in three days' time. Even so, at first he found it hard to fall asleep but, in the end, nature overwhelmed his anxieties and he drifted into a dreamless slumber.

*

It was a strange feeling of being dragged up, as if out of a well, that woke Ethelwulf. With full consciousness he realised how there'd never been a well and yet he was still moving. Finally he was aware of two pairs of hands yanking him to his feet. It was still dark, well before dawn and he heard the apologetic whispering of Leofwine, the useful mariner from Cowes, who'd occasionally doubled for Edwy as helmsman of 'Alsvid'.

"Good! We were afraid you'd never awake." Leofwine paused as Ethelwulf stretched the muscles in his arms. Perhaps the Wight man was half-expecting some cursing because he hurriedly continued. "We squeezed your nose to wake you up…. And that was no good…… but Guthrum here reckoned we should force you to stand up and - "

"It's the sentry, Ethelwulf," interrupted Guthrum, in his excitement failing to emulate the whispers of his companion. Ethelwulf, by now fully awake, blinked to focus on what little he could see of the features of the Derbyshire Dane by the dying embers of the fire. "He's not there!"

"What do you mean?" snapped his leader, all too aware the sentry should have been Guthrum himself.

Guthrum could sense the irritation and understood all too clearly what was passing through Ethelwulf's mind. "No, no! It's not me….. It's one of the Varangians…. I should be seeing him now and again as he patrols….. but he hasn't turned up."

"And we don't think it's just that he's gone to sleep," interrupted

, " because the whole area over there's too quiet."

Ethelwulf stared in the direction of where he knew the tent would be, but the glow of the fire made whatever was there seem even blacker than normal. He strained his eyes as if somehow they could boost his ears but could hear nothing. However, he was all too aware of the slight pattern of sound coming from the Vikings. Admittedly there were more of them but there was the odd movement, the sleep-filled murmurs and the occasional snore which revealed men at rest. There was none of that from the other side of the fire.

The three warriors quickly crossed over the fire and instantly realised there were no sleepers between them and the tent. Suspecting the worst Ethelwulf strode up to the tent and roughly tore aside the entry flap. It was empty except for all the various accoutrements carried with them from Holmgard. At that moment Ethelwulf knew he and Morkere had skipped around the truth without actually bumping into it; Oleg had eloped with Princess Olga. Even as that started to fall into place his military brain started operating at high speed. Leofwine followed him into the tent but Guthrum stayed outside. Quickly Ethelwulf turned to Leofwine and whispered he wanted Guthrum to arouse all the men as quietly as possible and get them ready for a fight.

Leofwine looked as if he were about to question the need for silence so Ethelwulf whispered, "We've been betrayed by Oleg into the hands of the enemy. Even now they're expecting to take us by surprise so this is our only chance to catch them out!" Leofwine nodded and left the tent. Within moments Ethelwulf had the pleasure of hearing the camp quietly come to life. Anyone at a distance might have wondered why there was more noise than usual but not realised every warrior there was arming himself as rapidly and quietly as possible.

The flap was pushed aside and Edwine, closely followed by Gunnar, entered. Edwine briefly looked around the tent, scarcely making out anything but proving to himself the report was true.

"I want you, Edwine, to take twenty men, armed with bows, and place them well into the woodland. Not too far because as soon as we can we're going to slip away. Give each man a number (one or two) so we can withdraw in order." Edwine nodded; he remembered past practice of using numbers to get individual men to move differently. Each could handle any number up to ten, beyond that might cause confusion. As Edwine turned and left, merely acknowledging the orders with a curt nod, Ethelwulf turned to Gunnar. "I want you to organise another twenty men into loading the three vessels with our goods. Don't bother with the princess's craft - she won't be needing it! Leave all the rubbish in this tent, it should serve to distract whatever visitors will soon be upon us."

"I'm sorry, Ethelwulf," began the Gall-Gael in obvious confusion.

"What is there to be sorry about?"

"I should've known," confessed Gunnar. "For days I've been trying to work out what was wrong. I knew that bastard was up to no good but couldn't quite - "

"Whatever you missed, Gunnar," interrupted the Saxon, "so did Morkere and myself." He clapped the giant lightly on the shoulder, surprised even now how small he sometimes felt besides the warrior from Lochlann. "But that's in the past and now we've to make sure there's a future - so get those boats loaded!"

Gunnar grinned sheepishly and stumbled in his haste out of the tent. In many ways he felt guilty, remembering how he'd noticed the Varangian's reaction to the arrival of the princess but had said nothing. Was it because he feared the Saxons would have laughed at him, perhaps sneering at him as a hopeless romantic? No! Everyone knew any such feelings in his chest had perished with the death of Deirdre. In some ways he longed to be with her and yet his Norse blood told him there'd be no room for any woman in Valhalla - and that was where he intended to go after death! Now he furiously picked on the closest men, some still putting on the last of their military equipment, and with a mixture of gesture and whispered command got them carry the food and other supplies towards the boats. A few resented being dragged away from the prospect of a fight but if any expressed such feelings Gunnar brusquely replied the longer they took the sooner they'd get their chance to meet Odin! Others found assembling supplies in the dark was not the easiest of tasks and became convinced they were abandoning through ignorance as much as they were carrying to the boat. They persisted in the task but, although working as quietly as possible, even a deaf man might have realised the camp had come alive in the middle of the night.

However, by now Edwine had selected his twenty bowmen, giving each an odd or even number with a brief explanation, and cautiously advanced into the woodland. At any moment he expected to stumble across some enemy warrior and for the fight to begin. But the area remained as empty, and strangely hostile as ever. He made sure the men were no more than three yards apart, so any orders could be easily passed along, even if death created gaps in the line. He knew his task was to prevent the enemy, whoever they might be, sneaking up and taking the Vikings by surprise. Like Ethelwulf he reasoned any attack must come from the land side; the enemy must be one of the Slav tribes of the regions and they had little skill - or confidence - in boats. Edwine also expected the original plan would be an attack at dawn, with the enemy coming out of the rising sun and so adding to the effect of surprise. Now the enemy must have realised something had caused the Vikings to awake; this might upset their plans but he doubted if there were any tribes in this country who objected to fighting at night. Perhaps they'd take the sounds of movement behind him as being one of panic. That might mean they'd attack hurriedly - and charge straight into his bowmen. Edwine lightly fingered the flight-feathers of an arrow, hoping Oleg might one day be within range.

Meanwhile his twin reported to Ethelwulf and together they assembled a force of seven men to stop any attack penetrating the bowmen defences - that is, while the men were loading the boats.

"Where do you think Oleg and his princess have run off to?" asked Morkere while they were supervising the general activity.

"I don't think they've run off to anywhere," answered Ethelwulf with his brow furrowed in fury. "In this miserable country nobody on foot survives for long. No, they've had help and it's all been planned from the beginning."

"Which is why Oleg was so protective about our charges," responded his cousin. "Obviously he didn't want any of our men catching any word which might give their game away -"

"And he didn't want us to catch a glimpse of the princess in case we became too interested in her!" snarled Ethelwulf.

"Yes. It wasn't even the action of a jealous lover," sneered Morkere. "He merely wanted to make sure we didn't watch her too closely in case we got some idea of what was up."

"Quite," agreed Ethelwulf. "That also explains his confusion about the riders, the bastard! I'm surprised he wasn't giving them some kind of signal!"

"No," corrected Morkere. "That would have been too dangerous. But it explains the urgency that's been there - up till yesterday."

"Quite. He was working to a schedule right from the beginning." Then Ethelwulf paused, looking at the surrounding trees as if passing through them to the wide plains he'd been told were there. "He needed to get to this place by tonight, not before or after."

"So we have to be eliminated as witnesses!" chuckled Morkere. "I shall certainly enjoy shoving my spear down his throat when we catch up with him!"

"Yes, cousin," confirmed Ethelwulf with a quiet determination. "We'll survive this treachery and come back for our friend!"

The first light of dawn brought clearer knowledge of how affairs stood. Suddenly they were interrupted by a cry from the trees. At first they thought it was the sound of one of their men being wounded then they realised one of the bowmen had caught sight of the enemy, loosed a shaft, and in his enthusiasm at a hit had yelped in triumph. So now all idea of secrecy was gone and each side knew the other couldn't be caught out. There were war-cries from the enemy who seem to have dismounted to penetrate the woodland and attack the Vikings. These were answered by shouts of derision as the Vikings took the would-be ambushers by surprise.

Ethelwulf turned to see how Gunnar and his men were getting on and was pleased to see the vast bulk of supplies had been loaded. Gunnar ran up, anxious to get into any fight before it was too late. Ethelwulf smiled at such desire to put his awesome axe into action.

"I want you to select ten men like yourself, Gunnar, and place them in front of the boats, making sure they're guarded by shields. First make sure the boats are free of any obstacles and ready to leave instantly." He looked up into the eyes of the giant knowing further explanation was needed. "I'm going to withdraw to the boats as efficiently as possible but the enemy may have the chance to attack our rearguard, that's you, before we can cast off."

"And the shields?" questioned Gunnar who preferred to fight without shield and wielding his axe with both hands.

"At first they'll try to overcome you with arrows. When they see the boats about to go they'll run at you, abandoning any attempt to kill at a distance."

Gunnar grinned. That sounded more like his idea of a fight. He turned and began to put Ethelwulf's orders into operation.

Ethelwulf now turned to Morkere. "Give Gunnar time to get that lot ready and then I want you to make sure every other bowman pulls back to the boats." He paused as he looked at the boats already being secured to the bank by single ropes. "They can give Gunnar and his men cover from there."

Morkere smiled, once again pleased how useful his cousin's reading of authors such as Caesar[50], Frontinus[51] and Vegetius[52] had proved, even though much of it had been done in secret for fear of censure. He could see how quickly Gunnar was carrying out the orders and again wondered how the effective killer they'd first met in the hall of Padric O'Mara half-a-dozen years before had been transformed into an effective lieutenant. Then he considered himself and his twin and realised Ethelwulf had that effect on so many of them; without that drive and military skill they'd have all perished long ago as miserable exiles.

Judging the time was right Morkere crept to where the bowmen were holding back the enemy. As he wriggled up next to Edwin he could see the enemy had been forced to retire behind the trunks and undergrowth of the woodland. He quietly repeated their cousin's orders and slipped back to the boats. Edwine called across that at a single whistle every second man should retire stealthily and that, with a subsequent double whistle, the remainder should withdraw, confident no enemy could understand the pure Norse he used. Edwine found himself fascinated by the problem of trying to spot the enemy. He caught a brief glimpse of a bundle of furs which was only half-concealed behind a bush before remembering his job was to secure the steady withdrawal of the bowmen. He let out one long shrill whistle and was pleased to detect movement to his right showing the plan was being put into action.

It didn't take long for Edwine to ensure the retreat of nine bowmen back to the boats. As they arrived they reported to Morkere who realised one was missing The tenth man was Alfred of Chester and Morkere scurried over to where Alfred should have been positioned. He assumed the bowman had been wounded and was unable to retire. Morkere had no intention of leaving any man to the mercy of the enemy. However, Alfred was past any rescue; Morkere broke off the shaft in his throat with the vague idea feathering might indicate the origins of the enemy.

Once the nine men were in position Ethelwulf ordered Morkere to repeat the process with the remaining bowmen. Morkere placed fingers to his lips and sounded a double long blast. Immediately there was a reaction as the remaining bowmen started to retire. Now would be the most dangerous time as the enemy realised that whatever had been pinning them down had gone away. The men were just crossing what had been their camp when the enemy found that out. There was a loud whoop and sounds of a charge.

As the first warrior cleared the trees he fell with an arrow in his chest and his fellows immediately halted and instead started firing arrows at the retreating Vikings. In no time, and yet in what seemed hours, the last of the bowmen managed to clamber aboard the boats, although Sweyn of Narvik found an arrow piercing his right shoulder stopped him pulling a bow, and so was forced to slump down in the gunwales of the leading boat.

Arrows started raining down on the rearguard of Gunnar and even the Gall-Gael was pleased with the shield providing some protection. However, one man fell with a shaft in his leg and Morkere who'd remained on the bank seized hold of Osric and started dragging him through the water to safety. Just as the warrior was being hauled into the boat a second shaft pierced his back and rendered the whole exercise a waste of effort. Yet the dead body was hauled on board as too many of the Vikings believed in tales of cannibalism among the Slav tribes to leave such temptation behind.

At a shout from Ethelwulf the rearguard began to walk backwards towards the bank. This provoked uproar from the enemy who dropped their bows and charged out into the clearing in sheer frustration at losing their prey. Two warriors were shot down before they'd covered half the distance separating them from the rearguard but the remainder drew so close that Edwine ordered them to cease firing. Instead the men put their trust in cheering on their comrades as the rearguard clashed with the enemy.

Gunnar found himself confronted by a slim youth, sporting a grey fur-hat with a tassel and a vicious curved blade which he swung in the direction of the giant with little hope of success. Gunnar laughed and, reversing the blade of his axe, smashed it into the skull of the enemy. However, some instinct caused him to moderate the force of the blow at the last moment so that the youth, instead of being sent into the realm of the dead, merely lost consciousness. Even before the youth had fallen Gunnar reached forward, seized the lad and, in the same movement, threw his inert form over his shoulder. Then he turned and plunged into the water. By some miracle none of the arrows which still came from the trees struck him and he was able to throw the lad into the second boat before clambering in himself. At the same time the rest of the rearguard turned and headed for the boats. One, however, was cut down by a club before his legs had carried him halfway to safety. Another was pierced by two arrows but still, somehow, managed to reached the third vessel, to be dragged aboard more dead than alive.

Now the boats were driven by the bowman who'd become rowers to edge the vessels into mid-stream. Yet they might not have got away if the enemy, scarcely outnumbering the Vikings anyway, hadn't decided plunder left on shore was worth more than the risk of crossing the widening gulf to reach the Vikings. A few from the woodland still tried to reach the boat with arrows but the effect was nullified as the boats rapidly drew out of range. Somehow most of the Vikings installed themselves into customary rowing positions and the boats were propelled out of all danger. Only after the enemy had gone did Ethelwulf think it safe enough to raise a sail.

*

It proved a relatively easy passage to Kenugard which they reached in four days. By that time Wulfstan who'd been struck by two arrows as he was hauled into the boat had slipped into the stage more akin to death than life. It was hoped with luck he'd be able to recover by the end of the winter which was fast approaching.

Ethelwulf admired the obvious strength of the citadel but realised that should the Prince of Kenugard choose to punish the Vikings for the loss of a bride there'd be very little they could do.

Vladimir Svyatoslaviski was not a handsome man but had the air of a warrior. From his youth he'd been forced to battle - against his brothers, against his nobles and against the Slavs. Only earlier this year he'd swept aside the paganism of his youth by dramatically hurling two idols off the cliffs into the river. Then he'd turned on the priests, some he'd simply expelled to the welcome of the Slav tribes surrounding his capital, others he'd forcibly converted to the ways of the Christ-king, and a hard core he had simply killed. Like most selfish men, and experience had made the Prince of Kenugard a very selfish man, he wanted both the white and the black, the Christian and the Pagan, the West and the East. So he'd allied himself with the sister of the Emperor of the Greeks for the wealth of the Greeks and the power that could bring; yet he still maintained a harem, insisting how in many ways it was forced on him by the need to maintain alliances with his neighbours. He kept a tight grip on his realm by the skilful application of terror while worshipping in a newly dedicated church to the Prince of Peace.

As he entered the throne-room of this man Ethelwulf realised he was before perhaps the most powerful ruler he had met - Mael Sechlainn had exercised little control over the sub-kings and freemen of his Gaelic horde, Harald Bluetooth wielded power largely through the strength of his will, and when that slipped he'd been pushed aside by his son - or so he had heard. This man combined the ferocity of his Swedish forefathers with the barbarity of his Slav ancestry to erect a system giving him absolute control. So, if only for a brief moment, Ethelwulf felt afraid as he explained the loss of the princess to her prospective groom. He well knew Vladimir had been briefed some time ago about his prospective bride, and he could guess he'd been looking forward to her arrival.

"You say you were betrayed," growled the Prince and the steel of his blue eyes burned through Ethelwulf's head as if he could pierce the very truth however it had been encased inside the skull.

"Yes, my lord," replied Ethelwulf, trying to return stare for stare. "Oleg Askoldsson conspired to steal Princess Olga away -"

"You are sure he CONSPIRED?"

"Positive, my lord, although as a stranger to your realm, I wasn't sure of some of the practices - "

"Such as?"

"Not letting any of my men near our charges nor his personal escort." Ethelwulf paused as he noted the Prince shifted his head slightly so he could survey their audience - but whether or not to convey the idea of amazement at such stupidity he couldn't be sure. "Then he never let anyone see the Princess - "

"So how do you know she was ever there?"

"Because once his guard slipped and we could see - "

"So you tricked him in order to spy on a princess?"

"Because we already believed that, for some reason, he was going to cheat your majesty-"

"Which, naturally, you were determined to prevent!"

The sneering tone in the voice was unmistakable and aroused Ethelwulf's anger. He was already furious with Oleg's betrayal of the Vikings into the hands of savages. "I don't know how Varangians consider any burden of trust placed on them, but in England we consider it a matter of honour - "

"Yes, yes," interrupted the Prince, obviously unused to finding anger directed against himself. However, there appeared a touch of respect in the tone which hadn't been there before. "And you say that after this Oleg had spirited away my princess, you were attacked by a Slav war-band."

"Indeed, my lord," replied Ethelwulf, desperately trying to regain a calm composure and all-too-aware of having risked the fury of the Prince already. "Evidence suggests they were Radimichi - "

"What evidence?"

"The formation of the flight on one of the arrows - "

"Not distinctive enough!" snapped Prince Vladimir, anxious to recover the obvious superiority with which the interview had begun.

"Perhaps," replied Ethelwulf, struggling to remain calm, "but we have a ring whose seven-points - "

"That may be Viatchian," interrupted the Prince.

"- point downwards unlike the Viatchians which have axe-like shapes,"[53] continued Ethelwulf as if he'd never even heard the interruption. Prince Vladimir for a moment felt at a disadvantage and slumped back on his throne. "The ring came with a prisoner- "

"Has he been questioned?" asked the Lord of Kenugard, his interest re-fired by this new perspective. A prisoner could be used as a bargaining-counter, as well as supplying information about the dispositions and intentions of the Slavs. Only a few months ago the questioning of prisoners had enabled him to drive off an attack on his capital by the Pechenegs. If only his father hadn't so hammered the Khazars.[54] His mind was jerked back into reality by the next words of the Saxon.

"He's talked, my lord, revealing not only his own race but also the plans of Oleg -"

"Which are what?" demanded Prince Vladimir.

"More or less as I expected," replied Ethelwulf, suspecting he now had the chance to secure for himself what he most wanted, revenge on Oleg Askoldsson. He sensed the princely impatience and so continued. "Firstly, the traitors deserted on the eastern side of the river and so, unless they retire northwards towards Gnezdovo, they must retire towards the east. Secondly, because I believe the princess would like to return to Pskov one day - "

"If she dare!" snapped Prince Vladimir, glaring round at the onlookers as if challenging any of them to expect such defiance.

"Perhaps she's hoping your marriage will allow you to forget - " Ethelwulf stopped as he perceived an unwelcome glint appear in Vladimir's eyes. "and, anyway, Oleg has only bribed the Radimichi and to proceed further east would find himself among the Viatchians or Mordva, or even the Volga Bulgars."

"I see you've mastered the names of some of our neighbours, Westerner," stated Vladimir, anxious to indicate he wasn't impressed by a litany of the tribes to the east of the river Dneiper.

"No, my lord," said Ethelwulf, lowering his eyes so he could better consider how to frame his plea. "I've sought the best of advice because, if my lord will permit, my honour demands the victims of Oleg pursue him to recover the princess and wipe out the insult."

"So you'd travel as far as the Salt Sea, would you?" asked Prince Vladimir, intrigued by the offer.

"We trust it wouldn't be necessary," answered the Saxon. "Oleg will consider himself safe because either we've been destroyed or, in fear of your anger, have fled northwards." He noted a slight smile had flickered on Vladimir's lips. "The prisoner said Oleg will hide somewhere in the Sozh river area, not far from Gomiy - "[55]

"Which our armies ravaged this very year!" burst out Vladimir.

"Indeed, my lord" agreed Ethelwulf," and so an area with no love for the power of Kenugard - and excellent water-links with Pskov."

"So," murmured the Prince of Kenugard almost to himself. "you want my approval to track down this traitor and bring me his head."

"And your princess," smiled Ethelwulf.

"Naturally," returned the Prince, as if that was but an afterthought. "So how many men will you need?"

"I know my lord's force are now hammering the Pechenegs so I'd only need about one hundred "

"Too many!"

"Then eighty will do," replied Ethelwulf and then added, "provided I've command of the expedition."

"Agreed!" answered Prince Vladimir of Kenugard, anxious to involve himself in further liturgical developments in his capital. "But I'll need you, and all your men fit for war, to leave within one week."

"Agreed, my lord," said Ethelwulf with a smile and bowed, knowing he had secured what he wanted.

*

The size of the force didn't worry Ethelwulf; but how was he going to get anywhere near Gomiy without news of his approach becoming commonplace among the Radimichi. There was no problem until the Sozh joined the Dneiper; then he'd have to branch off and suspicions would start. He decided to let rumour do its work and spread the tale they'd be going up the Beshed to attack the Viatchians. Of course, the Beshed left the Sozh just before they reached Gomiy but it was just a question of timing. First he had to spread rumour quietly but effectively.

The force had been assembled in five days with the addition of the eighty men donated by Prince Vladimir being made up almost entirely by the contingent delivered from Holmgard a few months before. Morkere found malicious amusement in the idea that should the whole affair turn out a disaster widows and orphans would be howling their misery well away from Kenugard. The Prince had supplied them with four large boats and three guides - although all three had had more experience with the Viatchians than with the Radimichi. Supplies were taken on board, at a more generous level to buttress the rumour necessary for the expedition.

At last all was ready and the expedition left at night. The departure was low-key as possible, giving the impression the whole affair was being conducted undercover - but inefficiently! All this had been explained to Prince Vladimir when Ethelwulf outlined his proposed strategy. The Prince of Kenugard had insisted on only two demands: the head of Oleg Askoldsson and the live body of Princess Olga. Two of the boats would be placed under the command of Varangians from Holmgard - Ivar Straight-Back and Njal the Fatherless - to encourage the active participation of that detachment. In fact, the last two vessels would be manned only by Varangians with the Vikings confined to the first two boats under himself and his cousins. Although he didn't mention it to Prince Vladimir Ethelwulf was determined to encourage the active blending of both units as much as possible.

The first night and the following day seemed a very long haul because whatever wind existed was a northerly and so of little use; all four crews had to apply themselves vigorously to the oars. During the second night Ethelwulf called Ivar and Njal to the side and quietly explained that whatever they may have heard in ale-houses and the like was untrue; the target for the expedition was Oleg Askoldsson. Ethelwulf noticed this produced a reaction in Njal the Fatherless and asked why.

"Because we served together in the west, against the Polochanye," answered the tall warrior and the clearness in his brown eyes indicated it was merely memories of past-shared campaigns.

"And do you know why we are attacking Oleg?"

"Yes," was the quiet answer. "He betrayed the lord of Holmgard and HIS lord, Prince Vladimir, and so he's a double traitor."

"So what will you do if you should meet on the battlefield?" asked Ethelwulf, confident of the answer.

"Kill him!" was the blunt reply.

Ivar Straight-Back smiled broadly and then added that, as he'd never met Oleg Askoldsson, he had no thoughts about the matter.

Ethelwulf explained how for a night-time stop they should aim to reach a point just past where the rivers Sozh and Beshed met. Then they'd send a force across country to seize Oleg and the princess. He didn't mention where they expected to find the fugitives; after all, trust only went so far.

*

It had been all rowing up the Dneiper and by the time they reached the branch with the Sozh everyone, including Ethelwulf, had taken their turn with the oars and cursed. When the weather was pleasant, even without a wind necessary for sails, rowing was not too bad, unless it was at the driving force of pursuit or attack. However, every day as they'd rowed up the Dneiper a bitingly cold north wind had battered their faces and chilled the knuckles of their raw hands. Winter was coming early and with it a reduced chance of settling accounts with Oleg. Ethelwulf knew that while Oleg was hiding somewhere in the Gomiy area he'd no idea exactly where. His only 'plan' was to seize some locals and persuade them to reveal the whereabouts of the traitor. Not much of a 'plan' really.

At the branch with the Sozh matters started to improve. Four days rowing had helped blend the expedition into a unit. Ethelwulf had ensured the rowing period still allowed time for the warriors to practise and exercise together. He'd been delighted with how easily both Ivar Straight-Back and Njal the Fatherless fell in with his basic strategies. He'd split the expedition into six units of twenty men with the remainder being either commanders or helmsmen. Each of the units had been drilled together; he'd been tempted to blend the Vikings in with the Varangians but was unwilling to break up old loyalties. However. he did insist on the units not establishing themselves in different areas of the camp; he wanted none of the exclusiveness with which Oleg had first aroused his suspicions.

As the expedition turned into the Sozh the wind slightly shifted direction and became useful instead of a hindrance. It was a great relief to hoist sails and settle back rather than slave over oars. As his mind had the leisure to speculate Ethelwulf wondered if news of his supposed attack had reach the Viatchians. If so, would the tribe decide to strike first? If that happened, what would he do? Retreat without a doubt and leave the whole campaign in ruins. He had to deal with Oleg before the Viatchians could react. Of course, if the Radimichi concluded the expedition was directed against them, they might well interfere. Perhaps they might warn Oleg - and he was convinced the Radimichi had been corrupted by the traitor - or hustle him out of the expedition's reach. More likely they'd launch an attack against the expedition, claiming they were acting in self-defence, either before or after he'd dealt with Oleg. Whatever way he looked the prospects didn't look attractive, but then that had been true almost the whole time since he'd witnessed the murder of King Edward at Corfe ten years before.

As the vessels were borne by pleasant winds along the Sozh the men had the chance to bask in the chill sunlight, escaping the harsh toil over the oars which had dominated their lives since they'd left Kenugard. However, with each mile Ethelwulf's anxiety grew; he desperately needed better information about the whereabouts of Oleg - and the only way of getting that was to lay hands on locals and squeeze the news out of them. He reasoned the arrival of a group of Rus in the previous week couldn't have failed to attract attention. Frantically, as they entered the second day of their progress, he started to search the land they passed for any sign of settlement, knowing that nearby he might come across the isolated peasant from whom he could get the information needed.

At last, as the sun began to sink after they'd spent an afternoon on the Beshed, he spotted the long house surrounded by a strong palisade which indicated shelter for peasants in a dangerous countryside. As he sailed past he was sure everyone in the settlement had been expecting an expedition on the way to the territory of the Viatchians. He hoped that, once they'd passed the next bend in the river, they'd pass out of local gossip and interest. As the settlement disappeared behind them, Ethelwulf eased his boat towards the bank, allowing a group of ten warriors under Gunnar to jump ashore. When he ordered one of the guides, recruited for work among the Viatchians, to join them the man started to protest. Ethelwulf stilled his protest by saying that, like any careful commander, he needed intelligence of everything going on around him. It should have sounded reasonable to any scout but the man started to protest again so Ethelwulf simply turned his back. The guide was seized by two of the Vikings and ruthlessly thrown on to the bank. Before he could stagger to his feet the guide was presented with Gunnar's axe as a means of persuading him to stop his jabbering and simply obey orders.

*

Oleg hadn't been pleased to hear a rumour the Prince of Kenugard had launched an expedition against the Viatchians. He was puzzled because, though being based at Holmgard prevented an accurate picture of the strategy of Prince Vladimir, it seemed all wrong. Everyone knew that, for the last few years, the Prince had been turning his eyes and ambitions towards the land of the Greeks. In the way were the Pechenegs, especially the clan called the Charaboi.[56] They'd already attacked his capital once and could do so at any time. If Prince Vladimir decided to attack anyone it should have been the Pechenegs. Besides the expedition was heading in his direction and that made him uneasy.

He was unable to sleep and raised himself into a sitting position. He wondered whether he should move further east but looked at Princess Olga sleeping so peacefully by his side and dismissed such a plan. Besides he felt safe enough in this village; admittedly he'd have felt safer within the settlement of Gomiy itself, with its strong palisade and one hundred Radimichian warriors within call. For some reason Ogluk, the chieftain who counted Gomiy as his capital, had rejected that idea. He hadn't answered when Oleg had asked why but the Varangian feared Ogluk didn't want news of his sheltering a deserting Varangian to reach Prince Vladimir and so provoke an attack.

Oleg was sorry the Vikings hadn't been destroyed by the war-party. For some reason they'd been prepared for the attack when it came and managed to slip away. Ogluk hadn't been pleased at the outcome, losing expected profit from the battle, as well as a respectable tally of heads. In fact, the booty had been largely made up of the discarded possessions of Princess Olga and these Ogluk had refused to return. The Princess had demanded them back and her fury provoked laughter among the Radimichi. Oleg was asked how long Varangians had stood by and permitted their women to challenge warriors as if they were men. Oleg recognised the danger that, good humour evaporating, the Radimichi would decide it was all a question of strength to settle who should dictate terms, and his Varangians were vastly outnumbered. In fact, even more since Erik Knutsson had cut down a Radimichian husband who'd caught him in bed with his woman. The Varangian had fled yesterday rather than face the judgement of the tribe, certain they'd rule only his death. Oleg hoped the man would be quickly tracked down and dragged back by the three Radimichi runners who'd set off in pursuit. It had been very difficult making sure none of the slur spilled over on to himself and the other men.

The attitude of the Princess hadn't helped; Oleg had to admit that, with all her beauty and connections with power, Princess Olga was not the best of companions in such circumstances. She had an amazing contempt for the Radimichi and their ways; amazing because her blood was only partly Rus and she had so much in common with these people. Perhaps that was the reason. Oleg looked again at the young girl sleeping so peacefully beside him. Who would believe anyone with such a face filled with innocence would have the gall to challenge so vociferously the decision of a Slav chieftain surrounded by his own people. In some ways he admired her bravery but then realised it simply stemmed from senseless rage, one stage removed from the tantrum for which, at home, she'd have been beaten. Perhaps he should beat her himself, but he couldn't bear the thought of damaging the purity of that white flesh. He knew he loved her, and was sure his love was returned, but wondered whether such feelings could ever survive any return they might make to the more amenable lands of Pskov.

For Oleg knew his time among the Radimichi must be brief. Not that he particularly feared discovery by the lords he'd betrayed; Yaroslav was still a boy with enough worries staying alive and in nominal control of Holmgard, and Prince Vladimir had changed since assuming the faith of the Christ-god. However, Oleg knew that any day might bring another incident like yesterday and gradually his band of Varangians would melt away. And he knew he couldn't survive alone among savages.

*

Gunnar couldn't believe his luck. He'd set out to find a peasant to tell all he knew about the whereabouts of Oleg, and had found a Varangian. In the gloom of the dying day he'd come across a strange sight, a Varangian with his back against a tree defending himself against attack by two Slavs, while a third already lay still on the ground. Certainly they'd been hunting Varangians but he'd not expected to have one handed over to him so easily.

Naturally his men killed the Slavs without a second thought - after all it was no more than slaughtering a couple of blood-crazed wolves. However, the Varangian was a different case. For a long moment the man stood defiantly pointing his sword at the closest of the Vikings. Then all resistance had collapsed and the man had shrieked out.

"Brothers! Don't murder me! I am of your blood!"

At that Gunnar had stepped forward with a cold glint in his eye.

"Why then did you choose to murder your brothers?"

At this the identity of his rescuers cut into the Varangian for the first time. He turned his blade towards Gunnar and, even in the failing light recognised the giant-form of the Gall-Gael. Gunnar was pleased at how even among the wastes of this barbaric land he could still arouse terror.

"We were told to go!" protested the Varangian. "We'd no idea - "

"I don't believe you!" snapped Gunnar. Then he lowered his axe and added. "But you're a Varangian and don't deserve the death of a wild dog." He paused and calmly looked from side to side at his men who'd by now completely surrounded the defiant but terrified man. "Lower your weapons, men. I feel he has some news for us."

As the Vikings lowered heir swords and axes the stranger debated within himself what to do next. For a brief moment he stiffened as if to launch himself in a last attack and die bravely. Then he must have realised he'd be dead before he got within sword-reach of the Gall-Gael. Perishing in such a miserable country had never been his aim so Erik Knutsson lowered his sword.

"I can guide you to Oleg Askoldsson," was all he said. Gunnar laughed and greeted the warrior like a lost friend. Of course he didn't believe the man for an instant, certain every one of the Varangians had been picked by Oleg as being able to throw away any principle if the price was right. Even so the wretch had a part to play, for a time.

*

Ethelwulf hadn't been too impressed by Erik Knutsson. Once the man had agreed to betray his leader the fawning to his new masters was almost sickening. Ethelwulf began to doubt the judgement of Oleg if this was the type of Varangian he'd considered suitable to accompany him on his adventure. Although the man appeared to offer all manner of cooperation he still denied any prior knowledge of Oleg's treachery. The Varangian admitted (how could he not?) that every Varangian had known of the "attachment" formed between Oleg and the Princess Olga. When Ethelwulf queried the use of the word "attachment" Erik insisted it had been the Princess who'd done all the pursuing. Ethelwulf inwardly very much doubted that, and instantly was on his guard as to whatever the Varangian might reveal.

Erik insisted that only on that final night had he and his fellows discovered the intentions of the pair. They'd been ordered to retire quietly from the encampment, being promised ponies to carry them well out of the way of the Vikings.

"And what did you suppose was going to happen to us?" asked Morkere, a disbelieving smile already playing on his lips. The others, including the two leaders of the Varangians, strained forwards in anticipation of the answer.

"We were told that when you awoke you'd be unable to follow us because you neither knew the country nor would have the will to leave the river."

"And who provided the ponies?" asked Ivar Straight-Back, scratching the lump on his left shoulder which had given him his name. For anyone who'd known the Swede over the twenty years he had lived in Kenugard this was a particularly revealing gesture. Ivar's hump irritated him when emotion was about to erupt. Njal quickly took his friend aside, unwilling to endanger the cooperation of their prisoner by the hostility of Ivar. Both Varangians had been instructed by Prince Vladimir that not a single one of the deserting Varangians should live; their shame should be buried with them well away from Kenugard.

"They were left by some Radimichi," admitted Erik and then thought it prudent to add. "Three of the tribe were there with the horses when we emerged from the woodland."

Ethelwulf wanted to ask what Erik thought would have been the payment for the Radimichi but stopped himself. Although, like the others, he felt no trust for the man, the captured Varangian could still lead them to Oleg, Only that was important.

*

Erik Knutsson had no idea how he was going to get away but knew he had to. His one idea was to stay alive until he'd the chance to leave the Varangians to butcher each other - and then he'd be gone. He was certain not one of the men listening to his tale believed him; but he wouldn't have believed himself. Still by guiding this force to Oleg Askoldsson he might give himself the chance to escape. He'd toyed with the idea of leading the whole lot into some kind of ambush but had quickly understood, when he looked around at the men relaxing over their camp fires, this force outnumbered anything Oleg could muster together. Besides he owed nothing to Oleg - nor that bitch, Olga; neither of them had stood up for him and kept one of their own away from the head-hunters. No, let this bunch of butchers deal with Oleg and the savages and in the chaos he'd slip away to the west as he'd planned to do.

The expedition reached the outskirts of the village but Erik insisted they shouldn't close in until the last moment. There were at least three dogs which could raise the alarm, and he was sure there'd be probably about the same number of human guards. Erik proved most informative as they drew closer to the village; there'd be ten Varangians there and about three times that number of savages prepared to resist. He added the savages were brave enough but lacked the weapon skills to put up much of a fight. From his description it appeared Oleg occupied a long-house near the centre of the village. There were six other such buildings in the cluster. In answer to the question as to how they'd know which one was occupied by Oleg, the prisoner contemptuously replied, "Because that's the one the Varangians'll be pouring out from!"

Ethelwulf marshalled his force on the basis of the information given by their prisoner. Two units would attack from the west, two from the east and two more from the south. He didn't bother with the north because the prisoner said there were marshes in that direction which would be difficult to cross at night. Each unit would give a single owl-hoot when in position, when they heard a double hoot in reply they were to attack.

*

It seemed a very long time before Ethelwulf heard a single hoot from the east and another from the west which showed all units were in position. He gave a double-screech of an owl and began trotting towards the village. The warriors had been ordered to charge as quietly as possible but to try and reach the village before anybody could emerge from the huts.

Just before they charged Ivar slit the throat of their prisoner. After all his job had been done and they didn't want to lose him. Erik had just been deciding to slip away to the west when he was seized from behind. He had no chance to struggle and heard the words, "Enjoy Niflheim"[57] as the knife cut into his throat.

Before Ethelwulf had travelled thirty yards he heard a dog howling danger, the cry was instantly taken up by two more; all three seemed tethered. Even as he worked that out there was a yelp as one hound died. By now both sentinels had died as arrows gave the first signals of attack. Other men were streaming out from one particular long-house and it was towards that building that all three groups of attackers headed. Ethelwulf had given orders the Radimichi should only be attacked if they attempted to interfere and he was pleased to see that both few of the villagers tried to come to the aid of the Varangians and those halting as attackers swept past them were not the victims of assault.

The deserters, however, were overwhelmed. One died before he'd drawn his sword and two more were hacked down almost immediately. Now there was a cry from the rear of the building as one of the attackers spotted figures climbing out through a window to make their escape to the trees. This caused the main thrust of the attack to change direction and the three escaping deserters were pursued; they tried to make some kind of stand as they reached the trees but were cut down by at least twenty Varangians.

Now, for some reason as the battle was virtually over, the villagers decided to intervene and some of the Vikings were attacked from the rear by Radimichi. Two men died before they were even aware of the change in the structure of the fight. However, this battle didn't last long because the villagers or, at least, those intervening, were fiercely attacked on all sides. Within moments this struggle was over and with four dead and seven wounded the villagers decided the original fight had nothing to do with them.

Ethelwulf was afraid the blood lust of his men might drive them to launch a general attack on the villagers but was amazed at the discipline which governed the warriors. One Varangian who'd seized a Radimichian girl was struck down both by a villager and one of his fellows at the same time. Varangians charged into the long-house and there were sounds of fighting from within.

When Ethelwulf reached what had been the home of Oleg it was all over; five deserters lay on the ground, four were dead and one nursing a savage wound across his stomach. Njal the Fatherless, who entered immediately after Ethelwulf, calmly approached and plunged his sword through the warrior's throat. Ethelwulf stepped forward to protest and the voice of Ivar Straight-Back stopped him by declaring Prince Vladimir had ordered none of the deserters should be brought back alive.

Njal furiously threw himself towards one of the windows as it became clear that neither Oleg nor the princess were there. The two female slaves were found hiding in one corner behind what appeared to be discarded baskets. For a brief moment it appeared the Varangians believed the capture of Oleg would be just as simple and hurled themselves into every corner of the building offering the remotest possibility it might conceal a human.

Morkere, on the other hand, took different measures. Grabbing one of the female slaves by the throat he threatened to hand her over to the warriors unless she revealed what had happened to her mistress. The terrified girl immediately confessed that, for some reason, Oleg had been awake and immediately a dog had howled had awoken her mistress and headed for a door at the far end of the long-house. Morkere realised the upturned baskets sheltering the two women had also distracted them from noticing the door. Clearly the slaves, faithful to their mistress, had shut the door after the fugitives, upturned the baskets to disguise the exit and sheltered behind them. Morkere admired the quick thinking and loyalty of whoever was responsible and immediately placed both slave girls under the protection of Edwy and three other Vikings.

None of this solved the problem of Oleg, without whose capture the expedition would be deemed a failure. Ethelwulf, placing himself in front of the door, ordered none of the Varangians to leave the building. It took some time, and the active assistance of Halfdan the Tall blocking the main exit with his bulk, for these orders to be carried out. Then he explained that, if any of them rushed out in pursuit of the fugitives there'd be little chance of tracking them in the morning. Instead, he explained, they should try to patch up some kind of peace with the villagers, see to their wounded and make sure no deserter remained at large within the village itself.

Outside an angry crowd of Radimichi had started to gather. About thirty Varangians stood in front of the building, their weapons ready to resist the villagers. Ethelwulf emerged and appealed to Halfdan the Tall to bring the tumult of complaint, threat and protest to order. At the top of his voice the Varangian, who even overtopped Gunnar, shouted for silence. Even though few in the crowd could understand his words they'd no doubt about the meaning of the armed warriors and were all too aware of their essential weakness. Gradually, starting with parts of the crowd furthest from the danger itself, the noise began to subside. At last Ethelwulf felt he could begin so he called Vagz to his side and the guide shambled over, somewhat reluctantly because his mixed parentage (Varangian and Radimichi) made his position a ready focus for criticism. However, he appreciated the need for an interpreter as Ethelwulf loudly called for the Head of the Village to step forward.

After some murmuring among the crowd, perhaps fearful an example was about to be made, the leading ranks gave way to reveal a short, broad-shouldered individual whose bulk and heavily rounded eye-brows gave the impression of both stolidity and stupidity; they also indicated an absence of guile. He looked like a man with whom the expedition could do business.

Ethelwulf began by explaining he was sorry he'd been forced to enter their village in search of a criminal and the escaping wife of the Prince of Kenugard. At this the chieftain, introducing himself as Pzmelka, declared the deserters had declared the woman was simply the lover of their leader who'd been accused unjustly of stealing the silver of Prince Vladimir. They'd been told the silver was part of the settlement the Radimichi had been forced to pay two years before. Pzmelka added that even though the man may have been a thief, the villagers didn't believe they could turn away someone accused of stealing what had been stolen from their people in the first place.

There'd been protest at this from Njal who insisted the settlement had been a fair one, levied on the Radimichi after one of their warbands had swept down and sacked a trading station on the Dneiper set up by Prince Vladimir five years before for the benefit of all. Ethelwulf insisted the origin of the supposed crime of the traitor was unimportant but, he told the whole village in clear tones, whatever Oleg had told them was a lie. He'd seduced the wife of Prince Vladimir, persuading her to desert her family and the duties of consort, and had then betrayed his fellows into the hands of the Pechenegs to conceal his escape.

Here were loud grunts and whines among the villagers and Ethelwulf wondered whether he'd gone too far. He was certain, from what Pzmelka had said, that no warrior from this village had been part of the force on the Dneiper; he also guessed Oleg had told them nothing of the attack. The reaction of the crowd showed both these surmises were correct, and also that the Pechenegs were both feared and hated by these villagers; if they raided the possessions of the Rus it was certain they'd show no respect for the property of their neighbours.

Pzmelka confessed all this was news to his people but still denounced the violence inflicted on his village. Ethelwulf apologised, insisting his men had tried to avoid injury either to the villagers or their property; he appealed to the villagers to recall how his men had first passed through them to attack only the deserters. There was a murmur of agreement about this and Ethelwulf followed up with an offer of compensation for any damage done to the village or its population. Njal almost protested at that but Morkere drowned him out by insisting that without such compensation they'd be unlikely to get away safely; beside, he added, the villagers can't expect us to pay up here and now. Njal nodded, understanding the strategy, just as Ethelwulf was promising Prince Vladimir would hear how the village had been caught up, through no fault of their own, in this apprehension of criminals and so would be most generous in compensation. He added that, of course, he'd need complete details of any damage to people or property to take back to Prince Vladimir.

At this there was further murmuring as villagers discussed among themselves whether they should accept such future compensation - and how much it should be. Ethelwulf managed to keep his features immobile as he'd no idea how Prince Vladimir would react to any promise given in his name. The chief point was that, if this ploy worked, he and his men could pursue the fugitives in safety.

Pzmelka thought compensation an excellent idea - perhaps because he reckoned that in any fight the villagers would end up on the losing side. Naturally he was unsure how far any promises this Varangian made would be honoured, but he had no alternative. So the matter was settled; both sides would restore order, look after the wounded, bury the dead and generally await the light of day.

*

Ethelwulf was delighted with how clearly the tracks of the fugitives were revealed in the morning; what was more he and his men had been able to rest and buy food from the villagers. For drink they'd been forced to make do with water, as ale might have led to the ruin of relations with the villagers. Close to the long-house, of course, the ground was in turmoil. It had rained the previous day and the rich mud was excellent in showing up how, in some cases, the attackers had savagely hunted down resistance and the defenders sold their lives as dearly as possible. Not that the losses had been enormous; four men had been killed and three seriously wounded, the other injuries were merely scratches which some of the Varangians had, at first, tried to exaggerate in hope of anyone promising compensation. However, they discovered the face of generosity displayed to some was not that shown to malingerers or those distorting injuries for the sake of gain; offenders found there was plenty of unwelcome work, making good damaged property and disposing of the dead, for those who attracted the displeasure of their leader.

Traces of the flight of two individuals had been discovered, leading into the woodland and these were followed by Ethelwulf himself and a patrol of twenty men. They moved with every attempt at silence, using signals rather than words to avoid alarming their prey - should they be close at hand.

But it quickly became apparent that terror had guided the fugitives towards the more difficult terrain to the north-east of the village. Ethelwulf considered using the villagers in hunting down the fugitives but rejected the idea as possibly too inconvenient as they approached Oleg and the Princess; after all, he had his orders.

*

Back in the village Ivar Straight-Back tried to form some kind of understanding with the chieftain, Pzmelka. Naturally it proved difficult as any communication had to pass through the lips of an originally-reluctant Vagz. Even so, Ivar persisted, partly because he realised trouble could still erupt, especially if Radimichi from other villages should appear upon the scene, and partly from the need for something to do.

Indeed strangers did suddenly appear within the village and the Varangians became alarmed. However, Pzmelka quickly indicted the Varangians were there only to hunt down traitors from among their own kind. One of the strangers had been told Radimichi had been killed the previous night and Pzmeka admitted this was true. However, he added it had all been done in ignorance and he'd already received an offer of generous compensation. At this another of the strangers seemed about to demand some form of payment for himself, whereupon Ivar stepped forward, holding his axe as if ready to strike off anyone's head. He loudly declared that, while Prince Vladimir could be generous with compensation, there'd be another response to any demanding what was not rightfully theirs. Vagz had problems controlling his voice when he translated these words to the strangers but the strain disappeared when they seemed to have the desired effect. The strangers shrugged their shoulders and, encouraged by Pzmeka, replied that any business done between the Varangians and the villagers was their own affair. With that almost as quickly as they'd come they disappeared. Ivar followed them with suspicious eyes. He doubted if that was the last they'd see of them, convinced that, whenever Ethelwulf returned, they'd have to fight their way back to the Dneiper.

*

Gradually the trees became wider spaced and the ground, unfortunately, harder so the easy trail near the village became one where a few traces led to nothing and the trackers, namely four Varangians with wide experience as hunters in the wilds of Gardarike, had to cast around repeatedly to pick up the trail again. Even so, the pursuit continued and the hunters grew near a rocky area which promised to offer shelter to the fugitives. For Ethelwulf reasoned that, however fit Oleg was, he'd be burdened by the princess; after the initial energy given by terror, tiredness and anxiety would take their toll. As neither fugitive could be properly dressed for journeying in the wilderness, the strength of the Princess Olga must dissipate. Ethelwulf was sure Oleg never would abandon his lover to save himself; the princess was his weakness.

By now the hunters had left behind virtually any vestige of the woodland and entered what appeared to be the foothills of higher land. Traces became fewer but Ethelwulf still insisted on silence as far as possible. The main party would hang back until a tracker picked up the trail and signalled them to approach. At last, tracks in a small patch of mud produced by water trickling down from a steep hill, appeared to lead into the entrance to a cave. Ethelwulf had no idea of the cave's size but he did know entering such a confined space might give Oleg the chance to inflict damage on his pursuers, and the treacherous Varangian had already caused him to lose enough men. He reasoned the lovers, if in the cave, must have been in there for some time, probably without food or water, and he doubted if either could have rested, waiting for the sounds of pursuit they knew must come.

Silently Ethelwulf signalled his men to retire from the cave entrance so he could give them orders. While one man watched over the entrance, the rest retreated to where human voice couldn't carry to the fugitives. Ethelwulf explained he wanted four men to conceal themselves around the cave entrance in absolute silence, two more were to stay below to prevent any escape back to the village. The rest should approach the cave entrance with the noise of hunters beginning to tire of the chase. They were not to stop at the entrance but continue along what appeared to be the well-used track passing further around the hill. The fugitives should hear them pass by and wait until they were sure the pursuit had passed out of sight or hearing. Then they'd emerge in order to slip away in another direction. Anticipating questions he added that, if the cave was small, they couldn't be comfortable, and they were certainly hungry. Also if they believed the pursuit was tiring they might believe it would soon abandon the chase and return to the village, possibly spotting the cave on its return. Of course, he added the 'cave' might actually be a tunnel through to the other side of the hill and the fugitives would escape; in that case, all their heads might be forfeit. Nobody disagreed.

Njal and three other men crept up to the cave, concealing themselves on either side of its entrance, far enough back not to be immediately seen by anyone emerging from such a hiding place.

Now Ethelwulf led the rest of the party up towards the cave; as they moved they deliberately straggled out so their leader felt it necessary to order them to close up. Those at the rear were panting heavily as they passed the cave entrance, without giving any sign they'd seen it. They passed further along the path for a short while and then stopped. Slowly and carefully they began to return to the cave.

*

Oleg had thanked Verdandi[58] for bringing them to such a hiding place, especially as, for the last mile, he'd been carrying his lover. With dawn her weakness had forced him to pick her up, knowing he must leave traces but hoping the increased rockiness of the terrain would make it impossible for them to be followed. Only sheer chance had shown him the entrance, low down and sheltered from the weather by an outcrop of rock. His back had felt near breaking as he'd eased himself and his burden through its restricted entrance because Olga had been unable to enter by herself.

She'd been exhausted, worn-out firstly by the alarm of being awoken in the middle of the night and then bustled out of the long-house, even before hearing the sounds of battle. Then as they ran for the trees he'd seen men on both sides of them moving swiftly towards the house they'd just abandoned. By some miracle they hadn't been spotted, probably because the attackers were too intent on overcoming his men who, half-asleep, staggered out of the long-house to their deaths. He hadn't dared look back, afraid one glimpse might cause him to abandon his lover and head back to die with his men. So they'd kept running, hand-in-hand, until first the trees and then distance hid them from the sounds of the fight. He never considered stopping and hiding, knowing all too easily they might be discovered. He knew night gave them concealment, hoping that somehow they might reach the river where a boat might carry them to safety. Then, with horror, he'd realised the ground was rising as they left behind the trees and so they must be heading away from the river. For a moment Oleg almost despaired but hoped somewhere they must come across Radimichi to take them to safety, perhaps at Gomiy. He knew Ugluk wouldn't welcome them, the Radimichian chieftain wouldn't dare hand them over for fear of his role in he attack being revealed. He might seal Oleg's lips permanently but the Varangian doubted the Radimichi would waste such an asset as the princess; at the worst she'd end up in the harem of some Emir to the south, but at least stay alive.

So Oleg had reasoned as they steadily climbed away from the trees. Only when his lover had stumbled had he realised they weren't going to escape that easily. They had to find somewhere to hide, hoping the Varangians would go back to their master with the false report of the deaths of himself and the princess. After all, why put themselves at continuous risk among savages in order to hunt down one of their own? Far easier to give up and go home.

Soon he'd been forced to carry Olga virtually every step of the way until stumbling upon this cave. Unfortunately they had no food, water or fire – and the cave proved to be very small. After he'd laid his lover gently down in its deepest recess he'd discovered that, apart from its narrow, winding entry passage, there was no room to spare. Oleg rested his back against the cave's wall and waited, knowing he could kill any warrior who intruded on their hiding place.

But nobody came and time went by. With it came hunger and hope. Oleg looked down at his lover, his eyes penetrating the gloom of their shelter to catch a glimpse of her face, and remembered how they'd realised their love even as he'd been ordered to carry her south to Prince Vladimir. At first they'd considered fleeing then and there, but realised there was very little chance of escape as long as they left a trail. So he'd determined to destroy that trail by pretending their deaths and, in achieving that, rid Holmgard of the Vikings who'd just stumbled in on their realm. Most of them had no right to be there. As Westerners they'd little idea of the manners and customs of the Rus. Perhaps they could be induced to pass into the realm of the Greeks, but probably not before they'd excited trouble within Gadarike. By being dupes in his plan, they fulfilled a purpose before being cleansed from his homeland. He'd been surprised how easy it was to contact Ugluk; one of his Varangians had married a Radimichian whore who turned out to be the chieftain's cousin. He'd promised the savages booty and the pleasure of destroying strangers from the North and the whole incident on the Dneiper had been arranged. A pity the Westerner and his followers had escaped.

Suddenly his ears detected sounds of humans outside. Somebody was trudging along the path and was not alone. Oleg glanced at his sleeping lover, drew his sword and prepared to defend their shelter. Whoever was outside passed the cave entrance without stopping and then suddenly came to a halt. Oleg tensed ready for a cry of discovery as other steps approached and passed the entrance. Then a voice called out. Despite himself Oleg moved closer to the passage, ready for whoever would try to enter. But nobody came near and the footsteps trudged by, slipping over the loose stones; he could hear the heavy breathing of some of the party as they hurried to keep up with the leader. At last the footsteps passed away into the distance and the silence which returned was even quieter than before.

Oleg knew that very soon, all too soon, the pursuers would abandon their march, turn and traipse back to the village. Perhaps they'd take greater care searching the trail as they returned and stumble across the cave entrance. Who knows where they might choose to pause, unwilling to return to the village without their prize? No, they'd be keen to leave the territory of the Radimichi and return to the welcome rivers carrying them back to Kenugard. Of course, they'd tell Prince Vladimir that he and the Princess had perished, carrying with them the heads of dead Varangians to show they'd caught up with the fugitives. What if the Prince asked for more details of the deaths of himself and his intended bride? Oleg considered there were a hundred ways to explain the absence of head or body; the fugitives had drowned and their bodies lost, they'd been burned in a fire breaking out during the attack, the Varangians had been attacked by savages and in the battle lost the evidence. He was sure any Varangian could spin out such a story to satisfy their lord. He was surprised Prince Vladimir had acted so promptly to hunt them down, but very soon they'd be forgotten as he turned to the exigencies of ruling Kenugard. Surely no Varangian captain, after making a decent attempt to hunt them down, would continue with a hopeless task. He decided to awake the princess and wait until he could be certain the pursuers were some distance away. Then they'd creep out from their shelter and carefully make their way to somewhere distant from this trail.

*

Svyatoslav detected a movement from deep within the cave and nudged his companion, Olaf. So the Westerner had been right; their quarry had sought refuge there. He wanted to signal the four men waiting silently, with a patience trained by years of hunting in the wild, on either side of the entrance. A warning he knew would be unnecessary but his mind, perhaps his pride, insisted he should call out. Suddenly Olaf lightly touched his shoulder and Svyatoslav realised his companion had sensed his tension and what could have been the consequences. A single finger paused at Olaf's lips to recommend silence.

The movement turned into a shape, vague in the darkness, and then into the figure of a man. The head and shoulders of Oleg emerged from the entrance. Now was the time to strike thought Svyatoslav but the hunters made no move. Had they heard or seen the fugitive? He was sure Oleg was still out of their field of vision - but then he'd was unable to see his comrades. Now Oleg rose awkwardly to his feet, using his sword as support for cramped limbs. He stepped forward to make way for another figure to scramble into view. Even from that distance Svyatoslav could appreciate the beauty of Princess Olga.

Just as she was straightening up from her crouched position Oleg seemed to sense danger. He'd been concentrating on whatever had passed along the trail, probably straining his ears to detect any sound of return. Now he sensed the closeness of a living creature and, stepping out to challenge whatever was there, came eye to eye with one of the hunters. Both Varangians made to charge at each other but even as Oleg moved behind him appeared two hunters. As if acting with planned co-ordination one leaped forward to grab the woman even as she screamed a warning, while his companion charged at Oleg from behind. The Varangian deserter, taken by surprise, tried to check his initial charge to turn and meet this new challenge but was too late. The new assailant's axe collided with Oleg's head and, despite the round helm which offered some protection, felled their quarry.

The woman's screeches had obviously reached the main body because Svyatoslav heard running feet as he and Olaf broke cover and ran to help. Indeed, aid was completely unnecessary as, after a bout of hopeless struggle and screams, the princess had fainted while Oleg lay prone on the ground. Thorkel, who'd struck him down, anxiously bent to examine the fallen captain, muttering he'd reversed his axe as advised by their commander. However, Oleg was merely unconscious and not dead. By the time Ethelwulf and the main party arrived his consciousness had returned and he was blinking up at the sky.

*

Ethelwulf looked at Oleg as the Varangian was dragged to his feet and his hands tightly bound behind his back. The coldness in his gaze outmatched the chill of the morning. "So, Oleg, we meet again," was all he said but the Varangian's mouth dropped open in surprise. Obviously he'd never believed Ethelwulf would either have sought or received the chance to hunt him down. "I can see you're lost for words," continued Ethelwulf, glancing towards the figure of the princess who, coming back to reality and recognising the Westerners, began struggling and screaming with renewed vigour.

Morkere interrupted. "Shut that bitch up!" he yelled and Thorstein clapped his hand over the mouth of the princess. Even as he did so he wondered whether violence towards a princess was the wisest thing to do. At least they were no longer distracted by the screams of a demented captive.

"Perhaps, Oleg, I should remind you of Alfred. Osric, Sweyn and Toste; but then they'd mean nothing to you now as they meant nothing to you when we were abandoned to the savages!" There was a venom in the words which the Vikings hadn't seen for some time and, to the Varangians, matched anything of which Prince Vladimir was capable. Oleg hung his head and refused to answer. Let this Westerner carry him back to face the Lord of Kenugard and whatever death awaited him. Perhaps he'd kill him on the spot, to save the bother of watching over him on the journey back to the Prince. In fact, Oleg had no intention of running away and leaving the princess to face the rage of Prince Vladimir so Ethelwulf need not be worried. He accepted the rage of the Westerner and was quite ready for torture; perhaps they might inflict on him the blood eagle.[59] So what? He could still find his way to Valhalla[60] and join the feasting and fighting there until the last call to Ragnarok.

Ethelwulf sensed what was passing through the mind of his prisoner and his eyes passed over the slumped head of Oleg towards a solitary tree; he nodded towards Edwy who quietly detached himself from the group.

There was a long pause as if Ethelwulf had used up all the venom he possessed and expected some response from his captive. Oleg was determined to say nothing, certainly not beg for mercy or even explain himself to this intruder into his land.

Suddenly Ethelwulf spoke in a voice more dead than alive, "Good, we're ready. Edred and Harold, take him!" At that Edred, who'd chosen to follow Ethelwulf in Finland rather than continue with Thorgrim the Short, and Harold of Furzebrook seized the Varangian captain from the men who held him and started dragging him backwards away from the main group. At first Oleg hadn't been prepared to struggle but as he twisted his neck and saw what awaited him he both screamed in anguish and used what strength remained in his body to resist the progress of his new guards. Twenty yards away loomed, in marked contrast to the harsh light of the late morning, a single tree and from it hung a noose.

The eyes of the princess followed those of the party and she bit into the hand of Thorstein so that it dropped from her mouth and she screamed. The sound of her horror momentarily dragged the attention of Oleg aware from the doom awaiting him and he tried to yell out some comfort to his lover but the words wouldn't come.

Suddenly his throat had gone dry and all he could summon up was a croak as they drew to the tree.

Ethelwulf smiled as he noted how the tree stood immediately in front of a pile of boulders. "Why nature seems to have provided you with a platform to leave this world," he remarked to Oleg.

The Varangian found himself begging to be spared such a death, reserved for slaves and captives who'd be denied entry into the Hall of Valhalla. He didn't fear death itself, confident he'd merited a place in the ranks of the warriors of Odin, but he dreaded the eternal night of Niflheim, reserved for cowards and those who failed to die like a warrior. So, despite all his resolutions when first confronted by the hated Westerner, he pleaded for a kinder death.

Thorstein, unable to still the screams of the princess, had knocked her senseless. Several of the pursuers, notably Varangians who'd not suffered from the treachery of Oleg, were standing back in horror, unwilling to intervene and yet unable to take part. Even Njal the Fatherless became rooted to the spot, his legs denied of any power to carry him to the dreaded tree so reminiscent of what he'd seen in his youth at Uppsala.

Ethelwulf had tired of he pleading of his captive and gave instructions to Edred and Harold to put him in place in whatever way they chose as the Varangian refused to face death with the courage of his race. Harold viciously struck Oleg a single blow which so stunned the Varangian that two Varangians, with the active assistance of Edwine and Edwy were able to half-lift and half-carry their victim to the top of the boulders. Oleg came back to consciousness as he felt the noose descend on his shoulders and be tightened by Edred. He started again to beg for mercy.

"Cut that wailing short!" snapped Ethelwulf and Edred pushed the Varangian captain into space so that he dangled at the end of the rope. For several moments his legs stumbled in mid air, as if trying to run away from fate and then suddenly his whole body went still.

"Is he dead?" was the curt question to Edred and was answered with a nod. "Then cut him down!" Ethelwulf was obeyed instantly and the corpse, once the pride of Holmgard, toppled down at his feet. Ethelwulf examined the dead features, twisted in the final agonised attempt at breath, and spoke quietly, "Gunnar, we have need of your skills."

Without a word, Gunnar stepped forward and swung his axe. The head of Oleg Askoldsson flew smartly from his body, rolling down the slope away from Ethelwulf.

"Pick it up, Gunnar!" ordered Ethelwulf. "We must take it to the Lord of Kenugard." The Gall-Gael grabbed their trophy and the whole party prepared to return to the village.

*

The Radimichi remained hostile but subservient as the war-party made their preparations to depart. By now Princess Olga had recovered consciousness and would have tried to summon the Slavs to her aid if she'd known her lover still lived. In his absence she assumed he was still dangling from a tree by their shelter and willingly drifted away from unwelcome reality.

The return to the boats was unremarkable although the journey back along the rivers to the Dneiper was tense as all knew accounts of their attack on the village must have circulated among the Radimichi. Particularly anxious was Ivar as he remembered the savage look he'd been given by one of the strangers when they departed from the village. He was sure that somewhere away from the rivers the Radimichi were trying to collect together warriors for an attack on the boats, confident they could squeeze silver out of the Prince of Kenugard if they managed to seize any of his followers. Perhaps Ethelwulf had been too generous in promising what he had no authority to offer, encouraging the greed of a savage people. Yet it had appeared a good idea and had certainly saved lives. Ivar searched the banks for any indication of Radimichi scouts. At any moment the boats could come under attack from a vengeful people. Nothing happened and even nature seemed supportive as the breeze gently drove their sails towards safety.

Yet the Dneiper didn't bring security, merely the greater confidence which comes with familiarity, if only for the Varangians. Princess Olga remained obstinately silent, confident she could explain her flight as one being forced and so secure the forgiveness of the Lord of Kenugard. She ate sparingly and accepted with scant grace the various considerations with which her captors tried to ease her situation. The two slaves captured at the village had immediately been returned to her side; encouraged by their ministrations the princess prepared for her arrival at Kenugard. Yet nothing the two slaves could do removed the misery which marred her features as the boats made their way steadily down the Dneiper, still assisted by considerate winds. Occasionally she'd look at Ethelwulf and none could interpret what thoughts passed within her head; at other times, she'd turn to look back up the river. Perhaps she was remembering her dead lover; if so, nobody could be sure as she never mentioned his name.

The Varangians themselves seemed happy enough. They'd penetrated the realm of the Radimichi and were going back home in triumph. None was happier that Njal the Fatherless as he clutched the bag containing the head of Oleg Askoldsson. Although he never attempted to show it to anyone when they all camped together at night, it was certain the princess learned of its contents. Njal, along with Ivar Straight-Back, had accepted somewhat unwillingly the commission to destroy the deserting Varangians and recover the Prince's possessions; now they would be reporting success bought at small price. Surely Prince Vladimir would be generous.

Njal looked ahead at the boat which contained Ethelwulf and found himself less certain of the welcome awaiting the Westerner. For himself he liked the Saxon who'd shown himself both brave and resourceful. Yet he knew whatever treatment the successful leader received depended on how the Prince received his bride. He knew Princess Olga wouldn't easily forget the death of her lover. Personally he felt Ethelwulf had been unnecessarily cruel, a speedy thrust from a sword would have been far more acceptable than the horror of a hanging. Of course, he'd not suffered from the Oleg's treachery; if he had been such a victim he'd certainly have provided the offender with a gruesome death.

That night as the fire died down the cousins were grouped together, sharing the last welcome warmth thrown out in defiance of the night's cold. Certainly the expedition had been successful; revenge had been secured and the Prince of Kenugard was going to receive both the heads of traitors and his runaway bride. They should be happy and yet they'd long before discovered nothing in this world was certain.

"What shall we do now, cousin?" asked Morkere as he noted the thoughtful look on the face of Ethelwulf. There was no reply but merely the lifting of an eyebrow which doubted any alternatives were possible. The Vikings were deep in the land of Rus, unable to return north without surety of pursuit back into the hatred of the Ladogans; on the other hand, the south meant the unknown and possibly an even more unwelcome fate. None of them could answer such a question about the future. Silently they gazed into the fire until all heat had slipped away and they snuggled down beneath furs for the night.

Of course nothing can last for ever. As they neared Kenugard they noted how the features of the princess began to lighten, as if shuffling off unattractive memories and preparing herself for her new role as the bride of a great prince.

"I wonder what will be our welcome when we bring this beautiful bride to Prince Vladimir," muttered Morkere almost to himself; but his remark caused Ethelwulf and Edwine to exchange glances.

*

The Wanderer 7:3

"Then possessing judgement's power;
Each man will judge as he deserves
For how he lived this too-brief life."
('The Dream of the Rood'[61])

Spreading the Gospel

Prince Vladimir was delighted with the heads the expedition surrendered. At first there was a twitch of resentment on his lips, clearly visible beneath the flowing beard, only recently flecked with grey, when he heard of what had been promised in compensation by Ethelwulf. But then he was advised such gestures might well bind Slavs living on the edge of his realm, making it more difficult for more hostile savages effectively to challenge his power.

When the princess was brought into his presence what had been delight was transformed into ecstasy. Whatever change had been produced in the personality of the Lord of Kenugard by his conversion hadn't affected his love of a beautiful face nor his lust for the female form. Clearly Princess Olga set out to seduce the Prince, employing a costume to show off her limbs while her features had been treated with the care bestowed on the members of the harem in distant Baghdad. Her efforts proved an instant success and from that moment Prince Vladimir was captivated. He shrugged aside her pleas that she'd been forced into flight by the wicked Oleg as if there was no need to justify what was obviously true; after all, God had intended her to be his bride.

This was bad news for Ethelwulf or other Vikings who'd chosen to enter the service of Prince Vladimir. Although the princess never betrayed any enmity towards them, nobody who'd tracked down her lover could believe she'd forgotten or forgiven. They remembered her distraught behaviour when Oleg had been hanged and were not surprised when, four months later, Ethelwulf was summoned into the presence of Prince Vladimir. From the start the Prince appeared unfriendly and Ethelwulf instantly suspected the princess had been poisoning the mind of his lord. He tried to spot her, certain from somewhere very close she'd be enjoying the interview, savouring in anticipation the supposed guilt which would wrack Ethelwulf's mind. From the first question he knew his suspicions were well-founded.

"So what happened to the traitor, Ethelwulf, when you caught him?"

Ethelwulf decided only truth would do, but he too could play at the game of tension.

"He was executed as you ordered, my lord." Ethelwulf wanted to ensure the princess, if eavesdropping, would be forced to recognise the Prince whose bed she now shared had ordered the death of her lover. He could see Prince Vladimir was unhappy with his reply and knew the interview was being spied upon.

"Yes, yes," agreed the Prince of Kenugard, anxious to shrug aside whatever personal responsibility he may have possessed. "But how exactly did he die?" He glared at his officer, making sure the man knew his Prince had been told about the death and so any attempt at lying would earn the severest punishment.

"He was hanged, my lord." Ethelwulf tried to reply in as casual a way as possible but he knew the Varangians, like their Northern cousins, viewed hanging as the most shameful of deaths. Of course ideas were different in the West but, as he had to recognise every day, he was not in the West now.

"Hanged?" There was a mixture of incredulity and anger in the tone. Ethelwulf knew the princess had enjoyed telling the Prince about the death of her lover, especially when, for obvious reasons, the full details hadn't been given in the official report.

"Yes, my lord," replied Ethelwulf and then the fury at the Varangian's treachery which could have so easily led to the destruction of his own force, broke out. "Like the treacherous dog he was!" Was that a gasp from somewhere very close by? He hoped so, but Ethelwulf contrived to keep a face firmly inclined towards that of his lord. Admittedly the Prince of Kenugard enjoyed the power of life and death throughout his domains but Ethelwulf wouldn't deny the truth whatever the threat.

"And what do you mean by that?" blustered the Prince, clearly taken aback by the force of Ethelwulf's words. Then he added, revealing even more how his hand was being forced by others. "How can you say that about an officer in my guard?"

"Because you yourself, my lord, dispatched me to bring back your bride who'd fled with him." Ethelwulf noted the quick glance to his left from the Prince and was satisfied the princess was listening to every word, but didn't pause, "after he'd conspired with savages to attack a body of troops sent by your son as an escort." It was good to remind the Prince whose troops had been betrayed and they both well knew Holmgard viewed Oleg Askoldsson in a different light to that presented by the Prince himself.

"Yes," agreed the Prince. "I'll never understand what drove such a fine officer to act against the interests of his Prince."

No, you never will as long as you're the slave of that bitch, thought Ethelwulf but kept his face calm, awaiting judgement from his lord.

"But that is all in the past," continued Prince Vladimir, "and I want you to know I had no desire for you to inflict such a horrible death on a man who'd once served me so well - whatever he had done!" Ethelwulf made no comment, content to let Prince Vladimir after putting himself into a corner manoeuvre himself out of it. At last the Prince added, "I suppose that what's done is done, and Oleg cannot be brought back." Ethelwulf had the irritating desire to add, "as his head was!" but refrained. Instead he decided to help the Prince out of his mire.

"If I acted out of order, my lord, I ask your forgiveness." He paused before adding, "Remember I come from the West where such deaths are common and not considered particularly shameful - "

"Yes," intruded Prince Vladimir, "We've heard of the barbarities practised in Western lands." Ethelwulf smiled inwardly at this expression of the complete reversal of how he saw the world. Even so he continued to listen. "So let us pass on to other matters," grumbled the Prince, as if to tell a listener he'd been satisfied with the explanation offered. "I've a new task for you and your men."

With that he was dismissed because Prince Vladimir considered it beneath him to explain in detail what would be his commands. An Advisor called Igor was given the task and attacked it with vigour, summoning before him Ethelwulf and his three principal lieutenants.

"I assume you know, Westerners, that our lord's domains stretch for many miles in every direction." he paused so that the Westerners could appreciate the immensity of the Prince of Kenugard's realm. "Twenty five years ago the father of our present Prince seized the fortress of Sarkel[62] from the Khazars. This fortress is on the Don, a mighty river which rivals the Dneiper itself. It welcomes into its walls traders from all nations and its riches are of the greatest importance to our lord. You'll find there followers of the Christ-God, Yahweh and Mohammed (as well as pagans and Rus) - all setting aside religious differences in their search of profit. There you'll find silk and furs, silver and slaves; everywhere is wealth. However, we've heard troublemakers are active in the town, persuading believers of different faiths to challenge each other and as a result undermine our control. Of course, others would like to see our control overthrown: to the south the Moslems, to the east the Bulgars. Above all, the Greeks want to take over the fortress as they fear our growing power in the region."

He paused and examined his listeners, The leader, Ethelwulf, had all the bearing of a warrior, with fair hair hanging loosely about his ears and grey eyes which displayed considerable intelligence; his tall body was strong and, with the practised eye of one who'd made a fortune in dealing in slaves, Igor estimated there'd be good profit in the sale of such a man. Next to the leader was a dark-haired warrior who, matching his leader in strength and height, out-shone him in looks; notably the man was left-handed from the way he carried his sword. Next to that man stood another, apparently his twin, but who resembled him but slightly; his hair was brown and his features more open, but he was still clearly a warrior. Behind all three stood a giant, dark-haired and black-bearded, who displayed an air of impatience with which he fingered the double-handed axe grounded in front of him. He alone seemed not to be listening and Igor dismissed him as a skilful fighter, but not really a leader. Overall he was impressed by his listeners but concerned by their lack of questions. He felt being toyed with, they were letting him to talk until he'd revealed all he knew without them displaying any interest they might have. This irritated him and Igor heard the hardness in his tone as he demanded if they had any questions.

Two of the listeners shook their heads and he noticed the dark-haired warrior merely allowed a cynical smile to play upon his lips. The giant cleared his throat to ask a question but then felt better of it. The silence in the chamber was oppressive and Igor felt increasingly uncomfortable.

"Do none of you want to know what are your orders?" he demanded

"I'm sure you'll get around to it," smirked Ethelwulf with calculated insolence as he added, "when you've finished with the lessons in history and geography."

Igor decided to shrug off the insult and continued as if there'd been no comment. "We're sending Amran Chat, a Khazar who is one of our most trusted agents, to identify these troublemakers and YOUR task is both to protect him as he goes about his business and to seize the people he identifies."

"Will we be under his orders?"

"Not completely," answered the Advisor with a knowing smile. "As you must realise, we're still assimilating the region, which is why this mission is necessary. So we'll not hand over complete authority to any person who might be tempted to......"

"....take a line not welcome in Kenugard." completed Ethelwulf.

"Exactly!" smiled the Advisor, warming SLIGHTLY to the Westerner standing in front of him. Sometimes he found it very difficult to get across subtleties of policy to recruits. Of course, when one was dealing with the Greeks subtleties sometimes got in the way of realities. As the first real contact he'd had with somebody from the far West he was impressed. He wondered how this Saxon's country was really governed, and that led one to wonder why he was here.

"So, when will we meet this Khazar?" asked the dark-haired warrior.

"Later today," responded the Advisor, pleased to be redirected back to the business in hand. He knew one of his weaknesses - inherited from his Greek mother - was the tendency to wander into the realm of speculation and not deal with the immediate.

What remained were basic arrangements for equipping a force - about thirty men was considered sufficient - and arranging for the Vikings to meet the agent who was to be their mentor in the ways of the Khazars. It was also considered essential that three guides, fluent in the language and customs of the Severians and Khazars, should accompany the expedition.

Amran Chat proved to be an instantly likeable fellow, short and plump with an air of grease about him stemming both from the fat with which he controlled his sleek black hair and the oil with which he cooked dishes consisting of rice, fish and cucumbers. It was exaggerated by the heavy sweat enveloping his face and neck as he moved with remarkable rapidity about the business of getting together everything needed for the expedition. Fortunately he'd acquired a good knowledge of Rus which, despite its variations from the standard Norse used around the Swedish Sea, made communication between himself and the Varangians possible. Also several of the Varangians, notably Morkere and Ethelwulf, had made great strides in mastering the peculiarities of the Rus dialect. Morkere began to explore the intricacies of the Turkic tongue used by the Khazars, but here his ambitions proved over-ambitious and he never achieved much fluency in the language.

Within a fortnight the expedition set off. The route had been carefully planned: east along the Desna and the Sejm; then a portage to the River Donets to carry them down to the Don south of the Sartov; and so on to the fortress itself. This way was considered the best means of keeping them away from the Pechenegs although the extent of that people's ravages had to remain uncertain. The whole expedition took up a single vessel, stronger-built than those used on the hunt for the princess, but no larger.

Trouble only began with the portage required to link the river Sejm and the river Donets. At first there appeared no tribes nearby ready to help. Of course, the Varangians could have struggled to carry the vessel by themselves but the effort might not have made it worthwhile. So, with suitable escorts, two guides, Gostyata and Sven, were despatched to find a suitable settlement. It didn't take Gostyata long to find a mir[63] and intrude himself to the extent of securing a special meeting of the local volost,[64] which involved no fewer than six such communities. One of the escort was sent back to summon Ethelwulf and other leaders while the Severian elders sent envoys to other communities to meet at the nearest goradichtiche.[65]

As Ethelwulf, Morkere and Gunnar marched into the goradichtiche they were discussing the carefully-laid fields outside the wooden palisade which seemed better organised than those found in England. They could see fields being ploughed. Just inside the gates of the stockade were large hives because the people were noted for their honey, much devoted to the production of a mead which could out-do that of England for potency. A large proportion of the population had been assembled and to the north of a large open area sat a group of seven elders - later it was revealed these represented the six communities of volost with an extra member to act as the senior elder, acting in rotation. To the left of the crescent of elders was a large mound, the kourgan or burial-ground of the clan which was guarded by a series of primitive statues of Voloss and Mikoula.[66] It was obviously going to be a very formal occasion and Ethelwulf was pleased he'd been reminded to carry in his boat a collection of presents for any of the tribes he might come across. He'd wondered what presents would be appropriate, realising the Severians possessed a reputation for sword-making and metal work in general and, through trade, had access to goods of probably higher value than any he could supply. However, he decided amber would be most suitable as Kenugard had access to a number of figurines made in a material abundant throughout the northern seas.[67]

Ethelwulf began by declaring how Vladimir, Kagan[68] of Kenugard, welcomed the good relations enjoyed between the Rus and the

Severians. He then produced seven amber figurines which he presented to the elders as a mark of the respect of his prince. These objects were carefully passed from hand to hand, except for one hastily returned to Ethelwulf, Gostyata hurriedly explaining it resembled a common image of Morena, the goddess of Death, and so would be considered bad luck if accepted. Ethelwulf hurriedly apologised saying the figurine, to the Rus, was a representation of Urd[69], one of the three goddesses of Destiny. He added they might see how closely Fate and Death were linked, hoping Gostyata would convey what he intended.

There were nods from several of the chiefs and the chief of the elders spoke to Gostyata who told Ethelwulf they accepted man's fate must be death and so the two goddesses must be linked. Ethelwulf nodded and began to explain his mission. He declared they were going to Sarkel on the business of the Kagan but had need for help in the portage between the rivers Sejm and Donets. Here the chief of the Elders, whom Gostyata said was called Tarkhan, asked if they intended to make war on the Pechenegs.. Ethelwulf hesitated in replying, uncertain as to which answer would be most acceptable to the Severians. In the end he said he hoped they'd not have to fight the Pechenegs but, if they did, he trusted his men could give a good account of themselves. This produced a mixed reception from the Elders, some nodding and smiling while frowns appeared on the faces of others. Ethelwulf asked Gostyata what had been wrong with his answer. Gostyata grinned and replied that, to the Severians, anybody making war on the Pechenegs, whom they hate and fear, must be the greatest of their friends; however, some thought your confidence in dealing with Pechenegs did you credit, even though they thought your youth was in danger of leading you astray.

Ethelwulf smiled somewhat sheepishly, admitting that although his men could account for the typical Pecheneg war-band, he had doubts they could handle the whole people. This provoked laughter among several of the Elders and Tarkhan replied such ambitions are often seen in the young and may not always end in disaster.

At this point, Ethelwulf thought it timely to return to his request and was pleased the Elders didn't reject the idea, as long as there was adequate payment. The Saxon asked if silver coinage was acceptable and Tarkhan replied he thought their Khwarizmian trade-partners were quite prepared to deal in that currency, although they preferred gold. At this Ethelwulf laughingly replied that obviously the labour of Severians must be very expensive indeed if they considered portage duties would warrant payment in gold. The Elders responded by smiling shame-facedly in their turn and the negotiations continued.

*

The Severians proved excellent workers and it was amazing how quickly a suitable number of lengthy logs were transported to the river bank, the vessel hauled out of the water (although this required crafty manoeuvring before it could be dragged prow-first on to land) and firmly placed on the artificial road. A team of four Severian oxen dragged the vessel over the next three days from one river to the other. Behind ambled a cart loaded with most of the vessel's contents followed by swaggering Vikings. Only Amran Chat seemed oblivious to the air of relaxation which ruled the day; his eyes flicked from side to side, noting the expressions of the Severians and the surrounding topography.

"It may appear a rich land," muttered Edwine, to the Prince's agent who was taking excessive interest in crops growing quite close to the river, "but I fear your master might find it hard to force the people here to pay more tribute."

"There comes a time when there's need for everything, young man," replied the agent for once without any expression on his fat features. "When Pecheneg war-bands are burning crops and raping women these people will turn to whoever can drive them out - and pay well for it."

"That may be so," answered Edwine, "if the Prince can drag his eyes away from whatever lies beyond the seas to the south." Like many others he was convinced the apparent preoccupation of Prince Vladimir with the affairs of the realm of Basil II[70] was distracting him from more immediate affairs.

"The Greeks have shown an unwelcome interest in extending their control up to our borders,"[71] replied Amran Chat, this time with an air of irritation." It isn't just vain curiosity that provokes that interest. If you Westerners knew enough about these regions you'd know the Prince has not deserted the gods of his fathers to follow women after the Christ-god!"

"So, is it all just a question of policy?" asked Edwine, and was somewhat amused, if not surprised, when he received no reply.

Meanwhile Ethelwulf was deep in thought as they marched along the river bank. He wasn't sure how far he could rely on Prince Vladimir, being certain that in Princess Olga he'd acquired himself an enemy. Much, of course, depended on how much influence she could exercise over her husband; so he found himself praying that Princess Anna, the bride from the land of the Greeks, might not only ensure the spread of Christianity among the Rus but also contrive to shut out rival attractions.

He was also puzzled by their mission, wondering what was the real aim of the Prince. Certainly Sarkel was an important centre, but not one of vital consequence, especially as the depredations of the Pechenegs at any moment could undermine any control the Rus could hope to exercise here. Was the interest of Prince Vladimir connected with his recent conversion to the Christian faith? It was possible, but then he'd heard the Khazars had accepted the faith of the Jews centuries before and he was certain they'd find little enthusiasm for any missionary activity. Then there were the Moslems. He'd only met one or two followers of the teachings of Mohammed before and was not proud of his ignorance. He was well aware that, along with trade, came influence and he wondered how the arm of the ruler of the Moslems might follow the trade of his subjects. Nobody had been able to tell him anything about that ruler but he was certainly powerful enough to cause the ruler of the Greeks trouble. One gap in his knowledge he had to fill was that of the faith of the Moslems for that was intruding as much into the affairs of the Rus as was that of Christ.

"I feel less happy as we march east," intruded the voice of Gunnar as Ethelwulf pondered on the clash of faiths. The giant was keeping a wary eye on the woods to their left as they marched along the bank, as if he expected at any moment to hear the war-whoop of savages pouring from the trees. Ethelwulf knew part of the Gall-Gael's insecurity stemmed from the differences of landscape from that of his native land; it was uncomfortably big, except when it shared with Ireland the closeness of tree-cover. As they marched east so the tree-cover grew less and the plains grew wider, and with that grew the insecurity of the giant. He wished he could say something to calm Gunnar but he was uneasy about their surroundings as well. Perhaps he felt Tarkhan had been too friendly, too willing to co-operate; as expected, the eyes of several Severians had wandered to the packs of the Vikings and Ethelwulf wondered if sheer greed might provoke treachery.

"Soon we'll be back on water and turning south," smiled Ethelwulf, well knowing that such was the direction he most dreaded because south meant going closer to the Pechenegs and, on all sides, it was that people which aroused fear.

"I'd rather we were turning north," growled the giant. "If only - "

"- We were still running from the Finns in the dark woods above Ladoga!" teased Ethelwulf as he deliberately finished the words of the Gall-Gael in a way unintended. Gunnar caught the mischievous glint in the Saxon's eyes and laughed. He'd been going to say, " - we had never left the land of our birth" but knew it would never be possible to return there. The past for all of them had died when they moved on, and in moving on they created a new past to be destroyed. When he thought like that Gunnar despaired and only a good draught of ale could either jerk him out of misery into merrier thoughts or plunge him into sleep; and on this march there was little chance of ale!

*

The fears of Gunnar and Ethelwulf proved completely groundless. Tarkhan's promises were upheld by his deputies who accepted the silver handed over with an enthusiasm bordering on rapture. Ethelwulf was surprised until he remembered the Severians were basically farmers, sharing only to a limited degree in the rich trade passing them by on the waters of the Dneiper, Don and Volga. Of course, some of their people had wandered to such centres as Sarkel but there had enjoyed mixed fortunes. Some may have profited but in their gains began to forget their kin; others suffered the extra burdens of failure in a foreign land and, if lucky, managed to scurry back home with tales of how such towns were so filled with thieves and cheats that no honest man could survive. But it made little difference, for among their audience lurked other young men who, sure fate would smile on them, would collect together a few possessions and wander off to the same towns.

Ethelwulf felt his mood lighten as he sat at the prow of their boat while it skimmed down the waters of the Donets, driven by a stiff breeze. Beside him Chorpan carefully scanned the banks with a quiet smile on his lips. As they had entered the Donets Gostyata yielded place to Chorpan as the chief guide for the expedition. Gostyata was a very likeable fellow, with a heavy growth of brown whiskers which never quite became a beard to mask the double chin that belied the slim, athletic frame he possessed. However, Gostyata was the offspring of a Severian and a Rus;

Chorpan was a pure Khazar whose parents had been enslaved over twenty years before when Prince Svyatoslav had carried the arms of the Rus into the remnants of the Khazar Empire and destroyed what independence remained. Chorpan had been carried north, in the womb of his mother, and from his birth had known nothing but slavery. However, he possessed a keen ear for language and a desire to escape from the drudgery reserved for slaves in the lands of the Rus. Quickly he'd mastered the alien sounds making up the language of his masters and found himself transferred, when scarcely fifteen years of age, into the service of Prince Vladimir himself. He'd already travelled on three expeditions to the land of his conception (if not his birth), proving himself both useful and resourceful for his masters. By now he enjoyed a status beyond anything which his parents, if they'd still been living, could ever have hoped; more importantly he'd managed to assemble, in a cache hidden somewhere among the back-alleys of Sarkel, an amount of silver surprising for one of servile rank. In appearance Chorpan had a wiry figure which culminated in a sharp nose, always on the look-out for information, and intensely-blue eyes which tested everything with a suspicion perhaps undeserved. Chorpan may not have been someone to be chosen for a bosom friend but rather for his expertise.

As the boat passed throughout the countryside of his people Chorpan sought to ingratiate him with his leader, as on previous expeditions, with descriptions of the life and history of his people. He told Ethelwulf how the Khazars had centuries ago ruled over a vast land,[72] so big that what now is called the Salt Sea was then styled the Sea of the Khazars.[73] Many peoples had been subject to their Kagans and those who resisted, such as the Bulgars, had been expelled from their lands.[74] They'd resisted the advances of the Moslems and adopted the faith of the Jews but, with a growing wealth from trade, they'd both encouraged the influx of people of every faith and undermined their own military power. So, a generation ago, Svyatoslav, the ruler of a city actually founded by themselves, had reduced them to the level at which they now lived. Ethelwulf argued that, from what he'd heard, the Khazars enjoyed a high level of prosperity due to the trade from east and south and north which met together in their realm. Chorpan agreed but added their warlike neighbours might so easily grab it all, so the Khazars lived in daily fear.

"Which is why we've been sent here," concluded Ethelwulf and was disturbed by the contemptuous smile of the Khazar.

"So we're told," muttered Chorpan adding, " but I wouldn't consider Amran Chat has the interests of the Khazars in his heart." He paused to see how Ethelwulf reacted and, seeing no objection, continued," He's been too long among the Rus, gained too much silver, to still yearn for a life among his people."

Ethelwulf glanced back at Amran Chat chattering away to Gostyata towards the rear of the boat and inwardly agreed. The agent of Prince Vladimir had shown no great excitement when they'd entered the lands of his ancestors and displayed little interest as they passed down the river Donets. His behaviour would have been no different if they'd been heading northwards into the lands of the Viatchians. Was Amran Chat the right man for the task? It depended on what was that task and Ethelwulf had no idea what that really was.

*

Chorpan's position at the prow of the boat was largely dictated by fear they'd sail past the confluence of the Donets and the Don on which Sarkel stood. When they reached that point the easy sailing, carried by a brisk North wind, was exchanged for the more arduous toil of rowing north-eastwards up the Don towards their destination. Fortunately Chorpan recognised key points in the landscape and so, just before the confluence was reached, they camped and prepared for the use of oars the next day. By mid-morning they found themselves proceeding in a completely different direction although the surrounding countryside hadn't changed, the woodlands of the northern Dneiper had been replaced by more open grasslands.

It took several days rowing, and signs of unhappiness among Vikings who'd been spoiled (perhaps) by the easy sail down the Donets, for the expedition to approach the township of Sarkel. Ethelwulf, like almost every member of the expedition, was impressed as they approached the white-blocks, forming its walls, which had given the town its name. Chorpan whispered to Ethelwulf it had been Greek builders who'd planned the town and Ethelwulf, even if he'd never laid eyes on a Greek town, was prepared to believe the town's origins owed little to a people content with the garodistiches which they'd passed. As they approached the town they could see how much it was dominated by the citadel, overtopped by its four towers, standing to the south-east. They noted the large number of houses clustered around the fortress, rivalling those of any city the Varangians had seen, which indicated some of the wealth flowing into the township.

Morkere made his way to the prow as the boat was guided into the mooring position at the foot of the hill to the north of the town. He seemed anxious to be the first to leap ashore, as if, in that way, he could acquire some form of 'ownership' over whatever would transpire. Ethelwulf smiled. In many ways the enthusiasm of his cousin resembled that of a young lad on his first trip to the local market. He remembered how his cousins had once looked forward to their visits to Wareham before they'd joined him in exile. Had he betrayed their enthusiasm? Many times he'd been assured it had been a free choice and that they'd rather wander throughout the world with him than wither away at home in Dorset under a King sitting on a throne that wasn't rightfully his. Of course, he believed them but when he witnessed the glint in the eye of his cousin approaching such a town he wondered if they were merely cheating themselves; perhaps a peaceful life surrounded by their family was the true destiny of a man. The soft bump of the boat against the dock woke Ethelwulf from his thoughts. They had reached Sarkel.

*

One of the first features striking Ethelwulf when they were installed in their houses was the position of the stove. Completely different from common western practice, it was placed in the corner where it not only failed to dominate the room but was less intrusive on other activities. In the centre was a low round table, highly suitable for Khazars who preferred to sit on the ground for their meals, but much less welcome to the Rus. On the walls were two large carpets adorned with insignia of which Ethelwulf recognised a Star of David in red and a chalice resembling the one he'd seen in Jersey seven years before. He hadn't come across the use of carpets in this way but was impressed by the way they shut out effectively the chill of the northern wind.

After making sure everyone had settled in Ethelwulf accompanied Amran Chat to the court of the local governor, whose name he'd discovered was Menashe Bulan. Somehow the Prince's agent had managed to smuggle on to their boat a brilliant emerald-green silk gown with which he hoped to impress the Governor. At the last moment Ethelwulf decided to take with him Chorpan as a personal translator, with the added advantage that the apparent enmity between the two Khazars might give him a clearer idea of what would take place during the audience.

On entering the chamber of the Governor Ethelwulf was impressed by the spectacular tables, whose decoration indicated a sophisticated origin beyond any known among the Rus, placed at the side with what was meant to appear careless abandon. He also was impressed by the magnificent throne placed to the rear of the room, whose arms were clearly of ivory decorated with silver. He was not so impressed by the throne's occupant, a small wizened figure whom he took to be the Governor. Menashe Bulan wore a turban decorated with thin strands of silver which matched the colour of his hair and the wispy beard which dribbled down his chin. He was hunched forward on the throne as if half-frightened a stronger individual might come and snatch it away. His caftan[75] was yellow with crimson lining exaggerating its edges and his trousers were of a black apparently out-of-place against an image so frantically trying to impress. The boots were largely hidden as the Governor tucked his feet firmly beneath him, but were exposed enough for Ethelwulf to appreciate, even at a distance, that they were made of the richest leather. In fact, Ethelwulf immediately wondered how Prince Vladimir, seemingly jealous of any display other than his own, would tolerate such gaudiness in what was after all only a relatively minor official.

Such thoughts were interrupted by a whine proceeding from the lips of the Governor, immediately translated by Chorpan in a hoarse whisper as a formal welcome to the envoys of the Kagan of Kenugard. Amran Chat replied in a like manner and immediately indicated Ethelwulf as the leader of a force sent by their lord to enforce whatever decisions he might reach. Ethelwulf bowed his head as, with the mention of his name, he acknowledged the curt turn of head from the Governor. However, he stiffened at how the agent completed the introduction, cursing inwardly that his lowered eyes prevented him noting the Governor's reaction to what could be seen as a usurpation of his authority. When he raised his eyes the Governor was squeaking out more formalities which Chorpan translated as being the promise to co-operate to the limit his authority allowed. Ethelwulf wondered whether that condition measured the maximum or minimum limits of that co-operation.

It seemed Amran Chat had left behind his friendly, casual manner in Kenugard because he now described in a brusque manner the commission from their lord to investigate rumours of troublemakers using differing faiths as excuses for promoting unrest in Sarkel. The Governor obviously disliked the implied slur that he was unable to control such elements but was forced to admit such troublemakers existed. He added that within the cells beneath his fortress was confined a priest accused of such mischief.

As the Governor paused Ethelwulf quickly insisted to the agent that he should interview the individual concerned. Amran Chat, apparently grown in self-importance since entering upon his mission at Sarkel, ignored the request and demanded from the Governor a list of all such offenders over the last year. Even before Menashe Bulan was able to reply Ethelwulf hissed in the agent's ear that, unless he wanted to be hauled back to Kenugard that very day, he should remember who commanded the basis of his power. Amran Chat turned pale and only half-heard the reply of the Governor, although Chorpan provided Ethelwulf with a suitable translation, having commendably shut out the Varangian's intervention. The Governor was willing to supply such a list but, deeply involved with several legal decisions at the moment, he'd have to delegate the task to others and could only promise the list would be available within five days. Amran Chat, harassed on both sides, could only accept the Governor's decision, with a graciousness whose insincerity could have been detected by the most barbarian Pecheneg, before he requested "his officer" be allowed to interview the trouble-making priest. Ethelwulf bridled at such a description of himself, almost missing Chorpan's translation of the Governor's permission for the interview. As Ethelwulf smiled his gratitude for the permission he detected a shrewd look on the face of the Governor demonstrating the man could detect a conflict between his visitors and was willing to exploit it. The Governor then asked politely if his guests found their accommodation to their liking, to which the only answer could be "most certainly". He then added that, perhaps, they should meet again the next day at sunset to consider how they would proceed. This last suggestion possessed the force of an order and Ethelwulf could see how quickly the Governor was reasserting his independence.

Outside Amran Chat tried to bully Ethelwulf, loudly denouncing his intervention as undermining his authority. The Wanderer replied that Prince Vladimir had sent him with his men not only to enforce the agent's decisions but also to make sure the Khazar authorities continued to be co-operative. When asked what that meant he roughly replied that, even as a stranger, he'd seen Amran Chat had been irritating the Governor enough to ruin any chance of co-operation. The agent sneeringly suggested perhaps the Varangian should assume the position of envoy for their lord. Ethelwulf replied he was only willing to assume the role of warrior and use his sword to cut into anybody's skull if necessary. Before the agent, assuming a deep shade of red with fury, could respond, Chorpan intervened by reminding them that Prince Vladimir had sent them both because he considered the mission would need two distinct skills and success depended on their acting together. Ethelwulf believed the Khazar enjoyed the humiliation of the agent but was prepared to use any dispute between the agent and himself to his own advantage. He recalled all three 'guides' had been selected by the Prince himself and given instructions in private. He hurriedly apologised to Amran Chat for any hasty words and was pleased to note the agent had enough control to see, like himself, that a quarrel between them would help neither. The agent, in his turn, apologised and asked Ethelwulf to provide him with a full report of his interview with the priest before the meeting on the next day. Ethelwulf agreed and the party broke up, with Chorpan scurrying alongside the Wanderer as he headed for the dungeons below.

*

The cell area, hidden away in the bowels of the citadel, were no surprise to Ethelwulf as he was conducted into its gloomy interior. Naturally the only light permitted was whatever filtered feebly through a small window into the corridor off which four individual cells existed. There was no direct external light into any of the four cells and the walls were dominated by large rings used to limit the mobility of the more dangerous inmates. Each cell was large enough to accommodate four prisoners, although if pressed probably five times that number could have been forced inside. Nevertheless, only five inmates occupied the attention of the two guards who half-snoozed their way through their period of duty. In one cell two bandits, caught stealing a skiff on the river north of the town, were awaiting their hanging in two days; in another a drunken Severian who'd dared challenge the local tough guy was recovering both from the effects of bad ale and the beating he'd suffered; in a third a Khazar convicted of raping a young widow, despite his plea he'd been invited into her house at midnight, was awaiting the date of his castration and execution; and in the last sat the priest whom Ethelwulf had come to see.

As the Saxon entered, the figure dimly visible in the corner of the cell hauled himself into reality. Chorpan had started to babble something in Khazar but stopped when the figure shambled into the light. Clearly the priest was no Khazar; his fair colouring and stature proclaimed his origins probably lay in the regions north of Holmgard. Ethelwulf ventured to ask in Rus the name of the priest and was pleased, and puzzled, when a hoarse voice replied, "Cyril." He'd been pleased because he could dispense with the services of Chorpan and puzzled because the name given was Greek and the face he could now see was clearly from the north. It was an old face, but appeared more aged than its actual years warranted. A beard more grey than its original brown consumed most of the features and the eyes lacked that glint produced by regular invigoration through sunlight. They were a clear blue, with an innocence underlining the quality of the figure standing there in the remnants of a brown robe.

After dismissing Chorpan who, deprived of the chance to spy on whatever was taking place, reluctantly shuffled out of the cell to join the guards, Ethelwulf turned towards the prisoner and smiled.

"Forgive me, but the name Cyril doesn't match your appearance."

The priest returned the smile, revealing a collection of badly-formed and broken teeth. "Certainly, stranger, I come from Holmgard - although your accent shows me you do not."

Ethelwulf gave his name and admitted his origins lay in the far west; the prisoner replied his knowledge of England was limited to having seen it once mentioned in a manuscript residing in one of he churches of Kenugard. Cyril went on to ask why he should be visited by a warrior from such distant lands. Ethelwulf explained the mission, as he understood it, and Cyril smiled with an air of somebody surprised it should ever be considered. Ethelwulf asked why the priest should be confined to prison in a land where, for many years, there'd been tolerance for differences in faith.

"I'm sure, Ethelwulf, you can discover why sooner than I can." Cyril paused and breathed out with a difficulty which seemed to stem from trouble inflating his lungs. He noticed the expression which appeared on the Saxon's face and added, "Yes, I'm suffering some pain following the nature of my arrest……. I made the mistake, you see, of questioning the right of any of the guards to lay hands on a priest of God…." He paused again, managing a faint smile. "Unfortunately, the guards, surely not by chance, had little patience with our faith, probably because of personal experience."

"But why did they arrest you?"

"I don't know," replied the priest. " I only know words had appeared on the walls of the synagogue - you know most of the people here profess a Jewish faith?" Ethelwulf nodded and the priest continued, having acquired more control of his breathing. "So, any attack on that faith challenges any form of authority within this land."

"What was written?" asked Ethelwulf, seeing the effort of explaining his arrest didn't seem to be helping the priest's health.

"I don't know," answered Cyril," and I swear by the Holy Trinity itself….. " He paused again, to master his breathing. "…. Even the guards would - or could - not tell me….. So after asking three times I abandoned the attempt because, "and here the priest again tried a smile," as you can see, breathing is not the easiest exercise for me - at the moment."

"Have you been seen by anybody who could help - ?"

"Don't be silly, young man, why would they do that for a prisoner," the priest replied sharply, and then corrected himself. "I'm sorry, Ethelwulf. You're a stranger here in the realm of Menashe Bulan - "

"But he's simply the Governor, answerable to Prince Vladimir!"

The priest gave a tired smile. "But one with such a degree of independence that he's almost come to think of himself as a Kagan!" Again there was a pause and a struggle to recover control of his breathing before Cyril continued. "I'm sorry, Westerner, talking has become too difficult for me..... Please ask questions of either Makarios or his sister, Elizabeth."

With that he turned away from Ethelwulf, indicating the interview was over. When the Saxon moved to protest, without turning back, the priest feebly raised one hand as if demanding peace, while using the other to support himself against the wall. It was obvious Cyril no longer had either the energy or even the will to continue the interview. Ethelwulf wondered whether he could get some improvement in the priest's condition, but instantly dismissed the idea as ridiculous. How could a stranger step into Khazar society and start demanding this or that change. It was possible Amran Chat might get somewhere but he doubted, after their clash earlier, he'd be willing to make any move to help either the Saxon or the priest. Before he could do anything - decide anything - he needed to find out the details of the case, what exactly were the charges against the priest. Quickly he made his apologies, feeling how inadequate he was when the figure simply retired even further into the recesses of the cell. So he loudly called out farewell and, not expecting or waiting for any response, turned and beat on the outer-door to be released into the freedom of the air outside.

*

Chorpan was delighted Ethelwulf needed his help to find either Makarios or the woman, Elizabeth, and elated that the whole business meant Ethelwulf had to tell him what had happened in the cell. He made no comment on the Westerner's failure to get any real information from the priest, inwardly assuring himself that a Khazar would have been more successful.

The priest, Makarios, proved extremely easy to find - in fact, he was waiting for them when they emerged from the citadel. Somehow he'd discovered the purpose of the visit and was determined to offer his help. He was a busy little man, with a manner which indicated more activity than was actually the case. His manner gave anybody the sense of time rushing past with a tendency to feel guilty for failing to keep up with him.

"How is Cyril?" he asked as soon as Ethelwulf had identified himself and Chorpan. Unfortunately, Ethelwulf recognised Makarios had but an indifferent grasp of Rus, his languages being confined to Greek and Hebrew, and so the services of Chorpan were essential. Briefly he outlined the description of the priest to his friend and noted the instant concern appearing in the eyes when he described the difficulty in breathing being experienced by Cyril. The little priest bustled into his next question.

"Can you get some kind of medical help to him?" Makarios noted hesitation in Ethelwulf and added, "The Governor would pay little attention to the likes of me, but would do anything for the agent of the lord of Kenugard." Ethelwulf explained he was merely the commander of the escort for the agent, and not the man himself. He noted the amused glint in the eyes of Chorpan as he described the position, for both recalled the argument between the agent and himself but a couple of hours before. Ethelwulf felt to add, more out of a sense of guilt than anything, that he'd try his best to get aid to the injured priest. He then asked, before the priest had a chance for another question, whether Makarios had any idea of what had provoked the arrest of his friend.

"Words had been daubed on the door of the chief synagogue," stated the priest and then, when Ethelwulf persisted by asking what words had been daubed, merely added, "'Let His blood fall on ourselves and our children!'"[76] Ethelwulf looked puzzled and the priest explained. "It was shouted by the Jews when it appeared Pilate was about to release Our Lord." He paused waiting for Chorpan to translate the words. "Christians hate Jews and say this."

"Does Cyril hate the Jews?" asked Chorpan, intruding his own question but instantly apologising to Ethelwulf. The Saxon dismissed the concern of the Khazar; after all, it was a question he might himself have asked. The negative answer was as expected, although a priest trying to proselytise among a people dominated by Judaism must be irritated by some adherents. Chorpan shared his scepticism and the priest was quick enough to spot the doubt.

"No! No! You don't understand," he pleaded. "If Cyril hated the Jewish faith he could never work among the Khazars - among the Severians or the Bulgars perhaps, but never a people who'd adopted such a faith generations ago." He moistened his lips as he looked from one to the other, worried his friend should be doubted. "Of course, he's met people for whom he found it difficult to feel that love which Our Lord demanded. We all do. But they're not just Jews; they can be pagans, Moslems or even, I'm ashamed to say, those who profess the same faith as ourselves."

"So why would the authorities arrest Cyril?" asked the Saxon.

"Because he was - is - the finest of our missionaries," declared Makarios. "He's not like me, sometimes so concerned with my own concerns and worries as to miss the needs of my hearers." He tried a weak smile, a gesture of apology which, though genuine, revealed no determination to eradicate such a vice. "Cyril, however, reaches into the hearts of men and women, whether pagan or Jew or even, cursed though they be, the followers of Mohammed."

Ethelwulf was intrigued by the vehemence which the little priest felt for the Moslems; he'd expected the strongest antagonism would be towards paganism but obviously Makarios had spent years among such people, perhaps looking on them as children stumbling in the darkness of their own ignorance. Obviously Moslems didn't fit into the same picture. The Saxon, with his very limited experience of Moslems, felt that was one area needing investigation; for if a Christian priest could feel so strongly about a Moslem, would the feeling be reciprocated?

"Why should they think he was responsible?" persisted Ethelwulf.

Instead of answering Makarios went on to something new. "After the words had been discovered there was found a dead animal - a pig - with its throat slit and hanging in mockery next to the door."

Ethelwulf looked questioningly when Chorpan translated and so the Khazar felt he had to add, "To both Jews and Moslems the pig is unclean. By hanging it there the synagogue became polluted."

Makarios understood words had been added and Chorpan found himself translating for the benefit of the priest. Makarios said, "Yes, the synagogue needed ritual cleansing and the Jews were furious."

"And so how did this affect, Cyril?" asked Ethelwulf.

"Two days later he chose to preach on a passage concerning Peter's dream in the book called 'Acts'." Makarios saw Ethelwulf was perplexed when his words was translated and explained with a smile. "I see Westerners are not readers of Holy Scripture! Those verses describe how the blessed saint, Peter, in a dream was presented with several animals thought unclean but God taught otherwise." He paused. "This passage occurs to introduce Paul's mission among the 'unclean' gentiles."

"So people came to link Cyril with the dead pig?" asked Chorpan, as much on his own behalf as Ethelwulf's.

"Yes," accepted Makarios. "My friend used Scripture to show God rejects no man, believer or not, who says Christ is the Son of God."

"I see," said Chorpan as if that ended the matter.

"But is that the only reason why they chose to arrest Cyril rather than - say, you?" insisted Ethelwulf.

Makarios grinned and nodded his head. When he'd heard of the arrest of his friend he'd first assumed it was just error, a mistake which the Governor would immediately sort out. But then Elizabeth, who'd been sent to the citadel, came back and reported how Cyril had been dragged out of the very pulpit and thrown into a dungeon because of the dead pig.

"But why did Cyril not protest - loudly!" argued Ethelwulf, shocked anyone could so meekly accept wrongful arrest.

Makarios himself had wondered that, concerned that possibly Cyril was seeking martyrdom because, until he'd heard of the priest's injuries from Ethelwulf, he hadn't realised his friend was incapable of protesting. Ethelwulf would have added that perhaps that was why Cyril received his injuries but decided to keep his mouth shut. Besides, tomorrow would see another audience with the Governor when he could try and secure the release of the priest.

*

Ethelwulf was shocked by the relative lack of enthusiasm shown by Amran Chat for trying to get the priest released; then he realised Amran Chat, despite his name might well be a pagan, but the vehemence with which the Agent insisted his father, and his fathers before that, had remained true to the Jewish faith took him by surprise. Ethelwulf feared there might be little prospect of the priest leaving his cell unless he could produce evidence against others - and there was very little chance of doing that.

It was then Chorpan and Sven, the third guide whom he'd tended to overlook, came up with the startling proposal that they should ask around the area because, as Sven remarked, even in a trading centre like Sarkel, anyone leading a live pig around the alleys at night might arouse suspicion. When Ethelwulf asked why he assumed the pig to be alive, he received the curt answer that obviously you'd tie the animal into position BEFORE you cut it's throat in order to make the pollution really effective. Ethelwulf realised he'd assumed the incidents had been directed against the priest rather than against the Jews of Sarkel. Naturally, Cyril hadn't been arrested until AFTER the pollution incident and so, whoever was responsible, couldn't have been trying to incriminate the priest. He also remembered Makarios hadn't volunteered any alibi for his friend. As he remarked to Chorpan he'd urgent need to discuss the matter again with the busy little priest.

*

Just as Makarios had approached Ethelwulf with ease so the Wanderer found it relatively straight-forward to find out where the priest lived among the alleys of Sarkel. He decided to take with him Morkere as well as Sven and Chorpan. After all, the reason why it was so easy to locate people like the priest and himself in Sarkel was that both of them stood out from the crowd, as foreigners. If that was the case, any visit couldn't be surreptitious so why not include another keen mind in the discussion.

Sven hammered at the cracked door of the small house next to a bakers in a side street to the north of the citadel. It was some time before the bolt was drawn back and the door cautiously opened.

An enormous pair of brown eyes stared up into Ethelwulf's face. For a second that was all he saw and then he saw the long, slender fingers of a girl gripping the side of the door with indecision.. Ethelwulf identified the girl as the sister of the little priest at the same moment she knew him to be the Westerner who'd met her brother a few hours before.

"You must be Elizabeth," he smiled and the girl nodded but made no move to open the door any wider. Ethelwulf was disappointed that he'd have to speak to the girl through an interpreter; he turned to Chorpan, who appeared at his side with a grin which threatened to break his face in two, and asked him to translate his words. "Is your brother in? We questioned him about the priest, Cyril, a little while ago." The girl shook her head and he was surprised how he took that as almost a personal rebuff. Even so, he decided to ask the question he'd intended. "Do you know where Cyril was on the night the pig was sacrificed at the synagogue?"

The girl hesitated, keeping a firm grip on the side of the door as if to buttress her answer. Chorpan glanced at Ethelwulf and then added, "We need to know this if we hope to get Cyril out of the rat-hole which is killing him!" The urgency in his voice unlocked the hesitation for the girl. She stepped out into the street and Ethelwulf was able to appreciate how petite she really was, she must have been gripping the door at an exaggerated height; if Makarios was small for a man he could never be described as slight, the girl, however, possessed a decidedly attractive air of fragility.

"I take you my brother," was all she said and set off at a pace which would have rivalled that of Makarios himself. It didn't take the group long to zigzag through the narrow alley-ways of Sarkel and reach the priest at prayer within the church of St. Methodius. Ethelwulf noted both Sven and Chorpan seemed unwilling to enter the building but Morkere didn't hang back and followed the girl straight into the small entrance. Within a moment or so Morkere and Makarios appeared and Ethelwulf noticed Elizabeth remained within the church.

"My sister say you question more," stated the priest as if irritated by a further interruption to his regular round of prayer, worship and other pastoral duties. Ethelwulf apologised and, through Chorpan, said he needed to know where Cyril had been on the night when the pig had been hung outside the synagogue. Makarios stood still for a moment and began nervously nibbling at the edges of his beard. He looked at the two guides, obviously Khazars, and then at Ethelwulf. It was clear he didn't trust the guides. Quickly, in West Saxon, Ethelwulf asked his cousin to go off somewhere out of earshot with Sven, adding it'd be best if only one possibly hostile pair of ears heard whatever the priest had to say.

Sven looked most unhappy to be ordered to accompany Morkere, refusing to accept the excuse they were required to stand guard outside the church. As soon as they'd gone, Makarios began jabbering at a frantic rate and Chorpan had to make him pause in order to translate for Ethelwulf.

"He no sure what his friend do, because he no like all his friend do. Cyril told by Eusebius – chief man for Christ in Sarkel - to be with him when he do special thing in secret place." The guide paused as he made sure he had repeated the words exactly for the Saxon. "Secret place in citadel and guard let him in. He – how say – make Christ follower daughter of Obadiah." Chorpan looked closely at the priest and rattled off some questions: finally he nodded his head and then returned to Ethelwulf. "This no good, Varangian. Obadiah is Kagan of Khazars in this land - he my lord before I serve Prince Vladimir. If what he says true soon big trouble here and he frightened Governor make it more bad." Ethelwulf began to show signs of impatience and so Chorpan felt he had to apologise before continuing. " He say Cyril change daughter of Obadiah into faith of Christ. This not true as she good in faith of Israel; she cannot - will not be traitor!"

Clearly Chorpan was distressed and Ethelwulf could understand the problems for Cyril in admitting where he'd been. Could he be persuaded to reveal the baptism? Chorpan asked Makarios to explain matters further and then turned to Ethelwulf.

"He say girl long time think about doing this but know father angry. Obadiah want marry her to Simeon son of big Kagan, Reuben. Girl frightened she have no chance of being Christ-girl in Itil; she think she can do this and run to our Prince Vladimir."

Ethelwulf could understand the princess might believe a powerful ruler, filled with a passion for expanding a faith he'd just accepted, would protect her from the wrath of her father. Obviously if she were baptised before leaving, if caught she'd have a better chance of appealing to the overlord of the Khazars. This business was getting more complex than anyone back in Kenugard could have guessed. He asked Chorpan to find out how Cyril viewed the situation and was told, as expected, the priest felt that admitting what had been going on would not only endanger the princess, Serah, but undermine what could become an evangelisation of the whole area. Makarios added his friend had declared a willingness to die rather than reveal the baptism; he himself was also reluctant to betray such a trust. Ethelwulf tried to question the use of the word 'reluctant' but Makarios altered it to 'refuse'.

Ethelwulf thanked the priest and with Chorpan paused before returning to the street. Before they rejoined his cousin and Sven he needed to consult Chorpan.

"Do you think we can get anybody to reveal the supposed baptism?" Ethelwulf asked, knowing the answer before he'd even finished the question by the expression of the guide. So he then moved on to the next question. "What would be the attitude of the Governor if we told him?" Here there was definite alarm.

"No, Varangian!" croaked Chorpan. "Governor like Kagan go war –"

"But why would he want to do that?"

"Kagan never say his daughter not want be Jew like father." Before Ethelwulf had the chance to answer he went on. "No! Kagan would want all think daughter made bad girl by Cyril for our lord. Kagan must fight our lord. Governor take Sarkel and hope be Kagan Menashe."

"But surely Prince Vladimir would not - "

"He'd like to take trade and get much silver," interrupted the guide. "No, Varangian. To free priest find true bad man - not easy!"

So Ethelwulf decided to send out Sven among the alleys surrounding the synagogue to see if anybody had seen anything which could be used to clear the priest. Unfortunately he'd need Chorpan when he attended again on the Governor. After all he had to make sure Amran Chat didn't proceed in any unwelcome directions. He delegated Morkere to supervising the collection of whatever information could be brought in during his absence.

*

The next day, the Agent was already outside the Governor's chamber when Ethelwulf arrived. As he saw the Westerner scurrying in his direction Amran Chat started to put on a display of impatience. He'd been talking quietly to a tall, wiry Khazar at the door; now his voice rose and he started to peer apparently in all directions at once, obviously slipping down the path of nervous despair. Ethelwulf couldn't understand what was being said as Chorpan had somehow become separated and was tailing along some distance behind. He felt it polite to apologise for keeping the Agent waiting but wasn't pleased at the snort of dismissal which his words prompted; it may have well been for the benefit of the Khazar, who bestowed on Ethelwulf a knowing smile, but Ethelwulf was certain Amran Chat had been luxuriating over some table while he'd been hard at work trying to carry out the commission of Prince Vladimir. Once Chorpan had arrived, calmed his gasping breath and straightened his brown cloak, which had managed to become askew in the rush, the deputation from Prince Vladimir was ready.

The thin Khazar, whom Amran Chat whispered to Ethelwulf was called Barjik, now gently pushed open the door and to an unseen audience announced the arrival of Amran Chat, Agent of the Kagan of Kenugard, and his party; Ethelwulf exchanged a glance with Chorpan as neither liked being so summarily dismissed.

Menashe Bulan didn't seem to have moved since the audience the previous day, except to exchange the yellow caftan for one of white which still possessed a scarlet edge. The Governor again appeared nervous but whether because he feared insurrection from the native population or investigation from the deputation was unclear. As the envoys entered he looked up from a document as if caught embroiled in yet another administrative task. He asked whether they'd managed to make any progress in their investigation of whatever was causing religious unrest among "his people". Amran Chat rather grandly replied that "his agent" had been assiduous in mastering the complexities of the current dissensions, but was interrupted by the Governor who, cutting him short, turned his eyes on Ethelwulf. Ethelwulf noticed the eyes of the Governor possessed a paleness of blue which was unusual and effectively disguised whatever thoughts were being marshalled behind them; now these twin orbs seemed to envelop him, with an encouragement to speak openly which he found disconcerting.

"I've spent the time, my lord, investigating the case of the priest, Cyril, currently imprisoned in your citadel, and coming to the conclusion he's innocent of the accusations made against him."

Menashe Bulan turned to his left where the gruff voice of an aide obviously reminded him of the details of the case. He then resumed his stare at the Westerner and asked how a stranger could so quickly reach conclusions at odds with those of his own officials.

"Perhaps, my lord," smiled Ethelwulf, determined to shrug off whatever distaste he might feel for the gaze of the man and talk to the Governor as a fellow servant of Prince Vladimir, "it's just because I AM such a stranger I can do that." He paused, too briefly for Amran Chat to do more than open his mouth to intervene. "I can see the charges stem from coincidence; somebody desecrated the synagogue and next day the priest seemed to challenge the strict dietary laws of the Jews."

"Have you looked at the priest's history?" The question was direct, even when passing through the massaging effects of translation. It threw Ethelwulf as he had to admit to himself that time had prevented such enquiry - and he'd never even considered it! "Can my lord enlighten me?" he found himself asking, not as a challenge, although Amran Chat seemed to consider it might be, by the way he appeared to withdraw himself from the Westerner emotionally if not physically.

The Governor was surprised at being questioned for he looked at the aide again. This time the gruff voice was less sure and the answer was less complete; Ethelwulf ignored the attempted translation of Chorpan as he concentrated on the Governor's face.

"Priest speaks bad words to Moslems and Jews."

"As one would expect from a priest who's taken upon himself the role of missionary," smiled Ethelwulf and then added, "Am I correct in assuming there was no link between the priest and the words earlier painted on the synagogue's doors?"

Again the Governor consulted the aide and confirmed no such connection had been made before the sermon.

"At this moment," answered Ethelwulf, "I've several men scouring the thoroughfares of your city for evidence against others - "

"Whom you've identified?" interrupted Menashe Bulan with a faint sneer on his lips, confident of the answer.

"Not yet, my lord - "

"Then, we'll give you five days to find the evidence, Westerner," stated the Governor, and he shifted his gaze so that it encompassed all three members of the deputation before him. "Otherwise, as you'll agree, we must proceed against the priest in the hopes we can satisfy the demands of our own people."

"As my lord commands," muttered Ethelwulf, already wishing himself outside the chamber and working to secure the release of the priest. He could sense the fury of Amran Chat beside him, knowing that whatever advantage the delegation might have initially possessed had been dissipated. As it was all three members sensed the audience had been abruptly terminated and silently withdrew from the chamber.

Outside Amran Chat ignored Barjik as he turned on the Westerner whom he considered had risked their effectiveness by apparently challenging the Governor. Ethelwulf simply smiled with an arrogance which further stoked up that fury.

"Perhaps we'll wait to see what five days can bring about?" Ethelwulf stated at last, with a confidence certainly not felt. He knew he'd pushed Menashe Bulan far too hard, especially as he knew so little about the customs and organisation of the Khazars. Perhaps he'd been too moved by the priest, Cyril; certainly the man was incapable of desecration.

"Yes, we shall!" snapped the Agent. "And I'm sure it'll lead to you being sent back in disgrace!"

*

Sven had good news; directly he saw Ethelwulf his mouth opened in an enormous grin revealing the wide gaps left by lost teeth, some due to decay but others to the frequent fights in which the guide had become involved in Kenugard. Apparently the unusual event of a group of three pigs being driven through the narrow streets and alleyways to the north of the synagogue had been noticed during the late evening. Before Ethelwulf could ask why THREE pigs were of such importance Sven's grin widened. He explained that, of course, several pigs would be a more natural sight than a solitary animal being driven for some distance, adding that market day had been the following day. Ethelwulf nodded, accepting that animals raised in all sorts of odd corners would have to be driven to market in the hours before trading began. Now Sven added his masterstroke by saying that a pair of pigs had been seen on their way to market later on the same evening.

"And you're interested in the missing pig?" asked Ethelwulf already knowing the answer.

"Westerner," replied Sven in the hoarse tones to which the whole expedition had become accustomed. "When three is two ask where other gone."

"And who was driving such interesting beasts?" smiled Ethelwulf, again confident of the answer.

"Who sell pigs I ask," replied the guide and, noting the disappointment in Ethelwulf's face, " Sure I have name soon."

Ethelwulf congratulated Sven on his good work and wondered if Chorpan would pass on word of the time limit imposed by the Governor. As it was he could do little so he decided to step outside their quarters and savour the delights of Sarkel.

He was amazed at the activity on almost every corner. Not only were all kinds of vegetables and fruit for sale but also the choicer items of barter - women's finery, jewellery and objects such as mirrors, knives and belts - were being exchanged with a good deal of noise and enthusiasm. In Sarkel trading was not limited to market-day but was a continuous occupation. He was certain the same items might be bought and sold several times in a matter of days before reaching their local value. On the faces of some he noticed an open friendliness, perhaps an urge to trade with a stranger, which was commonplace in other places, such as Visby and Waterford, where one of the leading occupations was that of trader. However, on the faces of many he detected a suspicion of his obvious Rus origins, not quite a hatred but a distaste for interference in the normal transactions of life. He found little difficulty in identifying some of the more extreme adherents to the different faiths which met and squabbled there, but often he'd have been hard put to distinguish a Moslem from a Jew or a Christian. Again he noted when trade was in the forefront of activities there was a tendency to gloss over too-obvious differences in order to maintain a clear flow of barter. A couple of the locals tried to speak to him but when they realised he had problems with their barbarous forms of Rus they abandoned the attempt, being content to offer trinkets with the broadest of smiles, and not appearing too heart-broken when their 'bargains' were declined.

At this point Ethelwulf suddenly realised he wasn't alone but had been joined by Morkere and Chorpan. It was clear the guide had told Morkere all that had happened in the Governor's chamber for his cousin didn't seem too happy. However, he cheered up when Ethelwulf told him of the optimism of Sven that very soon they'd have the names of possible offenders. Chorpan merely grunted, explaining Sven did have an irritating habit of anticipating success. Morkere and Ethelwulf exchanged glances as it was clear Chorpan didn't get on with either Sven or Gostyata.

"Perhaps you can introduce us to one of the finer taverns in your city?" offered Morkere with a wide grin as he clapped his arms around the hunched shoulders of the guide. Chorpan attempted a smile but it was a miserable failure. It was obvious he had little faith in Sven coming up with any useful information.

*

In this Chorpan was proved wrong because that evening Sven appeared with two names and descriptions for Ethelwulf.

"They Khwarizmian[77]trader, Marwan al-Tafiq and Haroun ibn Khalousi. I no know why they together. Perhaps nearby clans but long be together. They sell sable[78], amber and khutu[79] - "

"What's that?" interrupted Morkere completed bemused.

"Fish-teeth from ice seas," responded Sven, keen to carry on with his narrative. "Moslems like them but Khazars here no like."

Ethelwulf thought the cause may well have been their specialities, by shutting out local products, brought little profit to the traders of Sarkel, not making them the most popular merchants in the town.

"Look!" continued Sven, almost shouting as he saw the slight drift in the attention of the Westerner. "They have three pig late in night-"

"And were they in charge of the two pigs later seen?" interposed Ethelwulf.

"Maybe – maybe know men," confessed Sven. "Woman see men have two pig never see khutu traders before." There was a slight smile as he realised this was true of the Westerners before him.

"But it's strange to find two merchants dealing in fish-teeth taking an interest in pigs," remarked Morkere.

Sven nodded and rewarded the comment with a knowing smile. The transit of three pigs at such an hour could have been explained but his informants were positive the two men involved were Marwan al-Tafiq and Haroun ibn Khalousi, although, naturally, they'd employed a couple of Severians to actually handle the creatures. Neither Jew nor Moslem would willingly pollute themselves with close contact with pigs and so two Moslems dealing with such beasts were noted. The guide didn't bother to discuss the nature of religious taboos with strangers from the West; however, he did take up the point made by Morkere.

"That I think," he smiled before adding with an air of someone imparting an item of great confidence. "Men tell me they no know what men do but know they Moslem with pig."

"I think we need to do two things," interposed Ethelwulf. "Firstly we should ask both men - preferably separately - what they were doing with pigs." He saw the glee with which Sven agreed, noting the guide obviously had little love for followers of Mohammed. "Secondly we need to see if whoever saw the drivers of the pair of pigs can identify them."

"And they can explain what happened to the missing pig," stated Morkere and then added, "but how can we lay hands on the pair?"

"By appealing to their greed," answered Ethelwulf. He examined the features of the guide as he continued, "You, Sven, can carry one of our pieces of amber to each of these men and explain we've come from the far North, acting as agents for the Lord of Kenugard, but carrying with us - what did you call it, khutu? - which we're anxious to trade, privately." Sven nodded, his keen mind imagining the anticipation of the two Moslems at getting their hands on such a precious item." Stress the word 'privately'. We want to arouse the greed of the traders so they lose any sense of caution."

Sven smiled. He was sure both men would see a useful lever in what they suspected was the Westerner's need to keep such trading a secret from Prince Vladimir. Perhaps they might expect extra profit from the naivety of the Westerners when dealing with Khazar markets. Certainly if they believed rivals had heard nothing of a new supply of khutu they might anticipate even greater profit. The guide was surprised at the subtlety of the Westerner's mind - and noted he'd need to be careful when dealing with such a man.

Both traders should be approached separately with the bait of amber to meet the Westerners in a suitable location well away from the citadel. Sven was able to suggest a suitable spot where the ambush might be set up. He also undertook to make sure the women who'd seen the drivers of the pair of pigs would also be available to identify the suspects.

*

Marwan al-Tafiq was intrigued by the confident way in which the Khazar recently arrived with the strangers from Kenugard displayed the small amber figurine. He found the article attractive, but not overwhelmingly so; the reference to khutu had been far more exciting. At the right price a good supply of 'fish-teeth' could net him such a profit as would surpass two year's normal trading. Of course, the Khazar hadn't ACTUALLY said khutu would be there waiting but he stressed how several of the strangers, born in lands so distant they were the stuff of legend, had spent months among the Finns and Wends, certainly acquiring a suitable amount of khutu. The Khwarizmian trader agreed to follow the Khazar to discuss establishing a trading link profitable to them both. Before he set out he made sure the Khazar knew he'd very little silver in his purse, so there'd be no profit in a simple act of brigandage.

At last they came to a large building, constructed from the same materials which had given the citadel its name of 'white fortress', just as lengthening shadows reminded Marwan he'd almost forgotten about the practice of Salat;[80] he expected he'd just have time to complete business before bustling off to the nearest mosque. The door swung open after a vigorous knocking by the Khazar who, without a word, swept in, followed by the trader.

Suddenly the door slammed shut behind him and Marwan al-Tafiq found himself staring at the point of a broadsword in the hand of a Rus warrior. He was standing in the clear light of a torch but the warrior was partly in the shadows which encircled the light. Marwan wanted to scream but all he found he could do was to croak out the message he was carrying so little silver on him that robbery would be pointless.

"It's not silver but the truth," declared a voice to the left of the warrior. Marwan was puzzled and was about to question the meaning when the voice went on. "You were seen driving three pigs in the streets of this city two weeks ago. Is this true?" Marwan's mind was dragged back to that evening when, much against his wishes, he'd been carried along to place a slaughtered pig outside a synagogue. Haroun had declared it was an act of defiance against the locals trying to squeeze them out of legitimate trade. He'd protested but Haroun had said the result would so divert the attention of the Jewish traders that good Moslems would be able to snap up bargains before anyone else was aware of them. Besides he'd added the Jews practised a contemptible faith, shunning the true worship of Allah. He'd been assured he wouldn't have to soil his hands by even touching the unclean animals as pagans would be well paid to do what was necessary. Even with this memory restored to its key position Marwan was about to deny any involvement but the voice added, "We can produce witnesses so do not waste any more time!" Although still wondering what all this had to do with the Rus ruffian wielding the sword, Marwan hung his head and mumbled words to the effect they'd been driving the animals to market for a friend.

The response was a sneering laugh and the presentation of two old women into the light who simply stared at him before nodding their heads. The voice continued, "These witnesses identify you as someone driving two pigs through the streets directly to the north of the citadel. Do you deny it?"

Marwan tried to argue that others were doing the actual driving but this protest was mockingly rejected. "Do they speak the truth?" said the voice and the broadsword was silently advanced towards his throat. Marwan felt his throat grow big as dryness seemed to usurp his vocal chords; he again bowed his head and nodded three times vigorously.

"So what happened to the third pig?" asked the voice. It was the question which he'd known was coming and the one which he feared, just as the memory of the scene horrified the brain. A pagan driver had seized one of the pigs and with a skill gained by years of practice slashed its throat. Even as his companion continued to drive the remaining two pigs onward, the butcher had, with skilful efficiency, snatched from somewhere a hammer and with a single brutal blow pinned the pig head-downwards to the door. Blood dripped down the door itself on to the ground and Marwan, for the first time, had moved his head upwards and realised the building was a synagogue. Before he could protest the soft voice of Haroun had whispered, "Pigs decorate the house of pigs!" and hustled him on. In a daze he'd hurried along the alleyways before he caught up with the other pagan driver, only then noticing the butcher had remained at the scene of slaughter.

A prick from the sharp point of the sword brought his consciousness back to the here and now. Could he lie? No! Yes! The blade seemed to guess, to anticipate and he was suddenly terrified, feeling his bladder open as he knew a single wrong word would mean his death. Should he lie? Yes! No! Marwan described how the others had slaughtered the pig and stuck it up on the door. As he finished the blade was withdrawn and he heard a sound behind him before blackness snatched him from reality.

*

Haroun ibn Khalousi proved easier to lure to the ambush but much harder to extract a confession. He glared at the old women who identified him as a driver of the pair of pigs and denounced them as liars in the pay of the Jews. In fact, he spat at the Rus threatening him with the sword; at such an act of defiance the warrior had stepped forward and, with a lightening movement, reversed the blade so that its pommel smacked against Haroun's lips, before, just as quickly, assuming his previous stance. Haroun could feel a broken tooth in the mass of blood which now filled his mouth. Again he spat, this time aiming carefully and saw a mass of tooth and blood spill over the floor. Now he felt afraid, realising he wasn't meant for this world of violence. From the side came a movement and then Marwan's body was cast into the light. Haroun had to look very carefully to recognise signs of life in his partner.

Again came the questions and this time there was less resistance. Of course, Haroun's tale gave Marwan the leading role in the events of that night. However, he strenuously denied he'd scrawled "Let His blood fall on ourselves and our children" on the walls of the synagogue and had been believed.

So Ethelwulf was sure he'd secured enough evidence to get the priest released, but Chorpan had his doubts.

"You attack two traders," he insisted. "Maybe they say you lie."

"We have the witnesses to their driving of the pigs."

"Women! Man know women tell lies!" snapped Chorpan.

"Where did they get the pigs?" suggested Morkere. "And what did they do with the pair that survived?"

Ethelwulf looked at his cousin and weighed the questions in his mind. Neither answer involved criminal activity but would link a Moslem with pigs - unheard-of behaviour. Would it be enough?

"What did pagans do?" asked Chorpan suddenly. Then he answered his own question. "They Severian. Little Severians here."

"But are they still here?" doubted Ethelwulf and the guide stopped in full flight of his imagination. Severians wandered in and out of Sarkel every week. How could they find the men?

"Gostyata should prove useful here," put in Morkere and Ethelwulf slapped his cousin on the shoulder. Of course, the half-Severian guide had been wandering in and out of the area which made up the home of his people for the last few days. First they had to get a better idea of what the men looked like - as well as answering some questions about the trade in pigs!

*

Marwan al-Tafiq proved the more co-operative of the two prisoners. They'd bought the three pigs from a well-known Khazar trader, Kupin Shmuel, and sold the two pigs to another trader, a Severian trader called Khadir. Both men regularly appeared in the markets of Sarkel and both, apparently, had acted in good faith. Tracking down the pagans involved proved more difficult, although Gostyata shrewdly decided that at least one of the pagans must have been a herdsman or shepherd as butchery was unknown to towns as a trade. Accordingly he started asking questions, helped by a couple of Severians who swore they knew just about every Severian living in Sarkel. Unfortunately this didn't prove to be the case.

It was rapidly discovered there was a continuous drift in and out of Sarkel by people from the surrounding countryside, Khazars, Severians and others. Some came to the town for work, or to escape from problems in their villages; others came to Sarkel for specific reasons, such as bringing the fruits of a harvest or animals bred for the market. It was this latter group that Gostyata decided to concentrate on. Armed with a good description of the two pagans supplied, surprisingly, by Haroun ibn Khalousi, the guide passed among the traders dealing with animals and eventually came up with about three or four names, and their villages. Next he descended on the villages themselves and with a mixture of promises and threats managed to identify both of the individuals concerned. The two Severians were brought to Sarkel and willingly admitted they'd been hired by the Moslem traders to drive pigs through the streets of Sarkel in the late evening rather than the usual early morning. Papatzys proved most reluctant to admit killing the pig and nailing it to the door of the synagogue but, faced with the accusation of his fellow Severian and the promise of protection by Ethelwulf, he admitted what he had done. He was assured he could disappear back into the countryside once he'd given evidence. Of course, Ethelwulf doubted this would prove the case as the Governor would need to make an example to placate his

Jewish population; he hoped the example would include the two Moslem traders.

*

On the fifth day Ethelwulf felt confident as he approached the citadel with his prisoners and witnesses under guard by six men commanded by Gunnar. The Khazar guards at the doors of the Governor's audience chamber looked uneasy as they examined the axes of the Rus following Ethelwulf, Chorpan and Gostyata; Ethelwulf had deliberately selected six men who were tall and used to wielding the dreaded double-handed axe. For a brief period it seemed unlikely they'd be allowed to enter the presence of the Governor and there was further delay as about twenty Khazar warriors were summoned. It looked as if there was going to be trouble when Barjik, the aide to the Governor, demanded the Westerners lay aside their arms and they refused. Only when Ethelwulf suggested the Khazar warriors should enter the chamber first, surrounding the Varangians so they were no threat to Menashe Bulan was the matter settled, the doors opened and the parties filed into the chamber.

The Governor had changed his trousers to a dark brown and his caftan to a sky-blue, but he hadn't changed the suspicious glare with which he greeted the arrival of Ethelwulf. These suspicions were intensified when a somewhat breathless Amran Chat rushed through the doors unannounced, full of apologies and anxiety to please. The Governor said nothing but looked from the Agent to Ethelwulf and back again with a malicious smile on his lips.

"This matter doesn't concern my Prince's Agent, my lord," explained Ethelwulf, knowing Amran Chat, being in complete ignorance of how he'd gone about collecting evidence, would only get in the way when it came to proving his case. "You asked me to prove the priest, Cyril, was innocent of the offences against the community for which he's been imprisoned and that's what I've done."

"And is it necessary to come with such a large body of armed men?" queried the Governor and he wistfully admired the Rus warriors knowing that, as individuals, they were better than his own.

"Merely because we've brought into your presence, my lord, the actual offenders," came the answer. Menashe Bulan allowed his eyes to pass over the collection of civilians in front of him. Ethelwulf noted how he immediately dismissed the two women, paused when he examined the faces of the two traders, and almost licked his lips as his glance at last fell upon the terrified Severians.

Ethelwulf had no doubt the Governor was a cruel man who delighted in administering the punishments required by law.

At this point Amran Chat tried to intervene, asserting he was the head of the deputation to Sarkel. He stopped when Ethelwulf curtly invited him to describe the case against the people brought into the chamber under guard. The Agent's protests dried up as he realised ignorance wouldn't be tolerated before the Governor. If he tried to declare Ethelwulf had acted on his own in arresting Khazar subjects he would admit lacking control over his men; if he alleged everything had been done according to his orders, he'd have to outline the charges, and he knew he could not. Seeing his confusion Ethelwulf simply stepped in front of the Agent, bowed to the Governor and began to outline the case against the two traders.

He described the actions of the men in detail, periodically pausing to demand the relevant individuals should state what he said was true. As he spoke his words were translated by either Chorpan or (when he was dealing with the Severians) by Gostyata. He stressed the Severians had merely been hired by the Moslem traders and had acted with no intention of desecrating a holy place; even so, he could see Menashe Bulan was not impressed.

"So why did they butcher a pig and hang it from the door of a synagogue?" asked the Governor and Ethelwulf saw no explanation would be acceptable. However, the Severians were not so perceptive and blabbered about being told it was all a joke practised by the traders against some of their friends. Ethelwulf wondered whether this was what they'd really been told; it didn't matter because Menashe Bulan clearly didn't believe them.

As he described the role of the Moslem traders, backed by the reluctant admissions of both men, Ethelwulf could see the fury of the Governor growing behind the pale blue eyes. He wondered what were the links between Governor and Moslem community and, with horror, realised he had no idea.

Finally he presented the two women as witnesses to the connection between the traders and the pigs. He hadn't bothered to drag along the original vendor and purchaser of the animals; after all, the chamber was crowded enough!

At last, Ethelwulf finished by demanding the release of the priest and the silence which followed was almost threatening. Menashe Bulan simply sat and glared at Ethelwulf; Amran Chat started to bluster some kind of apology. His voice was stilled by a curt wave from the Governor.

"By what right do you demand the release of the priest?" asked the Governor, the squeak in his voice being more pronounced as his eyes narrowed to over-awe Ethelwulf.

"By the right of your own words, my lord," answered the Saxon, staring coolly back at the Governor. "You gave me five days to find evidence or you'd proceed against the priest. Having found such evidence I'd presume you must release the priest as the only alternative to proceeding against him."

"Not the sole alternative," contradicted Menashe Bulan with a sneer of superiority. "We could simply leave him to rot in our dungeon."

"And I could simply report to Prince Vladimir how a priest whose faith he now shares had been treated by the justice of one of his provinces." The silence now became chilling.

Menashe Bulan considered the words of the Wanderer and didn't find what he heard to his liking. "Why do you bother yourself with the affairs of one priest in one province of the Kagan's realm?"

"Because. like yourself, my lord, the Prince wishes to rule his people with justice, so the innocent can walk safely and the guilty tremble in fear of punishment."

The Governor came to a decision. He leaned back in his chair and withdrew the long talon which had been caressing his lips as he'd listened to the argument put forward by Ethelwulf. "Yes, we desire the guiltless to go free and so we order the release of the priest, Cyril, immediately." He turned to an aid. "Itakh, see that my will is done!" The aide scurried out of the room by some side door, ignored by the Governor who fixed his eyes on Ethelwulf. "You come from the edge of the world, Varangian. Don't meddle in customs of which you know little!"

"I had no such intention, my lord, "answered Ethelwulf smoothly. "I knew the justice of Prince Vladimir must be reflected in Sarkel."

"And so it is, Varangian," answered the Governor in a hiss which told Ethelwulf he'd found his measure for the future. "You'll now see how!" With that he rapped out orders which caused the two Severians to scream in horror, even as guards rushed forward to drag them out of the chamber. Ethelwulf looked around at Chorpan, completely at a loss at what had happened.

"They pig-stuck today," whispered Chorpan. Ethelwulf turned back to the Governor, prepared to declare both Severians had been promised immunity if they told the truth. One glance of the expression on the face of the Governor told him any appeal for mercy would be pointless; indeed, as he looked into the eyes of Menashe Bulan he knew he was being willed to protest so he could be accused of interference in the performance of justice.

"My lord acts with decision," he found himself saying, although his eyes conveyed a message of another sort. "May I ask what is to be the fate of the two who initiated the desecration?"

Menashe Bulan seemed to ponder on the punishment of the traders, although Ethelwulf was certain it had been decided for some time. "Their heads are to decorate the main gate of our citadel and their property absorbed by our treasury." At this Haroun ibn Khalousi fell upon his knees begging for mercy, but his fellow-trader merely stayed silent, perhaps confident that somehow the judgement might be altered. Four more guards stepped forward and seized both men - Haroun was dragged across the floor screaming for mercy. Amran Chat followed the exit of both men and appeared to shiver, perhaps remembering the limits to the power of Kenugard on the borders of the realm of his Prince. Ethelwulf kept his eyes fixed on those of the Governor and some message was exchanged.

"That is all!" snapped the Governor. "You are dismissed!" Ethelwulf bowed low, turned and led his men out of the chamber, followed by the scurrying feet of the two women, glad to get out while still free. Amran Chat hesitated, uncertain whether the order applied to him. "You too," screeched Menashe Bulan." Get out!" The Agent rushed out of the chamber to find Ethelwulf had already disappeared. Amran Chat determined to write a report highly critical of Ethelwulf to his master, confident he'd ruin this upstart from the West and hoping he'd soon regain the favours of the Governor of Sarkel.

*

The Wanderer 7:4

*"The days on earth for each is numbered,
Strive to gain renown before death -
The best memorial to any warrior
No longer in this world."* ("Beowulf")

Among the Khazars

Amran Chat was determined to separate himself as far as possible from the leader of the guards which Prince Vladimir of Kenugard had foisted on him. Naturally he'd never have admitted that to anybody but that was what he wanted. The Westerner had challenged the authority of Menashe Bulan, the governor of Sarkel, and had, unfortunately, got away with it. There was murmuring among the Moslem subjects of the Prince when the heads of the two Moslem traders convicted of desecration appeared over the gates of the citadel, and even more murmuring when the silver and trading goods amassed by the two men was seized by the Governor's warriors. Yet neither the Moslems nor the pagans, who had cause to mourn the barbarous punishment inflicted on the two Severians caught up in the affair, had enough power to defy the Governor. The bulk of the Khazar population, long followers of the Jewish faith, applauded the actions of the Governor; the Christians, welcoming back the released priest, simply breathed a sigh of relief that the eyes of Menashe Bulan hadn't turned in their direction..

Ethelwulf, the cause of Amran Chat's displeasure, seemed oblivious to the attitude of the Governor. Wiser men might have kept a low profile for whatever time remained for them in the territory of the Khazars but the Westerner seemed incapable of doing this. In fact, he was encouraged by reinforcements sent from Kenugard. The Varangians successfully rooted out a gang of brigands to the south of Sarkel who appeared to have an understanding with Pechenegs in terrorising the lower Don; for this they publicly received the thanks of the Governor but obviously he wasn't pleased.

For Menashe Bulan had never before been so challenged and was fearful others might see him as being overtaken by unusual weakness. He prided himself on the terror with which he'd managed to establish control over the region surrounding Sarkel. He had no intention of seeing all his work undermined. So he was determined to exploit the skills of the Varangians to extend his authority over the peoples to the east. He knew that originally the detachment had been sent as the bodyguard for the Agent of Prince Vladimir but, from discussions with Amran Chat, the Governor was convinced there was nothing the Agent would desire more than the complete removal of the detachment. Yet he knew he'd have to operate gradually; the first move was to get Ethelwulf attached to his own authority. Accordingly he sent envoys to Kenugard praising the abilities of the Varangians and begging that, since the threat of religious turmoil seemed to have diminished, he might make use of their skills in furthering of the power of the Kagan in the region. Much to his surprise his request was granted and he enjoyed the disappointment, bordering on distress, which took over the features of the hated Westerner when he informed him of the decision of the Kagan. Menashe Bulan knew there'd come a day when the Varangians would either disobey or fail to execute orders and then he could crush them. To his delight Amran Chat concurred.

At first, Ethelwulf had been appalled at his sudden change of masters. He'd rapidly developed a contempt for Amran Chat which meant he normally undertook independent action. He enjoyed the status with which he was perceived, especially by the Christian community within Khazaria. Now that would all go; for the only feeling Ethelwulf didn't possess for the Governor of Sarkel was contempt. He feared the power Menashe Bulan could wield, if given the opportunity; he hated the way the Governor almost abused the authority given him by Prince Vladimir; and he admired the persistence with which the Governor could set about a task and pursue it. The campaign against the Don brigands had been just an initiation in his new role. Ethelwulf suspected the Governor would have liked to use him against the Pechenegs but feared the immediate effect of such a war on his own position before the strength of Kenugard could be exploited.

It was, consequently, no great surprise when, soon after Christmas had been celebrated, Ethelwulf was summoned into the presence of Menashe Bulan to receive new orders. He was intrigued by it being, yet again, one of escort duty. Ethelwulf knew Menashe Bulan was irritated by the Kagan of Ithel[81] who retained a degree of independence from Prince Vladimir. Provided the Kagan of Ithel paid in full the tribute demanded by Kenugard and performed other duties, he was left to himself, although rumour suggested such payments might be stopped due to the growing influence of the Ghuzz.[82] Sarkel competed with Ithel for control over Khazar districts most in danger from Pecheneg aggression. Of course, one way of getting the backing of Prince Vladimir was to ensure a steady stream of taxation to be delivered from such areas - and that was why Ethelwulf had been summoned by the Governor.

As he entered, followed by the indefatigable Chorpan, Ethelwulf noticed Toghrul Beg, the huge Turkish mercenary employed to control those disputed territories. Ethelwulf didn't like the methods employed by the Turk and his appearance encouraged the feeling. Toghrul was as tall as Gunnar, that is about a hand's length taller than himself, but much bulkier. His hair had been originally black but was now grizzled; a thick beard of the same colour enveloped the lower half of his features, apart from a deep scar on his left cheek. His eyes were small, black and constantly shifting from left to right - the sign of a liar and cheat. They were obscured by bushy eyebrows but the sharp nose naturally pointed that way, as if to warn the innocent. Toghrul's mouth was big and his lips thick, behind which broken teeth revealed a life-time of neglect. He was probably aged between forty and fifty but moved with the surprising subtlety of a warrior almost half his years.

Toghrul was every inch a fighting man, protected by a studded leather hauberk which, as it was not yet summer, was cocooned in a thick shirt of marten skin. His leggings were made of similar material and his feet encased in strong leather boots. For weapons the Turk carried a long curved knife in the broad belt encircling his paunch and at his side a thick, heavy scimitar; he'd long ago abandoned the powerful bow common among his race as being worthy only of common warriors. For Toghrul was proud and with that pride came a cruelty and ruthlessness which had not only got him to the position of a leader among the garrison at Sarkel but kept him there. From the start he and Ethelwulf hated each other.

"I have called both of you here," interrupted the voice of Menashe Bulan as Ethelwulf and Toghrul Beg glared at each other, " because I'm despatching an expedition to villages lying to the south of Samandar on the Salt Sea."[83] Chorpan was maintaining a continuous whisper in Ethelwulf's ear as he translated furiously into Rus. Seeing there was no response the Governor continued. "For ten years we've issued demands for taxes from these villages which have been ignored."

Ethelwulf transferred his attention to the Governor and asked, through Chorpan, the obvious question. "Do the villages pay taxes to anyone?"

"We've heard they send irregular tribute to the Kagan of Ithel - and that he's controlled by the Ghuzz!" snapped the Governor. "We therefore think whatever money as can be raised from such people should be paid to ourselves and our lord of Kenugard." There was no comment on this although Ethelwulf wondered how much of the idea actually originated with Prince Vladimir. Again he cursed the limitations of language which meant he had to operate through Chorpan – loyal but with limited skills.

"So we'll send a force to ensure payment which our treasurer has calculated," resumed the Governor and he waited for any questions but there were none. He nodded, almost as a sign of self-congratulation and added, watching Ethelwulf for a reaction, "We'll place Toghrul Beg in command of the force." Seeing a slight tightening of muscles in the face revealing Ethelwulf's displeasure, Menashe Bulan continued, "Toghrul's command of language will help him negotiate with the heads of the villages."

If the Governor had hoped the explanation would be accepted he was disappointed. Ethelwulf largely controlled his reaction but inwardly fumed. The Governor should have appointed an official, well-versed in financial matters and the Khazar language, to command the expedition; if he really required both commanders he could have split their commands into different areas. The Wanderer was certain one motive for the Governor's decision was to underscore his control over the fortune of the Varangians and vent some of his pent-up irritation on Ethelwulf.

Toghrul grunted and what he presumed was a smile appeared on his lips. "How many men will we take, my lord?" he asked in his bass tones. The glare had returned to harass the Westerner, but now backed by a glint of savage amusement. As long as his force matched that commanded by Ethelwulf he was already dreaming of how to share out responsibilities, with the Varangians coming off distinct losers.

"You'll each take fifty warriors," answered Menashe Bulan before adding, "if Ethelwulf feels he needs help he may take two interpreters." The faint sneer in the offer was ignored by Ethelwulf, already planning to use Chorpan and Sven. "I expect you to leave Sarkel by next Tuesday." He waited to see if there was any problem with this but neither commander gave any reaction. "I'll see you both here tomorrow morning, together with lists of your needs, and then I'll detail your route and any other necessary orders."

Both commanders nodded, bowed and made for the door. Ethelwulf paused, stood back and let the Turk pass in front. There seemed an extra swagger in Toghrul's step as he left the chamber, which was just what Ethelwulf had intended.

*

Morkere was unsurprised by the violent language with which his cousin described the proposed expedition; although Ethelwulf had a cool head, especially on the battlefield, he let loose emotion when with people he could trust. So Morkere, Edwine and Gunnar had a description of the interview which certainly wouldn't have matched any report by Menashe Bulan himself.

"Should the Agent be advised to report the plans to Prince Vladimir?" asked Edwine and was somewhat taken back by the vehemence with which his cousin greeted the suggestion. Their lord might know little of the plans of his Governor but he might not welcome being told so by a Westerner. Even more, Amran Chat would probably go blabbing immediately to Menashe Bulan himself, and they wouldn't like whatever the Governor would do as a result. Indeed, would the Agent even pass on the report to Prince Vladimir? Amran Chat seemed to have settled into life at Sarkel so comfortably as to be almost considered a man of the Governor rather than the loyal servant of Kenugard. Edwine wondered how much of the fury was generated by sheer frustration.

Another cause was undoubtedly apprehension. They'd little chance of retiring towards distant Kenugard if anything went wrong. They knew little about the region and Morkere, already making good progress in the Khazarian language, was to find out as much as possible about the area and its people. Morkere wondered how far they should trust Chorpan and Ethelwulf insisted the guide shouldn't be told more than necessary, adding that, after all, the Khazarian elements in his personality might not see matters the way they'd prefer.

Gunnar was to assemble fifty men, properly equipped for the expedition and Edwine told to put together a list of food and other necessary supplies. "As for myself," grinned Ethelwulf, with a little of his more usual quiet good humour, "I'll receive instruction from the hands of the Governor himself and try to avoid scrapping with my fellow-pupil, Toghrul Beg!" This conjured up for the cousins memories of their hours of learning in far-off Dorset and how study was often punctuated by tricks and jokes which sometimes led to blood-letting; the resulting laughter transformed the mood of the meeting. Gunnar was completely perplexed; his schooling had largely consisted of practice with the long-handled axe which gave little opportunity for humour.

*

"First you should know," muttered the Governor directing his pale gaze at Ethelwulf, "that Samandar no longer exercises any authority in the area. It was the old capital of the Khazarian realm but long ago Ithel pushed it aside. Since its foundation Sarkel has proved the natural leader of the Khazars." He smiled softly to himself convinced he'd contributed much to the success of Sarkel, oblivious to the truth that only conquest by the Rus had put him in charge of the city. "So you might say there've been three centres of authority in Khazaria - Samandar, Ithel and Sarkel - and the former has lost its position."

The Governor now invited both commanders to join him at a table erected in the centre of his audience chamber. On the table was a map showing the full extent of what had been the Khazarian Empire. Menashe Bulan pointed out the three cities he'd mentioned, along with the original capital of Balanjar, which today was scarcely worth mentioning. Ethelwulf noted someone had added Kenugard to the map. Next the Governor indicated the three villages which most concerned him. They were situated like a string of pearls along the upper reaches of the river Kuma and Ethelwulf estimated they were unhealthily close to areas long accustomed to Pecheneg raids. He dismissed the idea the villagers might call upon such savages to help them resist demands for taxes. Menashe Bulan explained he wanted the commanders to advance between the villagers and Ithel, hoping they could cut off any interference from that quarter. The expedition would employ mules, even though the Varangians had never ventured near such creatures before. Ethelwulf's protests were stilled when he noticed the distances involved which prevented water transport being used; he stayed silent although he determined that his men should fight, as was their custom, on foot. He hoped it wouldn't come to that.

Toghrul Beg asked about any restrictions on his powers and Ethelwulf was amazed as the Governor gave the Turk more or less absolute authority. He denied any hope of appeal by any of the villagers to himself, let alone Prince Vladimir. As far as he was concerned, it was simply a question of collecting out-standing taxes and asserting an authority which had been allowed to lapse. He almost suggested the expedition should behave like a conquering army. The Turk's dark eyes glinted with delight as he realised the breadth of power this would give him. He avoided looking at Ethelwulf in case the Westerner should gain some inkling of just what he was planning.

*

Within hours of setting off many in the expedition were feeling sore. Perhaps some were irritated by having to be content with mules; this was certainly true in the case of Ethelwulf and his cousins. All in their youth had ridden horses, becoming inured to the pressure which hours in the saddle can have on the body and the legs. Of course, the years in between Dorset and Khazaria had given them little opportunity of extending their horse-riding skills, but it was the relegation to mules for all of them which was most upsetting. Then they noticed over half of the contingent directly responsible to the Governor rode the wiry ponies associated with the steppes. Calm consideration might have made them realise that such mounts were probably the personal property of Turkish warriors who supplied their own equipment under the conditions of service with Menashe Bulan. However, the calm voice of reason couldn't be heard among the Varangians trotting across the empty grasslands of Khazaria; instead the bitter tongue of resentment lashed them as they headed further away from the river which might, they still believed, carry them home. Ethelwulf and his cousins shared some of the resentment although their youthful riding experience meant at least they could control their mounts; Gunnar, on the other had, like many others, demonstrated the intractable reputation of mules was not undeserved. It wasn't just a question of keeping on, or even maintaining contact with the main body, it was the indignity of an apparently endless battle with a dumb beast - and, too often, losing.

At the head of the column trotted Toghrul, perfectly at home on the pony he'd owned for four years. It was a strong mount, taller and broader than the typical pony of the steppes, and one endured to hours of carrying the bulk of its master over the grasslands. Toghrul's heels almost touched the ground, often brushing against the blades of grassland found on either side of the vague track cutting across the plains; yet he took good care of Khatun, making sure she was always well-watered and fed before settling down for the night. Indeed care of his horse ranked far higher than concern for his men in the mind of the mercenary for he well knew that, in the vast expanses of Khazaria, possession of a horse could be more important than support of half-a-dozen men.

Ethelwulf positioned himself towards the centre of the column. In fact, the Varangians took up the rear section of the detachment, with the exception of a dozen men entrusted with the task of making sure no enemy had the opportunity of launching a surprise attack against the rear of the force. By Ethelwulf's side rode Chorpan who, by dint of enthusiasm and apparent loyalty, had installed himself in the affections of the Westerners; the guide confessed the region to which they were heading was new to him. He had to admit many of his people regarded such territories as better abandoned to the Pechenegs, whom he daily expected to attack. As they rode he tried to describe to Ethelwulf what made the

Pechenegs such formidable foes, stressing that a century before much the same might have been said about his own people, and before that others had been the terror of the plains. Immediately behind Ethelwulf rode Gunnar listening intently as he realised how different the whole situation was compared to that of his Irish homeland. Further back the twins tried to lighten the generally depressed mood by making sure there was occasional laughter as they told jokes or tales.

"Look, brother, how strange I appear," challenged Morkere suddenly throwing the hood used to shade himself from the sun over his head, thrusting up his arm like a snake so it reared above the mass. "How odd a servant to my neighbours. Can't you see how much I gratify a woman?" He wriggled his arm in a way provocative enough to rouse guffaws from his fellows. "I damage none except my slayer, for I grow very straight and tall in a bed." With that he used one hand to raise himself off the back of his mule while waving his arm around in an even more ridiculous manner; then dropped suddenly down. " I'm hairy underneath and, on occasions, some brave girl of a farmer grabs hold of me." One arm seized the hand that had been flapping through the cloak. "Rubbing my ruddy skin, she hides away my head and pops me in the pantry." The waving arm was suddenly jerked down beneath the folds of the hood where it's wriggling continued with vigour. "Then the saucy wench has good cause to remember me as moisture caresses her eyes." Morkere threw back the hood, revealing his laughing face. "Well, brother, who am I?" A flurry of suggestions were offered by all who'd watched his antics to the poser of the riddle. Each one was weighed and laughingly rejected, until two answers were accepted.[84] With a wink to his brother Morkere remarked, "Which one you prefer is up to you!" This produced applause from those around the twins and others volunteered riddles of their own.

The two sections of the column were separated by mules carrying supplies for the expedition - food, weapons and the various utensils which made existence bearable. These mules were in the care of a dozen Khazarians who made up a distinct group within this heterogeneous force. In fact, not even the purpose of the expedition united them for each detachment assumed its own interpretation of their orders.

By nightfall everyone had become resigned to their mounts and there was less murmuring. Even so the men didn't intermingle - partly due to language but chiefly on account of the resentment both sides felt for the other. The Turks believed the Varangians were intruders from an alien culture, even worse than the normal upstarts from Rus, with no knowledge or respect for local customs and practices. Of course, the Turks had little love for the Khazarians, especially as conversion to Islam and Judaism respectively was undermining the original unity maintained by paganism, but centuries of close existence, friendly or otherwise, had imparted some degree of understanding. For their part, the Varangians considered they were deliberately being under-valued among such peoples, being forced to fight in terrain unsuited to their skills, among people who'd no respect for such gods as Thor, and in a climate which put excessive strain on their stamina. So there were really two camps established - albeit side-by-side.

*

On the second day there was the first fight between the two groups and it arose from the morning call to prayer. As the Turks were prostrating their bodies towards Mecca the Varangians carried on getting ready. One of the Turks, rising to his feet, happened to bump against Ketil Grettirsson who was trying to push past with his arms fully laden. Instantly all the equipment was forgotten as Ketil threw it to the ground to swing a fist at the Moslem. The Turk dodged skilfully, went in low and up-turned the Icelander. However, Ketil was an experienced fighter and as the Turk attacked he found himself running on to the foot of his opponent. He swung to the side giving Ketil the chance of rolling to his feet. Neither man had yet drawn any weapon, each determined to prove that, as individuals, they were superior. Again the two warriors squared up to each other, slowly circling in search of some kind of advantage. The Turk possessed the more solid frame but the lean body of Ketil moved with the ease of a cat as he weighed up his opponent. The Icelander could see that, probably, the Turk would have the greater strength as he possessed the greater weight; perhaps he might win if it came to a lengthy fight but he had to expect the Turk might inflict sufficient damage as to make the Icelander dangerously slow.

The lighter man decided it'd be best to settle the matter as quickly as possible. Ketil lunged at the Turk who stepped smartly aside and managed to land a blow at Ketil's ear as the Icelander's momentum carried him past. Ketil stumbled but recovered his balance before the Turk could make full use of his advantage in weight.

Both men circled each other, still neglecting to draw the knives each carried in their belts. Ketil spat viciously to the right, expelling blood which started dribbling over his lips. He honoured his opponent with a strange smile; Ketil was a great survivor of such battles, never possessing the viciousness of Turgeis Silver-Tooth but revelling in the physical struggle. Never had he been defeated in the score of such conflicts over the last three years. Now he recognised yet another opponent worth his mettle; it seemed the Turk shared such feelings for he stepped back, stretched his body before settling again into a wary crouch, his head tucking itself into the strong folds of his shoulders.

By now both men were enclosed in a circle of cheering and jeering warriors; some of the more enterprising somehow managing to give odds and collect bets. Ethelwulf's first inclination was to stop the fight but Gunnar fiercely grabbed his arm as he went to approach the two men. He pointed out neither fighter had drawn a weapon and it was clearly a contest between experienced fighters, a fitting entertainment for the warriors and a way of releasing some of the tensions grown over the last two days. Ethelwulf looked closely at Gunnar; the advice he offered would have better suited the mouth of Morkere, offering a distant perspective on an outburst of emotion. Could Morkere have put the Gall-Gael up to this? Possibly, but Ethelwulf was certain Morkere wouldn't have used an intermediary. He looked across the circle of yelling warriors and noticed Toghrul opposite. It was obvious the Turk was savouring the fight, enjoying the spectacle and Ethelwulf realised how stupid it would be to try and put a stop to such entertainment.

Ketil extended his left fist slightly forward and the Turk obliged by charging at him. Ketil's straight left landed squarely on the Turk's nose, but his attempt to follow up with a swing from his right fist was woefully slow as the Turk managed to slip inside and grab the Icelander by the shoulders. Ketil mirrored the grip and for a moment both fighters simply glared at each other, trying to figure out a way of putting his opponent on his back. The Turk slipped his leg deftly behind those of the Icelander and tried to propel him backwards; he was surprised when Ketil swung his weight into his own and both collapsed to the side, with the Icelander on top. Now the Turk grabbed the tunic[85] of his opponent and easily swung the Icelander off him, but failed to roll on top of Ketil in the same movement as the lighter man slipped away.

Both men scrambled to their feet and as he did so Ketil aimed a kick at the head of his opponent, but only managed to slam into the bulky shoulders of the Turk. By now both men were starting to breathe heavily, eyeing each other up with obvious respect but still not reaching for their knives.

The Turk now swung his left fist at Ketil who stepped inside it, right on to the waiting right fist of the Turk. The nearest spectators hurt the crunch of a breaking-nose and the involuntary cry from Ketil. One of those onlookers was Ethelwulf and he saw the Icelander step backwards reaching for the knife in his belt. He rushed forward, putting himself between the two fighters as the Turk also placed a hand on his knife. Ethelwulf stared into the dead eyes of the Turk as the man tried to ease his bulk to the side to see what his opponent was doing behind the shield of the Westerner.

"Keep your hands clear of your knife, Ketil," ordered Ethelwulf, anxious to avoid the loss of one - or possibly two - good fighters. "I'm sure enough blood's been spilt today!" Out of the corner of his eye he detected a smirk on the features of Toghrul Beg but didn't care. If knives were drawn it didn't mean Ketil would be the loser, but he didn't want to take the risk. He had no sense of what Ketil was up to behind his back but he thought he heard a couple of other men enter the impromptu ring. A few of Turks started howling their derision and he feared his men might retaliate. As yet there was no sound from some of them standing there sullenly resentful at his intrusion. He raised his hand palm outwards as a gesture of peace, calling aloud for Sven.

Suddenly the squat figure of the guide was beside him, wearing a grin which Ethelwulf couldn't interpret; was the half-Severian actually pleased victory seemed to lie with the Turks? Ethelwulf explained he wanted Sven to declare there was no need for knives to be drawn, or further blood on either side to be shed. What he wanted was for the two groups to work together to ensure success and so he was ending the fight then and there. There were howls of protest on all sides and above the hubbub Ethelwulf then added, fixing his eyes firmly on the Turk, that if either man wanted to take the matter further they could fight him in person, with swords. The shouting ceased as eyes turned to both of the combatants, some willing either man to take up the challenge. Ethelwulf saw the smirk on the face of Toghrul Beg now widened into a grin; it was clear the Turkish leader believed Ethelwulf to be a fool. Part of his mind was gratified, remembering how often he'd been under-estimated; another part felt Pride tug at his desire to remove bad feeling between the two groups. He sensed the tension as Sven, after delivering his challenge, also looked at him as if he were mad. Perhaps he was, but it seemed to be working for he could tell the Turk was not keen on taking on any of the fearsome Varangians; as for Ketil, he was sure the Icelander wouldn't dare to fight his own leader and so provoke a blood-feud within their ranks.

The Turk spat in the dust and turned to face his nearest supporters, raising his arms as a claim of victory, backed up by an enormous grin. There were hisses of disbelief from the Varangians and, for a moment, Ethelwulf feared a more general fight would break out.

Then Gunnar stepped forward to his leader's left, in his hand was his axe as he calmly asked if any there would like to kiss 'Angrboda'.[86] The hisses died down but the howls of derision increased from the Turks. No leader from their side stepped forward to calm the warriors down - but it was the Turkish 'victor' who, by quietly turning his back on Ethelwulf and slipping back into the crowd of supporters, ended the confrontation. So the ring broke up, with obvious disappointment to some on both sides.

*

There was more tension the next day when scouts reported a band of Pechenegs nearby. Even as the report was being made a cry from one of the Turks signalled the appearance of Pechenegs on the skyline to the west. Instantly the Turks without orders began to form their horses in a loose battle information, some of the more eager reaching in their quivers to check they had a good supply of arrows. Ethelwulf was disappointed to see no such cohesive response from the Varangians. Some warriors scrambled off their mules and started to try and form a shield-wall, handicapped by their fellows who sat immobile on their steeds, getting in their way and, apparently, almost thinking they could act as some kind of cavalry. For a moment Ethelwulf was almost ashamed of his men but then realised whatever fault there was lay with him. In the north it was the custom to fight on foot. Warriors might ride to battle but they certainly didn't think of FIGHTING on horseback! They hadn't been trained to deal with such a situation; obviously, mounted on mules, they could not operate as a cavalry force - even if they had the appropriate skills. As soon as they reached their destination he must make sure they practised forming the traditional shield-wall again and again until they got it right. Even so, at this moment, he doubted if they would form an effective defensive unit with the Turks if they came under attack - and that was the fault of Toghrul Beg. He rejected any idea of approaching the Turkish mercenary immediately to sort out tactics. Ethelwulf just hoped the figures he could see along the skyline were only scouts.

Chorpan seemed to read his thoughts. "If many Pechenegs here you no see till attack," was his comment. "No, worry you," and then added with a contemptuous look at the confusion among the Varangians, "see how you fight!"

Ethelwulf grimaced, "Where we fall down!"

"They tell chief," answered the guide. "how when attack." He noted the alarm which passed across the face of the Westerner. "If ever!" Ethelwulf frowned in puzzlement and Chorpan laughed. "Sven tell you. Know Pechenegs good!" With that he nudged his mule and began to pass along the confused lines, encouraging the Varangians to recover their mounted positions; Ethelwulf made no attempt to stop him, confident the guide knew what he was doing. Instead he eased his mount along to Sven who was watching the turmoil with a mouth opened in either horror or surprise - or both.

"Pecheneg Kagan know enemy good before attack," said Sven in reply to Ethelwulf's questions. "Clan here Borotalmat,"[87] he continued, "but Kagan good look all places." He paused and sheltered his eyes as he tried to make out any details of the distant figures but gave up. "If more close, look colour standard. Borotalmat black-grey, but we go to sun. Then Boulatzoupon colour piebald." He smiled, mainly to himself as he continued in a murmur. "Pray clan no like clan. We fight two clan?"

Facing both clans was not a welcome prospect. Ethelwulf wondered if it made any difference which clan attacked but then thought the clans might use different tactics. He wanted to ask Sven but the guide had already turned to help Chorpan put the Varangians in some form of order. This was done with remarkable efficiency, although both Haakon Otter and Leif Olafsson had problems seating themselves properly on their mules, much to the amusement of their comrades. Ethelwulf was grateful both men had stable tempers, managing to laugh at their own awkwardness; if somebody like Turgeis Silver-Tooth had been exposed to such laughter blood would have definitely been spilt.

All that afternoon the distant figures shadowed the progress of the expedition. Toghrul made no attempt to communicate with Ethelwulf although it was certain he possessed intelligence to equal (and probably exceed) that of the Varangians! The Wanderer called over Sven the Far-Sighted hoping the Bornholm-man could detect the colours displayed by the Pecheneg scouts but the distance prevented identification. As evening drew on the scouts suddenly disappeared, so quickly that for a moment their re-appearance was expected. Once it was realised they'd gone the Varangians felt uneasy; rumour asserting they were scouts for a large force of Pechenegs advancing on them from the west. As the expedition set up camp by one of the small streams ensuring an adequate supply of water, Ethelwulf approached Toghrul Beg to work out a common strategy for dealing with the Pechenegs.

*

The condescending smile with which Toghrul Beg greeted the concerns of his second-in-command infuriated Ethelwulf.

"You'd better get used to keeping an eye on Pechenegs, Westerner," he advised, "because that's going to be your job while we're down here on the Governor's business!"

Chorpan tried to tone down the impact as he translated the words but the glint in the Turk's eyes gave Ethelwulf all the understanding he needed. He protested he'd understood his role would be to watch out for any possible interference from Ithel or Samandar. He was rewarded by a loud laugh.

"Don't think those weaklings'll do anything!" the Turk scratched his left ear vigorously and was rewarded by a large flea being pitched out on to the ground. "They'll just sit and wait behind their walls hoping the bogies will go away!" He laughed again at the expression of incredulity which Ethelwulf was unable to conceal. "The Pechenegs, Westerner! The Pechenegs!" A frown appeared as his own words vanquished the laugh. "Why do you think they can't properly collect tribute from the villages - and our Governor reckons he can!" He smiled cunningly as if, at last, anxious to share a secret. "I reckon that's why our Governor sent to the Kagan for warriors to help deal with a potential religious blood-bath. You've seen the state of Sarkel. Does it look like it's on boiling point with religious maniacs?" He paused before he answered his own question. "Oh, yes, we've the odd incident - like that stupid thing with the pig - but we're not going to have a civil war over religion."

"So we're only really needed for THIS?" said Ethelwulf with an open-handed gesture of dismissal. Inside his brain started to assess what the Turk was saying; and the answer was not one he wanted. He hadn't seen any signs of intense religious feeling in Sarkel; Christians, Moslems and Jews seemed, on the whole, to get on well with each other. After all, it was all a matter of business; when money was involved zeal went out of the window. All three religions felt some sort of contempt for the pagans, populating the surrounding countryside. Of course, there was always the zealot, like Makarios or Cyril, who took it into his head to start trying to win over converts, and, possibly, their activities upset zealots on the other side. But very soon business took over and others started calming the situation down - he'd heard Cyril was being sent back to Kenugard, just so he could cause trouble there!

Of course, being sent off to back up the collection of tribute was just the task he'd have expected to be given. He'd seen operations like that in Ireland and Finland, taking part in one or two. Nobody liked paying their taxes and anybody trying to collect whatever was meant to be handed over could expect some trouble. If the whole business was handled well then merely showing the collection was backed by force was sufficient to calm down all but the most suicidal, and he hadn't met any of those yet. However, what angered him was the dishonesty of the Governor - that is, if Toghrul was speaking the truth, and you could never be sure of that. Ethelwulf looked at the big Turk watching him with the eyes of a cat admiring a nearby bird. He knew Toghrul Beg was revelling in his discomfort, just looking forward to seeing the Varangians wriggle when stuck out in some exposed spot while the Turks got to work. He knew he couldn't do anything about it; if he'd been near a suitable boat he might have made a run for Miklagard or somewhere willing to pay for his services. Out here in the steppes he felt like a beached whale, and he'd seen the mournful expression on some of their faces in Iceland as they just waited for the butcher to arrive.

Ethelwulf felt he really needed to talk the matter over with his cousins or Gunnar or even men like Sven the Far-Sighted or Pekka whom he'd come to respect for their good judgement. He knew Toghrul was playing out the line but he just had to go along with the game. He shrugged his shoulders with what he hoped would be taken as nonchalance, and immediately realised it was not.

"So, Westerner," sneered Toghrul. "I see you accept your role in our enterprise."

"To watch out for Pechenegs?"

"To fight them - and die if necessary!" snapped the Turk, suddenly becoming tired of the game. Playing was good enough for the likes of the Governor, spinning their schemes in the safety offered by strong walls. Out here, on the empty grasslands, it was a different matter. Everyone needed to know their place and obey! He glared at Ethelwulf and accepted as a mere state of nature how much he hated the Westerner. Only the power of Kenugard enabled such creatures even to be seen in these lands. Of course, for years there'd been the odd trader, snooping his way along the Volga or the Don; but they'd known their place, not daring to come in force in case they met a grisly end far from their boats. Inwardly he smiled as he realised how isolated the Westerner must feel so far away from the river, let alone the sea. Perhaps he'd feel the same if he was separated from his horse - but then he wouldn't be so stupid as to let that happen! And this man was stupid, like all his kind; in their arrogance they strutted their way through the pitiful Slav tribes to the north and the west, not realising only peoples such as the Turks, the Pechenegs and the Cumans[88] deserved to dominate these plains. Even the Moslems to the south had taken into their armies such peoples, conscious the future belonged to their kind. If

Toghrul had ever known an emotion such as pity he'd have felt it for the Westerner at that moment; but the Turk felt no such emotion and so simply enjoyed the discomfiture of the stranger.

Ethelwulf recognised the triumph in the Turk's reply and made as if to comply, merely asking that he should discuss the matter with his men. Toghrul merely shrugged, noting the Westerner didn't have the self-confidence to command his men without advice; perhaps he'd been mistaken in him after all. The Westerner was nothing; he could be ridden underfoot whenever his usefulness had gone. In some strange way the Turk regretted the lack of competition.

*

"We're too far from water to have any chance of escape," stated Edwine with a gloom which reflected the general feeling among the Varangians. They all knew the only way to survive was to complete whatever were the aims of the expedition and somehow find their way back to Kenugard. Gunnar argued they should take on the Turks if that was the way to get out of this mess. Morkere laughed - not that he had much respect for the fighting qualities of the Turks, but because he knew that tackling the Turks would mean, almost certainly defying the orders of Prince Vladimir himself. Ethelwulf ended the discussion with a reluctant acceptance of their fate.

The next day they reached Samir - the first of the three villages which, supposedly, should be paying tribute to the Governor of Sarkel. Their arrival had been expected, but it was clearly most unwelcome. The whole population, just over one hundred, lined the one and only 'street' of the settlement in a silent alley of resentment. The Varangians found it particularly unnerving as they'd expected that, being selected to fight off the Pechenegs if required, the local population would welcome them as helpers.

In front of the large tent which made up the chief 'structure' of the settlement they were greeted by an old man, flanked by a rabbi and a small man who wore an antique leather cuirass clearly far too big for him. Ethelwulf glanced at it and then stared. He was certain he was looking at a piece of military equipment once used by the Romans. He longed to ask questions but had to stand back while Toghrul announced the purpose of the expedition. His words provoked such hostile murmuring from the population Ethelwulf was glad he hadn't even been introduced. The Rabbi said something in a high sing-song voice and Ethelwulf cursed he didn't have Chorpan or Sven next to him to whisper some translation of what was going on. Both guides, however, had been requisitioned by Toghrul Beg for 'special duties' as soon as they approached the first village. Ethelwulf suspected one reason may have been to isolate the Varangians from the local population.

After that brief ceremony of 'welcome' the Varangians were marched off to an area north of the village, unsurprisingly outside the flimsy palisade which formed what was styled the 'defences' of the Samir. Their guide was the cuirass-wearer and just as Ethelwulf had been struck by his body-armour so the man stole various looks at the weapons and kit of the Varangians.

At last their guide was moved to open his mouth. "Menakhem," he said, touching his chest. "Menakhem." There was a strange smile on his face as if he wanted to imply he was willing to introduce himself to them. Before Ethelwulf could utter a reply Morkere intervened with a stream of unintelligible words which transformed the smile of Menakhem into a broad grin. He replied in a flood of language which stalled when he saw Ethelwulf hadn't understood a word. Morkere waved his hand furiously, shook his head and, stabbing a finger at his own chest, spoke another series of phrases. Menakhem nodded and started replying but was immediately stopped by Morkere with a single word. The grin faded and the guide began to talk in a less violent way. He finished by gesturing towards Ethelwulf, clearly inviting Morkere to act as interpreter.

Morkere smiled and said, "I guessed our friend didn't like the Turks and when I remarked that neither did we he seemed delighted." He paused, nodded briskly at Menakhem, making sure a reassuring smile stayed on his lips. "He's clearly worried about what all this means. I think, but I'm not sure; he's saying the village have already paid one set of taxes to Ithel and haven't got much for us." He turned to Menakhem and asked a question - obviously a question as the little man began a long whine which had to be restarted several times by Morkere in order to be delivered at a slower rate. For years Ethelwulf had been surprised how quickly his cousin found his way around strange tongues. He'd seen Morkere in long conversation with Chorpan and had assumed he was trying to learn the language of the Khazars. Yet, he was surprised his cousin had managed to make so much progress since they'd known Chorpan.

Morkere at last turned to Ethelwulf, now joined by Edwine and Gunnar, and explained what he'd just learned, repeating several times that, perhaps, his limited knowledge may have produced some errors. It appeared that for three years nobody had been willing or able to collect any form of taxation from Samir - that is since a collector sent by Ithel had lost both the taxation and his head. However, the villagers hadn't been able to get away with a break in payment for they'd handed over some form of tribute to the

Pechenegs to keep them quiet. This year Ithel had sent another tax-collector, backed by a small force of Ghuzz archers, who managed to get together what was demanded and, presumably, get it all back safely to Ithel. Apparently the Ghuzz archers had scared the Pechenegs enough to make sure they kept well out of the way. In fact, they'd only spotted one of the Pecheneg scouts two days ago when they heard an expedition from Sarkel was on the way. You can be certain that didn't fill them with any enthusiasm. Menakhem swears the people around here don't want any fighting but they can't pay up three times over. As he finished Morkere said a few quick words to Menakhem who nodded.

"Well I got that right," stated Morkere. "They'd rather die quickly than pay up three times over and slowly starve to death."

"Would that be true of the other two villages we're due to collect from?" asked Ethelwulf.

Morkere frowned. "I can't ask that because I don't know the names of the villages." Ethelwulf realised his cousin was right; he was furious with himself for taking on such a dangerous role without proper information. He was sure Chorpan would know the names so he'd have to be patient. He hoped the Pechenegs wouldn't be anxious to collect their tribute.

*

Clearly nobody could monitor the activities of the Pechenegs without ponies so Ethelwulf soon found himself again confronting Toghrul Beg. The mercenary leader was obviously unhappy and distinctly unpleasant. He wanted to move on to the other two villages before they'd time to salt away whatever could be levied as taxation. He'd sent Chorpan and Sven, along with a couple of his own men as 'assistants', to spy out the land and see just how much potential there was before he made his formal appearance. However, he discovered the villagers had known about his approach almost from the day the expedition had left Sarkel. The arrival of his 'spies' had been treated with ill-concealed derision and Chorpan reported it was unlikely he'd be able to exact the amount of taxation he'd promised himself. Toghrul had arranged to farm the taxes from the Governor, an expected return had been agreed and Toghrul would be allowed to retain whatever he collected over that set amount. The 'spies' reported he might be lucky even to collect what he'd promised the Governor. So it was no surprise the Turk was very abrupt with Ethelwulf when he mentioned the need for horses to replace the mules supplied to the Varangians.

"Get some from the locals!"

"How?"

"Requisition them!"

Ethelwulf doubted whether such a policy would be acceptable to Menashe Bulan, especially if it provoked trouble from the villagers. He opened his mouth to protest but Toghrul got there first.

"You're going to have to dirty your fingers, Westerner!" he snapped. "If you need horses, take them and don't bother me!"

Ethelwulf could see it was no use trying to squeeze mounts out of Toghrul Beg. As he saw it the Turks would largely be based within the villages, collecting the taxes, so would have little need of their ponies. On the other hand, his men, despite their inexperience, would be expected to shadow an extremely effective form of light-cavalry, to stop the Pechenegs disrupting the tax collection. What could he raise from the villagers? Both guides had returned and he saw some very awkward negotiations in the near future.

In fact, Chorpan proved masterly in securing the cooperation of the villagers, helped considerably by Menakhem, determined to make himself of use. The village elder, Shmuel, spurned a simple deal offered by Chorpan. He agreed to lend the Varangians one pony for every two mules. When the Varangians finally left the village the property of either side would be returned. If any animal couldn't be returned then compensation would be paid. Both sides seemed happy and Ethelwulf was delighted. He'd gained twenty ponies in exchange for forty mules without upsetting the villagers.

When Toghrul was told of how Ethelwulf had acquired the ponies he almost collapsed on the ground with hysterical laughter. The Westerner appeared a weakling beyond even his expectations. Unfortunately he was leaving that day to move on to the next village, having squeezed out of Samir an amount just exceeding that promised to the Governor. When he returned he'd increase his profit at the expense of BOTH villagers and Varangians!

*

With the ponies Ethelwulf could set up two patrols, each under one of his cousins, to reconnoitre on either side of the village in broad crescents. Firstly Ethelwulf placed in each patrol his best bowmen, then over the next two days the men were vigorously trained in not only riding but fighting from horseback. The Pechenegs, like other nomadic people before them, had perfected the skill of striking at their enemies from horseback using the bow; Ethelwulf wanted his patrol to be able to fight back if attacked. Of course, the aim was to avoid such engagements but he expected the Pechenegs would waste no time in attacking any armed horsemen caught on the open plains. After two days he was pleased with the results and sent out both cousins on their patrols.

Meanwhile he was entertained by the appearance from the north of an Arab trader. A short man, with a girth to match his height, Ali ibn-Yussuf was a perpetually cheerful individual. He rode into the village one day followed by two mounted slaves and twenty sheep, apparently on his way home to Tabriz in Azerbaijan. He was in need of supplies to reach the Caucasus, the last major stop before reaching his homeland. His business was in herding sheep which grazed so successfully on the grasslands of Khazaria down to the less-hospitable lands of his own people.

"What about the Pechenegs?" was Ethelwulf's query delivered through Chorpan.

"The Borotalmat are my friends," he laughed loudly, exciting himself to even greater delight when he remembered how he'd helped cure the youngest daughter of their Kagan with medicines he happened to have bought in Baghdad. "Besides," he added after detailing this act of mercy which should have guaranteed him immunity for life, "they're like children. As long as you keep up a steady supply of presents they'll always welcome you." He reached for a small bundle tied behind his saddle. It was a small crimson bag decorated with strange writing in yellow which, Ali explained, came from the Word of Allah and said, "Your God, is the true God, besides which there is no other god."[89] Reciting further verses to himself Ali opened the bundle and drew out a collection of bright strings of beads. "These are inexpensive in the bazaars of Baghdad but here they cause eyes to open wide in wonder and the most threatening features dissolve in a grin." He slyly looked at Ethelwulf whose mouth had, without his knowing it, turned into a broad grin. "They work even with barbarians from the lands of mist and snow."

"My country is not one of mist and snow," responded Ethelwulf. "It's a land of warm sunshine fostering meadows of wild flowers and running streams and - "

"Sitting on the edge of the world!" laughed the Arab and Ethelwulf shrugged. Whatever he might dream of the beauties of England he knew he'd never return; for him home might as well be a land of mist and snow. "Ah, infidel," continued Ali," to see true beauty you'd need to wander among the gardens of the Caliph himself!"

"Are they really that beautiful?" questioned the Westerner.

"Assuredly!" was the answer. "For we true believers know that near that city was the first garden given to man, and so, we nourish nature to reproduce Eden in the modern world."

Now it was the turn of Ethelwulf to laugh. "Pechenegs would surely enjoy the beauties of such an enterprise!"

"I'm sure they would," agreed the Arab," but I have no fear of such warriors for their Kagan loves me, I have a bag full of trinkets and, above all, I have one final advantage which cocoons my life against the wiles of any pagan." He saw the puzzled look on the face of the Westerner and his loud, giggly laugh rose even louder. "I am the child of a woman who could claim descent from Fatima herself - peace be on her soul." He saw the complete bewilderment taking over the Westerner and his giggles turned into a shriek. "Oh dear," he mumbled, grasping his enormous stomach as it started to gyrate alarmingly." I should remember the supreme ignorance of you Rus." He paused and steadily brought himself under control. "Learn, unbeliever, and start your journey into the light here. Fatima[90] was the favourite daughter of the prophet, Mohammed - peace be upon him - who received from Allah Himself the meaning of life and how we might make our way into Paradise." Now he set off on another giggle and Ethelwulf waited patiently for him to explain just how, this time, he managed to keep himself so amused. " You see, my friend, 'Paradise' in Farsi means 'garden' and that's where we started, isn't it?"

Ethelwulf nodded, amused by how just going round in a logical circle had brought such pleasure to the little man. Even so he was not sure whether the confidence of the trader was justified and later asked Chorpan whether he believed the Arab would be safe.

Chorpan shrugged. "Yahweh alone knows, Westerner." He paused and then continued with a less fatalistic argument. "He trade long time no trouble Pechenegs."

"So perhaps his mother's ancestor is a lucky charm."

"Not all child lucky,"[91] muttered the guide but Ethelwulf didn't hear him. He couldn't protect the Arab and was equally certain the man would have spurned protection anyway. So reluctantly he bade farewell to the little man, perhaps not entirely flattered by being offered one of the necklaces reserved for pagans.

*

The next day Edwine rode in carrying the crimson bag with the strange letters on it that Ethelwulf recognised as the property of Ali ibn-Yussuf. Edwine said there'd been three corpses, minus their heads, abandoned in the sunlight and that was all.

"But the Pechenegs knew him," protested Ethelwulf. "He'd safely passed among them for some time."

"Perhaps he did in the past," declared Edwine," but it looks as if this time his luck ran out." With that he drew out from his belt the broken shaft of the arrow. "This was rooted in his fat stomach," he added, brandishing the shaft.

Sven reached forward and examined the feathering. "Yes," he explained, "his luck truly did run out, and so has ours." He held up the arrow so that both Ethelwulf and Edwine could examine it closely. "This shaft belongs to the Boulatzoupon - and they're far more dangerous than the clan your dead trader knew."

"But they're meant to be further to the east!" protested Ethelwulf, recalling the Boulatzoupon were the most easterly of the eight divisions of the Pechenegs and, after hearing about their ferocity, grateful he wouldn't be penetrating their territory.

"Unfortunately, Westerner," smiled Sven grimly, "the Pechenegs are the children of the wind. They wander where their horses can graze easily and where there are heads to be gathered!" He looked steadily at Edwine. "Did your patrol come across any other signs of Pecheneg activity apart from the dead?" Edwine shook his head. "We must hope they've decided to return to their more ancestral hunting-grounds," continued the guide. "I must carry the news to Toghrul Beg." With no further explanation Sven swung his pony to the west and galloped off. Ethelwulf wondered why he was passing on such intelligence to the Turks; he also wondered when Sven had acquired a horse.

However, at the moment he'd no time to worry about Sven and his loyalty; somewhere to the west of Samir was Morkere and the possibility of his meeting up with a Pecheneg war-band. Ethelwulf issued orders and Oleg, one of Edwine's patrol, galloped off in the direction of Morkere's patrol. Even as he went Ethelwulf wondered whether he was doing the right thing; he'd decided just to warn his cousin and not to call the patrol in. The reasoning appeared sound; the main purpose of the patrols was to give warning of the approach of any Pecheneg war-bands; by its very nature this task involved danger; consequently he couldn't run for cover at the mere hint of a threat. Should he venture out to give somehow support to

Morkere? Certainly not! Where would his cousin be? Where would the Pechenegs be? What if they decided to penetrate the village from the east while he marched his forces off to the west? Could he trust the villagers to act as extra look-outs? Above all, perhaps, what would be the reaction of Toghrul Beg when he heard of a Pecheneg war-band in the area?

Ethelwulf turned to Gunnar and told him to put the village in some sort of defensive position; it was no good assuming the Pechenegs wouldn't attack a village. The Gall-Gael nodded and quickly hustled warriors into closing off both ends of the main, and only, 'street'. Of course, the Pechenegs might attack from anywhere and so look-outs were positioned at intervals along the whole stretch of the thirty tents which made up the community. Gunnar got Chorpan to explain to the locals the immediate dangers of a Pecheneg attack and wasn't pleased at the reaction of some of the Khazars. Ethelwulf decided to take Menakhem and Shmuel into his confidence, using Chorpan to act as his interpreter.

"Some believe it's better to let the Pechenegs take blood occasionally than the constant bleeding ordered by the powerful elsewhere," answered the elder. Menakhem nodded in agreement.

"Why would you assume Pechenegs plunder only occasionally?"

"Because Pechenegs are constantly on the move and their needs are small," explained Menakhem. "They take from us what they may need for one moon and then pass on to exact from others what they need for the next."

Ethelwulf realised the more settled and cultured demands of Sarkel and Ithel, and behind them the even more advanced 'needs' of Kenugard, meant increasing tribute was needed to satisfy his masters. What must it have been like when Rome ruled the world? Immediately he realised the likes of Miklagard and Baghdad had replaced Rome with excessive demands. He could understand the logic of some of the villagers. Perhaps he should ignore the Khazars but concentrate on protecting his own men.

"I want you, Menakhem, to identify for me those you think may have such ideas." He saw the little man stiffen as being asked to 'betray' his fellows so he hurried on. "Nothing will happen to them, I can assure you. It's merely I want to use some of your people as look-outs and I'll only select those whom I can trust." This time Shmuel started to protest. "I'll not indicate why I choose one man and not another. There must be no finger-pointing at so-called 'traitors'. It must appear mere chance one man must do this unlike his fellow."

Both Khazars nodded but talked so rapidly to each other in their own tongue that Chorpan looked shame-faced at Ethelwulf and shrugged his shoulders. The discussion wasn't meant for his ears. Soon the jabbering stopped and Menakhem turned to Ethelwulf with a stern face.

"We don't like what you ask," he began, "but we understand why you ask it. We have to trust you but have learned not to trust agents from those claiming authority over us." Ethelwulf started to protest so Menakhem raised a hand in gentle remonstrance. "You appear to be different so we've agreed to trust you." He paused. "We'll talk together and give you some names you may find useful. Others may not be untrustworthy, they may be merely those who wouldn't be so useful."

Ethelwulf nodded, understanding the two men could then insist they hadn't handed over to strangers some of their fellows. He couldn't be sure how many of the men NOT selected would be willing to betray him to the Pechenegs. Only if he asked for more and more look-outs would he come up against the barrier of trust.

After further discussion Menakhem offered four names and Ethelwulf asked him to take the men to Gunnar to be given positions. He hoped Morkere hadn't come across the Pechenegs.

Edwine stood by while such decisions had been taken. Now he reminded Ethelwulf it'd be necessary for his patrol to return to their duties. Ethelwulf hesitated before he sent the men out again. What if the Pechenegs were out there waiting, watching? He had no choice. He ordered Edwine to resume patrol.

*

That evening both Edwine and Morkere returned with their patrols. There'd been no sign of the Pechenegs which could mean they'd passed on to other areas or had chosen to conceal their position. Although both patrols included men noted for their tracking skills, Pekka rode with Morkere and Jussi Samako rode with Edwine, nether had seen anything suspicious. Jussi's hoarse voice[92] insisted he'd seen Pecheneg warriors on the skyline for an instant but nobody else had seen the enemy so the Finnish trapper suffered mild teasing for seeing creatures that weren't there.

"These aren't the right conditions for Tapio[93] to be using his herdsman to protect his creatures," laughed Pekka and Jussi merely grunted he'd seen the Pechenegs, although doubt seemed to underlie his voice.

However, they were joined by Toghrul, accompanied by a grinning Sven, with all of his men behind him. He didn't look too happy but got down to business right away.

"Sven reports you've had contact with Pechenegs," he bellowed dismounting from his pony and approaching Ethelwulf. Of course, Ethelwulf only picked up the names 'Sven' and 'Pechenegs', realising the combination spelt trouble; Morkere supplied a rough translation. A breathless Chorpan, who'd been trying to get to sleep close by, came rushing up and Ethelwulf was grateful for his aid with translation as he no longer trusted Sven. Rapidly Chorpan was informed what had happened and launched into the role of interpreter, closely watched by a silent Sven.

"A trader has been murdered," answered Ethelwulf, "but our patrols have reported no sightings."

"Which doesn't mean they've gone away, Westerner!" sneered Toghrul. "When a Pecheneg wishes to cover his trail he makes sure none but those well-versed in the ways of the steppes can find it."

"Send out your own men, Toghrul, in the morning," answered Ethelwulf fiercely, resentful the Turk was belittling his efforts to perform his job." Perhaps they'll find what we could not see!"

"There's no need," answered the Turk with a self-satisfied smirk on his lips. "We've almost got all we came for." He lightly tapped a sack which hung from the saddle of the pony by his side. "The other two villages proved most co-operative when it came to paying up." He smiled broadly. "They knew what was good for them and we knew how to teach them their duty." The smile vanished. "Here, however, it's all been a different story." He thrust out a finger towards Ethelwulf. "You, Westerner, haven't been so vigorous in your duty towards our Governor!"

"I've carried out my orders," answered Ethelwulf, his temper rising even more, "despite non-cooperation on your part!"

"If you mean the horses," responded the Turk, "then any warrior of the steppes would tell you it's a warrior's own duty to look to his mount." He brushed that matter aside. "No. I mean you've done nothing to ferret out the silver these villagers have stashed away."

"There's no silver," said Ethelwulf, trying to stay calm. "They've paid off the Pechenegs and only have left animals or crops. Without that they'll starve!"

"And you believe such drivel?" scoffed Toghrul Beg. "Even when traders pass through your hands with herds of sheep or cattle you believe silver hasn't been hidden away here, concealed from authorised tax-collectors?"

"Any silver has been hidden away from brigands," replied Ethelwulf, "and I'm sure there's little of it!"

"Sven tells me differently," was the response and the named guide grinned broadly, delighted to have his usefulness publicly acknowledged.

"What would Sven know about such matters?"

"More than you've guessed," answered the Turk. "Sven, explain to the fool what you know and how you know it."

Sven stepped forward with a strange smile on his face. He started speaking in Rus and then paused, looking at Toghrul as if to get approval for such a use of a tongue unknown to the Turk. Impatiently Toghrul nodded and Sven began his explanation.

"You've made the mistake, Westerner, of believing that I am half-Severian and half-Rus," he paused, seeking approval and then enjoying the spectacle of surprise on the faces of his audience, including that of Chorpan. "In fact, I am half-Turk and half-Khazar. My mother yielded to the embraces of a Turkish warrior employed by Ithel and I was the product of such a union." He frowned as memories came tumbling back. "But my mother's family, once her lover had moved on, looked upon her as a harlot and drove her away from the family home. For months she wandered, defenceless and so often in terror of her life, northwards until she found shelter among the Severians. These pagans sheltered her, showing the kindness which her own religion refused, and I was brought up as one of them. Again fortune favoured me as I found employment with one of the Rus traders passing through the territory and, in his company, I made my way to Kenugard. By then my mother had died and the Rus, a kindly man called Olaf Svensson, being childless, took me in as his own, naming me Sven after his father." He smugly looked at the bewilderment on the faces of the Westerners, also realising Toghrul was gaining vicarious delight in his revelations. "With a natural gift for languages I could easily be accepted as the natural child of a Rus who traded extensively among the Severians. When my foster-father died it was even easier to assume to assume the identity which you knew. After all my own people had rejected me so I spurned them." A scowl replaced the smile. "I managed to conceal my origins from everyone, enjoying the secrecy which marked me as separate." The smile returned. "When we first arrived I feared Menakhem had recognised me - as he should have done because I'm his nephew. Of course, I didn't know anyone as I'd left this village when I was a tiny baby - with the taint of rejection."

"Why should Menakhem recognise you?" asked Morkere.

"Haven't you observed a similarity between his features and my own?" replied the guide. "Naturally, the fool couldn't think where he'd seen those features before - having little use for a mirror!"

Sven turned to Toghrul and they exchanged rapid Turkish - too fast for Chorpan to comprehend.

"Toghrul says I can tell you what he intends for we are as one in this matter," went on the guide, seemingly gaining in authority. "For I know these people as the liars they are. They burrow their silver in all sorts of hiding places, seeing it as a mark of their cleverness in cheating their masters."

"Why would you know all this?" asked Ethelwulf.

"Because of what my mother told me as we huddled down together among the Severians," replied Sven. "She wanted me to know I was a Khazar but rejected by my own people and dismissed like Cain to wander in the wilderness - but without the stain of his guilt!" He spat on the ground as if to expel the nasty memory of those days of coldness and poverty. "She knew how they hid away treasures so their wealth would grow amid their apparent poverty." He paused and looked towards Toghrul. "I told Toghrul this when I knew Pechenegs were near. For the silver is there to be had, I'm sure, and if we don't lay hands on it, the profit will fall to the savages!"

"So either way the Khazars will suffer!" stated Edwine.

"Exactly!" answered the guide. "They've brought their punishment on their own heads by their greed. Even as we speak Turkish warriors are seizing Menakhem and I'm confident it won't be long before he can be persuaded - "

"You'd hand your own uncle over to such as these?"

"No uncle of mine, except in blood which has come to mean nothing to me," dismissed the guide. "If he suffers I'll make sure he knows it's me, having suffered as an innocent child, who's brought this upon him."

"But there is no silver!" insisted Morkere.

Sven laughed. "So you've been told! So they'd tell any stranger but, and my mother well knew this, they're liars." Sven allowed a strange smile to caress his lips. "My Turkish comrades will get to the truth - and I aim to be there when the wretch comes to his senses."

"Where is all this taking place?" asked Edwine.

Sven looked at Toghrul and repeated the question. Whatever authority the guide might give himself, the Turks were giving him no real independence of action. Toghrul grunted out a reply and then added words which upset the guide. It was Chorpan who intruded a translation before Sven had the chance to recover his surprise.

"Menakhem where keep Torah. Toghrul wants you see man pain."

Ethelwulf realised Toghrul Beg was keen to display his superiority over both Khazars and Varangians. The Turk's respect for Ethelwulf and his men had declined the further they'd travelled from Kenugard. Probably he believed Varangians might be skilful in fighting from ships but their prowess declined away from water. Certainly his actions since leaving Sarkel might make the Turk believe he was dealing with a weakling. This suited Ethelwulf and he was keen to accept the offer, but not before he asked Morkere, in rapid West Saxon, to slip away and make sure the whole force of Varangians made their way to the same place.

"What did you say?" asked Sven as Morkere slipped away.

"I said Edwine and I would accompany you to the examination of Menakhem, to make sure what we believed was true. But he was being sent back to our men because he'd grown too close to the Khazars over the last few days."

Sven nodded. He knew the dark-haired Westerner had spent several hours talking to the Khazars, finding out about the customs of his people and developing a knowledge of his tongue. Certainly some relationship had developed between the Varangian and the Khazar. When he explained this to Toghrul he was surprised the Turk accepted it all quite easily, adding without Morkere the Varangians would be even more isolated. Sven understood that, without saying anything, Toghrul was expecting him to ensure Chorpan would be unable to translate for the Varangians. He glanced at his fellow-guide and noticed Chorpan was rapidly whispering to the Westerner. He knew he'd have to place himself between Chorpan and the Westerners, making sure such communication would be impossible. He baulked at simply knifing the guide, or handing him over to the Turks, because he recognised the man could be schooled to be of service to his new friends in the future.

*

Menakhem had suffered a long interrogation from the three Turks who bowed when their leader entered the tented area. The chest containing the Torah had been rudely pushed aside and a rough frame erected in its place. Menakhem had been tied to the frame and flogged for some time. The tent itself was encircled by Turks as a shield against the local population summoned by the screams of one of their number. As the Varangians were encamped at the far side of settlement they hadn't been drawn by sound, probably assuming it was a ritual practised by the Khazars. However, Ethelwulf was pleased to note that, even as he and Edwine arrived, some of his men were quietly sidling in among the surrounding population with the discretion he required.

Ethelwulf saw how the corselet of which Menakhem was so proud had been ripped off and flung into a corner; leaving a deep wheal over the left shoulder. However, that wheal was nothing compared to the marks of savagery which criss-crossed his back. His tunic had been torn down to allow the whips to cut more cruelly into Menakhem's flesh. Many of the cuts looked like deep ravines surrounded by long smears of dried blood. Menakhem himself looked more dead than alive; one eye closed beneath a mass of blood, his mouth open as he automatically gulped for the air which would allow his tormentors to apply their instruments even more.

As Ethelwulf approached Menakhem looked up and his serviceable eye tried to focus on a new tormenter. From somewhere deep down in his throat, long with the heavy pants of exhaustion, came a wheeze indicating internal injury.

Ethelwulf stepped forward and growled. "Tell him, fool, where you've hidden the silver and then I promise, they'll let you go." Suddenly he realised he'd spoken in Rus and doubted if Menakhem had sufficient grasp of the tongue. But he was wrong.

"No silver," gasped the bloody figure with a vehemence from the depths hidden even from himself. "No silver!"

Ethelwulf turned to face Toghrul with his face a mask of fury. "There is no silver! As I said; whatever silver these people had they've given to tormentors as savage as yourselves!"

Toghrul glared at the defiance and there was anger in his reply. "Get out of the way, weakling! You aren't worthy to be a Varangian. Let my men continue instructing the peasant in lessons of obedience." He looked to his right where one of the floggers was pausing for breath. "Carry on, Selim!"

Ethelwulf turned to face the man and recognised him as Ketil's opponent a few days before. In Selim smouldered a deep enjoyment in his task and he'd seized the brief respite to gulp down water to renew his energy. Suddenly he saw the Westerner step to his left, placing himself in the way of his target. Selim hesitated and looked across at his commander, after all in front of him stood a captain of the Varangians and he didn't want to be killed for striking an officer. Toghrul nodded, permitting him to strike a subordinate officer standing in the way of duty. Selim flicked back his whip.

Having fully committed himself Ethelwulf didn't hesitate; as Selim glanced at Toghrul for confirmation the Westerner grasped the broad-sword hanging from a baldric. As the Turk flicked back the whip, the blade was drawn and in a rapid lunge plunged into the shoulder of Selim. The Turk screamed, dropping the whip and chaos erupted.

Toghrul drew his scimitar to cut down Ethelwulf but collapsed with a spear hurled by Edwine. Sven drew a knife to dispose of Chorpan but found his wrist gripped and the two guides tumbled to the ground furiously struggling over the one knife, Now the second Turkish warrior with a whip acted, but mistakenly decided to abandon his whip in favour of his scimitar. Ethelwulf leaped across the space separating them and hacked the warrior down even as he drew the weapon. Meanwhile Edwine rushed forward, drawing his sword as he moved and plunged it into the heart of Selim. Chorpan rose from his combat with Sven leaving the treacherous guide in the dust with his own knife embedded in his chest.

Outside the battle between the leaders had been communicated to their followers and the villagers ran screaming for cover as the two groups of warriors attacked each other with all the hatred fostered since they'd left Sarkel. The Turks immediately realised they were at a disadvantage, unmounted and with their favourite weapon, the bow, of limited use in such cramped conditions. To make their situation even worse the more fool-hardy of the villagers attacked the Turks with whatever came to hand, realising the Varangians were fighting for Samir.

Gunnar's axe struck repeatedly at the Turks, smashing aside whatever defence - sword or shield - was offered. The other Varangians proved just as deadly as the Gall-Gael and within moments the Turks had been routed, Those trying to surrender were butchered even as they cast aside their weapons. Others saw what was happening to their comrades and ran for their horses pursued by a motley rabble of Varangians and Khazars, their blood-lust up. Only four reached the horses, leaped on to their backs and galloped out of the village. Morkere tried to organise some form of pursuit but found the victors were too occupied with either murdering those Turks still alive or despoiling their corpses. However, Morkere did seize all the remaining Turkish ponies, not knowing why but confident it was better to have the animals under his control than let them run loose over the steppes.

Inside the tent Ethelwulf cut Menakhem loose and Edwine gave him some of the water for which Selim no longer had any use. Even as they acted Ethelwulf and his cousin were considering their options.

"If any Turk gets back to Sarkel we can be sure the Governor will be sending a force to drag us back for punishment," stated Ethelwulf. He started looking around for the bag which Toghrul had so recently flourished, certain its silver would never be allowed to be far from the Turkish captain. He quickly spotted it behind the corpse of the Turk and laid his hands on it.

"You know that's the Governor's property," reminded Edwine, though anyone looking into his eyes would have seen how little he valued such claims.

"Only as far as a brigand captain owns the silver his gang has stolen!" snapped his cousin as his fingers tore at the string which secured the bag. For a moment Chorpan stood transfixed at what had occurred so rapidly and then let out a long wail of misery.

"What's wrong with you?" demanded Edwine and the guide started whining he'd face execution for what had been done here, along with the Westerners, although he'd taken no part in the fracas, except to defend his own life.

By now Ethelwulf had opened the bag and pulled out a handful of silver coins.

"You'd best vanish into the steppes, Chorpan," he advised, not really caring what the guide was going to do. "I'm sure you don't want to follow us!"

"And where are we going, cousin?" asked Edwine, relieving Ethelwulf of the bag so that he too could check its contents.

"To Miklagard, Edwine," was the reply as Ethelwulf recovered the bag and started to restore its contents. "This will get us there - or, at least, well on our way!"

There was a groan from Menakhem who was slowly recovering, so Ethelwulf hurriedly ordered Chorpan to get some help for the Khazar. Chorpan scurried off - and was never seen again by the Varangians.

*

The next day Ethelwulf assembled his warriors, finding out one had been killed and two wounded. Fortunately the wounded men could still travel for Ethelwulf had decided what they must do. The Varangians must head west until they came across the Kuban river. Somehow they'd secure transport - boats or rafts, it made no difference - to carry them down to Tmutarakan. There he hoped they could use the silver in the bag to purchase a vessel, preferably a longship, to carry them to the capital of the Greeks. Of course, planning was easy but not the execution of such a scheme. The Governor might guess their intentions and despatch a force down the Don to cut them off; the journey across to Tmutarakan would be through territory controlled by the Pechenegs; local Khazars might try to detain them, but that was doubtful. Certainly they had to buy supplies, for it would be far too dangerous to try and seize what was needed. There might be protests about the silver but Samir wouldn't bother about the other villages; Ethelwulf doubted if they'd even tell them what had happened. After all, they'd been saved from the greed of Toghrul Beg.

Shmuel proved most amenable, once he realised Menakhem was recovering from his ordeal and the threat to his people had been removed. Willingly, he exchanged some of the horses for mules, selling Ethelwulf the required supplies at reasonable cost. All knew there was no time to be lost, especially when news came in that the bodies of two Turks had been discovered not far to the north, victims of a Pecheneg attack. Nothing, unfortunately, was seen of the other two Turks who'd escaped the battle at Samir and Ethelwulf knew the Governor would hear of what had occurred.

The arrival of Aelle of Durham and Aldred the Eloquent gave further impetus to Ethelwulf's decision. Both men had stayed behind at Kenugard because they'd not been selected to be in the escort raised for the Sarkel expedition. However, both saw Thorgrim the Short arrive at Kenugard within weeks of the escort's departure. When Thorgrim had suddenly left Aldeigjuborg he'd not gone on to Kenugard as believed[94] but had returned to the court of Eric Sjersal at Uppsala. There he'd been promised much silver for the heads of Ethelwulf and his leading followers. On arrival at Kenugard he secured the promise of cooperation of first Princess Anna and, through her, Prince Vladimir – doubtless for a share of the bounty. Aelle and Aldred slipped away from Kenugard and, in the guise of traders, made their way to Sarkel and, from there, managed to reach Samir. However, welcome they might be, the Wanderer now knew the treachery of Thorgrim meant he had no choice but to escape to Miklagard.

So, with only two more days spent in collecting supplies and persuading one of the Khazars, a youngster called Aaron, to accompany them as guide as far as the river, the Varangians set off on their desperate attempt to escape the punishment of the forces of Kenugard.

*

The Wanderer 7:5

"Today and tomorrow
Will you be at your best; yet soon death
Will claim you, in bed or the fight;
The dread elements of fire or water
Will seize you, or you will fall
To a flashing blade or arrow's flight,
Or monstrous old age; then eyes
Once bright, will cloud over;
In no time, warrior, death will destroy you."
("Beowulf")

Escape from Gadarike

Much to Ethelwulf's surprise the ride to the River Kuban proved largely void of incident - indeed, Gunnar complained loudly of both soreness from riding and the monotony of the landscape.

"How different it is to the land of my birth," he remarked to Ketil Olafsson in a loud voice. "There, let me tell you, in the course of a day you can enjoy a pleasant stream, a delightful woodland glade and the comforting warmth of the sun on a gentle hillside."

"As well as a heavy downfall of rain, enough to force you to spend hours coughing over some smoky fire trying to dry out," laughed Morkere from nearby.

"Or the wintry blast of an icy wind that'll bury whatever landmarks you think you know under a hostile blanket of snow," added his twin, recalling to himself how Morkere had slipped away from Waterford under siege concealed by the wretched weather.[95]

Everyone laughed as Gunnar, shaken out of the delightful memories of his youth, was forced to admit that whoever directed Irish weather was not always in the best frame of mind. He adjusted the battle-axe strung over his back, telling himself that, but for its burden, he'd be in control of his horse. However, if he'd dared say that aloud the response would have been everyone knew he'd rather have the axe in his hand than be astride the most magnificent horse in the world.

Once or twice scouts patrolling the flanks of the Varangian column reported seeing Pecheneg scouts in the distance but nothing more came of it. However, Aaron pointed out the Pechenegs, having seen the scouts, had guessed a substantial body of fighting men were travelling westwards. Consequently, they wouldn't show themselves until they were sure of sufficient numbers to overwhelm the likely opposition. When Morkere argued the Pechenegs wouldn't know how large their force was, Aaron replied the number of scouts employed would reveal the size of the force. Instantly Ethelwulf increased the number of scouts, even though he was certain the gesture was futile.

*

One day two of the scouts almost captured a couple of Pecheneg riders - or it might well have turned out the other way. Hallbjorn and Thorgeir, the sons of Gudmund Olafsson from the Rangriver Plains in Iceland, had been resting in one of the few groups of trees breaking up the broad expanse of the steppes. It was cool there and they'd been remembering the excitement of racing each other in their own country when, as youths, they'd been entrusted by their father with some errand. Even then they'd been competitors, rivals and yet, to the outside world, allies and co-conspirators. Like many of the warriors under the command of Ethelwulf a petty dispute at home had driven them into wandering the lands and seas of the north. Like most of the Varangians there were times when they regretted their fate, but this wasn't one of them. The air was warm and they felt comfortable on their horses; they'd consumed their food with vigour and debated whether each of them, in turn, should enjoy a short nap. After all, from this position they could see the approach of any rider and well perform their duties as scouts without leaving the shelter of the trees for most of the afternoon. Then they'd have to retire to the river to link up with the rest of the force. They were congratulating themselves on their good fortune when they noticed a small disturbance to the north-west.

Only then did they realise the grassland had the ability to mask the approach of some riders due to occasional, easily-missed variations in the level of the ground. Even so, neither Icelander spoke as they waited for whatever was causing the movement to emerge more fully. As yet they'd nothing to report - the movement could be that of animals or men. So they patiently waited and were quickly rewarded with the sudden appearance of two Pecheneg scouts. The strangers were mounted on the dull-grey horses of the Borotalmat and carried lances and small shields, with a dark boss standing out in sharp contrast to the grey hide covering. Each carried on their back a curved bow of the sort unknown to the Icelanders; it was double-curved in shape and shorter than most of the bows with which they had experience. The strangers were surprisingly close and the Icelandic brothers were annoyed the Pechenegs had managed to approach without detection. In some way they felt ashamed and Thorgeir quietly suggested they could atone for such laxity by capturing one or both of the Pechenegs, who might be persuaded to reveal the plans or locations of their main war-band; perhaps it was simply the challenge which attracted the sons of Gudmund.

By now the Pechenegs were almost upon the two Varangians who'd slowly separated so they could attack from both sides. Years of acting together in pursuit of wild animals meant the brothers had excellent communication with few signals and no need for sound. The plan was simple; shoot the horses and before the Pechenegs could recover from their surprise make them prisoners. As the Pechenegs grew closer Hallbjorn found his mouth feeling suddenly dry. He knew the tension came from the excitement of the kill; his whole body was preparing for that sudden rush which would mean success or disaster. Slowly he notched his arrow, ready to bring down one of the Pecheneg ponies, confident his brother would naturally dispose of the other one. He looked across at his brother to make sure he was ready and suddenly froze as the whole situation changed.

About fifty yards to the west of the approaching Pechenegs and two hundred yards behind his brother another half-a-dozen Pechenegs were emerging. Hallbjorn realised he'd been so intent on the steady approach of their prey that they'd not picked up the larger group of enemy horsemen also making their way to the trees. Clearly this isolated spot of shade in the warmth of the day was most welcome and would attract others as well as the brothers. Frantically he released his grip on his bowstring and signalled to Thorgeir, still not making any sound to give away their position. He saw Thorgeir pause as he was about to focus on his target; somehow glimpsing his brother's gesture. Hallbjorn now repeatedly drove his finger into the air in the direction of the advancing Pechenegs. Thorgeir turned and saw the danger. With dramatic emphasis he shrugged as if to dismiss this unwelcome intrusion and turned back towards his target, bringing his bow up to the aim position. Hallbjorn guessed his intentions and copied his elder brother. Both released their arrows at the same time; one sped over the head of the advancing Pecheneg while the other brought down a horse. Neither Icelander, however, stayed to see the effect of their arrows; without even attempting to store away their weapons they yanked at the reins of their ponies and turned them hastily towards the river.

Immediately they were seen by the advancing Pechenegs who, letting out a clamour of war-cries, drove their ponies towards the trees with scarcely a glance at their two companion to the east, one of whom had crashed to the ground and disappeared beneath the grass. Neither Icelander cared to look behind as they sped towards the river, hoping that, as soon as they topped the slight rise in ground which hid the river from view, they'd see the column and, more importantly, be seen. If they had looked behind they'd have seen the Pechenegs divide on passing the trees, some reaching for their bows and others drawing sabres which were peculiar to their people.[96] As they rode the Pechenegs encouraged themselves and their fellows with yelps and screams of hatred, driving their horses with fierce pressure of ankle and knee. Two had iron helmets, the booty of previous kills, but the rest were content with leather caps. They were surprised to see strangers so far from the river, having been told a small force was hugging the river and going to the west.

At last, though, in reality, after only a few moments, the sons of Gudmund reached the crest of the upland and saw, making their way in ignorance of the drama on the plains, the column of Varangians. Hallbjorn let out a scream, willing someone in that force to turn and see what was happening behind them. Thorgeir tried to follow his brother's example and found his throat was too dry to let out any sound. At that point he forced himself to turn and saw how quickly the Pecheneg horsemen had narrowed the gap. Consciously he was aware he could only see four riders behind him but resisted the temptation to swing his head the other way to try and spot the others. To do that might slow down his pony and he already felt that, compared to the gallop of the Pecheneg steeds, his mount was capable of little more than a canter. Deep down Thorgeir began to despair but then heard the calm voice of his grand-father urging him to drop his head into the neck of his horse so he could whisper encouragement to the animal as it galloped. "Remember a horse is there to serve man. He knows it and expects you to know that. All he wants is the respect you can offer to his speed and strength." At the time he remembered smiling at the advice of the old man but now he felt his horse, recognising his desperation, would redouble its efforts. Now he regretted the times he could have fussed over the Turkish pony rather than merely making sure it had food and water. Had the pony come to recognise him as its beloved master and not just the latest owner? Frantically Hallbjorn started to pant all sorts of promises into the ear of his steed and the horse seemed to increase its pace.

Suddenly there was a shout from the distant column and riders detached themselves and started to move towards them, but to

Hallbjorn they seemed to crawl. He decided to glance the other way and so, with his head still firmly on the neck of the horse (like a lover reluctant to tear himself away), he glanced to the left and was horrified to see just how close three Pecheneg riders were. As if the sight of his face were a signal one raised his bow and fired at Hallbjorn. The Varangian tensed himself, ready to feel the arrow strike either himself or his horse, but the shaft fell short. He gulped for air and swung his head back to continue whispering prayers into the ears of his mount, half-thinking that merely looking at the Pechenegs drove them closer.

Hallbjorn could see the riders from the column quicken their pace but he didn't dare look back. He saw his brother look back and then almost stumble as he pulled his horse to a halt. Hallbjorn was past him before he dared glance back - at an empty sky-line. Soon they were joined by their comrades but nobody was keen on advancing over the crest to count how many Pechenegs they could find.

*

Nevertheless, without suffering loss, the Varangians did reach the river Kuban, at a point where it was flowing quite freely. Hiring the assistance of a small group of Khazar shepherds encamped on its banks, they immediately set about constructing rafts for themselves from the extensive woodland nearby. When the Khazars enquired if they'd employed rafts on any of the rivers within the realm of Kenugard Ethelwulf admitted they hadn't, causing the shepherds to laugh at the ambitions of these Rus who believed they were the masters of nature as well as of men. Ethelwulf didn't mention his men included some who had spent weeks wrestling with the waters of the fierce streams of Iceland, Norway and Finland. He was amazed how quickly five large rafts were constructed, each suitable for carrying at least fifteen men. By then he'd decided the ponies could not be transported by water so, rather than simply setting them loose to be the prey to Pechenegs, he gave them to the shepherds as a reward for their help. The shepherds were overwhelmed by the surrender of what, to them, was essential on the steppes. If they hadn't believed Ethelwulf crazy before, they did then. Such a collection was worth more than their whole flock and some were already calculating the profit they might make at Sarkel or closer settlements. When he heard the word 'Sarkel' Ethelwulf wondered whether his actions had been wise, but then considered Amran Chat would almost certainly have guessed their destination anyway. He didn't reveal to the shepherds that he expected the Pechenegs, after collecting a suitable force, to fall upon such booty, perhaps large enough to distract them from any other depredations.

Eventually, with loud shouts of good wishes and long life, the Varangians pushed off in the direction of the Sea of Azov and the city of Tmutarakan.[97] For several hours most effort was spent on acquiring mastery of the rafts. Although the river lacked the rapids which made the Dneiper so notorious Ethelwulf was sure that at some points they 'd have to manoeuvre their way through awkward situations. Several times they noticed large mounds[98] on either bank of the river and pointed them out to Aaron. The response was a shrug of the shoulders and the comment that ancient pagans had believed they could carry with them into the next world all they'd enjoyed in this. Ethelwulf thought pagan thinking hadn't advanced much, assuming the mounds were so ancient Aaron couldn't guess who had constructed them.

On the whole the Varangians relaxed as they'd seen no sign of any Pecheneg scouts and hoped this meant any war-band in the area had no wish to take on a heavily-armed group of warriors when, in the shepherds, much easier prey was at hand. As evening caused the light to fade Ethelwulf kept a good look-out for a suitable place to camp overnight. He commanded the leading raft, with Edwine in charge of the next one followed by another commanded by his twin, next Gunnar controlled a raft and the final one had been entrusted to Edwy, the helmsman of 'Alsvid'.

Finally Ethelwulf spotted a suitable clearing, largely masked from the steppes to the north by a long mound topped by trees. Placing sentries along the mound would provide sufficient warning of any hostile approach. The rafts were steered towards the bank, tied up and all the bustle of camp-making burst into action. Small tents were speedily erected while some men busied themselves with collecting kindling and more substantial fuel from the nearby trees. Two or three Varangians especially skilled in woodland craft were let loose to see what they could conjure up from the surrounding countryside. A few men, with the tents erected and fires started, produced fishing lines and tried their skill in the waters of the river. Morkere organised a rota of sentries before settling down, along with Ethelwulf and Gunnar and Aaron, to consider the general situation and their destination.

"This river is very long and rich in life," said Aaron, "It goes on for many days but lacks the fierceness of the Dneiper." He paused and looked almost conspiratorial. "No, its dangers come near journey's end, when the relaxed traveller thinks he's almost at the end of his labours."

Ethelwulf nodded as if he understood what was meant but was completely at a loss. For him at the end of the river Kuban was the town of Tmutarakan where he hoped to buy a ship capable of getting his men out of the grasp of Prince Vladimir. He had the vague idea this would mean a lengthy sea-crossing before he reached Miklagard. Once there he hoped there'd be a role fighting for the Emperor of the Greeks, of whom he'd heard even at his books at Wareham. Of course, when his teachers had described what had happened to such distant lands when the Empire of the Romans had fallen apart he knew they were describing events of which they knew little. Even so it would be an honour, and one not without profit, to follow in the steps of the heroes of his youthful books and serve such an Empire. He hoped to be more appreciated than in Ireland or in this God-forsaken land. His thoughts were interrupted by the continuing voice of the guide and he'd the irritating feeling he had missed something which might prove vital.

".... Near the sea this river becomes a monster, a creature with a thousand mouths as if uncertain how to spew out its contents. Each of these mouths is craftily hidden for the land changes from this open country to one so covered with reeds you can't tell where enemies, living or dead, may lurk."

"Dead?" asked Morkere.

"Yes," answered the guide. "Pagans and other ignorant people believe those meres and marshes are haunted by the wandering souls of the restless, creatures denied eternal rest because of the way they lived or how they died." He made a poor attempt at a smile. "Our people believe in the power of Yahweh, knowing that, as his servants, He will find a home for us in eternity. For others, however, the passage beyond the grave is one of darkness and horror. Some believe their spirit can be ensnared by whatever exists among the reeds and forced to feed on living creatures. Naturally, we Khazars don't believe such tales."

Ethelwulf didn't believe in such myths either, although he'd listened as a child to the journey of Aeneas into the land of shades.[99] He glanced at Gunnar and was sure the Gall-Gael believed such stories as he knew Gaelic tales of a separate existence for the soul.[100] Morkere rejected such ideas probably, like himself, believing stories were spread in the hope of shutting out the curiosity of strangers. He looked closely at the guide and thought he detected an air of doubt about Aaron's professed scepticism. Probably the closer the guide came to the source of his fears the less confident he became in his ability to overcome them. It did mean the chance of the guide deserting became more remote - important as Ethelwulf was sure the actual location of Tmutarakan was bound to be tied up with the myriad mouths at the delta.

"And Tmutarakan is located there?" asked Morkere. The guide nodded, unwilling to commit himself to a more precise description at that stage. For a moment Ethelwulf wondered if Aaron didn't know but immediately dismissed such fantasies; why should a young man set off into danger with a group of relative strangers unless he was confident of return.

The meeting was interrupted by the return of Pekka and the other hunters. While his companions carried their prizes, a pair of smallish antelopes, to the campfires, Pekka entered the tent and joined the conference. He reported they'd found definite tracks of ponies quite close to the bank, although the riders hadn't led their mounts into the water. He assumed the tracks indicated the presence of scouts, probably only a day or two previously. The Wanderer nodded, hoping that, having approached the river on one occasion, the Pechenegs would leave it alone for some time. But Pekka added that, with a fairly large number of tracks of varying age in the area, he'd argue the Pechenegs regularly explored the river bank, probably to check if any suitable prey was in the area.

Morkere and Ethelwulf exchanged looks. They couldn't conceal the remains of their camp on leaving enough to prevent any Pecheneg scout knowing how far they'd proceeded along the river. Edwine arrived, having supervised all the preparations for setting up camp, and was rapidly told of their discussion. He smiled at the tales of ghosts haunting the delta, whispering to his brother they'd never come across anything supernatural which lacked a human origin. With that, they joined the men, prepared for a dawn start.

*

The journey along the river during the next few days was very pleasant. The river was broad and the steppes on either side revealed no sign of danger. There was abundant game and, largely for the sake of morale, Ethelwulf would put into a bank where the skilful hunters among his men could exercise their talents. Even more abundant were the supplies of fish which seemed to throw themselves on to the lines put out. If it hadn't been for the ever-present danger of intervention from Sarkel or the Pechenegs the journey might have passed as idyllic.

The inhabitants of the occasional village they came across proved friendly, willing to supply fresh vegetables for the occasional game and more frequently silver. They told the Varangians about the journey ahead and it was clear, from the number of people who could speak some form of Rus, there was frequent contact with Tmutarakan itself. The villagers told Ethelwulf the river would suddenly narrow and then divide into numerous channels, with strong banks too often becoming treacherous marshes filled with disease and other creatures which they'd not describe.

As the river Kuban narrowed the confidence of their guide, Aaron, began to fall. Obviously what had been dismissed as, perhaps, a merely superstitious acceptance of the ghostly tales of the pagans, now became an obsession. Recently Ethelwulf had learned Aaron hadn't been the pure volunteer to join the expedition that had been thought. Apparently, Aaron had formed a relationship with an attractive young – and newly widowed - woman in Samir and she was found to be pregnant. What made matters worse was that Aaron had been attached to the widow before the death of her husband had been discovered. The husband had set off for Sarkel one day and disappeared - his body being soon found about a day's ride north of the village; his throat had been cut and his horse and other possessions stolen. At first, the villagers believed the unhappy man had been the victim of either Pechenegs or brigands but when the affair between the widow and the young man became known gossip piled on to rumour. At first tongues swore the expected child must be that of Aaron because of the question of timing. Then more malicious tongues pointed to the very convenient death of the husband, adding it had occurred at the very time Aaron was returning from Sarkel. What if the two men had met, the husband discovering he'd been cuckolded and the younger man deciding to be rid of a rival? When the baby was eventually born, it would be closely examined and if Aaron appeared to be its father there'd be an enquiry into the death of the husband. So Aaron had chosen not to await the birth but rushed to act as guide for the Varangians. Ethelwulf had been surprised the young man, instead of leaving them once they'd reached the river, had offered to stay with them as far as Tmutarakan. He hadn't believed the story that Aaron had simply tired of rural life and was seeking a new career among strangers. As the story had been wheedled out of the guide he'd first laughed at what payment the young man was enduring for his liaison with the widow. Then he wondered whether they were harbouring a murderer, but immediately dismissed the idea. Aaron seemed such an open young man he couldn't believe him a killer. The present mood change, nevertheless, did concern him.

Morkere reminded him of one belief of the local people that unhappy spirits made their way down the river to the open sea to seek rest. However, some of these sad wraiths were unable to find their way through the mass of rivulets, islands and marshes making up the delta. To sustain themselves while trying to escape they set upon unwary travellers, especially those who'd wronged them in life. Ethelwulf naturally connected this with the decline in spirits of their young guide.

*

One day Ethelwulf was standing next to Edwine Alfredsson who'd been given the task of scouring the steppes to the north for any sign of danger. Edwine, like so many others in the band, had joined Ethelwulf in Ireland. He was a dour warrior from Durham where he'd roamed the moors hunting for game and had acquired the ability to detect the slightest clue to such quarry. Unfortunately for Edwine he'd killed a Dane in holmgangr.[101] It had been fairly conducted - each man supplied with three shields and choice of weapon - and fought on an isolated island. However, the kin of the dead man didn't accept the verdict of fortune and Edwine had been convinced they'd never be satisfied with mere compensation. So to save his life he'd fled westwards to Ireland where he'd eventually joined Ethelwulf shortly before they'd all left for Iceland.

Suddenly Edwine cried out. "Look, over there!" He pointed towards the crest of the upland which gradually rose to the north. Ethelwulf looked to where he pointed and could see nothing, not even when Edwine directed his gaze by lining up the direction with one of the isolated trees on the bank. "No, wait for the sun!" he advised. "You'll see a glint which can only come from metal - and no animal uses metal!" So Ethelwulf screwed up his eyes and concentrated, to be rewarded with a brief flash of metal. He continued to look in the same place and could see nothing.

Ethelwulf told Edwine to bring Sven the Far-Sighted at once to see if he could make out what was there. All the while he kept his eyes fixed on the spot, partly for fear his senses were tricking him and he needed confirmation, partly because he was certain he wouldn't easily be able to locate the spot if once he broke his concentration. Suddenly he was aware Sven was standing next to him and so, not daring to shift his focus, he got Sven to line up his sight with the help of another tree.

For several moments there was silence as all three stared at what might be there and then Sven gave his verdict. "Yes," he remarked as if on any ordinary event. "I see three warriors, armed with spears and bows". There was a long pause. "They're riding dull-grey horses and - did you see that flash?" The other two nodded but none broke their inspection of the distant slope. "One of them has made the mistake of wearing a metal helm, the other two must have some kind of leather head-covering." Both Ethelwulf and Edwine concentrated but neither could see anything, although Edwine felt rather than saw some slight change in colouring which would indicate movement.

All agreed the figures could be none other than Pechenegs, but realised that, on rafts following the course of the Kuban towards the sea, they could do nothing to prevent the Pechenegs collecting together. From the description by Sven Ethelwulf assumed the scouts were members of the Borotalmat division - not that such knowledge made any difference, except that, perhaps, they had more contact with the Rus at Tmutarakan and so might be less hostile. Ethelwulf wondered if the Pechenegs would attack after they'd entered the area of the meres which made up the delta. Certainly, the nature of the terrain meant the Pechenegs couldn't employ their usual tactics of firing arrows from horseback, but it would provide them with more cover if they wished to ambush the force in transit. Suddenly he realised they'd not seen any other craft on the river, going either way, and that thought didn't add to his confidence. He knew relations between the Rus and the Pechenegs could vary from cooperation in trade - trinkets for supplies of mutton or beef - to outright hostility, and could change for apparently no reason and with bewildering rapidity.

*

That evening the leaders gathered and were told what the scouts had noticed that day. They agreed it couldn't affect their decision to reach Tmutarakan as speedily as possible. If they stopped - and even tried to contact the Pechenegs and make some compact - the delay might allow sufficient forces from Menashe Bulan or his master, Prince Vladimir, to cut them off from their one chance of escape. It might all end up as a question of luck. Edwine made a gallant attempt at cheering everyone by reminding them how often fortune had rescued them just when disaster seemed about to triumph. However, Morkere said, though true, such fortune normally demanded payment in a form often unacceptable.

At this Gunnar began to mutter away to himself and when prompted to utter aloud what was in his thoughts gave the following account.

"This is surely the country of the Vanir,[102] for look at all the mounds built to house such and their treasure until the end of the world." He silenced an interruption from Morkere by a curt wave of his hand. "You'll say mounds have appeared for some time, along the edge of the river but now it narrows and the countryside is more truly the realm of Odin.[103] The owners of the mounds, the children of the Vanir, want even more to hold on to what they held in life."

He paused and looked towards where he knew was the closest of the mounds. They'd camped, as usual, by the river, slightly to the west of a large mound which, Ethelwulf remembered, had attracted the attention of the Gall-Gael as soon as they had landed.

"In my country we've similar mounds and again it's not wise to disturb either the owners nor their possessions. Once there was a powerful king - not an Ard Ri[104] for in those times there was no such position - who was feared by not only his own people but by his neighbours. For not only did he command armies that could spread destruction even over nature itself but, people believed, his mother had been a witch who'd left him as a changeling in the cradle of the rightful prince of that land and had stolen the royal heir away. This king, from his very infancy, terrorised all who knew him; his foster parents never dared correct him and his slaves lived in terror of being summoned to do his will. So, when but a young man, he tired of his foster-parents and, one day, they were just not there."

Gunnar looked at Morkere whom he knew delighted in baiting him with questions difficult to answer. Morkere, however, seemed to have entered a dream state, listening not just to the speaker but to whatever sounds the night could offer. Gunnar continued. "This king went to war and expanded his realm for he was strong in battle and fortune, so it seemed, smiled upon him and all his works. He loved treasure of any kind and people rushed to surrender gold and jewels and all manner of riches so that he wouldn't turn his arms against them. The king managed to fill not one treasure house but two with the wealth poured upon him."

"Now when he was growing old he thought he should acquire a wife so that he'd have a child to take up his crown when he had gone. He looked beyond the boundaries of his realm and his agents reported that in a distant tower lived an aged lord and his daughter who, it was said, was the most lovely maiden in all Ireland. The king instantly marched against the tower, capturing it with ease, and, as the price of the life of the old man, demanded the hand of his daughter. The aged lord was most reluctant but his daughter used all her wiles to persuade him to agree."

Gunnar smiled directly at Morkere as if issuing a challenge. "Now why would any young maiden would want to marry such an ogre?"

There was silence for a few moments before Edwine suggested a reason. "You said the king was growing old and possessed mounds of treasure." Gunnar nodded. "Surely the girl could see he'd soon die and then she'd possess both wealth and beauty!"

Gunnar laughed. "Well done, Edwine," he said. " I can see a sharpness of mind has been given to BOTH the sons of Aelfhere. It was as you reasoned. The maiden had a cold heart within her beautiful frame and dreamed of the time when, as a wealthy widow, she'd have the pick of any youth in the land."

"So her father yielded and the wedding took place but, as I'm sure it will come as no surprise to any of you, the aged lord didn't long survive the wedding. The king sent slaves with poison in a bottle and they forced his father-in-law to drink it and die. When the queen heard of the murder of her father she hid her feelings but, instead of tolerating her husband, came to hate him; nevertheless, he was blinded by her beauty, showering presents on her and nightly tried to bring about the conception of a son. Yet the queen, unwilling to bring another such monster into the world, the next morning would go about those secret practices by which women know how to prevent conception. She knew that soon the king would tire of her and so, while his lust still clouded his natural suspicions, she contrived to poison her husband - to the great joy of his subjects."

There was a slight relaxation as Gunnar's audience thought he'd come to the end of his story, although they wondered what it had to do with the burial mounds they'd been passing. Gunnar coughed loudly to signal he'd NOT finished and they prepared for the remainder of the tale.

"The king had ordered his wealth should be placed within his burial mound as soon as he was dead. At first the queen demanded they should bury the dead monarch without his treasure, not daring to question of what value was such pelf to the dead. However, the priests replied that, until the king had been laid to rest on his throne in the middle of his treasures within his burial mound, his word was still law throughout the land and the queen had to give way. All the treasure was carried into the mound so that, as custom decreed, the king could be buried along with what was most precious to him."

"Finally the day of the funeral arrived. Many came from all over the land - not a few to make sure the old monster was truly placed within the mound. At the head of the procession came the priests chanting like priests love to do when the dead are being carried into eternity. Next came slaves carrying an ornate throne and sitting on that royal chair the dead monarch himself, dressed in all his finery as if on his way to a second wedding. Then came his queen, dutifully weeping for her dead husband, but at the same time making sure she had a true catalogue of whatever had been placed within the tomb. Finally came more slaves with the weapons of the king - his axe and spear with which he'd led his armies. Around the mound assembled his warriors ready to slaughter any who tried to interfere with the last rites of their dead master".

"Inside the mound at last the throne was placed in its central position and the queen looked at the high priest. Without her question he nodded, signifying now the power of the king was over and it was her word which was law. For a brief moment she considered ordering them to remove every bit of treasure from the tomb immediately but then remembered the warriors outside, whom she couldn't yet trust, and the mass of the people who might consider this act to be sacrilege. Better to let everything go ahead as planned and then later, more discreetly, reopen the mound and stealthily remove its contents."

Gunnar paused and smiled at his audience. "The queen had dreamed for months of this moment and she felt she must stamp her mark on this very hour so she brusquely ordered everyone to leave the mound so she could commune for one last time with her dead lord. Without a word they obeyed and the queen was left with the remains of her lord, her husband and her victim. She smiled and taunted him, asking which of his treasures should she take as a keepsake of their union. The silence of the mound muffling her voice was unwelcome so she soon brought her mockery to a stop."

"Then she saw on the middle finger of his right hand his finest ring, gold with a monstrous emerald. Reaching forward she touched the jewel and was amazed at the coldness, until she reasoned the chill must come from the dead body of the king. Quickly she grabbed his finger and began to ease off the ring, willing the finger to shrink so her task might become easier. Behind her she thought she heard a noise and dismissed it."

"But suddenly her neck was gripped in a vice formed by the dead king's left hand which drove her head down until her lips rested on his knuckles. She tried to scream but the pressure on her throat prevented any sound coming out. Instead she heard the voice of her dead husband whisper in its customary harsh tones above her head. 'I claim you, my darling, as my most precious possession to be with me for evermore.' With that the mound appeared to quiver as the queen found her lips kissing the dead knuckles as a sign of submission. Then the quivering became shaking and the mound collapsed within itself so that the entrance was completely filled in."

"Outside the people trembled until the priests declared the will of the gods had been done and their king had departed with his most precious possession. And the whole congregation marched away praising their gods."

Gunnar looked again at Morkere expecting a challenge but none came. Ethelwulf thought that, whatever the origin of the tale, it had to be a lie because who'd been in the mound to describe what exactly had happened to the queen. But he said nothing, recalling nature had the power to shake down hills and root up trees, so it was quite capable of covering up the remains of one dead monster and his heinous queen.

Finally Morkere spoke. "Thank you, Gunnar, for giving us the substance of peaceful dreams" and his brother joined in the laughter in which even the story-teller took part.

*

No ghoul merged from the burial mound during the night and nobody confessed to having a nightmare, whatever the actual state of their sleep had been. The following day they launched the rafts more quickly than usual, anxious to reach what they hoped to be the shelter of the meres and away from the wide plains which were perfect for Pecheneg tactics.

They were taken by surprise when the Kuban first divided and it was immediately clear Aaron had no more knowledge than they had as to which branch to take. Ethelwulf cursed himself for not getting details from the last village they'd passed but realised that was over a day's journey back and so out of the question. He decided to trust to luck and chose the northern branch.

After a while they noticed both the numbers of trees grew, blotting out the distant view across the steppes, and the amount of water around the rafts also seemed to increase. It became clear they might find it difficult to find a suitable amount of dry land on which to camp during the night so Ethelwulf decided to stop at the first likely spot, even if it was some time before sunset. They had to accept their watery path was but one of many snaking through what little dry land formed the numerous islands that surrounded them. Some Finns pointed out that what might appear as dry land from afar could prove treacherous, being a bog which would suck them quickly down into the next world. Ethelwulf knew Finland was a land of innumerable islands set in a myriad of lakes - although the Finns assured him their country didn't have the unhealthy air they sensed all around them. Meanwhile the rafts passed on, each vessel taking care not to run aground; this meant Ethelwulf's raft had the task of finding a way through the islands using whatever seemed the deepest channel. By the time they reached a possibly suitable area to camp he knew he'd never be able to find his way back to the broader stretches of the Kuban. In essence he was lost.

The Wanderer soon realised he had to make a decision - and stick to it. Only that way would he and his men have any chance of survival. So he determined to make for the rightmost channel whenever a choice was offered; also every time he did so he cut a notch on one of the timbers making up the raft. This way, if necessary, he could make his way back by taking the leftmost path; the only trouble was he was uncertain whether there'd been any consistency in his choice since first entering the delta.

That evening two men became delirious and Leif the Healer, an Icelander with some degree of medical knowledge, announced they must have contracted a fever from the unhealthy air surrounding them. Ethelwulf wanted to ask why, if that was the case, the rest of them hadn't been affected. However, he abstained, fearful the curt reply might well be, "Not YET affected." All night the sick moaned and whimpered in their unnatural 'sleep'; one of them, a Dorset man called Grim had been with Ethelwulf since their outlaw days in the forest of Arne. Both men died as dawn at last gave light to their surroundings. Ethelwulf mourned deeply for the dark-haired Dorset man, although he also remembered the playfulness of the other man, a Swede called Ulf. He ordered two graves to be dug on the island where they'd rested, the bodies laid therein and the smouldering ashes of the camp-fire placed on top.

By now the men realised they were starting to run short of drinking water. Although surrounded by water, none of the men cared to risk drinking what could easily have been tainted by the unhealthy air. After the deaths of Grim and Ulf some men took to masking their mouths with the edges of their cloaks, trying to shut out whatever poisons had been breathed in by the dead men. Nobody had either the energy or inclination to smile or even talk to their neighbour; one or two might point out, with a soundless gesture, a particularly handsome bird perched in one of the nearby trees which overhung the rivulets. No comment was passed; eyes scoured whatever land there was for Pecheneg activity but none was detected. Ethelwulf told himself that at least this passage through the meres had shaken off pursuit from the savages who terrorised the area.

Some started glancing at Aaron with suspicious malice in their eyes. Clearly the young guide, no longer of any use to them, was becoming a handicap. He'd become isolated and was normally found looking back mournfully as if joining the expedition had been the worst decision of his life. However, he found no sympathy among the Varangians but rather dark muttering about the guide.

One evening Sven the Far-Sighted took Ethelwulf aside and confided what he'd been hearing among the men. "Some of them say he's sold us out to the Pechenegs, leading us like lambs into the trackless wilds of the river so we can be more easily picked off!"

"So what do these men say should happen to Aaron?" asked Ethelwulf, irritated by the sheer stupidity of some of his followers. How could Aaron have made contact with the Pechenegs? Why would he risk his own life in reaching such a deal? What could the Pechenegs pay him? How would a force of light cavalry, such as the Pechenegs, be able to operate in a dismal swamp like this?

"They reckon that, since he's a lover of Pechenegs, we should finish him off here and now - and then leave his corpse to show the Pechenegs we know all about their games and aren't scared."

"And you share these ideas, Sven?" asked Ethelwulf, alarmed a man he'd come to trust might entertain such insane notions.

"No!" snapped Sven, all-too-aware of the thoughts which had passed through his leader's mind. "It's just I'm fed up with all this grumbling. If they have a complaint they should bring it out into the open, give us all a chance to fix it, before we all make an early trip to Valhalla!"

Ethelwulf smiled at how Sven contrasted 'they", the moaners, with "we", the decision-makers. Yet in many ways he was right. The expedition could only survive if they worked together, trusted each other. He was disappointed this trust seemed to have evaporated. After all they'd endured together he'd felt such trust could never disappear. Perhaps the grumblers were limited to those joining since he'd entered the realm of Prince Vladimir? He doubted it. He knew there were some among his warriors – the late Grim from Dorset or Pekka from Karelia - who delighted in looking on the black side of life. He thanked Sven and decided he needed to hold a meeting with the warriors that evening.

*

The men at first denied they felt any hostility towards the guide - except he seemed to have an unnatural reluctance to take his turn at the long paddles with which they propelled the rafts along. Aaron had been seized by Gunnar and dragged to the centre of the men. Ethelwulf didn't like making the guide feel he was on trial but had to bring matters to a head. He couldn't risk the guide hearing about what was being said and skulking off to join the Pechenegs.

Aaron readily admitted he knew nothing about the nature of the river at this point and then confessed the only time he'd been to

Tmutarakan had been as a child. At this a roar of disbelief and anger demanded why they were bothering with such a useless fellow. Aaron shouted that certainly he was running away from his village, but he'd been loyal and WOULD always be loyal to the Varangians. Ethelwulf demanded if any could deny this and no man stepped forward. But some protested the Khazar ate too much and spent too little time at the paddles. Aaron admitted he couldn't deny that charge but excused his greed by saying that, unlike his companions, he was still growing. There was laughter at this and Thorleif the Tall was roughly clapped on the back, for the warrior from Bergen was only one-and-a-half yards high and rumour cruelly said that was the reason he'd left his family six years ago early one June morning. Morkere was certain there'd been a darker reason but, as with others in the company, they were only expected to reveal whatever in their past they wished - and, anyway, Thorleif had a modest appetite!

Aaron said, like all his people, he'd no cause to love the Pechenegs who'd ruined the Empire once ruled by their Kagans. He declared his people had once ruled all these grasslands unchallenged until the savage Pechenegs had appeared from the east and spread terror among the trade-routes. He then asked the men how they thought he would be paid by the Pechenegs.

"With an arrow in your guts!" was the response from the back and there was loud laughter from many and nods of agreement from others. This enraged the young guide and he shouted abuse at his tormenters, at times abandoning Rus so that whatever insults or curses he uttered were completely lost on his hearers. In the end he became so emotional he simply broke down in tears. This provoked some shouts of derision but most of the company were somewhat nonplussed by this.

Ethelwulf stepped in and demanded they make a decision there and then; either they should execute the young guide as a traitor or accept him as one of the company. A few protested at this demand but they were soon quietened. It was agreed to put the matter to the vote and, by a large majority, Aaron was accepted as a full member of the company. Ethelwulf demanded Aaron should cut down on his food intake and increase his work output; the Khazar accepted both provisions with a smile. Yet some did not smile at the decision.

That same evening Ethelwulf introduced a system of rationing both water and bread. Each man was to be given his ration of bread at the start of the day and it would be up to him as to when and how to consume it. Water was the responsibility of each of the raft's captains and each received an equal amount for their men. They should decide how they allocated this precious commodity.

Nevertheless, that afternoon all these schemes came to an end as, without warning, the rafts burst into a wide lake. For once the air was less oppressive and with that both the water seemed clearer and the day brighter. Immediately the general mood rose and they decided to rest on the shore for at least the next day, after refilling their water-containers to the limit. Some of the more adventurous were even in favour of hunting both then and there and the next morning, sure that, just as they'd been invigorated by this sudden relief, animal life would have welcomed the benefits of the lake.

That evening their optimism appeared justified for the hunters returned with several birds and a couple of young deer. It was a merry time around the camp-fires and several of the men were in a playful mood, bringing up episodes of their fellows to provide tales to bring tears of laughter to their audience. Morkere went on at length about how moonstruck his brother had been about the daughter of the farmer Cynegils and was disappointed when his twin didn't deny it. Indeed Edwine declared he'd never met any woman to match Edith for beauty, intelligence or patience.

"That's because she had to put up with your boorish attempts at love-making!" teased Morkere and brought a blush to the cheeks of his twin. The blush reddened as it was noticed by his neighbours and brought about raucous laughter. Edwine would have given way to his brother, except that, from the moment they'd tussled over the skirts of their nurse, neither twin would willingly yield to another.

"True, Morkere, but we all have to learn - as you remember from Ireland and your adventures among the Finns!" Demands for Edwine to reveal the inadequacies of his twin were rejected by Edwine with a smug smile. Morkere seemed about to blush like his brother but suddenly shrugged his shoulders and laughed at himself, not forgetting to poke his twin in the ribs as a tacit acceptance of defeat. With that the talk turned to other targets and so the merriment went on until, as the flames of the three campfires started to die down, the men felt it time for them to sleep.

*

After dawn the next day the Pechenegs attacked. One of the sentinels had been knifed before he could raise the alarm but the other, detecting sounds of a scuffle, risked a false alarm by shouting for help. Even as he shrieked a warning he was jumped on by a Pecheneg. Somehow the knife-thrust which should have pierced his chest was deflected by the buckle of his cloak and Inar Eyjolfsson slipped away from the attacker, turning with the speed of a creature at bay, and had the good fortune of seeing his attacker run on to his spear. From then on he was known as Inar the Lucky.

The cries aroused the camp, helped by many of the men already getting themselves together in preparation for the pleasures of the hunt. So the Pechenegs found their surprise attack was met by unexpected resistance. Morkere knocked one warrior off-balance with his shield and his twin completed the move by burying his spear in the chest of the felled warrior. Now both the sons of Aelfhere stood at bay, back to back, armed with their favourite weapon as Pechenegs poured out of the woods, howling their hatred and determined to seize their due of heads.

Ethelwulf had been slipping his baldric over his chest when he'd heard the first cries of alarm. Drawing his sword he stumbled and had his quota of luck for the day when a spear whistled over his head. Only then did he realise he was without a shield but he brushed aside such shortcomings as he hacked at the ill-armed warrior confronting him. The man stepped nimbly aside and jabbed with his spear at Ethelwulf's exposed left-shoulder. The Wanderer tried to duck under the thrust, only dangerous because of the absence of a shield, and partly succeeded because the point of the spear merely grazed the exposed gap at the top of his hauberk. Even as he ducked, what had been a slash was transformed into a lunge at the exposed stomach of his enemy and, whatever pain he might have felt as the spear-point cut into his neck was masked by the elation of seeing his opponent crumple. Immediately Ethelwulf turned to face a new attacker, all too aware of the dampness of the wound in his neck; somehow he could smell his blood and this gave him battle-frenzy in a way he'd rarely felt before.

The warrior in front of him seemed enormous but ponderous in all his movements. Ethelwulf sensed an unusual lightness in his blade and an unnatural speed in his movements. He cut fiercely at the warrior and saw him collapse. Around him other warriors must have been engaged in fierce struggles but none registered in his brain. The rest of the world appeared entangled in a cloth and shoved away into some corner to play by itself. All Ethelwulf could smell was his own blood, all he could hear was the sound of his weapon striking whatever defences his enemies could offer, all he could see were the forms and faces of the warriors who dared to face him. 'Dared' was the word he'd have used if he'd been capable of any form of rational thought as he attacked the next Pecheneg appearing before him. This warrior was a slight man, carrying the small target-like shield beloved of horsemen but of little use when fighting on foot. His spear-thrust was hesitant as he seemed more terrified than war-like; with one cut Ethelwulf sent him to meet his ancestors. Now another two warriors seemed to melt away from before him, terrified by the blood-lust in his eyes. In fact, they were but part of the general retreat of the Pechenegs, realising too late they'd taken on warriors excelling their usual victims in weapon-skills. Edwine led the charge of a dozen men in hot pursuit as the enemy fled through the trees away from the lakeside. Only then did Ethelwulf begin to re-enter the realm of reality.

The clearing was littered with the bodies of the dead and wounded. Ethelwulf could see at least three Varangians were either dead or virtually so, another half-dozen were caring to wounds which varied in degree. Over thirty Pechenegs were scattered throughout the clearing. As he looked a couple of Varangians passed among them, checking on who was dead, and, if there was any sign of life, finishing them off. There could be neither booty or information gathered from such savages.

Hallbjorn Gudmansson approached him and quietly led him over to one body lying by itself in the shade of a tall tree. It was that of Aaron, the guide. Ethelwulf was asked to look at the wound and did so. In the back was an ugly hole which had released blood and so stained a large area of the guide's brown tunic. The blood had dried and he could see Aaron had died from a thrust in the kidneys.

"That wound was never made by a Pecheneg spear," commented the Icelander. Ethelwulf inserted his finger into the hole and realised the cavity should have been larger, should have torn more widely into the flesh. Perhaps it had been a sword thrust? Even as he considered that possibility it was rejected. As far as he knew the only swords the Pechenegs employed were long, cutting blades - most useful for being wielded from horseback. This was a smaller injury, more like that inflicted by a knife.

"I see you also think it was done by a knife," said Hallbjorn and added, "Who rushes out of ambush armed only with a knife?" Ethelwulf was about to say, "One who's lost his spear," but realised he was trying to explain away what both Hallbjorn and himself were thinking; Aaron had been stabbed by a Varangian blade.

"We could never find who was responsible," Ethelwulf said to the Icelander and the other man nodded. "And it wouldn't be worth all the risk of disturbing those elements within the force who - "

"-have proved increasingly awkward as the journey becomes more difficult," finished Hallbjorn. "Perhaps I could discreetly - "

"No!" interrupted Ethelwulf. "However quietly you go about asking questions somebody would get alarmed - and if they've done this once they'd do it again!"

"So we let whoever's murdered this miserable youth get away with it?" There was a tone of fury in the question. Hallbjorn hadn't consulted his elder brother, so confident had he been their leader would take the matter in hand. However, the Saxon must lack the sense of justice bred into Icelanders.

"Perhaps," answered Ethelwulf. "I'm sure we now have one less murderer travelling with us." He bent and rolled the corpse over so that he could stare into the shocked eyes of the dead youth

*

Time passed and morning dragged into afternoon and still the pursuers led by Edwine hadn't returned. Whatever had seemed pleasant and inviting about the lakeside turned into disgust and loathing. Ethelwulf realised the killing of deer should have warned him his camp could be approached by Pechenegs - and those savages had clearly followed the hunters let loose the previous day. Well, they'd paid for it and his conscience would ensure he'd continue to pay for years.

Suddenly there was a shout and out of the woods burst Pekka and ran straight up to Ethelwulf. It took some moments for the Karelian to recover his breath sufficiently to tell his story. Ethelwulf wanted to shake the tale out of him until he heard others making their way through the woods and then he relaxed.

Pekka destroyed all that mood with his opening words. "Edwine is dead!" Morkere had been casually making his way over from leaning against the tree when he saw Pekka arrive. Now, without a word, he turned and ran towards the sounds emerging from the woods. Ethelwulf this time did grab the surly tracker, determined to get the story immediately.

"We were ambushed," gasped the tracker. "A couple of the Pechenegs decided to drop back and pick off anybody who came after them..... They waited..... They were hiding on the top of a slope when Edwine - you know Edwine - always first - always sure of being there - " He looked into the face of Ethelwulf and saw no support from the cold grey eyes. If Ethelwulf could have sacrificed

Pekka at that moment for his cousin he'd have done so. "Well, Edwine charged up the slope - ahead of me because it wasn't a question - there was no need....... no need to follow tracks because of all the noise..... Anyway both Pechenegs had a go at him, one hit him in the chest and the other one ... got him in the throat." There was a howl of grief from the trees still masking the approaching warriors. Pekka looked over to those trees, as if some woodland spirit was out hunting for souls to carry off and was coming for his. Then he turned back, looking at Ethelwulf for support, but all his leader could do was order him to continue.

"There was nothing any of us could do!" protested Pekka. "He'd charged ahead .... We all thought they'd just keep on running .... I got one of the bowmen with my sword and Tosti got the other -"

"So you left him for dead?"

"No, Ethelwulf, no!" shouted the distraught tracker. "You know we'd never abandon a comrade - never leave Edwine to cling on to life-"

"You left him-"

"No!" screamed Pekka. "One glance told us there was no life in him and my people hold that - believe - a man needs the company of his killer to find his way into the after-life."

At that point several figures staggered into the clearing. One of them was carrying the body of Edwine over his shoulders and another was trying to stop Morkere throwing himself on to the body as it was being carried. Men who'd been listening to the account of Pekka broke away to flock around the dead Varangian, perhaps out of morbid curiosity, perhaps in the vain attempt to breathe life back into him. Everything seemed silent as Edwine was gently laid under a tree and, at last, his twin could take him in his arms. As if under orders every Varangian silently withdrew to the other side of the clearing to leave Morkere to mourn alone.

"What should we do?" asked Gunnar quietly and Ethelwulf didn't respond. His memory had just taken him back to his youth in Dorset when, on horseback or on foot, he'd compete against his cousins. Each would have their day, be unbeatable, and then the next week it would be the turn of another. Never was there any bad feeling, and almost never any arguments. Sometimes they'd wondered which set of parents would be most disapproving of whatever mischief they'd tumbled into, but it made no difference; they all stood together and took whatever punishment was handed out.

But all that had been when they were little boys - half-grown lads given the chance to ape their elders and felt that to be sufficient reward. Later they'd matched each other with sword, spear and bow and each had triumphed over the others at one time but the final verdict had been his own superiority with the sword while his cousins were his masters with the other weapons. He wondered what had happened to Edith Cynegilssdotter. How perverse that only yesterday Edwine had been teased about what had clearly been the great love of his life. And now he'd have no time - no chance - for love ever again.

"What should we do?" repeated Gunnar a little more loudly and this time was heard.

"You tell me," replied Ethelwulf. "Remember the pit of depression you were in when we discovered your dead betrothed."[105] Gunnar blanched as he remembered how they'd fought their way into Brian of Clonmel's wedding feast only to find his bride, his abducted betrothed, had already killed herself. Even the death of Brian had been no consolation and he'd turned instead to a wandering life with Ethelwulf - no real comfort but better than nothing.

"Each man must cross that chasm by himself and the rope bridge to be used is very finely strung and offers an unsure path."

"So we can do nothing?"

"Leave Morkere to himself. Let him make any peace he feels he has to make with Edwine. Above all, don't push him on but let him drain his grief until the waters of despair have been washed away."

Ethelwulf raised his hand to the Gall-Gael as he saw Morkere approaching. His cousin looked as empty and alone as ever he'd ever looked. Somehow his shoulders just sagged.

"What would our mother have said to know Edwine would never again sit at her table?" asked Morkere, more to himself than any other. Ethelwulf knew that neither Edwine nor Morkere would have ever returned to Dorset and so the question was ridiculous; besides he knew Hild Osbertsdotter had been dead for almost ten years now. "Why must I leave him in this miserable land, scarcely given Christian burial?" He stopped and glared at Ethelwulf. "Who is there, cousin, to give my brother Christian burial? Who is there to pray to God to let him enter the realm of Purgatory and await his chance of salvation."

"You know, Morkere, many men say that within ten years the gates of Heaven and Hell will be opened up as the Eternal Judge comes to bring about the final days,"[106] stated Ethelwulf, uncertain how much he believed in what he was saying but unable to offer any other form of judgement.

"But meanwhile, cousin, shall Edwine lie in this cold, wet ground deprived of the offices of the Church?"

"He will have our prayers - "

"Not enough, Ethelwulf, not enough!" shouted Morkere and grabbed his cousin. "Come with me and see how your cousin lies in death and remember how you brought him to it!"

Ethelwulf was forced over towards the corpse of Edwine, unwilling to resist the demands of his cousin even though he told himself the sons of Aelfhere were there by their own desire - and against his own wishes.[107] He looked down at his cousin and a tear appeared in the corner of his eye. Both arrows had been snapped off so the body could be more easily manoeuvred. Edwine looked surprised more than horrified or at peace; it would seem he'd died as BOTH arrows had struck him, with no time to cling to life.

"Would Edwine have even had time to repent his sins?" demanded Morkere and Ethelwulf felt himself shaking his head. "No, cousin, no indeed! And does not Holy Mother Church declare none shall enter into heaven with sin still upon them?"

Ethelwulf wanted to declare the Church had a whole system of dealing with the consequences of sudden death - a conglomeration of masses and prayers by which the Saints themselves could help such souls into Paradise; but he did not. He simply hung his head and was aware of his cousin ranting on about the injustice of it all, how Edwine had always had a purer soul than his own and now must tumble into Hell through lack of warning. Finally he finished by saying he himself would spend that night at prayer for the soul of his brother and he trusted his cousin would join him.

That evening, just before light vanished, a grave for Edwine was dug; graves for the other Varangian dead had been dug in the late afternoon and their bodies interred; the corpses of the Pechenegs were simply pitched into the lake. As night fell Edwine was solemnly laid into the ground, buried with his weapons and mail-shirt (at Morkere's insistence), his hands grasping his sword to make the sign of the cross over his heart. Morkere turned away as the soil was tipped in over the body. Then the surviving twin knelt in prayer, alongside him Ethelwulf. Much to their surprise they found themselves joined by Aldred the Eloquent, Edric, Edwy, Harold of Furzebrook and Wulfstan of Sherbourne, all original outlaws in Dorset. Others would have liked to have joined in the vigil but it was felt the night belonged to those who'd known Edwine the longest. For Edwine had been one of the most popular men in the entire company - rarely critical of another and always willing to help, ready to join in any fun and always reliable in a tight corner. Edwine's was a rare spirit that had walked upon the earth.

*

It took two days before Morkere was willing to be coaxed away from the graveside of his twin. When they did finally leave he was placed on the same raft as Ethelwulf, his place taken by Sven Haraldsson while Harald the Black took over Edwine's craft. When they passed finally out of sight of the lake Morkere suddenly tried to leap into the water. Fortunately Gunnar had warned Ethelwulf this was quite possible and two men immediately jumped on Morkere and held him down until the mood had drained away. Morkere then spent the next two days in silence either gazing into the water as it passed beneath or into the flames of the camp-fire at night. Following Gunnar's advice Ethelwulf made no attempt to intervene in what he saw as Morkere's penance; he knew Edwine's twin was recalling all the unthinking words which might have stung the dead man and for which there was no time to say sorry.

On the third day Morkere seemed to come out of his depression just as they emerged on to the Sea of Azov. Now the question was simply which way to Tmutarakan. Ethelwulf reasoned that, as they'd emerged on what must have been the most northerly exit of the river Kuban and as Tmutarakan must lie close to river access to the interior, the town must lie to the south. Accordingly he turned south and they paddled their way past the various mouths of the Kuban.

Suddenly he came upon a strange sight, on a sand bank lying between two outpourings of the river, lay a longship. It seemed clear that with a new tide the vessel should have gone its way over the sea but it hadn't happened. As they approached Ethelwulf hailed the vessel in the hope somebody on board could explain why the longship was so stranded. As his call died away a dozen heads appeared from nowhere, followed by several bodies all armed and ready for a fight.

"Who are you?" called Ethelwulf, assuming there weren't enough men on board to sail the vessel to the next destination. Obviously, it could mean the remainder of the crew were on shore somewhere and might return at any moment.

"I'm Halfdan Snorrisson," yelled a red-haired man who possessed a beard of the same colour which reached almost to his waist. "Who are you and what's your business?"

"My name is Ethelwulf the Wanderer, son of Edmund Ethelwoldsson, and we're journeying to Tmutarakan in search of a vessel to carry us to the land of the Greeks."

"Many men go there," scoffed the other, "but few return!"

"We don't intend to return," answered Ethelwulf, "for we've heard the Emperor of the Greeks has much silver but few true men in his armies, and so we intend to serve him." By now the rafts had grown quite close to the beached vessel and so Ethelwulf asked if he might land on the sand-bank.

"Seeing we are so few," replied Halfdan, "there's little we can do to stop you. For you are many and look as if you're brave warriors." He paused and looked around at the other men who listened keenly to all the said. "Besides you've asked permission which you didn't need to and so must be honourable men."

So the rafts were pulled up on the sand-bank and the Varangians approached the long-ship. Some of the crew scrambled up on to the gunwales with bows ready for action. Gunnar laughed and said if they thought he or any his fellows would be deterred by such a feeble display they were fools. Halfdan roared at the men to put aside the weapons for there was little chance of resisting a determined attack, and so both groups sat down together on the sand as if they were old friends who'd not met for years.

By evening both sides had learned much of the other - though not everything, for there was still a certain lack of trust between them. The vessel was really what the Greeks called a monoxyla[108] and under the command of Vagn Inarsson had been on the way to Tmutarakan with a rich cargo of furs and some amber expected to get a good price in the town. However, on leaving the Don they heard plague had broken out in Tmutarakan. For some time they'd been uncertain what to do and eventually Vagn decided to put into one of the mouths of the river and send ahead a small detachment to see if the rumour was true. However, Forseti[109] decided to punish their leader for, Halfdan confessed, much of their cargo had been plundered from a storehouse on the Don which hadn't been properly manned. Vagn had asked why spend weeks trading with the Severians and others when the gods had placed it all before them, almost as a gift. So they'd seized the skins and carried them off, laughing at the feeble resistance of the traders. At that hour Vagn's luck changed.

No sooner had they landed and made camp than they were attacked by a band of Pechenegs who must have been watching them for some time. Vagn died fighting three men and with him many followers. Halfdan collected together some of the crew and, while the fighting was still carrying on, attempted to put to sea to stop their cargo falling into the hands of savages. Ethelwulf's eyes narrowed at Halfdan's desertion while his comrades fought a losing battle on the shore-line.

However, complained Halfdan, the gods also wished to punish him for they struck this sand-bank and lacked the strength to shift the keel. They saw their comrades butchered on the shore and could do nothing to help; even so, the waters prevented the Pechenegs from approaching their vessel and that had been the situation for the last three days.

Ethelwulf was allowed to inspect the cargo which was as described. Hastily he consulted Gunnar and Edwy about what to do as Morkere refused to land on the sand-bank. They agreed Ethelwulf should buy the vessel and together with the crew sail it to Tmutarakan, sell the cargo and divide the profits between the two groups; so Ethelwulf should recover much of his silver. Any of the original crew wishing to sail on to the land of the Greeks should be allowed to join Ethelwulf's band. Halfdan said this was an excellent proposal as long as Ethelwulf realised how much effort might be needed to free the longship.

*

First they had to unload the furs and hides on to one of the rafts. Ethelwulf was surprised how long this took - a good sign of profit to come. Next they demolished one of the rafts and placed its logs in front of the longship to drag it towards water deep enough to float it off the sandbank. Halfdan remarked that the extra force supplied by Ethelwulf's men was just what had been needed. Anyway, the longship slid into the water fairly easily and Ethelwulf wasn't surprised at how the cargo was loaded more quickly than it had been unloaded earlier that day.

At last they were ready to sail and Halfdan undertook to guide them to Tmutarakan. On the way Halfdan explained that two years before the town had fallen under the control of Mstyslav, the son of Prince

Vladimir. This was not good news for Ethelwulf because he feared the arm of Kenugard might easily reach him in such circumstances. Tmutarakan was positioned on a virtual island, surrounded by swamps and with its obvious outlet being the open sea. Halfdan said the area had been granted to the Rus generations before by the Khazars because they believed the Rus would effectively be hemmed in by geography while acting as a suitable intermediary for trade. Nevertheless, with the town now under the control of Kenugard, some of the locals feared profits from earlier years might be dissipated in wars of no concern to themselves. Anyway, a gentle north-east wind drove them to the town later that afternoon.

At first sight Tmutarakan resembled a collection of hovels clinging to a pile of mud surrounded by unhealthy water. Not the most inviting prospect for men who'd spent some time lost among the pest-ridden mouths of the Kuban. However, the palisade surrounding the town on its eastern side seemed in good order and Ethelwulf was impressed by the solid looking quays constructed along the water-edge. He noticed three longships, one slightly smaller than his new acquisition already tied up. There were also a couple of squatter, fatter boats which ferried goods across the Kerch Strait to the Crimea. This aspect of Tmutarakan looked both busy and profitable. Ethelwulf believed he'd have little trouble disposing of his cargo.

As he stepped ashore he was greeted by a tall, thin man whose shoulders were bent by, as it turned out, long hours hunched over the records of all goods passing through the town. The new prince of Tmutarakan was determined to exact his share of any trade conducted in his realm, just as his father had secured a similar control on that carried up and down the Dneiper. The man introduced himself as Constantine, scribe of Prince Mstyslav, and Ethelwulf looked at him most closely for he was the first Greek he'd ever seen. The scribe wore a light blue tunic and high-laced sandals, over his shoulders he'd a caftan of sable and clearly, despite it being summer, wasn't happy with the temperature. He had a pointed nose, thin lips and eyes squinting from too many hours poring over documents by the light of candles. He looked an honest man but Ethelwulf knew appearances could be deceptive.

Ethelwulf instantly regretted having given his true name to Halfdan for he felt this town would have been a fitting place for 'Osbert of Middlebere.'[110] However, it was too late now and Ethelwulf gave his true name, explaining his men had travelled from Khazaria and were planning to move on to the land of the Greeks. This made Constantine stare closely at the longship but Ethelwulf was not drawn; he knew it'd take little time for the Greek to draw out the origins of the craft and he wasn't going to help Halfdan explain how he'd come into possession of longship and cargo.

"Why would you wish to journey among the Greeks?" asked he scribe in competent Rus, and Ethelwulf had he feeling that such would be the last wish of the man asking the question. He guessed Constantine was like himself, an exile; useful knowledge if it could be confirmed. He also considered the question implied surprise that, after leaving Khazaria, the Varangians weren't travelling northwards, back to the centre of Prince Vladimir's power. The newcomers could only have reached Tmutarakan via either the Kuban or the Dneiper, and the scribe was clearly intrigued as to why there was no desire to return north.

"I'm a Christian," answered Ethelwulf, staring resolutely into the eyes of the Greek as he then added a lie. "I've promised myself that, before I die, I'll journey to the land of Our Lord. I know the ruler of the Greeks has armies in that area and so I believe there'll be pay for my men and a chance for me to travel among such lands."

The scribe looked at Ethelwulf, clearly disbelieving him but unable to decide why. "Where do you come from, stranger?" he asked.

"From the far west, the land of the English," was the answer and Ethelwulf could see the scribe was puzzled so he added, "The land which the Romans called Britannia."

The Greek nodded. He'd heard about such regions on the very edge of the world, hidden by mists and a haven for the dead. It had been believed in Constantinople that bodiless souls were ferried over to such a land.[111] Certainly, this man was the first he'd met who admitted coming from there. He'd been fascinated by the Rus for years and was confident that once he'd returned to his native city he could settle down and produce an account of these barbarians. They'd been intruding into the affairs of the Empire for a number of years, offering the possibility through the spread of Christianity of creating a power to threaten the infidels of Islam.

Ethelwulf was amused at the obvious interest of the scribe, so he decided to reveal he'd travelled widely around the northern world. The scribe almost smacked his lips and Ethelwulf was certain he'd easily acquired one supporter in this new world. Now he decided to test out that support by humbly asking for permission to unload his cargo and sell it in the market place. The scribe asked to inspect the goods first and then he'd issue a warrant to allow the sale. This came as a great surprise to the Varangians and they found it rather hard to accept all this was happening within the realm of Prince Vladimir. Then he remembered hearing the Greeks had been in the area for centuries and their officialdom must have stamped their authority on how matters were conducted here.

The whole process of importing and selling the cargo was entrusted to Halfdan, although Ethelwulf made sure a couple of trusted Varangians watched every move. He was really missing the shrewd appraisal of Morkere but his cousin was still inclined to sit by himself, gazing out to sea, lost completely to the normal world. Gunnar whispered to Ethelwulf that such moods would pass, but Ethelwulf still found the whole matter distressing. He missed Edwine, more than he'd believed he could but his feelings fell far short of the distress that must be ripping apart Edwine's twin. Ethelwulf had by now brushed aside any idea of guilt for his cousin's death; free will had driven the cousins on, if not for him!

Edwy reported that, backed by a permit from Constantine, the cargo had proved most popular among the traders of Tmutarakan. The price had been excellent and Halfdan showed himself, to Ethelwulf's surprise, to act above suspicion. Within two days the Wanderer had recovered his outlay on the vessel and still made a profit which he intended to invest in a craft more capable of crossing the Pontic Sea.[112] He knew he had to give the vessel a name so that it became a real longship. In some ways he was ashamed it had originated in what the Greeks termed *monoxyla* and this vessel was going to sweep south across the Black Sea to unknown lands to the south. He had it; he'd call the vessel 'Brimfugol'[113] once it had been properly fitted out.

Gunnar appeared with news that lodging had been found in a tavern called *'Thor's Draught'*[114] which seemed both clean and reasonable in price. He dropped his voice as he added there were some Varangians there who seemed to be lost. He laughed at Ethelwulf's look of bewilderment.

"All I can say, Ethelwulf, is come with me, sit and listen, and then, if you wish, join in their talk."

Again he laughed as the bewildered look, if anything, grew deeper. Ethelwulf agreed to go with him and the Gall-Gael led the way with a knowing smile to *'Thor's Draught'*.

*

Later Ethelwulf confessed he'd been more than intrigued by Gunnar's invitation. *'Thor's Draught'* contained half-a-dozen men grouped in the corner loudly arguing about what they should do next. They'd ventured into Tmutarakan after working their way down the river Don on a voyage which hadn't proved profitable at all. They'd been forced to hand over a stock of skins to the Pechenegs after being surprised one morning on shore; at the time they'd considered they'd been lucky to escape with their lives but later believed they should have fought rather than hand over such booty to the savages. Then their bad luck had turned worse with the sudden death of their leader, a Swede called Eric Golden-Chain, of fever they believed he'd caught somewhere in the town. They were anxious to get away from Tmutarakan but had no agreed plans for the future; none of them wanted to try their hand again at trade on the Don and all swore Prince Vladimir was so tightening his grip on the passage of the river Dneiper that soon that river would cease to have worthwhile possibilities.

Perhaps, suggested one of the Varangians, a smallish man with grey-streaked red hair, it might be best to make their way back up the Dneiper to the lands of the Swedes. There was loud derision at such an idea, even though he insisted they could secure with ease suitable goods for trade here in the markets of Tmutarakan.

"Yes, and find ourselves stripped of whatever would be of value in Kenugard or Holmgard - both of them nests of thieves!" snapped a dark-haired Varangian whom some called Thorgrim Spear-Catcher.

"That's not taking into account all the toil of getting there!" added another dark-haired warrior who bore a family resemblance to Thorgrim. Ethelwulf knew the river Dneiper was notorious for the series of portages which entailed physically by-passing rapids using oxen or sheer muscle power. He'd experienced one extensive portage north of Kenugard and he'd certainly not have looked forward to a whole series of them.

Now he intervened, confessing he'd been interested in hearing their discussion. Thorgrim Spear-Catcher demanded the name of someone who listened to the private conversations of others.

"So private that the whole street could hear your babbling!" snapped Gunnar. Thorgrim looked at the speaker, measured the height of the Irish giant and the familiar way he caressed his axe, and decided he wouldn't challenge the interruption. Ethelwulf readily gave his name and that of Gunnar, adding they'd but recently arrived in town and would soon be heading south for the land of the Greeks. This produced a buzz of discussion from some of the Varangians but the smallish man who'd advocated a return to the Swedish Sea drew himself up to his full height and demanded to know what was so good about the land of the Greeks.

Ethelwulf smiled. "I've heard the Greeks have lots of silver, and even gold, for warriors to come and fight their battles for they don't know how to make war." He saw he'd made an impression and followed it up with a brief reference to the recent intervention of Prince Vladimir into the land of the Greeks.

At this another Varangian, who up till then had largely kept his thoughts to himself, said he'd journeyed south with the Prince of Kenugard and what the stranger said was true. The Greeks had buildings covered with gold and silver which quite spilled out from their purses. He added they must be weaklings for they wash their bodies at every opportunity and many content themselves with a single woman because they're ruled by servants of the Christ-god. There was loud laughter at that and Ethelwulf added that surely the women of the Greeks must be yearning to find themselves favoured by true men - and that, as a man only kept one woman, there must be women to spare for true warriors.

He could see that, by now, the Varangians were starting to see themselves enjoying the women and silver that was for the taking in the lands of the Greeks. Now it was Gunnar who interrupted by asking what had happened to their vessel.

"It's still in dock here," replied Thorgrim, "as we don't know which way to sail."

"How many are in your company?" asked Ethelwulf and was amused the calculation seemed to cause some dispute, based on a certain difficulty, with some of the men. At last they said they numbered twenty-four. He smiled and said he'd more than that but the Greeks would welcome two longships more than one. "For I've heard the ruler of the Greeks not only has savages such as the Pechenegs to take away his silver but worshippers of a man called Mohammed in the south would like to seize his whole realm."

"And" added the warrior who'd fought under Prince Vladimir, "he has constant revolts from his subjects, which was why he paid us richly to join him in war - as well as sending his sister northwards to marry Prince Vladimir so he can readily call on such fighting men!"

Ethelwulf considered he'd done enough to arouse the interest of the Varangians. He said he'd be staying at this tavern while his own vessel was being fitted out. He expected to leave Tmutarakan within a week and hoped they could merge their companies. They had to decide where their best opportunities lay.

*

As expected, the next day Ethelwulf received a delegation led by Thorgrim Spear-Catcher and his half-brother, Thorstein Gerdasson, along with the smaller man, Kalli Hallbjornsson, who proved to be the spokesman for the company.

"We put your offer to our men and, but for three men wishing to return to Kenugard where they'd left women, the company voted to join you and seek our fortune among the Greeks."

Ethelwulf smiled broadly and welcomed the men into his force. He discovered their vessel was called 'Niflheim's Envoy'[115] which was, perhaps, in recent circumstances, an apt name. It was further agreed Gunnar should be put in charge of the vessel, along with three other Varangians, to replace the men who didn't want to go south. He thought very carefully about the original crew of the 'Brimfugol' and decided none of them would be acceptable for the voyage. His chief reason was their decision to leave their comrades to the Pechenegs and steal away with the cargo; he was certain that with a few more men, and better luck, they'd have reached Tmutarakan and disposed of the cargo without another thought of the men slaughtered or captured by the Pechenegs. He had no need for men he couldn't trust and so decided to pay them off, at a generous rate. Yet he decided to delay making his decision public for as long as possible, not wanting to risk some kind of brawl.

Meanwhile work was going on at a tremendous pace refitting the 'Brimfugol'. They'd first checked the keel which was found not to have suffered from its enforced stay on the sand back. There was slight damage to one of the twelve strakes just above the water-line; in rough seas that could be dangerous but it was speedily replaced, with new rivets and plates applied to keep it in place. Ethelwulf noted the strakes below the water-line had been tied to the frame by whale-bristle, a substance which at first he hadn't recognised. Some of the nails securing the above-water strakes to the crossbeams had to be replaced. Caulking was reworked to make the vessel more sea-worthy. It was decided to replace half of the twenty pairs of oars which drove the ship as damage to the rowlocks on the starboard side might have weakened their strength. The sail too had to be largely replaced, parts of it having been allowed to go rotten, so fresh strips of dyed wool were carefully interwoven with others to produce a fine sail of brown and grey stripes. Next the 'old woman'[116] was closely inspected and found to be sound but above it they replaced the mast partner for greater security. Naturally, after its adventures in the Kuban delta, they replaced the reefing lines and also the beitiáss.[117] The side rudder was also replaced as it had been split when going aground. Also the vessel had lost its small boat somewhere during the passage down the Don; this was replaced and a new tent added. All in all the 'Brimfugol' was ready for a sea-passage by the end of the week.

Several times Constantine visited the work being done on the 'Brimfugol' and expressed his admiration at the workmanship of the fitters. It was obvious he wanted to expand his knowledge of the northern world and so Ethelwulf spent several hours describing whatever aspects of life there interested the Greek, which mainly seemed to be relating to government. Constantine had become well-versed in the ways Prince Vladimir ran his realm and was amazed when told about the authority of the Icelandic Althing; for him such delegation of power to the general community seemed highly irresponsible. Perhaps long ago the writer, Aristotle, had held Democracy was the least bad of political systems[118] but he argued the problems of the modern world made such ideas impossible to introduce. He pounced on the relative isolation of Iceland as the reason why the experiment worked. Constantine compared the system of Irish kings and kinglets to what he'd heard existed in the land of Italy now the power of his Emperor no longer had much effect there. The Witangemot in England he compared to the Senate of Rome which, in theory, still guided the destinies of the Empire long after real power had moved elsewhere. In his turn he told Ethelwulf about how the Empire was governed, as well as tales of some of its neighbours, especially those to the south.

Such discussions were interrupted by the arrival of a new longship. It had a blue sail and fifteen banks of oars, which seemed to revel in the freedom of the Sea of Azov after the rivers Dneiper and Donets. Directly its master stepped on to the quay Ethelwulf recognised him as Thorgeis Green-Eye, a dangerous warrior from Kenugard. He'd avoided the red-haired warrior, noting him as a man as swift to anger as Gunnar but without the excuse of the effects of ale. He wondered why Thorgeis should have appeared at just that time, but immediately put such suspicions aside when he realised Prince Vladimir would have scarcely heard of the slaughter of the Turks let alone have had time to despatch an avenging force.

Immediately Thorgeis turned he spotted Ethelwulf and, although he shouted out a greeting, there was no warmth in his eyes as he approached. He'd actually left Kenugard before Ethelwulf, journeying down the Dneiper to make his way to the land of the

Greeks. However, he'd tired of the effort of the series of portages and been easily persuaded by one of his men, Ragnar Ringed-Beard, that readier profit was to be found further to the east. So he'd undertaken one great portage and transferred his vessel, 'Ran Cheater',[119] across to the river Donets. They'd discovered greater thieves already plundering the district and had been forced to fight the Pechenegs. In the end they'd seized a shipment of honey and wax being transported by Khazar traders but it hadn't been worth the effort. When he'd said this to Ragnar the fool had dared disagree and so his head had been left as a parting-gift to any Pecheneg war-band in the vicinity. Certainly, from then on, his luck had changed because he'd overtaken another longship bearing south carrying hides and had the good fortune to triumph in a little dispute of passage. So he'd added hides to his cargo which he expected to sell at good profit in the town before going on to the land of the Greeks.

Thorgeis cast envious looks at 'Brimfugol', remarking luck seemed also to have come the way of the Westerners. He laughed when told how Ethelwulf had not only recruited the crew but also acquired 'Niflheim's Envoy' to add to his fleet, remarking there seemed more fools here in the south than in the rest of Prince Vladimir's realm. Ethelwulf frowned at this because he'd never intended to cheat Thorgrim Spear-Catcher and his comrades, but he kept his thoughts to himself. He then had to fend off questions from Thorgeis as to how and why he'd left Khazaria. In the end he remarked that, like Thorgeis, he'd tired of the small profit and loud complaints to be found among the Khazars, and so had come to Tmutarakan intending to travel to the land of the Greeks.

Thorgeis laughed and suggested they should travel together, sharing the dangers and the profits, but sensed a reluctance in Ethelwulf. The Wanderer asked bluntly how many men Thorgeis commanded and the reply was thirty-two. Ethelwulf stated that, as he commanded twice as many, he should enjoy double the profit. At this there was a glint of rage in both the green eye and the brown eye possessed by Thorgeis, but he quickly mastered himself and agreed to the division - adding the proportions should change along with circumstances. Ethelwulf looked somewhat askance at that deep comment but let it pass. So a fleet of three vessels would set out to seek their fortunes in the land of the Greeks.

Ethelwulf still expected daily the arrival of a force from the Governor of Sarkel and wondered if his new allies would stand by him in any dispute with the Governor, if not Prince Vladimir himself. He toyed with the idea of telling them the truth but decided publishing such information could do nothing but harm. Besides, he'd enough trouble in having to dismiss Halfdan Snorrisson and his fellows.

Ethelwulf called them into *'Thor's Draught'* and started by saying how profitable everything had turned out. He then proceeded to describe how, nevertheless, with the arrival of Thorgeis he seemed almost to have a surfeit of men. So he was handing them the bulk of what remained of the profits of their cargo as a fitting start to their trading ventures in the area. At first they'd not understood him and he felt guilty at provoking such bewilderment in men who were probably honest and brave but had given way, on a single occasion, to temptation. Bluntly he then stated there'd be no room for them on his expedition. He was surprised how well they seemed to take the news. One of the men started protesting silver was of little use in this town where it could be so quickly frittered away. Another declared he could see little profit on the river Don when the Pechenegs seemed to be in such a dangerous mood. A third started to beg to be allowed to go south and then, realising the sullen eyes of his comrades were fixing him with contempt, stumbled into silence. Ethelwulf answered he was sure other vessels might arrive, short of crew and anxious to travel south, which would be pleased to recruit new warriors. Halfdan looked as if he was about to throttle Ethelwulf but one glance of Gunnar's axe changed his mind. In the end argument ceased and each man accepted the purse of silver offered and trudged out of the tavern. Ethelwulf wondered how long they'd keep their silver and what success they might meet trading in Gadarike. Then he realised he didn't care. He couldn't risk desertion in the land of the Greeks.

The next day three longships turned south ready for service across the Pontic Sea.

*

Gardarike Afterword

Apart from Prince Vladimir and his son, none of the characters described here are factual. Vladimir of Kiev (980-1015) fully established his realm within the sphere of Greek influence and thereby earned sainthood. Yaroslav I seized Kiev from his brother, Svyatopolk, in 1019 and ruled there till 1054. He strengthened the links of his realm with the west and, by curbing the depredations of the Pechenegs, improved trade along the Russian river system. He earned the title of 'the Wise'. Kiev essentially lost its dominance with the Mongol invasions of the early 13th century, after which power moved to Moscow.

Much of the description of the society of the Rus comes from works basing their accounts largely on Arab travellers such as Ibn Fadhlan (c.925). However, the accounts given of the Khazars and Pechenegs, apart from employing historical studies of such peoples and the results of archaeology, are pure fiction. After over a century of pillage the Pechenegs were driven westwards by the Cumans and ceased to be any threat by the 12th century

The description of the general environment and the life style of the various peoples then occupying what is now Russia and its neighbours is accurate. Perhaps the action of leading characters is too calculated but it was certainly a region in turmoil whose organisation was still not completed when the westward expansion of the Mongol Golden Horde effectively delayed matters until the 15th century.

The Wanderer 8:1

'Never is aught easy in this world,
This earthly state is tightly held by fate.
Here fleeting goods and fickle friends
Ensures the world's a wilderness.'
('The Wanderer')

Imperial Favour

The dwarf blinked up at the brilliance of the light reflected from the white-washed tower above his head. Why had his master placed him up here, so far away from the bustle and the magic of the streets below? What good would it do to keep him here, staring out westwards up the Bosphorus towards the home of those half-heathen devils? Still any order of the Quaestor[120] John had to be obeyed. The dwarf nervously fingered the lobe of his left ear; he wouldn't like to lose an ear for disobedience.

Of course, his master was interested in anything those barbarians might do. Ever since the Autokrator[121] had sent his reluctant sister, Anna, into the wild northern wastes his master had been interested.[122] His master had been there when those barbarians stood firm against the onslaught of the double-damned Phocas[123] and so had given victory to the Autokrator.

Nicias had to admit he'd not chosen to be there on that glorious day. What good would his stunted form have been in preserving the sanctity of the throne. No, he'd spent a very pleasurable time among the ladies of the alley-ways near the Hippodrome. There he could discover all those little secrets and whispers which oiled the process of court. He'd known the Autokrator had had enough of the Grand Chamberlain,[124] even before the Autokrator himself had. That had been several years ago; now his master wanted to know how placed was the City Prefect[125] to wield power through the young Autokrator.

The Autokrator had been showing disturbing signs of independence lately. For most of his life he'd been content to follow the will of others.[126] However, for the last few years he'd started upon a risky course; the destruction of the power of his uncle had been one thing, how he disposed of the office of Grand Chamberlain was another. Nicias knew how anxious his master was that any responsibilities connected with the central office of administration should be shuffled into the control of the Quaestor and not go to bolster the regime of the City Prefect.

For a time Nicias had considered slipping across to the quieter waters of the household of Alexius Euergetes, but his subtle hints had been rudely snubbed. So be it; let the City Prefect look to friends among the Guilds. He had helpers among the alley-ways and quays of Kynegion.

The dwarf brought his mind back to reality as his keen sight caught a glimpse of three sails coming from the north. Lately travellers and traders had arrived in growing numbers from the territories of Kenugard and Novgorod. Nicias didn't like their stories of dark, snow-covered woods and months of icy darkness. They were a cruel and barbaric race, scarcely fitted to walk the streets of the New Rome. However, their weapons had proved useful in the past and they'd the naivety of the innocent clamouring for guidance from those wise in the ways of world. Nicias knew his master would welcome early news of three such boatloads of potential allies. Besides, it'd get him away from this infernal roof and down among the cooler shade of the streets and alleys below.

*

Morkere looked mournfully northwards, towards where the body of his twin had been laid to rest in the borders of the land terrorised by the Pechenegs.[127] Ethelwulf didn't like seeing his cousin in such a black mood. He'd left part of his own heart up there among the labyrinth of the Kuban Delta. They'd been forced to escape from the power of Kenugard and gambled on the Pechenegs' movements taking them well away from the river. They'd believed Pechenegs could be given the slip among the rivulets, islands and marshes of the mouths of the river Kuban. In all this they had been wrong.

Morkere had scarcely spoken to his cousin since they'd burst out into the open sea several weeks ago. It had been an easy voyage - that is, as far as the weather went. The wind had been brisk and steadily driven them south-east towards Miklagard. They'd scarcely bothered to stop at Bosporus[128] being so anxious to quit those regions of the north which had held such disasters. With hindsight he regretted their haste; at that outlying possession of Miklagard they should have picked up an interpreter or two. Sven might know the way to Miklagard, but he didn't know the ways of Miklagard. Such ignorance could lead to catastrophe.

Now they'd left the open sea itself for the more restricted approach to Miklagard. He looked suspiciously at the hills on either side as the three ships passed unchallenged through the sea-way separating Europe and Asia. If only Edwine had lived to share in this approach to the Queen of Cities!

Ethelwulf looked across at Gunnar leaning forward towards the prow of 'Niflheim's Envoy' to his right. Now there was another moody one; dangerous when drunk and silent and not much safer when sober. Ethelwulf had cherished a great affection for the lean warrior since the days they'd battled against the wild Gaels in the Hall of Clonmel.[129] Even so, he'd rather have left Gunnar behind in the fens of the Kuban and had Edwine with him now.

On his left 'Ran Cheater' cut through the waves with careless ease; its commander was Thorgeis Green-Eye, a fearsome red-bearded Varangian whom Ethelwulf had first met at Kenugard. He'd no love for Thorgeis and knew the feeling was returned. However, he was a natural fighter with either hand and there'd never be any fear of desertion as long as he gained enough silver.

It was good to have a fine vessel beneath one's feet, even though 'Brimfugol'[130] was not the equal of 'Alsvid'. Never again would he trust himself or his men among marshes and rivers. He smiled as it seemed his whole life had been directed towards this journey to Miklagard. Would he be welcome here? Vladimir's expedition two years before had returned to Kenugard full of tales of the wealth, the luxury (and the treachery) of the Greeks. Some, usually with minds befuddled by the strong beer brewed in Holmgard, had muttered about taking their swords there to seek employment.

"Greeks like other men to fight their wars," sneered Snorri Green-Cloak, spilling the last of his draught down his chin. "For that they'll pay gold - " there was a murmur of surprise from some of his hearers who hadn't heard his tales before. "Yes, gold not the silver pennies which the kings and jarls of the north think are worth a brave man's life!"

Ethelwulf had put the information to the back of his mind. To know where weapon-skills could earn good pay was useful, but it was far away and there must be many weary miles and hostile tribes in the way. Then he'd felt safe and secure in the stronghold of Kenugard – confident that Oleg, Lord of Aldeigjuborg, would have too much to busy himself with in Karelia than seek revenge.[131] Then he'd been forced to break with Prince Vladimir and flee south chiefly to put off pursuit, partly due to the treachery of Thorgrim the Short but chiefly the result of events in Khazaria.[132] Only later did he recall Snorri's words and use them to keep his men going. Thorgeis had already planned to serve the Greeks; raiding Pecheneg villages or robbing Khazar traders had little to recommend it.

Three days ago they'd left the open sea and entered the narrower sea-space that Sven said the Greeks called Bosphorus. Soon according to the promises of Sven they'd come to Miklagard itself. He was pleased Sven the Far-Sighted had followed him from Finland; the little man had earlier journeyed south to trade with the Greeks. He was a shrewd fellow, constantly keeping eyes and ears open for useful information; a perfect spy.

Ahead of them lay - what? Perhaps he'd made a mistake, another error of judgement. Something, however, told him there'd be work here for any force of nearly one hundred warriors. He knew the Greeks had given such fighters a name "Varaggoi," he smiled. The word meant 'men who have given their word' and somehow the Greeks had picked it up from the followers of Svjatoslav years ago.[133] Strangely that gave him some form of comfort. The Greeks obviously expected men from the north to give their word and keep it. Well, he'd served in too many armies to have any second thoughts about making promises.

Now he could just make out buildings, white and gold in the sun It wouldn't be long before he was among them.

*

The Gate of Hebraike had been a surprise. After their ships had put in at the Harbour of Phospherion, Ethelwulf found himself hustled along by persistent men dressed in the azure-striped uniforms of customs officials through the Gate of Hebraike into one of the older parts of the city He'd secured the company of both Gunnar and Thorgeis - the latter insisting that as an independent captain he should know all decisions immediately.

Ethelwulf had tried out his half-remembered Latin but had been shrugged away by a fat, bald-headed man. Life would have been impossible had not a wizened trader, whom Thorgeis instantly recognised as one of those "whining Khazar thieves" stepped forward and offered to interpret for the newcomers. He introduced himself as Yakub in a strange, tuneless variation of Rus,[134] but seemed able to be understood readily by the fat official and that was all that mattered.

Thorgeis was against trusting the man, but Ethelwulf insisted they had need of an interpreter - and this man was the only one readily available. Unfortunately, the discussion between the two captains took place in Rus. So Ethelwulf was not surprised when, after agreeing to accept the services of the man, he was promptly told the charge would be five ortug of hack-silver.[135] At this Gunnar gripped his axe more tightly and promised to give the Khazar enough metal in his skull to satisfy the greed of even such a thief as himself. Yakub blanched at this threat, for nobody who stared into the blood-shot eyes of the Gall-Gael[136] fighter could doubt savagery was only just controlled. He hurriedly cut the price to three ortug.

The newcomers had no choice but to pay the sum. The fat official started fidgeting, sensing the squabbling developing in front of him would prove an unnecessary distraction. Ethelwulf promised to hand over the sum AFTER the interview. For a moment the yellow-skinned trader wondered whether he could accept the word of this tall stranger; then he caught sight of Gunnar's fingers tightening on his axe and knew he'd no choice. He offered his hand to the barbarian from the north; after a puzzled half-smile the newcomer grasped it. Yakub was not sure whether he relished the strength of purpose the grip conveyed.

Ethelwulf was concerned to find the trader walking ahead of the three newcomers in animated conversation with the fat man. He didn't like the way the trader pointed to the ships and then to the south; the squeaking tones of the unknown tongue of Miklagard set all sorts of anxieties going somewhere in his stomach. Ethelwulf determined to start learning Greek before he was much older.

*

The slim aloof official greeting them in the large building just within the Gate of Hebraike proved surprisingly friendly At first he found something at which to snigger when the fat official ushered in the trader and the three strangers. Then catching the glare in Gunnar's eyes he glanced nervously at the four Tagmatikoi[137] who lounged discreetly in the background. For once he was glad the Eparchos[138] had such an suspicious nature; having an ever-present coterie of spies sometimes had its uses.

John Angelus found he could listen with surprising patience to this barbarian's offer of military service as transmitted through Yakub. At least that was the way he'd understood what the skinny intermediary had whined into his ears. He noticed it took the barbarian three attempts before he was satisfied the Khazar had properly conveyed what he was trying to say. What strange sounds the barbarian used. However, he liked the keen-eyed honesty that commandeered his features; and he looked admiringly at the broad sword which hung so confidently over the stranger's shoulder. The Quaestor glanced across at the Prefect's spies, straining to hear the ill-phrased jabbering of the Khazar interpreter. These warriors from the north could have their uses.

Meanwhile Ethelwulf casually dismissed the four heavily-armoured strangers who so clearly had a keen interest in what was being said to this grey-haired official sitting in the silk-cushioned chair He listened carefully to the Greek used by the merchant, surprised at the variation of sound and language which seemed to form each of the virtually identical statements in Rus. Was the Khazar cheating them? Ethelwulf doubted it; the man seemed to be honestly concerned at getting across the request. He noted the answering sounds from the official seemed to differ; with time and practice Ethelwulf had acquired an excellent ear for tongues.

The Quaestor found himself naturally giving the answer everyone expected - wait and see. He then turned to the Khazar and spoke rapidly to him. The trader blinked rapidly, clearly not too happy at these new instructions from so powerful an official of the Empire. At first he made no attempt to translate. Thorgeis spotted the blatant failure on the part of the interpreter and loudly remarked to Gunnar that clearly the Khazar had used up whatever value he had. At this the Khazar turned and fixed Thorgeis with a contemptuous sneer.

"The Quaestor John has graciously offered to pay for you to learn to escape from the fetters of your barbarian tongue," he coldly remarked, but then added. "However, he insists the Imperial Treasury can only pay for one week of my time."

Yakub paused, awaiting for a rush of enthusiasm from the three Varangians and was disappointed when none was forthcoming. He could have pointed out they would get nowhere - NOWHERE - if they continued to gabble in that noise they called language in the north. However, he didn't for he had other work to do, and the Quaestor was noted for being neither prompt nor generous in his payments. Both he and the Quaestor knew the Postmaster General[139] had his own staff of interpreters that could solve the problem; however, it was clear the Quaestor wanted to delay any firm communication between the strangers and others in the imperial government.

Ethelwulf turned to Gunnar and deliberately shut out both Thorgeis and the Khazar by speaking rapidly in that version of Norse which was the common means of communication in Ireland.

"This would be a great advantage to us, Gunnar," he paused. "However, we must ensure that at the end of a week we'll be able to talk to these Greeks as they would wish, even if as little children."

Gunnar coughed and glared at the Khazar trader. "You might well pick up a smattering of words, Ethelwulf," he conceded, "as we all know you've an ear for strange tongues but..."

Thorgeis grew ominously silent after failing with Rus and Swedish to grasp what his two companions had said.

"That's enough!" cut in the captain of 'Ram Cheater'.

Ethelwulf turned to Yakub and bluntly said, "Please thank his Excellency, the Quaestor John, for his kind offer. We'd like to accept." Then he added in a quieter voice. " If you can enable one of us to speak to the Quaestor in his own tongue, however simply, in that time we'll add ten ortugs to whatever the Greek pays."

He saw the Khazar's eyes glint briefly with greed. He was sure no mention would be made of this second source of income. Hurriedly Yakub blurted out the acceptance by the strangers of the kindness of the Quaestor. John Angelus didn't like the man, rejecting the too-obviously assumed confidentiality of the Khazar. The sooner he could dispense with the trader's services the better. He found himself drawn to these strangers and that was just why he didn't want any of his colleagues to get involved - yet. In the end the Autokrator would welcome these men, he was sure of it; however, he wanted to ensure they'd be introduced through the offices of the Quaestor and no one else.

The three strangers and the Khazar found themselves ushered out of the room, noticing one of the lounging eavesdroppers also slipped away. As they walked slowly out into the sunlight, Ethelwulf turned to the Khazar and solemnly handed him the promised fee for his services. Without a word of thanks Yakub quickly thrust the silver into his purse; only then did he promise to meet the Varangians for their first lesson later that day, after he'd taken the opportunity to put his brother in temporary charge of his business. Ethelwulf breathed his thanks for the man's efforts and then smoothly commented, "If, Khazar, we fail to talk to the Greek at all in seven days, you'll receive payment in axe-silver from Gunnar."

The trader stopped and his mouth fell open. Was this barbarian threatening him? If so it would be the easiest of actions to disappear into the alleys of the city and never be seen by such ruffians again. Then he remembered he'd accepted the commission of the Quaestor; he couldn't abandon these strangers. He may not like his new pupils, but he'd certainly have to make sure they passed their examination.

*

The Khazar proved to be a good teacher, or rather Ethelwulf made an excellent pupil. In the last ten years he'd acquired a good knowledge of the variations of Norse heard in Waterford, Breidavik, Hedeby, Ladoga and Kenugard; in addition he possessed a smattering of Norman, Wendish and Rus.[140] The trader's other pupils, however, proved less adept. Gunnar remained limited to a collection of nouns and Thorgeis simply grunted some distortions of stock phrases. Morkere had been added to the class and showed a facility with the tongue of the Greeks which surpassed even that of his cousin.

Within a week the small party, with Morkere replacing the reluctant Gunnar, returned to the Tribunal of the Quaestor and was greeted by the official with seeming impatience.

"We say some words now, "said Ethelwulf, and he noted the quick exchange of glances between the Quaestor and their teacher. "Again I say we want your soldiers be."

A slight smile appeared on the face of John. This was certainly not good Greek, but quite creditable for a barbarian with only a week's practice. He asked who the newcomer was and was surprised the barbarian leader answered before the Khazar had a chance to translate.

"He name Morkere. I name Ethelwulf. England come. No Rus."

This last statement was a surprise. The Quaestor John had assumed all such barbarians came from the domains of Prince Vladimir of Kenugard. Where was this "Angleland" he asked and received another surprising answer.

"Rome call England Britannia. My people take country. Long way." There was a pause as Ethelwulf noticed the Quaestor was trying to come to a decision. "Morkere tell more."

At that Morkere stepped forward and said, "We fight like Rus but we not Rus. If we promise we your soldiers we always fight for you."

Interesting thought the Quaestor, especially that more than one has started to learn Greek, even if he murders the language slightly less than his leader. Like other citizens of the Empire he'd been impressed by the fighting abilities displayed by the followers of Prince Vladimir when they'd helped the Autokrator smash the forces of Phocas. However, he'd also noted an independence of spirit; one didn't want too much independence in hired-soldiers, they had to take orders without question. Quaestor John Angelus began to form some idea of how to make use of this gift of God; however, he didn't notice one of the ever-present watchers slip off.

"Would you take my orders - acting on the authority of the Autokrator, of course?" he added, giving half-a-glance to the spies of the City Prefect. He frowned as he realised there were only three there now. His frown deepened as he noticed the look of incomprehension on the face of the barbarian leader; however, he saw the one called Morkere whisper something rapidly to him even as the Khazar began a translation. Perhaps that other one could be trained further; he liked the dark looks of the young man and a question about the sadness of his expression came and died on his lips. It was the leader who spoke first.

"We fight for you; we fight for emperor. We good fighters!" and he glared at the three eavesdroppers as if daring any of them to challenge that judgement.

Quaestor John summoned the Khazar closer and rapidly settled his account. He didn't want any more ears than necessary to take in the rest of the conversation. It was a risk but once he'd enrolled these men - he suddenly stopped, realising for the first time he actually didn't know how many barbarians there were. He fired this question to Yakub who was securing a purse to his belt. The Khazar admitted he didn't know, and, without asking permission, turned and asked the barbarian leader. Quaestor John was annoyed; that information would be better kept to himself alone. However, he was pleased when Morkere indicated ninety and seven. Almost enough for three Pentekontarchies.[141] Could he get more, perhaps enough for a whole Bandon? He asked this question and there was some confusion among the barbarians. Quaestor John's suspicions were aroused. Why did they hesitate? Surely they could simply send back to Kenugard and bring more warriors like themselves. He nervously drummed the fingers of his left hand against the arm of his red-upholstered chair, while the barbarians all seemed to try to speak to the Khazar at once. The trader was obviously at a loss as to what to say and nervously looked at the door, wishing he'd been able to escape before this problem had come up. He saw the Quaestor stiffen, looking from the barbarians to the interpreter and back again.

At last Yakub started nervously trying to explain; interrupted now by one barbarian then another. He pointed to Thorgeis glaring up at the imperial official as if challenging him to question his honesty. "This man insists, Nobillisimus, there'd be no problem." He rapidly questioned the red-bearded barbarian and was answered in a flood of unintelligible gibberish. "He says he could send messages to his cousins in Kenugard and Holmgard and within a year could get whatever men you require."

Now the Khazar found himself grabbed by Ethelwulf who, thrusting his face very close to the alarmed trader, bluntly stated, "Don't you realise, you load of ass-dung, we can't contact Kenugard at all." He paused, forgetting how much or how little the trader knew of their background. Then he decided on the truth; better that than caught out later. "We - we quarrelled with the Lord of Kenugard and -"

" He doesn't know we've come to Miklagard!" finished Morkere. A thin smile flittered across the features of the Khazar. Knowledge was power; perhaps he could find some way of turning that titbit of information into silver the next time he travelled to the Cherson. Ethelwulf noted the brief light in the eyes and his grip on the trader tightened. "Tell the Quaestor what I've just said, son of a toad!"

Yakub shook himself free from the Varangian's grasp and faced the Quaestor once again. Quickly he explained it appeared that some of the barbarians were running away from Kenugard. John frowned; he didn't like news like that. Any further discussion was prevented by the noisy arrival of the absconding "spy". The man swaggered into the room, gave a curt bow to the Quaestor and then loudly demanded the barbarians be taken immediately to the emperor. John cursed, realising that by the emperor was also meant the City Prefect. However, he could still save some recognition by a slight distortion of the truth.

"These men have offered me their swords and I've accepted them," he paused noting the disappointment on the braggart's face with some satisfaction. "I intended to form a small corps of these Varangians and then offer them for service with his imperial majesty." An unbelieving smirk began to appear on the lips of the messenger. John killed the smirk, "I'll take these men myself to his imperial majesty so I can offer him their service immediately."

With that he turned to the Khazar, ordering him to stay for the interview as a required witness. He then told him to instruct the barbarians to be silent and follow him to the emperor. He was pleased the Khazar's interpretation of his words seemed to find favour with all the barbarians.

*

Ethelwulf was struck by the blueness of the ceiling and the gold of the angels disporting themselves in various attitudes above his head. He'd seen wondrous illuminations in the manuscripts at Wareham and in Waterford but they'd been nothing to this. Even the ikons which the Princess Anna[142] had brought to Kenugard as part of her bridal-price couldn't match the strength, the majesty of those figures His mouth fell open and he suddenly felt his cousin's elbow in his ribs. A procession was entering the chamber.

First came two guards, dressed in the gold and purple tunics of the Arithmos.[143] Without deigning to look at the three barbarians, Yakub or the Quaestor, they separated, making their way to either side of a high-backed ivory throne on a low dais in the middle of the room.

Behind walked two men talking quietly to each other. One was dressed in red with a fine cloak laced with gold and a belt which drew Thorgeis's eyes by the glitter of the precious stones it contained. After a brief final word with his companion he made his way to the throne and firmly sat down. Ethelwulf was aware of a sharp intake of breath from the Quaestor to his left. He was about to comment when John Angelus began to explain his actions, justifying his recruiting of barbarians from the north.

The tall, black-haired man adjusted his position on the throne and asked for confirmation that the Quaestor John had actually recruited these men. As the Quaestor started to reply there was a cough from the smaller man, who'd taken up his position to the right of the throne.

Ethelwulf looked in the direction of the unknown figure and found himself seized by the gimlet-stare of the man's brilliant blue eyes. He realised the Quaestor had come to a hesitant halt and then restarted. What was going on? He cursed for not positioning himself close to the Khazar. Then he realised the trader was at as much a loss at what was going on as he was.

John Angelus was furious, but dared not show it. How could the Autokrator allow Alexius Euergetes to play the part of Basileus![144] Did he not know the rogue already had the ambition of Phocas? He'd started to protest at how the upstart had seated himself on the imperial throne, but a warning cough from the Autokrator himself had made him bite his lip. Why was the Autokrator playing these games? Did he fear the barbarians? Was he testing out their loyalty - and then a more pleasant thought sidled into the Quaestor's mind, or was he really putting the loyalty of the Eparchos to the test. Yes, that must be it. John felt more prepared to go along with the game.

He was aware of the Eparchos Alexius pontificating from the throne, warming to the task of playing emperor. Somehow the

Quaestor managed to grasp what the man was saying - no, ORDERING him to do. John Angelus turned his worried face towards the Autokrator, but the black arched-brows remained firmly positioned over the clear blue eyes. He dared not disobey.

The Quaestor found himself agreeing to hand over his new recruits to the Eparchos to try them out on a special mission. The nature of this task would be more clearly explained in private, and here the Eparchos glanced at the Khazar nervously looking down at his foot, shuffling from side to side.

The trader seemed relieved when actually given the task of interpreting by the Quaestor, and carefully explained the new orders to Ethelwulf.

"But why does the Emperor want us to undertake some special mission -" he began, but was rudely silenced by Yakub, anxious both to hear whatever else the Quaestor had to say and to show everyone he exercised some control over these barbarians.

However, the Khazar hadn't reckoned on the tenacity of Morkere who loudly blurted out to the Quaestor, "Why we go for emperor? Do we fight enemies?"

There was a gruff laugh from the brown-cloaked man to the right of the throne. John Angelus was told he hoped no fighting would be required. He suddenly paused and looked towards the occupant of the throne.

The Eparchos took his cue and brusquely ordered the Quaestor to dismiss the barbarians and their interpreter. As the orders were being carried out he ordered the Quaestor to contact the Postmaster General and obtain an imperial interpreter to improve the barbarian's lamentable Greek.

The Khazar bit his tongue as he translated the Quaestor's orders to the three barbarians. In a strange way he was sorry to see himself excluded from the activities of these barbarians and resented the criticism of what he'd achieved in one week's tuition. However, the Quaestor himself murmured his thanks, promising to remember the trader in future, as he ushered the barbarians and their interpreter out of the imperial presence.

*

Ethelwulf couldn't understand why he and his men had been selected for the task later described by the Quaestor. He sensed his new employer was also somewhat puzzled by the orders. Yet, however the official may have queried the original instructions in private, he'd no hesitation in passing them on to the barbarian leader. At the same time the Quaestor introduced him to Leo the Pamphylian who'd been loaned by the Postmaster General to act as interpreter. John Angelus was slightly consoled by the obvious irritation of Isaac Ducas at having to hand over an increasingly-valuable asset to the Quaestor with no time-limit.

The barbarians instantly took to the grey-haired Chartularius.[145] John Angelus allowed the man to introduce himself to them in that yelping which they dared call a language. He didn't know Leo began by apologising for the many new sights which must cause strangers such bewilderment. He added he'd also been amazed at seeing the washing habits of the Rus traders.[146] Ethelwulf laughed, at the same time realising the honest features of the man masked a degree of shrewdness. He must have been told none of the barbarians were actually Rus, otherwise he wouldn't have dared comment on such behaviour.

In his turn Leo felt drawn to the barbarians. When he'd been summoned from his office he'd nervously fingered the blue-stripe on his tunic on his way to the Quaestor's tribunal. He didn't like getting out of routine, although he had to admit enjoying the four years spent in Cherson trying to establish some form of customs duty on the trade brought down from the north by the Rus. He'd liked their roughness, after his initial fears, realising that honesty and openness were two virtues to be seen there and not in the capital of the Empire.

Briefly he translated the Quaestor's instructions, adding without prompting a brief explanation so smoothly the Quaestor was unaware such information had been passed on. One third of the Varangians were to act as an escort to bring the defeated rebel, Sclerus,[147] from his exile near Ancyra[148] to the capital. The emperor had heard the old rebel was engaged in treasonable correspondence with nobles at the capital. He was to be questioned about these matters.

Thorgeis asked why they were being used as gaolers instead of fighters. Leo answered him with a quiet smile and explained that between Ancyra and the capital the country was difficult and there'd plenty of opportunity for attack by both friends of the rebel and apelatai.[149] Thorgeis was cheered by that news. He remarked casually to Morkere he felt his axe had been going blunt since throwing in his lot with Ethelwulf the Wanderer.

Leo noted there were two groups at least among the barbarians; his master would welcome whatever news he could supply about these new arrivals from the north. He smiled inwardly at the comment on the axe, knowing such words were commonplace among the Rus where men were expected to live by their boasts.

Ethelwulf was to entrust his three vessels to the care of the Custodian of Phospherion with only a light guard of fifteen men to keep away the inquisitive (and thieving) hands of Greeks. Fifty of the Varangians under the command of Thorgeis were installed in barracks near the palace. Despite his earlier boast, Thorgeis clearly preferred the chance of being in command of what could become a key unit in palace defences. Ethelwulf noted he could scarcely bother to wish them luck for their journey.

The remaining thirty-two Varangians, together with Leo the Pamphylian and the Chartularius Aximander of Pergamum (acting as both guide and agent of the Eparchos) would set off for Ancyra in three days time. Aximander took upon himself the task of getting together supplies and transport for the expedition. Leo locked himself away with Ethelwulf, Morkere and two other Varangians for several hours in a frantic attempt to improve their knowledge of the Greek language.

Gunnar and the others were left much to their devices and Leo considered it a sign of God's grace that in that time only three were thrown into gaol for brawling and another two slightly wounded in scuffles with local ruffians. He laughingly secured the immediate release of the three imprisoned barbarians. So the party was still complete when it set out for Ancyra which lay over two thousand stades[150] away.

*

The journey proved surprisingly uneventful, considering the dangers of apelatoi with which Leo had entertained his pupils for the last ten days. The horses proved very manageable, even though one or two of the Varangians had scarcely ever sat on any saddle before. Some initial tumbles provoked laughter silenced by threats of murder, but, on the whole, the men worked well together.

Aximander proved to be a surprising guide. At first he explained in detail to Ethelwulf some of the history of the regions through which they were passing, patiently putting up with awkwardly-phrased questions. He was initially shocked that none of the barbarians had ever heard of the council summoned at Nicaea by the founder of Constantinople itself;[151] especially as some of them professed to be followers of the Lord Jesus. However, he reasoned that being both barbarians and entrapped by the errors promulgated by the Bishop of Rome,[152] there might be a reason for their ignorance.

Accordingly Ethelwulf was not too surprised when their guide sought to usher them away from the old town of Nicaea itself. The group left the main road just west of the town with its white sun-baked houses, skirting north on the instructions of their guide to avoid putting extra burden on the townspeople. Ethelwulf could appreciate the sudden influx of over thirty armed foreigners might cause alarm, and produce a fresh barrage of required authorisations from the capital. As his knowledge of Greek grew he understood the power for good or evil exercised by the Imperial Administration. He easily managed to convince his men the problems from delaying in the district easily out-weighed any attractions the local inn might hold.

As the journey continued, nevertheless, Aximander took to going off for hours at a time. Always saying he had to pass on messages from the Sacellarius[153] and other officials of the capital to the village chiefs and elders. Ethelwulf didn't like the idea of their guide being so keen to disappear. Morkere suggested they should detail two men to follow the official; but Ethelwulf pointed out that, not only would they both be conspicuous and at a loss in unknown territory, but their ignorance of language would prevent them learning anything anyway. He saw Morkere bite his lip as he accepted the dangers of unknown territory, remembering only too well the death of his twin among the Pechenegs. Even so, Ethelwulf was pleased Morkere seemed to have shaken off the depression which had inflicted him for several weeks.

Leo, on the other hand, proved increasingly valuable as the journey progressed. The slight Chartularius appeared as ill-suited to riding as many of the Varangians but, unlike them, never complained. Indeed, his cheerfulness and constant willingness to expand the vocabulary and grammar of his pupils at any opportunity was much appreciated. Words and phrases learned from Leo were passed on to any men wishing to overcome their total ignorance of the Empire. Morkere continued to be the most adept at the language of the Greeks, although Ethelwulf soon began to manage some form of conversation with Leo, and their guide - when he was there.

Leo proved a source of information about everything from the ruling Macedonian house[154] to what could be expected to be the tariff for any whore at one of the bath-houses in the capital.[155] Gunnar showed most interest in Leo's description of the scandalous career of the late empress[156] and loudly regretted he'd not been available to take his chances at gaining a throne. Remembering the events in Clonmel[157] Ethelwulf didn't share his enthusiasm. He was also pleased Gunnar's comment was made in a form of Norse of which Leo remained in total ignorance.

In the late morning of the tenth day after leaving the capital, Ethelwulf gazed up at the fortress dominating the little town of Ancyra.[158] Leo told him it had been built nearly two hundred years previously by the emperor Michael II. The Chartularius added that those had been difficult times for the Empire before it had been rescued by the ancestors of the present Autokrator.

Ethelwulf noted the strength of the tower to the east. Whoever held that tower would hold the town itself. Not that the town seemed to have anything of value. He was glad they were to ride east towards Charsianum. Leo, however, was anxious to point out they'd not have to venture beyond the boundaries of the Bucellarian theme. To do so would require further authorisation from the capital. Fortunately the estates given to the defeated traitor Sclerus were only one day's further ride.

Gunnar remarked it was about time they rested and suggested they camp just outside Ancyra for the night. For once Aximander seemed keen to let the Varangians get in touch with local people and readily agreed to the idea. Ethelwulf wondered why their guide even encouraged some of the men to make their way into the local inns to buy wine considered 'essential for bedding-down' in the country, only insisting they return to camp before curfew.

Several of the men took the chance of striding off to town and two hours later staggering back with leather wine-bottles, fresh bread and a goodly supply of the local brew already in their stomachs. As Thorgrim of Birka loudly remarked, "This Greek wine may be more like urine than good honest ale but at least it helps you forget the flies!" Ethelwulf was amazed they all got back safely before curfew.

*

Bardas Sclerus proved to be a very tall and austere figure. Old age and arthritis together, however, made it impossible for him to stand unaided for very long. His iron-grey hair was cut fashionably short and he must have been a handsome man in his youth. His cloak of light azure was etched with gold and his belt was of the finest Pisidian leather. On the third finger of his right hand he flaunted a thick gold ring holding a large blood-red ruby. He was also blind.

This last fact pushed all else into the background when Ethelwulf was led into the marbled hall where the exiled noble proudly stood, supported on either side by Saracen slaves. The blindness of Sclerus poured out from burned-out eyes; a mutilation the Varangians had first witnessed exacted as legal punishment two days after their arrival in the capital. Yakub had explained, with malicious amusement at the distaste his words aroused, that civilised peoples shunned the taking of life, preferring to give criminals time to repent their sins and opportunity by removing the distractions of sight or speech. Gunnar had grunted Valhalla had no seats for the deformed.

Ethelwulf whispered to Leo he doubted this could be the man who'd twice threatened the Imperial House. Leo hushed away the enquiry as Aximander stepped forward and read the formal summons from the emperor. Sclerus showed little reaction except for the tightening of his long fingers on the forearms of the slave on his left. In a high-pitched quivering voice he thanked Aximander for delivering a chance for him once again to pledge his loyalty to the Autokrator.

Aximander relaxed slightly and then went on to introduce Ethelwulf as the leader of the escort to conduct him to the capital. Sclerus smiled grimly at the mention of a barbarian name and asked Ethelwulf to step closer. Sclerus then quickly raised his right hand to Ethelwulf's face and lightly explored his features. At first his fingers had touched Ethelwulf's chin as he hadn't expected the barbarian to be almost his equal in height. Ethelwulf felt a strange sympathy for the fallen noble as he gazed into those sightless sockets while fingers delicately tried to 'picture' another's features.

"So the Autokrator has taken warriors from the Rus?" Sclerus asked softly.

"I from far west travel, sir," replied Ethelwulf quietly, "but for two years I live among Rus."

The other smiled at the oddly-phrased but comprehensible Greek. "Perhaps there's hope for you yet, stranger," he smiled, "as long as you escape your barbarian tongue!" He paused and moistened his lips as he lightly placed his fingers against the cheek of the Varangian leader. "Do you know our Saviour, the Lord Jesus Christ?"

Ethelwulf replied he'd been brought up in a Christian household, and Aximander interrupted to say that, unfortunately, the barbarian had been raised in the errors of Rome.

"But there still might be hope for his soul!" countered Sclerus. Ethelwulf appreciated the defence, despising the imperial envoy for intruding upon a private conversation. Leo now stepped forward and introduced himself to Bardas Sclerus, irritated by the way he'd been so ignored by his fellow Chartularius.

Aximander brusquely stated they'd have to start their journey to the capital the next day as the Autokrator was insistent on speedy obedience of his orders. This produced a quiet and knowing smile from Sclerus. He did, however, get Aximander to agree he should be accompanied by his two Saracen slaves. The imperial envoy obviously felt such a concession might usefully buy time.

Sclerus now asked his escort to camp near the house that night, repeating recent rumours of large bands of apelatoi in the district. For once Aximander had no interest in supplying the answer and shrugged off the decision to Leo and the Varangian leader. Ethelwulf wondered whether the request stemmed from a desire for more warriors to protect the estate or fear for strangers in the area. Anyway Sclerus promised them ample supplies of vegetables and wine to make their night more comfortable so his request couldn't be turned down. As they left the old man Ethelwulf smiled as he could already hear Gunnar's complaining, "Two warm peasant-girls will make me comfortable enough; not a cart-load of turnips!"

*

The next day Bardas Sclerus solemnly bade farewell to his household. The slaves were to be sold off to neighbours, but the servants were to maintain the house ready for the return of their master. None really expected to see their lord again; to fail in two rebellions and then be summoned to the capital was to expect no forgiveness.

Sclerus was helped into the saddle of a beautiful grey horse and positioned himself craftily by the side of Leo. His knee was so close to that of the Pamphylian that he could tell the direction and speed of the party, even though sight was denied him.

Ethelwulf was relieved at the apparent emptiness of the streets of Ancyra as the party passed close to the north of the city. Although on imperial business he'd had enough experience of such small town mentalities in the past to know central administration's decisions were always the subject of critical debate - which had a nasty habit of turning into resistance when least wanted.

Ethelwulf was accompanied at the front of the returning party by Aximander. On several occasions he tried to engage the Greek in conversation but every time was met either by apparent incomprehension or misunderstanding. In the end he gave up and the pair rode together in silence. Unlike Sclerus and Leo who rapidly developed a warm understanding. Ethelwulf wished his companion had been Leo, or even Sclerus. At least he wouldn't have felt so shut out.

*

For the first four days the journey proved uneventful. Aximander was completely uncommunicative, and Ethelwulf looked forward to the evening's halt when he could again talk freely and feel the warmth of another human being.

On the fifth day, however, Aximander began slipping off again, giving as an excuse the need to forewarn the authorities so that transport could be arranged over the Bosphorus. When Ethelwulf happened to mention Aximander's excuse that evening he noticed Sclerus stiffen and asked Leo, in Rus to ensure privacy, to ask the old rebel the next day about his opinion of the government guide.

Leo reported the following evening; and his report did nothing to calm Ethelwulf's anxiety. Sclerus had pointed out no prior provision greater than forty-eight hours could be made for transport across the Bosphorus. He could see no reason why Aximander should be trying to contact anyone on the business of the Autokrator. Of course, Sclerus added, he had several bitter enemies in the region; people who wouldn't want him to have his last words to the Autokrator before being sent into exile.[159] Here the old man paused, remembering that dreadful day when four men had arrived at his estate with the authority of the Eparchos in the name of the emperor to put out his eyes. He'd been expecting the decision, but for each day his eyes survived he had thanked God, knowing it was more than he deserved.

Ethelwulf didn't like the thought of personal enemies encouraged to act out vengeance on a prisoner in his charge. He was tempted to challenge Aximander when the envoy returned late that night. It was very late, however, and the man was as distant as ever. How far could he trust Sclerus anyway?

*

The next day Aximander disappeared immediately after breakfast and by noon the party were wearily preparing to enter one of the small canyons which shuffled the road to Constantinople as it edged its way towards the sea. Suddenly Ethelwulf found himself joined by Hallbjorn who urged him to look ahead, to a collection of dark trees growing just as the canyon began to narrow into a gorge.

Ethelwulf stared at the trees, squinting his eyes and putting his hand up to supply shade as he thought he could detect a glitter of reflected sun. He ordered the party to halt and waited for Gunnar and Sven the Far-sighted to join him. He asked the latter to describe what he could see among the trees.

"Metal!" was the curt reply. The man gulped as if to take in fresh air for an assault on his vocal chords. "Possibly armed men - possibly something else."

Certainly armed men, thought Ethelwulf and began to look around for some more-easily defended position. At the same time he detailed Leo and one of Sclerus's slaves to ride quickly back towards the last settlement they'd passed and use the imperial warrant to summon assistance if they could. No sooner had the two men turned their mounts and scampered back down the road, than Ethelwulf led the party off the road and towards the protective overhang of an isolated cliff. He could find shade there as well.

Gunnar turned and noticed movement among the distant glitter of metal. There was more of it and he hurried forward to report to his leader. Gunnar was forced to hustle their old prisoner along as Sclerus had simply halted his magnificent animal at the sudden departure of Leo. Rather brutally Gunnar cursed at the man to move on quickly. There was no response, but then the one remaining slave gently led his master towards the cliff, saying they were seeking shade from the noon-day sun.

"Don't lie to me, Abdul!" snapped the old rebel. "I know when there's alarm; I've heard the reassuring gripping of weapons and the half-mutterings of scarcely-remembered prayers before a battle. Are we about to be attacked?"

Ethelwulf nearby replied they were simply taking precautions as he feared local nobles might be seeking revenge on their prisoner. He gratefully realised that what had appeared a slight rise in ground towards the cliff was, in reality, a fairly steep slope. This would help them hold the position.

"Yes, and not just LOCAL nobles," sneered Bardas Sclerus and coughed. " Alexius Euergetes has reason to fear I might open my mouth to the Autokrator about rumours I've heard throughout the theme." And then he stopped, suddenly realising he'd already said too much - and the barbarian couldn't understand words or content.

By now the party had reached the shade beneath the cliff. To their immediate relief they found a small stream trickling its way down through a deep cleft in what had appeared a solid wall of rock. The horses were collected together and made secure under the care of the Arab slave and two of the less experienced Varangians. Sclerus was led to a large rock near the stream, close to his Arab slave, and made comfortable. The Varangians drew their weapons, ready to link shields in the traditional shield-wall.

The glittering metal moved down from the hillside ahead. Soon the Varangians could see they were about to be attacked by a large force of Greek troops. Sven the Far-sighted shouted to Ethelwulf he could see Aximander riding in the middle of the advancing line of heavily-armoured warriors.[160] At this there was a general roar of derision from the Varangians who loudly banged their shields. Morkere whispered to Edric alongside him that if he wanted one man to die that day it'd be Aximander.

Suddenly there was silence as a tall, black-armoured warrior rode forward from the Greek side until he stopped a short distance from the closely-packed Varangian band. He shouted out several sentences in a deep menacing voice, and Ethelwulf looked round for Leo to shout out a translation. Suddenly he realised their interpreter should be well on his way to get assistance.

It was Morkere who volunteered an attempt at translation. "He says they only want Sclerus!" he cried out so all the party could hear his words "He promises we'll all be allowed to live if we hand over this traitor to the Autokrator."

Ethelwulf was never to know how accurate Morkere's translation had been. Certainly it produced an immediate effect among the Varangians. There was a loud murmur of disgust which swept along the whole shield-wall; to break their given-word to the Quaestor to deliver Sclerus in safety to the capital would make them unworthy to be called "Varangi". Ethelwulf didn't bother to ask Morkere to yell back a reply; he summoned up the few words of obscenity he'd so far garnered from the Phospherion beer-houses and was pleased to see that the message got across.

Without a sound thirty cavalrymen charged up the slope towards the shield-wall. However, as Ethelwulf had noted when selecting this defensive position the slope was deceptive, growing steeper as it toiled up towards the waiting axes and spears. By the time the enemy reached the shield-wall their over-burdened mounts were barely at walking pace; they proved easy fodder for the vicious swing of battle-axes which downed both horse and rider. Once down the rider had scarcely disentangled himself from the useless mount before a second blow removed him from the fight. Only a few of the cavalry were able to evade death and recover their position.

Immediately on their withdrawal enemy archers poured arrows at the shield-wall, but a slight-repositioning of the shields gave adequate protection, thanks to a combination of distance and elevation. Now Gunnar started beating his shield with his war-axe, screaming abuse at the enemy. Although the tongue was Norse the passion was there and there were reciprocal boasts and threats from the other side.

Ethelwulf smiled and whispered to Morkere that standing and shouting at each other would suit him very well; every hour passed was an hour nearer rescue. Perhaps the enemy leader realised this as he despatched forward about sixty lightly-armed warriors against the Varangian lines. The result was slaughter. Some were cut down by javelins and thrown war-axes before they even reached the shield-wall; others pressing on were sliced in half by the practised axes and swords of the barbarians.

By now the enemy had lost almost one half of its fighting strength and gained nothing, apart from one Varangian killed by an unlucky arrow in the throat and two wounded by spear-thrusts. So the Varangians had to face a second hail of arrows. Then the enemy withdrew to reconsider their position. Ethelwulf ordered his men to relax and, for the first time, noticed the slave caring for Sclerus who lay on the ground among the horses. Quickly the Saxon made his way to the fallen pretender and immediately realised Sclerus was past any comfort, from his chest protruded a grey-feathered shaft. Bardas Sclerus had at last found peace.

Ethelwulf shrugged and made his way back to his position in the shield-wall. Now the battle no longer had a purpose; should he tell the enemy? He stared across at the Greeks still trying to summon up the energy and courage needed for a new assault. No, Sclerus might be dead but his body could be taken for burial at the capital; besides, he was absolutely certain none of his men would be given quarter if they surrendered. Both sides watched and waited.

With the evening Ethelwulf ordered three Varangians to prepare some sort of warm meal for his men. If another attack came they'd have to break off from eating, and that would give them even more fury. There was no attack and evening passed into night with the

Greek force still poised menacingly a few hundred yards from the shield-wall. With night Ethelwulf positioned look-outs and ordered the rest of his men to rest where they were. Used to snatching sleep at the oars or on the damp plains of the Dneiper, the Varangians found no problem resting with the threat of sudden death so near.

*

With morning the enemy had disappeared, slunk away during the night so quietly the look-outs hadn't even noticed. Gunnar was displeased and wanted to make the negligent sentries suffer. However, Ethelwulf refused, grateful the enemy had apparently given up, being reluctant to lose any more men!

He also refused to move forward. If the enemy had disappeared they could be simply waiting in a more advantageous position further on. Indeed as Sclerus was dead there was no hurry; a corpse could get to trial in whatever time it needed. So Ethelwulf ordered his men to pitch camp where they stood; ordering some to bury the enemy dead, collecting whatever distinguishing features they could find. With that he waited for the arrival of reinforcements.

Leo returned the next day with two hundred men despatched by the local governor. Only then did Ethelwulf consider it safe to proceed with the remainder of the journey to the capital.

*

Bugles and drums were not welcome to the ears of the Varangians. They far preferred the quieter pipes and harps of the north. Nor did they like the fine brown cloaks with which they'd been presented by the Quaestor on their return to the capital. But then there was much they did like in their new life in the capital.

They'd been treated like heroes. It was true Sclerus had been killed on the journey, but there were several among the imperial service who welcomed the opportunity to silence what could have been embarrassing revelations of past promises and understandings. The Quaestor made it clear the death of Sclerus couldn't be blamed on the Varangians and enthusiastically enrolled them among the imperial guard. To distinguish these new recruits he supplied fine brown cloaks and large gold rings; the men cherished the rings, for gold like fame lasts for ever; the cloaks, however, were less popular as many complained they'd impede good axe-work. Ethelwulf managed to get the Quaestor to accept the cloaks would only be worn on ceremonial occasions. Unfortunately this was one.

Today was the birthday of the co-Emperor Constantine, the younger and less influential partner in the control of the Empire. The Imperial Family would thank Almighty God for success and life in the holiest shrine in Christendom, the church of St. Sophia.

Ethelwulf had assembled a guard of ten men, including himself, and they were positioned with their backs towards the Weeping Column, just inside the magnificent Imperial Door. He remembered how terrified some of his men had been when they'd first marched into the centre of this magnificent shrine and stood beneath the awe-inspiring dome. They'd all been told by Leo gleefully how several times the dome had needed repair and support, and had been known to crash its way down on to the ground below.[161] Seeing the delicacy and refinement with which it had been constructed Ethelwulf wasn't surprised. He was glad his men weren't positioned under its threatening beauty.

When the doors were thrown open and the guards passed by, Ethelwulf was surprised to see the skinny lesser emperor, Constantine, walking side-by-side with the short, unimpressive individual with the magnetic blue eyes. Was this man Basil the Autokrator? If so, who'd been the man daring to seat himself on the imperial throne and lord it over all as if he were the anointed of God? He'd question Leo when this magnificent celebration was over; he'd enjoy wringing the Pamphylian's neck to encourage him to spill out the truth. No, the man was honest; they'd not discussed whoever had given the orders, merely the instructions themselves. He was certain the Quaestor had known the truth and had smirked inwardly at how easy it was to deceive a barbarian. Ethelwulf made a silent resolution to wrong-foot his ex-master in the near future.

The party following the service of thanks to the Pankrator[162] was extraordinary. Nothing he'd seen in Ireland, Jelling or Kenugard could match the sheer extravagance and voluptuousness of the affair. Perhaps his men had no love for the rather thin wines of Anatolia, but they certainly disguised the fact magnificently.

Only Gunnar passing out between the legs of one whore brought in for the occasion prevented what could have been an awkward confrontation. He and Thorgeis had been loudly comparing their ability to "ride the Miklagard mares", and after the third successful mounting Gunnar had been definitely weakening. A failure would have made him reach for his war-axe to silence any sniggers. Fortunately his incapacity was immediately followed by his lapsing into unconsciousness. Ethelwulf had the drunken man safely tucked up with the rather intimidated Bulgar whore in a small bedroom nearby. When he awoke in the morning it'd be time for him to continue the game.

It was just when Thorgeis was starting to crow after a fourth mounting that Sven spotted a fierce light in the sky to the north. Thorgeis was left to roll off his whore by the sudden rush of men towards the balcony which looked out over the Golden Horn. There could be no mistake, to the north belched fire from the crowded alleys of Galata.

Without thinking those Varangians still capable of action rushed towards the few boats loosely tied up for ferrying traders and others across the narrow waterway to that part of the city dominated by Jews and other barely-acceptable traders. Ethelwulf found himself squeezed in between fat Thorkel Iron-Hand and Ubbe of Grimsby. Only when he was halfway across did he start to wonder why he was there. It'd have been so much easier to have stayed in the ale-house near the Perama Gate; yet, like other barbarians from the north he both loved and hated fire, fearing its destructive force which could end everything. He pulled himself together and started urging his men to pull at the oars in some kind of unison. After a few drunken sallies, soberer hands took charge and the wide, flat ferry-boat made its way across the fire-lit waters.

Galata itself was in chaos. Too late it appeared the resources of the fire-brigades, the fund-starved responsibility of the Eparchos, had been thrown into action. Why there'd been such a delay was uncertain; perhaps because the befuddled heads of the imperial court were still celebrating their master's birthday, perhaps because the area was simply the home of Jews and other less-welcome inhabitants of the capital. Whatever the reason delay had ruined any hope of controlling much of the conflagration.

Water wagons dragged by terrified horses and driven by no-less terrified slaves virtually abandoned any attempt to save those houses clustered between the Galata Tower and the synagogue to the north-east of it. Here were concentrated the shops and factories of Jewish enterprise. Ethelwulf and the crew of his boat found themselves drawn towards the heat and flames ripping open the night from this district.

Only a warning yell from Ubbe prevented Ethelwulf from walking into the path of a careering water-wagon, spilling its cargo as it surged through the streets in a frantic effort to get involved and yet stay safe. Morkere bent down and flung a piece of broken timber after the disappearing vehicle, loudly regretting he'd no spear to teach the driver how to handle his horses.

By now the small group of Varangians had reached the street whose Hebrew name glinted above their heads in the unnatural flicker of the inferno. Opposite them a large house had fire belching out from three windows and blackened smoke from its door. Then they heard a scream and for a moment glimpsed through the distorting haze of smoke and fire a woman's face at a first-floor window. Morkere turned to his left, ripping off his fine brown cloak and wrapping it tightly around his mouth. His action allowed Ethelwulf to plunge into the house yards before him.

Once inside Ethelwulf found he could see nothing; smoke filled his eyes, stuffed up his nose and battered its way down his throat. He coughed loudly and turned back towards the door, his eyes screaming for relief and pouring out frustrating tears. Somehow he turned to his left and his body banged against a large barrel just within the door. He ripped at his cloak and plunged it into its contents and then wound the sodden mass furiously around his throat. For a moment he was both sickened and invigorated by the fragrance of a sweet wine from Andalusia. He dabbed his eyes and began to recover some vision. Seeing Morkere and Ubbe he croaked to them and was pleased they quickly followed his example and wound damp materials tightly around their faces.

Ubbe led the rush up the staircase towards the trapped woman but Morkere's shoulder smashed down the door which blocked the way to the front of the house. There on the floor lay a female figure, motionless and abandoned. Morkere reached down and easily scooped the shape over his shoulder before heading for safety.

For some reason Ethelwulf chose not to follow Morkere and Ubbe back down the stairs. By now his eyes had begun to sting again and the protection given to his throat by the wine-soaked cloak was starting to fade. Even so, he ran along the short corridor towards the rear of the house. Entering a room where already flames were starting to eat up floor-covering and floor-boards in the far corner, he almost tripped over a body lying slumped against the upright. He quickly bent down and stared into the strangely-peaceful features of an old man unconscious to approaching death, but somehow still breathing. As Ethelwulf started to drag the body through the doorway he noticed an ugly wound on its left temple.

Suddenly he felt a light tap on his arm and looking up, recognised the narrow, blood-shot eyes of Sihtric, the fletcher from Gunnar's vessel. Without a word the man seized the legs of the inert man and Ethelwulf found himself heaving up the torso as they headed towards the stairs. At the top he felt like pitching the old man down to make his own way to safety. His lungs shrieked for moisture and he could no longer sense anything in his throat; his eyes were filled with tears and he felt flattened by exhaustion. He was pushed aside by Sihtric who started half-dragging and half-carrying the unconsciousness man downstairs; Ethelwulf simply prevented the man's head from smashing against stair and wall as the body was transported to safety. Outside, in the cleaner, softer air Ethelwulf sank down next to the unconscious man, feeling his cloak loosened from around his throat and then himself drifting off into oblivion.

*

Simeon the Jeweller was embarrassingly profuse with his thanks to his saviours. Loudly he called upon the God of Abraham and Isaac to bless these strange men from the north who'd saved both himself and his daughter, Rachel. He even continued to shout praises to the Varangians when his daughter slipped away into death three days later. It was the will of God; she'd been too good for this world, like her mother, Rebekah.

Only on the cause of the wound to his head was the Jewish merchant silent. Whenever Ethelwulf raised the question, Simeon decided there was something of greater importance to discuss. Other members of the Jewish community got together a petition to the Autokrator, complaining of the timidity and inaction of the fire-brigades when their homes were being destroyed. Simeon, however, refused to have anything to do with such complaints; instead he delighted in showing off Ethelwulf as his brave rescuer and mourning for the daughter dragged alive from the flames but whom God had still taken to Himself.

For a time Ethelwulf and Morkere were paraded around the neighbourhood of Simeon as heroes. The Quaestor was not too pleased, not liking to have warriors he'd recruited linked too closely with what many in the capital viewed with distaste and suspicion. Loudly Simeon promised that if ever his rescuers needed help then his house and all he possessed would be theirs. Morkere dryly remarked that clearly a promise of future wealth was cheaper than ten miliaresions[163] now. Ethelwulf shrugged; who knew what the future might hold. Besides, he didn't mention the large emerald Simeon had declared would be his, if ever he had need of it, before putting it again firmly under lock and key. Ethelwulf's only regret was that the girl had died.

Even so, within weeks Ethelwulf was summoned before the Eparchos. He stared coldly at the Nobilissimus, this time seated in an ornate chair; he didn't like the unpleasant taste of the memory of when he'd first met the official. Now he felt hostility in the narrow brown-eyes scrutinising him.

"Your men are growing restless, barbarian," snapped the imperial official. "Only yesterday my police had to arrest two trying to set fire to a bath-house." Ethelwulf tried to protest the men had been set upon and robbed while still revelling in the effects of the baths. Only after drinking several large bottles of coarse Thracian wine had they set off to get their revenge. The Eparchos brushed aside the excuse; he regretted the Autokrator hadn't let him to pitch this menace from the north into the Bosphorus when they'd first arrived.

Unfortunately the barbarian had proved to be a menace, with the terrible combination of luck and ability. He'd developed the habit of getting in the way and, without realising it, of upsetting schemes in total innocence. Ethelwulf's rescue of that miserable Simeon, for instance, had meant the debts of the Eparchos hadn't been purged by fire; he couldn't blame Psellus, the captain had obeyed orders and left Simeon for dead before putting torch to the merchant's home. It was unlucky this barbarian had blundered in and rescued the old man before the fire had done its work.

Aximander, however, had proved a different case. The man had made a serious mistake in not insisting on a more vigorous assault on the barbarians. Certainly Sclerus had been removed before he had a chance to reveal certain unfortunate letters; but then, the letters still existed - somewhere. What was more, the death of Sclerus and the destruction of the barbarians would have been blamed on the Quaestor for interfering with the imperial will. As it was, the Eparchos had been fortunate in placing the blame wholly on local troublemakers; Aximander had been forced to eat a suitable dish of toadstools and so HIS mouth had been shut.

The Eparchos stared at the open countenance of the barbarian in front of him. Did the man not realise how he'd ruined such precious schemes? Probably not, he was still innocent of the ways of the capital of Constantine and Justinian. Anyway now he'd get rid of the man and be seen to serve the Autokrator at the same time.

Briefly the Eparchos explained to the barbarian that his force was to proceed south to the island of Crete, recently seized by imperial forces.[164] The island was being harassed by Saracen pirates and the barbarians would form the nucleus of a naval force to strike back against these enemies of the Pankrator.

The Eparchos sneered inwardly at the pathetic enthusiasm with which the barbarian welcomed his despatch to destruction. If things went better this time Saracen pirates would receive a body-blow before they destroyed this barbarian interloper. Then his agents might profit from the trade of the southern seas.

For his part, Ethelwulf looked forward to the chance to escape the noise and smells of the capital. The task would expand his knowledge of the Aegean and see how 'Brimfugol' would handle in action.

So both Alexius Euergetes and Ethelwulf welcomed the commission – but for very different reasons.

*

The Wanderer 8:2

"I can sing about myself a song that's true,
Of my travels, how in troubled days
Often I have endured a time of hardship,
How my heart sheltered bitter sorrow
And learned just how often ships foster sadness."
('The Seafarer')

Crete

"'Niflheim's Envoy'[165] is failing to keep in its proper position," complained Sven the Far-sighted as he looked to the east. The three Varangian vessels had left the imperial capital three weeks before and slowly made their way southwards towards the island of Crete. Ethelwulf deliberately made slow progress to accustom himself to the tides and currents of the unknown Aegean Sea.

Gunnar at first had been pleased to escape from the inaction of the capital, but grew increasingly resentful of the slowness of their passage south. Now he was definitely driving his vessel forward ahead of both 'Brimfugol' and 'Ran Cheater'. Ethelwulf didn't like to see his formation start to break up just as they were nearing the dangerous waters to the north of Crete. Perhaps when they reached Chandax he'd try to talk Gunnar round to being more co-operative; perhaps by then he'd have forgotten all about such blemishes of order. Ethelwulf knew he'd rather have Gunnar straining at the leash, resentful of inaction, than Gunnar besotted and debauched, miserably sobbing out his memories of far-off Ireland in the dying lights of a feast.

Ethelwulf was about to signal Gunnar to pull back into line when Sven the Far-sighted yelled out he could see two sails further to the east. Immediately all eyes turned in that direction and Ethelwulf quickly signalled to his companion longships to steer towards the new arrivals. Thorstein grunted and swung the tiller of the 'Brimfugol' towards what still appeared as two dots on the horizon.

The Varangians were certain the two dots were not from the imperial bases in Cibyrrhaeots.[166] The more likely explanation was they were Saracen pirates, who still operated off the smaller islands of the Aegean and even Crete itself. It would pay to make sure of their identity before going further south.

*

Ali abd-Kadir was not unhappy. His capture of the rich Thracian[167] galley off the coast of Chios had proved Allah had forgiven his sin of the previous year. He smiled remembering how the Greek captain had almost foundered his vessel in his frantic attempt to escape the attack of three Saracen galleys. It was a pity Haroun al-Bekr had grounded his own craft while keeping their quarry off the rocks. Imsh Allah - it was the will of God that Haroun would be humbled and forced to beg for help from his leader He'd been given the 'Heraclius' (renamed the 'Abu-Bekr'), after its crew had been given the customary choice between conversion and death. The entry of sixteen unbelievers into the faith of Islam must surely count in the judgement of Allah that awaited him.

Yet Ali abd-Kadir knew no mortal could bargain with the One and Only; he'd murdered his brother - no, he'd killed his brother over the diamond bracelet which clung reassuringly to his wrist. He'd soon be home in Maks[168] where he had more work to do for Allah. He knew there were those at court who needed him to persuade their master from taking on those violent hirelings from the east.[169]

His thoughts were interrupted by a cry from the look-out; three small ships could be seen coming quickly from the west. Ali abd-Kadir bit his lip; the wind was all wrong, favouring these newcomers. If only Haroun hadn't been sent off with his prize as a gift to his master! Ali abd-Kadir quickly ordered his helmsman to shift course from south to south-east in order to try to snatch some of the wind from these newcomers. Part of him wasn't afraid, confident in the power and strength of Allah who'd look after his servants; part, however, still saw his brother's face as he tumbled backwards into the sea, his screams blown away by the breath of God.

The race, for such it appeared to both sides, went on for three hours, with the three strange vessels from the west ever-gaining on the two Saracen pirates. Ali abd-Kadir had never seen vessels like these newcomers before; long, low in the water, driven by huge striped sails. They were smaller than either of his vessels, but they moved through the bright-blue waters with a confidence unknown to any Saracen. Ali abd-Kadir knew how much Saracen success at sea depended on unbeliever skills, many of them repelled by the dictates from the imperial capital as to how to fashion their Christian faith.[170] In return for a degree of toleration, and a fat share in profits, seamen from Crete and Cyprus and other parts of the unbelieving Empire were happy to sell their abilities to Fatimid sea-captains.

By now Ali abd-Kadir could make out some of the figures carried towards him by those three strange craft. They were certainly not

Greeks; their hair was fair and their skin pale in the Mediterranean sun. He turned to his second-in-command, the massive renegade-Jew, Yussuf. The giant spat contemptuously over the side in the direction of the approaching vessels.

"They look like the mother of our master,"[171] he grinned. "Perhaps they'll fight like her!"

Ali abd-Kadir tried to smile, but doubts about his worthiness before the One and Only brought no mirth. If only he could out-sail these strangers, but it looked as if nothing but Satan himself or one of his Djinn[172] could fly before their vessels with success. Perhaps he could tack before the wind and bring into effect his ram? No, the wind was too strong, as if the elements had decided he couldn't fight as he had been trained to fight.

He heard Yussuf urging him to abandon sail and rely on the strength of the slave-oarsmen waiting expectantly in the deck below. Could he do it? For several precious moments his precious 'Jewel of Hisham' would be helpless, deprived of the power of wind while the oarsmen were driven into the proper rate to turn the vessel and send it smashing into the bow of one of the attackers. He didn't like the idea but there was no choice. Quickly he told Yussef to order Abdul-Aziz in 'Dream of Fatima' also to turn his vessel and attack.

For what seemed like hours the 'Jewel of Hisham' sat motionless in the water while the sail was quickly put away, the mast lowered and the oarsmen whipped into thrusting out their heavy oars into the sea. At last all was ready and with relief Ali abd-Kadir felt his command lurch forward into the direction of the enemy. He could see them clearly; fierce, ugly barbarians reaching for javelins and bows as they prepared to attack his vessel. The 'Jewel of Hisham' was beginning to make speed. Below he could hear the grunts of effort and the crack of the whip on the shoulders of the slack.

The Saracen galley sped through the bright-blue waves powered by eighty oars straight at 'Ran Cheater' . It seemed inevitable the vicious prow of the larger vessel would smash into the bow of the Varangian longship and send everything to the bottom. Saracen attack was based very much on manoeuvre and ram; the imperial navy in the past had sometimes saved itself by the secret weapon of Greek fire. On occasions, however, as off Chios, the enemy had no such defence; then they were easy prey for the viciousness of such an onslaught.

Ali abd-Kadir could see 'Dream of Fatima' turn too late to meet the attack of the other two longships. Well, Abdul Aziz had enough practised fighters on board to handle this unknown enemy. He could see one longship violently crash into the side of 'Dream of Fatima', smashing into pieces the oars of his partner. The other longship buffeted into the side of its fellow and warriors began streaming out, using the first longship as a bridge.

Yussuf screamed a warning and Ali abd-Kadir turned to see the Varangian ship ahead suddenly swing to port and start an insane, crashing assault against the oars of his vessel. As it broke every oar in its passage the progress of the Saracen ship was slowed. Ali abd-Kadir heard himself screaming abuse at the murderous attack on his vessel. Below he could hear the screams of slaves as the impact of the collision smashed oar-handles into their throats and chests. He could imagine the scene; already some of the slaves would be throwing aside their oars, ignoring the threatening presence of the overseer and terrified by imminent drowning.

The Saracen captain saw his second-in-command gather together ten lightly-armed fighters and charge screaming towards the side under attack. Over his head the giant waved a monstrous scimitar, shouting out a mixture of Arabic and Yiddish curses. Ali abd-Kadir was less headstrong. He quickly collected a group of Saracen spearmen to resist the invasion he knew would come from over his bow. Both vessels were slumped together in deadly embrace as one war-party led by Yussuf hurled itself over the side of the 'Jewel of Hisham', while another, led by Thorgeis, swarmed into the bow of the Saracen vessel.

Thorgeis smashed his axe into the skull of one hapless seaman who'd been frantically trying to clear space to allow escape from below. As the Saracen lurched to the floor, the red-bearded Varangian shrieked his triumph of Odin, waved his bloody weapon aloft and turned to urge his followers on. A spear narrowly missed his left ear and Thorgeis narrowed his eyes and ran furiously at the knot of Saracens advancing along the deck towards him. With a violent swing to the right he swept aside the leading spears and then, in a single movement, cut his axe back towards the leading Saracen. The fighter stepped back and, tumbling against his advancing companions, caused the Saracen defence to lose cohesion. Other Varangians ran past Thorgeis screaming hysterically and thrusting with swords and spears.

Ali abd-Kadir found himself hemmed in by his men who instinctively gave way to the impetus of the attack. He cursed as a man's body forced his scimitar aside as he was about to slash at one of the barbarian invaders. Then he felt a sharp pain in his side and was thrown against the very man who'd impeded his blow. In his fall he dropped his scimitar and, glancing down, saw a monstrous red mess where his side had once been. Before that glance he'd felt winded, now he felt sick and dizzy. He found himself dragged down towards the floor of the deck by the mass of men and the sheer weakness tearing through his limbs. He screamed as trampling feet snatched the last clutching at life from him.

The Saracens started to turn away from the fury of the Varangian attack. Some attempted to put up resistance, others simply to push their way back towards amidships. Here they found themselves suddenly crushed by a battling mass of retreating Saracens and yelling Varangians swept over from the deck of 'Ran Cheater'.

Yussuf yelled out his men were to give their lives for Allah as he cut at the head of a short, black-bearded Varangian. His words were ignored by several Saracens, throwing down their spears and scimitars and then themselves to the deck, beating their foreheads on the planks in submission. Others formed a tight circle around Yussuf, prepared to enter Paradise fighting for their faith.

Thorgeis called his men off and, breathing heavily, they surrounded the defiant knot of pirates with eyes filled with hate. Thorgeis looked across at the other two longships and saw Ethelwulf had managed to sweep away all resistance off the other Saracen vessel. Good, now they could relax. He inclined his head and listened to a splatter of words from Bjarni Strong-arm. As he listened a strange smile spread over his lips, almost wolfish in anticipation. He barked out a brief order and Bjarni and two other Varangians rushed to the hole which led to the quarters of the rowers.

From below Thorgeis heard a horrible scream and then a growing murmur of anger and excitement. Within moments three slave-rowers appeared on deck, the leading one brandishing the scimitar that had once adorned the waist of Mu'awiyya, master of the slaves. Seeing the tight defensive group around Yussuf, the new arrivals gave a scream of exultant hatred. Quickly they armed themselves from the dead bodies of Saracens, and thrust weapons into the hands of other slaves who appeared on deck, blinking at the sunlight and the scene of carnage they witnessed.

Without a sound the Varangians gave way to the new arrivals who started baying at the surviving Saracens, shaking their broken chains and new-found weapons. Suddenly a tall, black slave, armed with a heavy spear, lunged towards one of the Saracens. The thin pirate taken by surprise was pierced through the chest by the spear and the slave, withdrawing its point, howled in triumph. This was the signal for a general rush on the Saracens by the maddened slaves.

The Varangians stood gawking and commenting on the weapon-skills and ferocity of both sides as that area of deck-space rapidly became obscured by the bodies of dead and dying. At last only Yussuf and two slaves remained. Yussuf parried one blow with his scimitar and then virtually cut one naked opponent in half; the other flung himself screaming at the wrong-footed Saracen. Without a sound Yussuf took the plunge of a long knife in his upper torso; he then twisted the slave's wrist and, with no pause in movement, forced the man to thrust the dagger into his own throat.

Covered with blood Yussuf looked round at the gaping Varangians and spat out blood on to the deck. Then, with a triumphant prayer to his Maker, the giant renegade took one powerful stride to the gunwale and launched himself into the middle of the sea. His head never re-appeared above the surface.

For a brief moment there was silence and then Thorgeis burst into song.
> "The ugly giant gave milk.
> Then bathed his heart
> In blood-red seas."

There was a clamour of support from his crew as they brandished their weapons in the direction of the other victorious Varangians. It had been a profitable morning.

*

Two days later five vessels carefully made their way into the harbour of Chandax. There was no challenge from the tower protecting the approach as they flew aloft the flag of the Autokrator.

"Do these Greeks feel so safe," frowned Ethelwulf to Hallbjorn, "that they allow entry to pirate craft without challenge."

Morkere made no reply but pointed to the north-west. Around the headland were emerging eight sails.

Ethelwulf laughed. "Perhaps the Greeks are not so trusting!" He paused. "Do you think they're there just by chance?" Morkere gave no answer but concentrated on the task of placing 'Brimfugol' smoothly next to the quay. After it had been made secure he leaped ashore, being immediately followed by his cousin.

By now a small group of imperial officials, guards and curious bystanders had appeared from the bottom of the main street of Chandax. They stood talking among themselves while the other ships were also brought into dock. Only then did a grey-haired man with sloping shoulders step forward and loudly demand the business of the strangers.

Ethelwulf reached into his tunic and withdrew the despatch of the Eparchos; at the same time he introduced himself and briefly explained the presence of the two Saracen vessels. There were smiles all round, which grew wider as he asked if the eight warships slowly making their way into the harbour behind him were all part of a reception committee.

The grey-haired official, who introduced himself as Artemides of Lesbos, grinned and explained they'd received advanced notice of the arrival of three vessels filled with barbarians from the north. Not sure of such unknown visitors the governor of Chandax, Michael Theophilus, had daily sent a squadron of war-galleys to wait off Agia Pelagia for the expected arrival. The orders of its admiral were simply to overawe the strangers when they arrived.

Morkere nodded in the direction of the Saracen ships and remarked that doubtless the coming of five ships had given some cause for alarm. Artemides brushed aside the criticism with the assurance that God would protect his people.

By now they'd been joined by Thorgeis and Gunnar together with Bjarni Strong-arm and Leofwine who'd been put in charge of the 'Jewel of Hisham' and 'Dream of Fatima' respectively. Ethelwulf ordered Leofwine to remain in charge of both vessels while the other three, with Morkere, made their way to the governor. Thorgeis loudly asserted he didn't want to visit some oil-coated Greek before he'd had a chance to get the taste of salt and spray out of his mouth. Fortunately he spoke in Rus, and so Ethelwulf found no problem in giving way. Not for the first time did he fear Thorgeis was not the best of companions in a strange land.

*

Michael Theophilus was a sick man; the pain in his stomach came and went in intensity, but it was always there. Theophano, his beautiful black-eyed daughter, tried to bring him comfort - warm, drugged glasses of wine had proved the most successful. Even so Michael knew he was dying, and felt he'd failed his emperor. He'd kept the powerful families that dominated the town of Chandax in check - just; however, he'd lost control of the eastern part of the island. In that he had failed.

He remembered coming ashore with the general, Nicephorus Phocas, and being welcomed by the inhabitants whom they were freeing from a century of Moslem rule. Even then he hadn't been too sure of the local inhabitants. Had they not failed to warn them of a Saracen relieving force? Only the brilliance of their general and the strength of the Tagmatikoi had saved their lives. Yes, some among the locals had certainly sweated at the circle of heads which Nicephorus placed around the Saracen defences.[173]

Michael coughed and clutched at his stomach as pain ripped through his entrails. Some of those locals now lorded it over the good immigrants from Anatolia which their general had brought in to replace the slaughtered Saracens. Why did the Autokrator allow these pigs to plot and wait for the return of the old times? His mind tried to shut out the pain by concentrating hate on those whom he knew waited for the return of the profits of piracy and a cut in taxes.

Nobody liked paying taxes, but they were needed to keep the Empire strong, to shut out the barbarians from the north and the nauseating Bulgars. Yet these pigs preferred to follow - to follow Peter the Left-handed in insurrection against the Anointed of God.

At last the pain was fading away and Michael pressed his lips together as he thought of the welcome the Autokrator would give to anyone sending Peter to the capital in chains. The man had defied imperial forces for two years, making it impossible to collect taxes in any of the coastal villages between Gouves and Agios Nikolaos, let alone those of the Lasithi Plateau and the surrounding mountains. If only he could send in troops capable of seizing the traitor and dragging him out to face justice. However, to send a large force into those mountains would be a waste of effort, and those Banda he'd sent against Peter had been destroyed.

For a long time he'd been promised help by the Eparchos and the Quaestor and none had come. At last he was about to receive fresh troops from the capital. The Eparchos had specifically ordered him to send these new soldiers, barbarians so expendable, immediately into the mountains. If they succeeded in capturing Peter then the Autokrator would know how to reward his faithful servant; if they failed and finished up like others before them then the Eparchos would not be unhappy. The governor knew the Eparchos had no love for the barbarians from the north; he was sure he was right.

A slave warned him of the approach of the newcomers who'd entered his harbour that morning. Michael hastily had another slave dress him in the gold-edged tunic of a Nobilissimus. He hoped these barbarians could recognise the proper trappings of authority.

*

"I tell you that stuck-up Greek is a proper son of Loki,"[174] snarled Gunnar after the Varangians had come away from their first audience with the governor. Ethelwulf didn't know how Gunnar reached that decision since his knowledge of Greek was decidedly limited and so the whole interview had been unintelligible to him. Still he had to agree with Gunnar, surprised at the alacrity with which the governor had urged them to crush the enemies of the Autokrator in the east of the island. Morkere had persuaded the governor eventually to let them rest for five days while they recovered from the sea-voyage.

Even so, nobody could find fault with the quarters allocated to the Varangian leaders. They lay to the west of the town, just inside the Hanion Gate. Their men were given rich tents just outside the walls. Food was plentiful and, more importantly, there was no stint of wine. By now Gunnar had become reconciled to the absence of proper ale, and found some wines had an equal capacity of bringing about oblivion. Thorgeis particularly was impressed by the prompt payment of the wages promised by the Quaestor two months before. Anyone who paid his troops so readily must be a good leader to serve. However, Morkere noted the payment must have been authorised actually by the Eparchos and, more strangely, none was made to Ethelwulf's men. It was explained as an oversight, but the shrewd Varangian had his doubts.

Ethelwulf shared Morkere's suspicions of the governor. Perhaps it was the way he managed to keep firm control of his beautiful young daughter; Ethelwulf noticed the looks which passed between the pair. Maybe it was that Morkere had developed an understanding of the subtleties of Greek language and diplomacy. He'd come to rely increasingly on Morkere's judgement; almost as if the good sense of his twin had passed with Edwine's death into Morkere.

The five days spent in the ale-houses of Chandax didn't pass too slowly. The Varangians were allowed very free access to all parts of the town. Despite their lack of language they managed to pick up the general atmosphere. They reported many among the local population regretted their move from the more remote hills of Anatolia. Ethelwulf established himself at a tavern called 'ptomaine The Silver Chalice' and began to acquire a thorough knowledge of the surrounding countryside by examining maps loaned by the governor, talking to local peddlers and the like, and (above all) in making short expeditions after nightfall out of the Hanion Gate and towards the villages of Kolivas and Goumes.

The Wanderer found much to admire in the surrounding defences constructed by the Saracens a century before. He found less to admire in the murmurings and complaints of peasants dragged in from the surrounding hills to answer for taxes before imperial officials. Anathasius, a Chartularius assigned to help (and spy on) the Varangians, tried to explain how the governor needed to recoup the enormous expenditure lavished on the imperial navy to protect islands such as Crete. Ethelwulf doubted very much whether the imperial squadron ventured much out of port. Certainly he hadn't taken to the standard of discipline and organisation witnessed on those vessels based at Chandax. Except for the imperial standard they'd little in common with the galleys he'd examined at the capital.

Eventually it was time to move and Anathasius ushered in a peasant farmer called Cleon professing to know the whereabouts of Peter. Ethelwulf asked why he was willing to lead them to the man claiming to lead Cretan resistance against imperial tyranny. Cleon ignored the diplomatic cough intruded by Anathasius and poured out a hatred for the rebel based on the burning of his farm and the slaughter of his goats. Morkere closely watched Cleon's animated features as he supplied a list of injustices, frequently interrupted by Ethelwulf with pleas to slow down and speak more clearly. At the end Morkere whispered he felt they could trust the man although he'd omitted the most obvious inducement of the large reward on the head of Peter the Left-handed.

So it was settled. Peter would be staying at the house of his mistress in the village of Gouves, a night's march to the east of Chandax. Cleon explained he knew this because his cousin regularly visited the community, trading in olive oil and keeping his eyes open. By now, however it appeared too late to start so Ethelwulf stated the expedition would leave immediately after dusk the following evening. He then dismissed the two Greeks and turned to confer with his leading followers. After a short discussion Gunnar was told to assemble fifteen reliable men for special duty that same night. Gunnar slipped out with a strange smile playing on his lips; they'd already discussed one possibility of how to exploit their minimal numbers and yet succeed in capturing or killing Peter. The plan appealed to him, although he hoped to catch up with lost sleep the following day.

*

Anyone watching the exit to the port of Chandax soon after dusk would have seen two of the barbarian longships quietly make their way out to sea. During the day it had been rumoured they'd be setting up camp near the village of Mallia, as this provided a better means of access to Peter's stronghold on the Lasithi Plateau. Ethelwulf was gambling that, if he heard of the move westwards, Peter wouldn't be tempted to retreat further into the interior.

Hidden in the middle of 'Brimfugol', and disguised in a grey cloak and Varangian helmet, slumped Cleon. He'd never been out to sea before and just as they turned westwards he vomited over the side. After that he started to feel better, and even offered a feeble grin to the grizzly Bardas ordered to guide the vessels to Mallia. For a brief moment Bardas looked puzzled as clearly this man was a Greek like himself. Then he shrugged his shoulders; he'd spent the last twenty years fishing off the northern coasts of Crete and had been promised a year's respite of taxes for a night's work. Now a bargain like that could not be turned down!

After two hours 'Brimfugol' and 'Niflheim's Envoy' reached a point on the coast opposite the trackway branching off towards Galifa and Kastelli, hidden somewhere among the hills and mountains. Here the Varangians silently swung overboard from both vessels and hastily ferried ashore a party of fifteen men led by Ethelwulf. He hadn't liked leaving Morkere back at Chandax, but felt someone with a good knowledge of Greek would be needed to prevent Thorgeis producing a riot.

Stepping ashore Cleon immediately put himself at the head of the group and trotted off up the trackway. With clear reluctance the Varangians following him shifted into a shambling trot. Hallbjorn imagined how Gunnar must be quietly laughing at the physical exertion he'd escaped by volunteering to command the two longships. Having deposited the small force the longships began to make their way slowly further westwards along the coast. Gunnar was to position the two longships as close inshore as he could near the trackway which led up to Gouves. After waiting two hours he was to land two boats and await developments. Meanwhile Cleon was to lead the small landing party into the foothills so they could circle around Gouves and approach the village by a small path from the south-west. Ethelwulf estimated that whatever guards Peter used would be posted to the north of the village, guarding the main approach from the coastal road.

*

During that strange period of night called the "false dawn" Cleon led the Varangian war-party along the narrow path to the south-west of the village. Once they all stopped and listened as they heard the distant wail of goatherd pipes. As they approached the village they could see no lights anywhere; Ethelwulf despatched Hallbjorn and two men to circle around the village and investigate the condition of the track leading northwards to the coast.

After waiting a few moments he slipped into the village, past two small stone-built huts, surprised how little noise his feet made on the stony path. and into the open space which formed the centre of Gouves. Cleon lightly touched Ethelwulf's left shoulder and pointed towards a larger hut to the south of the space. It looked a grim-faced white in the feeble light; on its roof Ethelwulf knew olive leaves would be waiting to dry further in the sun.

At a signal from their leader two Varangians crept towards its large oak-door half-hidden in shadows sprayed out by moonlight. The Wanderer thought he could hear Bjorn's thin knife as it began to work at the lock on the door. He trusted no lock in the village would be the equal of those he'd seen in the imperial capital. He heard a sound and, almost at the same moment, saw Bjorn disappear into the shadows. Quickly Ethelwulf ran across the open space; as he did so he heard a single scream from the house followed by the sound of a table being pulled over. Five Varangians formed a defensive barrier around the doorway as Ethelwulf scrambled into the building, over the body of a naked old man on the floor.

It took a few moments for his eyes to get used to the darkness in the hut, moments when he could hear the village outside coming to life. hen he saw a man swing a club at Bjorn, catching the Varangian heavily on the left shoulder and smashing him against the wall. Thorkel was turning from the bloody female shape which was huddled near the far wall. Ethelwulf saw the club-wielding figure shriek with hatred as it hurled itself at Thorkel. As Thorkel raised his arm in a forlorn attempt to protect his head, Ethelwulf threw himself on the maddened figure. Thorkel collapsed from the powerful blow to his skull but the force of Ethelwulf's charge thrust his assailant's body on top of him. Before the man could move Ethelwulf smashed his face into the rush-strewn floor. The man pushed violently and Ethelwulf found himself falling to the side; then he felt fingers clawing at his face, his throat. He brought his knee up violently into the man's stomach. Somewhere he made contact because he heard a grunt of pain and, for a brief moment, the fingers left his throat. Then he saw another figure and an axe descended rapidly on to the head of the man.

Ethelwulf started to protest and there was harsh laugh from Harold of Furzebrook. "I know when to give a little tap and when to kill," breathed the former outlaw of Purbeck Isle. He helped his leader to his feet, but Ethelwulf immediately sank to one knee and examined the unconscious form. Outside he could hear the clamour of mingled shouts of men and yelps of dogs as the village pushed itself into rescuing the rebel leader. Where were the other rebels Ethelwulf wondered, and then smiled. He remembered Cleon had said that Peter liked to keep his business with the daughter of John secret; the man knew how rivalry between villages and settlements could undermine any insurrection. Well, he thought, looking at the female carcass in the corner, Peter didn't need to worry any longer!

Already Harold had grabbed the unconscious man and roughly thrown him over his shoulder. Ethelwulf hoped this was indeed Peter the Left-handed. Where was Cleon? He stepped out into the open and a large stone whistled past his ear and ricocheted off the lintel. He could see Njal Hammerhand had set fire to three huts to the east of the village. The inhabitants were torn between trying to save these buildings and attacking the ring of armed men which guarded the entrance to the hut of John the Smith. Fortunately they were ill-armed and could cause little damage to determined men.

Bjorn appeared at his side, muttering Thorkel could stay and rot for all he cared. Ethelwulf turned to help the warrior who'd joined them in far-off Dublin but Bjorn hastily added Thorkel was dead anyway. At that Ethelwulf ordered a steady retreat in the direction of the trackway to the sea. Some Varangians offered protection from shields, others charged at the villagers and gained them precious moments as the hate-crazed people scurried for cover. Ethelwulf hoped Hallbjorn had secured the trackway; he didn't want to be caught here as dawn finally broke.

Suddenly he heard Cleon's voice and saw the agitated face of the peasant to his right. Where had the man been just now? It didn't matter. He heard Cleon jabber that two of the villagers had slipped past him, up the way they'd come. So reinforcements were on their way, were they? Ethelwulf ordered his men to start trotting towards the trackway which descended towards the coastal plain. He sensed the remainder of the war-party group behind him as he trotted past what he recognised to be the local cemetery on his left. Now the earliest traces of dawn were showing him the clear and welcoming view of the sea and safety.

Hallbjorn stepped out from behind a tree and shouted the way was clear. Ethelwulf ordered him to stay there and delay any pursuit; at the same time he told Harold to make his prisoner more secure before the man woke up. At this Cleon rushed up to the tall Saxon and yanked up the unconscious head so he could peer into the face of their prisoner. His laugh told Ethelwulf there'd been no mistake; Peter the Left-handed was their prisoner. All they had to do now was to get him to the longships.

As they hurried down the stony path towards the sea Ethelwulf hoped Gunnar had placed the boats in readiness. He didn't know how long Hallbjorn could hold off any rescue attempt; it depended on how many of Peter's men arrived and how many were prepared to risk death at the hands of barbarians.

By now he judged they were half-way to the sea. Behind him there was an outburst of shouting and he was tempted to send back some of his men to help Hallbjorn. No, he remembered Hallbjorn in the forests of the Wends;[175] the man could look after himself.

Soon the trotting Varangians stumbled on to the coastal road between Chandax and Mallia. By now it was clearly daylight and, with great relief, they could see Ulf and Eynar already preparing to push the boats back out to sea.

As his men tumbled into the boats Ethelwulf looked back towards the still burning village of Gouves. Where was Hallbjorn? He ordered Harold to see their prisoner was handed over to Gunnar and helped push one boat out to sea. There were enough spaces in his boat for Hallbjorn and his two men when they arrived.

Suddenly they saw two figures appear from under the scanty trees and shrub which masked the trackway to Gouves, running towards the coastal road. Behind them were at least twenty armed, shouting men. As they watched one of the running figures collapsed with a light javelin in his back. The other one didn't give a second glance at his fallen comrade but dashed across the coastal road and began weaving his way across the broken ground which separated the road from the beach. Now the pursuers saw the longships riding at anchor off the beach and suddenly stopped, screaming abuse at the solitary retreating figure.

It took several moments for Uffe to gasp out that Hallbjorn, after conducting a slow and steady retreat down the trackway to safety, had been caught by a sudden attack from the flank and killed before he could do anything. At that he and Ubbe had run for their lives. Here Uffe paused and a great sadness came into his eyes as he looked back to the crumpled figure lying in the dust on the wrong side of the coastal road. Ethelwulf gently coaxed Uffe into the boat and they set out for 'Brimfugol'.

It was clear Peter was in a bad way. From what Ethelwulf had already learned of Greek manners he knew the Autokrator would prefer to have Peter placed into his hands alive. The prisoner was showing no sign of recovering his conscious state. Reluctantly Ethelwulf decided to put into the port of Eraklion on his way back. He was surprised how, with difficulty, he established some form of communication with Cleon. His knowledge of Greek had grown considerably, and one or two of his men could help out when necessary. Provided Cleon could be persuaded to calm down, repeat phrases, use alternative vocabulary (to by-pass Cretan dialect) and reduce his language to what he might have considered 'baby-talk', reasonable communication was established between Greek and barbarian. It took a little time but Cleon declared he was certain to find a doctor at Eraklion able to ensure that, at least until the official hand-over, Peter would survive.

A small tower on the dock offered a feeble attempt at defence for the port. As it was dawn there were few people around. In fact, the Varangians quickly discovered, through the excited reporting of Cleon, the absence of people was due to a disaster which had occurred the previous evening. There'd been a minor earthquake in the area immediately to the south of the town. It took some time for Ethelwulf to get Cleon to concentrate on the purpose of their detour, the care of their prisoner.

Eventually Cleon located a doctor and the Varangians, shrouding the unconscious form of their prisoner as much as possible, made their way towards the house described to their guide. Ethelwulf realised how impossible it'd have been for them to make their way to such help without the assistance of Cleon. For a moment he wondered why the guide was willing to help the man he hated and had betrayed; then he realised that, in imperial eyes, if matters went wrong, all involved would pay for failure.

The doctor, Leo, proved most uncooperative, declaring he'd enough injuries caused by natural events to care for without having another brought about by human hand. Harold of Furzebrook threatened to use his axe on the doctor, despite Ethelwulf's remonstrances, but the doctor detected the reluctance of the Varangian to carry out any such threat. At this point, Cleon began jabbering and the doctor's mood changed; he leaned forward and, for the first time, closely examined the man on the temporary stretcher of two spears and a spare sail. He brusquely ushered the Varangians and their prisoner into the back room. Cleon whispered to Ethelwulf he'd revealed who the patient was, adding that, if he died, the doctor could expect imperial interference in the affairs of the town for some time. He'd stressed discretion was important as Peter might have supporters in the town who'd attempt a rescue. Ethelwulf nodded and Harold was placed at the door as a sentinel.

The doctor carefully examined Peter and, at last, stood again erect with a satisfied look on his face. He explained, through Cleon, that there was no serious injury; carefully cleaning of the area around the wound should aid recovery and that was what he proposed to do. With a day's rest, Peter would be able to continue his journey.

He was interrupted by a fearful howling and sounds of confusion from the entrance. Harold was just about blocking the entrance of two Greek men screaming for Leo. A small child was missing; Cleon seemed to use the Greek words for 'boy' and 'girl' in different sentences so it was uncertain as to the gender of the child. Anyway, the men were demanding the strangers lounging around in the town with apparent time on their hands could help search for the girl; a more accurate translation might have been 'lazy barbarians help find child' but Ethelwulf avoided being so accurate when he explained the problem to his men. It was agreed Ethelwulf and Gunnar should lead a dozen men to help the locals find the child; Harold of Furzebrook should supervise whatever was done to bring Peter back into a state of consciousness. Ethelwulf hope to distract the inquisitive from the doctor's house while their prisoner recovered. So the detachment was assembled and set off guided by the excitable Greeks.

*

The earthquake had opened up ground just over the hills behind Eraklion. A couple of holes resembling caves had been created and the child, a little girl called Euphemia, had been seen wandering very close to these new 'caves' shortly before she'd disappeared. Obviously curiosity had led the girl into entering a 'cave' and something had prevented her from re-emerging.

"Why you no look for her?" asked Ethelwulf of the large peasant with a grizzled beard who'd been introduced as the girl's uncle.

"Spirits there," answered the man, after failing to communicate with a torrent of Greek. "Want girl, keep girl."

Ethelwulf nodded, disappointed anyone could so easily abandon a loved one. Apparently, the actual parents of the child were still too distraught to be of any use to anyone. He approached the 'cave' and looked inside. Immediately to his left and right the hard ground had been ripped apart. He stepped inside and suddenly felt nothing ahead of him. He paused, foot in empty air, and then hastily withdrew, calling for torches to be brought so he could enter the 'cave'. Meanwhile his men were given the task of exploring other fissures which had suddenly appeared in the area.

At last a torch was brought, lighted and, with it held ahead of him, Ethelwulf re-entered the 'cave'. He discovered the drop into nothingness was a mere yard's depth, not enough to cause much worry to even a ten-year-old girl. He dropped down and was amazed to find himself on a level surface, ducking his head under a chunk of ground which hadn't given way, he was able to stand and became even more awe-struck. He appeared to be standing in some kind of passage and on either side he could see what looked liked dark figures painted on the walls.[176] At first glance they resembled some of the wall paintings which had adorned the cathedral at Winchester. Ethelwulf stopped and returned to the outside, deep in thought, extinguishing the torch as he climbed out of the 'cave'. Immediately he was surrounded by babbling locals whom he shook off.

Gunnar looked at him and Ethelwulf managed a quiet smile.

"Have you ever heard of the Minotaur, Gunnar?" he asked and the Gall-Gael shook his head. "It's a very old story, "explained Ethelwulf," which I was told as a boy." He paused, making sure he had the tale correct in his head as he briefly described how Theseus had travelled to a palace in Crete, killed a monster that lurked there, won a princess and returned home. "Now the monster, half-man and half-bull, lived in an underground maze." He saw the bewildered expression on the faces of Gunnar and the two other Varangians who'd been drawn to the story. "That's a series of passages which so twist and turn people can become easily lost, and so they couldn't escape the Minotaur."[177]

"Is this true?" asked Thorgrim Spear-Catcher.

"Perhaps," answered Ethelwulf. "It was all so long ago that truth and lies mingle together into legend." He looked back at the entrance to the 'cave'. "But there was a palace on this island, belonging to a king called Minos - of that I'm certain. And I think God has opened up an entrance to that palace to us."

"Is the monster still there?" asked Gunnar, almost relishing the task of tackling such a creature.

"I doubt if it ever was, Gunnar," answered the Wanderer with a quiet smile, "Can you imagine bull and woman copulating to produce such offspring." One look at Gunnar's face showed Ethelwulf the Gall-Gael could indeed imagine such a coupling so he didn't pursue the matter. "Anyway, if I've stumbled on what remains of that maze the girl may well be lost in its coils - and we have to look for her!"

There were nods from Thorgrim and Wulfstan, though Gunnar seemed less enthusiastic about that than tackling the monster which, suddenly presented to him, had been snatched away.

"I'll want another four men," said Ethelwulf, "and, at least, five long skeins of different coloured wool." He saw the bewilderment on his men's faces and laughed. "The way Theseus got into the maze and out again was by marking his path with a long thread of wool, which the princess had given him."[178] He saw the men grin and nod. "He was going to one place, the centre where the monster lived. We may well have to go different ways looking for the girl." The men didn't look so enthusiastic about that. "Don't worry, lads, if the monster ever existed he'd have died a long time ago!" His laughter died as he suddenly realised other dangers might be hidden away in the maze. "However, we must take care because I'm sure creatures such as snakes might well have found the open spaces of the passages welcome retreats from the heat of the sun."

*

It didn't take the villagers long to collect together what Ethelwulf required, although none volunteered to accompany him under the earth. They'd all been well-schooled into how ghosts peopled this whole site and humans had been suddenly snatched away before and never returned. Ethelwulf gave a skein of blue wool to Gunnar, a green skein to Thorgrim, a white skein to Wulfstan and kept a red skein for himself. He explained each of them should pick one other warrior to work with; whenever they'd cross a passage which went off in another direction one pair should branch off and follow that passage, using the wool to mark their trail. Once they'd reached the end of the wool they should stop and return. He certainly had no intention of losing any men!

"What about the fifth skein?" asked Wulfstan and Ethelwulf said the black skein would be used to mark the main route back to the entrance. Each leader should take a smooth stone as an anchor for their skein when they left the main path, while the black wool would be anchored to a rock at the entrance. "Remember, men," he concluded, "we don't know what's there, so be careful."

"How will we tell the others we've found the girl?" put in Bjorn.

"We won't! Just make your way back to the entrance with the girl and wait for the rest of us."

With that he lowered himself back into the passage, followed by the others. At first there was an excited chattering as they looked at the figures painted on the sides of the passage; tall slim figures standing, crouching, jumping; sometimes there were pictures of what looked like bulls; usually, however, decoration consisted of mere patterns, picked out in red and black against the dull grey of what felt like plaster.[179] As they made their way along the passage, with only the torches of Ethelwulf (at the front) and Gunnar (at the rear) alight, the men became used to the figures which attracted less interest. What did attract attention, however, was the occasional rustle from ahead of them, presumably caused by whatever small creatures had settled in these passages and were having their world invaded by men. Periodically Ethelwulf would stop and call out "Euphemia" but there was never any reply.

At last they came to a turning to the left and Ethelwulf detailed both Thorgrim and Gunnar, with their partners, to go down that passage, explaining there almost certainly was some division to be explored. He waited as they disappeared into the darkness ahead. Some time after what light came from their torches had vanished he thought he could still hear them shuffling along the passages and certainly heard the gruff voice of Gunnar as he called out for the girl.

At last the black skein gave out and Ethelwulf was forced to start using the red skein as their guide. Almost immediately a passage appeared on the right and Wulfstan was directed along it, first anchoring his white skein to a stone which he deposited in the main passage. Again Ethelwulf waited as he heard Wulfstan and Bjorn disappear into the unknown. Eventually he heard Wulfstan cry out the girl's name but there was no reply. Ethelwulf shrugged and turned to Njal Hammerhand.

"So Njal, we're left by ourselves to find the lost Persephone!"[180] Njal looked perplexed but Ethelwulf merely laughed, judging he'd had enough explaining of classical tales for one day. They carried on in silence, given scant comfort by the flickering light illuminating the designs on the walls which had ceased to be of any interest to them. At last they reached a junction between two passages and Ethelwulf had to decide which way to go. He called loudly down both passages in turn waiting for any response; there was none, merely his voice gradually being muffled as it echoed down each passage. In the end he took the right-hand passage and they stalked along it until the skein ran out. Then Ethelwulf shouted again 'Euphemia', but without result. So they returned to the fork, recovering the wool as they went. Here Njal suggested they now try the other passage to see if the girl had gone that way. Reluctantly, as he could see the torch was starting to burn down, Ethelwulf agreed. They followed the other passage until again the skein ran out, but without success.

Now they turned back, frustrated at their lack of success and Ethelwulf urged Njal to make all speed as he could see the torch was clearly beginning to flicker out. They moved into a trot as they retraced their passage along the path shown by the red skein. Of course, they only had to be careful when they came to any junction and Ethelwulf considered he should have merely placed strips at such spots, thereby saving much of the skein and so enabling deeper penetration of the passage structure. Nevertheless, he immediately realised the life of the torch wouldn't have allowed them to explore much more of the passages anyway.

At last they reached the black skein path and continued trotting, not daring to stop to call out Euphemia's name as the torch was definitely flickering to extinction. They reached the junction where Wulfstan had broken away and continued without even pausing to see if the white skein remained in position. Soon afterwards the torch flickered out of existence and they were in total darkness.

Immediately they both stopped. The only sound they could hear was their own breathing, coming in bursts as they recovered from their rush towards the entrance. Furiously Ethelwulf tried to remember where Gunnar and Thorgrim had turned off and realised he couldn't even recall on which side of the main passage the new path had lain. He asked Njal but the Varangian had no idea. They called out for anyone to hear them but only heard their own voices disappear into emptiness. They felt very alone.

At last they recovered their breathing and Njal suggested they slowly make their way along the passage, beating the walls to discover where the turning lay. Fortunately Ethelwulf had immediately ordered Njal NOT to turn round when the light failed, so they knew in which direction to go, otherwise they might have gone AWAY from safety. Slowly they crept, like two blind men, whistling to keep up their spirits as they rhythmically beat the walls to ensure they didn't miss the passage. At last, Njal yelled out he'd found the turning and they froze, furiously trying to ensure they remained on the correct line and didn't wander off on to the passage explored by Gunnar. As they stood there Ethelwulf yelled out but there was no reply. Both men were sweating - and not just because of whatever heat was underground. It was like a nightmare.

Having decided on their path, they carried on, beating the walls, increasingly disorientated, unsure of whether there'd been another turning between them and the main entrance. They stopped, uncertain where they were and terrified by the slight sounds around them as whatever life had made its home in those passages accustomed itself to their presence. Ethelwulf realised that whatever protection their swords might have offered them when they could see had disappeared in the blackness. Again they yelled out and there was no response. Should they stay where they were and await rescue? Were they in the right passage? If they'd taken the wrong turning they'd never be discovered. Ethelwulf regretted ever undertaking the search for Euphemia; then found himself regretting ever entering the Empire of the Greeks. What a way to perish! Nearby he could sense Njal and was certain the Varangian shared what amounted to his anger.

Again they cried for help and, to increase the volume, shouted together. Once more their voices were muffled in the darkness but they thought they heard an answering cry. Ethelwulf shouted again and was certain he heard a sound that could be no echo. They waited for what seemed hours and then shouted again. As they did they saw light entering the passage. Within moments they'd been found by Gunnar and others with fresh torches. They were saved.

*

A couple of hours later, back on the surface and having gulped down what seemed the most beautiful water they'd ever drunk in their lives, they were told of the experiences of the others. It had been Thorgrim, with his brother, who'd discovered the body of the missing girl She must have encountered a snake sheltering in the darkness underground. It was amazing the girl had travelled so far before she'd met death. Ethelwulf could easily imagine the terror as the child had stumbled on lost and in darkness, not knowing whether she was going towards or away from safety. He looked at her features which showed little alarm as death had snatched her - perhaps it had been a relief from the terror along the passages.

Once recovered he advised the locals to fill in the 'cave', assuring them there was no treasure to be found but merely death. He was tempted to delay departure so he could supervise the operation, to prevent another tragedy, but decided he couldn't afford the time. Quickly he made his way back to the main town of Eraklion where he found Peter had returned to consciousness. Ethelwulf was delighted. At least something had turned out right!

*

The absence of Morkere on the quayside as 'Brimfugol' and "Niflheim's Envoy' made their way slowly into Chandax was worrying. Ethelwulf knew his cousin should have been there as arranged, making sure Thorgeis was in order. In fact, as Ethelwulf stepped on to land Thorgeis swaggered drunkenly into view. He couldn't bother to try and hide his glee at Ethelwulf's discomfiture.

"Looking for your little cousin?" he laughed and swayed from side to side as he made sure his laughter was taken up by the half-dozen men who accompanied him. Ethelwulf made no response but turned and waited for Gunnar, Bjorn and Leofwine to join him. Seeing the murderous glint which crept into Gunnar's eyes he hastily stepped close to Thorgeis.

"I did expect Morkere to be here to receive me," he paused and fixed Thorgeis with a cold stare. "I felt that perhaps you might have more urgent business -"

"Than to welcome back our heroic - our ever-victorious captain?" sneered the drunken Rus, leaning so close to Ethelwulf that alcoholic fumes poured into his face. Ethelwulf recoiled and stepped back; Thorgeis turned and laughed at his audience. "Wait till that crafty Greek governor tells you what he's done to your precious Morkere - " He said no more as Ethelwulf's left fist thumped into his stomach. As Thorgeis slumped forward, badly winded and his face reddened, Ethelwulf seized his belt and pitched him straight into the sea.

Now it was the turn of Gunnar and Leofwine to roar with laughter at the spluttering, struggling figure in the water below. Two of his companions rushed to the edge of the quayside to offer help, and Gunnar pushed both of them off dry land to join their leader.

"It seems there's great need for sobering treatment," he laughed, and then added grimly, "both here and at the tribunal". Ethelwulf frowned; let Thorgeis and his men make their own way ashore, he needed to know what had happened to Morkere NOW!

Ethelwulf quickly ordered Leofwine to take 'Brimfugol' back out of the harbour with Peter the Left-handed on board. If there was any need to negotiate with the governor about anything then his prisoner might be a key factor. He looked down at Thorgeis grabbing at a convenient rope trailing down into the water. Could he trust Thorgeis? No, but it would take time for him to get together enough force to give him the courage to act. Bjorn was despatched to the camp outside the Hanion Gate to bring the crews of 'Brimfugol' and 'Niflheim's Envoy' to hold the quayside.

Now it was time to find out what had happened to his cousin. Followed closely by Gunnar, Ethelwulf hurried to the tribunal of Michael Theophilus.

He pushed his way past market stalls as he headed for the tribunal near the Gate of Jesus. On his left he noted a leather-seller spitting in his direction but he shrugged off the temptation to draw his sword and cut into the man's skull. This was not the time to start a riot. Ahead a small number of stall-holders had deserted their living and seemed about to oppose his progress. Ethelwulf was just in the mood for a fight and he could sense his fury was shared by the Gall-Gael at his side. Instantly he realised that if he was on the point of exploding into violence, there was a far greater chance of Gunnar resorting to mayhem. Ethelwulf stopped and lightly placed his fingers against the arm of the giant. He could feel the Gall-Gael was barely in control of himself.

"No, Gunnar!" he whispered and sensed the Gall-Gael relax. It took some time for the mood change to take effect and Ethelwulf was concerned the small huddle ahead might decide to move on to the attack. However, they seemed to have thought the better of taking on armed men with their bare-hands and dispersed. The Varangians passed on, trying to stay calm. Everything appeared normal - still hostile stares and the occasional muttered remark. Beside him Gunnar tightened his grip on his axe.

Nobody dared to stand in his way as he stormed into the tribunal, shouting for Michael Theophilus. He heard a movement in the balcony above his head and looked up to see the supercilious face of the governor looking down at him.

"How dare you so rudely enter our tribunal," Michael struggled to keep his voice even.

"Where is Morkere Aelfheresson, Greek?" bellowed Gunnar, fortunately in unintelligible Norse, and threatening to mount the stairs leading to the balcony. Ethelwulf restrained his rush, aware suddenly of three guards who'd rushed into the hall behind him.

"We have the warrant of the Eparchos," stated Ethelwulf rapidly calming down. "We've been acting on imperial business -"

"Yes, Greek," screamed Gunnar, again in words unintelligible to anyone but Ethelwulf. "Have you turned traitor to your emperor?"

"Watch our backs, Gunnar!" hissed Ethelwulf and then turned his attention again to Michael. "Where is Morkere Aelfheresson? " he paused and his voice was scarcely above a whisper. "We've been told you would know -"

"And do your imperial orders permit you barbarians to rape our virgins?" sneered the governor, his hands gripping the balustrade.

"What?" shouted Ethelwulf. What did this haughty Greek mean, with his ill-disguised contempt for anyone born outside the Empire?

"The one you call Morkere was seized four hours ago in the bed of my daughter, Theophano -"

"But you said 'raped'-" interrupted Ethelwulf, desperately trying to work out how things could have gone so dramatically wrong in a few hours. He knew Morkere had been drawn to the girl, and she'd clearly returned his feelings. There had been many women in the life of the black-haired warrior in the last ten years; Ethelwulf was sure the governor's daughter would be no different.

"No daughter of mine would willingly soil herself with a barbarian, " spat out Michael, his long nose sniffing out the disdain felt for those not sharing the blessings of civilisation. Michael paused and fixed his angry brown eyes on Ethelwulf who'd taken two steps up the stairs towards him." This morning we'll give him a fair trial, much more than he deserves, and he'll be blinded and castrated tomorrow as the law demands -"

Ethelwulf half drew his sword and made to rush up the stairs. Michael yelled to his guards for help, but their eyes were focused on the war-axe which Gunnar teasingly swung before him. Michael decided to retreat towards his bedroom door, perhaps it could be barred and more help summoned.

Suddenly Ethelwulf laughed and pushed his sword back in its scabbard. "If you do any such thing, Greek," he spoke, with a horribly-pointed gentleness," I'll return Peter the Left-handed to his friends in the hills -"

"Traitor!" spat out Michael, knowing it would only be a matter of time before Peter battered his way into Chandex itself. Then a worse thought struck him; what if this barbarian really did turn traitor, become the pirate all these creatures really were? He'd five ships already within the harbour itself. What damage could he cause? Would he call in Saracens to help in the pillage? For the first time Michael was struck by the potential threat in Ethelwulf's position and his mouth suddenly went dry.

Ethelwulf sensed the hesitancy, the weakness of this popinjay above him. He didn't waste time but baldly offered Michael an exchange, Morkere for Peter - providing both men were unharmed.

"And what will you tell the Autokrator?" asked Michael, realising here might be a way out of his difficulties, but still anxious to get some revenge on this barbarian.

"Nothing!" answered Ethelwulf and Michael held back a smile from his lips. So he'd be able to report to the Eparchos this barbarian had offered to join in rebellion against the Empire; he was sure the capital would know how to deal with such treason. Michael found himself almost too eager to agree, insisting the Varangians should provide an escort for the captured rebel to the Autokrator.

Ethelwulf hesitated; why was this Greek being so eager to compromise? He'd already learned that what passed as honesty in this Empire was simply a mask. Perhaps the man was genuinely frightened - but surely he didn't imagine he'd join the rebels in an attack on Chandax itself. He stared hard at the governor, trying to penetrate the facade of superiority which was taking over. Anyway there was little else he could do; Morkere had to be freed and, if it meant pandering to this Greek, so be it.

*

The deal was made and Morkere quickly released from the prison cells of the governor's tribunal. He didn't seem at all put out by his experiences and, when Morkere even suggested Theophano had been worth it, Ethelwulf was almost tempted to return him to the governor. Instead he handed over Peter to four guards sent by the governor. There was a strange pitying look in the tall rebel's eyes as he stared at Ethelwulf during the hand-over. Did he somehow sense the deal which had been struck; perhaps seeing the compromise would bring the Varangian no good? Whatever it was, he made no sound as he was manacled by the guards and then bustled away in the direction of the governor's tribunal.

Thorgeis sulked in the Varangian camp for two days and then hurried off to the governor. What he managed to communicate in his minimal Greek Ethelwulf didn't know, but the next day Thorgeis re-appeared, sporting a long blue robe of silk, and announced the governor had decided to accept his crew into his personal guard, so they'd be staying at Chandax. Ethelwulf was delighted - mainly because it removed one problem from his return to the capital.

*

Three days later Ethelwulf was making the last preparations for the return to the capital of 'Brimfugol'. They'd escort the 'Eudocia' under Theophanes of Samos, a loud-voiced honest sailor, who was anxiously awaiting the arrival of the prisoner for take to the capital.

A flurry of noise from the main street caused both captains to turn in that direction. A squadron of guards, Varangians headed by Thorgeis himself, were rapidly approaching. In their midst was Peter the Left-handed. However, when they halted at the quayside, everyone could see Peter was no longer the proud, defeated rebel they'd last seen. The man dragged forward by two Varangians was a broken, frightened wretch; one whose sightless eyes betrayed some of the suffering endured over the past three days. Ethelwulf stepped forward as the prisoner was brutally pushed up the ramp leading to the 'Eudoxia' but stopped at the unearthly gibberish which poured out from a mouth deprived of a tongue. Why did the Greeks have to do this? Why not simply kill a man, not mutilate him and leave him to rot in some obscure hole in the Empire?

As Peter fell on to the deck of the 'Eudocia' his grunts became more insistent. Theophanes turned his back and glared at the gawking Varangians as his prisoner was dragged below to be chained near the slaves. Ethelwulf heard Morkere whispering curses by his side and almost snapped out the order to get ready to leave for the capital. He'd had enough of Chandax.

*

The voyage to the capital was without incident and, despite occasional thoughts drifting across to the cargo of the 'Eudocia', pleasant. No Saracen pirate appeared to try and intercept the convoy and by the time the Harbour of Hormisdas came into sight, Ethelwulf was shuffling off Chandax as a rather nasty memory.

The Quaestor seemed pleased to see them, and almost desperate Ethelwulf should be present when Peter the Left-handed was presented to the Autokrator. He was being plagued by an irritating cold but, in between sneezes and attempts to free phlegm from his throat, he told Ethelwulf of the arrival of fresh strangers from the lands of the Rus. John Angelus was somewhat put out Ethelwulf didn't appear so enthusiastic about newcomers from Kenugard.

However, the newcomers had merely passed through the territories of Vladimir on their way down from Sweden. They had known little of the ruler of Kenugard, just wanting to keep themselves to themselves. However, they did bring welcome news of further humiliation for Sweyn Haraldsson and his jackals, the Jomsvikings; this time at the hands of the men of the western lands.[181] Some of the arrivals were willing to join Ethelwulf as a fighting force at Miklagard; most, however, merely wanted to complete their business and then travel home. Ethelwulf trusted they wouldn't spread word among the Rus of his whereabouts; pressure from Prince Vladimir of Kenugard might still force him into further flight.

One day, however, a summons arrived to attend the imperial palace of the Mangana; with the message came from silver-edged blue robes to be worn when they entered the presence of the Autokrator. Rather awkwardly Ethelwulf and Morkere tried on the new robes; apart from the length they found them quite acceptable, although not as workmanlike as their normal tunics and leggings.

Gunnar was adamant at first against even trying on such "unmanly" garments. Only when Ethelwulf threatened to teach him respect with 'Claw'[182] did Gunnar stop laughing at the appearance of his companions, mincing his way up and down their quarters like a whore skirting the puddles of the city. Morkere pointed out the imperial practice to give largess personally to trusted followers;[183] if Gunnar wasn't present he couldn't expect to share in any reward. This changed Gunnar's mind; silver was silver, but he still refused to try out his new robes beforehand.

*

Two weeks later the Gall-Gael stood nervously fingering the silver-edging of his robe. Steadfastly he kept his eyes on his sandaled toes so as to avoid the malicious glint which refused to desert Morkere's eyes. Neither of his companions said a word as he joined them at the entrance to the imperial quarters.

When they heard the silver trumpets blast out the fanfare compelling silence as the imperial procession entered, Ethelwulf remembered how he'd once mistaken the Eparchos for the Autokrator himself. How innocent he must have appeared in those days! Even so, the Eparchos did look more majestic than his master, though now his robes were easily outshone by those of both the joint-emperors.

Alexius Euergetes looked down at the three Varangians standing quietly just inside the entrance. How ridiculous barbarians looked in the trappings of civilisation, even robes of mere Clarissimi.[184] How right Michael was to report their disgraceful conduct; yet the man was a fool to send Peter to the Autokrator in that condition. Indeed, it made sure Peter's earlier friendly discussions with the governor wouldn't be mentioned, even with the help of imperial interrogation. However, it resulted in the Autokrator giving exaggerated credence to the account of the Quaestor of the seizure of the rebel, especially when supported by the comments of that fool,Theophanes.

The Eparchos offered a slim smile to Ethelwulf as he felt the Varangian's gaze on him. "Oh, I've such matters to settle with you," he thought, remembering how the blundering of these men had ruined earlier plans. If only he could make the Autokrator understand how they'd challenged imperial authority in Chandax; nevertheless, the possession of Peter standing there before him silenced all comment. Indeed, the Eparchos was forced to spend most of his energies countering the Autokrator's suspicions at the mutilations of the rebel. Finally he managed to get Peter the Left-handed hustled away to the monastery of St. Mark near Nicaea; later, perhaps, the man would be permanently silenced.

The Autokrator and his co-emperor graciously acknowledged the short anthem by the Kractae[185] especially produced by the Praepositus Manuel.[186] The Eparchos recalled how he'd endured a private rehearsal three days ago. The obese composer had been so proud of the allusions to "light to the Gentiles" and "light coming to those embroiled in death."[187] Naturally. the Basileus knew that through him barbarians might come to know the Lord and salvation, but the words had been used before when that monster from Kenugard had dared demand an imperial princess for his bride. Indeed some barbarians already claimed to be Christians, although shrouded in the perversities of the bishop of Rome.

The Eparchos was suddenly aware of the imperial eye fixed on him; he'd been dreaming, forgetting to hand personally to the Autokrator the illuminated scroll to make these barbarians members of the Tagmatikoi. Blushing he surrendered the document and was rewarded by a cold stare from his master. He must explain his abstraction as being due to affairs of state. The Autokrator would appreciate the alarming news from Berrhoea; it was time the so-called Tsar of the Bulgarians[188] was brought to order.

Constantine was content to let his brother hand over the scroll to this tall, handsome barbarian in front of them. He liked yielding to his elder brother, to make him feel important so he could while away the hours at the theatre or even better at the table or with those hordes of women who suddenly discovered his attractions.

He smiled at the barbarian in front of him, admiring his strength and wandering how such a warrior would have fared in the gladiatorial contests one thousand years ago. If only he'd been alive then; able freely to indulge his passions without the restraint of the church. Yes, the man looked strong but so did they all; how pleasurable it would be to challenge just one of them to a mock combat. He glanced aside at his brother. If only Basil would agree to re-introduce the gymnopodia[189] and let the citizens see the war-like skills practice in the Hippodrome.

Now the barbarian was reaching forward and taking the scroll from the imperial hand. He was mumbling some sentence or other in abysmal Greek. If only, thought Constantine, he could be taken in hand and schooled in the art of declaiming the words of Homer or Hesiod. No, better perhaps to learn from the barbarian the skill of handling a war-axe like his companion was so fiercely holding. Now that was a weapon to use on your opponents. Constantine imagined using height and reach to beat down any opposition one of his "play-mates" might offer. It was a pleasant thought.

Constantine was jerked back into reality by a whispered comment from his brother. Of course he'd join his brother that evening in a private dinner to honour their triumph. He wondered who else would make up the twelve places at the table.[190]

*

John Angelus was horrified to receive an invitation to dinner for himself and his three barbarian protégés. He knew how to behave in front of the Autokrator, but did the three barbarians? Quickly he called them into his chamber and, despite the protests of both Ethelwulf and Gunnar, deliberately schooled them in the art of civilised dining. If Morkere alone had been invited, then the Quaestor would have been more confident; the dark-haired warrior had rapidly acquired an appreciation of both Greek language and manners. With a little more practice he would be almost worthy of dining with the emperor. However, there was little hope for the other two, and the Quaestor even toyed with the idea of inducing sickness so that they'd be unable to attend; yet to do that might invite critical scrutiny from the Eparchos, and that could mean ruin. John was sure the Eparchos had suggested the small dinner party; he was equally sure the motive had been to bring down imperial wrath on himself. If only he could be sure of all three barbarians.

The Quaestor managed to get promises of good behaviour at the meal from all three men. Gunnar even offered to avoid any wine, but John hastily pointed out that only followers of the enemy of God avoided that gift of the Almighty. Morkere intervened by saying he'd make sure Gunnar wouldn't undermine his obvious appeal by drinking too much. Ethelwulf asked for suggested topics on which the Quaestor believed it would be safer to talk. After the Quaestor had briefly described the interests and passions of the co-emperors, between them they managed to list three such topics - none of them included Crete which John felt might hold too many opportunities for the Eparchos to raise embarrassing questions.

When the Quaestor and his protégés entered the gold-ceilinged dining room at the Mangana he was further alarmed by the other guests who made up the twelve at table. Naturally he'd expected the Autokrator to have invited his brother and the Eparchos to the meal; he had not, however, dreamed that seated there would be the three daughters of Constantine.

The eldest, Eudocia, was a sullen young woman, embittered by the ravages of smallpox which had lessened her opportunities for marriage with one of the more powerful families of the state. The youngest, Theodora, was still a child and so liable to burst out with any pointed question which might provoke an unguarded reply. The most dangerous of the three was the beautiful and spoilt Zoe, already capable of playing along a man until he'd said or committed any stupidity. And his three charges would be fitting playthings for her venomous mix of flirtatious wit and shrewd interrogation.[191]

Fortunately the other two guests were the Drungarius,[192] Nicephorus Ducas, and the Orthanotrophus,[193] John Palaeologus. Neither of these men posed any threat; indeed the bluntness and innocence of Nicephorus might well act as a diversion for the spite of the young Zoe.

The Quaestor was also pleased Morkere was placed between Zoe and Eudocia; he could rely on the young man to be discreet. Ethelwulf was manoeuvred between himself and the Orphanotrophus, a reasonably safe position. At the risk of leaving the Eparchos reclining next to the Autokrator, the Quaestor managed to position himself opposite the dangerous Zoe. The most seriously exposed risk remained Gunnar who'd been positioned opposite Morkere; the Quaestor trusted he could head off any queries by Zoe and rely on Theodora to be so over-awed by the occasion as to keep quiet. What conversation Constantine might choose to make could never be foreseen; the one advantage being that the rapid speech of the co-emperor might completely defeat Gunnar and allow him to be dismissed as an ignorant fool.[194]

As it turned out, Gunnar proved to be an unexpected success at the meal. Too far away to be exposed by questions from the Eparchos or Autokrator, he delighted Constantine by a description of the technique of fighting with the war-axe, all delivered in execrable Greek. John sensed Eudocia was quietly amused by the clumsiness of the language and Theodora clearly horrified by the image of the wounds inflicted by the weapon. Her horror almost seemed to excite Constantine who took the unusual measure of slowing down his words so that his questions could be grasped by the barbarian. Twice Zoe tried to intrude into this conversation but was successfully side-tracked by Morkere into describing the standards of conduct expected of an imperial princess.

The Quaestor was intrigued by Zoe's fascination with the warrior sitting on his left. Ethelwulf had become quite animated as he described barbarian naval tactics and asked about the imperial weapon of Greek fire.[195] Their discussion clearly interested the Autokrator and John was pleased to see the Eparchos was forced to stay largely silent during the discussion on account of limited knowledge. The Orthanotrophus was content to concentrate on the marinated poultry and extravagantly-garnished vegetables placed before him.

John found he was able to attend properly to the delightful morsels offered at the meal. However, he made certain he constantly monitored the conversations going on around him. He also contrived to limit Gunnar's intake of wine, with the amused assistance of Morkere.

All in all, by the end of the meal John Angelus was feeling much more relaxed. He smiled as he heard Gunnar volunteer to demonstrate the power of the war-axe to Constantine and nodded agreement as Ethelwulf asked for a chance to see Greek fire in action. A frown only appeared on the Quaestor's face as he failed to overhear the whispered comments by Morkere in Zoe's right ear which seemed to give her so much amusement. Perhaps he'd been wrong in being so confident in Morkere.

*

The Wanderer 8:3

"A moth eating up words?
Hearing this I wondered
How a moth could consume
A man's song; a thief munch in darkness
Fine words of a great man.
The thief was no wiser
By his meal of words."
(Exeter Riddle Book: A Book Worm)

The Missing Manuscript

The Eparchos was furious. How had any idiot let a manual produced by a dead imperial cretin be stolen? Fortunately, he'd a very good idea of the identity of the thief – and had decided on who should recover the document. Michael Bryennios was a member of one of those aristocratic families which he so despised. Even so, the young man was fuelled by an ambition which made him a serviceable tool. Of course, the diplomat would require protection and that was where the Varangians came in.

He'd already explained matters as fully as he intended to the young aristocrat; now he intended to supply a cut-down version for barbarian minds. Alexius Euergetes, although officially the City Prefect or Eparchos for the capital of the civilised world, was much more than that, thanks to the efforts of the last few years. Whatever shouldn't have been his business BECAME his business; the Eparchos was determined his influence should be seen wherever imperial power existed. So he had involved himself with the disappearance of part of the *'To our own son, Romanus"* by the grandfather of the Autokrator.[196] It was an interesting work – he'd already made extensive use of its ideas – and quite well written. However, it had been designated as TOP SECRET because, above all else, of comments about some of the peoples on the imperial borders. Why should the Autokrator worry about the barbarians? Because the whole aim of the book was to help the Empire play off one barbarian power against another, exploiting its geographical and diplomatic advantages. For this to work the barbarians had to be kept in a state of ignorance; and now the book had been stolen!

In front of him stood two of the imperial servants he most hated: Ethelwulf and his cousin, Morkere, had already interfered in his schemes with ghastly results. Fortunately for THEM, he hastily added in his thoughts, they'd blundered into his schemes and still seemed totally unaware of reality. Ethelwulf was tall and strongly built, his handsome features marred both by a scar along his jawline and an usually doleful expression. His cousin was slightly shorter, though still much taller than the typical Byzantine subject; his mastery of the Greek language had secured him more friends, despite also possessing frequent bouts of depression due to the death of his brother in Russia. Thank God, Our Everlasting Lord and Master, added the Eparchos to himself, realising three meddlers would have exceeded the intrusion of two.

Outwardly, however, he smiled with the oiliness of a practised snake and began by congratulating the Varangians with their successes in serving the Empire. Of course, he didn't speak the sentences with any sincerity but then he could be sure neither of the men in front of him believed a word.

"We're faced with a crisis," he admitted. "Our servant chosen to deal with this crisis is an administrator, and not a fighter, so he needs protection." He leaned forward as if to impart some dark secret with his long neck resembling that of a vulture about to feast on its prey. "The Autokrator himself insisted you two would be the best for the task." Actually he himself had suggested them, though the Autokrator, after a slight hesitation, had been most supportive.

He noted the effect of flattery passing over the features of Ethelwulf, clearly the man yearned to be valued and such men were riddled with weaknesses. However, as neither Varangian said anything, the Eparchos felt obliged to carry on. "A valuable, and most secret, book has been stolen from the Imperial Library and must be recovered." He noticed the look of puzzlement appearing on Ethelwulf's face. "The work was produced by the Autokrator's grandfather, as advice for his successors." He felt the need to add, " – and very good advice," just to show his loyalty.

"Why would it be stolen?" asked the dark-haired Varangian.

"Not because anybody could sell it or pass it on as an heirloom," scoffed the Eparchos, almost letting his guard down. "No, it's merely its author was too honest, too open in his judgements."

How unlike yourself, thought Ethelwulf but said nothing. It rarely paid to ask questions when dealing with the Eparchos. The answers were either lies or liable to be superseded without notice.

"So we should consider who would most like to examine it," asked Ethelwulf but delivered the question as if it were really a statement.

The Eparchos was irritated. Barbarians weren't supposed to think; they were there to obey orders and save Greek lives by sacrificing their own. If he answered that question he'd be forced to reveal more about the loss than he wished, so the Eparchos ignored it.

"You'll be assisting Michael Bryennios," he explained," and he alone is authorised to examine the work when it's recovered."

"So it's not for our eyes," stated Morkere and the Eparchos nodded. That means, thought Morkere, we'll have to persuade this 'Michael' to reveal details the Eparchos has withheld.

"When do we start?" asked Ethelwulf and the Eparchos smiled; that was more like it, a request for orders.

"You'll meet Michael Bryennios in the Imperial Library at dawn tomorrow morning." The Eparchos loved the ill-disguised half-protest forming on Ethelwulf's lips. "You'll have much to do and little time to do it in." There was a brief pause before he concluded, "You are dismissed."

*

Michael Bryennios didn't look at home in the Imperial Library. Perhaps the pallor of his skin and the slight hunch in his shoulders might have resembled the appearance of scribes busying themselves in odd corners, but the slanted, cat-like eyes and the harsh mouth were truly the inheritance of generations of privileged inbreeding. His welcome was affable while retaining that air of superiority the Saxons had come to expect in dealing with members of the upper echelons of the Imperial Administration. Michael's dress revealed him to be a Spectabilis, reasonably elevated in the administrative hierarchy but not awe-inspiring. However, clearly he thought the Varangians serviceable but not really worthy of respect.

Ethelwulf's attention was drawn to the bewildering array of materials stored all around them, some bound and some in manuscript form. The Imperial Library possessed a dreadful history of damage by fire[197] and he was amazed at how much had been preserved, forgetting the repeated requisition of copies from all over the Empire to make up for losses. Fortunately, Morkere's attention was focused on their companion because a slight cough from his cousin dragged Ethelwulf's attention back to the official soon after the Spectabilis had started speaking.

"........ Your task will be simply to ensure my personal safety. I've been advised the thief may well be an Apokrisiaros[198] called

Theodosius Phocas as he was the last individual with recorded access to the missing volume."

"Why would he need to access the book?" asked Morkere and his question was rewarded with a glare from the Spectabilis.

"You are not to ask questions but merely take orders!" the bureaucrat snapped. "As this is the first – and only – occasion for you to breach that rule I'll answer. He informed the Assistant Librarian, who has since been disciplined, that he needed to research imperial relations with the non-believers during the reign of the founder of the present glorious dynasty."

Michael noted a slight stiffening in the stance of the dark-haired Varangian but was gratified no protest followed. He didn't realise Morkere had excellent access to the gossip-factory which riddled the lower levels of the Imperial Administration. Knowing the name of the suspect and the area of concern should make it relatively straight-forward to fill in the details without resort to this buffoon.

Michael continued, "I know the address of this individual and we are to go there this afternoon. As far as I'm aware, the man hasn't left imperial employment and is awaiting his time to profit from the crime." He failed to see the sceptical look on Ethelwulf's face.

*

During the morning Morkere discovered Theodosius Phocas had been born in Sicily, just before the island had been lost to the Saracens. When he heard the missing section was about the Moslem neighbours of the Empire and how they should be treated he linked the two together, sure that Theodosius must be planning to flee westwards – assuming, of course, he was the culprit. But Ethelwulf insisted the Spectabilis had made it obvious that any thinking to be done was not for them; they were merely barbarian muscle standing by as he led them up one blind alley after another.

Morkere started to protest but instead muttered, with a shrug, "After all, the Greeks have always insisted our swords are valued rather than our brains."

"Although I'd like to see Sicily rather than the miserable gorges of the Bulgar realm," mumbled Ethelwulf to himself, unaware Morkere had heard the words and just managed a smile. He too would like to see what had been the most western outpost of the Empire but accepted they were bound by whatever ideas their Greek superiors might conjure up.

Theodosius Phocas, despite his illustrious name,[199] had been forced to live in a run-down street to the north of the Cistern of Aetius but not right up against what survived of the Walls of Theodosius. Miklagard was easily the largest city the Varangians had seen and they wondered how its inhabitants kept their sanity. Everybody's life seemed to intrude on their neighbour and the chance of getting away to be by oneself was denied to most. Indeed, both looked forward to campaigns as an escape, even though the Varangians were somewhat sheltered from the mass of citizens.

The Apokrisiaros had been forced by financial pressures to rent a small apartment on the third floor of a grubby tenement in a street which had probably seen its best days under the Isaurian Dynasty.[200] Naturally outside it had three members of the begging community, two of whom claimed to be monks. None of them dared challenge Michael as he bustled his way through the entrance to the tenement, followed by two armed and tough-looking barbarians.

On the way the Spectabilis insisted the suspect had been rumoured to have money-problems, debts left by the insane speculations of a father squandering a fortune (largely not his own!) on the family trading venture in Syracuse,[201] and ruined when the city was recaptured by the Saracens. Phocas, as a young man, had fled with his father to the capital, abandoning all their property to the victors. Somehow the Varangians managed to avoid betraying their own investigations as Michael Bryennios hinted the suspect was likely to flee westwards.

"Would that be possible?" asked Ethelwulf with as innocent a face as he could muster. The Spectabilis glared at the question, then felt the urge of demonstrating his superior knowledge by explaining the overland route would be extremely difficult due to Bulgar attacks. Neither Varangian looked at the other as both knew about such campaigns. However, the Spectabilis explained, there were still limited trading contacts between .the Empire and the Emirs controlling the island. The Autokrator had been encouraging diplomatic contacts, knowing they could be most useful in dealing with enemies clearly on the verge of internecine war.

By now they'd reached the second floor and the Spectabilis fell silent, placing his finger against his lips. He casually waggled his finger in their direction, indicating they should draw their swords to meet any danger. Morkere glanced at Ethelwulf as both drew their weapons and glanced back the way they'd climbed. The Spectabilis looked puzzled and the Wanderer passed his open hand across his face as if stilling any protest. Obviously if the suspect had friends in the block they'd be charging up the staircase to rescue him once an arrest was attempted. Michael nodded although a frown clouded his pinched features. They crept up the stairs until they reached the home of Theodosius Phocas.

With a bravado resting on the backing of two Varangians the Spectabilis hammered on the door with an energy fit to knock it in. Even somebody fast asleep on the ground floor would have been moved to answer the door. But nobody from Theodosius's apartment bothered to react.

"Break it down!" ordered the Spectabilis and, when Ethelwulf hesitated, added, "This is a matter of state, Varangian!"

Before he'd finished Morkere had leaned back and driven his foot against the door just below the lock. The door shuddered but didn't fall open. Ethelwulf smashed his shoulder against the weakened door and, this time, resistance collapsed. The Wanderer half-tumbled into the apartment.

The interior of the home of the Apokrisiaros matched its exterior. It had two rooms, opening out on to an almost-non-existent balcony. It contained one table, two stools, an unmade bed and a body. One glance showed the body was a corpse and a second enabled Michael to identify the corpse as that of Theodosius Phocas.

"Too late!" he cursed, rather unnecessarily. It appeared Theodosius, in the absence of any shelves or cupboards, had been in the habit of stacking his few possessions against one wall. His property was scattered all over the floor, a couple of pieces of ostracae settling in the pool of dried blood which had poured from the wide gash in his throat. The murder weapon, a Saracen blade, lay conveniently by the side of the wound. From the glazed look of shock in the eyes it looked as if Phocas had been taken completely by surprise. "Whatever was here has been taken," grunted Michael, almost moved to kick the corpse in frustration.

"Perhaps the manuscript has been hidden," suggested Ethelwulf and was rewarded with a look of contempt by the Spectabilis. In a room with four pieces of furniture there wasn't much hope of concealment. "It could have been hidden under the floorboards!" responded the Wanderer.

Morkere moved forward to see if any of the boards had been tampered with but was restrained by Michael. "We must be careful. We must report this murder but give nobody cause for curiosity."

The Varangians understood this. Clearly none of the upper echelons of the Administration wanted the Autokrator to know security had been breached. They didn't have much time as the noise of entry must have provoked a call to the agents of the Eparchos[202]. It was clear the Spectabilis didn't welcome the interest of Alexius Euergetes – doubtless to avoid a charge of incompetence. Quickly they ran their fingers along the edges of the boards, testing for any sign of removal. Although a few splinters were collected between them, and the roughness of edges made their fingers sore, no hidden cavities were discovered. They stopped on hearing the heavy tread of police boots on the stairs.

It took some time for them to convince the police, noted for both their suspicious nature and limited intelligence, of their innocence. Finally, the dried nature of the blood and the evidence of noisy entry allowed them to slip away from the scene of the crime.

*

Michael admitted not being happy because, if the Apokrisiaros had been the thief, he must have been working for somebody else who'd secured the document while silencing his agent's mouth. He ALMOST revealed the document concerned the Saracens but simply declared the answer must lie in Sicily. "We know the wretched man never recovered from the losses of his family a generation ago on the island. How he hoped to profit from his crime I don't know – "

"But he was not the instigator," suggested Ethelwulf and instantly regretted his intrusion.

"You've been warned, Varangian!" snapped the Spectabilis. "I've only to say a word to the Chartularius[203] Psellus or his master, the Logothete of the Praetorium and you'll be in serious trouble." Ethelwulf knew the Logothete of the Praesidium,[204] Bardas, was directly responsible to the Eparchos, whom he'd already upset to the point of needing support from the Quaestor to prevent disgrace.[205] He hung his head, not letting Michael see the resentment he felt; disgrace would probably mean finding himself in one of the remote spots used to imprison those out of favour.

Michael chose to see the gesture as recognition of his power and smiled. "I'll need to travel as speedily as possible beyond the limits of the Empire to the west – and I'll need protection so you two must accompany me." Both Varangians acknowledged the command and Michael's smile broadened. "Of course, travelling overland in such times as our Master is waging war against the pagans to the north will be impossible. We'll go by sea."

Again both Varangians lowered their heads in submission but, this time, Morkere gave his cousin a most decided wink.

*

Standing on the deck of 'Pearl-Bearer' Ethelwulf realised he'd never been on a Byzantine merchantman before. The first thing that had struck him, even while still on shore, were the two masts, each with a lanteen sail. So he was surprised to realise she wasn't much larger than 'Brimfugol', probably not much more than twenty yards from bow to stern and six yards across the widest beam. However, she was much higher and had an extensive hold for merchandise.

The Wanderer was approached by a rather large individual, oozing the sweat of the universal unwashed and a general air of neglect. He introduced himself as the Master of the vessel, Constantine Eumenides. Before he could say any more the Spectabilis stepped forward with remarkable speed, thrusting into the open hands of the master a sealed letter.

"You are expecting us," intoned Michael with the confidence of years of dealing with subordinates in the bowels of Imperial Administration. "I am Michael Bryennios, Spectabilis on special business of his Excellency, the Eparchos. These," he added with a vague flourish of his hand, "are my escort, Varangians, and are of no consequence." Michael's eyes flickered back in a look of dismissal at the Saxons before continuing in rapid Greek. "As Master you're under orders to interrupt your voyage to Venice in order to put us ashore at Taormina."

Morkere failed to follow this rapid stream of Greek except for the single name of 'Taormina'. Where was Taormina? He was certain they'd been going to Syracuse because that was where the dead suspect's family had lived. Perhaps he was wrong. Morkere's speculations were interrupted by the arrival of two strangers, differing in physique, costume and, as it turned out, purpose.

"My name is George Tornices," stated a tall, thin individual with an ingratiating smile which reached no farther than his lips. "It is my merchandise which has given place to your passage." Having failed to arouse any feeling of guilt among the newcomers, he added, "This is Leonardo Tiepolo from Venice." His companion, short, with black whiskers sprouting from his chin and almost every other orifice, bowed.

"I am honoured to make your acquaintance," his hoarse voice stated in very formalised Greek.

Ethelwulf looked closely at him, intrigued by the appearance of the first Italian he'd ever met. Leonardo wore a gown longer than was fashionable in the capital and his hair exploded from his head in a manner never tolerated among the privileged classes. His eyes were shrewd, calculating as if evaluating the equipment of the newcomers. George had given the Varangians scarcely a glance but his companion's eyes examined the weapons and appearance of the Saxons. Ethelwulf was sure that If Leonardo was the first Italian they'd met, the Venetian certainly had never before met any warriors from the north.

"You understand," remarked Michael, "I've been instructed to travel to Sicily on affairs of state."

"And that the authority of the Autokrator can determine whatever is carried by vessels leaving his capital," replied George, clearly irritated by having three strangers thrust upon his business.

"But we're able to accommodate you in the – what do you call it? – stern," croaked Leonardo and there were attempts at smiles from both Greeks. At that point Constantine Eumenides intervened with a curt reminder they must catch the tide, adding the newcomers should stow their possessions in the stern and avoid coming out on deck until his ship had left harbour.

Morkere and Ethelwulf exchanged glances, fully aware of how strangers could get in the way as any vessel performed all the operations required to get out to sea. Michael was not so accommodating, making his way towards the stern quarters with mumbled protest.

*

During their enforced isolation neither Varangian spoke and Michael, having seized the only lockable chest available for his own possessions, pointedly ignored them. It was obvious the Spectabilis regarded them as little better than slaves, perhaps even lower than the freedmen pandering to the whims of the Greek aristocracy. The Saxons didn't mind as they were absorbed in the Harbour of Theodosius as it slowly drifted away. They'd almost forgotten the immensity of Miklagard's access to the sea which had first struck them three years before on arrival from Gadarike. Distance removed the stench of so much of the city and the oppressive effect of so many thousand strangers. Neither cousin had that love of the sea possessed by so many Vikings; for them it was an inconvenient bridge between one land and another, an attitude shared by more in the far north than often realised. They wondered how soon they'd be allowed out on deck, knowing 'Pearl-Bearer' might well put into port at the other end of the Sea of Marmora before setting out on the awkward crossing of the Aegean Sea – 'awkward' because the prevailing wind was a northerly[206] and merchantmen had abandoned the use of oars centuries before.

In fact, both Varangians dozed off and failed to notice Michael slip out of the cabin, making sure he didn't disturb his two bodyguards. By the time either Saxon was awake he had settled himself down in a corner and was rapidly writing on a small piece of parchment.

He noticed Morkere looking at him and frowned. The dark-haired barbarian was the one who could speak Greek but he was certain he couldn't read the language – indeed he probably couldn't read in any language. Even so, the Spectabilis disliked having to put down instructions to prevent eavesdropping because of the natural bureaucratic fear of finding such written instructions used against him in the future. He tried to smile at the Varangian, irritated he needed to make the effort.

"We are now free of the Sea of Marmora, not bothering to touch land, so you may wander outside." There was a significant pause. "Make sure you don't get in the way of the sailors nor ask too many questions. Remember I must report back to the Eparchos on my return." Ethelwulf nodded acceptance but Morkere grinned. In Crete he'd discovered that asking questions was just the way to find out what was really going on behind the mask of Greek manners.[207]

Both Saxons staggered outside, momentarily put off by the unaccustomed effect on their movements by the swell of the sea. Outside they soon bumped into the Master who immediately decided his instinctive dislike of the Spectabilis made both Varangians his friends for life. Rapidly he described their route to carry his vessel back to Venice.

"...... for it is not the first time I've travelled among Westerners," he explained. "Fine seamen they are, but also crafty traders and I'm not sure our new agreement with them will be to our advantage."[208] He paused, perhaps considering his words might appear critical of the Autokrator. "But who am I to say?"

He explained how they'd be passing south of Lesbos and then, risking a stretch of open sea, making for Negropont. He'd then slip due south, keeping clear of Athens – "because the last time we put in near there we ran into a lot of regulations we could have done without." However, he'd no plans for landing on Crete, except to take on fresh supplies – "because there's too much thievery there after generations of harbouring pirates." He'd then sail westwards before striking land at Syracuse in Sicily, despite it being in the grip of the infidel. "At the moment, the Autokrator's got his eyes on the Bulgars so this might prove tricky. It all depends on how Yusuf al-Kalbi fancies himself."[209] That allusion was beyond the Varangians but they said nothing, merely nodding as if they agreed with his assessment. The Master concluded by saying he'd finally reach Venice and deposit the two merchants along with their wares.

"We've never been to Sicily or Italy – " began Morkere, anxious to get on even closer terms with the Master, but was interrupted by Constantine with a chuckle.

"People there didn't enjoy the last time your type were in the area!"

The Saxons laughed but had no idea of what the Master meant.

"Where is Taormina?" asked Morkere suddenly and Constantine Eumenides blushed.

"Why should you ask that?" was the reply as the merriment disappeared from the Master's face.

"No reason," said Morkere. " I just heard it mentioned with Sicily."

Constantine Eumenides grinned again. "It's a small town some distance to the north of Syracuse, famous in Sicily for being the last town to surrender to the infidels and also for existing so close to a volcano called Etna."[210]

Both Saxons nodded, remembering the volcanic activity on Iceland. Morkere, however, remained puzzled. He was certain he'd heard the name 'Taormina' spoken by the Spectabilis but the Master had stated their only landing would be at Syracuse.

At that point they were joined by the Byzantine merchant, George Tornices, anxious to snatch the Varangians away from the Master. For his part Constantine welcomed the loss of Ethelwulf and Morkere so the Saxons found themselves conducted down a narrow ladder into the hold.

"You can imagine, Varangians, that space is very precious on a vessel this size." The merchant paused until he'd detected both his listeners nodding in agreement. It was clear he wanted to communicate to the Varangians the problems their intrusion had produced. "Of course, you'll see a number of amphorae scattered throughout the vessel, helping to stabilise it in case of rough weather. In those amphorae you'll find wine and a little olive oil; on the return journey the proportions should be reversed for, at the moment, there's little taste for Sicilian wine in our capital." He gave a crafty smile. "But it will change, I can assure you, and then merchants such as myself will see profits soar."

"As long as Saracen pirates aren't a problem," interposed Ethelwulf.

The smile vanished but the merchant insisted he'd been assured by the highest authorities that the imperial Ousiakons, Pamphyles and Dromons[211] would see off a threat. His voice dropped as he added, "I can tell you there're many seeking to turn the eyes of the Autokrator westwards so he can restore the realm of Justinian."[212]

"I think the Saracens are quite capable of putting up a good fight," argued Morkere, remembering the battle with the 'Jewel of Hisham' and 'Dream of Fatima' on the way to Crete.

"They don't have Siphonarioi nor our deadly weapon!"[213] snapped the merchant and then hurriedly shut his mouth as he realised he was referring to a state secret. The Varangians laughed and Ethelwulf explained they'd already seen it in action.

"Anyway," said George Tornices, anxious to turn the conversation to other subjects, " over there you can see some of the high-grade silk we're taking to Venice. They can't make it themselves and can't get enough of it. As I am a member of the Metaxopratai[214] I both supply raw silk for the imperial factories and deal in the unrivalled finished product." He paused and a sly look came into his eyes, not detected by his hearers in the semi-darkness of the hold. "You can be certain that for whatever they pay us, they collect double from the barbarians further west."

Ethelwulf would have agreed. He could count on the fingers of one hand the number of silk gowns he'd seen in the western lands. However, he said nothing but, by turning his back on the silk, forced the merchant to continue his commentary.

"Over there we've some of the finest ceramics you'll ever come across." He paused and, even in the poor light they saw the grin as he continued. "Next to them you can see some of the furs and amber we've traded with your fellows from across the Pontic Sea."

Ethelwulf laughed. "I know – we helped send them to you!"

"And we'll trade them on to Venice at a good price!" smiled the merchant. "Don't let my friend, Leonardo, know their original price – please!"

They all laughed at this, wondering at how objects which cost so little in one place could be a king's ransom in another. Such was the way of the world.

*

Leonardo made no attempt to interrogate the Varangians about prices when he encountered them emerging from the hold. It was a relief on both sides they could converse in Latin, with the bonus nobody else on board could understand their words. "I can see you've been examining how far my Greek friend is deceiving me!" he chuckled as George Tornices scurried off. "But I tell you for every nomisma[215] the fellow gains from me I'll gain two in the fairs in Lombardy!"

He stared at the two Varangians with obvious admiration. "I wonder what my Doge would make of you." Leonardo said softly. "I could promise a fine wage, especially if, as I've heard of your kind, you're able to fight on water!"

"We're content in the Imperial service," replied Morkere, unsure of the Venetian's intentions.

Leonardo Tiepolo smiled. "I'm not trying to recruit you, my friend. I know you're with the Greek envoy - or whatever he is!" he added the last words with a crafty look at Morkere.

"Why should you doubt he is an envoy to the Saracens in Sicily?"

"He doesn't have a rank fitting to deal with the rulers of the island," asserted Leonardo. "Besides, if he was going to talk to their Emir he'd be off to Palermo[216] with a fine collection of trade-gifts and not what he manages to squeeze out of my colleague!"

True, thought Ethelwulf, but they knew the Spectabilis was hunting down stolen property, not trying to secure some treaty with a foreign power. Let the Venetian fish as much he wished, he'd say nothing. Leonardo seemed to realise he'd gone too far and there was an embarrassed silence. Then the merchant started to ramble on about his city, whether to gain the sympathy of the Varangians or out of native pride was uncertain.

"Our city may be said to have sprung from the ocean itself – and certainly its prosperity and greatness is linked to the sea. When I was a young man our Doge, that's the name of our elected ruler like the Romans elected their consuls, became a dictator, abusing his authority and trying to ensnare us in the squabbles of our neighbours. I should point out Venice, astride several islands, lacks interest in the petty wars on the mainland as its destiny lies across the sea. So we – and I can say 'we' because I wasn't the fat old fool I am now – we drove him from power and began to rebuild our city.[217] Now we've a new young Doge, Pietro Orseolo, who's already secured one favourable treaty and will, I'm sure, make us even richer and more powerful than we dreamed."[218]

He suddenly stopped and looked at the Varangians. "But I'm being rude, taking about myself and not about you. You're certainly a long way from your homeland of ice and snow, for I've heard the land of the Rus has plains made of ice like oceans and men sometimes find themselves existing for months in darkness." He grinned. "But I don't even know your names." Leonardo stopped here to give his companions a chance to introduce themselves and Ethelwulf, whose command of Latin was better than that of his cousin, responded.

"I am Ethelwulf of Arne, in England, and this is my cousin, Morkere. Our land is rarely covered with snow, although we've been forced to travel in lands ruled by ice for months. We did live among the Rus, trapping for skins and fighting for our employers. We came to Miklagard three years ago and are content to serve the Autokrator."

Leonardo confessed he'd misjudged the Saxon, excusing himself on the grounds of ignorance. "I'm sure," he concluded, "any warriors like yourselves would find employment in Italy, if not in the service of my own fair city."

"Why would your city not wish to employ us?" demanded Morkere in a tone as if he'd been insulted.

"Because our battles are at sea –"

"Have you not heard of Vikings?" interrupted Morkere, anxious to stress a difference from the more usual Varangian. "They can fight on land and ship with equal vigour. We are Vikings!"

Ethelwulf smiled, thinking how much Morkere's mother would have hated that description. However, the memory of a long-lost life destroyed the smile and Leonardo noticed the sudden melancholy.

"Why the sadness, man from England?" he asked.

"Because we miss our homeland to which we can never return," was the reply. Leonardo was about to ask why but changed his mind. He was still in awe of the Varangians, thinking he'd never seen such fearsome warriors.

*

'Pearl-Bearer' dropped anchor off the western tip of Crete while boats ferried fresh supplies from the shore. Ethelwulf's attention was drawn to the six anchors, of equal size and shape; Constantine Eumenides explained that the size, number and structure of anchors were controlled by Imperial decree, experience showing such dimensions to be the most effective. Morkere noted the Spectabilis rarely appeared on deck and when he did, displayed such a sickly pallor that he was clearly intended never to be a seaman. Neither Varangian showed any sympathy for the Greek who never showed them any consideration.

One incident, however, did earn the respect of everybody else on board for the Saxons. On the last trip ashore four of the crew were seized by locals, clearly expecting to extract some kind of ransom from a ship deprived of key sailors. Ethelwulf and Morkere were rowed ashore one night and next morning appeared as arranged with all four sailors. They were taken back on board and 'Pearl-Bearer' rapidly put out to sea before there was any more trouble.

"One moment there's a guard at the door and the next he's on the ground with his head nearly cut off," said Thomas, "In his place was the yellow-haired one and before the second guard – him that had been tormenting little Leo there – could yell, he's clutching at a knife stuck in his chest."

"Then we heard some kind of scuffle outside and his dark-haired mate sticks in his head and gabbles something," added Black Peter, a runaway slave from Egypt. "So the fair-haired one gives me a kick and drags Leo to his feet."

"'Come!' was all he said," interposed the slightly-built Pamphylian, "and we didn't need to be asked twice. Even George managed to get a move on for once!" George, a sturdy Thracian with a greater tendency to sleep than bestir himself, simply grunted his feelings.

"Outside there's a third of the bastards on the ground. He didn't look dead but he certainly wouldn't be happy when he came round," continued Thomas. "Anyway we slunk away as fast as we could -"

"Though the lookout wasn't going to do any more spying!" interrupted Leo.

"Not with the rope I saw around his throat," murmured George with what, for him, was a grin.

"I don't think I bothered to look," said Mark. "I didn't want to hang around 'cos the locals'd skin any of us alive if they laid hands – "

"But they didn't!" stated Thomas and the others nodded. They'd all tried to express their thanks to the Varangians but it had been shrugged off with the simple words of the dark-haired barbarian. "We do what we do!" "And they certainly do it well!" commented Thomas and the others grinned.

*

Naturally the story of the rescue went around the vessel and the Varangians found not everyone shared Leonardo's open admiration or the Master's gratitude. Michael Bryennios hissed his disapproval at the Varangians – hissed because he realised how their actions had endeared themselves to the crew.

"You're here to protect ME! Not go off, killing subjects of the Autokrator and risking disaster for us all!" Michael's green eyes flashed hatred. "I was warned about you both, but I didn't have any choice. I was ordered to track down the thief and I needed swords!"

"We would have been delayed here for weeks if they'd kept hold of our men," was Ethelwulf's answer.

"Don't answer me back, barbarian!" snapped the Spectabilis. "I'd have gone to their village with the Autokrator's rescript!"

"And found nothing!" interrupted the Wanderer, his temper refusing to let the Spectabilis suggest a solution which would never have worked. "They might have hidden the men somewhere in the mountains – "

"Or cut their throats!" added Morkere, not wishing his cousin alone to suffer the fury of Michael Bryennios.

"Don't YOU interrupt me!" screeched the Spectabilis, forgetting their voices could now be heard through a good part of the vessel. "You've murdered imperial subjects! Even now a complaint must be on its way to the capital!"

"Yes, I'm sure Michael Theophilus isn't very happy," grinned Morkere. "That is if he's still alive!" He remembered the cell in Chandax and the cruelties of a sick man, terrified of disgrace.

"I'm well aware how you've disgraced the imperial service on this island!" snarled the Spectabilis.

"The Autokrator didn't seem to think so," responded Ethelwulf, recalling how the censures of the Eparchos had been largely rejected by the Autokrator. The Spectabilis fell silent, recalling gossip about how the barbarians were entertained by the Autokrator and his brother as if they were heroes. He'd heard how the Eparchos had stood on the brink of disaster – and survived. Perhaps these barbarians had powerful protectors.

"You still risked death and disaster for our mission for no good reason," hissed Michael. "How could I succeed without your swords?" Neither Varangian spoke; if the Spectabilis was trying to be conciliatory then he shouldn't be interrupted. Morkere was tempted to ask about Taormina but decided now, if ever, wouldn't be the time. Ethelwulf was certain he'd made a mistake; Theodosius Phocas had come from Syracuse and so it was logical they'd be going there. Yet, both agreed that whoever had murdered Theodosius wouldn't necessarily go to his victim's home city! What had the thief stolen? Why? How much did Michael Bryennios know? There were too many questions, too many questions!

*

Nobody was aware of the storm until it struck them; then everything was turned upside down. The Master decided to run before the storm but, it being night with little chance of accurate navigation, that involved a distinct risk. Yet the winds were northerly and 'Pearl-Bearer' had just veered northwards so the odds were the vessel could be propelled halfway up the Adriatic Sea with little risk of shipwreck. Even so, the value of the amphorae as cargo became immediately apparently as, strategically placed, they helped retain stability on the vessel in the plunging seas. Ethelwulf had thought their repeated use on voyages was for reasons of cost,[219] now he realised there was another purpose; he also identified how several had become battered and chipped, and why the damaged vessels were not simply discarded.

Naturally there was a call for everybody to help preserve the ship, although the Spectabilis, with a complexion of violent green, contrived to stand next to the helmsman operating the double-tiller, to the base of which he firmly strapped himself.

The Saxons were surprised at how much they understood the instructions being passed back-and-forth among the crew,[220] some swarming up the masts to adjust the lanteen sails, others making sure every bit of cargo was secured. Philip and Stephen, two slightly-built seamen from Rhodes, rushed into the merchants' quarters amidships to make sure everything was secure and then repeated the operation in the stern quarters. John and Paul, both from Cilicia, climbed down into the hold to batten down any loose trading objects. The importance of this was shown when an amphora was wrenched loose from its position and swept one unlucky sailor overboard before smashing itself to pieces against the bulwark. Luckily most damage, shattered glassware and spices tipped out, took place in the stern hold and so did little to impede the task of managing the vessel as it was battered northwards.

Nevertheless, before long a voice from the amidships-hold announced water was starting to seep through just above where the keel joined the side of 'Pearl-Bearer'. The two Saxons immediately volunteered to help bale out whatever was leaking in. They were joined by Leonardo, but he spent much of his initial effort in trying, with mixed success, to move his cargo away from the damaging water. Meanwhile both Ethelwulf and Morkere applied buckets to scooping out water, at first with little effect as they were hampered by swords dangling from baldrics. Once the weapons had been discarded their efforts proved more successful. For a time it looked as if the ship might be overwhelmed by water as Ethelwulf passed a half-filled bucket by way of Leonardo to Morkere who scampered up the half-dozen steps and cast the contents into the sea. After some time the Saxons changed places to give Morkere a rest but still the sea remained a threat.

Then, just as slyly as it had begun, the storm ceased and everyone on board was almost alarmed at the silence. However, parts which never should have creaked now did so and water continued to push its way into the hold. The Master knew he had to make for land to repair the caulking of his vessel, restore order in the holds and give an exhausted crew rest. By some miracle the storm had carried away the clouds obscuring the stars and with their aid Constantine Eumenides steered a course for Taormina.

When they heard that name the Varangians looked at each other. Had chance determined their port of call or was the Master exploiting their need in order to satisfy the Spectabilis? Certainly they couldn't expect an answer from either the Master or Michael Bryennios. So they turned to Leonardo, slumped in a corner trying to pretend his goods had suffered no damage.

"I thought we were bound for Syracuse?" asked Morkere and the Venetian wondered why they'd believed that.

"Because we're part of a diplomatic mission," lied Ethelwulf and Leonardo grinned.

"If that were true you'd be heading for Palermo because that's where the Saracens hold their court. " He paused and recognised the confusion on the Saxons' faces. "Neither Syracuse nor Taormina are what they were a century ago - too Byzantine and so weighed down with all the restrictions and rules which their new masters impose. Of course, there's been a lot of trouble on this side of the island but the locals know when they're beaten – or rather when they aren't going to get any help." The last words were whispered as Leonardo didn't want to quarrel with either of the Byzantine passengers.

None of that helped and so Ethelwulf decided to ask the Spectabilis why they were heading for Taormina. The Byzantine sniffed as if something had just intruded into his nostrils.

"It's not for Varangians to ask questions, merely to obey orders – as I've told you before!" the stress on the last phrase was meant to be threatening but the farther Ethelwulf was away from Miklagard the less patience he had with Byzantine obscurantism. He said nothing and made no attempt to move, simply willing the Spectabilis to carry on and, in this battle of wills, he proved victorious.

"Before we left I was told there is evidence Theodosius Phocas had been in contact with somebody in Taormina." He paused and glared at the Varangian. "Before you mention the word 'Syracuse' let me say I can say no more without revealing the object of our search. Now go away before you test my patience too far."

Without a word Ethelwulf left, certain the search would be for a missing manuscript possibly now in Taormina. He was only mildly irritated by not knowing precisely what manuscript.

*

Taormina proved an impressive town. A small quay was linked to the town itself by a steep path and above the town towered a citadel by which the Saracens hoped to intimidate their subjects.[221] As 'Pearl-Bearer' slipped alongside the quay soon after noon Ethelwulf was shocked by the overwhelming silence, almost as if the town was in mourning.

Michael Bryennios had urgent business to discuss with the local qadi and wasted no time in ordering the Varangians to accompany him as he paid his respects to the most prominent member of the diwan[222] of Taormina. Both were to wear the scarlet cloaks he'd especially brought with him, making sure the rest of their outfit was neat and clean.

So in mid-afternoon three figures began the steep climb to the seat of power in Taormina; no mounts were available from a population cowered into identifying any help for Christians as almost an act of rebellion. As the Saxons wore byrnies, leather with limited metal protection, leggings and swords in baldrics, they were just able to keep up with the Spectabilis who appeared to have acquired fresh energy from being once again on land. However, by the time they reached the mosque, formerly a church, just inside the city gates, all three needed a rest.

The Spectabilis suddenly felt the need to reveal his purpose to the Varangians, but, they noted, in doing so kept his voice low to prevent any passer-by overhearing him.

"I carry with me a small gift from the Autokrator to the qadi as a form of introduction." He licked his dry lips before continuing. "If I feel the qadi is supportive I'm authorised to make him presents from some of the stock of George Tornices. Of course, he's not happy about this, especially as the price of my requisitions will merely be offset against future tax demands. Anyway, that will be done tomorrow but it's important my credentials are presented at once."

Michael failed to convince the Varangians but they gave no sign, simply sipping a few drops of water from the water-bottles which, despite the dark looks of Michael, they'd insisted on carrying with them. Inwardly both cursed the Spectabilis for forcing them to climb such a hill during almost the hottest part of the day.

"I hope, cousin," muttered Morkere, "the fortress has some of the traditional welcomes of the infidel."

Ethelwulf grinned. "By that, I suppose, you mean water fountains, delicate food and dancing girls."

Morkere didn't reply because of the glare from the Spectabilis as he realised their conversation, in West Saxon, was gibberish to him. Michael stood up and set off, not even bothering to ask if his escort was ready. Nevertheless, progress up the hill to the citadel became ever slower as whatever energy they'd possessed at the quayside was sucked out of their legs by the sun.

At the main gate the pretensions of Michael Bryennios were shown in their true light when the guards denied them admission and appeared completely ignorant of Greek. For a few moments the Spectabilis appeared on the point of collapse from a combination of physical exhaustion and frustration but then a dwarf-like creature scurried forward, offering assistance.

"I am John Mekros," he announced in an unexpectedly loud voice but with a strangely-accented Greek. "I am the official interpreter of His Excellency, Yussuf ibn Ali, to whom has been entrusted Taormina by the Grand Emir." He paused to examine George Bryennios with deliberate calculation, not bothering to give the Varangians a second glance. "I can see you're a Roman official and doubtless an important one, I'm sure." Was that a look of insolence as he spoke?

"I've been ordered by the Autokrator to negotiate business of a delicate nature with the Qadi," replied the Spectabilis in a voice matching the dwarf's. "I trust you'll admit us into his presence."

"You are fortunate," was the reply. "The Qadi has rested and is about to attend court. He can spare you a brief audience." He glared at the Varangians, obviously angered by their height if not by their armed presence. "However, these two armed ruffians won't be allowed into our citadel."

The Spectabilis shrugged and declared his escort could stay outside as the matter was too delicate for crude barbarian ears. Whatever irritation was felt by the Saxons was not revealed as their expressions didn't change – although Michael was all too aware they'd understood every word.

*

"I can't see any dancing girls, cousin," grinned Ethelwulf as they sat side-by-side on a broken wall looking out over the sea. Pity we aren't looking the other way and then I might see England, he thought but said nothing.

"So what do you think our friend is up to?" asked Morkere, kicking a nearby rock at the word 'friend' just to emphasise his feelings.

"If he wasn't a Greek, I'd put it down to mischief," was the answer. "However, we've learned that's all normal behaviour here."

"Oh, yes, it's all snobbery when he's dealing with us 'barbarians' but he seems a bit devious when he's dealing with his own kind."

"True," agreed the Wanderer, "but he's working for the Eparchos so you can be sure he's not used to being straight." There was a pause. "He certainly was in a hurry to see the boss of this place."

Morkere kicked another stone before he replied. "You think he intended to come here all along?"

"Certain of it," said Ethelwulf, "and I reckon all that evidence linking the suspect with this place is a product of our friend's imagination!"

"We're still left with a 'why?'," was the response of his cousin, casually getting to his feet. "Sitting up here's so peaceful it's hard to think that inside the Spectabilis could be putting us in danger."

"Now I think, Morkere, you're being too suspicious. We've been shut out here because that's the way the Greeks do things." There was a brief pause. "Have you ever been invited to a planning conference anywhere in the same way as in Finland or Ireland?"

"No," was the reply and with that the conversation closed as Morkere went off to stroll around the circuit of the walls. In doing so he provoked suspicious stares from the Saracen sentries but nobody made a move to stop him. On his return Morkere said the walls looked strong and the soldiers fit.

"So let's hope we don't get into a fight," smiled Ethelwulf

*

Some time later the Spectabilis reappeared and immediately said they'd be returning with various diplomatic presents. Neither Saxon spoke as they wondered if George Tornices would resist seizure of his property. As it turned out, he didn't, apart from loud protests. Leonardo watched as his colleague had several choice items removed, in return for an imperial promissory note. What the Venetian made of it all was kept to himself.

However, within moments of entering his cabin, the Spectabilis rushed out, screaming, "It's gone! Where's the thief?" Suddenly he was aware of the shocked silence of the Varangians and the two merchants who'd been discussing the possible virtues (or rather vices) of Taormina.

"A special document which I had for the Qadi has disappeared." He paused and glared at the Varangians, about to accuse them of the theft before realising neither had been near their quarters for some time. "You two, search the ship! Check if anyone is missing!

Search everyone's belongings!" Then he decided to add, "Check first with the Master!"

Constantine Eumenides was furious. It was bad enough to have had imposed, at the last moment, three non-paying passengers. Now one was insisting he'd been robbed. So he called together the crew and discovered that Stephen, the Rhodian with the pointed ears of a goblin, had disappeared. A few questions revealed that Stephen, although recruited from Rhodes, belonged to a family from a small village on the way to Etna. The Master also discovered Stephan had been injured in the recent storm, aggravating the effect of a fall several months before; so his hip would sometimes seize up and make it very painful even to walk, let alone run.

"Good!" snapped the Spectabilis. "We must make sure we know his destination and track down the thief." With a stream of Greek he dispatched one seaman up to the citadel with an urgent request for help, while sending three others to trace the route of the missing man. It didn't take long to learn that Stephen had headed up past the Saracen citadel. By then Michael had collected mules for himself and the Varangians, rid himself of his fine garments in favour of rough travelling garb. Indeed he was a picture of energy and organisation, no longer the languidly haughty bureaucrat.

"Our friend seems a different man after being robbed!" whispered Morkere to his cousin; even though he spoke in Saxon he half-expected the Spectabilis to be angered by his words.

"Perhaps Greeks should be robbed more often."

"Then there'd be less need of such as ourselves," grinned Morkere. Although neither mentioned it both Saxons wondered about the missing 'document'. Why was it so important? Why had the Spectabilis not taken it with him to the Qadi earlier? However, there was no time for discussion as they were to be quickly carried up the hill towards the citadel. Once there they were met by a patrol of nine Saracens. The Varangians closely examined the fursan,[223] noting the length of their spears and the small targets which were their principle form of defence. They looked tough enough.

The next surprise was how easily the Spectabilis communicated with the Saracens. Although neither Varangian understood a word of what was going on, a guide for the region around Mount Etna had been produced and the patrol split into two – four warriors under their leader were to follow the track around the mountain and hunt down the thief before he reached his native village of Ragalna – at least, that's what Morkere understood by the name being repeated so often. The Varangians and Michael, with the guide and the remaining four Saracens, were to find their way directly across the crater region. Ethelwulf doubted if anyone troubled by a damaged hip would try to make his way by the rough paths he expected ahead; Morkere, on the other hand, was certain any thief knowing the area wouldn't expose himself to easy pursuit along a proper track. The debate was confined to the few moments spent watching the patrol disappear along the trackway. Then the guide headed south-west for the volcanic mass ahead of them.

*

If either Saxon was perturbed by the gusts of smoke rising from the mountain dominating the skyline they didn't show it. Both had seen volcanoes before in Iceland, appreciating that some were always 'alive', although of limited threat – more often causing locals to resort to rituals to keep themselves safe. They were impressed by how far they seemed to progress, before they realised how far they still had to travel to reach the crater. Ethelwulf was amazed how readily the Spectabilis adapted himself to the hunt and how little he seemed concerned by the crater. How he had misjudged the man!

Nobody spoke as they followed the guide along an almost non-existent track. Soon on either side were small heaps of discarded lava, once black but now more likely covered by moss or primitive vegetation. Apart from the crunch of the hooves of their mounts no sound interrupted the peace of their surroundings; even birds seemed uninterested in such a barren hunting-ground. As the path steepened Ethelwulf wondered how any man, burdened by an injured hip, could make his way over such terrain. Even if mounted the irregularity of movement must be crippling.

As they got higher, progress became more difficult, everyone finding it harder to breathe in the thinner air, except for the guide, untroubled by whatever the mountain could throw at him. He showed no hesitation at pressing on, somehow detecting a path when untrained eyes saw nothing. None of his companions was prepared to give up although the Varangians found themselves slipping past two of the Saracen riders. Nothing to be surprised at when dealing with men unsuited for such a journey, but disturbing when immediately both Saracens quickened their pace.

Soon they found the territory behind them hidden by mist and the Saxons started to be afraid, unable to talk as they rode in single file, and certain they could never find their way back down from this monster. Ahead the way appeared clear, although vegetation had given up its attempt to conquer the mountain. On both sides of the route lay piles, depressions or level stretches of coarse, black stones. The Varangians had seen volcanic activity but this was different, never had they experienced such a desolation in nature – even the snow-covered steppes of the land of the Rus hadn't appeared so abandoned. Ethelwulf ran his hand lightly over 'Claw' and felt comfort. And still they climbed.

The Spectabilis eased his mount alongside the guide and with a mixture of words and signs was trying to find out – what? Ethelwulf had believed he understood the Spectabilis and had been wrong; the shallow, arrogant bureaucrat had become the eager, tireless hunter, and the change was unwelcome.

Suddenly there was a cry from the front. It was the Spectabilis and his shrill voice yelled out words which caused the two warriors in front of Ethelwulf to surge forward on their mules. The figure ahead must have heard the shout for it turned and tried to scurry off the path up towards one of the craters of Etna. Ethelwulf, along with everyone else, urged his mount forward, uncertain why he was in such a hurry. Ahead the figure fell once, picked itself and, clearly in pain, tried to drag itself to safety. Safety? There was no safety; no hiding place in the bleak landscape. As the figure attempted to get away from the path it fell again and this time there was a considerable delay before it could get to its feet.

The Saracens reached the point where the figure had left the path. Both quickly dismounted and, throwing aside the spears, ran up after the figure. Even though fitter and faster than their quarry they also stumbled among the old lava rocks, one clearly cutting himself by the way he paused to examine his palm and tried to bind it in the ends of his jerkin. His companion rushed ahead and caught the fugitive, smashing his quarry to the ground. Then he seized hold of the figure, whose pleas for mercy could be clearly heard by the advancing party, and started to drag him over the rocks. He was helped by the second Saracen, abandoning attempts to stem the flow from his own wound in the fiendish desire to inflict even greater punishment on the fugitive.

The main party reached the Saracen mules and dismounted. The Saracens were dragging the fugitive back to the path, ignoring his screams and shouting their triumph to their companions. What had been a sombre, silent atmosphere was transformed. The Spectabilis stepped off the path, unable to control his impatience. Morkere also left the path as he noticed something not blending in with the general rock-strewn surface.

Once Stephen, for it was indeed the runaway seaman, had been dragged before the Spectabilis, Michael opened proceedings by striking the seaman in the eye and screaming what, to Ethelwulf, was gibberish. Stephen slumped to his knees, scarcely supported by the Saracens. Michael yelled, "Where is it? Where is it?", and, before Stephen could answer, drove his knee into the face of his victim. Stephen was pitched backwards and the Spectabilis threw himself on the fugitive, grabbing a lump of lava to smash it into his face. One of the Saracens who'd ridden behind Ethelwulf stepped forward to stop the Greek battering Stephen but his comrade grabbed him, hauling him back with a meaningful look at the Wanderer.

Stephen had slipped into unconsciousness and Michael threw the bloody rock aside. He turned to the nearest Saracen and spat out an order. The warrior sheathed his scimitar and drew a long knife, grabbed Stephen's head and, in a single stroke, sliced off his left ear. The pain brought the seaman back to consciousness and Michael, seizing Stephen by his tunic, started to shake him. Now another of the Saracens joined in, supplying a couple of kicks to the exposed areas of Stephen's back. The seaman tried to scream something but his words, probably in some obscure dialect, were unknown to his interrogators so the shaking and kicks continued. At last Michael seemed to have had enough and cast aside the half-conscious form.

A cry from Morkere made everybody look away from Stephen. "I believe you're looking for this," he shouted, holding above his head what looked like a thin manual. In his left hand he held his sword and Ethelwulf knew there was trouble. The Wanderer stepped back so that he was level with the Saracens.

"This is the stolen book, Ethelwulf!" Morkere shouted in West Saxon. "So we've found our murderer!"

Even though the Spectabilis knew not a word of the barbarian's tongue he guessed what was being said and screeched out an order to the Saracens. As Michael opened his mouth, Ethelwulf was already drawing his sword and cut down the Saracen to his right before the man's scimitar even left his belt. The second Saracen was almost quick enough but the Wanderer swung round and stabbed the warrior in the kidneys. The two Saracens who'd captured the fugitive were further away from the Saxons; for a moment they hesitated as they were between the two Varangians, then they moved away from each other to take on each of the Saxons.

One Saracen cut at the head of Morkere who parried dropping the book in the process. The Saxon jabbed at the Saracen's stomach who parried and then cut again at Morkere. A duel was in progress.

Meanwhile Ethelwulf was equally engaged by the Saracen who'd first caught Stephen. Both were well versed in sword-craft, displaying mastery according to their different styles. Quickly both realised footwork had to be kept to the minimum, moving on the rocky surface was too ungainly, and here the Saxon's greater experience proved advantageous. Although he suffered a slight wound to the knee he sliced through the Saracen's sword-arm and then skewered the helpless man.

Ethelwulf turned to help his cousin, just in time to see such aid was unneeded as Morkere drove his sword into his opponent's stomach. The Wanderer switched his attention to the other humans present. The guide was riding furiously back down the path, dragging with him three of the mules. Stephen was hovering between life and death, staring up into the sky and mumbling what could only have been words of a prayer. The Spectabilis was running away from the path, by chance on the same route taken by Stephen; in Michael's hand was the book. Why had the fool not grabbed a mule and escaped along with guide? Because the book was invaluable.

"Grab the mules, Morkere, and see to Stephen!" yelled Ethelwulf as he rushed after the Spectabilis. The Wanderer was certain Michael had probably hired the thief and then murdered him. It had all been done before he'd taken the Varangians to the tenement. Why had he brought us with him, Ethelwulf asked himself as he panted after the Greek. It was clear Michael knew Sicily and possibly had some prior agreement with the Qadi. However, a lot could go wrong before then and the Spectabilis needed protection, to be abandoned as required. Why had Michael stolen the book in the first place? He didn't know, but he was sure he was gaining on the Spectabilis; after all a Varangian was expected to keep fit but a Greek bureaucrat had a life-style most unsuited to physical effort!

Michael reached a small rise and disappeared over it. As his pursuer reached the crest he paused to rest, glancing back at his cousin who'd collected the scattered mules and was bending over the fugitive. He again turned his attention to his quarry, approaching the crest carefully. Crouching low, Ethelwulf slipped to the side in order to confuse an opponent possibly waiting there with a rock to knock him down. Suddenly he ran over the crest and a rock flew over his shoulder. Michael had been waiting with lump of lava, ready to hurl it at his pursuer. But Ethelwulf appearing at a slightly different point had made Michael redirect his throw and miss.

Michael turned and ran on with Ethelwulf in pursuit. The Wanderer was now aware of a strong stench[224] that before had been weak enough to ignore. He also heard a noise like a sword-smith's bellows, a horrible gasping that might have belonged to a creature from hell. For a moment he was confused but then Icelandic memories told him he was nearing the crater of an active volcano.

The Spectabilis was approaching another crest, ignoring sound and stench in his efforts. He turned to see the Saxon again narrowing the gap between them. With a cry of fear he turned and launched himself over the crest. Suddenly the cry was transformed into such a shriek of horror that made Ethelwulf even increase his pace. Mounting the crest, half-expecting Michael to be waiting in ambush, he saw what had happened.

Michael had tripped as he surmounted the crest and been pitched head first into a river of molten lava being pumped out of the volcano. His head, shoulders and arms were in the lava but the rest of his body had stayed out. Obviously he was dead, drowned in a river of molten debris. Fortunately, Ethelwulf noted he'd dropped the book as he'd pitched forward.

*

Morkere had used some of their precious water to bring Stephen back to the state in which he could be tied on to a mule. Only by promising freedom could he be persuaded to guide them back to Taormina. While Morkere sorted out their new recruit Ethelwulf used two of the mules to ferry the bodies of the Saracens to the lava flow. The four bodies, along with their equipment and the remains of Michael Bryennios, were dropped into the boiling fury. Ethelwulf trusted nature would destroy evidence, if not he calculated sufficient damage would be done to make recognition impossible.

Exhausted, he returned to find Morkere and Stephen talking quietly. It appeared Stephen was not the simple seaman everybody had assumed. In youth he'd been educated in Sicily but had slipped away because of the increasing Islamic control. He described how his mother and sister had both been forced to appear veiled in public, stand in subservience to any Moslem and hear their religion daily denounced. Neighbours converted to Islam rather than pay the poll-tax levied on all non-Moslems. So he'd travelled eastwards, gaining passage by becoming a sailor and then earning a living that way. Once back in Sicily, and so close to his native village, he'd been tempted to desert and, in doing so, steal from the haughty Greek who must be carrying riches. He'd forced open a box, seized a small jewel and then noticed a manual. Opening it he only had to read the name of the author, Constantine Porphyrogenitus, to realise its value. Clearly it had been written by an Emperor and so must contain secrets the Emir at Palermo would like to know; perhaps he could use the work to buy for his family the chance to emigrate. He concealed both book and jewel in a small satchel, slipped on to the quayside and started climbing towards Taormina. At first he'd planned to go to the Qadi, throw himself on the mercy of one in charge of the law and try to gain his family's freedom. Then he remembered the Greek would be there and so turned off, aiming to reach his home village and get help from his family to travel to the capital.

Then everything started to go wrong. He'd injured his hip on board some time before and it received fresh damage in the storm. The climb up the hill proved too arduous and the pain refused to go away. In agony, he decided to cross over Etna, instead of using the main track circling the mountain, in case his theft was discovered. His choice had been disastrous and he'd nearly lost his life.

"So how did you recognise the book?" Ethelwulf asked his cousin.

Morkere laughed. "I didn't. My Greek isn't that good but, like Stephen, I was able to spell out the name of the author and knew who he was!"

"And gambled on Michael revealing all?"

"I could see how worked up our friend had become, so I reckoned, if I was right, he'd blurt out the truth and if I was wrong – "

"We'd simply be lashed by his tongue yet again!" The Wanderer grinned. "Very clever, cousin, very clever." He clapped Morkere on the shoulder and they both climbed into the saddle. With Stephen they should find their way off Etna before darkness came.

*

Stephen guided them successfully off the mountain, seeing them to within sight of the Qadi's citadel. There the Saxons agreed to let him go, deciding they'd insist they'd been attacked by brigands and they were the sole survivors. Obviously, the Qadi would despatch a relief force but Ethelwulf was sure they'd find nothing. Anyway by then they'd be long gone.

As they said farewell to Stephen, Morkere suddenly thrust over his shoulder the satchel with which he'd carried his spoils, saying he'd need something for the journey. The runaway seaman grunted his thanks and drove his mount down towards the road to Syracuse.

Seeing the surprised look on his cousin's face Morkere explained that, with a Saracen patrol looking for him on the main Etna track, it was best if Stephen made his way first to Syracuse.

"But why did you give him the satchel?"

"We've got the missing book and we didn't want the rest, did we?" grinned Morkere.

Ethelwulf frowned for a moment as he realised what Morkere meant. Inside the satchel must have been the missing jewel. He smiled. He also believed the seaman had suffered enough.

*

With the aid of John Mekros the disappearance of the Spectabilis was explained away. The Qadi had enough to concern him without bothering about an unwanted visitor. The four Saracen guards were simply put down to losses to brigands, a growing problem. There was no news of the suspected thief and nobody asked about the missing property, leaving Ethelwulf to wonder how much Michael Bryennios had really told the Qadi.

Passage on 'Pearl-Bearer' proved a more difficult problem. Without the Spectabilis the Master was unwilling to accept the Varangians on board. Ethelwulf couldn't reveal the recovery of the book because he'd then have to explain the disappearance of Michael Bryennios. Their passage had been authorised by the Eparchos and so Ethelwulf lied by saying they'd been only loaned to the Spectabilis and would be required for the spring offensive against the Bulgars.

The Master accepted this but the two merchants insisted the vessel carry them first to Venice before it transported a couple of Varangians back to the capital. As Constantine Eumenides had accepted their silver, he accepted their argument. Ethelwulf and his cousin were forced to continue their journey to the trading republic at the head of the Adriatic.

*

The Saxons had never seen a city like Venice, perched on a group of islands at the head of the long strip of sea styled the Adriatic Sea which separated Italy from Dalmatia. Hundreds of years ago the survivors of the Roman Empire had sheltered from barbarian invaders among such islands and from it had emerged Venice. Low wooden houses, at first simple but gradually with a claim to opulence, were constructed on the reed-infested islands. Swamps were drained and wooden piles rammed into mud to give a firmer basis to this product of man's ambition. After the houses came the churches, the Saxons were impressed by one of the oldest on the island of Torcello.[225] Stone structures had appeared on Olivolo[226] and other islands but they were a rarity; most building was in wood, with thatched roofs, so that the minimum weight was placed on swampy foundations.

Most movement took place on the canals but meetings and business were conducted in an open area (called a *campo*) or even in the narrow streets winding their way through the mass of houses. The Varangians could see the pitiful remains of the destructive overthrow of Pietro di Candiale a few years before. The luckier buildings, such as the Palace of the Doge, were being rebuilt, the less fortunate were awaiting their turn.

'Pearl-Bearer' docked against the waterfront near the Palace and Leonardo clapped his hands excitedly as he stood on the fondemente which ran along next to the water.

"Home at last, my friends," he laughed as he seized with each arm one of the Varangians. "You'll find my city has the potential of surpassing all you may have seen." A passer-by called out and Leonardo returned the greeting. Ethelwulf turned and saw George Tornices was less enthusiastic but disguised such feelings by scrupulously monitoring the unloading of his merchandise. Now and again he'd step forward and gruffly order porters to carry or stack objects in different ways. Leonardo laughed at his concern, assuring him Venetians knew very well how to handle other people's property. Then the Venetian turned to the Varangians.

"We must go and announce our arrival to the Giudicii."[227] He saw the puzzlement of his companions' faces. "They advise the Doge and so must know immediately anything affecting our city. It's both polite and wise to obey the rules here, my friends, as you'll discover." There was a slight pause ended by rapid instructions to porters standing near by. Leonardo glanced at the Byzantine merchant still closely supervising the unloading of his merchandise. "I can see George doesn't trust my countryman so let's leave him to tire himself out! Come, let us go the Giudici and then I must take you home to meet my wife, the most beautiful woman in Venice!"

The Varangians found it very hard to keep up with Leonardo as he scurried in and out of the alleys but eventually they arrived near the rather rundown church of San Salvatore. In one campo there was a grove of elders and in their welcome shade sat three men, dressed alike and with grey beards that made them look like brothers. Leonardo hurried over and bowed low before them. He spoke in his native tongue but gestures showed he was explaining the presence of the strangers to the Giudici. Ethelwulf noted the looks they received were more those of curiosity than hostility.

"Come forward, my friends, and address the Giudici," said Leonardo as he returned, adding in a lower voice, "Remember they, and not the Doge, decide whether you stay here in peace or not."

Ethelwulf and Morkere strode forward and, in unison, bowed to the three men sitting under the trees. One of the Giudici welcomed them in somewhat halting Greek and it was Morkere who answered, choosing Latin as being a more convenient tongue. Immediately they noticed a relaxation in the manner of all three men and the original speaker replied in Latin so rapid that both Saxons, unused to the language for many years, found it hard to follow. However, the meaning was clear. The Giudici welcomed soldiers of the Ruler of the Greeks but hoped they'd soon be able to return to their homes.

"Unfortunately, sire," replied Ethelwulf, " that's impossible as we come from the land of the English and have been wandering for fifteen years."

This produced discussion among the Giudici and one at last replied they'd meant the New Rome built in the east. The speaker ended by entrusting them to Leonardo while they were in the city. Leonardo bowed low and was followed by the Varangians, well practised by their years at Miklagard in ceremonial leave-taking.

As they walked away Ethelwulf asked Leonardo what the Giudici had said among themselves before they had ended the audience. Lorenzo laughingly replied that one had suggested perhaps the land of the English might be open to trade with Venice but the other two had scoffed because they doubted if there was anything the barbarians possessed worth the effort.

*

Over the next few days the Varangians passed the time mainly with Leonardo Tiepolo as he disposed of the goods he'd brought from Miklagard. Occasionally they saw George Tornices trading with Venetian merchants, although his business lacked the briskness of the native Leonardo. Some of the Greek goods, especially the fine silks, were in great demand, not for the Venetians' own use but for resale in the markets of northern Italy or, over the Alps, in the developing trade systems of central or western Europe.

George spent more time, or seemed to, in buying up exquisite examples of glassware from the nearby island of Murano – especially popular being glass beads.[228] Another popular item were the slaves, chiefly Magyars, who'd been carried over the Alps from the wars which had plagued southern Germany for many years. George showed little interest in the wood for sale, mostly cut from the pine forests of northern Italy; this was essential for the continued existence of the imperial navy but its bulk meant George left it for others. However, he was interested in honey from the Lombard Plain and spices acquired by Venetian merchants thanks to their close contacts with Moslem powers.[229]

Everywhere the noise and energy rivalled any to be found within the Empire of the Autokrator, and certainly exceeded whatever the Saxons had seen in Russia or Ireland. They were assured that, further inland, the occasional markets appearing throughout the lands of the Franks or the Empire of Otto would soon be surpassing even this activity. This they would not believe.

It wasn't long, however, before new stock had been carried aboard 'Pearl-Bearer' for transport to Miklagard. The amphorae had been emptied of their contents and filled with the oils and wines of northern Italy. The Varangians, with little silver to spend, made no purchases but put themselves on board in good time. Surprisingly George Tornices announced at the last moment he'd not be returning to Miklagard but intended to tour markets further inland trying to identify the origin of the intricate metalwork from Bavaria which made occasional appearances in Venice.

Within ten days 'Pearl-Bearer', with George being replaced by his cousin, Leo, set sail for Miklagard, carrying back two Varangians with the task of explaining what had happened to the envoy of the Eparchos and return the missing manuscript.

*

The voyage proved completely without incident and, for once, the meltemia[230] proved helpful to the Master as he attempted to get home by the day promised. Ethelwulf thought it be best to report to the Eparchos before news of their arrival reached him. In this he proved over-ambitious because, somehow, the Eparchos was impatiently awaiting them as they entered his audience-chamber.

Alexius Euergetes immediately expressed surprise at the absence of the Spectabilis. "I expected a report from the trusted envoy I'd despatched, not to be faced by two barbarians," he sneered.

Ethelwulf described how they'd been attacked by brigands in Sicily and Michael Bryennios killed.

"So you've failed in your mission!" interrupted the Eparchos. The frown appearing on his features predicted both difficult explanations by himself and punishment for the Varangians.

"No, sire," answered Ethelwulf, putting forward a distorted version of events. "We caught up with the thief, largely due to the excellent intelligence of the Spectabilis and recovered the missing manuscript. However, the thief, one Stephen of Ragalna, had allies among the local brigands and they tried to rescue him. During the struggle both the Spectabilis and Stephen were killed but we managed to escape."

"Ran away, you mean?" sneered the Eparchos, thrusting out his hand for the missing manual without expecting to ask for it.

"No, sire, "replied Ethelwulf. "It was what the Domestikos[231] would call a strategic withdrawal. We needed to ensure we recovered the document – and here it is." Ethelwulf passed the manual into the hands of the Eparchos who acknowledged the act with a curt nod.

"I presume you've stuck your nose into this," accused the Eparchos, stating what he'd have expected the Spectabilis to have done.

Ethelwulf flushed but kept his temper. "Certainly not, sire." After a pause he added, "As you know, sire, we barbarians are unable to read the Greek tongue."

Eparchos narrowed his eyes. He certainly knew the dark-haired Varangian had acquired a good knowledge of Greek in a short time but could he read? Immediately he rejected such a ridiculous idea. Of course, barbarians had neither the will nor ability to master such a skill. He was pleased the Spectabilis had perished on the expedition, otherwise he might have needed silencing. Michael Bryennios would have read the damn manual and tried to wheedle some privilege out of him. At the moment, only the librarian knew the manuscript had been taken in the first place, and that fool had been packed off, minus his tongue, to a remote monastery. Not that he really thought the document would have been of any use to the infidels. He was certain they knew already what the Imperial Administration thought of them. Whatever the Autokrator's grandfather had written down as advice was commonplace among the security systems of both the Empire and its enemies. No, but the Autokrator would have seen the theft as a breakdown in security and, even if he'd placed most of the responsibility on the Logothete, the Eparchos would have been held to blame. As it was, it had all ended well with the recovery of the document.

Suddenly the Eparchos was aware of the barbarian's eyes on him and realised his thoughts had left himself unguarded for a few moments. Naturally, like all his kind, he 'd be expecting a reward. He should have it. The Eparchos reached down, seized a pen and scrawled a few words on a sheet of palimpsest.[232]

"Take this to the Largitionalos[233] you'll find lolling about in my antechamber. It's your reward but will also buy your silence." There was a pause. "Do you understand?"

"Yes, sire," answered Ethelwulf in a clear voice and his cousin mumbled an echo.

"Good," said the Eparchos. "Then we've finished our business. You may go."

Without a word the Varangians saluted, turned and left the Eparchos already planning how he must visit the Library and restore the manuscript without arousing the suspicions of the new Librarian.

*

On their way to the Varangian camp Morkere asked Ethelwulf why he'd failed to name the true thief to the Eparchos.

"The Eparchos would have never believed a barbarian accusation against a Spectabilis, unless we could prove it - which we can't. So it was easier to blame Stephen, who, by now, must have scurried off with his family to safety. It was also easier to pretend ignorance of the manual's contents because I think knowledge would have led to our being silenced."

"So we're safe?" asked Morkere in doubtful tones.

"Not quite! I never believe what the Eparchos says and I doubt if he thinks I tell the truth. But he can never prove it."

They looked forward to telling Gunnar all about the dancing girls at Taormina – even if they were only the figment of a frustrated mind!

The Wanderer 8:4

"Exurgent enim pseudochristi et pseudoprophetae, et dabunt signa et portenta ad seducendos, si fieri potest, etiam electos" (Mark XIII:22 – Vulgate)

"For there will arise false christs and false prophets, and they will give signs and portents to lead astray, if it can be done, even the elect."

Revelation

In five years the Varangians had managed to become men of substance within the territories of the Autokrator. Ethelwulf had proved highly successful in campaigns in Thrace. He'd also managed to help Prince Vladimir preserve the friendship of the Autokrator during a dispute over the substantial trade through Cherson – and so re-established his own good standing with the ruler of Kenugard. No longer did he fear discovery in Miklagard by any traveller from Rus; indeed, he actively tried to set up contacts with the northern world through the trade routes of the Dneiper and Don. So he'd learned of the death of Byrhtnoth[234] and the gradual disintegration of the English kingdom before the onslaught of increasing Viking attacks. He remembered the crime which had provoked his loss of home and country and felt God must have withdrawn his blessing from the King of the English.[235] Ethelwulf also heard of the success of Olaf Trygvasson,[236] the Christian warrior who still spread havoc throughout the far west.

For the time being he was content to soldier in the armies of the Autokrator and had looked forward to the dispatch of the Varangians to Antioch. The Autokrator was determined to assert control over Aleppo. As a boy he'd listened to the stories of the conquering usurpers[237] and longed to see his own standard flutter from lands regained from the Saracens.

The Autokrator had received an appeal for assistance from the Emir of Aleppo and, with the failure of local imperial forces, he was determined to rescue his subjects.[238] With typical speed of decision the Autokrator returned to the capital, not bothering even to visit his co-emperor. Immediately he put into effect a long-planned means of transporting his army rapidly to Syria.

Ethelwulf was somewhat irritated to be given two mules by order of Nicephorus Comnenus, the Paymaster-General. Irritation was replaced by amazement as he realised the same equipment was being issued to every one of the 40,000 men who made up the imperial army.[239] Once again he was impressed by the forethought of the Autokrator, who must have issued the original requisition orders at the same time as he ordered the governor of Antioch to stop the Saracen invasion. Had defeat been anticipated? Possibly; but Ethelwulf also thought the Autokrator had been planning to lead an invasion to rescue the Holy Land itself.

Like Ethelwulf, Morkere was initially disappointed they'd have to leave their horses in the capital and take to mules. Then it was pointed out that, from what travellers reported, mules were far better in the type of country through which they would be travelling. They recalled their use of mules in Khazaria and understood. Sven Haraldsson added that any good Varangian fought on foot anyway, so how they got to the battle-field didn't matter.

Gunnar was appalled by the rapid pace set by the Autokrator after crossing over into Anatolia. He complained to the Strategos Peter and was nearly sent back to the capital in disgrace. So he shut his mouth, tied his war-axe to the saddle-bow transferred from his horse, and kicked the mule into a faster trot.

The Autokrator had decided to lead his army by the unwelcome, but more direct, route straight across Anatolia. From Nicaea he'd advance to Malagina and then to Dorylaeum, where the river Tembris would be crossed. Soon afterwards he'd pass into the Cappadocian theme by way of Amorium and Laodicea skirting to the south the impossible route through the great salt desert south of Lake Tatta. This would mean a stiff march to Heraclea, leaving Iconium to the south, which would allow entry through the Cilician Gates between the Taurus and the Antitaurus mountain ranges. There might be a chance of a brief rest at Mamistra to allow stragglers to catch up or to send out spies south to discover what was happening in the area threatened by Saracen invasion. The army would then have to force its way through the Amanus Mountains by means of the Syrian Gates. It would be an easier stage to Aleppo, or, if (heaven forbid) it was too late, to Antioch from where the conquest of the Holy Land could be undertaken.

By the end of the third day over one thousand men had been abandoned as the army rode into Dorylaeum in hot pursuit of the Autokrator. Ethelwulf was determined none of his Varangians would be left behind. When Njal Hammerhand protested one hand made it very difficult to keep up with such mad progress, Gunnar merely tied Njal's ankles together firmly by a rope reaching under the mule's stomach. Others who might have protested took one look at Gunnar and changed their minds.

By now the army was entering perhaps the most difficult stage of the march, the march to the south of the central Anatolian salt desert. Further to the north would have been impossible for even the lightly provisioned and mounted force. Even so water was scarce and, although it was only April, already the hot sun tormented thirsty and tired troops.

Still the Autokrator pressed on, determined to reach Aleppo and preserve a useful pawn from the grasp of the Saracens. By the seventh day, as the exhausted army slipped inside the friendly walls of Iconium, another two thousand had dropped behind to stagger on in hope they might arrive in time for the confrontation between Empire and caliphate. Less than one third of these stragglers ever made it to Iconium; most died of thirst or exposure on the hostile Anatolian hillsides, while others turned around and headed back for the more welcome delights of the capital.

Only two Varangians no longer rode with the army; both had slipped away through the Cappadocian highlands to the west of Lake Tatta, hoping in mad desperation to reach Ancyra and then make their way somehow to the sea to take them home to Gadarike. Ethelwulf resisted demands to dispatch a patrol to drag them back for punishment; better lose such wretches before anyone's life depended on their courage in battle.

By the eleventh day the army passed through the Cilician Gates and left the ravages of Anatolia behind them. For a time some of them even tried to sing a chorus or two, but then the shock of the nature of the country still to be crossed closed their mouths. They looked to their Autokrator for inspiration and he firmly set his mind on the planned halt at Mamistra.

Here the Autokrator graciously allowed the weary army to rest for a whole day, fearing that to delay longer would undermine the impetus and determination which had carried them successfully over the terrible trackways to the north. Spies went southwards to discover whether the rescue of Aleppo were still possible, or the army would have to settle for the longer-term base at Antioch.

Gunnar spat into the dust at the entrance to the crude stable Ethelwulf had commandeered and so uttered his opinion of the Autokrator and the court and the whole sorry drive across the Anatolian barrenness. Morkere chuckled and commented that waste of spit might prove troublesome if they were to have any further deserts to transverse.

"Why any man should want to even piss in this miserable hole I don't know," growled the Gall-Gael, leaning heavily on his war-axe.

Alexius, the small balding owner of the stable, looked timidly at the axe as if anticipating Gunnar demolishing his livelihood. He rushed up to the tall warrior, vigorously jabbering in some dialect unknown to them all and furiously pointing his fingers to the ground outside.

"I think," smirked Morkere, "our little friend is telling you to sleep outside if you feel like swinging that axe of yours."

Gunnar glared at the little man and slumped down next to the open doorway. Within a few moments he was asleep, his mouth drooping open and loud snoring coming from the depths of his throat.

Harold of Furzebrook busied himself, drumming up bread from somewhere and distributing it among the Varangians. Most of Ethelwulf's men contented themselves with snuggling down next to the three campfires they'd built, trying to keep out the biting cold of the April night which had followed the heat of the spring day. A few of the more adventurous wandered into the sleeping town of Mamistra in search of women or wine; they found neither in abundance as they'd been forestalled by other members of the imperial army. So disgruntled men trudged back to firesides later at night and tried to ease their way in besides snoring companions.

*

On day sixteen the advance guard of the Autokrator's army finally reached the walls of Aleppo. The troops of Manjurekin melted away towards Damascus and the inhabitants of Aleppo hastened to persuade their rescuers to retire to Antioch.

The Autokrator needed very little urging to transfer his headquarters to the imperial city of Antioch where he could plan a series of raids into Syria which might force the withdrawal of the Saracens and so open the way to Jerusalem itself.

Ethelwulf found the Varangians were little used in the days which followed the relief of Aleppo. He never liked periods of inactivity when a combination of boredom and sheer perversity could lead any of his men into trouble.

The danger was increased by the rich and unusual environment of Antioch itself, offering the temptations of this world and competing access to the next. For Antioch contained a wide range of followers of Our Lord, as well as Jews and Saracens. For centuries it had been the centre of commerce and communication from all parts of the East. Its richness was overwhelming.

*

One day, weeks after the Autokrator had returned to his capital, Ethelwulf was wandering alone among the shops and alleys near the Tower of the Two Sisters in southern Antioch. To his right he could admire the slopes of Mount Sulpius as he carelessly made his way towards the cathedral of St. Peter.

Suddenly he heard a scream ahead and, without pausing, drew his sword and rushed to the end of the alley. A half-starved youth was wildly waving a staff to ward off the advance of a noisy mob of traders and customers. He realised the youth had been caught stealing the large orange nervously clutched in his left hand. Ethelwulf started to sheathe his sword; let the justice of the streets take its course, a thief's life was forfeit the moment his fingers closed on the prize.

"Are you going to let the justice of the imperial throne be usurped by this rabble?" hissed a voice in his left ear and he turned to stare into a pair of burning black eyes. The glare of a bent old man demanded action from anyone wearing the insignia of the Empire.

"It would seem nothing will save -" Ethelwulf began, making as if to retreat back down the alleyway.

"Coward!" snapped the brown-cloaked figure. "Let true servants of the Autokrator show a barbarian how to behave!" With that Ethelwulf was thrust aside against a wall and the old man moved vigorously towards the mob, screeching at them to stop in the name of the Autokrator. For a moment there was silence and several members of the pack started to withdraw with hung heads. Then the young thief chose to snatch at the chance of freedom and run for an alleyway opposite. At this one trader stuck out his leg and tripped up the fugitive. With a scream of rage the nearest traders threw themselves on the half-starved body sprawled in the dust.

The old man rushed forwards, grabbing some of the assailants and trying to drag them away from their victim. As he yanked one man away another screamed abuse and swung at the interfering nuisance with a hammer; the old man collapsed without a sound.

Ethelwulf drew his sword and ran to rescue the fallen hero. Let street violence take care of thieves but any man should help the brave. As he charged forward he screamed a common war-cry. A face turned towards him and he slashed at it; there was a scream of pain and the face was swept backwards. An iron bar swung towards his head and he ducked and thrust at a fat, bare-chested man. The man cried out in pain as he tumbled back over the prostrate body of the old man.

Now the mob had two outlets for its passion. Some kicked and pummelled the lifeless body of the thief, others turned to meet the intrusion of the Varangian. One man tried to seize Ethelwulf from behind and was lurched off his feet as the armed man turned. Another shoved a tray hurriedly in the way to fend off the downstroke of 'Claw'. A third succeeded in landing a vigorous kick into Ethelwulf's thigh causing him to half-stumble. A hammer crunched into his left shoulder causing him to yelp with pain; as he turned to meet this attack a noose looped over his head from behind, he felt a sudden theft of air as his head was yanked backwards.

Suddenly he was on his back, his eyes misty and his sword blindly swinging above his body to keep his attackers at bay. From the corner of his eyes he saw a club descend vigorously in the direction of his bare head. He tried to move his sword to intercept the blow and failed. There was no more light.

*

Ethelwulf screwed up his eyes to shut out the bright morning sun attacking his eyes. How long had he lain here, in this chamber of shadows away from the noise and excitement of the world? He could remember nothing - no, he could recall from somewhere gentle hands and a soft voice and the loving caress of lukewarm water on his brow.

Where was he? Ethelwulf tried to nudge himself up on to his elbows and his body creaked protest. He gave way to the pain and sank back, relieved at the wisdom of his decision, on to the simple bed. If sitting up was too much, then his eyes should explore. He turned his head to the side and part of the world moved and the rest stayed still. Giddiness made him feel helpless and nausea awoke somewhere in his guts. He closed his eyes to get time to think, to wrestle with weakness, to put the world back into order in his head.

He remembered the mob - the club - the noose; his throat hurt and he tried to lift his right hand to bring relief. The muscles in his shoulder ached with the effort and his fingers, when they reached his neck, seemed to be without any feeling. He closed his eyes and again reality circled inside his head.

A sound to the left told Ethelwulf a door was being unlocked and opened. Unlocked? Was he a prisoner? Ethelwulf closed his eyes and concentrated all his other senses as he heard two people enter the room. They approached his bed and he resisted the urge to open his eyes and see his visitors. He heard the hurried muttered conversation between a woman and a man. From the voices he guessed the woman was young and his nostrils detected the soft fragrance of hillside flowers; the bass tones of her companion he naturally associated with middle-age, but he could be wrong. The language spoken was new to him and as he listened to the voices he found himself drifting away from this room, back to the meadows of Arne and the gentle laughter of Elfgivu and his mother.[240]

"How long can the stranger stay here, father?" asked Lydia, her grey eyes longingly resting on the sleeping form in the corner.

Epaphroditus saw the look and frowned. How weak was the flesh! How short-lived the temptations given by the Demiurge! The stranger, whoever he was and wherever he came from, must be a heretic - perhaps a pagan or, worse still, an ignorant believer in the dual-nature of their Saviour.[241] For his daughter there could be no happiness with such a man, better to welcome the suit of Timothy to enjoy these few years before the return of Our Lord in glory.[242]

The preacher looked down at the sleeping man and his features softened. Perhaps there might be a chance for this stranger to know the true nature of their Lord before the destruction and desolation promised in the Apocalypse came about. He frowned at the handsome face betraying both violence and suffering. He knew this man was a creature of the heretic in Constantinople, that city of vice, a barbarian from the north foretold by the prophet -

> " Raise a banner before Zion,
> Flee for safety, do not delay,
> For I bring wickedness from the north
> And great devastation."[243]

Monsters to destroy the lambs of God before the idols of the children of Antichrist enthroned at Constantinople.

Yet Epaphroditus could see a use for these tools; they were close to that mother of harlots, the imperial throne and ideas planted there could be nourished and spread throughout the Empire.

"We must care for those whom God has sent until they are able to undertake the work of the Lord", he smiled at his daughter who seemed warmed by the duty of caring for this wounded soldier. Epaphroditus remembered stories of how long ago the Emperors had listened to the promptings of the Holy, Universal and Apostolic Church and torn down the idolatry throughout their realm. Yet the world and its minions had proved too strong for the work of the Lord and they'd turned their backs at last on the keepers of the Key of Truth,[244] rejecting light for the darkness of damnation.[245]

Lydia made a move towards the sleeping figure and was restrained by her father. She shouldn't get too close to a man locked in the embrace of the Evil One. When Life would re-awaken their guest, pushing aside its sister, Death, there'd be time to talk and, with God's will, bring him to see the Truth.

For Epaphroditus really did see God's purpose in bringing to his house this soldier of the Autokrator. How else could one explain the sudden panic and flight of the mob at the sound of approaching soldiers and yet the failure of the squad to enter the alleyway and discover their wounded officer. Epaphroditus had emerged from his home, noting the mangled corpse of the thief and the badly injured bodies of old Silas and the young officer. He'd recognised the accoutrements of military authority worn by this barbarian and so, while others cared for their battered fellow-in-Christ, he'd quickly had the wounded soldier brought into his house.

That had been three days ago and the man hadn't awoken. His daughter had sat for hours by the bedside waiting for the barbarian to return to this world until exhaustion had driven her to her own bed. Epaphroditus had been glad of that; it was not proper for a young virgin of the True Way to wait upon a man still ensnared in the fetters of the Evil One.

Timothy yesterday had reported his uncle, Silas, had recovered from the blow which had knocked him unconscious. He'd upbraided the old man for daring to intrude in the fracas and so provoke more trouble. However, the oil merchant had been adamant, arguing it was wrong to stand by and watch the destruction of flesh which hadn't yet received the sanction of true belief. Epaphroditus had laughed at the innocence of the old man; how could he expect Our Lord to open the eyes of an alley-thief? This soldier was different; the preacher was certain God had drawn the barbarian to the Empire for a purpose and, as the will of Our Lord could only be for the triumph of the True Faith, He had led the soldier into the house of His true servant.

Epaphroditus ushered his daughter out of the room and carefully locked the door. No man dare release a prize offered by God Himself and Epaphroditus found himself muttering quietly, "*yield yourselves to God as dead men brought back to life, and your limbs to the Almighty as the tools of righteousness.*"[246] This man would be brought back from death itself to do the work of the Lord; but first he'd have to be shown what that truly was.

As he heard the key turn Ethelwulf allowed his eyes to open again but didn't turn his head. He'd sensed the approach of the woman, and then her rapid withdrawal. What did it all mean? Now he must rest, restore his body.

*

Two days later Ethelwulf was sitting up in bed, reluctantly sipping a vegetable-based gruel. What he wouldn't give for a good hunk of meat but these people didn't choose to eat of the flesh of animals. They weren't poor - and they could speak Greek fortunately. He discovered that yesterday when he dared speak to the shy young woman who'd brought him some well-cooked vegetables floating around in a soup. His request for meat was politely rejected, though he almost felt guilty for wanting to eat animal flesh.

These people seemed to be Christian and yet no ikon was in the room. When he crossed himself in giving thanks to God for his salvation the young woman reddened and turned her back. By now he was able to stand and he managed to stagger over to the door; he hadn't been mistaken, it was locked and he was a prisoner. He dragged himself over to the window and looked out. About three yards opposite was a window much like his own; by squeezing against the wall he could just make out part of the alley below. Ethelwulf thought he was in Antioch still but couldn't be sure. He looked forward to the return of his nurse in order to get more details of his surroundings.

As he heard the key turn in the lock, Ethelwulf returned to the bed and awaited his nurse. He was disappointed to see enter a tall, upright man in black-and-white robes. The man had a black beard heavily-tinged with grey and a commanding manner. His brown eyes glowed as he saw the Varangian was seated on the bed.

"Good! I'm pleased Our Lord has brought you back from the shadow of death to do His work," he stated in faultless and clear Greek, as if expecting an automatic acceptance from his audience.

"Why am I a prisoner here?" demanded Ethelwulf and made as if to rise. The newcomer waved his hand in a dismissive gesture.

"No man is a prisoner but merely a small leaf on the tree of life." Here the newcomer paused and looked steadily at the wounded man on the bed. "Don't you know that Tree of Life has almost grown to its full height and will be cut down by the axe of the Lord before our tiny span on earth has passed?"

Ethelwulf well knew many expected the world to come to a pre-ordained end before ten years had passed. He'd come across the idea in places as diverse as the bogs of Ireland and the woods of the Dneiper. It came as no surprise such ideas blossomed on the heady banks of the Orontes. Even so, he was a prisoner whatever this man might say!

Seeing the wounded man made no response Epaphroditus introduced himself as a "humble preacher of the Holy, Universal and Apostolic Church" and quietly asked the name of his "guest". Ethelwulf felt lessening hostility at the warm and friendly tones and readily gave details of his name and purpose in Antioch. Soon the two were in earnest and friendly conversation. Finally Epaphroditus withdrew - making sure he locked the door behind him.

Ethelwulf now knew he'd fallen into the hands of one of the religious groups most hated and feared by the Imperial House. The founder of the present ruling family[247] had carried out ruthless persecution and removed the sect as a threat throughout the Empire. However, from what he'd been told by Leo the Pamphylian this man wasn't content with the normal ideas and practices of the sect; he clearly burned with a passion for the immediate Second Coming. Ethelwulf wasn't happy about such passions, knowing how it could shroud more earthly ambitions and petty frustrations.

Even so, as he picked at the bread and vegetable soup which the man had left Ethelwulf felt more relaxed. He was certain his release wouldn't be long delayed. A light smile played around his lips as he imagined the irritation of Gunnar, even now hunting through the alleys and taverns of the city for his missing leader.

*

Ethelwulf's next visitor said nothing as she hurriedly retrieved his empty plate. She kept her black-haired head averted as she retreated to the door. However, he was certain she'd almost given an answering smile to the broad grin which he'd given her entry.

Soon Epaphroditus returned and was met by a warm smile, but began, "Your master has condemned himself before God because, as Scripture says, ' *he has hindered us from speaking to Gentiles to bring them salvation.* '"[248]

Ethelwulf decided discretion dictated silence. The preacher knew he was an officer in the imperial army and had to recognise treason for what it was. Nevertheless, these people had helped and sheltered him; they didn't deserve the mutilations prescribed by imperial law for such utterances. Observing the silence, and taking it to be acceptance, Epaphroditus placed some more food on the small table below the window and sat down on the bed next to the recumbent Varangian.

"Do you not know your immortal soul is in danger?" he hissed reaching for the hand of Ethelwulf. "The heavens are full of news of the frantic strivings of the Evil One to deceive all *'men about to perish for spurning the love of truth and so their salvation.*'"[249]

Again there was no reply; Ethelwulf felt unable to withdraw his hand while his eyes were gripped by the brown eyes of a fanatic. "For you are in deadly peril, my son, for the *'spirit of Antichrist is in the world already'*[250] and is enthroned in the city of Constantine, the Babylon of our age -"

Ethelwulf felt moved to protest but his objection was hurriedly brushed aside by the preacher.

"Did not the inspired writer of the Apocalyptic Vision say that he "saw *another beast arising from the earth which had two horns like a lamb and spoke like a dragon'* ?[251] And are there not two so-called joint-emperors in that pit of abomination?"

"My master worships God with all his heart," protested Ethelwulf.

"No - no, my friend, not the true God," interrupted Epaphroditus, moistening his lips as he tightened his grip on Ethelwulf's wrist. "'*He is the antichrist, denying the Father and the Son'.*[252] Has he not set himself up above the proper level of a ruler of this world? As Scripture says *'the son of destruction, opposing and raising himself above every so-called god and idol, will be seated in the temple of God, proclaiming himself God'.*[253] Do you not know this vile creature orders men to believe Our Saviour was truly made flesh[254] in this creation of the Demiurge —"[255]

" But Christ was made flesh to save us from our sins -"

"Oh, my poor son," wailed the preacher, raising his eyes to heaven. " You're in danger of eternal torment. Again Scripture has stated that *'God sends to men to make them believe what is false, so that every man may be condemned who spurned the truth but wallowed in unrighteousness.'*[256]

Ethelwulf remembered the warnings of Father Wilfred about the dangers of false teachings. Yet he'd heard in Miklagard matters which would have shocked the Dorset priest. He'd listened to priests who declared that all he'd been taught as a boy had been in error, that he was still a child of darkness. In his heart Ethelwulf felt unease, a knowledge that the time of this world was almost up and he still had to save his soul. Could this man be right?

Epaphroditus saw the hesitation in his prisoner's eyes and pressed home his advantage. "*'For we believers have entered into that rest*[257] promised by Our Lord - a peace which is freely given to all who come to believe, even at the eleventh hour." He paused seeing something of the anxiety leave the eyes of Ethelwulf. " *'Our realm is in heaven and from there we await the coming of a Saviour, the Lord Jesus Christ',*[258] who will sweep aside the tyrants and children of darkness who govern this world!"

Ethelwulf suddenly felt very tired, almost at peace and made to withdraw his wrist from the preacher's arm. Epaphroditus smiled; reassuring his prisoner he was among those who wanted to save him from damnation and telling himself very soon an instrument would be forged to help bring about the destruction of Antichrist. He got up from the bed and silently retired from the room. The sound of the key turning was the last thing Ethelwulf remembered before he slipped into the world of dreams.

It was dark and yet he could see the miserable blue of tempestuous ocean; the seas were like those off the eastern shores of Iceland, fiercer and more untamed than those he'd seen for years. A greenish glow was spreading out over the waters which suddenly broke just like the lake-waters had been breached when they'd seized the Teardrop of Morrigan in that other world so long ago.[259] This time, however, a two-headed scaly dragon erupted from the deep and, even as it emerged, ripped the storm clouds with a burst of flame from the jaws of one of its two heads.

As Ethelwulf's gaze was dragged towards one head, he could see the serpent assume the features of the Autokrator and as his eyes were sucked into the beast's eyes he saw his longship tossed on a sea of corpses imprisoned within the very eye of the dragon.

Then the heavens erupted with a piercing white light and the clouds turned into the gates of a fortress. From out of the gateway rode a single rider on a pale horse, armed and waving aloft a glittering javelin. With a fierce cry the rider launched his weapon at the very eye of the dragon which held his longship.

Like a fiery missile from heaven the javelin sped towards his doomed ship. He turned to urge his men to jump overboard and saw the crew was made up of skeletons dressed in the armour of Morkere and Gunnar and yet lacking any hold on life. Still the fire came down from heaven, slowly spreading light as it fell; there to the west he could see Corfe, black and threatening against the horizon; to the north he could see the dreadful forests of the Wends and to the east the miserable waters of the Kuban.[260] Only to the south could he see a pure, white-stoned city. He tried to turn his vessel towards the city but suddenly it was blocked by the javelin from the sky. As he looked at the approaching head of the javelin it became the face of Epaphroditus and he woke up and screamed.

He was in darkness; outside was the silence of a city at rest. He lay there, thinking of the end of the world and the dangers to his immortal soul. For some reason he was unafraid, almost lovingly making his way towards salvation. He leaned his head back, closed his eyes and relaxed; he felt happy.

*

The next morning his beautiful but silent food-bringer performed her task and slipped out of the doorway before Ethelwulf could ask her name. Soon the door was unlocked to admit Epaphroditus. The preacher looked at Ethelwulf's empty bowl and smiled.

" Have you thought on my words of how you can *'eat of the Tree of Life'*?"[261] he asked, positioning himself against the window so that much of the morning sun was blocked out from the room. Ethelwulf squinted at the silhouetted form of the questioner and nodded silently. "Then you should know that *'God is light and in him darkness is unknown'.*"[262]

Ethelwulf heard the words coming from a distance, as if carried on the wind but with a clarity of a voice next to his ear. Epaphroditus was surrounded by the bright sun-light, throwing into fierce contrast the blackness of his body. He wanted to hear the words of the preacher, but then he remembered the key and asked again why he was being kept prisoner.

"Because you are still a servant of the Antichrist," said the soft tones of truth," and *'we struggle against the rulers of the darkness*[263] to whom Satan has given dominion over this world."

"But the Autokrator has respect throughout the whole of the Christian world, even from the Holy Father in Rome and his son among the country of the Germans,"[264] protested the Wanderer, recognising the preacher's words challenged what had become his life for the last five years.

"Do you not recognise the signs of the Second Coming?" countered the preacher. "It is the time when *'the Lord Himself will come down from heaven with the voice of authority, with the shout of the archangel and the call of the trumpet of God...'*." The dark shape in the window seemed to grow as the voice rose in volume."'*...The dead will be the first to rise, then we, the living, will be gathered with them to meet the Lord in the air.*'"[265] The voice stopped and the light peeping through the window recovered some of its brilliance.

"How can you be so sure?" croaked the prisoner, raising a hand to try and shield his eyes from the brilliance of the sun.

"Scripture itself points the way," answered the confident tones of the preacher. "'*For the wrath of the Almighty is revealed from heaven against mankind's ungodliness and evil in wickedly suppressing the truth'.*"[266] Epaphroditus paused and moved away from the window, approaching the bed." The end has started; ' *the followers of Egypt will fall and her haughty power be humbled*'[267]; God *'will stretch out his hand against the north and wipe out Assyria, destroying Nineveh and making it a desert waste'.*[268] Soon an angel will appear *'holding in his hand the key of the bottomless pit and a great chain'*[269] to bind Satan for ever." Epaphroditus leaned closer to his prisoner and his hot breath somehow appeared deliciously sweet and calming.

Ethelwulf was surprised he felt no need to withdraw from the fierce gaze of the preacher. "And the servant of Satan sits enthroned in the city of Babylon for God Himself has promised that He '*will give the land of Egypt to Nebuchadrezzar, king of Babylon, to carry off its wealth, despoil it and plunder it –*'" [270]

" But who is Neb- Nebuch ?"

" But another name for the Beast, the Antichrist, the limb of Satan that holds the throne of Babylon and is your master," Epaphroditus thrust his face closer to that of his prisoner," or is he?"

Ethelwulf found himself stammering out he didn't know – wasn't sure - needed time to think. The face was withdrawn by a triumphant Epaphroditus. There was a strange smile caressing his lips as he murmured, almost to himself, "You don't have much time, my friend." With that he abruptly left the room, again making sure the door was locked behind him.

The prisoner sank back and closed his eyes. He felt peaceful, at ease; apparently at the end of his path of wandering. He heard the key in the lock and didn't open his eyes; let the preacher come into the room once more and warm him with the news of salvation.

He was aware of the fragrance of his beautiful turnkey and quickly opened his eyes and swung his head in the direction of the door. The girl was standing there, one finger placed against her lips willing him to silence. In her eyes was alarm. Quickly she crossed to his bed and lightly placed her thigh down next to his. The warmth and softness of her body expelled the memory of the preacher's eyes and he could only see the large violet orbs of his new visitor.

"Don't speak," she whispered, huskily, " for I don't have long and my father might return at any moment." Ethelwulf made to sit up but she laid a restraining hand against his shoulder and he felt relieved to submit to her will.

"You must get away from here before my father lures you into danger," she paused, seeing the puzzlement in his eyes. "Yes, young man, my father needs you to carry out his dreadful purpose, one that will bring dishonour and destruction on our family." Ethelwulf started to protest and the fingers were switched to stifle his murmurings. The hand was soft and gentle. "I love my father dearly but I realise that lately he's acted strangely," she smiled and added. "Don't deny you find his words unusually -"

" But he's telling me -."

" About the Second Coming of Our Lord," interrupted Lydia. "Yes, I know. What was a hope became a dream and has now become an obsession." The fingers were withdrawn. "He's certain he must help Our Lord bring about the pre-ordained end - "

"But he's told me - ."

"My father will tell you anything - especially as he sees you as an instrument brought into our house by God Himself -"

"Why? For what purpose?"

"My father has come to believe the signal for the end will come when the Antichrist (and he is convinced, I'm afraid, the Autokrator is the Antichrist) is struck down by one of his servants -"

"Murder the Autokrator?"

"Yes," insisted the girl, still trying to keep her voice scarcely above a whisper. "He believes the forces of the Beast will be unnerved by such an act and lead to the even swifter triumph of Our Lord -."

"I don't believe that such a good - "

"Oh, yes," she countered, "you'd find even Satan himself good if you continue to consume the soup I bring you!" She rose from the bed and walked quickly across to the window; again the bright sunlight framed a dark silhouette. Her voice continued in the same soft way. "Don't you feel strange? Have you not had dreams that were different?" She crossed quickly back to the bed and retrieved her seat. "Well?"

"Yes," confessed Ethelwulf, feeling his throat unnaturally dry and wanting, even as he spoke, more of the sweet-tasting vegetable soup. "I had a frightening dream last night and yet your father -"

"My father has mastered the skill of adding special mushrooms to such soups to bring the fiercest of men to total submission."

"But why -."

"Why you?" Lydia smiled. " From the moment you told my father you stood guard so close to the Autokrator he was convinced you were the one he needed - "

"I don't remember - "

"No," Lydia anticipated, "you wouldn't remember half of the things you told my father." She paused for effect. " About a castle and a murder; a wedding which ended in butchery; a mockery of the cross in northern forests.[271] Yes, you start - but how would I know these things if you hadn't told my father?"

Furiously Ethelwulf searched his memory for what he'd told the preacher. He couldn't remember much; most of the time he'd been listening enthralled to the words - yes, enthralled was a good description. So he HAD been drugged. He'd heard of potions and concoctions in the capital; there men used such tricks to dispose of unwanted rivals or bring an object of desire to bed.

"Don't worry," smiled Lydia. "I shall bring you no more drugged food, though I betray my father - "

"Why would you want to go against the will of God?"

"No!" she hissed in alarm." Surely I'm not too late! Do you not understand? It is NOT the will of Our Lord but the fantasies of my father." She hastily checked the rising volume of her voice. "If you go along with my father's plans, whether you murder the Autokrator or not, our entire family will be destroyed!" She paused, furiously scanning Ethelwulf's face for any sign of agreement, but all she could see was confusion. At last she made up her mind. "Look, next time he visits you, pay close attention to his words. I'll make sure your mind isn't too drugged to think straight. See if he doesn't talk about death and sacrifice and doing the work of the Lord - "

"And then?" queried Ethelwulf, wondering whether this whole episode was but a fantasy conjured up by a weakened brain.

"I'll come again and - and, if you wish, help you escape."

"But - " Ethelwulf's question was cut off by a quick movement of a hand against his lips. Then the girl arose from his bed, hurried to the door and, almost in a single movement, opened it, disappeared from view and turned the key.

Again Ethelwulf was alone, but this time he was no longer relaxed.

*

That afternoon food was left as before, without a word or any indication that anything had been altered. This time Ethelwulf dipped his spoon into the soup and sniffed it suspiciously. There was nothing unusual in the odour, but the very action made him long for a good hunk of beef to give a man proper nourishment. Make do with what you've got, he thought and gulped down the warm liquid.

Epaphroditus entered, glanced at the empty bowl and smiled.

"I'm pleased your strength is returning," he said as he made his way once more to his favourite perch by the window. "Are you yet ready to 'take your share of suffering as a good soldier of Jesus Christ'?"[272] He paused and Ethelwulf almost saw the smile broaden; now the backdrop of the evening light appeared to make the features of his gaoler so much clearer. Or was it, perhaps, that previously the food had been drugged?

Epaphroditus took the look of bewilderment he saw as alarm at his words. " No, don't fear suffering, my son," he urged softly, " *'for the conqueror will not be hurt by a second death'.*"[273] Epaphroditus allowed the words to take effect before he continued. "You are the chosen one, my son; the one longed for by the Psalmist who said *'the righteous will rejoice at the sight of vengeance; he will wash his feet in the blood of the wicked.'*"[274]

So the girl's warning had been proved correct - so far. Ethelwulf masked his feelings as he gazed into the eyes of the preacher. For a brief moment a frown appeared on the face of the gaoler. Was there life in those eyes which shouldn't have been there? NO! The soup had been consumed and with it the mushrooms which gave the peace of acceptance. Epaphroditus peered again into the grey eyes of his prisoner and saw a curiosity which made him hesitate; what should have been there was submission, not questioning.

"How can I carry out the will of the Lord? "gasped the Saxon and Epaphroditus breathed more easily. The man was searching for a way to perform the will of God.

"You've been chosen, my son, to wear the seal of Our Lord on your forehead as one who has *'come out of the great tribulation'*[275] and scripture declares that *'the sword is to be polished to be given to the slayer '*[276] You will be the slayer of the Antichrist that will bring in the angel of death mounted on a pale horse[277] and the angel armed on a white horse[278] and the servants of the Almighty to bring about the destruction of desolation."

Ethelwulf started to protest but Epaphroditus waved his hand in annoyance at the interruption. "At this moment " he declared, "You don't know the destiny laid out by God for you - but I do. I know the time foretold for the destruction of that harlot Babylon is drawing near; even as the forces of Antichrist are destroying the armies of Egypt Our Lord is about to return in triumph -" He raised his hand and retired rapidly to the door. "But I see you are tired, overwhelmed by the glorious honour which God has offered you. I'll return when you've thought about these things."

He quickly left the room and the key was firmly turned before Ethelwulf could even move. Now he knew the girl was speaking the truth he had to find a way of escape. He quickly got up, surprised at the strength in his legs compared to yesterday, and crossed to the window. By craning his neck he could only just see part of the street below. He looked rapidly around his prison; there was nothing that could be used as a rope. Ethelwulf knew he'd need the help of the girl if he was ever to slip out of this trap.

*

The girl returned at the usual time the following morning and shrugged aside Ethelwulf's gratitude. Again she urged him to keep his voice down while they discussed the means of escape from the house. She pointed out her sect had long and careful training in the arts of war so that even if Ethelwulf could overcome her father, he could never get past the three men on guard in the passage.

What about a rope for the window then? There was a dreadful silence and then a mischievous smile appeared on the girl's lips.

"I carry such a rope with me always, " she said, almost laughing at the bewilderment that appeared on the Saxon's face. "Look at my robe," and she flourished a fold of the brown homespun in Ethelwulf's face. "Supposing you were to take it off me - "

"But how ? "

"Of course, I'd protest but you'd first knock me unconscious," smiled Lydia. "Then you'd tear it into strips, link them together and lower yourself down into the street."

Ethelwulf had to grin at the sheer audacity of the plan, but it raised several problems. How was the first tear to be made? "I'll catch it in a doorway before I arrive" was the answer. Where would he go after escaping through the window? "Turn right and go along to the square, then take the second left and the alley will take you to the Tower of the Two Sisters." When should the attempt be made? "This afternoon because my father will be late returning from a meeting with the Elders, and I can arrange to be early."

So it was agreed and Ethelwulf settled himself down to await the arrival of his gaoler for the last time.

*

Epaphroditus was excited. It was now some time since the soldiers of the Antichrist had stopped hunting for the missing officer and he'd heard the barbarians had returned to the capital. So much the better; when his prisoner re-emerged into public gaze he'd be sent immediately to the capital to rejoin his troops. Once there the Lord's chosen one could strike down the Antichrist.

Today he'd reveal his plans to his fellow Elders. Perhaps old Silas might bring up his usual questionings of the will of the Lord, but surely even that old fool would have to admit God had led him to intervene in the fracas and so bring about the barbarian's capture.

For days he'd put off any visit of the old man to his prisoner, not wanting any distraction from the purpose of hastening the Second Coming. However, this afternoon Silas would be welcome to expound how God had brought about his intervention. Surely the old man would bow to the will of the Almighty, rejoicing in the role he'd played in bringing about the destruction of the limb of Satan!

Because of his own excitement Epaphroditus failed to detect the tell-tale liveliness in the eyes of his prisoner. If he'd seen that strange glint would he have assumed it was growing enthusiasm for God's plan - or something else?.

Ethelwulf expressed himself humbled by the role he was to play in the events of the last days.

"Yes," agreed the preacher, " for Scripture says that *'when the thousand years have ended, Satan will be set free from his prison, coming out to lead astray the peoples at the four corners of the world.'*"[279] Epaphroditus paused and gave his prisoner a sharp look. "And did not the Antichrist send one of the deceivers of mankind among the barbarians in the north?"[280]

Ethelwulf agreed Christianity had begun to spread among the Rus. He added he'd heard that in the distant frozen north others were being brought to Christ by a new king, Olaf Trygvasson.

Epaphroditus leaped upon this information to point out that what was being taught was not the true faith of Jesus Christ but heresies long ago exposed but maintained by the cohorts of liars in the service of Satan. Ethelwulf's silence was taken by the preacher to be assent and he hurried to make his departure. Obviously this barbarian had been won over; perhaps tomorrow they'd baptise him into the true faith. First, however, he had to win over the other Antioch Elders of the Holy, Universal and Apostolic church.

With relief Ethelwulf heard the key turn and he was left in peace.

*

Lydia was as good as her word and arrived earlier that usual. Ethelwulf noticed a jagged tear in her robe below her left breast. She advised him to escape at once, not even bothering to consume the soup she'd brought.

"For, after all," she smiled, "would I have stood here while you gulped down that soup?" She paused and carefully began to unwind her robe, keeping her eyes averted from the lustful gaze of the Saxon as her nakedness was revealed." Please," she finally added, "strike me from behind quickly - so I neither feel pain nor suffer injury to my face."

No sooner had she finished than Ethelwulf struck her once, sharply across the back of her head with his hand. The bowl couldn't be used as any soup splashes might reveal the blow followed the removal of clothing. He gently caught and laid her on the bed, delicately turning her to face the wall as a gesture to her modesty.

He set about tearing the robe into long strips and tying these together, having to interlace several strips to form a single strand to produce sufficient strength to take his weight. The task took longer than he expected and Lydia was already beginning to stir as he finally fixed one end of his "rope" to the bed. Softly he whispered his thanks and slid out of the window.

Leaning out into the open air Ethelwulf braced his feet firmly against the wall of the house and started to descend into the alleyway. He could see the "rope" dangled several yards above the surface of the alleyway so he knew he'd have to jump in the end. Ethelwulf cursed himself for not having checked on the alley being empty, but then realised that would have proved impossible anyway.

The actual descent proved easier than he'd expected. Fortunately there was nobody around to see the tall figure rapidly make his way down the "rope" and jump the last three yards to the street below. As he landed he glanced up and thought he saw a head quickly withdraw into the room. If Lydia had tried to look down in the street he was sure the angle of the building would have kept him invisible.

Ethelwulf turned and awaited attack from the house. None came so he quickly took off in the direction described by the daughter of the preacher. He saw nobody until he reached the square that Lydia had described. Even then no one showed any interest in the tall lean figure striding towards the Tower of the Two Sisters.

It didn't take Ethelwulf long to reach the Tower but he did have trouble gaining entry. The sentry recognised immediately he was a barbarian, but then the Varangians had returned to the capital two days before so what was this man doing here? Ethelwulf saw the sentry's eyes harden as the suspicion of desertion flickered across his mind; he clenched his fist preparing to knock the man down.

"What are you doing here?" sang out a clear voice and Ethelwulf saw the surprised face of John Talamides appear behind the shoulder of the sentry. "We thought you were a goner," laughed John, pushing the sentry aside. "Come in and tell us all about it."

Ethelwulf found himself ushered past the sentry and into the mess-room of the Akritai.[281] He laughed at the look of incredulity which appeared on the face of Zeno Parmenides; a third man in the room was a stranger and promptly dismissed Ethelwulf's arrival as unimportant.

It didn't take Ethelwulf long to describe the events of the last few weeks. At the end John Talamides called in a young junior officer and ordered him to take six men to arrest Epaphroditus for treason. Ethelwulf was certain that, by now, his escape would have been discovered and the preacher and his family would have slipped out of one of the gates for shelter among their fellow Paulicians to the north around Edessa.

Ethelwulf wasn't pleased to hear the Varangians had been summoned back to the capital. Reluctantly Morkere had abandoned the search for his cousin among the dirty and hostile alleyways of Antioch and taken charge of the return. He'd left money with the commander of the Tower of the Two Sisters to help Ethelwulf's prompt return to the capital – if he ever reappeared. The next day Ethelwulf left for Miklagard.

*

The sea voyage from the mouth of the Orontes to the Golden Horn was completely uneventful. Ethelwulf concentrated on food and exercise to recover his physical fitness. By the third day he regretted he hadn't decided to stay in Antioch and help in the hunt for Epaphroditus. He'd have liked to have given the preacher some lessons in theology of his own. He regretted the loss of his sword; it was true that another would immediately be found to replace it, but he felt every lost sword somehow separated him from his first weapon in Dorset and with it the peace and security of his youth.

The captain of 'Penelope' proved an amusing liar. At first he claimed to have visited Cherson and was full of wild tales of Pechenegs and Rus. However, his stories first became quieter and more restrained when he realised that at least one of his passengers had travelled among the Rus; finally after two days he stopped telling any stories at all. Ethelwulf said nothing and made no comment. He liked to think he'd travelled in lands where man and horse were joined at the waist or slave girls gang-raped as part of funeral games for a Rus hero.

Miklagard had lost none of its smell - but then he'd only been absent from the capital for months, and not the years which had seemed to intervene in his prison in Antioch. Ethelwulf glimpsed a grey strand among the yellow of his hair which he was certain hadn't been there when he'd last sauntered among the streets of the capital. He regretted he'd not been able to match arguments with Epaphroditus a second time.

With scant patience he watched while the captain of 'Penelope' matched wits with the customs officials of the Nobillisimus, Philip. The captain brushed aside their growing interest in the area towards the bow of his vessel and ushered them towards the aft. A few glasses of Syrian wine later (and possibly an exchange of a small bag of Nomisma) and the customs officials laughingly returned to shore.

Ethelwulf lost no time in following them. Quickly he left the bustle of the Harbour of Hormisdas and made his way north towards the palace. It was strange how safe he felt here among the squalor and activity of Miklagard compared to the alley-ways of Antioch. One beggar stretched out to clutch at his legs as he made his way past the rags which made up bed and shelter for some of the recipients of imperial largess. Ethelwulf swung his fist and the lice-ridden cripple lurched himself back against the comforting shadow of the wall. The Varangian didn't hear the hissed curse which floated in pursuit as he hurried out towards the more open areas next to palace of the Autokrator.

A burly member of the Arithmos thrust the haft of a long spear across his path and spat out an order to stop. For a moment fury made Ethelwulf reach towards his missing sword. Didn't the lout recognise him? Had the world so changed that a captain of the Varangians was denied admission even to the outer courtyard of the palace? Then something made him stretch his legs to add height to his riposte of authority.

"How dare you question an officer of his Imperial Majesty's guard!" He looked into the man's brown eyes and then slowly passed his own eyes down towards the sentry's boots, as if storing away every detail for future reprimand.

"Nobody is allowed to pass this gate, by order of the Eparchos himself," snapped the man and pushed his bulk between Ethelwulf and the gate. There was no point in trying to push his way through. It was obvious no Varangian was within the precincts of the palace, or else he'd never have been challenged.

Yet if that was the case, there certainly had been changes. Although the co-ruler, Constantine, had occasionally showed a dislike for the crudities of the barbarians from the north, the

Autokrator had revealed increasing trust in their loyalty and devotion. This hadn't proved popular with the Arithmos who saw their traditional role of guardians of the palace and its occupants being handed over. Only fear of imperial anger and the common sense of commanders such as Ethelwulf and the Arithmos captain John of Tarsus had prevented some kind of bloodshed between the two groups of soldiers.

Where had his men gone? Why weren't they here? It was no good asking this brute. With a calculated sneer Ethelwulf turned and strode off towards the *'Virgin's Well'*. If there were any Varangians alive and free in the capital they'd be trying to drink the stocks of Theophrastos Eumenides dry.

*

The tavern-keeper was brutal in his summing up of what had gone wrong.

"You'll find your cousin in the prison close by the Hippodrome." The inn-keeper paused to allow half of a malicious smile to dart across his lips. "It appears he had the nerve to go and demand the Paymaster-General should hand over back-pay to your troops!"

Ethelwulf was surprised Morkere could have been so foolish. Of course, the Varangians were owed almost one year's wages, but that was the way of the Imperial Treasury. Morkere above all people would have known you always got your money out of skin-flints like Nicephorus Comnenus by going through even bigger rogues like the Eparchos or the Quaestor. Why hadn't he acted through them? Why was he suddenly so keen on getting paid?"

He glared at the fat tavern-owner and any sign of amusement vanished from the greasy face.

"So it was the Paymaster-General who personally gave the order for the imprisonment of - "

"Well, I heard," volunteered the Greek, "he'd no choice, seeing as how your cousin threatened to install barbarians in the Treasury itself until his men got paid."

No Greek had any patience for any barbarian; even those exacting a profitable income from the open-handedness of the Varangians felt little sympathy for these threatening strangers. The Empire had for centuries depended on the war-skills of barbarians from beyond its borders; but its citizens felt only a mixture of fear and contempt for their protectors. Ethelwulf was lucky Theophrastus had told him where to find his cousin. He was even more fortunate in extracting the information the Varangians had been posted away from the palace itself on the personal authority of the Eparchos. The tavern-keeper was not certain, but he believed they'd set up camp to the north of the city, near the Gate of St. Romanus.

Ethelwulf brusquely thanked the man, remembering to shove a miliaresion[282] into the clutching palm before hurrying out of the door and turning left towards the Amastrianum. From there he turned south-west towards the Forum of Bovis, crossing the river Lycus. He then made his way north-west towards the Gate of Romanus.

It was mid-afternoon when he emerged from the shadows of the gateway and saw ahead of him the military camp which now contained his followers. The first Trapizita[283] asked about the whereabouts of the Varangians merely spat in the dust and turned his back. Ethelwulf reached to teach the man better manners and then felt better of it. Anatolian mercenaries were jealous of the privileges wrung out of the Autokrator by the barbarians from the north; he understood the hostility. He passed deeper into the camp.

Carefully skirting past a latrine at the corner of one of the lanes carving their way through the mass of tents, Ethelwulf decided to head north. If his men were there, they'd be the newcomers - and so get space farthest away from the city gates and the source of consolation from the monotonous regime which made up camp life.

At last he could see the open countryside beginning to appear ahead. Now he had to make a decision; turn left or right. Suddenly he heard softly through the air the strange thin notes of the bone flute. It came from the right - and it was no sound common to the alleyways of Miklagard or the hills of Anatolia. Hurrying towards the sound Ethelwulf could remember the cold, cheerless dawns a decade before in Iceland. He'd been struck by the way the notes clawed their way upwards.[284] from a tune played by northern fingers.

Then he saw Ulf Ragnarsson sitting next to the remains of a camp-fire with a pipe to his lips, trying to revive the welcome memories of home in Uppsala. As he played a dreamy mist clouded his eyes and his mind wandered far away from the murmurs and scrapings of camp-life and back to the peace and tranquillity of home, when the only company were the wolves and birds. He could feel the beautiful chill of the first kiss of morning just before the spring dawn hustled off the cold of night. He could smell the trees and the moss and purity of the forest air.....

"I see you still keep those fingers nimble." The voice yanked the slight, balding northerner back into reality and as he looked up his face burst into an enormous, gap-toothed grin.

"Why, cap'n. None o' us ever 'spected to see you agin!" He stuck the pipe back inside his jerkin and, clambering to his feet, shouted Ethelwulf was back and everything would soon be put to rights.

Within moments Ethelwulf was in deep discussion with Gunnar, Edric and Harold the Black. He was told how Morkere and the others had planned to leave Miklagard and go westwards towards the lands of the Franks. Some Varangians had visited the territories of the Holy Father and the lord of the Franks and described the opportunities there - without having to mumble through alien prayers or put up with the heat and dust of Anatolia. Morkere had volunteered to go to the Paymaster-General for their back-pay. With that they'd be able to sail westwards by the next spring.

"You see," added Harold, nervously scratching at the prematurely-white hair which had earned him his name in youth, "none of us ever believed you'd emerge from that hole in one piece!"

Ethelwulf felt a cold shiver touch his spine as he remembered that in the lands of the Autokrator a warrior could live, die or exist as a mutilated half-man. He knew they'd never have left Antioch unless convinced his chances of survival had disappeared.

"Anyway," grunted Gunnar. "We heard that little runt of a Greek didn't bother to listen to more than a few words before he had his guards throw Morkere into some miserable cell - "

"And immediately we found ourselves transferred out here," added Edric. "Before we even knew what had happened to Morkere we were ordered to move out - "

"They even tried to put Olaf Blue-cloak in charge of us," sneered Harold, "but we soon told him to piss off - "

"And he did to, "chuckled Gunnar, "but then Olaf was never one for standing up to true men."

"So we decided to move out here double-quick," explained Edric, "and then nobody could come down on us for being mutinous."

"It seems to have worked," spat out Gunnar. "They haven't paid us - but they've left us alone up here!"

None of them had made any attempt to reach Morkere - so none of them even knew whether he was dead or, worse still, had been subjected to the barbarous imperial practice of mutilation. The three Varangians looked shame-facedly at the ground but Ethelwulf couldn't blame them. Morkere had only been seized two days ago and they'd been waiting for some kind of retaliation from the Eparchos or Paymaster-General.

In the embarrassed silence Ethelwulf began to plan out his campaign. It would be useless to storm into the presence of the Paymaster-General; all he'd probably achieve would be a set of manacles next to his cousin. However, in imperial politics he'd learned little men jumped when bigger men barked; and Nicephorus was a little man in every way. Somehow he had to get the support of the Eparchos. For a moment he considered getting back-up from the Quaestor, but knew John Angelus was fully taken-up with resisting the expansion of the powers of the City Prefect. The Quaestor would never give his rival the chance of labelling him a friend of traitors.

Then a solution came. All imperial officials had a constant need for money - they needed it to buy the luxuries that public life required, and pay-off both those below and those above them. The Eparchos was no different. Offer him the chance of wealth and he'd be your man, for a moment at least – and that was all he needed.

Ethelwulf knew where money could be found - but he didn't want the likes of Gunnar to blunder in behind him. So he rapidly explained he'd secure an audience with the Eparchos personally and try to get Morkere released, with or without their back-pay. Harold expressed the view that nothing would be gained by crawling before that stuck-up Greek, but Edric countered that nothing would be lost either. So Ethelwulf was to go and beg help from the most powerful official in the Empire.

*

Ethelwulf was surprised how quickly the Galata alley-ways had re-acquired the squalor and dinginess of before the fire. He'd no trouble finding the house of Simeon the trader in jewels. To look at the white-painted frontage no one would have believed that only three years before the whole building had been gutted by fire. Ethelwulf remembered Morkere trying to save the trader's daughter, and how he'd managed to drag out Simeon from the inferno. He hoped the Jew would have an equally-good memory.

The hunch-backed assistant scurried off to fetch his master as Ethelwulf entered the ante-room where jewels were bought and sold. It was hoped the man had recognised Ethelwulf and not simply run away at the approach of imperial livery.

Simeon pushed his way through the curtains which concealed the rear of the building and the enormous smile which sprang into life showed he remembered his rescuer.

"Greetings, young master," he uttered as he hobbled forward to welcome the Varangian captain. "It's good to see that Jehovah has kept you safe from infidel weapons - "

"So you know I've been serving in Syria? " smiled Ethelwulf.

"Naturally," chuckled the old man. "We traders need to know where the imperial eye is turned to make good business." His grip tightened on Ethelwulf's forearm. "Besides, I must pay special attention to the affairs of one to whom I owe - "

"So you've heard of what has happened to Morkere - my cousin," began Ethelwulf, and instantly realised the trader's spies had let him down there. Certainly Simeon remembered the dark-haired, handsome rescuer of his daughter, but news could be more easily gathered of the movements of leaders. As Ethelwulf explained how his cousin had been imprisoned for demanding what was their due, the features of the old trader took on a murderous glint.

"It's never wise to demand what is one's due in this Queen of Cities," he sneered, remembering how the Eparchos had bluntly refused to repay a loan and had sent soon afterwards two ruffians to eliminate the debt. He'd never told anyone how he suspected the fire had been started in the rear of his shop to disguise the assault made upon him. None of his neighbours questioned his story that he'd tripped and, in so doing, dropped a candle among the coverings at the rear of his premises. One day he'd repay the Eparchos for the murder of his daughter and the destruction of his property. In the meanwhile he had chosen to forget about the debt.

Now he remembered the bravery of these barbarians - and his promise of future help. The young warrior didn't have to ask. He knew how to open prison-doors in the city of the Basileus. "I still have that emerald if you have need," he almost whispered.

Ethelwulf nodded and followed Simeon into the rear of the shop.

*

The Eparchos was most sympathetic. When presented with such a beautiful addition to his collection of emeralds he agreed the Paymaster-General had been hasty in his imprisonment of the Varangian. He knew how much the Autokrator valued his loyal warriors from the north, certain the Treasury would immediately honour the debts to such brave men. Ethelwulf thanked the official for his confidence and asked for an order to the Paymaster-General for the release of both his cousin and their back-pay.

"Such instructions are the prerogative of the Autokrator," confessed the Eparchos. "Humble officials such as myself have no authority to interfere in the workings of the Paymaster-General - "

"So I must lodge an appeal with the throne - "

"No, "snapped the Eparchos. "Their majesties need not be bothered with matters such as this." He paused and his fingers irritably tapped on the arm of his chair. "I'll have a word with my colleague this evening." He paused, to make sure the Varangian knew what was expected. "I'm sure that when you approach the Paymaster-General tomorrow morning you'll find him most sympathetic -"

"And if my cousin has already been - "

"Subjected to the legal prerogatives of imperial justice," snapped the Eparchos. "Then that will be unfortunate, but nothing - nothing - can be done!"

So if Morkere had lost his tongue or been blinded, Ethelwulf was expected just to pick up the results of such mutilation and go off without complaint. Well, any Greek laying hands on his cousin....

Ethelwulf repeated his gratitude to the Eparchos and quickly left the room, before words were spoken which might be regretted later.

*

The Paymaster-General was full of oily self-importance. He regretted the imprisonment of Morkere but the young man hadn't appreciated demands for back-pay should only be raised by the commander of the bandon. He had refused to listen to reason and, unfortunately, had to be restrained by his guards.

Ethelwulf's eyes hardened and Nicephorus hastened to add that the force used had been minimal. He'd been assured the young man had been well-treated in prison. By now, he was sure, he'd calmed down and, if prepared to submit a proper apology for his breach of etiquette, he'd be released.

There was a nervous pause while the Paymaster-General waited for the Varangian captain to take up his cue. Ethelwulf took a deep gulp of air before he hoarsely promised Morkere would be sure to recognise his failings and apologise to the Paymaster-General for any embarrassment he'd caused.

Nicephorus smiled. It was good to make these barbarians realise how good behaviour was practised in the Empire. Now and again they had to be taught the virtues of civilised conduct. He looked up into the eyes of the Varangian, coughed politely and continued.

"Of course, now you've been restored to imperial service by the intervention of Our Lord Himself, I'd be most willing to listen to any suitable request you might make for promised emoluments."

There was another pause. Ethelwulf moistened his lips before he said a formal request for the payment of moneys owing to his bandon had been submitted that morning to the office of the Chartularius. One day this little toad would be taught honesty.

*

It took Ethelwulf some time to persuade his cousin to allow a Chartularius to draft a suitable apology to the Paymaster-General. The document expressed sorrow that the Paymaster-General had been threatened by the violent words of one inexperienced in the sophisticated ways of the Empire. It explained that, at the time, Morkere had been mourning the supposed loss of his cousin and had given insufficient regard to the proprieties expected of a servant of the Empire. When the document was brought to Morkere for him to scrawl a cross, to be witnessed by the Chartularius Philip, the Varangian argued he couldn't be expected to agree to what he could not read. Ethelwulf pointed to the insect-infested corner of the cell and asked bluntly if his cousin really did prefer his new companions to his friends outside. Morkere took the stylus in his left hand and furiously made a mark on the parchment.

There'd been a strange smile on the lips of the Mysticus [285] John when he took the document out of Ethelwulf's hands. For a moment there was a temptation to force it down the Greek's throat, but the mood passed. It was helped by John remarking his master had accepted the petition for agreed payments to be made.

So Morkere was restored to his friends - and silver was soon to pass swiftly from Varangian purses to bath-house owners and inn-keepers. However, there remained other debts to be paid.

The Wanderer 8:5

"Omnis plaga, tristitia cordis est:
Et omnis malitia, nequitia mulieris."
(Ecclesiasticus 25:17 – Vulgate)

"(The worst) woe of all is sadness of the heart:
Of all spite, the wickedness of woman."

The Whore's Murder

"The Lord, Jesus Christ, and all his angels be praised! The upstarts of the west, [286] falsely claiming to be the heirs of Constantine and of Theodosius, have been moved to seek the hand of one of the Imperial House for their barbarian prince."

The Quaestor seemed delighted at the latest news from beyond the western borders of the Empire. At last those barbarians claiming to be the heirs of that traitor to the Empire, Charles of France,[287] were prepared to make submission to the true ruler of Christendom.

As a young man he remembered the embassy of that Italian who'd squawked so much when they'd confiscated those bales of cloth.[288] He recalled being despatched by the Patrician Christopher (may he burn in deserved hell-fire) to add this final humiliation. The Italian had, for once, lost his sickly paleness [289] as he even physically tried to keep hold of the cloth. All to no good. What poisons had the fool poured into the ears of the Bishop of Rome on his return. He hadn't revealed the diplomatic insult provoking the incident.[290]

Anyway that was all in the past. Liudprand seemed to have got over his treatment as he'd joined in another embassy which had secured the Princess Theophano for his master. The Quaestor recalled the old man had even been able to get his precious purple cloth at last.

Now there were new supplicants from the West. This time they included someone who could be expected to treat the Autokrator with due reverence.[291] He was sure they'd learned from the past. The attempt by the last king of the Germans to seize imperial lands in Italy had been a disaster.[292] The present king was supposed to see himself as a worthy off-spring of the Imperial Family, destined to re-unite the lands of the ancient Roman Empire. Perhaps - if the Autokrator had no direct heirs, the seed of his father would someday govern from the distant western seas to the Caucasus.

The Quaestor pulled himself back into reality. It was treason to even think the Autokrator would die childless. Banish the thought. Whatever veneer of civilisation this king of the Germans contrived to assume he was still the child of a barbarian father, sprung from a land where there was no sun and little culture. He must ensure he had private conversations with the German envoy; unfortunately, he'd good reason to believe the German had already been won over by the promises of the Eparchos. Yes, Nicias must let the German see how civilisation entertained its visitors.

*

She'd smiled at him. He was certain of it. For a moment their eyes had met, locked, cavorted with each other and then she'd smiled. Ethelwulf ran his fingers lightly through his hair and frowned. Was he some half-grown lad to be ensnared by a smile? He recalled the Queen long, long ago at Corfe. She had smiled like that, he was certain of it. It was the gesture of the seductress, the Jezebel.

No. Zoe wasn't like that. She liked men; he knew that. The whole court knew she toyed with lovers as her sister still toyed with dolls. Only her father and uncle preserved the illusion their heiress retained the modesty of a virgin and the piety of a nun.

She'd smiled at him and it had been an invitation, a challenge not to be ignored. No man could escape his fate. If he was doomed to perish at the hands of Greek executioners then let it be so. It didn't have to be like that. He knew the captain, Michael Comnenus, and the Deputy-Chamberlain, John Phocas. Both had been lovers of Zoe for a time, until she'd tired of them. Both still enjoyed the profits of her favour.

Besides to bed a princess was not knew to him. Had he not enjoyed the body of Gormflath on the banks of the Liffey - and survived the enmity of her husband-to-be?[293] He remembered the surprising softness of Skuna and the gentle cooing as he carried her back to her father.[294] He was certain Morkere wouldn't hesitate - and yet his cousin's relationships with women had often led to trouble.

But she had smiled at him, a Varangian from a world outside her dreams. He had to find out more about that smile.

*

"Do you think he's stupid enough to think he'd ever couple with a daughter of the Imperial House?" tittered the maid, Anna, as she carefully arranged the hair of her mistress in the Aphrodite style then sweeping the boudoirs of the New Rome.

Zoe allowed a small smile to flit over her lips. Oh yes, she was certain the barbarian fool was already dreaming of climbing into her bed and penetrating her Imperial Treasury. As if she'd even dream of it. She could never do that with anyone who smelled as he did! He was a barbarian; fitting for Pechenegs or Rus or Saracens, but not for the child of an emperor.

Still it'd be amusing to play with him for a while. To let his mind slip into forbidden dreams. Just, just tantalise him with what could be - and then take it away. She'd no dislike for the barbarian. He had the good looks many of his sort had; but they were charms one might relish in a well-groomed horse or a prize boar. Yes, that was it. These warriors from the north should be put out to stud among the Bulgar and Slav women of the Hippodrome, to breed a future fighting force for her family. Perhaps this could be an experiment to test the virtues of such a mating.

Then the smile re-appeared as a grin. She swung her head around so quickly that Anna was forced to apologise for dropping one of the curls about to be inserted in her hair.

"What was the name of that whore Michael said bore a passing resemblance to me?" she asked.

Anna was shocked. No woman of the Hippodrome could look anything like a daughter of the Imperial House. Michael couldn't have been serious. It had been an insult.

However, Zoe insisted. She wanted Anna to get the name from Michael, find the woman and bring her to the palace. She had an idea which would liven up the tedium of palace life.

*

Morkere grinned when his cousin confessed his feeling for the second child of the emperor. She was the only beddable one of the girls - though Theodora might have possibilities in a year or so.

"In a year or so we may not be here," dourly commented Ethelwulf. Already he'd spent longer in Miklagard than in any other place since his flight from Corfe seventeen years before. He was tired of wandering. Perhaps a princess might find him a suitable post.

"In a year or so the whole world may not be here," laughed Morkere, scoffing at the growing belief that within a decade Christ would come again to bring about the end of the world.

"Don't scoff at what God may have in mind," answered Ethelwulf, surprised at his own abruptness. Perhaps Epaphroditus had managed to worm his way deeper into his mind than he'd believed. In a way he was glad now they'd never caught up with the madman, he wouldn't like Lydia to mourn the loss of her father.

"What are you dreaming of now?" smiled Morkere. He was worried about his cousin, in many ways changed after his return from Antioch. Always he'd believed in destiny, but now he assumed the passive role of simply waiting to be tossed and carried as fortune decided. The men were less happy as well. Gunnar was muttering about returning to Kenugard where a man knew where he was - and could be sure of what he drank!

"But I must wait for her to make her move," mused Ethelwulf, more to himself than to his cousin as they sprawled in the gathering dusk overlooking the streets leading to the Harbour of Hormisdas. He'd got his men restored to their duties at the palace and nothing more had been said about back-pay since the release of Morkere. In fact, payments had been more prompt since then.

There was a growing mood among the troops, however. A restlessness after the spluttering out of the campaign in Syria. The older hands increasingly looked to the north and the rumours of ambition among the Bulgars. The Autokrator had decided to cut down the power of those Anatolian lords who'd conspicuously given little help to his march on Aleppo. He'd imprisoned the Patrician Constantine Maleinus and seized his estates. Other Anatolian nobles had lost lands acquired in the previous half-century of imperial weakness.[295] For a time the Varangians had expected trouble - a profitable rebellion to crush, but nothing happened. So now all hopes rested on the simmering state of the northern frontier.

Morkere realised part of the trouble lay in the effect of the monotony on his cousin. Ethelwulf didn't have the ready outlet of Gunnar of boozing and brawling. This might get the fierce Gall-Gael in trouble again and again; however, what Ethelwulf had in mind could have far worse consequences.

*

Zoe was pleased. The courtesan Theodora had been brought from the Hippodrome by her master, Nicias. At first she'd resented the insistence of the balding Thessalonican on referring to the girl as a "courtesan". That title should be reserved for those allowing their bodies to be monopolised by the wealthy and the powerful in private apartments hidden away in the alleys by the Aqueduct of Valens. Gradually, however, the princess came to admire the girl; perhaps helped by the strong resemblance to herself.

Directly the whore opened her mouth the princess had been disillusioned. Instead of the pleasing accents of the palace she'd endured the coarse distorted language of Taron. The girl had been born in a village to the east of Mus and been both enslaved and deflowered by a pillaging band of Turks. On the destruction of the band by an imperial force she'd fallen in with the Thessalonican, after passing through a number of hands. Fortunately, up to this moment, her master hadn't realised the extra profit to be made by the strong resemblance between his chattel and a daughter of the Imperial House. Zoe decided to make sure the rogue had no chance to act on the glimmer of an idea she detected in his eyes during that audience. Two days later Nicias was set upon in one of the alleyways between the palace and the Hippodrome and beaten to death. His killers weren't caught and his possessions, including the terrified Theodora, smuggled into the palace.

It took two days of intense, and impatient, coaching for the girl to start learning her part. The matter was complicated by the need to ensure very few even knew the girl existed. Zoe was forced to play an active part in the rehearsals and training herself. At first she was amused, indeed intrigued, to see how the frightened slut was taught to whisper hoarsely rather than employ her usual whining voice. Michael was not gentle in his methods. Zoe noted a cruelty she'd never believed existed in her former lover; obviously his way with underlings was very different from how he courted a princess. The girl was brusquely told that if her voice rose above a whisper an operation would produce the same effect permanently. She was allowed to wear one or two of Zoe's robes and have her hair carefully washed, cut and styled by the zealous Anna.

Zoe felt her plans were moving well. The barbarian would be smuggled into the palace to share the bed of a princess and so would be mated with the impostor. Zoe was confident barbarian ignorance and Michael's training would prevent the discovery of the trick. When observation had lost its fascination, Michael would rush in with the guards and seize the couple. Zoe wondered how the barbarian would react to find he'd been making love to a whore and not a Byzantine princess. Anyway, it didn't matter. The whore, if willing to keep her mouth shut, could be packed off to the brothels of Corinth or Nicopolis. If the barbarian proved apologetic for even contemplating touching a daughter of the Imperial House, he could be despatched to Kars or Taron, somewhere he could cause no trouble and never be heard of again. If he proved truculent, and Zoe hoped this wouldn't be so, he'd have to be silenced and hidden away in one of the monasteries in Anatolia.

Of course, there remained Anna and Michael and one or two servants. The princess was certain every one of her servants wouldn't like to lose their position; as for Michael, Zoe had begun to feel a renewed interest in the handsome Syncellus.[296]

*

The invitation was discreet, whispered by Anna, the personal maid of the princess. Even so, there could be no mistake. He'd been asked to attend on the Princess Zoe in her private apartments at midnight in two days time. Ethelwulf, although he'd promised discretion, was impelled to take his cousin into his confidence. Hadn't Morkere scoffed at the 'randy delusions' of his cousin? Ethelwulf had stayed silent, unable to counter the sneering demand to prove the alleged passion the princess had for a Varangian. Of course, he couldn't make the first move - that would lead not only to punishment for himself, but disgrace for the whole Bandon. So he'd sat during their rest-periods overlooking the Harbour of Hormisdas enduring the mockery of his cousin. At least they'd kept any word of his dreams from Gunnar. The cruder onslaught of the Gall-Gael would have produced either a fierce quarrel between the two or Ethelwulf driven beyond the limits of caution.

Now that would all prove unnecessary. Zoe had opened contact herself. Naturally he knew he was being summoned merely as an imperial plaything, just as she might send for a magnificent stallion or a performing dog. But that could be changed. He was certain that, with careful strategy, a princess could be won - and when that had been achieved, who knows what could happen?

Morkere was surprisingly suspicious of the whole affair. He didn't believe a princess of the Imperial House would dream of being bedded by a barbarian. Ethelwulf reminded his cousin of John Phocas and Michael Comnenus.

"But they're both Greeks!" protested Morkere. "Can't you see how much these Greeks pride themselves on what they call 'civilisation'?"

There was a contemptuous grunt from Ethelwulf. Of course, the Greeks enjoyed a culture more refined than anywhere else in the known world, but that made them dependent on the swords of real men from the north. Besides he didn't like Morkere being so dismissive of his attractions. He'd never, in the past, found women looked on him without favour.

Morkere laughed - cruelly. "Idiot! You're talking about a princess, one who claims she has the blood of Justinian flowing in her veins."

Their discussion had become so heated their voices had risen above the customary soft tones of their mid-afternoon musings. What made it worse was they'd somehow slipped into Greek – often used by both as useful practice for the world beyond the parade-ground! The voices attracted the attention of Psellus, a Chartularius in the department of Bardas, the Logothete of the Praetorium.[297] As he listened from behind the curtains, shutting off the verandah from the palace, a frown of puzzlement appeared on his face. Gradually this was replaced by anger as he realised the identity of the woman under discussion. How dare these barbarians even think of a princess of the Imperial House in such a manner. Did they think she was no better than a whore from the Hippodrome?

*

"And you say the barbarian will be sneaking into the palace in two night's time?" checked the Eparchos. There was a deep frown on his forehead. He had no great love for the Macedonian House. Was not his mother a descendant of the great Theophilus[298], robbed of her birthright by the bloody crime of the peasant, Basil? [299]Even so he was appalled that a barbarian wretch should even dream of raising his eyes to a princess of the purple.

Psellus had hurried into the private apartments of the Eparchos only moments before. He'd decided his news was more suitable for the Eparchos himself than for the Logothete. The Eparchos was a man of action, whose family had been prominent in the affairs of the Empire for centuries. He'd appreciate the insult about to be offered to the Empire itself.

At first the Eparchos had resented the intrusion of the secretary and been about to order his ears clipped for intruding on the privacy of an overworked servant of the state. However, the first words delivered in the man's squeaky voice captured his interest. As he listened a frown appeared and grew in intensity. He couldn't believe that even that shameless hussy in the palace would so belittle the pride of the Empire. Of course, he'd heard tales of her growing lusts, but that was what one would expect from the child of such a family, unless they were held strictly under control; he doubted whether Constantine had either the time or the will to control his favourite daughter. As long as she betrayed the Imperial Family with a member of the nobility, such as Michael Comnenus or John Phocas, it could be tolerated. After all, just like her aunt, Anna, she had value in the diplomatic schemes of the Empire. Barbarians, such as the German Otto, would be pleased with an imperial princess, even if somewhat tarnished beforehand. However, the Eparchos feared even a German king wouldn't welcome a woman shamed by an affair with a barbarian soldier.

Naturally the offender had to be that meddler from the land of the Saxons. As soon as he'd seen the man years ago he'd put him down as a threat. Even though the barbarian had known none of their language, he'd shown no fear before the Autokrator himself - and he'd learned quickly. The mouth of Alexius Euergetes tightened even more as he remembered how often this man had blundered across his schemes. He must have the luck of Satan himself. Well, this time his luck had run out.

Quickly he ushered Psellus out of his chamber, promising him a rich reward and expressing his eternal gratitude. The man might have further uses in the future, as a means of controlling the Logothete from below. Now, however, he had to deal with the barbarian as quickly and effectively as possible.

Alexius looked out into the blackness of the night. It wouldn't do to have any Roman too closely involved in his schemes. He knew how Romans loved to talk, and he wouldn't like any unwelcome stories getting back to the Autokrator. One could never be sure how the Autokrator would react. He'd be angry at his niece, but then she'd won him over repeatedly in the past. He might even see the action of the Eparchos as somehow directed against his family. No, the Eparchos realised he'd have to remain detached from any action, and yet close enough to profit afterwards.

Just a hint after her lover had been butchered in her bed would be enough to bring the young hussy to order. Perhaps she might be persuaded to marry into his family. It'd be a pity to waste her on a barbarian when his nephew, John, could be presented as an eligible suitor. The Eparchos allowed a half-smile to flit across his lips. Perhaps there might be a way he could restore the promise lost when Anastasia's claims were pushed aside by Michael the Drunkard and his family shut out from power.[300] Perhaps a grandchild could sit upon the imperial throne. For a moment the

Eparchos allowed himself the unusual luxury of dreaming; then his mind returned to its normal calculation.

The barbarian had to be eliminated and Zoe terrorised into bowing to his demands. He was certain that if she were compliant neither the Autokrator nor his brother would stand in the way of a marriage with such a noble house as his. And only last week a likely tool had landed at Hormisdas. The Almighty must have decided the Eparchos would get his deserts.

Alexius Comnenus clapped his hands together once to summon a slave and rapidly issued orders. He gazed out into the night as the instrument for achieving his aims was brought to his presence.

*

Thorgeis still stank. He might wear the flowing robes of an imperial officer but he hadn't acquired the civilised custom of bathing. Even so, the Eparchos was pleased to see the red-haired barbarian as he strutted into the room and waited impatiently for his orders.

Alexius had heard all about the quarrel between the two barbarians in Crete two years ago. Although despising this braggart in front of him, he'd long been worried by the success of Ethelwulf in the capital. It was his good fortune that just as he had the chance to rid himself of the meddler from the north, he had the very tool to hand.

"I've read the report of George Eumenides," he paused to let the barbarian wonder about the contents. Unfortunately he was only rewarded with a sullen glare from the mercenary. It was obvious the wretch had lost none of that resentment towards his betters he'd shown when he'd first arrived in the capital. "I'm pleased to see he writes most highly of you." There was no response from the barbarian. Did the idiot not understand Greek? "He says you do well," conceded the Eparchos and was rewarded with a grunt. Good. The less the ruffian could blab to anybody close to the Autokrator the better. However, he had to make sure the creature knew enough to play his part.

"Ethelwulf' still here," offered Alexius and noted the fierceness which took over the eyes of the barbarian. Did he really have one green eye and one brown eye? The Eparchos caught himself squinting in the half-light to confirm the peculiarity and immediately swung away towards the cleaner, fresher air of the city. He heard a movement behind him. Let the barbarian wait, he must learn who were his masters. Michael Theophilus, and his successor, had been too conciliatory to the barbarian. He may have been useful in recovering control over the villages of the Lassithi plateau, but standards should have been maintained. The barbarian should have been made to bathe at least daily!

The Eparchos turned again towards the Varangian with a forced smile. "You not like Ethelwulf?"

"Yes," grunted Thorgeis. What was this Greek up to? Why had he been dragged away from the dice at "*The Black Horse*" - just when he'd started to win back some of the kerations lost to those slimy Greeks the night before? It had clearly been important; he could tell that from how that fat fool, George, had turned pale and bustled him out of his tavern. Somehow he'd understood the Eparchos wanted to see him immediately. He'd tried to turn back into the tavern and found George summoning two ugly-looking oafs to propel his difficult guest towards the house of the Eparchos. Behind sauntered the little runt that had started it all. At first he'd been tempted to turn around and throttle the half-starved fool, but the slave made damn sure he stayed well out of reach - and the lout who'd volunteered himself as a guide had a very powerful grip of the Varangian's elbow.

At last they'd reached the home of the Eparchos and the lout shuffled off into the shadows. Thorgeis had pushed his way past other slaves and found himself facing the Eparchos. He'd had little time for the Greek in the past; but now they shared an enemy, and it was good to get to know an ally. Still, Thorgeis didn't like the way the Greek turned his back on him, a trusted emissary of the Governor of Crete deserved better than that.

"Ethelwulf has many friends here," stated the Eparchos, and Thorgeis was certain he wasn't facing one of them. Why couldn't these fools stop whining in that language of theirs?

 "He even go to palace." The Eparchos paused to make sure the Varangian had taken in the meaning. Oh, if only the barbarian had bothered to learn Greek like Ethelwulf had done. No, such ignorance could have its uses. "He now good friend of Princess Zoe". Alexius was pleased the barbarian obviously had heard some of the vulgar gossip circulating in the capital about the pastimes of the emperor's daughter. "He VERY good friend of princess," added the Eparchos, allowing a sneer to pass across his lips. Yes, the man understood.

Thorgeis swallowed hard. What was this Greek playing at? He didn't want to hear the Saxon was worming his way into imperial favour. If half the stories he'd been hearing about this princess Zoe were true, he was sure Ethelwulf would be having the girl on her back by now. Which little trollop was she? Surely not the one with the pock-marked face?[301]

No, he knew Zoe. She was the one who'd tarted herself up when they'd all left for Crete two years ago. Thorgeis bit his lip as a horrible thought stumbled through his mind. Had the whore been making eyes at the Saxon even then? He looked across at the Eparchos. No, if she had been this bastard'd have been up to mischief long before now. Well, my skinny friend, he mused, what are you up to?

The Eparchos was content to wait and revel in the obvious twists of realisation trooping into the barbarian's mind. How plain was the hatred - and how useful! The meddler was as good as dead.

"You want speak Ethelwulf about what he do to you?" ventured the Eparchos. The Varangian made to move closer to the Eparchos and for a brief instant Alexius thought he'd pushed the barbarian into violence. He'd heard how Ethelwulf had pitched this fool into the sea two years ago. The Eparchos looked the ruffian up-and-down; Ethelwulf must have been lucky to have caught this man off-guard. All the better. In two night's time it would be a different story.

"He see princess at night soon," added Alexius, enjoying the pain entering the warrior's eyes. "Maybe you see him there alone?"

So that was it. Thorgeis could almost laugh aloud. This Greek was giving him the chance to settle matters with the Saxon. Good. He didn't like owing debts of the kind he owed Ethelwulf; for months his mind had savoured the pleasure of their next meeting. When he'd heard Ethelwulf had disappeared in Antioch he'd felt cheated of his revenge. By now that incubus for revenge had sucked out almost everything else - but not quite. His eyes narrowed in calculation.

"What I get for doing what you want?" he growled, and was pleased the Greek recoiled from the answer. Did the slimy toad think he was going to do all the dirty work for nothing? He'd better make the price worthwhile because Thorgeis knew if he ever got rid of Ethelwulf he'd have to arrange for the removal of other members of the Varangian guard. Perhaps this Greek could fix that.

Alexius bit his lip. He didn't like openly stating he wanted Ethelwulf assassinated; he knew better than anyone how the odd word could drift its way along corridors into the ears of enemies. To plot murder was punished by loss of tongue and eyes - and entombment in one of the less-fashionable monasteries on the Anatolian mainland.

Could he trust this barbarian? Perhaps for a time, until he could arrange a suitable accident. In the meantime it would be necessary to find a suitable bribe.

"I'm sure the Imperial Treasury would realise it owed you... let us say .. perhaps five hundred nomisma in gold?" He paused, pleased to see the nervous moistening of the lips and the glint of greed which showed the bait was being accepted.

"Others must be killed," ventured Thorgeis, pleased the Greek was giving ground and anxious to bind the Empire fully into the conspiracy. " Gunnar ... and Morkere."

The Eparchos nodded curtly. He could well understand why this barbarian wanted others dealt with. He'd heard one barbarian would die to avenge another. It didn't matter. Morkere could be seized, blinded and thrown into one of the convenient gaols for riff-raff in the capital. He knew the man could be dangerous, so he had to disappear. The Irish madman could be removed as part of a drunken brawl. Let this barbarian remove the keystone and he'd demolish the rest of the arch.

"You help me meet Ethelwulf," grunted Thorgeis, relishing the chance to settle matters with the Saxon.

"Servant Papias[302] help you," answered the Eparchos impatiently, anxious to rid himself as soon as possible from a link with murder. "He take you Ethelwulf in two night's... " He paused, and changed his mind. "No, Chartularius Psellus meet you by gate in Street of Wineskin Makers at midnight."

Thorgeis frowned. Why had the Greek so quickly changed his mind? Was he planning some treachery? He squinted at the calm features of the Eparchos. I wonder what's going on behind that mask you call a face, he thought.

The Eparchos had decided to limit his involvement. Psellus knew too much already, so he may as well take on a new role as well. It would be easy to silence his tongue later. Now he just wanted this barbarian out of here.

"You may go," he dismissed the barbarian and turned back towards the pure night of the capital. He'd not have liked the strange look which flashed into the green eye of the Varangian.

*

Morkere smiled at the obvious excitement of his cousin as the hour of his arranged visit approached. Ethelwulf was content to sleep-walk through his duties at the palace. Fortunately, they were the simple placing and changing of sentries and the supervision of weapon practice for the second and third Pentekontarchies.[303]

Ethelwulf showed little patience with how Harald Broken-nose marshalled his defences to withstand the attack led by Gunnar. He too-readily allowed Gunnar to feint towards the left before using ten warriors placed on the right to storm up the artificial mound used for the sessions. Although all weapons were scrupulously blunted there could still be the occasional broken limb or nasty wound to teach a Varangian the value of a sound defence. Certainly Harald was too-easily deceived by the feint, but he rapidly recovered and fought the third Pentekontarchos to an exhausting draw by regrouping part of his company on the top of the mound itself. It was a good recovery.

"If you'd have let any Bulgar get that close he'd have wiped you out," snapped Ethelwulf and Harald simply glared back resentfully. Of course, he'd made a mistake - but had recovered quickly enough to stop Gunnar in his tracks. He looked across at the Gall-Gael breathing heavily at the foot of the mound. There was a malicious smirk on the face of the Varangian. He knew he should have driven the second Pentekontarchos off the mound with that charge by Ubbe and Ragnar, but he hadn't reckoned on Sigurd Croaker going berserk on them. The man had simply hurled himself at Ubbe and smashed him clean off his feet before felling Ragnar. If any man deserved a public reprimand it was that crazy Orkneyer. It was generally agreed berserk moods should be vigorously held in check in practice session. Too much damage could be done by a single act of craziness. Ubbe was lucky to escape with a broken shoulder.

Morkere steered his cousin away from the incident and towards the planned parade next week before the visiting envoys from the German king. He knew how anxious they all were to show the westerners just what proper fighting men could do. It was the only time Ethelwulf showed any real enthusiasm for duty. Morkere couldn't wait for the appointed time to come, simply to get his cousin back to normal.

*

Shortly before midnight Ethelwulf arrived alone at the side-gate to the palace where the maid Anna had promised to meet him. Something in his stomach told him she wouldn't be there, that it was all a mistake. However, she was waiting; as he reached the welcome shadows of the porch a soft voice whispered, "Come,

Varangian!" and he found himself being led quickly, and silently, through the twisting corridors of the private quarters of the palace. Once he tried to ask the maid how far they had to go and she simply turned and vigorously hushed him into silence. He felt the comforting hilt of his sword as he followed as quietly as possible the spare, blue-gowned figure, distorted by the inconsistent light of occasional illumination.

At last the maid reached an open doorway which led into blackness. "Your desire lies within, barbarian," she whispered and melted into the shadows before Ethelwulf could offer any question. Ethelwulf didn't like the abruptness of her disappearance. He tightly gripped his sword and started to pull it from its scabbard. Then he stopped. If enemies were here now he wouldn't be quick enough. He relaxed and tried to still his breathing so he could catch any sound coming from within the room.

For a time he heard nothing, and then he detected (or thought he heard) the soft pant of a sleeping woman followed by the languid rustle of a body turning in bed. Could that be the princess? Why were there no lights? He hesitated and then decided discretion required the minimum of light and the absence of witnesses. He stepped into the room and stopped, willing his ears to take in more of the sounds coming from the bed.

The sleeper seemed to awake and he heard his name, or thought his name whispered. He took several steps towards the bed and could smell the occupant. The fragrance was one he'd sensed before in the audience-chamber of the palace, a product of the distant estates of the Empire. It was a perfume not to be had in the capital for anything short of a fortune. That settled it. Quickly he unbuckled his sword and stealthily laid it beside the bed, half-frightened any noise would shatter the dream and he'd find himself back in the barracks.

The occupant of the bed slithered over and pressed itself close to his body. For a moment fingers clutched at his tunic and then he found it being quickly, and expertly, removed. Ethelwulf sensed softness and passed his hands lightly over the shape in the bed. There was no doubt it was a woman, but was it THE woman.

"Zoe?" He was amazed how hoarse was his voice as he tried to whisper the question. There was no response from the figure that by now had half-removed his tunic. He repeated the question and was rewarded with a muffled, garbled response before soft lips stilled a further enquiry.

By now his right hand had brushed aside the night-gown and could feel the hardening nipple of his companion. He found his whole body responding to the kiss, as he passed his hand downwards towards the stomach of his princess.

There was a soft murmur and he felt her breasts rub eagerly against his chest. As her fingers started to explore his body any doubts persisting in his mind were expelled by the luxury of feeling desired. He found his response strengthening and moved to explore further the pleasures of his companion.

*

Zoe was pleased with the report of her maid. Anna had returned stealthily to the princess's bedroom a few minutes after guiding the Varangian there. She reported the only sounds were those of two people exacting the supreme pleasure from each other. Her mistress found herself moved to question closely exactly what the maid had heard and almost regretting the whore was being enjoyed and not herself. That could not do. A princess of the Empire of East Rome should be above pandering to the lusts of a barbarian - and yet she felt drawn to try out the stallion before it was sent off to war.

In the meanwhile she must make ready for the rest of the night. Michael would arrive shortly, together with a small trusted detachment of Arithmos. They'd be necessary in case the barbarian should prove difficult - not that Zoe intended him to come to harm. Together she and her re-installed lover would savour the grunts and whimpering of the lower orders. This would prove an additional wrapping for the later pleasures of the night. To make love to a prince of New Rome on a bed already warmed by the brutal lusts of barbarians! Zoe moistened her lips at the novel smells and sensations that could be explored when in the arms of her Michael.

First, however, they'd capture the pair of lovers in bed - like Ares and Aphrodite ensnared.[304] She smiled as she imagined the shock and disappointment seizing the barbarian's features as he realised how he'd been deceived. Perhaps if he was good she might, just might entertain him later. No, better to enjoy the caresses of a noble in the folds made by a barbarian. One never knew what dreadful disease could be caught by mixing with creatures just above the level of the beast.

*

He was glad he'd forced the Greek to bring a torch as they'd been smuggled into the palace by one of the agents of the Eparchos.

Thorgeis had no love for the twisting and winding of Greek buildings. He remembered the ruins of long dead Greeks he'd visited in Crete.[305] There his guides had seemed amused by the bewilderment of the barbarian; later Thorgeis had taken them aside to teach them respect. He'd vowed never again to put himself at the mercy of half-men in such terrifying darkness.

Psellus started to whine as Thorgeis insisted he should lead the way with a lighted torch. He wanted to get as far away from this stinking lout as soon as possible. By now he was regretting ever passing on to the Eparchos what he'd overheard. Certainly the princess should be stopped from disgracing the honour of the Empire with one of those savages from the north. However, to send another of these brutes was verging on madness. He'd not liked the coarse ruffian from the start. He'd been frightened and intrigued, by the strange clash of one green and one brown eye giving the barbarian such an odd appearance. He liked even less the brutish way he'd been hustled along the alleys of the capital to the palace. Now he needed to find some corner to slink into until the barbarians had butchered each other.

It may have been a good idea of the Eparchos to set one brute to kill another, but some vestige of loyalty made Psellus fear for the safety of the princess. But then the trollop had already put herself in danger by being on heat for a savage. Should he stay and try and protect the niece of the Autokrator? Could he count on a reward? Only the loss of his tongue to keep him silent for ever; the princess would take active measures to revenge herself on whoever had brought about her disgrace. Better to take the gold already paid by the Eparchos and the position promised in far-off Nicosia.

Psellus stopped suddenly and could feel the brute grunt behind him. He was frightened to turn around and face this monster he'd smuggled into the palace. Perhaps if he didn't look back he could pretend he was alone. A prick from a sword in the back of his neck ended such a delusion.

"Move on, Greek!" hissed the barbarian. Thorgeis wanted the corridors and halls to float away straightaway. He yearned to plunge his sword into the throat of the Saxon and revenge all he'd suffered in Candia. This craven toad wasn't going to get in the way; but he had to be on hand until they'd been restored to normality outside this rat-hole. He smiled as he imagined asking the Saxon if a quick coupling with a royal slut was worth dying for. Perhaps there might even be time for that extra pleasure.

Psellus scurried forward, so quickly the Varangian was almost left behind. Only the sharp tap of a sword on the shoulder of the slightly-built guide slowed the terrified Chartularius to a more sensible pace.

At last they reached the bedroom of Princess Zoe and Psellus made to move aside. Suddenly he felt his arm seized and wrenched in the direction of the room.

"No, Greek!" hissed Thorgeis, so close Psellus almost fainted from a mingling of growing terror and the stench of bad breath. "You take me to Varangian."

Psellus tried to resist but was helpless. He paused and listened carefully before he stepped through the doorway into the darkened room. All he could detect was the faint sound of a breathing sleeper; surely there were two. There must be two! Had he been mistaken all along and led this monster almost into the bed of his princess. His throat seemed clamped by terror and he couldn't breathe. For this he'd lose both tongue and eyes. What had he done? Then he heard a second sleeper breathe and felt the clamp on his throat lessen. Oh, the beautiful freshness of air. The Chartularius stepped into the room, followed by the Varangian.

*

Ethelwulf heard a noise. From somewhere outside the fulfilment of his dreams had come a hiss, a whispered voice. He opened his eyes slowly and gradually clawed his right hand towards the sword abandoned by the side of the bed. Then he froze. Next to him the princess enjoyed the sleep of the lust-satiated. Her quick breathing gave him some grip on reality. Elsewhere the room was gradually becoming lighter. His mind tumbled into life. Someone was coming into the room carrying a torch. The stealth of their movements told him they came both uninvited and with no good in mind. His fingers found the hilt of his sword and closed on it. A steely comfort was carried up through his right arm into the rest of his body.

By now the light was rapidly approaching the bed. Slowly Ethelwulf began to ease his body up, taking his weight carefully on his left arm and drawing his sword up from the floor. The figure next to him stirred uneasily and started to wake up.

There were two figures and as Ethelwulf strained to search the shadows past the flickering torchlight his companion tried to scream but only a hoarse whimper emerged. A figure, made even more huge by the savage distortions of the torch-light, stepped forward and with a roar of triumph slashed viciously at Ethelwulf. With a single movement the Varangian intercepted the blade in mid-air and the clash of steel was drowned in the gasp of Psellus and a second whimper from the woman as she scrambled to leave the bed. Ethelwulf tumbled sideways into its welcome shadow. Psellus had moved towards the opposite side of the bed and started to back away from the battle.

Thorgeis snarled and yanked the torch out of the Greek's hand, thrusting the torch furiously in the direction of his quarry. It was then the woman caught her right foot in the bed's covering and lurched towards Psellus who'd slipped into a daze. Thorgeis sensed the movement and the accompanying threat of intrusion. He thrust out his fist to stop the flight, oblivious of the torch in his hand. In some way a human face and fire clashed and this time the woman shrieked and the sound somehow cut through Psellus's stupor. The princess had been injured! He yelled and tried to grab the Varangian's arm.

A battle lust tore into the red-bearded Varangian's mind. He swung his sword wildly in the direction of the Greek and its edge cut deeply into the neck of Theodora. Her second scream was silenced forever. Now Psellus let go of the Varangian's arm and shrieked in horror at the murder of a princess. As he threw himself to the floor, Thorgeis slammed a foot into the side of his head and turned to hunt down Ethelwulf.

There he was - naked, standing horrified with his back against the wall. Why had Odin allowed the fool to wake at that very moment! With a malicious grunt of triumph Thorgeis charged at his victim. Ethelwulf leaned towards the right and thrust his sword up to parry the onslaught. Baulked, Thorgeis swept the torch in his right hand to scorch his enemy, but found the Varangian turned his left knee inwards to lose height and slashed his sword towards his attacker's exposed stomach. Thorgeis had to cut the sweep of the torch closer into his body to counter the attack. The action threw him slightly off balance and he had to give ground. Ethelwulf ran out of the trap.

Why hadn't guards responded to the screams? Ethelwulf realised the princess would have wanted no witness to her meeting a Varangian lover. He threw a glance at the lifeless form slumped over the corner of the bed. And then Thorgeis was on him again.

As Ethelwulf steadily gave ground he tried to manoeuvre himself towards the door and safety. However, a series of fiercer thrusts from Thorgeis turned him back towards the wall. He was helped by the semi-darkness and hindered by the feeling of inferiority produced by his nakedness.

Should he yell for assistance? How was he to explain the dead princess? No, he had to concentrate and keep himself away from the bed. He didn't want to get boxed in again. Ethelwulf was surprised how far he'd calmed down and accepted the sudden carnage in the bedroom. Vaguely he was aware of the other assassin starting to come to his senses. There might be the answer. Certainly the second man had been of no assistance to Thorgeis; with luck he might even bring about disaster.

As he parried, Ethelwulf cut down the blade towards the arm of his attacker. Thorgeis moved his arm away and exposed his chest. Ethelwulf lunged viciously at the throat of the Varangian and Thorgeis stepped back towards the bed. By now the Varangian was realising the torch illuminated himself more than it did his opponent. As he tried to thrust it more in the direction of Ethelwulf he only succeeded in sucking out distorted shadows from his naked opponent. Perhaps it would be better to fight in complete darkness? No, the Saxon would be quicker without a shirt of mail and he couldn't be sure of cutting off retreat through the door.

Why had it all gone wrong? It was all the fault of that miserable Greek. As if in answer to that thought he heard a groan from somewhere behind him; and the resulting hesitation almost resulted in Ethelwulf's sword severing his leg. A deft movement meant the blade merely sliced through his leggings and Thorgeis swung the torch at the head of attacking Varangian. He was rewarded by a yelp from Ethelwulf as the torch singed his left arm. Then he found he was harried by two violent cuts at his head. Without thinking he stepped back and swung the torch at the Saxon's head.

Ethelwulf crouched lower and smiled. The second man was slowly getting to his feet behind the Varangian. Would he manage to distract Thorgeis a second time? He thrust at the Varangian's stomach and Thorgeis stepped back yet again.

Ethelwulf rapidly passed his sword into his left hand. For years he'd trained with his left-handed cousin to expand its use. Gradually he'd acquired considerable skill fighting this way. Now he realised Thorgeis had weakened his right-side by filling his hand with the torch. The Varangian could not switch hands easily, without abandoning his light. Clearly he was reluctant to do that as it would offer Ethelwulf a chance to slip away in the darkness. On the other hand, a torch offered neither the secure defence of a shield nor the precision of a sword. Thorgeis might well be able to fight with sword in either hand, but by abandoning his useless accomplice he'd put himself at a disadvantage.

Ethelwulf slashed at the Varangian's left thigh and Thorgeis made an awkward parry. Swinging his sword in an over-hand arc Ethelwulf cut at the neck of his opponent. Thorgeis moved his sword to parry but the direction of the attack had been unanticipated and Ethelwulf was able to bounce his blade up past the guard of the sword and cut into the forearm of the Varangian.

Thorgeis grunted, dropped his arm and stepped back. As he did so he stumbled into the rising form of Psellus and was propelled unexpectedly to his right. As he fell Ethelwulf lifted his left leg slightly and skipping forward on his right launched his sword at Thorgeis's unprotected throat. The blade tore deeply into flesh and was harried by a torrent of blood as it withdrew. Without a murmur Thorgeis collapsed in a dying heap.

Ethelwulf stepped forward, grabbing the torch almost as soon as it struck the floor. At the same time he dropped his sword and seized hold of Psellus who'd been petrified by the sudden end of the fight.

"Quickly, Greek!" snapped Ethelwulf, "Or do you want to lose your eyes when this butchery is discovered?" He pushed Psellus back so that the Chartularius found himself sitting on the bed, still in a state of shock. By the light of the torch feebly held in the hand of the Greek Ethelwulf grabbed his clothes and then his sword.

"Well, butcher?" snarled Ethelwulf and raised his sword arm to pummel the Greek into life. Psellus recoiled from the blow and, in doing so, his face was brought up close to that of the murdered woman. There was a strange yell from the Greek and Ethelwulf dropped his clothes again to yank the Greek's hair so that the little man no longer faced the corpse.

"What are you blabbering about?" he hissed, abandoning his hold to retrieve his clothes.

"It's not her Highness!" squealed the Chartularius, almost allowing himself to laugh in triumph." It's not the Princess Zoe!"

"What?" yelled Ethelwulf, as he pushed aside the Greek and stared into the frozen features of his lover. The man was right. This was certainly not the Princess Zoe. Somehow, for some reason, he'd been the victim of a trick. Why?

Psellus made to squirm past him and slip out of the door.

"Not so fast, my little runt", gasped the Varangian, bringing up his sword as if to chop the Greek in half. Psellus abandoned all thought of immediate escape. "You're going to show me the way out, so that we can both shake off this madness together." Ethelwulf was breathing heavily, but there was an anger growing somewhere in his inside. Had the princess planned for him to be murdered here, in her bed? What had he ever done to her to provoke such a crime.

The little man was scrambling to his feet and Ethelwulf ordered him to pause while he resumed his clothes. In a moment he'd done so and they both hurried out of the room. Not a word was spoken until Psellus had led the Varangian safely back outside. Then he felt Ethelwulf's fingers tighten on his throat.

"And now, my little runt," stated Ethelwulf, "You're going to tell me how you brought Thorgeis along to murder me."

*

Michael brought two trusted guards with him and Zoe made sure she was dressed in the full grandeur of imperial purple to cower the barbarian into submission. In a way it was unfortunate the fool would be humiliated, but then he should never have raised his eyes in her direction. Perhaps, later, if he were very submissive, she might have some reward for him; but the very thought of those barbarian hands on her soft limbs made her tremble with distaste.

It was Michael himself who held the torch to guide them through the deserted corridors of the palace. Her uncle had gone off to visit his troops facing the Bulgars to the north and her father to watch the revival of the Hypsipyle.[306] So it had been easy to make sure no guards were in the immediate area of her bedroom. She'd told the Arithmos officer she would be spending the night with Theodora in another part of the palace. How fortunate the whore was called Theodora. She didn't like to think she'd told an absolute lie.

It was amazing how still and unfriendly these passages were after dusk. Michael said nothing and the two guards simply followed as if on parade. Perhaps this wouldn't prove as amusing as she'd hoped. She scurried to catch up with Michael. Why was he so unfriendly? Did he really believe she would think for a moment of inviting a barbarian into her bed? Well, he'd soon see how a princess of the Imperial House could reduce such a wretch to absolute submission. She consciously stretched her neck to prepare for looking down on the barbarian fool.

Now they were at the entrance to her bedroom. It was strangely quiet. She looked at Michael and he signalled the two guards to halt. They could almost hear the flames of the torch breathing in the night air as their ears searched for the sound of resting lovers. Nothing.

Michael lightly placed his hand on her arm in restraint and then stepped forward into the darkened room, holding the torch ahead of him to illuminate the scene. It took them some moments to overcome their surprise. Draped half-across the foot of the bed sprawled the huge body of a red-bearded stranger. By the side of the bed lay the whore, her features distorted into an image of horrified surprise by the flickering light.

Zoe felt sickened. She wanted to scream and no sound would come. Michael quickly summoned the two guards and without a word the lamps, carefully positioned in different points of the room were lighted. With their glow came a sense of reality - just. The princess and her lover were anxious to get rid of the two guards. These men had been told they were going to seize a Varangian who'd dared seduce a maid of the princess and insult an imperial bed. Nobody had expected to come across two bodies.

"They must be moved - at once." Zoe was surprised and impressed by the way Michael so easily took charge. She found herself nodding as he signalled the two guards to remove the dead stranger. Who was he? Neither asked the question as the body was dragged out of the room and hauled into a nearby closet. The two members of the Arithmos silently re-entered and one gently picked up the dead whore in his arms. The other looked at Michael.

"Make sure neither is found anywhere near the palace," ordered Michael. "This is all a horrible surprise." The soldier dared raise an eyebrow in question. "Say nothing to anybody and report to me personally at the end of duty tomorrow," Michael paused, significantly. "You'll both be amply rewarded - if you obey orders." The princess turned away as the guard saluted and withdrew. At last the lovers were alone together.

"Where's the barbarian?" asked Michael, more to himself than to the princess.

"Certainly not in this slaughter-house!" snapped Zoe and shuddered. "Anna must make sure all the linen is burnt in secret and the room scrubbed."

"Who was that man?" persisted Michael.

"This room must be scrupulously clean before either of my sisters has the chance to enter," murmured the princess, turning as if to assess the size of the task.

"Did the barbarian kill them both?" asked Michael. He firmly placed his hands on the shoulders of the princess - and rapidly withdrew them as he took in the venomous fear consuming her eyes. She's frightened of him, he thought. She's terrified that somehow the barbarian will get at her.

"I'll have the barbarian taken care of - immediately," he promised and was surprised the princess shook her head.

"No," she hoarsely murmured. "I must first know why this all happened." She paused and then re-assumed her control of her lover. "Then we'll decide whether he should live - or die."

*

Psellus had poured out the full story of the plot against the Varangian in return for a free passage on a trading vessel for the west. Somewhere he'd lose himself in the alleys of Palermo before agents of the Eparchos could shut his mouth for ever.

Ethelwulf hadn't been surprised at the Eparchos. He'd long known that, unwillingly and unwittingly, he'd become an obstacle to the ambitions of the most powerful official in the Empire. On several occasions he'd been moved to make his peace with the man, but somehow had never known how to approach the Eparchos. He'd never been sure of the ambitions of Alexius Euergetes and hesitated to declare himself an opponent of imperial schemes. For that was the problem. Nobody was sure where the plans of the Autokrator and those of his minister parted.

Morkere advised his cousin to disappear as quietly and quickly as possible either to the west or else back to the land of the Rus. He was still preparing to follow Psellus westwards, leaving his men to make their way later, when George Epiphanies, the personal bodyguard of the princess Zoe, bustled into their presence.

"You are summoned immediately to attend Her Highness," he barked. The balding Arithmos officer had the customary arrogance which came with years of authority. He'd been raised from the ranks by the Autokrator after an act of insane heroism in the Bulgarian wars. Now he was content to strut around the palace and leave the thrill of risking head and hand to others.

Ethelwulf looked at Morkere who nodded grimly. Too late to run now. He had to brazen out whatever the princess would do, relying on homicide remaining the ambition of the Eparchos and not of Princess Zoe.

"I'll see you soon, Morkere," smiled Ethelwulf as he grabbed his brown cloak and prepared to follow the imperial officer.

*

It was a short walk to the palace and an uncomfortable one. George made no attempt at conversation, simply striding ahead of his charge, confident the Varangian would meekly follow him. When they at last entered the quarters of the princess, Ethelwulf noted she was accompanied only by the nobleman, Michael Comnenus.

It was Michael who spoke first. "We've heard you dared to enter the private quarters of Her Highness without permission."

"I had to -", began Ethelwulf, glancing rapidly between princess and nobleman. Behind him he could sense a slight movement as George Epiphanies unsheathed his sword.

"Had to, barbarian?" interrupted Zoe and looked with disdain at this savage who had the effrontery not to lie in her presence.

"Yes, Highness," answered the Varangian. " I servant your family and I love - "

"Love?" sneered Michael, "What does a barbarian know of anything above the lusts of the woods?"

"Silence, Michael," ordered Zoe, colouring and determined not to let Michael take charge of this interview. Surely this Varangian knew better Greek than this? How could she have ever considered him? She shivered at the thought. Let this barbarian condemn himself for effrontery out of his mouth.

"Yes, Highness," resumed Ethelwulf, moistening his lips to stop the first lie burning them. "I see man - a killer - go palace; so I follow."

"Why did you not summon the guards?" questioned the princess, knowing the answer before the question was even finished.

"Highness," breathed Ethelwulf, as if brushing aside the awkward questionings of an infant, "I no guards see."

"And who was this rogue you so fortunately happened to observe enter the palace?" asked Michael determined to resume the pressure on the Varangian. Like everyone else he knew how all barbarians clung to each other, wallowing in their ignorance. Many of them served unheard-of creations of Satan, conjured up in the dark forests of the north. From childhood they were pledged in blood to bind one with another even beyond death.

"He Thorgeis Green-eye," dismissed Ethelwulf," – left Varangian join Governor Chandax."

"So you met him when you brought back that Cretan rebel?" offered Michael. Zoe, however, added, "And that gave you reason to sneak into our quarters?"

"No! No, Highness," protested Ethelwulf. "I call guards, but none come, so quiet I follow bad man down one... two ..... passage. He go in dark place."

Zoe almost smiled. The barbarian was proving an accomplished liar. She could almost imagine two stealthy figures making their way along the dark corridors - if a word of it had been true.

"I follow and...and.." here the Varangian's story seemed to falter. He didn't know who the victim was. How was he to explain her sleeping in the bed of a princess? He could almost feel the breath of George behind him. Let them worry about who the woman was and why she'd been there.

"And see him woman frighten ..." Ethelwulf looked from Michael to the princess Zoe and back again. There was no response from either; or rather there seemed a glint of malicious pleasure somewhere in the eyes of the princess. "Hear woman cry. Is she lady of Autokrator?"

"Why?" The question from Michael was coughed out. He didn't like barbarians and Zoe was playing with this one for far too long. Why did she not have his tongue cut out now, so they'd not have to endure his murder of their tongue for any longer?

"Who sleep in palace?" Ethelwulf turned the question. He was sure Michael knew the identity of the victim, just as much as his royal mistress. He looked into Zoe's eyes. "I kill man before kill woman."

"But, unfortunately, my loyal barbarian," smiled the princess. "You failed." She paused. How was she to explain the woman. "The poor girl was the sister of my maid who'd dared profit from my absence by tasting the luxury of my bed." Again she hesitated, certain the barbarian was believing none of this and daring him to challenge her. "Our maid has been punished - and has lost her sister." Anna had been packed off that very morning to the borders of Armenia. She'd felt it fitting her maid's tongue should be silenced by adding another inmate to the brothels of Trebizond.

Was the maid the same one who'd ushered him into the palace the night before? Probably. If so, he still didn't know why the princess had lured him into her bed with - . He still didn't know who the girl had been, although he was sure she'd certainly not been the sister of an imperial maid.

"Why did you not summon the guards after you'd killed the man?" asked Michael, determined not to let this barbarian slip out from under the net. He didn't understand why Zoe was letting this man tell lie after lie and not simply having him punished for violating the sanctity of an imperial bedroom.

"I not know," mumbled Ethelwulf." I not know girl, why Thorgeis kill her." He looked for assistance into the face of the princess." I frighten and go back to friends."

"Have you told anyone of this?" questioned Zoe sharply. Ethelwulf shook his head furiously in denial. The princess turned away from Michael and said - half to herself. "So we've a strange girl murdered in our bed and a murderer killed in the act - and all with our guards away...." She dared the Varangian to ask why the guards had been absent and was pleased at his continued silence. Perhaps the man would be able to keep quiet. Certainly she'd find it hard to explain to her father or uncle what had happened. She was also certain the barbarian had told someone of what had gone on; so simply to remove this source of embarrassment might cause other questions.

"Tell no one," she tried to offer a smile, but what emerged was a grimace. "Go in peace and join our uncle in his struggle with the enemies of the faith to the north."

Ethelwulf breathed a sigh of relief and Michael snorted with irritation. Without Zoe's co-operation he could do nothing. He looked across at the guard, George, and was met with a blank wall of bewilderment. Perhaps it was best to leave things in darkness.

*

The Wanderer 8:6

"Where has the horse gone?
Where the man?
Where the treasure-giver?
Where the place of feasting?
Where the hall's delights?
I mourn the gleaming cup,
The warrior in his hauberk,
The prince's glory.
How time has passed away,
Darkened under night's shadow
As if it had never been."
('The Wanderer')

The Bulgar Hoard

The army was making its way with difficulty along the river Maritza. Scouts had reported the Bulgar horde, satiated with its winter-raiding plunder, had retreated northwards two days previously so that there was little need for speed. Even so the Autokrator was furious. He hated to think of the ikons of the Holy Mother pillaged from the shrine at Rhaedestum being slobbered over by the enemies of Our Lord.

"This army moves like a snail," he grunted to the Philip Palaeologus, Domestic of the Scholae.[307]"I remember how quickly Roman soldiers can march when they know Our Lord is with them."

"And when your majesty has carefully laid the way with mules and wagons," smiled the black-bearded veteran of the Anatolian campaign. The relief of Aleppo three years before had been a master-stroke of imperial planning and resource. However, both he and his master knew how much the effort had taken out of the imperial coffers - and this was going to be a far more difficult struggle. Even so all their efforts had only ensured about one third of the force actually arriving at Aleppo.

The Autokrator was still displeased at the speed of the imperial army as it made its painful way northwards in pursuit of the Bulgarian raiders. If only the Kleisurarch [308]Leo had been quicker to block the narrow gap through the mountains at this very pass they'd have had the savages bottled up and waiting for the slaughter. As it was he'd delayed, collecting together outlying detachments of his forces before daring to try and bar the road north to the raiders of

Thessalonica. By the time his troops had approached these narrow jaws his quarry had slipped north.

Within two days the Autokrator himself had arrived and dismissed the incompetent general on the spot. Leo hurried south to secure the support of the emperor Constantine and so acquire some compensation in the newly-won provinces of Anatolia. Basil despatched a messenger immediately to the capital advising his brother not to entrust in such doubtful hands the gains of the Aleppo campaign. If Constantine really did want to win over the man, and his connections with such families as the Ducas and the Comneni, then he should give him a position in far-off Erzerum or Kars where there was little challenge to the rule of New Rome.

The Autokrator remembered how he'd made the fateful mistake, years ago, of pausing after breaching Trajan's Gate on his way to smash the Bulgarian stronghold of Sardica. The delay had enabled the Bulgars to establish control over the surrounding mountains, from which they couldn't be dislodged. The mistake had cost the Empire the campaign and the war. The Autokrator was angered by Leo not learning from so recent history.

Now, by pressing on, the Autokrator hoped to catch up with the retreating Bulgars. Their Tsar, Samuel, had been a threat to the Empire for nearly twenty years. This time he'd catch and destroy the enemy of the Christ.

The army advanced in constricted order, basically a column following the advance scouts and largely made up of alternate divisions of cavalry and infantry, with more scouts on the flanks. Of course, the employment of scouts was considerably restricted in some passes through which the Autokrator drove his men.

*

Somewhere in the middle of the column Gunnar rode awkwardly, in gloomy conversation with Morkere. The hills that hemmed them in from the north closely resembled the hiding-places of the Gaels who'd plagued the raiders sent by Kjartan Ulfsson to get supplies from Wexford.[309] Bandits prospered in such hiding-places, ready to fall on unwary and helpless travellers and then evaporate in the mountains before any decent force could be assembled.

"Not bandits, Gunnar," smiled Morkere. "Apelatai.[310]" In districts like this it is a profession worthy of a man with an eye for profit."

"Yes," grunted the Gall-Gael. "Whatever cattle can be reared in such a countryside as this must really be worth grabbing!"

"Which is why the Empire places such value on the Akritai,"[311] interposed Ethelwulf, remembering the skirmishes in far-off Anatolia. Like all troops from the capital he'd tended at first to question the strange dress and the even-odder tactics employed by commanders like Anastasius. However, within days he'd discovered methods used to confront Saracens couldn't be used in the foothills of Bucellarion. When they did come together to fight in the open, like in the attack on Sclerus,[312] they could be beaten by more orthodox tactics. Usually, however, the arrow in the back or noose from an adjacent bush began and ended brigand onslaughts.

"Yes," agreed Morkere, "out here different values rule." He nodded in the direction of Thomas, an officer of Akritai whose leather tunic offered little protection but greater mobility than the mail-shirt favoured by the Varangians. The Thessalian had the nose of a stoat and the eyes of a snake; he smelled danger, ever-alert, lightly caressing the bone hilt of the long knife at his hip.

Ethelwulf observed the tension in the face. It was clear the Greek was very unhappy about the surrounding hills. His eyes searched the undergrowth clinging to the bare sides for any sign of danger. Every time there was nothing there he seemed disappointed and turned to the next clump which could hide an ambush. Somewhere up there some of his men were toiling from hillside to hillside, but he couldn't see them. And if they so easily escaped detection what chance was there of even glimpsing danger before it launched itself against the army passing beneath.

*

That evening the Domestic Philip realised the need to supplement the provisions carried by mules with supplies extracted from the local peasantry. By now they were entering regions which had deserted to the Bulgar Tsar in the previous ten years. It was fitting the inhabitants should come to realise the enormity of their mistake. It was right the blood and silver sucked out of imperial farmers and traders to the south should be repaid with interest.

He sent for Ethelwulf and brusquely ordered the Varangian to detail a foraging expedition. His lips narrowed into a bitter smile. "And if you're weary of all this marching and waiting, barbarian, it would only be proper you should lead a Dekarkhos yourself!"

"Nothing would please me more," the Varangian's smile was as cold as his general's. A small force of ten men would be large enough to seize provisions - and small enough to escape detection from bands of both retreating Bulgars and Apelatai.

"Don't wander away too far," warned the Domestic. "Our Autokrator wouldn't like being forced to send out a search party for a missing barbarian." He chuckled. He had a respect for the Varangians, but, like so many others brought up in the traditional regimes of the Empire, was jealous of the growing influence of mercenaries from beyond the borders of the Empire.

"Don't worry," answered Ethelwulf, as he looked at the mountains vaguely outlined against the moonlighted sky. "No warrior from the north would want to rest his bones in hills such as these!"

Ethelwulf would lead Morkere and eight other men into the countryside to the west of the army in the early hours of the next day. They'd adopt a broad sweep and intercept the army before the following evening. As well as securing provisions they'd try to make contact with possible scouts and spies. Other foraging parties would be sent out to the east.

*

There was no sound from the village. The half-dozen mud and straw huts looked as if they hadn't been inhabited for a long time; however, smells betrayed the recent presence of peasants. Morkere was sent up-wind to the north with six of the party. After a suitable wait Ethelwulf began to close in, carefully.

A light touch on his arm from Sven the Far-Sighted alerted him to a movement from the farthest hut. Ethelwulf stopped and signalled his advancing men to widen the arc. There was a long pause, as it produced no response. Then they moved forwards again.

The first hut was entered. Its darkness yielded a few handfuls of grain and half-a-dozen carrots. Fine pickings Ethelwulf approached the second hut and pushed aside the crude covering which concealed the interior. He listened carefully to silence; not even birds seemed to want to sing on this miserable, sunless day. He stepped into the darkness. It was empty, with signs of panic and the frantic gathering of possessions as people scattered to the holes and caves of the neighbouring mountainside.

From outside he heard a shout and rushed out to find Morkere wrestling with a tall, skeletal figure. The wretch seemed half-starved and it was no contest. The stranger was floored by a blow from Morkere and quickly surrounded by three other Varangians. For several moments he lay there gibbering. Then he calmed down and the whines and grunts turned into distorted Greek words for mercy. Olaf thought a good kicking would be the best means of getting better sounds from their captive but was restrained by Morkere.

The dark-haired warrior knelt down next to the writhing figure and firmly, simply, commanded silence. There was a series of sighs and then the whimpering shrivelled up into a long plea for mercy.

"Be good to a poor slave of these savages," croaked the man. "Have mercy on an old man who's spent twenty years the captive of pagans, unloved by his people and unmourned."

"Who are you?" snapped Ethelwulf, quickly glancing around at the surrounding mountains. He didn't like the idea of being detained in the open by this creature, but he'd been ordered to make contact with anyone who might be of use.

"My name - my name is Nicholas," stammered the man, for the first time daring to raise his face from the mud and look up his new captors. "I was born in Thessalonica long before any of your kind dared intrude on the Empire." His eyes had narrowed as he recognised the unusual dress of the men surrounding him.

Morkere was the first to sense the hesitation and hurried to calm the man down. He explained they were part of the army of the Autokrator himself.

"Is the Lord's Anointed, John,[313] at last turning his armies away from the infidel?" asked Nicholas. Morkere chuckled and informed the man the Autokrator was, in fact, Basil. For a moment their prisoner was confused, then there rattled a strange and unearthly laugh emerged from his throat. "Yes, yes....I understand....the young Basil has grown to manhood while I've been enslaved here among savages." He started to scramble to his feet and Guthrum Crooked-Knee stepped forward to stop him getting up. Ethelwulf waved the Varangian aside and Nicholas managed a feeble half-smile of gratitude. Guthrum spat into the mud to express his distaste for showing clemency to slaves and turned to forage in one of the neighbouring huts.

"Where are the people who lived here?" asked Morkere, allowing his eyes to search among the surrounding hillsides for any sign of life. Had the inhabitants been warned? If so, by whom and why?

"A scout came rushing through the village, shouting imperial raiders were on their way to ravish their women and steal their food", sneered Nicholas. "So they made off as quickly as they could, forgetting to take ALL their property!" He cackled at his own joke as he pointed to his chest.

"Will they return soon?" asked Ethelwulf, taking the Greek's elbow firmly and shaking him out of his self-amusement.

"Oh, yes," smiled Nicholas, allowing a glint of superiority to pass across his eyes. Here it was Nicholas who knew the answers and these soldiers, with all their weapons and commissions from the Autokrator, who depended on him. Ethelwulf could see the return of something of the arrogance of the man before his enslavement twenty years before. He guessed Nicholas had been a member of the imperial civil service, probably collecting imperial assessments, before robbed of status and liberty. There was a contempt there which all Greeks shared for barbarian mercenaries. Still, as long as escape from these hills depended on co-operating with such mercenaries he could be expected to keep this superciliousness in check and answer questions. And if he were to prove too awkward they could always leave him again for the Bulgars to look after.

Perhaps Nicholas sensed the threat of being abandoned. Anyway he hoarsely urged the Varangians to seize whatever they could find and burn the village before escaping back to the safety of the imperial column. He pointed out they lacked the skills to survive in these hills, easy prey for brigands who'd grown old in murder and cattle-thievery. Certainly there must be need for haste when peasants could combine with brigands and return in force.

Very quickly they set light to the crude dwellings of the natives, and hauled on to their backs what remnants of food and equipment had been abandoned by the peasants. The expedition had been a failure. The only certainty being that nothing done by the imperial army could be accomplished in secret.

*

Nicholas proved a very eager guide, even though he'd wanted to retire south rather than press on as if on the trail of the elusive villagers. However, Morkere brusquely informed him they needed to intercept the imperial column on its way north. Nicholas sullenly accepted the decision, and then brightened up as he assumed control of their march.

They'd only been trudging along in silence for a hour or so when the Greek urged them to stop. His ear leaned towards the sharp breeze starting to chill their faces. As Guthrum adjusted his pack Nicholas furiously shook his head and willed him to silence. They all strained their ears to penetrate the comforting background of nature. There was the faint sound of movement on the path up ahead, the trudge of feet of many men making their way rapidly towards the village. Ethelwulf looked questioningly towards their guide. Nicholas sidled close to the Varangian leader so that he'd no need to speak above a whisper.

"There are many caves to the north," he said, waving his right hand broadly in the direction of the dark-grey hillside. "It's best to stand aside from danger rather than confront it."

Ethelwulf nodded and ordered his men to follow Nicholas as he broke into a trot and left the path for the unwelcome hills. Morkere stopped to try and scrabble out the prints of feet in the mud of the trackway, but quickly gave up the impossible task. They'd have to rely on the barrenness of the hillside to destroy signs of their passage - or the incompetence of their enemies. From what he knew of Apelatai they must trust to the rocky nature of hills.

It didn't take them long to reach the shelter of the nearest hillside. Nicholas, without stopping plunged through the rough scrubland which barred the entrance to a narrow gap between two rocky faces. Then he paused to catch his breath and smiled knowingly to the Varangians.

"Look around and see your salvation!"

The Varangians looked at the steepness of the hillsides on both sides. Here and there they could detect points of blackness which could only be holes or entrances into the hillsides. How deep were these caves? Could they conceal eleven men? Could they find a hiding-place before their unseen enemies were upon them?

Sven the Far-Sighted began scrambling up the hillside, dislodging small stones as he furiously tries to get a good grip. Ethelwulf ordered him to stop and carefully make his way back down.

"Don't leave such an easy path for our enemies to follow," he said and turned carefully to the other side of the gap. Carefully he made his way up and away from the rest of his men. After a few paces he softly ordered them to follow, making sure they didn't dislodge stones. Morkere laughed and charged up the opposite slope, releasing a flurry of grit and small pebbles down on to the trackway. Then he followed the rest of the men up the hillside.

It took Ethelwulf several moments to reach the first black scar on the hillside. He looked inside and was disappointed how shallow was the opening. He carefully made his way up to a larger, more-promising entrance about twelve yards to his left.

This was much better. He had to bend his head to clamber into the hole, kicking aside some loose stones just inside the entrance. The dampness and peace that whispered out from the depths drew him on. At first he could see nothing and relied on the fingers of his left hand to trace a passage along the moss-covered walls into an ever-promising hiding-place. Behind him others entered the passage.

By now his eyes were growing more used to the dinginess of his surroundings. He could see the faint outline of walls and a rough path which beckoned him towards a narrow gap, partly obscured by a large, bone-shaped boulder. Without speaking he passed through the gap and was instantly forced to his knees by an abrupt drop in the level of the ceiling. He seemed to crawl for ages through the narrow gap, occasionally pausing to test for open air above his head. At last he could feel nothing and tentatively straightened up. With relief he stretched his aching back and enjoyed the grunts and curses of his men as they crawled after him.

As Guthrum straightened up in the darkness he struck a light and the damp walls eerily reflected the feeble-glow of the primitive torch hastily made at the entrance to the cave. Ethelwulf was surprised how large the cavern was. He was tempted to stop there, safe in the surety he could hold the entrance against any crouching approach. However, if they were discovered their enemies simply had to wait outside, safe in the knowledge that starvation would eventually drive them out.

It was better to go deeper into the darkness so that no sound could betray their presence to searchers outside. He was confident they'd left little sign of entry. It'd be bad luck if any enemy decided to follow them in here.

Carefully the Varangians made their way deeper into the cave. At last they came to a narrow opening. Guthrum was the first to squeeze his way through, taking with him their only source of light. For a few moments the Varangians stood in darkness, straining their ears to catch any sound of pursuit. There was none. They were alone in a damp, chilled darkness.

At last Guthrum returned and reported the gap led to an even larger cavern. More importantly there was water there. From somewhere clean, refreshing water dripped into a small pool. Without any discussion the men made their way through the narrow cleft in the walls into the larger chamber.

If only there was another source of light! Morkere started to explore the cavern systematically in the vain hope of coming across something to burn. His search was made more difficult by having to be conducted in darkness.

His first feeling was fear as his foot struck something which clearly wasn't rock. For a moment he wanted to cry out but then mastered his dread, reached down and his hand brushed against an old branch of a tree. There was no doubt about it. In his left hand he was gripping what had once grown outside! He couldn't help calling out to Guthrum to bring the light.

As Ethelwulf followed the light-bearer he felt angry at his cousin. Was Morkere mad? Didn't he realise his cry could alert any enemy on the prowl outside. Who knew how far sound travelled, echoing and distorted among these caverns? However, when he realised what had provoked the shout, he almost laughed aloud. Here by the wall was a small pile of firewood, including kindling, as if some friendly spirit had decided to set up quarters for them in the depths of the hillside. So men had been here before.

Some of the wood was detached and set alight, after Sven had carefully secured his cloak over the narrow cleft with the aid of two swords to prevent any trace of light drifting out into the world. Once a small fire had set its glow against the surrounding dank walls the men's spirits rose noticeably. It'd be easy to wait here till nightfall and then sneak out and find their way back to the army. Easy? Not quite, but light and a little warmth does wonders for optimism.

It was Harald Long-Arm who found the skeleton. He was nosing about in the corner largely hidden by the pile of wood and at first thought the white bones sprawled against the wall were merely scattered odd branches. Then he looked more closely and saw the skull. He was a brave man but he couldn't stifle the gasp of horror which drew the others quickly to his side.

The skull was lolling loosely against the left shoulder bone sunk back against the wall. Sven pushed aside the others and quickly bent down next to the remains. He'd seen many such bones in the land of the Rus, the remains of the struggle for mastery between

Varangians from the north and the native population. It was almost a medical eye which examined the skeleton.

At last he rose to his feet and coughed loudly. "It's obvious why he never left this cave," he affirmed, pointing down at the left femur; a good, clean break separated the bone into two unequal parts.

"Poor devil," muttered Ethelwulf and made to straighten the remains. Then he stopped as his fingers rubbed against a sack which he'd first taken for the wall of the cavern. Gently he eased the skeleton away from the sack and drew it out into the open.

It was a coarse brown sack, like one carried by travellers to store rations for the journey. This one looked old but the dryness of the cave, despite the supply of fresh water, had kept it from falling apart. Ethelwulf noticed a cord holding secure the bag's neck and tugged at the knot. The cord chose to snap rather than the knot unravel. As it did so some of the contents of the bag spilled out into the comforting light from Harald's torch. The Varangians were looking at the cold, mocking glint of gold and silver coins. There was a gasp of surprise from the company as Morkere squatted down next to his cousin and reached towards the half-a-dozen coins which had tumbled out of their hiding place.

An unpleasant cough from Harald made Morkere pause and look round at the torch-bearer. Even though most of Harald's face was hidden in half-shadow as he'd thrust the torch towards the coin, Morkere detected a glint of resentment. He looked at Ethelwulf and laughed. "Let's see if Nicholas can tell us anything about gold which lies hidden away from the eyes of men."

By now the whole company had grouped itself around the discovery and Nicholas was thrust forward by several hands before he had a chance to respond. He joined Morkere and Ethelwulf in their examination of the coins. Carefully he picked up one of the coins and brought it closer to his face. After squinting at its face for some time, ignoring the shuffles of impatience around him, he swore softly to himself before offering a loud judgement.

"This coin bears the image of Leo the Saviour[314]- dead for ten generations." He flicked aside the coin and grabbed another, subjecting it to a close scrutiny. "And this was made by his son!"[315]

By now both Morkere and Ethelwulf were taking it in turns to drag out more coins from the bag. As they tumbled out on to the cavern floor more fingers reached to examine the mixture of gold and silver coins. Suddenly Ethelwulf rose to his feet, swept his arms wide and ordered everyone to step back.

"These coins should be properly examined by somebody who might be able to tell us why they're here." He paused and glared at Harald who'd managed to grab two coins and was trying to examine them without too-obviously adjusting the position of the torch. "Perhaps they're the property of us all - and so every coin must now be returned to the bag!"

"And if it is not our property?" questioned Ubbe Crack-finger.

"It may be judged to belong to the Autokrator." There was a loud murmur of disapproval. How could gold hidden away in some cave in this Bulgar wilderness be the property of the Autokrator. Ethelwulf hastened to calm his men. "I don't say it is," he conceded, and then looked fiercely at Sven who still mumbled dissent. "But remember we are sworn to follow the Autokrator - "

"And we're alone in an Empire of his subjects," interposed Morkere with more meaning. This brought about a fresh bout of muttering but several coins were thrown down back on to the pile on the floor.

"Why not make our way north, away from these Greeks and their fancy ways?" suggested Sven, producing a loud oath from Ubbe Crack-finger.

"Oh yes, fool?" he sneered. "And how are we to pass through hordes of savage Bulgars and after them Pechenegs and -"

"After them, who knows what?" finished Ethelwulf. He looked around at several faces in turn. How did they think they could find their way back north, across lands they didn't know and tribes of which they were scarcely aware?

"What about making a run for the west?" offered Harald and was greeted with a murmur of support. That was better. However, to the west lay more lands of the Empire and beyond them the unwelcome attentions of Frankish kings. Ethelwulf knew he'd have little hope of keeping the band together as they escaped from imperial lands towards those of the Holy Father. It was easier to stay here, hide the gold and slip away legally from imperial control.

As if reading his cousin's thoughts, Morkere urged they should stay in imperial service until the present campaign was over and then get permission to retire back to the land of the Rus.

"But then we'll have all the others wanting a share of our gold!" protested Harald. Ethelwulf didn't like the use of the term "our gold". Perhaps it'd be best to share out the coins immediately they reached imperial lines. No, his men would be unable to keep the coins to themselves and very soon imperial agents would find out about the theft. Better to keep the gold together and share it out when back in the capital. There the sudden appearance of old coins would produce little comment. He knew one could even come across coins proclaiming the triumph of an Empire recovering the Holy City.[316] In the markets of the capital any amount and type of coinage could disappear. First, however, to find out how many coins there were - and how they'd found their way into the cave.

*

It was some time before Nicholas managed to complete an inventory. The task hadn't been helped by constant interruptions and attempts by different Varangians to pick up one coin or another for closer inspection. However, at last it was done and the sack was completely turned inside-out and thoroughly shaken. There in front of the circle of Varangians, now forgetful of any danger from the outside world lay several neat piles of coins. Over half were gold and there were four hundred and nineteen coins in all.

Nicholas had grouped them according to the head of the ruler on the obverse. The largest pile, made up of fifty six coins of various sizes, belonged to the reign of Constantine V; the next largest was that of his son and namesake.[317] The most recent coins dated from the reign of his mother, the Empress Irene.[318] There were twenty-two of these. The oldest coins dated from the tenth year of the emperor, Constans II.[319] So the hoard encompassed over 150 years of imperial history.

What was most interesting were the ten coins from the reign of Abd-al-Malik[320] and another twelve coins issued by his Umayyad successors.[321] Ethelwulf noticed several of these coins were almost copies of imperial issues, distinguished by Arabic script. The latest dated from the reign of abu-Jafar[322] over two hundred years before.

There was a chuckle from Morkere as he recognised two small crude coins put aside by Nicholas unable to decipher their inscriptions. "These were issued by Pepin, lord of the Franks,"[323] he stated, lightly tossing them up and down in his hand. "I wonder how they came so far east."

"Who was that barbarian?" asked Nicholas, with minimal interest.

"I've heard he was a great king," answered Morkere, " and the father of Charles, the greatest king who's ever lived." He recalled the stories of the sacristan, Gregory, in Jersey. He'd liked to hear of old times when men valued honour and the king of the Franks was held the lord of Christendom.

Nicholas sneered. "There you're wrong, barbarian, for the greatest of rulers have been sent by the Almighty to guide the people of New Rome." It was Morkere's turn to smile quietly as he laid down the coins. He'd heard of such emperors as Constantine and Justinian but they'd never had to face an attack from even fifty berserks.

There was an impatient movement from some of the onlookers. Most of them knew some Greek but much of what was being said was beyond their comprehension. It was Ethelwulf who put the question all wanted to ask.

"So, Nicholas, how did all this gold end up here, deep in the earth, clutched by a dead man?"

Nicholas was silent for several moments, fingering some of the coins as if to tease out their story. Then he turned to Ethelwulf and began a slow, painful story. His words were translated conscientiously by Morkere.

It was a tale of imperial disaster. Long ago the Empire had been threatened by savage hordes of Bulgars. Imperial forces under the emperor Nicephorus Phocas[324] had trudged north to destroy the wild forces of Krum, the heathen Tsar of the Bulgars. At first they'd forced the Bulgars to seek peace, but, driven on by ambition, they'd determined to hunt down the Tsar himself and destroy the Bulgar power for ever. However, they'd neglected to position scouts properly and, in their haste, to get to grips with the Bulgars, had passed through the pass at Verbitza. The imperial army had been massacred and the haughty emperor's skull employed as a drinking-cup by Krum himself.[325]

As for the skeleton, Nicholas was certain the man had been an agent for the Imperial Treasury. During their initial success the imperial troops had sacked the capital of Krum, which must have contained the plunder of earlier Bulgar raids. The variety of the coins themselves argued they'd come from different origins. The age of the coins meant the man had hidden here about the time of the imperial disaster. Probably the damage to his leg prevented a more successful escape from these mountains.

Yes, escape was the next objective. By now it must be nearing night. Ethelwulf decided it was time to slip out of their refuge and make their way northwards to their imperial master. Sven would take charge of the hoard until it could be shared out. It would be up to Sven to make sure the bag was adequately concealed from both the attention of imperial officials and the envious greed of their fellow Varangians. Nicholas was willing to keep his mouth shut for a proper share of the treasure.

*

Carefully they made their way back through the narrow gap and into the outer chamber. They didn't dare to use the remains of their torch for fear of hostile eyes outside. Sven grunted with the effort of pushing the bag ahead of him through the gap. However, it was noted he didn't offer to let anyone else share the burden.

Harald slipped ahead and looked out into the night. There was no sign of any enemy. Without a sound the Varangians passed out into the chill freshness of the darkness. Silently Ethelwulf signalled them to follow as he turned right and made his way north.

He hadn't gone far before he realised something was wrong. The night was too quiet. There was no sound of normal night-time activity; more an air of expectation. Suddenly the chill of the weather was replaced by the cold of knowledge they were being shadowed as they stumbled along stony paths.

Ethelwulf stopped and signalled the surly Karelian, Pekka, to make his way to his side. The man had survived for several years in the wilderness to the north of Ladoga, making a living out of trapping animals (and others would have added his fellow-humans). Long ago he'd proved his worth when there'd been the need to amass the international currency of the north - slaves.[326] He was a lonely man who never seemed to want the company of his fellows, but he also had the ability to disappear into natural surroundings with unnatural ease.

A few whispered instructions and Pekka slipped away from the path. As they passed into a dark shadow cast in the moonlight by a huge tree he was there, and as they emerged again in the moonlight he was not. Only Sven seemed to realise the Karelian was no longer with them, and he only gave Harald a light tap on the elbow and a sharp shift of his head. Harald followed the direction indicated and frowned in surprise. He never liked the way the old man slipped off when trouble seemed to be coming. Trouble? Harald tightened his grip on his axe.

A few moments later Pekka was back again, by the side of Ethelwulf as if he'd been there all the time.

"There was a spy," muttered the Karelian, "but he won't be seeing any more."

"Why didn't you take him prisoner?" asked Ethelwulf. He needed to know how many enemies were out there and when to expect an attack.

"I did," grunted Pekka, " but the man somehow slipped out of my grip and started to make off." He paused as if a not-unpleasant memory intruded. "Fortunately he wasn't quick enough for my knife!"

There'd been no sound from the trees and rocks that flanked the pass. Ethelwulf well knew the accuracy of Pekka's knife throwing. The spy hadn't had a chance - and it was a good sign he'd not tried to call for help. The enemy couldn't be near, yet. However, the enemy knew the direction of their march and their destination. They also knew the best place for an ambush. Somewhere up ahead he was sure a band of Apelatai were settling down to await the arrival of their prey.

He stopped suddenly and the men protested as the comfort of steady progress was brought to brutal halt. It took but a few sentences to explain the problem. Harald shrugged off the danger. A man was given but so many years on this earth and when he must go to meet his fathers nothing would get in the way. Till then he should fear nothing for death had no claim. Ethelwulf was pleased such fatalism had little support. There were grunts of disapproval as Harald urged them to go on even more quickly and take any ambush by surprise. Pekka brusquely denied ever any need to hurry to one's death, let Hel[327] work for her kingdom.

Morkere turned to Nicholas and asked if there were any paths leading east or west. That way they might be able to by-pass any ambush. Nicholas strained his eyes to pick out any features of their surroundings to remind him where they were. He'd endured twenty years in these hills and had long become accustomed to the paths and trackways cut into them. At last he knew where they were.

"A little way ahead," he ventured, seeking support for Ethelwulf. "There's a rough track to the west - but it doesn't turn north!"

That was no good. How could they hope to get back to the main army. Ethelwulf had no wish to spend the rest of what life remained wandering round in these miserable hills.

"Where does this path take you then?" snapped Sven adjusting their treasure on his right shoulder. He didn't look forward to lugging this bag along what this Greek called a "rough trackway". As far as he was concerned the path they were on was rough enough. His shoulder ached and there was a soreness caused by the shifting of the mass of coins within the bag. At first he'd ignored the discomfort, telling himself that soon they'd be resting by the fires of the army, ramming bread into their mouths and trying to fend off awkward questions from their fellows. As the soreness had grown, he'd wanted to stop and insist someone else should take their turn at carrying their treasure. Then he'd looked at Harald Long-Arm and changed his mind. Better to put up with discomfort than give that one a chance to dip his hand into their store of coins. Now it looked as if life was going to get nastier.

Ethelwulf sensed the hesitation and quickly ordered the lean Ketil Kolbeinsson from Skejjar[328] to take up the burden. There was a shrug from the black-eyed Icelander as he entrusted his spear to Harald so he could more easily take over Sven's burden. Harald's eyes followed the transfer, as if checking the weight was the same as it had been in the cave. With the bag on his shoulder Ketil retrieved his spear and completed the operation by spitting into a nearby bush.

*

They soon found the promised trackway and Ethelwulf didn't shorten his stride as he led the band westwards, away from the imperial army. Nicholas had been persuaded to admit he only knew the trackway led to somewhere on the river Vardar.[329] Guthrum Crooked-Knee had brightened at that. He'd crossed a river with a name like that as a member of an expedition despatched to deal with a Bulgar raid against Thessalonica. He insisted that, once they reached that river, if they turned south they'd find their way back into imperial territory. But did they want to go there? Harald's weren't the only eyes which glanced at the bag carried by Ketil as if making sure it wasn't a dream. Surely if they reached that river it couldn't be much farther to get to the lands of the West. How far away was the river? No one knew - and certainly none could even guess at the distance beyond.

*

The trackway proved as bad as feared but no worse. Sven started to feel life coming back into his shoulder just as Ketil felt unusual resentment start growing somewhere deep inside. 'Unusual' because it wasn't the nature of Ketil to experience such feelings. His uncle, Thorolf, had beaten him regularly but had defended him in the Althing.[330] His neighbour, Njal the Sharp-sighted, had tried to cheat him and only laughed at the clumsiness with which the farmer tried to manoeuvre their neighbours into backing him. Since then he'd travelled far, much with little complaint, and felt he'd profited from the skill of his leaders. Now growing stiffness just below his neck forced his mind into unknown emotions. Why had he been chosen to carry this burden?

He tried to adjust the weight of the bag and his problem was noticed by Morkere. With a slight smile Morkere called out for Ethelwulf to stop and when the small band shambled to a halt breathing heavily, without a word he reached for the load. Ketil started to protest and then caught a look of authority in the man's eyes and handed over the burden.

"We must all take turns to carry our treasure," stated Ethelwulf as everybody took the opportunity to grab a short rest. "This trackway makes its weight seem even heavier - "

"Why not share it out now," snarled Harald.

"And where would you put your share, donkey?" sneered Guthrum, between his gasps for breath. There was a general murmur of amusement among the band. Nobody had anything which could be used to hold so many coins. Whatever pouches they had were filled with grain, beans and whatever else they'd managed to grab before setting off the day before.

Harald glared at the grey-haired man - but had no answer. After all every step they made brought them closer to somewhere they could share out the booty.

*

Morkere only managed to carry the bag for a few miles and then was forced to hand his charge over to Harald. At first Harald Long-arm enjoyed the comforting caress of the coins against his shoulders. However, very soon the caress changed to assault and then he felt it biting into his skin. Surreptitiously he tried to manoeuvre the weight so it was evenly spread between his chest and his back. It didn't work. One stumble and the weight lurched forward and scraped against his throat. He thrust it back on to his shoulder and caught a malicious smirk in the eyes of Sven as the smaller man glanced at him.

Thorgrim Spear-Catcher carried the bag for some time without complaint, revelling in the toughness of Icelanders. However, at last the burden proved too much for him. The next to carry the weight was Pekka and the task was done in a manner to show that Karelians were a match for men from Iceland. There was the faint light of the false dawn in the sky before Pekka was induced to hand over the bag to Ethelwulf. Still they trotted on in silence, although Nicholas had long started to feel his legs had deserted his body and were somehow gambolling along besides him. What was left just felt heavier, yearning to bury themselves in the ground. Years of drudgery had toughened the muscles so that the imperial financial official who'd have collapsed after the first mile or so refused to give ground to these barbarians. Grimly he bit into his lips to bring blood and so some kind of moisture. Several times he was about to cry out for mercy, ready to go back and eat scraps from the Bulgars and toil among their savagery if only he could rest. And just as he was about to collapse the party paused while THE BURDEN was changed. Nicholas felt the Pankrator must be watching over him, preserving him in the midst of barbarians.

At last they came to a river. They'd splashed their way across two streams during the half-light of dawn. This, however, was definitely a river. It must be the river Vardar. They'd reached the end of the first part of their journey. First they had to cross this barrier. There was no possibility of finding a passage to the east of the fierce torrent of water. It cut too steep a path through the sharp hills.

However, the trackway led into some kind of ford. Beneath the clear waters they could dimly see the outline of large boulders breaking up the light-brown mixture of gravel and mud which formed the river-bed. Carefully stepping from one boulder to another Ketil made his way across the river. As he went he dragged a train made up of twisted belts, cloaks and baldrics. In his native land it wasn't unusual to be forced to overcome such obstacles. This barrier was no problem - the waters were not fast-flowing nor muddied by sediment. However, this wasn't the case with others inexperienced in crossing such open country and was no reason to take chances. After reaching the other side he tugged at the line now spanning the river with Guthrum holding the other end.

Ethelwulf reluctantly laid aside his shield and then took a firm grip on his sword. Clinging on to his sword and firmly gripping the line with his left hand, he confidently made his way across the waters. He was quickly followed by the rest of the band. Guthrum was the last to cross the torrent. Before he did so he threw the spears, axes and swords which had been abandoned across the water. He tried to throw across Morkere's shield but had the frustration of seeing it fall short and be carried along to a battering by the rocks downstream. Shields were too heavy and awkward to be successfully thrown across the torrent. Ethelwulf ordered Guthrum to throw them into the stream. Let them be battered into uselessness rather than abandoned to a future use by the enemies of the Empire. Finally Guthrum tied the line around his waist and joined his fellows on the western bank.

On the other side of the river confidence grew. They'd only to turn south and make their way back to the confines of the Empire. It never occurred to any of them to turn north and try to make their way towards the army. Who knew what lay to the north? The Tsar might even be regrouping his army behind the barrier of the Vardar.

*

By the evening spirits had risen considerably. Somehow the sun seemed warmer and the path easier as they made their way southwards. It was then an arrow caught Ketil in the throat and he was dead before his body slumped into the dust.

Ethelwulf and the rest of the band threw themselves towards the scrubland which grew by the side of the trackway to avoid further loss from the shower of arrows from both sides of the path. No longer did some of them carry shields and only Pekka had elected to retain his bow as they'd crossed the Vardar. Ubbe fell in the open with an arrow in his leg and, before any attempt could be made at rescue, two more arrows ended his life. Thorgrim charged into the undergrowth as if he'd spotted one of their assailants. He swung his axe but before it landed he crumpled with a spear in his guts.

By sheer chance Nicholas tumbled on to one of their attackers and a furious tussle broke out. Nicholas was no fighter, and hadn't shown himself to be a brave man, but he was infuriated by such an unexpected onslaught. Before the surprised Bulgar had managed to scramble to his feet Harald had smashed in his skull with his axe.

Now the Varangians realised they were largely shielded from attack from the opposite side of the trackway both by the undergrowth and the existence of enemies in their hiding place. One Bulgar tried to cross the trackway and was downed by a javelin cast by Sven.

Morkere found himself facing a bow-legged opponent. The man frantically threw aside his bow and drew a sword. However, he was unable to parry the thrust of Morkere's weapon as it passed through his sheepskin coat and into his lungs. Guthrum also made short work of skinny peasant who tried to escape into the scrubland.

In a matter of moments the scrubland on one side of the trackway was silent as the Varangians breathed uneasily watching for any further attack. The other side of the trackway was also without movement as the local attackers considered whether to call off their attack. After all they were peasants not experienced warriors. It had been too good a chance to strike a blow against the Empire, and get some booty at the same time. Now, however, it seemed best to wait for darkness when they'd have the chance to slip away back to their village. Both sides waited for the light to fade.

*

By the unfriendly light of the moon the Varangians scrambled further south, away from their attackers. It was several miles before anyone spoke and then only Harald again suggested division of the treasure. He pointed out each man's share would be larger now - although there were fewer men to carry the burden.

Morkere, whose turn it was to be weighed down by the heavy sack, suddenly stopped and threw THE BURDEN on to the trackway. The crunch of muffled coins against the ground appeared to scoff at the harshness of the moonlight.

"If Harald again whines about getting his hand on what I'm carrying," Morkere snapped, "I'll increase all our shares by getting rid of him on the spot."

Harald reached for his axe and Sven hurriedly placed himself between them. There was a twinkle in his eye as he ventured to suggest to Ethelwulf that perhaps Harald should be given his share now - and left to look after himself. There was a murmur of approval from the others.

"Then, of course," grinned the little man, "Harald can be sure no one else is going to get their hands on his share - "

Harald insisted he'd no worries about dishonesty, being only concerned about the general well-being. There were a few jeers from men glad to seize the chance of a rest. Ethelwulf stopped further discussion by stepping forward and swinging the sack on to his own shoulders.

"I suppose it's my turn to carry our treasure," he admitted, "and I don't want to be on this trackway when daylight comes." With that he set off down the path confident no man would hesitate to follow. Having been ambushed once on this path he was anxious to get to more open country. Perhaps they might reach a settlement and find out where they were. Surely they must have crossed into imperial territory by now.

*

In fact, they'd been within the province of Thessalonica for some time, but it was only in the late afternoon they came upon peasants who told them they were within one day's march of Petrisk. Approaching the village what would they do with their treasure?

Morkere was for burying the hoard there and then but Harald was equally adamant they should immediately divide it up among the remaining Varangians.

"Who can tell what the Autokrator will decide to do with us?" he insisted and there were several grunts of support. After all they'd been missing from duty for several days and their master had little love for runaways.

"So you're going to walk into camp with a pouch of gold coins at your belt," sneered Ethelwulf and there was a cackle from Sven who again proposed a medium course. What good would it do any of them to bury the treasure out here in the wilderness? When could they ever hope to come this way again?

Even Morkere had to grin at the use of the word 'hope' as regards this meandering along rocky paths. So he supported Sven's insistence that any division here would undermine the need to stay together as a fighting group. Yes, even Harald, having once been threatened with expulsion from the group, could see the power of self-interest there.

"So let's keep the treasure in one bulk until we actually get near the imperial camp - and then we'll hide it on one of the supply wagons!" There were several grins at the impudence of stealing from their master and using the Autokrator's own wagon to carry their hoard for them. Every one of the party had experienced the awkward weight of their common treasure, and none wanted to carry on like that indefinitely. First get guidance from villagers back to the imperial camp, then conceal their loot until it was safe to smuggle it aboard one of the wagons. Once safely hidden there they could take turns to make sure it remained undiscovered until their return.

"...And then we can share it out." concluded Ethelwulf and grinned at Harald who was forced to agree to the wisdom of the plan. First they had to hide the coins before they entered the village.

*

It was surprisingly quiet - frighteningly still. Having abandoned so much of their equipment in crossing the river Vardar. Sven slipped into the nearest hut and re-emerged immediately shaking his head in disappointment.

"I suppose they must think we're some thieving imperial tax-collectors come to fleece them," he grunted and spat in the mud before glaring at Nicholas. The Greek pretended not to have understood the comment and turned towards the large hut in the centre of the village. As he did there was a shriek of hatred from the nearby trees and about a dozen men charged the Varangians.

Before he could even move Nicholas was smashed to the ground by a club wielded by a tall round-shouldered peasant. The man then swung at Morkere and found the skilled warrior easily swung under the blow and slashed with his sword at the man's throat. The peasant jerked his head to the side and the blade cut into his cheek, baring the bone. With a scream of agony the man threw himself on Morkere. As his body smashed into his opponent the man dropped the club and his fingers clawed at the Varangian's eyes. Morkere collapsed under the momentum of the attack and dropped his sword as he lunged for the peasant's fingers. With a yell Guthrum buried his spear in the back of the enraged attacker.

Immediately an arrow struck Guthrum high in the back and he half-turned to meet this new attack. As he did so a second arrow struck him above the left knee and he sank down. Morkere grabbed his sword and, pushing aside the inert body of the peasant, struggled to defend his rescuer. However, he was too late. A third arrow hit Guthrum and without a sound Guthrum Crooked-Knee keeled over into the mud.

Ethelwulf found himself under attack from two men and a large hound. His sword bit into the throat of the dog as it leaped in attack and its falling body impeded the onslaught of one of the peasants. His companion thrust a home-made spear in the direction of Ethelwulf without making contact. The Varangian leader stepped forward and thrust at the man's face and the peasant slipped in the mud as he lurched to avoid the blade. Meanwhile the other peasant had recovered his footing and slashed with a knife at Ethelwulf's body. Somewhere he felt contact but no pain, battle-lust was pushing aside all feelings and fear. Ethelwulf turned and half-severed the man's head from his body. He screamed hatred and leaped towards his first attacker. The man turned and fled.

Olaf died miserably and quietly smothered by the bulk of a grease-smeared peasant who'd smashed him to the ground. Even as cruel fingers squeezed the last life from his body Olaf sensed his knife bite deeply into the groin of the giant. The peasant attempted to rise and then slumped back on to the lifeless form of his victim.

Meanwhile Pekka was struggling to fight off two assailants. As he swung his sword one of them grabbed his arm and yanked it upwards. He heard the bone break and his useless arm dropped his weapon. At that very moment the other man shoved a broad knife into Pekka's stomach and he started to feel his entrails uncurling before the darkness of death ended all sense.

The peasants had no time to enjoy their triumph as one was felled by a blow from Sven's axe and another transfixed by a vicious thrust from Morkere's spear. The other peasants now realised they were fighting men driven beyond pain and human feeling by the fury of battle. They'd heard tales of such demons who'd appeared in the armies of the Autokrator. Never before had they seen such violence and they turned in panic and fled from the scene. Ethelwulf hurled his sword in useless venom at the fleeing men and Morkere chuckled as reality again flowed through his veins.

"A good sword is hard to come by, cousin," he laughed, running forward to retrieve the weapon, "even among the Greeks."

Ethelwulf sank to his knees simply happy to be still alive. Sven busied himself by scrutinising the bodies of their companions. None still breathed; half of the original force of eight had perished. Sven had the pleasure of slitting the throat of Olaf's killer; none of the other peasants he came across had still been alive.

By the time Ethelwulf was more aware of his surroundings Sven and Morkere had collected together several spears and swords. Harald Long-Arm had sloped off somewhere.

Morkere frowned. Where had the man gone? Before he even asked the question, Ethelwulf supplied the answer, "The gold!" He struggled to his feet but wasn't quick enough for his cousin who rushed off in the direction of their buried hoard.

Harald had indeed gone off in search of plunder. He'd had enough of fighting. Somehow he'd managed to kill one assailant and frighten another into flight. As he glanced around the clearing he could see his fellow-warriors were managing to hold their own. Let them scrabble with these swine in the mud, he had better things to do. If he could get his hands on the hoard and make his way south Harald was certain he could find a ship to take him west.

The hoard had been quickly buried near a large moss-covered boulder before the Varangians had entered the village. The size of the boulder and the peculiar greenness of the moss made it stand out from its surroundings. Harald found the site easily and savagely used his sword to dig into the ground. Fortunately the hoard hadn't been buried deeply and the ground was still loose. As his sword cut into the ground Harald remembered Sven giving the soil a heavy press of his heel "for luck" as a completion of the operation. Among the Rus it was usual to bury weapons or furs in different caches all over the countryside; a final heel-print set the seal on the act and ensured the owner would return to recover his possessions.

Now Harald threw down his sword and used his fingers to quickly tear aside the loose earth. At last he could feel the hard, comforting shape of the bag. The back of his right-hand smoothed aside the remaining earth and his fingers clutched at the bag. He was surprised how numb his fingers felt, it hurt him to grip the bag and yank it from its hiding-place.

"Thank you for finding our money, Harald," spoke a harsh voice behind him. Harald dropped his treasure and reached for his sword even as he turned. Morkere buried his spear so deeply into Harald's body that its point emerged to pierce the abandoned bag. Pain passed quickly across Harald's face before life left his body. Morkere chuckled as he released his hold on the spear, at the same time twisting it so that Harald's corpse slumped to the side. "I always said you were too closely attached to those coins!"

Brutally putting his left foot against the dead man, Morkere firmly gripped the spear-haft and pushed. The corpse was propelled up the shaft and off into the mud. A quick movement released the point from the hoard. Morkere rubbed the weapon against the corpse to remove the blood, looking up as Ethelwulf and Sven appeared.

"Harald always did want to cut down the number of shares," croaked Sven and he spat into the face of the dead man. Bury a man with your spittle and he'll never come back to haunt you.

Ethelwulf reached forward and retrieved the bag. With a slight grunt at the effort he swung it on to his shoulders. "It's a pity greed destroyed a fine warrior," was his epitaph as he turned away. "We can't stay here, even to bury our dead."

His two companions agreed. Nothing could now be done for the dead, but their enemies might return at any time. All they could do was head south and hope that sometime, soon, they'd stumble across the sea. Once there they might feel safe for with the southern sea was civilisation and not the savagery of the frontiers of the Empire.

*

John Phocas didn't known what to do. His instincts told him something was hidden by the Varangian's grey eyes as Ethelwulf calmly answered his questions. He could accept the patrol had been cut off by Bulgars and forced to seek an alternative escape route. He knew the three men had reported to imperial agents at the small village near the mouth of the Vardar. They'd raised no protest at the escort sent to accompany them to the capital.

He'd heard of this Ethelwulf and, apart from some ugly tale about an intrigue with her Imperial Highness, liked what he heard. He also knew the Varangian had crossed the Eparchos on several occasions and survived. That warmed the Deputy Chamberlain to the barbarian. However, he dared not give the Eparchos any chance to whisper any hint of treachery to the Autokrator. Worse, he'd no idea how the Princess Zoe would react if she ever found out he had this particular barbarian lodged in the cellars beneath his mansion. Of course the man was treated well, although kept within the house. One never knew how the subtleties of imperial politics would make the strangest of allies useful. At the moment, however, he could see little use for the barbarians.

"We only wish to rejoin our army spreading civilisation among the Bulgar dogs," interrupted Ethelwulf. He didn't like the hesitation of the official. No wonder Zoe had tired of the man. He might come from one of the noblest families in the land but his lack of decisiveness must have irked her character. Yet the man was honest, or appeared to be, and that was unusual in the imperial capital these days. Ethelwulf remembered his first master, the Quaestor; John Angelus had managed to hold out against the Eparchos for several years but in the end had been destroyed. He'd last been seen on his way to spend what few years would remain to him in an obscure monastery in the south of the Peloponnesus. A pity. The Quaestor had possessed imagination - and the ability to see how barbarian arms from the north could revitalise the weakening Greek forces.

"Yes," agreed John Phocas, almost to himself, "yes, any of us would seek to join the Autokrator in his triumphal progress in the north." He paused and a strange smile appeared on his lips. "Perhaps you should travel as part of the escort to the latest payment to the imperial forces." The smile broadened. Where would be the last place the Eparchos would look for the barbarian than among the escort of his own convoy. He was certain news of the barbarian's presence in the capital would soon leak out - and then spies would be kept busy gathering intelligence. Perhaps he'd delayed too long already?

With difficulty Ethelwulf managed to keep calm. What could be better? He needed some means of transporting the hoard back north with him; he couldn't trust anyone in the capital and knew too little of its alleyways and bath-houses to risk stashing it somewhere. However, put one more sack with others carrying the imperial seal and none would look too closely. He closely watched the official. Was John Phocas going to change his mind again?

*

It was two days later that three extra riders might be found among the Company of Tagmatikoi sent north as escort for the army's pay. There were some resentful looks and whispering at the intrusion of three barbarians among their numbers, but no soldier reported the presence of strangers to the officials who bustled around making last-minute preparations. Although there was envy of the growing privileges of the Varangians they were still good soldiers - and any soldiers was worth five pen-pushers!

As they trotted out through the Gate of St. Romanus Ethelwulf glanced around and his eyes for a moment met those of the Eparchos. The City Prefect was standing on a balcony overlooking the city gate, idly watching the convoy as it made its way north. Ethelwulf immediately reached forward and adjusted the bridle of his mount, imagining the eyes of his enemy boring into his back. But there was no outcry, no official pushed his way forward to stop the escort and demand the arrest of the three intruders. Had the Eparchos really not recognised him? Slyly he glanced over his shoulder and was pleased to see the Eparchos in bored discussion with Nicephorus, the Paymaster-General, probably discussing the amount of profit they'd make on the transfer of pay to the north.

Soon they'd passed out of the city and Ethelwulf felt able to relax. He glanced at his cousin, but Morkere was sullenly looking towards the clouds to the north. Since the death of his twin there were increasing bouts of depression, based on the guilt of being still alive when a worthier brother had perished in a strange land.

"Did you see the Eparchos?" whispered Ethelwulf and Morkere answered with a contemptuous look. Why worry about any Greek when they'd soon be making their way out of this accursed land? Ethelwulf tried a half-smile and failed. In silence the cousins rode north to rejoin the army.

*

It was two days later that Morkere saw the dwarf and Nicias saw him. Nicias had long ago realised service with the Quaestor couldn't match the rewards offered by the Eparchos. At first he had to suffer repeated humiliations as the Eparchos tested out his potential loyalty. However, the travesty of the attack on Sclerus[331] had settled the matter. The prompt report from Nicias allowed the Eparchos to maintain his position and shut the mouth of Psellus before it had been too late.[332] From then on Nicias remained within the household of the Quaestor but his skills were employed by the Eparchos.

Nicias quickly realised the venom consuming the Eparchos for the newcomers from the north. However, the Quaestor had all too quickly lost control over the employment of the barbarians, undermining the value of much of the dwarf's intelligence. Now, however, he spotted one of these very men in the baggage-train of the Eparchos himself. What was the man up to? Nicias was certain the City Prefect would pay highly for this information. Quickly he melted into the crowds which had turned out to gawk at the imperial baggage-train going north.

Morkere wanted to rush after the dwarf but was unable to break ranks. Instead he whispered to Ethelwulf they'd been spotted. Neither doubted that within hours the news would be well on its way to the capital. Sven was brought into the discussion when the force paused for rest an hour later. He was in favour of retrieving their hoard and disappearing into the countryside.

"No," rejected Ethelwulf, his eyes furiously checking none was close enough to overhear the conversation. "If we did that we'd be labelled thieves and deserters and would stand very little chance of ever getting away from the Empire."

"If you really want to leave imperial service," sneered the pilot from Gadarike. Long ago he'd had enough of the Greeks and all they stood for. His spirit longed for the crisp winters of Kenugard before his bones were too old; the chance to sit and doze by a huge fire as slave-girls pandered to whatever one desired. Somewhere in the back of his mind there was a laugh. Nowhere in the Empire could you find a woman to make you truly happy. He'd tried girls in Syria and whores in the capital, but they were all the same. None of them had that toughness which came with wintering in Gadarike. He had to get back there before it was too late.

"I, for one, would like to slip away from all this intrigue and lies," confessed Morkere. He was alarmed how his moods increasingly swung from happiness to misery. Nothing had gone right since Edwine had left him in those marshes in the north. For a time he'd managed to quieten the tensions the death of his twin had left by plunging into learning to play the Greek. He'd been surprised how easy it had all seemed, but then it had started to fall apart. First there'd been his arrest by Michael Theophilus [333] and then the growing realisation that none of them would ever be accepted by the Greeks. As he saw the growing resentment of the Eparchos his alarm had increased. His cousin was too ready to shrug off the antagonism of the most powerful man in the Empire outside the Imperial Family. He'd come to realise the fatalism always in Ethelwulf's personality was taking control, especially after his cousin's disappearance in Antioch.[334] Now the only way to escape disaster was to leave imperial service. Even so, he had to agree with Ethelwulf that sudden desertion wouldn't work. The Greeks had the most amazing intelligence system and he was sure no port would provide a safe route back to the north. No, they had to leave the army openly and with honour.

"We must make sure the gold is very well hidden," he affirmed, "and hope we manage to get to the presence of the Autokrator before we're placed under arrest."

The others agreed and Sven undertook to make sure the hoard was well concealed on the second wagon. It was the one driven by the friendly Thracian, Nicomedes. Sven made great efforts to become very close to the little man, especially during drinking bouts. Somehow he managed to start the habit of sleeping off the effects of the rough local wine cocooned among the sacks on the back of the Thracian's wagon. It was comforting to sleep near one's hoard.

*

Ethelwulf's hopes proved unrealised. First a bridge decided to collapse under the weight of the leading wagon and two days were wasted recovering the ejected sacks and repairing the bridge sufficiently to allow the convoy to pass over safely. No matter how much Ethelwulf cursed at the delay he could do nothing to speed up the process.

Then there was a mysterious fire in the barns used to store the convoy's food supplies overnight. Two good men died putting out the flames and Morkere was convinced that somehow the hand of the dwarf would be found in the disaster. There was no time for investigation - and no breakfast for the exhausted and depressed men who tried to get the convoy together the following morning. The result was much slower progress that day, which meant the imperial logistics service was thrown into uproar. From somewhere agents found shelter for the convoy from the harsh elements which provided an unwelcome accompaniment to the trudge northwards.

Finally John of Cappadocia, who headed the convoy, was persuaded to launch an attack at the growing number of brigands hovering within scent of the gold being transported north. He knew the loss of any of the pay would mean his prompt despatch to an obscure house of religion, probably with the reminder of a slit nose. After fifteen years of faithful service in the palace guard he'd no intention of letting slip the chance of honourable retirement.

Ten trusted men were sent out one night to harass the brigands who, with growing confidence, were brazenly encamped close by. The Varangians were not selected for the expedition and Morkere almost believed this was because of the suspicions of the imperial officer. Ethelwulf was more logical, insisting a Greek would naturally employ an all-Greek force to operate in such country. Even so they were all pleased when the patrol returned the next morning with four heads. After that the brigands took to camping farther off.

All this produced delay and it caused no surprise to the Varangians when the Eparchos himself furiously rode into the camp one morning and promptly ordered their arrest. At first John of Cappadocia hesitated. After all the Varangians were tried soldiers and he'd no love for the Eparchos. However, he quickly thought of his pension and any doubts were flattened by the frightening coldness in the eyes of the Eparchos.

*

"Surely you didn't think traitors like yourselves could hide from imperial eyes?" demanded the Eparchos. He was savouring the sight of seeing the three Varangians manacled in front of him. The only disappointment being none of them bowed their heads in submission. At first he'd believed the beating his guards had given Ethelwulf would have brought about that submission. The

Varangian had fought back but couldn't stand up against the onslaught of three graduates of the fighting-schools from the alleyways of the Hippodrome. One half-closed eye still stared impudently into the face of Alexius Euergetes; the other eye was merely a mass of damaged tissue.

"We're no traitors to the Empire," croaked Ethelwulf. His mouth hurt; his lips swollen from the fists of the thugs and cracked with dried blood. "We merely became separated from the army and were making our way back!"

"So who helped you carry out this little performance?" sneered the Eparchos, ignoring the answer. It was obvious no traitors would be making their way BACK to the army. Yet there must have been a reason why these men hadn't simply tried to rejoin the Autokrator in the north. Why had they travelled back to the capital - and who'd helped smuggle them among the convoy? He'd been delighted with the report of the dwarf, but had immediately sent his agent among the taverns and brothels that held all the secrets of the capital. Someone was prepared to act against his authority. Not since the Quaestor had anyone dared interfere with his activities. If there was a potential rival somewhere in the capital he needed to dispose of the danger NOW.

None of the Varangians had offered any names, and stuck to the same carefully-prepared story. They'd been cut off from the main army and sheltered in a cave. A local peasant had guided them south away from the Bulgars because he feared reprisals for his treachery. Too late they'd realised they were heading away from the army. So they'd killed the peasant and trudged southwards to re-enter the territory of the Empire. There they'd been attacked by local inhabitants and their companions killed. It had been Sven who'd suggested the admission of killing their peasant guide; it was just the sort of detail to make their story more believable.

When they reached the capital their story became more confused. All insisted they'd simply presented themselves to John the Cappadocian and been accepted as useful additional soldiers. Ethelwulf insisted John had believed they'd merely been on some mission to the capital and were anxious to return to duty. Nobody offered any answer to the query as to why the captain hadn't demanded an imperial authorisation for travel.

Alexius knew they were lying; all barbarians lied, being the natural children of the Dark One. Yet their story seemed to have enough truth about it to pass the Autokrator. He couldn't allow that to happen. Further investigation was required in the capital and so the

Eparchos decided to ship the three Varangians south. Who knows what nasty accident could happen on the road to the capital?

He was surprised at the effect his decision had on the prisoners. For the first time he sensed a crack in their resistance and it pleased him. Why did they so want to reach the Autokrator? He looked at the slightly-built grey-haired man in front of him. The Eparchos had been surprised by the toughness of the pilot from Gardarike. The special attentions of Demetrius had worked no miracles. The barbarian merely cradled three broken fingers in his left hand and glared at the Eparchos. If such treatment failed to work with the barbarian from the north, Alexius was certain time would be wasted on trying out such tactics on the two from the far west. Besides Ethelwulf might get away with it after all - and then he could expect revenge.

The Eparchos looked at Morkere and saw a cold sullenness which offered no answer. Why did these men want to get back to the army? But no, that couldn't be true. Why had they wandered back to the capital instead of immediately making their way across country to the army? Alexius guessed the Varangians didn't want to leave the convoy and decided to test out the thesis. He suggested that, on second thoughts, they'd not be sent back to the capital. He was pleased to see Ethelwulf start to relax and then added they should be rushed forward to the judgement of the Autokrator himself. The tension came back into the hated Varangian's eyes.

So there was something here with the convoy. The Eparchos knew he'd no chance of any of his agents ferreting out the secret without setting the whole convoy on its guard. Much better to let the three barbarians have one last chance to see reason and cooperate. The Eparchos announced the three prisoners would be transported northwards to the Autokrator in three hours time. In the meanwhile they were to be returned to the hut which served as their prison.

*

Morkere quickly persuaded his two fellow-prisoners that no treasure was any good if they were dead. All three were certain they'd never reach the Autokrator alive. The Eparchos wouldn't resist the chance to get rid of all three that such a journey offered. Morkere was sure the Eparchos could be bought and Sven agreed, although he was reluctant to see ALL the hoard being used to buy their freedom.

Ethelwulf was not so sure of the avarice of the Eparchos. Greed was certainly there, but so was ambition and a heavy layer of bitterness. He'd seen that in the brown eyes of their captor when he'd failed to break their stories. Even so, Ethelwulf had to agree they'd be dead men once they left the convoy. Reluctantly he agreed to hand over the hoard, hating to think of the Eparchos profiting from their bad-luck.

Morkere now proposed they should get the Eparchos to surrender them into the custody of John the Cappadocian. Under escort they'd retrieve the sack from the wagon and hand it over. After all, Sven had taken to sleeping in the wagon and they could say they were merely recovering their property. No one would question them if the Eparchos was present. Later the hoard could be handed over to the Eparchos, when there were no prying eyes around.

When the suggestion was made to the Eparchos they could see greed triumph over vengeance. All he wanted to know was where and how they'd come by the hoard. Ethelwulf insisted it was the profits of a raid on a Bulgar village when they'd first become separated from the main army. He neglected to describe the contents - or even the outward appearance as he didn't want the Eparchos to perform his own recovery operation.

So the agreement was made and the three Varangians were handed over to the custody of John the Cappadocian. With the Eparchos the four men strolled over to the wagon where the hoard was hidden. The Eparchos and Ethelwulf were apparently discussing intelligence of the backstreets of the capital; this served to explain the continued presence of Alexius Euergetes. It also justified to the captain the sudden release of the three Varangians into his custody. He was told the Varangians must be taken to pass on their intelligence to the Autokrator himself - meanwhile the Eparchos would send agents back to the capital to act against the traitors uncovered by Ethelwulf. Hidden among one of the sacks on the wagon was evidence of this treachery. It was to be retrieved and handed over to the City Prefect.

Later that evening Demetrius, acting on the orders of the Eparchos, came to return the sack to the wagon. There was no reason to doubt his honesty.

*

The Autokrator was furious. His blue eyes flashed vehemently at the Varangian who towered over him. He'd trusted this barbarian, had allowed him even to dine with himself.[335] Now the man was shown to be nothing but a traitor. It was true the Eparchos reported the three men had been caught coming north, but there'd been a hint the scheme had been to slip away once they approached the borders of the Empire.

"After all, sire," had confided the City Prefect. " These barbarians know how little chance they have of slipping out of your realm without notice. Once, however, in this place of desolation..." and there was almost a sigh as he neglected to finish the accusation.

Could this all be true? The Autokrator had taken to the barbarians from the north. They'd shown themselves to be excellent fighters and thoroughly loyal. They'd not been called upon to fight their own kind but he was certain the time would come when the Rus would launch another expedition against his capital. Meanwhile he'd heard the man confess to wandering around somewhere in the west instead of immediately returning to his unit. Only two things stood in the barbarian's favour. Nowhere was there a suggestion he'd been tempted to slip off to that upstart claiming to be the successor of Constantine.[336] Nor was there any doubt he'd been arrested while openly part of an imperial force heading north.

"The Eparchos believes you and your companions would desert once you got closer to the barbarians - "

"Then the Eparchos is a liar, sire," burst out the Varangian, brushing aside the shock the interruption had produced on the Autokrator's features. "...and he's also very ignorant of geography!" Puzzlement replaced shock and Ethelwulf could see a strange interplay of curiosity and irritation cover an undertone of fury on the Autokrator's face. Quickly he explained no one wishing to travel back to the land of the Rus would think of leaving from anywhere but the capital. The only sensible means of travel was by water and the only reasonable source of shipping was the capital. Only a fool could dream of passing through the territories of Bulgars and Pechenegs to reach Kenugard.

By now the Autokrator was calming down, remembering his earlier thought that there'd been no attempt to escape to the west. Ethelwulf saw the chance to deal with the Eparchos, especially as the imperial official was trying to convict him of desertion.

"I trust the Eparchos has handed over to the Imperial Treasurer what I recovered on my way back to civilisation," he said with as much display of innocence as possible. He was certain the Eparchos had never intended to hand over the hoard, confident no one would see any discrepancy between the imperial manifest and the actual amount of pay which arrived at the camp.

The Autokrator sharply demanded an explanation and Ethelwulf described how the Varangians had come upon the hoard and brought it with them out of Bulgar territory. The Autokrator was certain there'd never been any intention to surrender the treasure to the imperial authorities but he didn't bother to press the point. Ethelwulf then added the Eparchos had insisted on the surrender of the hoard as the price of submission to imperial judgement.

The Eparchos immediately admitted there was such a sack of coins. However, he insisted Ethelwulf was lying as the sack was merely a contribution from the Isaurian and Cappadocian provinces. Ethelwulf must have seen the sack in his quarters and concocted the story of having retrieved the treasure for the Autokrator.

"Where are the receipts for the money?" asked the Autokrator, prepared to admit the "contribution" had been extorted from Anatolian peasants. If that were the case then there'd be no receipts, but he'd have the money and that was all that counted.

There was a slight hesitation as Alexius Euergetes admitted the receipts had been retained at the capital. Both knew there'd be plenty of time to "discover" the relevant paperwork if any investigation was ordered. The Autokrator was prepared to let the matter rest. The Varangian had made a serious accusation, probably in an attempt to win back imperial favour, but there was no proof either way. Perhaps they should pack the Varangians off again to Syria, well out of the way and ready for another push towards Jerusalem. But Ethelwulf refused to back down.

"Sire, is it true the Eparchos declares I only saw the sack of coin, lying unopened in his quarters?" He looked intently at the Autokrator, deliberately shutting out the Eparchos from the query. The Autokrator raised a questioning eyebrow and his official nodded agreement.

"Yes," he stated, "and on that basis you've dared to try and malign the good faith of one of the most loyal of my servants."

"Then, sire," and Ethelwulf paused for effect. "Can the Eparchos explain that I know that the sack contains two coins minted by Pepin, lord of the Franks, ten coins produced by the Saracen ruler called Abd-al-Malik and fifty six coins of your ancestor the emperor, Constantine V?"

There was a heavy stillness in the tent. The Autokrator looked questioningly at his minister and the eyes of the Eparchos bored into the soul of the Varangian. Ethelwulf persisted. "Perhaps the

Eparchos can tell us whose are the latest coins in this "contribution" from the provinces?"

There was a heavy mockery in his voice. As the Eparchos started to splutter that, of course he couldn't know the nature of every coin handed over by the loyal subjects of the Empire, Ethelwulf added with purposeful quietness, "I can tell you that they date from the reign of the Empress Irene."

The Autokrator broke the silence by clapping his hands to order a guard to bring from the quarters of the Eparchos a sack of coins in the charge of the slave Demetrius. Nobody spoke until the soldier reappeared with the bag loosely slung over his shoulder. Carefully the man placed the sack on the table in front of the Autokrator and then awaited further orders.

"Is this the bag?" asked the Autokrator, aiming the question at both Ethelwulf and the Eparchos. Both nodded but there was a nervousness about the official which hadn't been there moments before. The soldier was ordered to fetch the Chartularius Peter who distributed pay to the troops. After thirty years working in the Imperial Treasury he had a knowledge of coins second to none.

The Chartularius entered almost immediately and was ordered to carefully open the bag. Nervously the man's thin fingers picked at the knot securing the bag and finally worried it loose.

"Now spread the contents over the table and organise them according to their origin," ordered the Autokrator. A frown appeared on the forehead of the official but he quickly set about the task. Within moments the coins had been divided into distinct groups.

The Autokrator stepped forward and picked up a coin from the largest pile. He carefully examined it and then turned to Ethelwulf. "Who issued this coin, barbarian?" he snapped.

There was no hesitation. "The Basileus Constantine, sire," stated the Varangian, "and you will find there are fifty-six of them!"

A quiet smile appeared on the lips of the Autokrator. "Count them!" he snapped and the deft fingers of the Chartularius tore through the piles of coins re-ordering them into tens.

"Fifty-six there are, sire," admitted the official looking with awe at the barbarian as if the man possessed some magical knowledge.

"Are there any strange coins there?" asked the Autokrator and, seeing the look of incomprehension appearing on the official's face, added, "I mean coins originating from outside the Empire."

The thin fingers lightly touched small piles of coins on the right of the table. "These coins were produced by the unbelievers in the east, " he whispered, as if almost frightened that contact with them could snatch his soul away. Then confidence appeared. " I have some knowledge of the Arabic script, sire, and many such coins have passed through these fingers after your triumphs in the east."

"There are ten coins issued by Abd-al-Malik," stated the Varangian and the amazed official nodded in agreement before confessing that there were two coins there he didn't recognise.

"Only two?" smiled the Autokrator and the amusement vanished as he turned to face the Eparchos. "Perhaps the Eparchos knows they were issued by Pepin, lord of the Franks!" The astonishment of the Chartularius was even increased as he heard the Autokrator order the immediate arrest of the Eparchos.

Alexius didn't even have the energy to protest as he was hustled out of the imperial presence, not seeing the Varangian crudely kneel before the Autokrator and kiss the imperial foot.

*

Convicted of treasonably attempting to steal recovered imperial property the Eparchos was stripped of all authority. The Autokrator recalled the insistence of Alexius that the traitor Sclerus should be blinded so he should never again enjoy the beauties of nature. He ordered the disgraced official should also suffer that fate.

The Autokrator hesitated about what to do with the Varangians. He had no doubt Ethelwulf had been planning to steal the hoard but couldn't prove it. It'd be wrong to punish a man on suspicion, and also inexpedient with action demanding every soldier available. However, the man couldn't be trusted not to slip away back to the west or the north. The answer suddenly came to the Autokrator. The Varangians would form the advance guard for the reconquest of the Holy Land.

"Just like the old days," grumbled Gunnar and affectionately stroked the edge of his battle-axe. It hadn't been the same when Ethelwulf and the others had disappeared into the hills of Bulgaria. When they'd not returned he'd tried to shrug at the tampering of Urd but something kept telling him Ethelwulf was still alive. Wherever he'd gone was beyond the help of man, certainly a Gall-Gael from the distant shores of Ireland. Gunnar had set his mind to staying alive in the vicious campaign which the Autokrator launched to try and drive the forces of the Tsar Samuel into submission.

With the Saxon back, life could return to what it always should be - fighting, drinking and whoring.

*

The Wanderer 8:7

'For every warrior death outweighs a life of disgrace.' ('Beowulf' paraphrase)

The Turkish Horsemen

"I don't want to have to drag the swine halfway across the Empire with me," protested Morkere. He'd just been told that, on their way to Antioch, the Varangians would have to escort the mutilated Alexius Euergetes to exile in northern Syria. However, whatever he wanted was ignored. The Varangians had been ordered to march across the Empire once again and set up camp near Antioch.

Gunnar laughed grimly. It'd be pleasant to have that stuck-up Greek in his proper place. Nobody was going to show any sympathy because of his mutilation; the Eparchos in all his power was too recent an event. Gunnar didn't know Ethelwulf had protested vehemently about transporting his old enemy across the breadth of the Empire. The Autokrator had insisted it would be a good test of the loyalty which the Varangians were supposed to have.

"After all, " he added, and there was no amusement in his blue eyes. "You prided yourself on defending one traitor from attack years ago.[337] Let us see what you do for another!"

To question the Autokrator in such a mood was pointless. Ethelwulf curtly bowed and withdrew. They'd allow one month for the transfer of the prisoner, it would be good for his immortal soul to tolerate the presence of the wretch for such a short time.

*

The journey across Anatolia was very easy, so unlike the rush of the campaign three years before.[338] The Varangians took their time, although they welcomed the chance to cross the wild hills mounted on horses. Of course, it meant a longer period spent in the company of Alexius, but he could be ignored. The disgraced official rode glumly on, his sightless eyes staring into the hills ahead and his lips held tight against any temptation to talk to barbarians.

Ethelwulf at times felt some pity growing for the man and quickly pushed it aside. If the Eparchos had succeeded he was certain all the leading Varangians would have suffered even harsher mutilation before being sent back to Gadarike, if they were lucky.

Yes, the Empire would have revelled in giving such a lesson to barbarians in imperial justice.

By now they'd entered the borders of Seleucia and Ethelwulf was inclined to pause to meet the governor of the last imperial province before they entered the war zone of Antioch. He'd been ordered to deposit Alexius in the monastery of St. Chrysostom outside Germanicea. To get there he could take the longer (and safer) road by Augustopolis; or he could venture on the shorter route through the Cilician Gates. This might prove dangerous as rumour in the capital said Turkish mercenaries in the pay of the Caliph in Cairo were terrorising the region between Antioch and the Gates. It was said the Saracens were trying to get together a force sufficient to recover northern Syria. Internal wrangling, however, was making it difficult.[339] The governor of Seleucia should know the situation and be obliged to offer advice.

Accordingly, it was a relaxed group of Varangians who rode into the small coastal town of Seleucia. They were all pleased to be nearing the end of their journey. Certainly Alexius seemed pushed into some kind of enthusiasm when told they'd nearly reached Antioch. He smiled that all-too-familiar cruel smile when informed they'd report to the governor and get directions on how best to proceed.

*

The Governor, Philip Ducas, seemed particularly unhelpful at their first meeting. Of course he didn't refuse help, but stressed the need to update his intelligence before he felt able to offer the Varangians proper guidance. Ethelwulf realised that, like all lesser governors, the man was frightened of losing what little power he had. He noted the green edge decorating Philip's white robe, revealing he held a modest Patrician rank.[340] Better to be patient with the man. Once an imperial governor had made sure there'd be no comeback for mistakes they could be cooperative.

In fact, the next morning the atmosphere changed completely. The Governor greeted Ethelwulf with a warm smile and offered him a goblet of the local wine, which the Varangian declined.

"Well, you need to rest before you and your men tackle the Cilician Gates," advised the Governor, beckoning him to take a seat. Ethelwulf started to protest but Philip hastened to give an explanation. "My agents have.....have reported there are no hostile forces between here and the Gates."

"Naturally, no enemy would dare penetrate so far into imperial territory."

"No," the Governor shrugged off the interruption. "but the Gates are but halfway to your destination." He paused and glanced out of the window, as if checking on the accuracy of his statement. "Even now my agents are exploring the roads to the east of Gates. In two days they'll report back."

"We've been commissioned by the Autokrator to press on to Antioch - "

"But not to risk not arriving at all!" The Governor cut off all argument. Without his support either road would be difficult. Certainly the road to the north would add at least the two extra days to the journey. It would be better to delay here, rest and give his men a chance to acclimatise to the more pleasant temperatures of the Mediterranean coast.

*

Two days later the Varangians were released by the Governor. He offered the support of a company of Cappadocian spearman under the Pentekontarchos,[341] Alexius Thadeis. These men were being despatched to support Antioch to resist the coming Fatimid attack. It would be best for both detachments to march together; a force of nearly one hundred men could deal with anything the scouts had missed. Ethelwulf was surprised how easy it was to agree. These men were experienced soldiers used to fighting in this region.

He wasn't alarmed at the hurried conversation between his prisoner and the Pentekontarchos. After all, word had soon got around the small town he was escorting the fallen Eparchos. For years the man had been one of the most important figures in the Empire. It was natural provincials would try to approach men who'd once controlled the destinies of thousands.

The order of march was soon settled. An advance guard, made up of one of the four Cappadocian dekarchies,[342] led the way; followed by thirty Varangians under the command of Gunnar. Next came the core of Varangians, led by Morkere, in charge of their prisoner. These were followed by twenty Varangians, under Ethelwulf; finally the rear was controlled by the remaining thirty Cappadocians under Alexius Thadeis. One point that concerned Ethelwulf was the Cappadocian insistence on marching under a battle standard of their own province.

At first progress was good. The Cappadocian advance guard set a good pace and within hours the Gates came into view. It was a peaceful day, with a cold, clear blue sky and a bright golden sun. Ethelwulf decided to press on through the pass before they rested for the night. He felt the Cappadocians to the rear slightly increase their pace as the pass came into view.

It didn't take long to reach the pass. Normally Ethelwulf would have detached scouts to examine the surrounding hills for danger before venturing into a confined space. The slopes of the pass gradually rose until merging into the sharper inclines of the surrounding mountains. The Pentekontarchos, however, assured him that, not only had the pass been thoroughly examined by scouts within the last few days, but even then the slopes were concealing only the friendly eyes of imperial soldiers.

Ethelwulf remembered the last time he'd passed through the pass. Then imperial scouts had made sure no enemy was within days of the army; now the whole area was subject to depredations from wandering bands of brigands or Turks. Two years ago the imperial armies had loosened their grip on the area surrounding Mamistra and allowed an influx of Turkish mercenaries from over the river Euphrates. The failure of the Imperial Treasury to maintain payments to frontier troops had led many to desert and scavenge an existence as brigands. It was time the Autokrator re-appeared to bring order to the region. For the first time Ethelwulf began to see a purpose in this expedition.

By now the column had trotted into the rough pass. Somehow the ground seemed stonier and more difficult. Behind him Ethelwulf felt an edge creep into the Cappadocian spearmen. No soldier liked to expose himself to fighting off a surprise attack in a confined space.

From somewhere up ahead Ethelwulf heard a loud shout and instantly raised his hand to halt the column. Behind him he felt the reluctance of the rear to come to a halt and he ordered Haakon Slit-Eyes to gallop ahead to find out the cause of the disturbance. Haakon nodded and swung his horse out of the column to by-pass the troops ahead who hadn't come to a halt. As he did so there were more cries and an arrow struck Haakon in the shoulder. By chance the Varangian kept his seat but, even as he turned in question towards his leader, his mount started to gallop.

By now it was obvious there was an attack emerging from somewhere ahead. Ethelwulf ordered the Varangians to dismount. No Varangian would want to fight from horseback. He started to group his men into a tight phalanx to advance up the pass, assuming the Cappadocians would be taking on a similar formation. Suddenly behind him one of the Varangians screamed and pitched forward with a javelin in his back.

*

Haakon found himself carried forward past the patrol Morkere was hastily forming into a loose circle around their prisoner. However, the Varangian had no time to notice details as he struggled to drop his shield from his good arm and take over control from its useless fellow. Haakon had never been a horseman, half-apprehensive of creatures that seemed so amenable and yet full of power. Given the choice he'd have preferred to trudge across the Anatolian wastes and feel more secure. Now, he felt terror grow as the horse started to gain speed, picking its way with unwelcome skill past the confusion of men and horses. Suddenly a warrior stepped forward and swung a war-axe; the blade sank into the side of his mount's head and with a squeal the animal was thrown to the ground. Somehow Haakon managed to pitch sideways before the horse's body crashed on to the stony ground. Despite the searing pain that passed through his entire right arm Haakon laughed; at least he felt master of his fate again!

Ahead Gunnar was shrieking at his men to close ranks. Some of them were dismounting, allowing their horses to mill around and add to the existing chaos. Others tried to retain control of their mounts and peer over the heads of the Cappadocians in front at what had caused the turmoil.

From out of the dusk came a burst of about sixty Turkish horsemen; wild men, using their short bows with powerful effect as they charged towards the surprised imperial troops. Gunnar wondered how long, if at all, the Cappadocian spearmen would be able to resist the onslaught. At this point in the Gates a solid line of ten men could force lightly armed horsemen to swing into the more-restricted paths to the left or right. Once there progress would be less sure because of the unevenness of the ground.

By now Gunnar had thrown himself to the ground, slapped his horse off in the direction of the charging Turks and got a firmer grip on his battle-axe. From his throat came the savage war-cry of the Waterford levies. He remembered the fury with which his father, Thorgeir, had dragged three Gaels down with him as he'd been pitched over the edge of the Eagle Falls. Since hearing about that he'd never liked fighting beside a steep drop. This was different; here a man could stand and fight in a shield wall.

Suddenly in front the Cappadocians melted to either side. Gunnar cursed them for their cowardice as the Turks were given free rein in the centre of the pass. He started to order his men to form a tight formation in the middle to break up the rush. Then he saw the Cappadocians turn and charge at his own men. As the Varangians turned towards the middle they were attacked from the side of the pass. From out of nowhere more figures launched themselves on the unordered Varangians.

Gunnar swung his axe and one brigand was almost cut in two. As blood spouted over his right fore-arm Gunnar yelled in triumph and stepped forward. This was the way men should act; this was why man had been born from a fallen tree.[343] Now a second brigand was coming from the right. Gunnar turned to meet the fresh attack. As he did so a rock struck him from the other side and he was knocked off balance. The brigand thrust a spear deep into Gunnar's thigh.

"Sharper than Erin's dew,
My life-pool flows out
To lick the evening air."

He struck viciously at the man and the attacker crumbled before him. Gunnar felt the wounded leg suddenly lose all strength as if his body was aware of the damage. He violently sank down on one knee and a shudder passed through his body. A Cappadocian spearmen stepped from somewhere in front and lunged at the wounded Varangian. Gunnar swung his axe and the force of the blow lifted the spearman off his feet. Then Gunnar slumped forward, groaned once and lay still.

By now the Varangians had been pushed aside by the combined onslaught of Turkish horsemen, Cappadocian spearmen and brigands. The attackers passed on to the waiting shield-wall of Morkere, already under attack from ambush at the side of the pass. By chance Morkere had drawn up his force to the right of the gap, allowing free passage to the Turkish horsemen. With derisive cries they passed by to leave the ten Varangians to deal with the surviving Cappadocians and brigands. Some distance away Ethelwulf had managed to reverse his battle-formation and steadily advance to attack the Cappadocian spearmen. He was unaware Gunnar's force had been so quickly swept aside; he only knew he couldn't safely advance further up the pass while a hostile force controlled his rear.

As the formation charged at a jog-trot towards the Cappadocian spearmen brigands poured out from both sides of the pass. The Varangians were already outnumbered two-to-one before the

Turkish horsemen struck at their rear. By then the battle had been fiercely joined. Ethelwulf cut at a thin spearmen and his sword bit deeply into the man's shield. The counter-thrust of the spear was easily parried by his shield before a second sword-lunge ended the life of the spearman. However, this merely allowed a second man to step forward and thrust at the Varangian leader. As he ducked below the spear-point, Ethelwulf glanced towards the left, just in time to see Alexius Thadeis felled by a blow from Ubbe's war-axe.

"Let his soul rot in hell," the thought almost became words as he lunged at the Cappadocian and missed. However, the man was wrong-footed and Sven by his side pierced him with his own spear.

"That's the way to skewer Greeks!" he laughed, and the sound changed to a scream as a Turkish arrow struck him in the nape of the neck. Ethelwulf glanced behind him at the unexpected intrusion. He wanted to yell out a warning to his men but saw they were already under enough pressure. From both sides the wings of the line were starting to curl inwards as the Varangians defended themselves against the onslaught of the brigands. What had been a steady line became a sharp echelon and was in danger of becoming a static ring. To stop here was to challenge destruction.

Ethelwulf yelled to his men to close up and charge the centre of the Cappadocian line. He formed the arrowhead of the formation as it tore into the enemy. An angular figure stood in his way momentarily and was cut down by a sweep of his sword. A second went to take his place but was thrust aside, with a savage yell of victory, by Harold of Furzebrook.[344] Now there was an open gap and Ethelwulf turned to his right to strike against the exposed side of the nearest Cappadocian. Harold turned to the left and was challenged by a giant spearman. Both struck with their spears at the same time - and both died at the same moment. Ethelwulf hacked at a spearmen and saw blood spout out from a severed limb. Behind him he could sense the Varangians beginning to turn the Cappadocians against themselves.

At this point the enemy found themselves under another threat. Turkish horsemen ruthlessly charged into the melee. For them any foot-soldier was a target. Some Cappadocians screamed at them to stop, but their cries were either misunderstood or ignored. In panic the Cappadocians tried to break out of the chaos, escape from being pressed against the walls of the pass. This gave them a chance of safety and they fought a rear-guard action against both Varangians and Turks.

The Varangians were now more exposed to the onslaught of the Turks. Ethelwulf was challenged by a grey-cloaked horseman and cut at the rider's legs. He missed and the next moment was pushed off balance by the buffeting of the warrior's mount. The action caused the stroke of the scimitar to swish past his head. As Ethelwulf started to recover his balance a large rock struck him just above the left eye and he was pitched senseless into a growing pile of corpses. For him the battle was over.

*

Morkere revelled in the fury of the battle. Odds of four-to-one simply added to the exultation. He'd ordered Alexius to be removed from his horse and thrust under a bundle of camp impedimenta. Thorstein guffawed as the disgraced official shrieked as the dregs of the morning's breakfast were poured over him.

"For once I'm pleased menials skimped their duties," he laughed and crudely rammed the pot firmly over his victim's eyes. "Stay there, and stay quiet, while men deal with these turncoats." With that he turned and resumed his place in the Varangian shield wall, standing as firm as when he'd guided 'Brimfugol' into the harbour of Eraklion ages ago.[345]

Brigands launched an attack against the left of the wall. Two Varangians were felled by a fusillade of missiles. Sensing the weakness several of the enemy charged for the gap in the line. With a yell the gigantic form of Eric the Little[346] filled the gap, swinging an enormous axe to cut the legs of one man before it smashed against the shield of a second. The man staggered back, even though his dying comrade had taken most of the force of the blow. The attackers paused at the vehemence of the defence.

Now Cappadocians pierced the left of the wall as Uffe was smashed to the ground by a large rock hurled by a spearman driven insane by a fearsome blow to his head. The spearman died the next moment but his fellows rushed into the gap. Morkere turned to face the new threat and found his spear snapped in two by a savage swing of a brigand's club. He stepped back quickly as the brigand swung the weapon again. As the club whistled past Morkere pushed forward his shield and had the pleasure of hearing its boss crack open the man's nose. By now he'd had time to draw his sword, but the brigand turned and ran. Morkere stepped forward and didn't see the Cappadocian to his left swing his sword until it was too late. The blade bit deeply into his neck beneath his chin. Just as Morkere sensed the blood surge out he felt his legs give way and dropped his shield to save himself from falling. A

Cappadocian spear was buried into his chest below the collar-bone and Morkere was driven back on to the stony ground.

Lying helpless Morkere saw a figure step forward and cut down the Cappadocian. "Edwine!" was all the sound which came from his lips as he closed his eyes and died. Njal Hammerhand at other times would have laughed to have been mistaken for the dead Varangian; now he was engrossed in withstanding an attack by two Cappadocians. One he felled with a broad sweep of his sword, the other knocked him over by the sheer force of his charge. Before Njal could fight back the Cappadocian's knife had been driven into his throat.

*

The Turks had regrouped around Alexius Euergetes who'd been dragged from his shelter. "I don't know why the Seleucians are willing to give so much gold for this heap of dung," admitted Selim Urq to his follower, Tutush. Doubts were unimportant as long as the Governor paid up. If he didn't they'd have to kill the prisoner; a blind man had no value in the slave markets of Jezireh.[347] He'd been disappointed in the number of prisoners they'd taken; ten Varangians left alive were no real profit. He'd expected some losses but eight dead men and another fifteen wounded was unacceptable. Perhaps he shouldn't have listened to the envoys from the Governor Philip, but the temptation had been too great. A straight bounty of gold for the safe return of the prisoner being transported eastwards, the possibility of slaves for the forces of his master, Samsan-al-Dawlah,[348] and a chance to practise brigandage for three days west of the Cilician Gates. Such had been the terms he'd been unable to resist.

Tutush was now ordered to escort the blind prisoner westwards to the outskirts of Seleucia. He was given strict instructions neither to enter the city itself nor to hand over the prisoner until the bounty was paid. Nicephorus of Tarsus, who'd assumed the leadership of the Cappadocians, volunteered as intermediary. Although Selim didn't trust the Cappadocian, he'd no desire to risk to attack in Seleucia itself. Even so, he'd have liked to have known what was the interest of the Governor in this disgraced official. Of course, he'd quickly discovered the blind man had once been second only to the Roman Sultan himself; but that was in the past. As his family said "A dog is only a cur even if sired by the Caliph's lapdog itself." What was true NOW was important, not what once had been.

Selim turned his attention to the ten prisoners. None of them could speak Arabic of course, and only two some crude form of Greek. A

Cappadocian had been detailed to stay with them as interpreter until they reached Edessa. If the man was cooperative he might let him have his freedom, otherwise he'd have eleven prisoners.

Gunnar looked at Selim and hated the barbarism of the horseman. It was the way he strutted about as if in triumph over the Empire. Only treachery had defeated the Varangians. There'd be scores to pay in the future; the deaths of so many warriors – Ethelwulf, Morkere, Uffe, Njal. Gunnar looked at the Turkish chief as he'd looked at Brian of Clonmel so many years ago, and saw the man lying dead beneath his war-axe.

> "Dead are the fighters
> Beloved of Thor
> Let the daughters of Urd[349]
> Shed tears and sharpen
> Death-bringing thorns
> For when Verdandi[350] nods."

"What is that brute mumbling about?" grunted Selim.

"I don't know, sir," answered the Cappadocian nervously. "It's not a civilised language but a tongue bred in the wilds of the north."

You had better improve, thought Selim, or not even the prospect of a price in Edessa'll keep you alive. But he said nothing and merely rode back to join the main body of the Turks.

*

Luke the doctor was drawn to the battlefield by the need to help the wounded and the dying. He'd been visiting his widowed sister on her holding near the mouth of the Cilician Gates. For years he'd worried about how she continued to work the small farm with the help of the strong and stupid Zeno and the wiry Leo. He'd spent many hours trying to persuade Zenobia that thirty years effort in keeping on the dead Gabriel's herd of goats and scratching a living from the dust was enough. Today had been no different; friendly but fierce disagreement.

Then Leo had run in with the news. He'd seen a detachment of imperial troops while narrowly avoiding a band led by the Armenian brigand Thoros near the pass. He expected Thoros would make sure his men kept out of the way of the advancing troops, but they might be caught and there'd be a fight.

"May Christ bring judgement on the doers of evil," affirmed Zenobia as she bullied a broom into a corner. Luke smiled quietly to himself.

His sister's words might be equally applied to the Armenian brigands and the soldiers of the Empire. For him, however, any suffering imposed a duty; the Almighty would call to judgement those for whom their hour had come, for others there'd be the need for a physician's skills. It took some time to get his sister to agree.

*

Luke had started to question the wisdom of his rush to help the wounded. There were so few - and when he'd found one Turks or brigands had been upon him instantly to plunder the wretch. In fact, the badly wounded were finished off by some of the more ruthless victors and the less injured carted off to the slave markets. What was the point of it all?

Somehow he wandered over close to the cliff which flanked the entrance to the gates. One reason for such movement was to get away from the misery and despair of what was happening elsewhere in the aftermath. Then he heard a slight noise.

At first Luke could see nothing; then he saw from behind a rough hawthorn bush a foot. Quickly he passed behind the bush and came upon a man gradually coming back into consciousness. As he recovered a low moan came from cracked lips and the body started to twitch. Luke glanced in the direction of the Turks and saw nobody had noticed his disappearance. He had to make the man more comfortable - and keep him quiet. He knelt down and thrust his mouth close to the man's left ear.

"Be quiet! There are enemies all around!" From somewhere he sensed the man wanted to respond. "Don't try to reply. Just lie here still until it's safe and I'll come again!" He paused and gripped the man's left hand. "If you understand and will do this grip my hand!" With relief he felt the comfort of pressure on his hand. Then he stood up and passed in front of the bush. Somehow he had to try and keep any Turk from coming over here. How? He didn't know. He realised the Turks were anxious to leave the battlefield; some were collecting together prisoners, others waiting on the orders of their leader. The brigands were already disappearing back into the hills, weighed down with spoils. The Cappadocians had regrouped and ridden off in the direction of Seleucia.

Luke found he was slipping back towards the main group of Turks. Not too close, just enough to distract any who started to move in that direction. So far this day had been a failure; now he'd the chance of at last helping one survivor.

*

Two hours later Luke made his way back to his hidden survivor. The Turks hadn't wanted to stay but the potential slaves had been difficult to manage. One of them had tried to resist the binding of his arms and had to be killed; no, thought Luke, murdered would be a better word. The man had been unarmed and outnumbered among his enemies. It hadn't been necessary to kill him but it had been easier. As he thought, the Turks were in a hurry.

The wounded man had deteriorated under the growing heat of the morning. Luke found it hard to put only a little water between his lips. Grey eyes opened and a hand feebly tried to force more water into a dry throat.

"Easy, my friend," smiled Luke. "Too much water can do you harm, and after all this I want you well!" The hand relaxed and Luke gently moistened the neck and forehead of the man. With excruciating care he wiped clean the wound above the left eye. The man whimpered softly at the contrast between the cool water and the sun-dried blood concealing the injury. Luke was pleased the wound seemed less than he'd feared at first. As he dipped the cloth into the small leather flask, Luke stood up to make sure no one was in the area. It was amazing how empty and desolate the mouth of the Gates appeared. Here and there a plundered corpse remained to feed the creatures of the wild. There was no sign of any human.

Gradually Luke got the survivor back into full consciousness. Only then did he help the man crawl further under the bush to get shelter from the sun. As an afterthought he placed next to the man a heavy sword, so unlike any Greek would have carried. With that achieved Luke hurried back to get a mule from his sister's farm in order to transport the survivor to safety.

Ethelwulf sank back in the shade and dreamed of when his Varangians had marched together.

*

It was very hot and Gunnar had almost given up trying to moisten his lips with his tongue. He glared at the back of the Turk in front of them and remembered how Grim had died that morning. The young Varangian had spent too many weeks in an imperial dungeon for brawling to welcome the prospect of captivity. Something within the Dane had snapped and he'd tried to throttle the Turk who was binding his wrists. In doing that he'd ignored what they'd all agreed to do, wait and seize their chance when the odds were better.

Perhaps it was for the best that Grim had died so quickly because it prevented the rest of the Varangians launching a doomed attempt at freedom. Even so the Turk in front was the one who'd stabbed the young Dane and Gunnar never forgot his debts.

Next to him Thorolf started singing and others took up the mournful song of Hermod's ride to Eljudnir.[351] The words offered little comfort to the Varangians marching off into slavery, but it helped keep them bound together, separated from their surroundings by culture and belief. Even the description of winter and darkness marked the gulf between them and the world of Greeks and Turks. Somehow Gunnar found himself croaking in chorus as Hel scorned the approaches of the gods.

For hours they trudged through the bleak countryside, ever eastwards away from hope. Gunnar found it surprising none of the Varangians dropped in the dust permanently. Some slumped down as exhaustion and heat cut into their minds. However, a few kicks from the Turks and words of encouragement from their fellows got them back on their feet. By the time they finally made camp there were still nine of them, and three guards which put the odds distinctly in the Varangians' favour. Of course there was the Cappadocian - but he was treated almost as if he were a prisoner and Gunnar was well aware of his growing resentment. George Critas didn't understand why he'd been selected for such an unwelcome task, unless it stemmed from the petty-mindedness of his leader. Naturally he could speak the Greek of the capital, but so could a dozen others. He'd been chosen because he irritated Nicephorus of Tarsus.

George rode most of the day next to Magnus and, with a little difficulty at the effort of an exchange between mounted and walker, managed to communicate. Magnus had been one of the quicker learners of the argot of the capital's alleyways. Since leaving Trondheim fifteen years before he'd acquired a strange knowledge of several languages - the German spoken in Koln and the Lombard in Pavia. Then when the old empress had died,[352] he'd drifted down to Bari and entered the service of the Empire. Three years later he'd joined the Varangians. Now he wished he'd stayed in the west and, while trying to concentrate on all the Cappadocian told him, planned their escape. Apparently their route would pass close to the town of Sis in two day's time. After that, another five day's march would bring them to the south of Germanicea and the limits of any pretence of imperial control. From there the journey to the destination of Edessa would take another eight days, if they survived it! So Magnus concluded any escape must take place in the next two days. If the Cappadocian admitted imperial control was weak beyond Sis then it was certainly non-existent. Besides every day made them weaker and lowered morale. Somehow he had to get Gunnar to lead an escape.

*

That night the Turks made the mistake of allowing the prisoners to be herded together, too late realising they'd no control over communication conducted in Norse.

Somehow Hjalti Egilsson managed to worm his wrists free of the rope and yet contrived to give the appearance of captivity. Still, it was his fellow Icelander, Kol the Quick, who decided to make use of the opportunity. Anybody not knowing Kol would look at his apparent bulk and see the typical northern sense of irony in the nickname. Others, who knew better, held Kol had got his nickname from his ability to run fast over a distance of one hundred yards. Those more informed, however, knew Kol's talents for rifling the belts and pouches of others had given rise to the name. Certainly they'd caused him to leave his home six years before and somehow find his way down to the capital of the Empire.

As the light from the campfire started to fade Kol staggered to his feet to relieve himself in the shrub-land on the edge of the camp. Two of the guards looked sharply in his direction and reached for their bows. They relaxed, however, when he turned towards the fire and wearily crunched his way back over the stones to his companions. For an instant he stumbled, cursed and cannoned into George. The Cappadocian was unbalanced and tumbled on to the ground to the derisive hoots of the Varangians. One of the Turks rushed towards the sprawled Varangian and smashed his bow viciously against Kol's back. The Icelander offered a feeble grunt, recovered his feet and, without looking at his assailant, staggered back to the rest of the Varangians.

As he eased his way back on the ground next to Magnus he whispered, "Now let's see if the Greek will scream thief!" His yellow teeth formed an enigmatic grin as he passed Magnus a knife.

Magnus used it to slash through the bound wrists of the thief and then returned it without a word. Kol rolled carelessly over and freed Einar Gunnarsson, before passing the knife on. In this way all the Varangians were soon free. Magnus waited for George to discover the theft and rouse the Turks. There was no sound from the Cappadocian who sullenly made himself comfortable on the other side of the dying fire. Magnus was certain the man knew what had happened to his knife. Why was no alarm raised?

"Gunnar says wait till he gets up to go and piss in the darkness," whispered Kol. "That should lead off one. You and me have got to take care of that squint-eyed bastard." and he indicated the smallest of their captors. Magnus stared up at the stars and wondered who was going to deal with the Greek.

It seemed hours before Gunnar slowly dragged himself to his feet and stumbled off into the darkness. There was a yell from the older Turk who drew his scimitar and rushed after the Varangian. For a moment there was silence and then a sound of a struggle. Melik, the shorter Turk, started to run towards the sound and was tripped by Magnus. Kol threw his bulk on the helpless guard and rammed the man's face in the ground. A scream was choked off by the sound of breaking teeth and then a furious struggle for air. Kol didn't release his hold until the sounds had ceased.

Meanwhile Cnud and Hoskuld attacked Tutush who'd been asleep when the disturbance had occurred. Somehow, he managed to escape from their attack and drew his scimitar with a shout to Allah. The next instance he'd been felled to the ground by a blow from George. The Cappadocian hadn't waited for Eric to reach him. Directly the Varangian had awkwardly risen the Cappadocian rushed off into the darkness. It had seemed like years since he'd noticed his knife had been stolen. For a moment he'd considered calling on the Turks for help. Then he realised he was just as much a captive as any Varangian, with no hope of getting back to Seleucia. So he'd decided to keep his mouth shut and await events.

Immediately he ran off into the darkness George realised he'd made a mistake. He had no weapons, no equipment and was alone in hostile territory. His only chance would be as a guide to the Varangians. In a moment he'd re-entered the fight and downed the Turkish leader.

By now Tutush was recovering from George's attack and was starting to struggle to his feet. Suddenly the figure of Gunnar appeared from the darkness and with a cry of "Remember Grim!" severed the Turk's head from his body with one blow of the scimitar. It was no match for a war-axe mused the Gall-Gael but it would serve a turn.

For a moment the Varangians considered killing George but Magnus pointed out they'd need a guide if they ever hoped to get back to Seleucia again. None of them had any real idea of where they were and all had been long enough in the service of the Autokrator to know guides were vital to survival.

*

The next day the Varangians could just see the Cilician Gates in the distance. They'd taken turns in riding the horses, but even those on foot felt less exhausted than at the prospect of marching away from slavery. As the day wore on they started to look suspiciously at George. Once back among his kind how would he act? After all, he'd have no wish to be labelled traitor by his fellows - and certainly the Governor Philip wouldn't welcome the return of the Varangians. Perhaps it might be best, after all, to dispose of him - now they could see their way back to safety.

George sensed the feeling and so, with the help of Magnus, during a short break from the march, explained he had no intention of returning to Seleucia himself. No Cappadocian wanted to spend the rest of his life among Greeks. Once they'd passed through the Gates he'd branch off to the north, and join up with the forces operating in the Charsinian theme.[353]

The Varangians appreciated his fears. Neither Cnud nor Bjarni had any wish to return to Seleucia. Surely the Governor would have them silenced. Hoskuld, however, argued an open return would give the Governor little chance of silencing them. Of course, they might be forced to pledge their silence to escape his control.

"Why should we traffic with Greeks?" snapped Eric, remembering the furious battle in the pass which had cost them so much.

"Because we're in the land of the Greeks," countered Gunnar and most of them were surprised at the calmness of the Gall-Gael. Since the deaths of Ethelwulf and Morkere, he'd assumed the leadership of the Varangians. With his new position came a willingness to compromise which none had ever seen before. How long it would last once he was back in the capital was another question. In the meanwhile they could see he was right. To get back to the true safety of the Varangian force in the capital they'd need to pass through the whole of Anatolia. There'd be many chances of a Greek ambush on the way.

Far to the north Cnud could see a dust-cloud and George instantly ordered them to pack and hurry towards the Gates. He explained it was very unlikely any imperial force would be operating to the north of them out here. This left three possibilities for the identity of the unknown force - Turks, brigands or Armenians. None of them would think twice about attacking a small, badly-armed force. The Varangians agreed reluctantly, wishing they'd somehow managed to recover their arms.

The Varangians passed through the Gates before the dust cloud grew any larger. Some of them wanted to search for any survivors but George insisted on hurrying them on. He brusquely reminded them that they'd seen Turks and brigands butchering the badly wounded; as for the dead, they could suffer no more. Even so several of them keenly looked on both sides as they made their way past the site of the recent disaster. Nowhere was there a sign of life, everywhere a morbid silence. They were glad to pass out of the Gates and feel properly on imperial territory at last.

*

"What am I expected to do with a dying barbarian?"

"He's not dying," answered Luke to his sister's protest, "and, given but a few days' rest, he'll be back serving our emperor."

"And, in the meanwhile, he'll be gorging himself on our food!" snapped Zenobia and glared at Ethelwulf who was ravenously consuming the leg of goat her brother had decided they could spare. Perhaps they did have plenty of meat but God hadn't been kind this last year for everything to be squandered on a barbarian.

Luke dropped his voice and whispered in even more-rapid Greek. What he was about to confide to his sister he didn't want the barbarian to even guess at.

"I'm puzzled by why Cappadocians in the livery of our Governor were acting as confederates of the Turks." Zenobia glanced at the barbarian and saw him pause between gulps at the meat. She gestured her brother to silence and approached the table to see if there was anything else the barbarian required. Ethelwulf shook his head and Zenobia explained she and her brother had to examine some damaged equipment outside. They wouldn't be long. The barbarian belched and resumed his attack on the meat.

Outside Luke explained there'd been a large party of Cappadocian spearmen still there when he'd arrived at the sight of the battle. There'd even been Armenian brigands skulking around doing their petty murders for trinkets and trivia. He hadn't dared approach the Cappadocians to find out why they'd helped slaughter a detachment of imperial soldiers. Then they'd all trooped off surrounding a tall man, apparently blind by the way he clearly depended on the assistance of others. One of the Cappadocians had gone off in the opposite direction with a group of prisoners.

"To join some infidel slave-hole, I shouldn't wonder," murmured Zenobia in pity at the fate of even barbarians at the mercy of Turks.

"At least they still live," interrupted a voice and both brother and sister reddened at the appearance of the barbarian. There was a quiet smile on the lips of the stranger. "I must apologise for pretending to know so little of your language," he paused and the smile shooed off the embarrassment of his hosts. "It's just I had to be sure you could be trusted and when you -"

"Yes," admitted Zenobia," it might well look as if two conspirators were off to sell your head."

"No," countered the barbarian. "I didn't see you as traitors, for if you had been I wouldn't still be alive." He sank down on to the ground at their feet, as if to demonstrate physically his trust. "Rather I felt you'd say more to each other than you ever would to me."

"How long have you been there?" asked the brother.

"How right you were!" confessed the sister at the same time and knelt to check the effort hadn't over-tired her guest.

"You're right, my friend," said Ethelwulf, looking up into the eyes of the physician," in believing we were betrayed." He paused, as if to check once again the facts. "Why I don't know, but can only say we were escorting the disgraced Eparchos into exile in the east."

"And there's your answer," interposed the eager voice of Luke. "I've never met the man but I do know our Governor owed his appointment to the good offices of his cousin, the Eparchos!"

Ethelwulf bit on his lip and gazed hard into the distance, as if trying to winkle out the intriguers of the imperial court. "And none of them was able to give us any warning - "

"No, my barbarian friend," answered Luke. "There you misjudge them." He paused and also looked towards the west. "How could they remember every relative of every governor in this Empire?"

"But they knew!" insisted Ethelwulf between gritted teeth, remembering the distrust of the Autokrator over the gold. Would that be a reason for treachery? He well knew the Autokrator had no time for any offender. Back there, surrounded by the rest of the Varangians and other hired troops of the Empire it might have been considered inadvisable to strike at him. Here, in an obscure district of the Empire where he was unknown he could be disposed off, quietly. Yes - but why his men?

"How many prisoners did you see go east?" he snapped out the question to the physician and Luke blurted out "Ten" before he realised what he'd said. "So few...so few!" muttered the barbarian as he considered his next action.

Further thoughts were interrupted by the warning of Zenobia she could see horsemen approaching from the north. Luke and his sister looked at each other. What were they to do? Hand over the barbarian if these horsemen were acting on imperial orders? Who'd know this barbarian still lived? It was Zenobia who reached a decision first. "Take him to the old grain pit, Luke!" she insisted and both men found themselves hustled towards the rear of the cottage.

The 'old grain-pit' was merely a hole, lined with crude bricks to try and insulate the contents from any dampness which might filter through the ground. It had been built by their grandfather in the days before the White Death[354] had driven the infidels so far away that homesteaders here could expect some peace from attack.

Now Ethelwulf was pushed down into the hole and an old, heavy door thrown on top of him. Attached to the door were several dried shrubs and furiously brother and sister swept loose sand and grit over its entrance to hide any trace of the pit. With a sudden thought Zenobia swept away their footprints, then both rushed into the cottage to remove any traces of their barbarian guest.

*

Inside the pit Ethelwulf heard the scraping of sand and stones over the entrance but remained in darkness. He'd been thrust into this gloom before he'd had a chance to protest. Now he realised he didn't have enough room to stretch out his legs. With the realisation came a cramp in his left leg and he wanted to cry out. With difficulty he massaged the limb and fought off some of the pain. Thrusting his cool sword next to the flesh eased the discomfort.

Now he felt short of air and every breath he took made the pit seem smaller and dingier. He pushed his left hand up above his head and felt the door. Although he'd no idea who or what was outside he had to get out. He pushed against the door and found he couldn't move it; perhaps he was weakened by the effects of his wound. Just rest for a while and then try again. Yet even as he told himself that lie he recognised the falsehood. The door was too heavy; bulky to start with and now weighed down by sand and stones. He made two more attempts to push up against the obstacle and then gave up. It wasn't worth the air.

After a few moments, or maybe hours, he thought of sliding the door across to let in more air. But he couldn't get a grip on any part of the door. The cross-beam was far too wide to be gripped by his fingers and there was nothing else to serve as a handle. By now air was escaping - somewhere. It couldn't be his lungs! His lungs couldn't hold all that air, could they? He panted several times as if to empty whatever was in there out into further use in the pit. It was no good. It merely made what was hot, dry and uncomfortable even more nauseating. From somewhere he could smell dead goat - and then remembered his last meal.

His last meal? No, that had been with Morkere and Ubbe, camped by the tiny stream to the west of here. Morkere had picked up a small stone and challenged Ubbe to hit a lump of rancid fat discarded into the stream. Ubbe had taken up his challenge and before any stone had struck the lump of fat, seven or eight Varangians had joined in the game. It was if they were a collection of half-grown youths by some shady stream far-off in England. For a moment he half-saw Alfred Bat-Ears[355] screaming abuse and then he'd gone and so had the glimpse of a sluggish Dorset stream.

Then he saw Morkere, grinning at his brother's embarrassment at being discovered on top of Edith Cynegilssdotter.[356] She'd been a pretty girl - long, long ago. He closed his eyes against the darkness and tried to doze.

*

It was still dark and his limbs ached. His throat was so dry but he dared not cough for fear of polluting his home. Yes, he mustn't make a sound or his enemies would rush in and murder his mother. Was that her head, staring at him from a perch on his toe?[357] He reached towards the illusion and it dissolved. Now there was a terrible itching at the top of his back. His fingers clawed at his back, over his neck but couldn't find the source. Something was dancing, cavorting on his back. He was alive with creatures, vermin. Nature was breeding inside his clothes; no, some had burrowed deep down beneath his skin and was setting up home in Arne.

He was a hall, wide and warm, with shields on the walls and filled with laughing men. There sat the awful king of the Danes[358] joking with the fat Frenchman.[359] In disgust the Frenchman turned towards Ethelwulf and changed into the fur-trader, Aslak.[360] The man smiled knowingly and pointed his finger somewhere behind Ethelwulf's left ear. Without turning he could see the figure of Maija emerging naked from a sauna. "It's not true," he croaked and the finger turned into the smile of the Eparchos. Alexius nodded in confident authority and Ethelwulf recoiled from the smile which detached itself and floated gently towards him. He turned his head aside but the smile came and kissed his lips. He wanted to scream.

*

Nicephorus of Tarsus wasn't satisfied with the answers Luke gave. The man had readily admitted he'd visited the site of the recent battle, giving as an excuse the desire to ease the suffering of the dying. Possible, but something about the edginess of the physician made the Cappadocian uneasy.

He hadn't been pleased to have been despatched immediately by his master back to the Gates. Everything had gone well until the blind man had interrupted his account of the battle to ask what had happened to the captain of the Varangians. Nicephorus had honestly admitted he didn't know and a loud wail had broken out from the man. His master had ordered him outside and had been urgently questioning the blind man before he'd even left the room. Within moments he'd been summoned back into the presence of his master who was now alone. He'd been asked if the Varangian captain had been one of the prisoners taken east and had replied no. His master had breathed deeply at the news and had then ordered him to return to the Gates and bring back the head of the Varangian captain. Nicephorus had started to question the order.

"Silence, dog!" His master glared down at him and Nicephorus could see the burning tongs of the inquisitors in his eyes "Without that man's head we'll not be satisfied." There was a pause as if the Governor considered giving an explanation and rejected the idea. "We must have that man dead!"

Without a word Nicephorus left the room and collected together fifteen spearmen from the nearest tavern. It hadn't been a happy group which had left town at dawn and reached the Gates over two hours before, spent the heat of the noonday sun scouring the crevices and shrub-land of the pass for the remains of the dead Varangian. One or two peasants from neighbouring estates had wandered out on the off-chance of picking up some easy loot. It hadn't taken very long to discover that Luke, the son of Simeon, the son of Nepos, had been poking around the battlefield. He was the only scavenger not accounted for; Nicephorus felt he could discount the brigands and the Turks. So he'd ridden here to question the mysterious physician and hadn't been pleased with what he'd heard.

While they talked his men conducted a rapid search of the cottage and the two outhouses nearby. Zeno had scampered around, offering help and generally getting in the way. Zenobia had merely stood, threatening retribution of any who'd break or damage her property. Nicephorus was surprised Gabriel had actually managed to live five years with such a harridan. A good hiding was what she needed - but she wouldn't be worth the trouble.

When his men reported finding nothing, Nicephorus had to give up. The simplest tale would be to insist he'd heard the Turks had come across the barbarian after he'd left and taken him east with the others. The barbarian certainly wouldn't turn up to contradict him and any story a Turk produced would be ignored. At last he felt satisfied; he even started to smile before he noticed Zenobia scowling at him. How he'd like to teach her proper respect!

*

When the door was finally thrust aside, with the help of Zeno, they first thought the barbarian had perished in that cramped hole. Then Zenobia noticed he was still breathing and the two men somehow managed to manoeuvre the unconscious barbarian out of the pit. The man started babbling away in one of those horrible tongues never heard in the Empire until these last terrible years. Gently the man was put on a crude bed in the quarters of Leo and left. It was already dark and Luke had enjoyed enough excitement for one day.

Three days later the barbarian woke up and started to babble again in that miserable tongue of his. Luke insisted in talking Greek and, after several frustrated attempts to lure the barbarian back into civilised speech, communication was at last resumed.

Even so, the barbarian looked oddly detached. There was no smile when Zenobia tried to persuade him to consume some broth with all the coquettishness of a young whore. Luke was shocked but his sister insisted play-acting was one way of getting through to the mad, and she was sure the barbarian had lost his reason. Luke was forced to agree. At first he put down the air of desolation to exhaustion but then he saw the limbs of the barbarian strengthen and recover with rest and nourishment and the mind still stay shut. The man could talk, insisted on asking questions again and again about which of the barbarians had marched east. Gradually he noticed the barbarian marking off names as each telling seemed to answer further questions. The list lengthened with time. "Gunnar

....Einar .... Thorstein ...no, Magnus....Sven...". Only when he could not describe a gaunt, black-haired warrior was there genuine emotion, a tear in the eye and the whispered name of "Morkere!"

Zenobia didn't like the way the barbarian continued to mutter away to himself and carefully sharpen the sword brought from the battlefield. Almost lovingly the man tended to the weapon, singing strange songs from unknown lands. She hated sharing her home with a madman, but pity stilled her tongue.

At last, Ethelwulf announced his intention to leave for Seleucia. When asked why, he would only say it was to deal with the children of Loki.[361] For a moment Luke started to protest and then saw a look in his sister's eyes and shut his mouth. He even agreed to take the barbarian to the provincial capital in the family ox-cart. Ethelwulf readily agreed and in the early hours of the evening the two men left. Zenobia had a strange mixture of relief and regret as she waved farewell to the disappearing figures.

*

It was surprising how quiet the side entrance to the palace was. Although it was just past midnight Ethelwulf would have expected more than one sentry to have been on duty. However, he thanked God for his luck and whispered instructions to the doctor, Luke. The physician had wanted him to denounce the Governor publicly and appeal to imperial justice. Ethelwulf, however, had argued that without evidence there'd be no chance of getting justice, and whatever evidence existed was within the Governor's palace. Quite simply he proposed to hunt for the evidence at night among the Governor's private papers before appealing publicly for justice. Certainly there lay there a copy of the imperial rescript authorising his passage to Antioch. That would show he was under imperial protection when attacked and so had been the victim of treason. That was what he said, but what he planned was to settle accounts with those responsible for the deaths of so many brave men.

Luke hadn't been deceived, doubting the stranger's ability to read Greek. He'd seen the wild look in the Varangian eyes and had refused to help. Ethelwulf brusquely stated he needed no help to carry out his plan and Luke recognised the determination of a madman. With help the barbarian might get the evidence he needed; without help he'd recklessly charge into the palace and be killed instantly. Luke had been told the Governor had left that evening for Tarsus, taking with him his cousin, the deposed Eparchos. That should make this expedition easier to carry out.

Reluctantly he agreed to accompany the barbarian and been horrified to discover how poorly protected the palace was. He realised he'd been hoping the strength of the guard would deter any attempt to penetrate the palace. Now his hopes were frustrated and he could only assume the lightness of the guard was due to the earlier departure of the Governor.

Luke smashed a bladder of pig's blood against the crown of his head. A mass of blood would distract any guard, but he had no intention of risking permanent injury to help out one mad barbarian. With a brief grip of the Varangian's hand as a gesture of good luck he staggered into the street, uttering sounds which passed for groans and sobs. As expected the sentry stepped forward as he stumbled towards the entrance. The soldier lowered his spear in challenge and stepped into the stream of moonlight which revealed a wounded man. He didn't notice the figure which slipped through the dark entrance behind his back.

Ethelwulf was surprised within the courtyard to see the office of the Governor betray some kind of light. That wasn't good news; it could mean a Chartularius still at work and able to interfere in the defence of his master. The Varangian carefully mounted the staircase. Near the top he could see the shaft of light from a lamp and then heard a familiar voice. There was no mistaking the hoarse tones of the deposed Eparchos. In silence Ethelwulf was drawn to the sound, unsheathing his sword as he drew closer.

"It's a pity the barbarians escaped the infidels' chains," complained Alexius. That afternoon they'd heard from spies in the capital that Gunnar had arrived there and denounced the Governor for treason. In days imperial agents would arrive to investigate the matter.

All their plans had been upset. Alexius had promised his cousin they'd share the treasure hidden safely in Tarsus. He'd concealed it there ten years ago, just as there were similar amounts stored in other remote parts of the Empire. As a careful man he'd prepared for the day when his power was destroyed; as a frugal man he'd amassed considerable wealth, none of which he desired to hand over to the Imperial Treasury. Of course, his cousin wouldn't have dared risk imperial displeasure by even communicating with him if it hadn't been for the treasure. Philip had known a portion of the loot from raids into northern Syria had been stashed away somewhere. He'd been offered the chance to share in such wealth, and so family loyalty had come to the fore.

Now they had to both hide and fabricate evidence quickly. The Cappadocian captain had been arrested immediately and placed into secure confinement. Tomorrow he'd be schooled in the story for the imperial agents, after a warning of what alternatives existed. The Governor was producing a document describing the sufferings of his cousin at the hands of the barbarians. The poor man had fallen seriously ill and been handed over at Seleucia to rest before later transportation to his exile. Three witnesses had already given written testimony as to the state of the disgraced minister and the handover to provincial custody. No barbarian would be given credence against such evidence.

Later, when the imperial envoy had been packed off to report, both would make the journey to St. Symeon where Alexius would spend his last years. By doing this the Governor would acquire credit in heaven, and on the way a share of the treasure at Tarsus. Yet, it was surprising how the former Eparchos still dominated his cousin. Even in his mutilated state, the energy and ruthlessness which had made him the near-master of the Empire for over ten years gave him this last authority.

The failure to find the corpse of Ethelwulf had alarmed Alexius on his return to Seleucia. He'd screeched at the soldiers who reported failure. Now he was terrified that, like the other Varangians, Ethelwulf would appear and denounce him to the Autokrator. Experience had shown that, unlike other barbarians, Ethelwulf might well obtain the ear of the Autokrator. He needed proof the meddler was really dead.

As a first step, Alexius secured the arrest of the Cappadocian. There was much the man needed to learn before interrogation by the imperial envoy. The former Eparchos sent out a stream of agents to scour the district between Seleucia and the Cilician Gates for any news of the missing Varangian. He despatched a specially-trusted envoy to Selim to question him about the disappearance. Another agent went into the hills to hunt down the brigands and find out whatever news they had.

Now Alexius was organising this hurried concoction of evidence to give themselves time to complete their schemes. Documents had to be produced, even if in the Governor's own hand, allowing digression from imperial orders.

"Nobody will listen to the words of a barbarian once we've eased our arguments among the powerful," confided the Governor.

"You forget, cousin, the leader of those who escaped has the especial support of the Lord Constantine," countered Alexius. There was a pause as if sudden despair had terminated activity.

"They share a love of taking life," sneered the fallen Eparchos, and then cackled," but Constantine is not the Autokrator."

There was a rustle of parchment as the Governor resumed his secretarial activities. An inaudible mumble accompanied the task.

"Don't complain, Philip," snapped the disgraced minister. "Just because the barbarian escaped the arrows of the Turks doesn't mean he can escape a knife-thrust in the capital."

"That would be just what anyone would expect," stated Ethelwulf as he stepped into the room. He saw the Governor drop his pen and, instinctively, move to conceal his handiwork. Alexius was sitting with his back to the entrance so the Varangian had no chance to see his face. He was sure surprise had immediately been replaced by calculation. Already the blind man would be working out a solution. "I'm pleased to hear Gunnar, at least, survived your treachery," added Ethelwulf and moved quickly towards the desk. As he did so Philip snatched up the papers and thrust them into the folds of his robe.

"How are you still alive?" was all he could ask, mesmerised by the physical presence of a man he'd been sure had died days before.

"God moves in mysterious ways," smiled Ethelwulf and reached with his left hand for the documents. His right hand itched to swing the sword and hack off the Governor's head but somehow the news of Gunnar's survival was clawing into his rage.

Suddenly he heard Alexius shriek, "And answers prayers!" and felt a cold, searing pain penetrate his back. A blackness clutched at his vision and he staggered forward with a thin blade jutting from just above his waist. His legs seemed to lose their strength and he felt himself falling. The Governor turned to run and the sword swung as if compelled by its own momentum, virtually severing Philip's head as it completed the movement.

Suddenly there was a confusion of sounds. The Governor collapsed backwards against the wall. The sword clattered to the floor as Ethelwulf felt unable to maintain his grip. The Varangian slumped to his knees, clutching at the desk in a frantic attempt to keep his balance. The blind man rose to rush for assistance and started to scream for the guards. Somehow Ethelwulf managed to grab the legs of Alexius and drag him to the floor. The terrified man kicked out and a sandaled foot crunched into his attacker's nose.

The blow cut through the growing weakness and dark forces erupted in Ethelwulf's brain. His fingers clawed at the body of his prey and dragged the blind man towards him. The strength which terror gave Alexius was out-matched by the power that insane lust for revenge gave the barbarian. His fingers clawed their way along his victim's body towards his throat. Alexius slithered and kicked and pummelled to force himself free, without success. Gradually, remorselessly, he was sucked into the grasp of his enemy.

At last Ethelwulf's fingers were round his throat and in his blindness Alexius felt the hatred in the barbarian's eyes. He tore at the bands squeezing out his life; he spat at where he sensed his enemy; he kicked savagely at the bulk which was smothering out his life. Still the fingers tightened on his throat, shutting off air, starving him of life. He wanted to cough, to break out from the grip, to take in that beautiful air. Life was sweet, even in blindness, life was sweet. Weakness was growing. In his blindness Alexius saw a tumult of colours; magnificent shades that no human could ever see. From outside came the grunts of his assailant as energy drained but hatred maintained his hold. Alexius felt his fingers grow cold and his other limbs slip away from his brain's control. He remained a brain starved of air, cut off from reality. From somewhere he could hear sounds of approaching help.

There was a stillness between his fingers. Beneath his body the blind man had ceased to twitch. Suddenly Ethelwulf felt a flood of exhaustion rush through his body and started to slide off the dead man. He felt his hair fiercely gripped by someone and he was yanked half to his knees. Such pain, such exquisite pain!

*

From somewhere in the grime came the anguished scream of a being in torment. Ethelwulf raised his head to penetrate the gloom.

"So you've come back to your senses," croaked a voice and Ethelwulf could just make out a figure chained to the wall opposite. He squinted and thought he recognised the speaker. "Yes, barbarian," cackled the figure, "the last time we met we were on opposite sides!"

Ethelwulf knew Nicephorus of Tarsus and made to get at the Cappadocian. Something yanked at his shoulders and he realised he also was chained to the wall. Why was he here? The effort caused a cutting shiver of pain to leap from his back and he remembered the Eparchos. At least his debts to Morkere and the others had been partially paid.

"You've been hanging there for nearly two days now," commented another shape to his left. He turned his head and saw a skinny figure stuck to the wall by a large rust-layered chain. The man spat into the dirt at their feet and laughed. "It's a wonder you've still got any life left in those arms of yours, seeing how long you've been strung up." As the creature spoke Ethelwulf felt an ache fill up his arms and start to intrude into his mind.

"Even then you didn't start off in very good shape," sneered the Cappadocian. He tried to smile and Ethelwulf could see that several teeth had disappeared. "You certainly gave the Governor and that nasty toad of a cousin of his what they both deserved!"

Ethelwulf tried to moisten his lips and found there was nothing there. A dryness from deep-down inside had come with consciousness. He felt old and used-up, finished. He tried to look up and found he lacked the energy.

"Still," conceded the Cappadocian. "We all thought you a goner the moment you were dragged in here - "

"Not that your moaning and whining helped us feel any sympathy," concluded the skinny man. He glared at Ethelwulf. Leo, who'd hung for weeks before being taken out and executed, had been a good mate, someone you could share a joke with at the gaoler's expense. It had been a pity Leo had to be carted off. For a morning he'd even hoped they'd forget about it and someone would botch things up and they'd get extra rations. Some smart official, however, had done the calculations and they'd found the food for the cell cut accordingly. In fact, the only good thing about this barbarian was the food had gone up again - and all three of them had had his share. Now he was awake, so even that benefit had gone! He squinted into the corner and made out a vague shape hanging there. Perhaps that pig from Armenia would drift off permanently; then they might get HIS share.

Ethelwulf was introduced by the Cappadocian to the other two prisoners. With suitable mockery he was described as a barbarian who'd so upset the Governor there'd been a full-scale battle to get rid of him. He'd finished with the ironic comment that it was the Governor who'd been finished off instead.

".....And next to you is Nicomedes, once the finest pick-pocket and scavenger in Cilicia and now a bit of dung helping to hold up this palace." There'd been a cackle from the corner and Nicephorus indicated Thoros from Armenia. "He's a brigand who's seen better days and can only see worse ones coming!" was the comment which roused a grunt of satisfaction from Ethelwulf's skinny neighbour.

What was to become of him? He'd murdered two men, somehow he remembered all that. He could recall the reason and savour the pleasure of the act; he couldn't deny the crime and for that death must be the penalty. Both Thoros and Nicomedes also had histories which merited execution but the Cappadocian had surely acted in the service of the Governor? Nicephorus anticipated the question and explained it had been necessary suddenly to forget past services and rewrite the events of a few weeks ago. The Varangians had been attacked by a large force of Turks and brigands and had been overwhelmed. The Cappadocian spearmen had done their best to support the barbarians until the death of their leader had forced them to retreat. He added it was now widely known that the Governor's cousin had been removed from the custody of the barbarians after complaints of bullying and cruelty.

"No imperial envoy will ever believe that!" snapped Ethelwulf, knowing that indeed they would. The whole capital had known the reason for the fall of the Eparchos and no Greek failed to live in terror at the vengeful nature of the barbarians from the north.

"Should any envoy bother to penetrate down here," confided the Cappadocian, "I will, of course, tell him the truth." He paused and looked stolidly at the Varangian. "We were carrying out the orders of our master, after being told of the treason of you barbarians."

"What treason?" croaked Ethelwulf, alarmed at the prospect of fresh accusations against the survivors of the battle. The Cappadocian explained that evidence had been produced to show leading Varangians had been in correspondence with the ruler of Edessa to plunder the province of Seleucia and then retire across the Euphrates. If Ethelwulf had possessed the energy he'd have laughed at the sheer monstrosity of the lie. How could any of them have communicated with the ruler - and who was he anyway.

"Before you scoff, barbarian," smiled the Cappadocian, "let me tell you I've seen the documents and I believed them. "

It seemed time only for silence.

*

Two days later the great door was thrown open and Gunnar marched noisily into the cell. It took him a few moments to get adjusted to the gloom before he saw Ethelwulf and ordered the gaoler to release the prisoner instantly. As he was hustled out into the bright air of freedom Ethelwulf heard the despairing cry of the Cappadocian to remember him - and then the great door was shut.

Outside he was amazed how fit and strong Gunnar appeared. Beside him Ethelwulf felt small and weak and dirty. A good bath and a long sleep in the Governor's bed changed all that. On the morrow Ethelwulf almost felt himself a Varangian captain again. At the last point, however, the identification broke down.

Gunnar explained that in the capital he'd managed to get to the emperor Constantine and been remembered. His story had aroused imperial fury and for once normal lethargy had been abandoned. Messages had been sent to the Autokrator, an investigative mission organised and Gunnar put in charge of the escort. His orders had been simple; arrest both the Governor of Seleucia and the deposed Eparchos. What hadn't been said was whether they should reach the capital alive or dead. He'd brought with him Hjalt Egilsson and Hoskuld and they'd saved him from being unceremoniously strung up by the Governor's guard. Unfortunately, for the sake of appearances he'd been forced to go along with the decision to place Ethelwulf in detention for his own "protection".

Now fresh orders had arrived from the capital. The Autokrator had been furious at the treachery of the Governor of Seleucia. He understood the action of the barbarian in exacting vengeance for the deaths of his companions. When he came to accept the only true way of Christ he'd see how wrong such vengeance was. Ethelwulf was to return to the capital and await further orders.

Ethelwulf said nothing. He'd seen enough of the mercy of the Greeks and had no wish to suffer future mutilation. In fact, he'd wearied of his life of wandering and warfare and felt a strange draw from the south. So close to the land of His Saviour and yet so far away from His Grace. Somehow he had to make up for the evil he'd done and witnessed since that great act of treachery twenty years before at Corfe. He'd only two years left before the world would come to its preordained end. He remembered how Willibrord [362] had told him of the approach of a darkness the northern world vaguely identified as Ragnarok. At the end of a thousand years Christ Himself would return to judge all alive in this world and the millions of dead souls. Perhaps Epaphroditus[363] had got hold of something and misread the runes of fate.[364] It was all too close to shrug off such ideas. He'd made his decision: he'd leave the service of the Empire and go, as a humble pilgrim, south to the Holy City and await the end of the world.

At first Gunnar laughed at Ethelwulf's schemes but then a shrewder voice told him of the danger of returning accompanied by a man who'd displeased the Autokrator in the past, and was sure to do so in the future. Perhaps it'd be best if Ethelwulf were allowed to slip away during the night after leaving Seleucia. It would be best to tell Hjalti and Hoskuld the truth - afterwards. Naturally there was a regret at the departure of a friend of fifteen years, a battle-companion who'd never let him down. But time severed all friendships in this world; as for the next, who could tell?

So the first night after leaving Seleucia Ethelwulf quietly rose from his sleep, gripped Gunnar's arm in silent farewell and without even a glance at the sleeping Varangians led his horse southwards towards Jerusalem.

*

Miklagard Afterword

Miklagard was the Viking name given to Constantinople or Byzantium, the capital of the Eastern Roman (or Byzantine) Empire. The ancient Roman Empire had been divided in 395 but the Western Empire disappeared in 476.

The only historical characters appearing in this section are the imperial family. Basil II (976-1025) smashed the Bulgar threat and proved one of the greatest rulers of the Eastern Roman Empire. However, his efforts so weakened the Empire that, under the chaotic hands of his successors, Byzantium proved unable to challenge the rise of the Seljuk Turks. Basil's niece, Zoe (1028-50), with three husbands and a collection of lovers, was but one of the destructive forces at work. The picture of the imperial family given here is largely backed by historical sources.

The bureaucracy, with its myriad of titles and mode of governance which have given us the term 'Byzantine' are represented according to the evidence. The wealth and complexity of so many aspects of the Empire easily surpasses what this novel describes. However, the system was in a state of terminal decline despite the efforts of such rulers as Basil II and later Alexius I Comnenus (1081-1118) and Michael VIII Palæologus (1261-82). It was finally shuffled out of existence by the Ottoman Turks in 1453. Its claims thereafter passed to the Russian Tsars.

Warriors from the Viking realms make their appearance as Varangian Guards in Byzantium in the years before 1000. After 1066 the unit was dominated by Saxon exiles following the Norman Conquest. The Varangians continued to be a key military unit in the Empire until the seizure of Byzantium in 1204 by the Fourth Crusade.

Seljuk Turks made their appearance within the Islamic world during the tenth century, quickly dominating the Abbasid caliphate of Baghdad. By the mid-11th century they controlled a strong realm which threatened to overwhelm the struggling Byzantine state after the destruction of the imperial army at Manzikert in 1071. One of the reasons for launching the First Crusade in 1095 was to prevent this happening.

The Wanderer 9:1

*'The brave man who clings to his beliefs,
Shall never show his heart's misery until
He hopes to cure it.'* ('The Wanderer')

Awaiting Eternity

There was dust and heat and a long road clawing its way down from the mountains. Nowhere was there movement except for one small figure painfully labouring down over gravel and dust away from the hateful mountains of Anatolia.

The figure paused and rubbed a sweaty forearm across his grimy forehead. The other hand felt for the long sword which swung loosely from his neck. His lips were casually moistened by his tongue and there was a sigh which slipped out into the friendless Syrian air. Somehow he detected a sound of hoof-beats from behind him; instantly he turned off the road and plunged into the nearest clump of thorns. No scratch could stop the furious drive to hide himself from whoever was coming along that road. He settled himself down lower, under the scrub so that his mouth almost sucked in the dust - and waited.

Three horsemen came down the road, riding quickly and confidently. They wore the insignia of the imperial guard. Since the defeat of the infidel five years ago there was little to harm imperial envoys on the road to Antioch. Yet there was an air of uncertainty in the manner of their leader. Nicephorus Psellus had no love for his mission. The orders had been quite firm. He was to hunt down the traitor, Ethelwulf, and bring the fugitive back to the imperial capital itself. That was within reason; what was beyond the ability of man was the Autokrator's personal order to bring back the treacherous Varangian ALIVE. He knew the stranger from the north and feared him. What was more he knew the Varangian had been driven insane by the slaughter of his followers and had murdered both the prisoner entrusted to him and Philip Ducas, Governor of Cilicia. The murder of the Eparchos could be ignored; indeed, there were several in the intimate circle of the Autokrator who welcomed the convenient removal of an awkward reminder of past intrigues. The killing of the Governor was different, however; only the imperial court could remove one entrusted with the care of an imperial province. Even then, the removal of eyes or tongue was preferable, as Scripture taught, to the removal of the divine gift of life.

The murderer had been seized even at the scene of his crime and placed in chains. His escape from the custody of Gunnar Thorgeirsson was very suspicious. The two men had been battle-companions; it was natural for the new commander to have shared the hatred for the old Eparchos. This didn't, however, excuse the treachery of letting loose a traitor. Though nothing could be proved, Gunnar had been arrested and was on his way to the imperial capital to explain how a prisoner could have so easily got away.

Nicephorus had been entrusted with the task of recovering the disgraced Varangian. It wasn't difficult to work out where he'd have fled. No man, not even one driven into insanity, would have travelled north or west, back towards a betrayed master. Perhaps he'd have trudged east; but there Turkish horsemen terrorised the roads, murdering or enslaving any who came from the imperial dominions. No, Ethelwulf would never have journeyed that way; if he had, he'd be dead by now - as would be anyone who attempted to follow him! To the south, however, lay the city of Antioch where the traitor was known to have friends. The whole territory was bristling with heretics who defied the True Faith and its imperial mouthpiece. Then to the south of that lay the border regions between the Empire and the lands controlled by the infidel regime of Cairo. If the traitor had a conscience he'd be heading for the Holy City itself, perhaps to seek forgiveness for his horrible crimes.

There were some who'd have turned their eyes away from the search, ridden south, seen nothing, reported failure and returned to their military duties. Perhaps that was what was really expected; perhaps there never was any intention to recover such an awkward prisoner. With the Autokrator one could never be sure. If the fugitive was killed few would be sorry; if he was brought back in chains perhaps there'd be criticism. Yet the orders were quite precise. The fugitive was to be seized and sent back alive to the capital; if he died "*imperial pleasure would be lessened and the guilty would have to answer for their deeds.*" What did that mean? He'd wanted to ask but the blue eyes of the Autokrator had ordered silence. Only the grin of the inn-owner, Theophrastus,[365] had shown Nicephorus just how impossible his mission was.

The two troopers with Nicephorus had no such doubts. To them the Varangian was a heretic from the north, a dabbler in the occult and a seducer of their women. Whatever passed for religion with such a man could never be the True Faith; only full acceptance within the folds of the Apostolic Church of the City of Constantine could be that. From the moment this man and his followers had come from the north they'd been trouble. Always they'd been the favourites of somebody or other within the imperial circle; how else could their long catalogue of crime and disorder have been glossed over? At last they'd got their deserts and been butchered by those enemies of Christ from the East. Those who survived were learning how to behave properly within the capital. They were no longer able to strut around in their brown cloaks, brandishing their fearsome weapons and lording it over the followers of the True Faith. Both Thomas and Markos were certain the fugitive, if ever within the range of their arrows, would die. They'd never try to take the madman alive, as their commander had ordered. One didn't give a mad dog the chance of biting off your hand.

The riders passed by the figure concealed by the thorns without a second glance. It was hot and Antioch itself lay three hours riding away. The figure lay in the dust for several moments, breathing in the sound of the disappearing troopers. He'd no doubt he was their quarry but equally sure they wanted to avoid him as much as he wanted to elude them. All that was necessary was time. He'd no wish to return to the power of the Autokrator. If the horse given to him by Gunnar hadn't broken its leg within a day's riding, by now he'd have been in Jerusalem, hidden away from imperial power. However, for days he'd been forced to trudge along unfriendly roads ever southwards and always on his guard.

Time passed slowly while Ethelwulf rested, sheltered from the heat of the sun by the dappled shade of the thorn bush. Finally he decided it was safe to continue; the imperial troopers had long ago passed through the gates of Antioch itself. A grim smile appeared as he recalled how easily he'd been hidden away there by the fanatical Epaphroditus.[366] Had the madman ever been captured by the security forces? He didn't know; why not? Was he simply not interested or had it been hidden from him? Probably the answer was straightforward; the preacher had escaped and was still sheltered among the dim alleyways of the city. If the city could hide that madman then he might find shelter there too. Why? He'd little silver, no friends and no cause. There was no coterie of madmen working together for the end of the world ready to help a runaway warrior from the north. Of course, many would hide anything (or anyone) from imperial eyes - but at a price. He'd so little; just a few coins, the remains of the rags they'd thrown over him in prison and a sword conveniently lost by Gunnar.

Why was he going south? What were the alternatives? North and west lay the realm of the Autokrator and a nest-bed of enemies and former friends anxious to shut up any awkward secrets forever. East were the awesome lands of Islam where any infidel could only expect death or slavery. To the south lay chaos and therein safety; a means of getting hidden away perhaps until a berth could be found on some trader heading for Italy. Then it would be back home to - what? England was still ruled by a man whose throne rested on a murder he'd witnessed twenty years before;[367] not a hopeful sign of welcome. Perhaps trudging south would let him be sucked into the chaos and disappear forever.

Two hours passed and as evening came on he could make out ahead two still figures by the road. For a moment he hesitated; were they waiting for him. Only two? His eyes scoured the rocky desert on both sides of the road and could detect no movement. He withdrew his sword from the scabbard tied to his back and tramped on.

Gradually the figures became more distinct; but neither moved. One looked like a woman or a child; the other looked like nothing but a bundle of rags thrown aside in the dust. He paused, rested and again looked around. Night was rapidly approaching. Soon he could slip away from any threat with ease into the surrounding desert. He took a deep breath as if trying to suck in any sign of danger. There was none - no sound, no movement, just the eerie silence of the sand and rocks.

He reached the figures - a woman and the body of a man. The corpse lay on its face, a dusty blue cloak covered its form except for one ankle sprawled out into the dust. A sandal was half-on the dead man's foot. The hair was grey and thick; the blood next to it had dried into a dull-brown mess. There was no sound from the woman. Indeed she'd not moved although she must have heard his steps.

Ethelwulf stretched out his sword and rested it on her shoulders, the edge touching her throat. Still no movement so he moved the blade against the throat, under the chin, and with the flat surface forced round her face.

He knew her; behind the tear-stained grime was a face from his past. At the moment he recognised her he knew Epaphroditus lay sprawled in the dust and was glad. He remembered the misery of his drugged nightmares, the hectoring of the madman as he tried to urge him towards murder; above all he remembered the terrible feeling of loneliness which had been with him day and night in that Antioch room. With that memory his face softened and Lydia knew him. There was a visible start as she knew the Varangian prisoner and instinctively her body moved to protect her father from revenge. Then she remembered he was past all danger and let out a new howl of misery.

Ethelwulf gently laid aside his sword and knelt down to comfort her. If he hated her father, he owed his life to this beauty now worn so frail by the hardships of the road. Gently he extracted her from what had been her father, reached for the water-bottle which tumbled into view and allowed her one, cool draught. She coughed and tried a smile which came out as a grimace.

"Peace, my angel," he whispered. "Rest and God will bring you back into life - "

"There is no God," snapped the girl. "No Almighty could let my father die like this; no Lord would desert a servant who'd given so many years of loyalty." Reluctantly she gobbled at fresh water poured down her throat. Her face relaxed, her eyes closed and she slipped away into oblivion.

*

When Lydia came back to the world the sun had long gone to rest and the night was cold. She turned her head towards the brisk fire which teased a flame-backed sparkle into her eyes. Where was she? Next to the fire sat a hunched figure, his back towards her. Was it her father; had it all been a nightmare? She remembered the rapid advance of imperial troopers across the desert. They showed no sign of slowing down as they rode up to two lonely figures. A cry from the officer in front made father threw her out of the path of the rushing horse. Why hadn't he moved himself? Was he too old and too tired to cling to life for another year when the Lord would return?

She'd never know; indeed she wasn't even sure what had happened to her father. Had he lunged at the hated officer, trying to yank him from the saddle? Certainly, the past months of hiding and skulking from one shelter to another among his fellows must have turned her father's mind. Before the barbarian had come he'd been strange, his talk full of prophecies and his mind dominated by the vision of the Autokrator as the Antichrist himself. Only with the help of Silas had she smuggled her father away before the guards could come as she knew they would once he'd gone. He? The captive who'd come to imprison her dreams. She'd known it meant ruin for her father; but success for her father would have destroyed her faith. So she'd let him slip away and bring the soldiers.

Had her father ever guessed? She couldn't be sure. He'd been furious to discover his stripped daughter in the empty room; but his fury seemed against the man who could strike down a girl and use her very clothing to escape doing the will of the Lord. It had taken all the authority of Silas to persuade him to go into hiding. She'd been told of the roughness of the soldiers as they ransacked first one house and then another. Fifteen men had been dragged before the Governor; five had denounced the Antichrist that sat on the imperial throne and lost their tongues. Silas had said they'd been lucky to keep their lives - a remark which had roused her father to even greater passion. He'd been tied down on a bed for three days before the fever left him; gently she'd fed him, begging him to await the Second Coming with patient humility. In the end he'd softened into the shell he became; with the loss of his hatred for the Autokrator went the spirit which had driven him for years.

Epaphroditus was content to pass from one house to another throughout northern Syria. Everywhere she heard whispers; her father no longer believed Christ would return in triumph to destroy the ungodly. Lydia knew it was a lie; her father still dreamed of that Day when all accounts would be settled but knew he was unworthy to help bring it about. Had he not sinned? Had he not let his daughter be despoiled by a stranger, an unbeliever, a barbarian from the north? He should never have allowed her even see the wild man. Lydia had denied again and again being raped; local women had tested her, proving her virginity to be intact. But her father would not listen. Her nakedness had been enjoyed by a barbarian and it was all his fault. *"The enemy has covered with his hand all her delights."*[368] God would turn His Face away because he'd betrayed his daughter. He wouldn't listen. What lay ahead for his child but a life of whoredom among the unbelievers. Gradually hysteria gave way to depression and her father became sullen; she alone gave thanks to the faithful passing them from house to house, risking their lives in devotion to the cause. Epaphroditus merely sat and scowled and softly cried in the night. In betraying his daughter he had rejected God. No longer would the Millennium bring a New World to him; he was ensnared in the chains of Satan.

Finally they decided to leave Antioch and journey north into Anatolia. There fresh converts were daily turning to the Lord as the Final Day approached. At first Epaphroditus was dismissive: *"there shall come in the last days scoffers, living according to their own evil desires."*[369] Then he realised there was no choice. With every day the imperial searchers grew closer; every day brought fresh arrests. Only would his appearance in Anatolia end the persecution of the Faithful in Antioch itself. By such sacrifice might he secure the forgiveness of God. So he was persuaded to leave, accompanied only by his daughter.

The road was long and hard, but her father grew more companionable with every stade[370] separating them from the scene of his shame. Lydia came to believe they should have chosen exile months before. Her father was becoming the man he'd been before she'd let the barbarian destroy their world.

Then the imperial troopers appeared and he changed. Never would he step aside for the minions of Antichrist.

"*This is the Way, keep to it,*"[371] he muttered and turned to face the approaching horsemen. Lydia was pushed aside as the preacher raised his arms to call down curses on the spawn of Satan. "*Be you cursed with a curse, even as you despoil me.*"[372] he screamed as the horsemen rode him down. Lydia scrambled over to her father abandoned in the dust as the troopers rode on. Gently she raised his battered head and held it in her arms. He opened his eyes and gazed fiercely at her; there was no love only despair. "*Where is the God of justice?*"[373] he asked and slipped into death.

For an hour she sat in the dust, holding her father close, thrusting his lifeless lips against her breast as if she could pass on some dregs of life into his corpse. Then reality came and enveloped her in the despair of loneliness. There she was alone in the desert, defenceless, with a dead man as a companion and no hope of the Second Coming.

*

He turned and she abandoned the past for the present. He knew her just as she recognised him. With that thought a gentle crimson touched her cheeks as she remembered the last time he must have gazed on her, naked and unconsciousness in that Antioch room.

"I'm pleased you've come back to life," he smiled. There was a warmth in the lined face lit by the flickering fire. He reached forward and gently placed a blue cloak around her shoulders. Only when his hands released their hold did she realise what had been offered to warm her. Furiously she shrugged off her father's cloak and looked for his body.

"He'll have no need for it where he's gone," muttered her companion. Then he saw the look of horror on her face as she took in the implications. "Before the throne of God at the Last Judgement there is no heat nor cold."

"Nor justice either, "she sobbed as she remembered the last words of her father. Where indeed was the God of Justice? Her people had been harassed and tortured, driven from their homes and denied any appeal by the very authorities her father had seen as the agents of the Enemy. Seeing the puzzled look on the face of her rescuer she repeated the last words of her father and found they were received coldly.

"Whatever was stolen from him couldn't have been more than he tried to take from me."

She wasn't going to see her father maligned by a man who'd brought down so much mischief on the heads of her family and people. If only she hadn't helped him, what would have happened? She stated baldly her father had lost his position, his home, his security and finally his life. She was irritated by the quiet smile which slowly appeared on his face - and he hastened to apologise.

"It was just that the defence of your father has brought back life, and I am pleased." She abruptly turned away from him, partly to hide the glimmer of amusement which appeared in her violet eyes. He coughed and moved over to her. "I'm sorry. Every child must defend a father; no man can judge from the outside what passes between father and child."

The flicker of amusement died as she recalled her father's fury at her despoliation by this man. She'd asked him to strike her, had offered her dress to him and allowed his eyes to scan her body. She'd brought despair on her father; she was responsible for the misery of the last months. A tear trickled down her cheek. " I'm to blame for his misery and the pain of my people."

"Nonsense!" was the brutal response. "If I'd been led against the Autokrator, by now your people would have been no more." He paused and kicked at the fire. "Don't you know the Autokrator is a much kinder ruler than many who'd like to sit in his place." He remembered the dead Eparchos; that fiend hadn't been without the ultimate ambition. "By saving your father from his folly you preserved your people." He turned and looked gently at her. "Of course, you also saved me and, for that, my life is yours." There was a moment of awkwardness between them which he ended by a sharp cough. "Meanwhile it's late and we're both tired. Tomorrow will bring better decisions."

That was true. Lydia curled herself up in the cloak, feeling once again those fatherly arms which had shielded her as a child. He was gone to meet his Maker; she still had work to do. She remembered her father's dream of destroying the Autokrator. He'd seen this man as a useful tool and had almost succeeded. Her people had suffered for nothing; that was wrong. The Second Coming demanded a second attempt.

*

The morning gave them no hope. They had food and water; but the desert was wide and all around were enemies. Lydia had sensed yesterday the barbarian was no longer a favoured soldier of the Autokrator. Of course, his ragged costume might be just a disguise to penetrate the trust of those resisting imperial tyranny. However, his manner revealed a tension not seen before; even during the nightmare captivity imposed by her father, his self-confidence had both alarmed and attracted her. Now that had gone; she sensed only the shell of a man wearily rose and looked towards the south.

"We must go on to Antioch," he mused, shrugging off her protests. "To go north would be to place ourselves ever more-tightly within the grasp of the Autokrator." He paused and half-smiled down at her. "Life has been unfair to me in the last few months, as it has been to you."

Where was her father? What would he have done? Lydia frantically looked about her, again feeling deserted in a hostile land. He saw the look and guessed the cause. The hated fanatic was dead; he was part of the past. It was his daughter who now needed to come to terms with...... What was he saying? He'd destroyed whatever position he might have had within the Empire, shrugged off responsibility for other Varangians attracted by the richness and promise of Miklagard. He'd given up the future and almost abandoned the present. He had no idea where he'd go or what he'd do. He only felt an ache within, that life was pointless and death an unknown horror; somehow he had to shuffle along a narrow track until he could recover the right path.

The girl, however, was different. She'd none of the blood and guilt dragging him down. Whatever had been the sins of her father had left her unblemished. His sole memory of her was one of goodness and kindness. Whatever the girl was fleeing had died with her father. He pointed quickly to the left and saw his gesture drag the eyes of the girl to the simple grave of her father.

She half-ran, half-tumbled over her feet to a small patch of disturbed sand, three large stones and the crude cross formed from the branches of a thorn bush. Here would lie her father until the Day of Judgement; perhaps that would be next year, perhaps it wouldn't come for an eternity. She didn't know, perhaps she didn't care. Gently Lydia touched the cross and whispered a simple prayer to her Lord. "Master and Lord of Creation, ...have pity .... look mercifully on this soul who left us.....was taken.... before Your return for which he'd struggled so long. Keep him in peace... that true and blissful sleep.... until he can enter into Your Kingdom. Amen."

A tear slowly formed and trickled down her left cheek. Her father had been so close to the triumphant return of the Master; if only he'd lived but a few months he would have joined the Elect of God. "*And I heard the number of them who were chosen; and there were chosen a hundred and forty-four thousand of all the tribes of the children of Israel...*"[374] Lydia could hear the voice of her father so close that she could almost feel his breath. "*No more shall they hunger nor thirst; nor shall they feel the light of the sun or heat. For the Lamb in the heart of the throne shall feed them and take them to the living springs of water; and God shall wipe the tears away from their eyes.*"[375]

She smiled and felt her father's warmth; she knew he had so little time to wait for the Promised Return. Now he was at peace, soon he'd be in triumph. She heard a movement behind her revealing she wasn't alone. Even in that God had given His protection and comfort. The barbarian had been sent to her for a purpose.

Lydia turned back towards the barbarian. Why had he suddenly appeared, just when she'd sunk into the despair of failure? She knew he liked her; she'd longed for him so many times in her dreams. She bit her lips. The pain squeezed out such carnal thoughts and an innocent face smiled at the barbarian.

"Thank you for giving him even this simple burial," she murmured. "I know you....he ..... you had no reason to love him....I know...."

"....That you helped me when I had need," he interrupted her confession." When I was in the depths of misery you came to lift me up." He paused and there was a slight tremor in his voice which hadn't been there before. "Perhaps....perhaps God decided I should help you in your darkest hour."

She stepped forward and, grasping his hand, slid to her knees. With her head brushing lightly against his thigh she repeated the words of Ruth: "*Tell me not to go from you, or stop following you; for wherever you go, I will go; and wherever you stay, I will stay.*"[376]
He didn't see the turmoil in her eyes as she spoke these words. Why did she say them? Was it love for this stranger? Was she, like her father, determined to use him to bring about the destruction of the Anti-Christ? Was she simply terrified of being left alone?

He gently stroked her hair; bemused, concerned, alarmed at the trust of the girl. What would he do with her? He didn't know what life held for him; even less could he be sure what fate held for her. Firmly he grasped her shoulders and raised her to her feet. One hand turned her towards Antioch, the other hand firmly gripped their provisions. His sword clanked against the buckle of his pouch and he remembered the tedium and tension of the drill exercises in the capital; tedium because so much of the polishing and cleaning was irrelevant to real fighting; tension because all had known that failure to reach the standards of the Paymaster-General[377] could mean loss of pay or liberty.

Lydia looked back over her shoulder at the grave of her father, alone and abandoned by the side of the road. Her legs trudged in the direction of Antioch while her heart stayed in the wilderness. Part of her died with her father. She pulled his cloak more tightly around her shoulders, just to feel his comforting warmth. Of course, he wasn't there - could never be there again - but in the cloth she could sense his sweat, his hopes, himself.

*

Once past the extensive cemetery to the north of Antioch, Ethelwulf and Lydia crossed the Bridge of Boats, which was surprisingly quiet, and headed for the Gate of the Dog. By now they'd caught up with a mass of travellers. Ethelwulf bent low, dragging his body wearily along with the help of a staff; his sword had been surrendered to Lydia who hung it from her neck. By thrusting her head forward she countered it weight and managed to stay upright, supported by the right arm of her companion. Both looked weary and dust-stained, as they were; both seemed confident and open, which they were not.

The Gate of the Dog was one of the least-guarded entrances to the city, unlike the Gate of St. Paul through which passed the road from Aleppo or the Gate of St. George which straddled the route to the coast and Lattakieh. The rather restricted entrance was crowded with the hubbub of commerce, very useful to the two weary travellers from the north. In front a rickety cart over-laden with jars of oil had caused the two sentries to jump into activity. Had an excise certificate been issued at Emessa? No? Why not? The driver tried to explain he'd been forced to by-pass the advanced imperial base because of rumours of bandits near the road. The sentries were now even more suspicious - and excited. If they could frighten the driver into accepting a transit warrant issued locally he might be induced to supply a "gift" for their cooperation. An amphora of oil sold on the open-market could equal their pay for one month; sold among the stalls of the dingy alleyways of the city (and so without the heavy imperial sales tax) it would be even more profitable.

They were immersed in persuading the driver to contribute to the imperial taxation system when Ethelwulf and Lydia slipped past.

A few moments effectively put the two fugitives beyond the ready discovery by imperial forces. Simeon ben Joseph proved a cooperative landlord. In return for a couple of coins they were given an obscure room at the rear of his dingy inn overlooking the dismal alley of Basil Epiphanes. Who were these strangers? Obviously runaway lovers whispered Simeon's wife, Sarah, noting the absence of any rings indicating marriage. Her brother, Samuel, disagreed; there was no sign of affection between the pair, although the man carefully guided the woman as she staggered up the stairs. Sarah noted the stiffness of her back and wondered if she were with child; nobody could be sure because of the thickness of the cloak smothering her limbs. That must be the explanation; lovers guilty of escaping a family's curse would hide away anywhere. So what if neither were children of Israel? The man was a barbarian from the north, but they'd become less unusual in the last few years. Some belonged to the imperial garrison, others were traders.

In their room the two fugitives glanced nervously at the single bed and then at each other. It wasn't right; Lydia was certain her father would have denounced it as a trick of the Dark One. To be alone in a room, let alone in a bed, with an unbeliever in the house of a Jew! How could she ever again feel clean! Ethelwulf guessed the distaste of his companion and felt cold. Certainly she'd have been desirable in another life but not now; what had been his heart had been torn apart in that final battle. Whatever energy he still possessed had trickled away in the final assault on the Eparchos and his cousin. Now he was worn out, an old man.

"Have no fear," he murmured. "Your chastity will stay untouched even if we do share the same - "

"I have no fear of you, barbarian," was the reply and he looked down into the hostile eyes of the East. "We virgins of the Lord are protected against the lusts of creatures such as yourself." She turned her back so that he could not see the hesitation which flickered across her face and showed the depths of her lie. Yes, she wanted him at that moment. She needed the warmth and comfort of arms around her, shutting out the miseries of the last two days. If only he'd hold her, shield her in a chaste embrace! She gulped as a thought of horror struck her. Was that what she really wanted - was it? She dared not turn back to face the barbarian; afraid of what she might feel and what he might see. The man was a fool; had not her father said he was a fool, an idiot useful only in carrying out the will of the Lord. Yet he'd not touched her in those final moments in that room so long ago. Yes, he was a fool.

Ethelwulf looked at Lydia's back and remembered what he'd abandoned months ago. Perhaps hope survived somewhere. Why had she been slumped there by the roadway when he'd trudged south? Why here the girl to whom he'd been drawn when captive but who'd seemed so untouchable in her very purity? Why had their paths crossed just when she'd lost all hope and he'd left hope behind? Had fate given him one more chance to climb out of the pit of despair? Could this virgin somehow lead him back to life? No, she was like her father; her whole purpose was fixed on the dreamed-for return of the Saviour, so close and yet so far. She'd never want him, never want a barbarian, when in months she'd join the virgins in welcoming the Everlasting King. Did he believe that? Could he be sure Christ would return to earth within twelve months?

Could he be sure He would not? Would it be fair to Lydia? He smiled grimly; such arrogance. Why should a pure young girl even look at an old man like him? What did he have to offer; no gold, no favour, no position. A fine prospect as a bridegroom; hunted the length of the Empire and beyond. Yes, that was another risk. To leave the Empire was to place himself in an unknown world. Islam offered slavery or death; perhaps Italy might offer a chance to recover. Recover? Did he honestly think he could live again? Was this all the impact of a pair of bewitching eyes?

Without a word Lydia snuffed out the candle; a soft moonlight revealed some pattern of movement. Quickly she turned her back on the barbarian and removed her top garment, retaining the dark woollen under-garment as a shield for her modesty. Silently she slid under the blanket which covered the simple bed, hugging its side with both hands so as to lie next to the edge without toppling over. Ethelwulf stripped and climbed into the other side. If the girl wanted to be modest, so be it; he'd enough to tax his brains without worrying about the temptations of the flesh.

The night grew colder and Lydia felt her fingers loosen their grip on the edge of the bed. She tried to relax and failed; her legs felt heavy and ached. She eased the muscles in her back and found herself edging towards the centre of the bed. She paused, took a deep breath and listened. She could only sense the sound of heavy breathing' "sense" because she couldn't be sure she did hear breathing. She relaxed further, sliding back as she did so.

Suddenly she felt back touched by a warm, solid object. It was the barbarian's back; it could not be anything else. She listened closely but could hear nothing. Suddenly she felt a heavy weight as an arm slumped over her thigh. She opened her mouth to cry out but her throat was too dry. She made to push off the arm.

"Calm yourself, Gormflath!"[378] hissed his voice in an unknown tongue. "I'm no Olaf,[379] needing violence to bring a maid to bed." Lydia felt the shape swing over so that they were no longer back to back. Why could she not cry out? Why did she not scream and jump from the bed? Now the whispering became more passionate, but still in an unknown tongue.[380] "Darling, I love you.... You know that! Not even the apples of Idun[381] are more beautiful than your breasts." [382] With that her companion turned over and Lydia's nipple was caressed delicately by a thumb. She froze in horror but did nothing; wondering why she was allowing her body to be so abused and do nothing. Was she terrified of the man? Was she frightened of discovery? Did she feel gratitude?

No! Horror of horrors! She could feel some yearning within her body for his touch. Softly she could hear his voice chanting, this time in the Greek of the alleyways, the song peddlers sang out to any foolhardy maid who dared wander among them without an escort.

> "Sister of the wind, daughter of the sun
> Give unto your servant, the fruit of your loins!
> Bind him up in chains of love,
> Smother him with grapes of joy
> Fill him with fragrant...."

The rest was lost in incoherent mumble.

Somewhere she could hear her own voice give out an answer:

"*Awake, wind of the north; come, wind of the south; blow upon this garden of mine, gushing out its spices. Let my beloved enter his garden and gorge on his pleasant fruits.*"[383]

Could this be possible? She was melting herself into his sleeping form. Her lips sought his and she was overcome by the tang of the unknown pressure of the kiss. This was not the kiss of peace with which the faithful greeted each other in the Assemblies of the Lord but the fruit of Eden, the taste given to Adam by Eve[384] after the first disobedience. So pleasurable! Her finger sought his neck and she touched his ear.

Suddenly Ethelwulf's whole body stiffened and his grey eyes opened wide. He was awake. What was happening.? All he could feel was her softness, so wound up in him; a pair of hands so close and fervid. His hands slid down her back and felt the tension. He felt a tightness within himself. A feeling of ecstasy flowed into him, through him and out again.

*

Afterwards there was mutual embarrassment. For Lydia the shedding of virginity had not been without pain, but that had been nothing to the pleasure. Now she felt ashamed, used, humiliated. She hated the large barbarian; he'd taken what was hers to give but once. It should never have been a matter of shame and darkness

Ethelwulf sensed her awkwardness. How had they come to be embattled in a conflict of love? He remembered drifting into the arms of that witch, Gormflath; feeling her hair, smelling the scent of the woods of Ireland when they'd once entwined, out of the reach of her son.[385] Then somehow he'd been in those terrifying Wendish woods, secure in the arms of his lover, Skuna, the loyal daughter of a treacherous king, Mistivoj.[386] Others he'd preferred to have forgotten - like the Byzantine princess, Zoe,[387] a flagrant whore, or the unresolved passion for that royal murderess, Queen Elfrida.[388]

Something had to be said; perhaps an apology, perhaps a promise. He opened his mouth to speak but Lydia was the first to break the uneasy gulf between them.

"It's just as my father foretold," she stared into his eyes with a dead resignation that cut more deeply than hatred. "He guessed I'd helped you, but said nothing." She paused as she remembered the speed with which they'd abandoned home and friends before the arrival of the imperial guards. "He said barbarians took what they wanted and when they wanted it - and left without payment!"

"That's not true!" Ethelwulf snapped. Why did the accusation so hurt? How much truth lay behind it? What would he have done for the girl if her father had been seized and executed by the authorities? He bit his lip as he realised the answer would have been 'nothing'. Yes, he'd have wanted to supply, perhaps even have given, silver; but then the imperial trumpet would have called and there was only room for whores in the train of Varangians.

Now he was no longer a servant of the Autokrator; he'd renounced his allegiance and simply wanted to leave the Empire. So what difference did that make? He looked at the girl - beautiful, helpless and dependent. To travel fast was to travel alone, but did he need to travel fast? As far as the court was concerned he was best forgotten, perhaps they already believed him dead. In a month or so any hunt would be abandoned. It would be best not to attempt to cross any frontier till such a search had been forgotten. Where was there any hope for safety? Perhaps one of the ports such as Acre or Jaffa handling pilgrims and trade from the West. His eyes moved slowly down towards the girl's feet. She fitted into this world so naturally; however long he stayed in the east he'd always stay the barbarian, the outsider, the object of curiosity. That could be dangerous. This girl, apparently so defenceless, could protect him - and his sword would keep her from harm. Would she stay with him? He reached forward and lightly touched her cheek with his left hand; the softness of her flesh made his own seem callous.

"Your father was mistaken, Lydia," he whispered. "The West teaches us to care for women; it's a lie we take without payment - "

"I - ", her voice was bitter and she moved her cheek away from his hand.

"I'd have you as my wife," he continued, scarcely knowing what he said and almost as shy as a young lad. "That is if you'll have me."

She smiled at the tremor in his voice and her fingers reached up to touch his hand. Her eyes searched his for sincerity - and found it. Ethelwulf would never know why at that moment he wanted to marry a young heretic, a refugee like himself in a hostile Empire; never before had he offered marriage to a woman; now it came so naturally he was swept along with his own need. He stepped forward and felt her drift into his arms. Her warmth took over his whole body and her softness gave him strength. Somewhere next to his heart he felt her smile and the stupidity of his offer was wiped away by hope.

*

They were married in Lattakieh, in a tiny chapel dedicated to St Cyricus[389] on the saint's day. Ethelwulf carefully hid the smile that mocked the tale of the awkward brat. In Jersey Guibert of Falaise had believed the holy mite could work miracles, but that hadn't secured him the succession at St. Helier for long.[390] However, that was in another world when so many good warriors had been alive and well. The priest coughed politely and the barbarian blushed as he heard his prompt repeated. Yes, he did promise to have only Lydia Epaphroditou as his wife until Christ would come again. He smiled down at his bride. He was but two days journey from the limits of imperial power; all he had to do now was wait.

Lydia had already shown her usefulness by guiding him to the home of a distant cousin, George. Perhaps this cousin had been why they'd headed for Lattakieh rather than stay in the safer hinterland; he couldn't remember.

George was a fanatic, mutilated by the imperial authorities for daring to speak out against the tax impositions of two years ago; as the imperial army had just recovered the city they'd been merciful and George had merely lost one ear. However, George was prepared to do anything against the child of Satan installed at the New Rome; helping the daughter of the saintly Epaphroditus would merely gain him extra blessing when Christ Himself returned within the next eighteen months. He'd given the barbarian a surly look as one who'd wielded the sword for the Anti-Christ, even if he now saw the truth. Lydia, of course, was well aware her future bridegroom was still as unsaved as when her father had tried to use him to destroy the Anti-Christ; however, she made no move to correct her cousin, merely smiling and announcing that she and the tall barbarian wished to be married as soon as possible. Helena, George's grey-haired wife, raised her eyes to peer knowingly at the young girl at that news. Good Christian girls only rushed to the altar when they had need for carnal sin to be washed away; Lydia caught her look and forced herself to smile. It was a weak smile; she knew what Helena was thinking and it was largely true. She did feel polluted by the barbarian and was ashamed of that weakness which had given him the chance to wreak his lust. However, she knew he was a good man and she trusted his word. Of course, if she was honest with herself she could do nothing else. The Second Coming was so near that marriage was the only refuge for one who'd so readily abandoned her maidenhead; perhaps she loved him, possibly he loved her. It didn't matter.

With the ceremony over they returned to the small room behind George's leather shop for the wedding feast. As the imperial tax collectors had plundered George's savings as part of the enormous fine accompanying the loss of his ear, there was little left with which to celebrate. The meal consisted of a few honey-cakes dipped in spiced wine and matched with the yoghurt produced in the hills which hemmed Lattakieh to the sea. It was enough. George insisted on rising to his feet and raising his cup to the downfall of the Anti-Christ in the capital. His wife looked anxiously at the barbarian when her husband made his outburst, but there was no sign the ex-Varangian still felt any loyalty. Of course, nobody knew Ethelwulf had been that officer responsible for the ruin of their cousin. Lydia decided the past should stay buried; Ethelwulf was introduced as a fellow-refugee who'd protected her on the road.

Her cousins were told he was a refugee because a religious conversion had caused him to leave the imperial service.

It was agreed the barbarian would help George with his business. He'd travel up into the hills to collect the hides used by the small leatherworker to make pouches, belts and other articles sold in the markets of Lattakieh. For a moment Ethelwulf hesitated, and then realised such absences in the hills would reduce any chance of discovery by the imperial security system. Besides it made the pretence of heresy easier to sustain. Lydia too was pleased; she was both drawn to and alienated by her barbarian husband. All she could hope for was release when Christ returned next year.

Not that Ethelwulf and Lydia were unhappy. Perhaps both entered into a conspiracy of mutual deceit but their lovemaking at night grew in passion as week followed week. Lydia's feelings for her husband were fanned by his absences. It was hard to be so dependent on such a mean-spirited woman as her cousin, Helena; repeatedly Lydia was informed that charity had its limits and only the Final Judgement would balance the books. This attitude lessened as Ethelwulf proved increasingly useful in the risky trade with the hinterland.

*

The road was dusty and the sun hot. Ethelwulf allowed both mules to saunter over into the shade of the tall shrub by the side of the road. The air was so quiet as to be suspicious. Years of fighting had given Ethelwulf a good sense of danger and he wasn't happy. He glanced at the second mule laden-down with the hides he'd bought from the brothers Nicias and Nicephorus yesterday. He'd never taken to Nicephorus but George had used Nicias for years and insisted the brothers had proved very useful as agents in the past and would continue as long as there was need for trade. Of course, neither brother was a true believer but belonged to the Nestorian heresy; they shared a hatred of the Anti-Christ and from that shared hate had come a profitable business arrangement. The brothers collected hides from cows, sheep and goats which roamed over the hills under the loose control of the villagers; they stored the hides away from the prying eyes of the tax-collectors and then sold them to George. When Ethelwulf was first introduced by George as his agent neither brother had been enthusiastic. Nicephorus showed his feelings by spitting into the corner of the hut; George stopped Ethelwulf reaching for his sword with a warning look and the tense moment passed off. On the next occasion Nicephorus was absent and on the next three visits, when Ethelwulf had come alone to the isolated hut over the muddy stream some joker had called 'Brightwater', Nicias had acted on behalf of the brothers.

"Nicephorus....he busy in hills..... Me do deal....You come see good skins....." In the absence of Greek, Nicias resorted to the local patois and made sure it was so simple no man could accuse him of trying to cheat a stranger. On this last trip Nicephorus sat in the corner, silently watching as a mixture of bronze and silver coins had been handed over. Then he suddenly stepped forward and offered Ethelwulf a drink from an earthenware flagon. Ethelwulf declined and could see the flicker of hateful disappointment which appeared in the dark eyes of the Syrian. Nicias said nothing, merely silently counting out the money and sorting the coins into the different types. He didn't look up as the barbarian departed.

That had been two hours ago and now Ethelwulf took a long draught from his own water-pouch. It was hot and still too silent. Quickly he made his way into the shrubbery; to any watcher the barbarian was leaving the road to relieve himself but Ethelwulf quickly slid into the dark shadows of the cliff. There was almost a cave here and it was beautifully cool. Out on the road one mule nuzzled the other as they feasted themselves on the rough brambles. Now was the time to be patient.

Time passed and the larger mule started to get restless; Ethelwulf had tied both to the same clump of shrub but now the larger mule started to tug at the leather thong. Then there was a sound from immediately above him and Ethelwulf pressed back against the rock. Already his sword, normally concealed under cloth covering the larger mule, was in his hand. In front he was masked by a large shrub. A pebble pattered down by his head and he heard a few whispered words in an unknown tongue. Somebody was scrambling down the rock to his left; he couldn't see but sensed there were two of them, and had a very good idea which two.

A figure detached itself from the shrubbery and crept across the road towards the mules. Nicias! Where did they think he was? Ethelwulf slowly pushed aside a branch so he could see more clearly whatever was on this side of the road. For a moment he could see nothing, except a thorn which threatened to gouge his cheek. Then the opening cleared and he saw Nicephorus. The man was standing on guard as his brother approached the mules; in his hands was a short bow with the arrow already notched. His eyes were keenly scanning the bushes opposite. Ethelwulf smiled, so the brothers had made a mistake; they'd guessed he'd choose the wider, denser expanse of brambles opposite. Of course, if his reason for leaving the mules had been so natural that would have been the way he'd have gone; even now he'd still be crouching down among the shrubs somewhere. However, his motive for leaving the road had been an instinctual sense of danger. Slowly, he reached down to his belt for his knife.

Nicias reached the mules and paused to look around. For a brief moment he stared at the shaded spot where Ethelwulf stood - and then his eyes moved on. There was no sound as the Nestorian's hands reached to release one of the mules; then he paused as if hesitating to steal both hides and mule. There was a sharp hiss from Nicephorus. How could his brother think twice about despoiling the barbarian? From the first moment he'd seen the unbeliever he'd hated the man; once a tool of Anti-Christ always an instrument of Satan. *"For they despoil those that despoiled them, and rob those that robbed them,"*[391] he whispered to himself; for years he and his brother had scraped together a living only to have it stolen by some tax-collector, Fatimid or Greek it made no matter. Now was coming the triumph of the Lord and of those who sincerely believed in Him. To take back what was rightfully theirs was no sin. Why did his brother hesitate? He smiled as Nicias unhitched the first mule and moved on to its companion. For a moment he relaxed.

Ethelwulf stepped out from his cover and Nicephorus heard a sound to his right, only about twenty paces away. He swung round to face the danger; at the same moment Ethelwulf's left hand went back and he hurled the knife. It caught Nicephorus high up in the chest, just beneath the collar bone; he shrieked with pain as he dropped his bow. Nicias turned at the scream and saw the barbarian leaping towards his brother. He started to run towards Nicephorus to help him face the onslaught, and then realised it was too late; Nicias turned to run back towards the hills. By now Ethelwulf was on the wounded brother who was just tearing the knife out of his chest with one horrendous effort; after the blade blubbered his blood. He looked up and saw against the sun the silhouetted barbarian raise a long sword; his eyes were drawn to the dazzling blade as it began its descent.

Almost as 'Ban-bitar'[392] cut into one brother's neck, Ethelwulf turned his attention to the other's retreating figure. He dropped his sword and grabbed the discarded bow and arrow. With almost a single moment he notched the arrow against the string and aimed at the running figure. Although Nicias was over one hundred paces away, the arrow from his dead brother's bow still felled him when it tore into his thigh. With a desperate effort he rolled over to face back down the road as his hands grabbed at the shaft. The pain as he tugged at it almost wiped away all consciousness; certainly the scream as he saw the nightmare figure running towards gave him the strength of desperation. The arrow-head was torn out of his flesh and he staggered to his feet - or rather to one knee as the barbarian reached him. Nicias startled to gabble out a prayer for mercy and then realised the barbarian in his haste had left behind his sword. For a brief second hope awoke in his mind and his right hand clutched for the small knife which was tucked in his belt.

"Thank you for giving me a second chance to use this," grinned Ethelwulf as he reached down and seized the blood-stained arrow. Nicias shrieked once as the barb was thrust into his neck and then he lay still. The Wanderer looked down at the slight body in the dust and took several deep and savage breaths. Perhaps he was getting old; two years ago he'd have struck Nicias squarely in the back and there would have been no need for all this effort. As the blood-lust drained away so did the energy. A sudden alarm made him glance along the road in both directions. Here in the East he couldn't afford to be discovered with two dead men; a barbarian fugitive would have no chance.

Quickly he dragged the still warm body of Nicias to the side of the road. Then he ran back towards the dead Nicephorus. The corpse was off the road but already attracting the interest of flies as the hot sun rapidly dried the pool of blood. A movement made Ethelwulf realise one of the mules was loose and he hurried over to tether it again. Now he'd the chance to look around he could see a suitable spot for the last resting place of the brothers; it was a large area of scrubland, where they'd thought he had gone. Quickly he seized hold of Nicephorus and threw him over his shoulder. About twenty paces into the scrub was enough; he pitched the body down and turned to get the other corpse. Fortunately Nicias was lighter than his brother and soon had been tumbled down next to him. The Wanderer returned to the road and recovered his weapons. His sword opened up the hard ground and then Nicias's knife and his hands were used to make a shallow hole, big enough to hide two bodies from the attention of insects and animals which might provoke human interest.

By the time both corpses and their weapons had been safely stowed under a loose mound of sand Ethelwulf felt tired. Even so, he knew he couldn't stop now. Several moments were spent collecting stones of varying sizes to be placed over the grave; then he lightly trod down the rocks into firm position. Finally more sand was thrown over them to make the whole area look less like a grave. One thing remained. How had the brothers reached this spot? Presumably they'd used mules; but where were they? Abandoned mules would attract attention, loose mules would simply be added to the finder's collection; after all, any mule could wander off from a careless owner without causing suspicion. However, he couldn't take long.

Quickly he scrambled up the escarpment from which the brothers had emerged. There was nothing there. Now he had to guess the direction from where they'd come. He headed back along the high ground paralleling the track which passed for a road. After a few moments he came across two mules, resting in the shade. Quickly he released them and turned away. Mules had the common sense to head back home; their return would raise questions but nobody would bother to hunt for the brothers in such a barren area. Anything could have happened to them. Neighbours would quietly appropriate whatever property the brothers possessed, thanking God for such unexpected bounty, and Nicias and Nicephorus would slowly vanish from human memory.

It was mid-afternoon before Ethelwulf could set out again on the journey home. As he rode perched high on the back of the larger mule he decided to say nothing to George and Helena. Information could be given by anybody to the authorities; the same could be said for Lydia. Ignorance would protect her from any enquiry.

*

One month later a surprised Ethelwulf brought back news that Nicias and Nicephorus had disappeared weeks ago. George cursed, blaming bandits for forcing him to find somehow new agents with the herdsmen of the hills. Of course, it meant he had to accompany the barbarian back into the hinterland which he found increasingly embarrassing. As the Second Coming approached his patience with Lydia's husband lessened; he was by no means certain the barbarian was a true believer and he wondered if sheltering anybody with doubts about the Return of the Lord would threaten his welcome into the New World.

Fortunately for George he found a shepherd quickly enough who was willing to act as an agent regarding the collection of hides. Thaddeus seemed surprisingly friendly towards the barbarian, then revealed his cousin kept a tavern in Antioch very popular with the troops of the Empire. Ethelwulf didn't like that news, until Thaddeus admitted the cousin never ventured far away from the city as he'd grown soft with the years.

"A pity," smiled Ethelwulf. "I may even have drunk his wine when I was in the service of the Autokrator." He grasped the shepherd's hand as he and George prepared to leave. Any acquaintance from his past could be most inconvenient, but it was nice to think a supposed contact in the past had eased a deal in the present.

However, on their return George and Ethelwulf found other news to occupy them; Lydia was pregnant. Helena seemed remarkably unenthusiastic. Perhaps the Lord would return before the child was born. "*Whosoever is born of God does not sin; the child of God protects himself, and the wicked cannot harm him,*"[393] she muttered as she comforted Lydia while glaring at the barbarian. It was obvious she felt the father of the unborn child would be numbered among the ungodly and be doomed for eternal death; perhaps it was better that way.

Ethelwulf wasn't pleased by the news. Already he was considering slipping away from the hateful world of the East when he had the chance. To leave behind Lydia would be bad enough: to leave behind his child would be even worse. However, he contrived to hide such anxiety and tried to show enthusiasm at the news. Lydia was not deceived but considered her husband had been affected by the mumblings of Helena. Later when the two women were alone she challenged the right of anyone to question the Mercy of the Lord. Of course her child would inherit the New World; so would her husband. Helena had agreed, but her eyes said no.

George, however, was full of joy at his cousin's pregnancy. For weeks he'd feared the barbarian would desert Lydia and leave her as a charge on his charity. Not that he didn't love his cousin; but life was hard enough with only a dependent wife. Hearing of the child to come reminded him of the rumoured devotion of barbarians to their sons; if only Lydia would produce a son everything would be all right. Meanwhile his wife should ensure Lydia had absolute rest.

He even called in the Jewess, Sarah, half-feared as a witch and doomed for perdition the next year, to examine his pregnant cousin. Sarah arrived with a smug smile and an air of importance. Though her neighbours were cheerfully writing her destruction when their God would return, she knew it wouldn't happen. The Messiah was yet to appear, and when he did he'd come to free the Land of Israel for His own people.

"*I have surely seen the affliction of my people in Egypt, and have heard their cry because of their oppressors; for I know their sorrows. And I am come down to rescue them from the land of the Egyptians, and bring them out from there to a good and large land,* flowing with milk and honey,"[394] had stated Rabbi Symeon. Every child of Moses knew the time of suffering dating from the sack of the Holy City by the Romans would soon come to an end. A thousand years had nearly passed; a millennium of misery for God's chosen people. The four beasts[395] which would oppress the people had been seen in the Empires of Rome, Persia, Egypt and now the New Rome; with their destruction the children of Israel would recover Jerusalem.

Now Sarah came and laid her ear to the stomach of the pregnant Lydia. She could hear the movement of the child within; its movements were strong and arrogant, like those of a boy. George beamed when he learned the child would be male. Now the barbarian would stay - at least until the Second Coming; after that there'd be no need for worry.

*

What Ethelwulf had feared for months happened in the third month of the New Year. He'd just walked through the gateway of Heraclius when he saw a familiar face approaching. It was Jacob Ben Isaac who'd occupied the shop opposite that of Simeon the Jeweller in the city of Autokrator. After Ethelwulf's rescue of the old man and his daughter from a fire,[396] the Varangian had been marched around the neighbourhood as a hero. He'd met Jacob ben Isaac who'd shrewdly assessed the value of contacts within the imperial palace and so forced on Ethelwulf the gift of a fine, silver-mounted dagger. Unfortunately the weapon had been removed by Epaphroditus five years later and probably had been traded in the alleys of Antioch. Yet if he knew Jacob, Jacob would remember him. He quickly ducked down an alleyway and heard from somewhere behind him the cry of "Varangii! Varangii!"

A breathless Ethelwulf slipped into the rear of George's shop and slumped wearily into a vacant chair. Lydia, in the last days of her pregnancy, arose in alarm at his appearance.

"Have you been seen by imperial agents?" she gasped and he shook his head in reply. "Have you been attacked by those who don't like true Believers?" She whispered and he made no reply. "I'll tell George. He'll get us some defenders – we'll not be destroyed - frustrated - in these last few weeks. We-"

"No," he mumbled. "I wasn't attacked; I was recognised!"

"By an agent of the security - "

"No, " he snapped. "By an old friend...." He saw her start to relax and became angrier. What right had she to be so helpless at this time. If only she'd have his son soon he might try to smuggle both of them out of the city before it was too late; if she hadn't been expecting his son he'd have quietly left in the night. He approached her and tightly, almost cruelly, gripped her forearm. "Don't you understand? This friend, this Jew, will ask others why I scurried away." He allowed the word "Jew" to do its work. Every Jew knew every other one's business; there were not many ex-Varangians in the city and he'd soon be identified. All it then took was for one person to mention his name to the imperial spies and the hunt was up. Perhaps he had twenty-fours before they'd push their way into George's home and drag off his barbarian guest to prison. He could see the tension appear in her cheeks. Lydia knew enough about gossip among the Jews to know they didn't have long. "We must get clothes and food.......and.....money, yes, money.....George will give us money..." She rose awkwardly to her feet. Where was George? Just when you wanted him he wasn't there. Perhaps Helena would give them money - just to get rid of them.

"George'll be here by the morning," he spoke slowly as he took her arm to help her to the door. Whatever George might do, they had to get away by midday tomorrow. One word to anyone outside the Jewish community and he could expect imperial agents to be battering the door within a day. Once out of the city he might be able to lose any pursuit; perhaps he'd go east, as if to Damascus, and then circle round to meet his wife just over the border.

They reached the door and he started to bundle Lydia up the stairs to the small room which they shared. As he did so Helena came in from the courtyard and one glance showed her something was wrong. The problem was quickly explained and Helena took charge. Lydia must go upstairs now instantly and rest; meanwhile she and Ethelwulf would collect together clothing and food for the flight. It'd be no use trying to leave before George arrived in the morning; only George had the money which could bribe their way across the frontier. When Ethelwulf started to protest she harshly remarked that George would arrive by dawn and it would take that long for "your Jewish friends" to work out who he was.

*

That evening had been one of relentless packing until screams from Lydia interrupted everything. Helena rushed upstairs and returned immediately with news that all this panic had brought on the birth. She glared at Ethelwulf whom she held responsible both for her cousin's condition in the first place, and then for this current crisis.

She didn't know what he'd done, but she was sure it was enough to secure a large reward. Once the child had been safely born she'd make sure the authorities got their hands on this barbarian troublemaker. The reward would compensate them for any inconvenience Lydia and her child might cause. Perhaps they'd marry her off to some old Greek who'd not ask too many questions.

Now Helena said she was going to get help and brushed past Ethelwulf before he'd a chance to protest. Very soon she was back with two of her neighbours in attendance. One started to boil water at once; Helena and Eudocia rushed up the stairs to where Lydia had started screaming again. Ethelwulf went to follow them and then changed his mind. Up there was women's work; he would be unwelcome. It'd be better to pass the time making sure they had enough food for the journey. At least there'd not be the problem of Lydia suddenly producing their son in the middle of the desert!

Now the other neighbour, Maria, rushed past him with a bowl of boiling water. "Don't stand there, you useless hulk!" she snapped, "Get clean cloth - anything......And start boiling more water!" Like any well-trained slave Ethelwulf rushed to the kitchen to boil water and immediately realised that more had to be brought from the small well at the end of the street. A frantic rush along the street brought him to the well with a large bowl in hand. One Greek was bundled aside and two women quickly made way - perhaps alarmed at the look of desperation or simply forewarned.

Another frantic rush back to the house, spilling water all the way and Ethelwulf was able to pour enough into the large cauldron hanging over the fire to warrant the effort. He moved towards the stairs as the screaming continued. All his life he'd endured the screams of the dying and the wounded; some screams of the tortured still haunted his dreams.[397] These screams, however, were different. Why? Did he love Lydia? No? He wasn't sure; he only knew he wanted the screams to stop ripping into his head.

Suddenly they stopped. The silence was worse than the screaming. He waited for the cry of an infant to signal his son had been born. There was none. The silence went on, twisting his ears with the dread that the silence wanted but a moment before - was now the silence which terrified him. Slowly he started to climb the stairs, looked up and saw a grim-faced Helena standing there.

"Behold your son!" she snapped and held out a lifeless form towards him. He pushed past her; where was Lydia, his wife, the sharer of his misfortunes. Inside the room one woman had just covered the face of the pale, still form on the bed. Everywhere was blood, saturating the bed and dripping on to the floor. Maria turned and hustled him out of the room. Vaguely he heard her whisper Lydia had joined their Saviour early and would return in weeks to share in the triumph of the faithful. Without seeing Helena he trudged back down to the pathetic bundle on the floor below and sat down, his head in his hands.

*

Two hours later George arrived and the first words were spoken in that silent house. Tragedy was described very simply. His cousin, Lydia, had died in bringing into the world a feeble child, already dead before it left the womb. Why had the Almighty so punished a house of Believers? Perhaps it was all the fault of the barbarian who'd bustled his way into their cousin's life, forced them to enter into a conspiracy against the Empire and then, in one last bout of panic, inflicted such anxiety on their cousin that she'd miscarried. Nothing could have been done to prevent tragedy; now the only thing to do was to rid themselves of the barbarian.

George agreed. Before his cousin, and her child, could be laid to rest to await their Lord, the barbarian had to be removed. At any moment imperial agents might force their way into their home and drag them off for harbouring a refugee from justice. Ethelwulf was bundled out of the door before the shadows of the narrow street had given way to the brightness of a new day. Nobody offered him a chance to say goodbye to his dead wife; nor had he asked to see either her, or what should have been his son, again. Nothing remained for him in Lattakieh. With a bundle of food and clothing, a few coins in his purse and his weapons in his belt he turned his back on the True Believers and headed south.

*

The Wanderer 9:2

*"I must mourn all my afflictions alone.
There is no one still living to whom I dare open
The doors of my heart."*(The Wanderer)

The Centre of the World

A bright sun warmed the orange groves to the north of the Holy City; its heat penetrated whatever cover was offered by the trees and stirred into life the lonely figure slumped by a small pool. Somehow Ethelwulf forced open his eyes and saw nothing! At first the mixture of dust and sweat masked whatever existed out there. Behind the eyes the mind was numbed by the sudden demolition of his family just as it seemed a new life was about to be added. Life was unfair; not to him, for he deserved whatever misery God had in store; rather the innocent had suffered yet again as payment for the misdeeds of the Wanderer from the north. For a moment the Wanderer dreamed himself back into the comfort of a Dorset morning, and then the oppressive heat pushed him back into reality.

He'd almost no recollection of his journey south after the death of Lydia and what would have become 'Edmund'; whatever anybody else would have styled his son, the boy would have been a reincarnation of his own father, but born in a foreign land and probably destined to die far away from the heartland of his forefathers. Yet it hadn't happened; a premature birth and a tragic death had spun Ethelwulf out of whatever shelter he'd enjoyed in Lattakieh. Somehow he'd smuggled his way down to Tortosa, paying his way with the few coins George had handed over simply to get rid of him. As for food - he'd been forced to beg, grateful the charity of Islam extended to the unfortunate of any race. Of course, he'd appeared mad, perhaps he was insane, as a Varangian to wander out from beneath the protection of the imperial arm and into the uncertainty of the tiny states which clung between the rival powers of Cairo and Miklagard.

First he'd joined a caravan heading for Baalbek - and a miserable journey that had been for one placed in charge of the camels, laughed at for his foreign ways, and fed on scraps; yet, none laughed too openly for all saw the long sword strapped across his shoulders - not as efficient as the scimitar but just as frightening. The caravan had been almost glad to depart so early one morning as to leave the stranger from the north still snoring alongside the dung of his charges; one kindly soul had left a few coins of silver on the madman's chest, perhaps as a parting gift, perhaps as an invocation against the Dark One. When he awoke Ethelwulf had staggered into a nearby stream and thoroughly washed off whatever taint camels could leave on the skin of a warrior. A cleaner, and happier, man had chased away the laughing children attracted to his rags and sword.

*

It was at that point he stumbled across the Benedictines from St. Augustine's at Canterbury. It'd have been difficult to decide which side was the more delighted to find a fellow-countryman in such a distant land. Obviously, Ethelwulf neglected to give his true name; once more he became 'Osbert of Middlebere' although he decided to drop his links to the Irish fur trade.[398] Now he was a Hampshire pilgrim fallen among thieves on the borders of the Empire but still determined to be in the Holy City for the Millenium.

"So you believe Our Lord really will come again in this holiest of years and begin His Eternal Kingdom from the Holy City itself?" The air of scepticism in the words of Brother Theobald intrigued Ethelwulf. For years he'd come across Christians who believed the return of Christ as predicted in the Revelation of St. John would take place in the city which had denied Him in His last days and had seen His shameful death.

" And I John saw the Holy City, the new Jerusalem, descending from the Father out of heaven, made ready like a bride dressed for her groom,"[399] muttered Brother Wilfred, quietly as if to remind his Brother the Word of God itself had promised what would happen.

"Yes," smiled Brother Theobald as he held the grey eyes of their new companion in a gaze filled with the peace Ethelwulf had lacked for so long. "What you say is perfectly true. However, I feel Our Lord still has much work for us to do in this world of sin - "

"Hasn't it been said these last days will be dominated by a dragon *"which gave power to the beast, and they worshipped the beast*[400]?"persisted Brother Wilfred, but was interrupted.

"And hasn't the beast been likened to the Autokrator, who controls New Rome[401] and hungers to secure the Holy City for himself." The words were muttered in a hoarse whisper and Ethelwulf closely scanned the faces of the English monks for any reaction. There was none. Those who'd abandoned the world had no wish to become embroiled in the politics of a distant land.

However, Brother Theobald had to add gently, "I trust you've not taken up with one of the many heresies which bedevil this land."

Ethelwulf hastened to assure him his interest in such matters was simply as an observer. He remembered the fanaticism of Epaphroditus, so cocooned in the alleyways of Antioch he could believe he could bring about the Second Coming through murder. Inwardly he shuddered, not only with the nightmare of the father but the fading memory of the daughter. Brother Theobald sensed the mood behind the eyes and said nothing. Was their new companion lying? He looked at the muscular body, adorned by the long sword, and knew that whatever the truth was none of the brothers could wrestle it out of the stranger. Perhaps they should call for help but they'd be lucky to find any here who were not either the followers of Mohammed or - even worse - of some perverted cult.

It was clear the Brothers of Canterbury had need of the strong arm of a warrior, and he had need of the anonymity brought by the robes which they willingly loaned him to cover his existing rags. So the party moved south, deciding to avoid the Islamic centre of Damascus in favour of the more diverse one of Tyre. From there they moved on to Tiberias where Ethelwulf proved his worth by discouraging the too-pressing attentions of a small group of Qarmatians.[402] These had passed them on the road to Nazareth and then turned, moved as if by spite to attack the infidel. Their leader adopted a surly posture in the centre of the road; Brother Theobald slowed as he realised the Brothers would soon have to step on to the unwelcome rocks which flanked the narrow path. Suddenly, he felt a body brush past him and saw 'Osbert of Middlebere' advance fiercely against the Qarmatian, shouting in Arabic. The Moslem seemed rather shocked and Brother Theobald hoped their companion uttered such language in ignorance. The Qarmatian, however, didn't move. Without pausing, Ethelwulf's left fist knocked the Moslem from the path into the gorse which cluttered up one side of the path. Even as the Qarmatian screamed a long sword appeared in the Englishman's right hand and its point pressed against the throat of the felled opponent. Moslem hatred confronted Christian vehemence; a whispered threat made the Qarmatian wince and his followers hesitate to draw their knives.

The Qarmatian leader spat out a few words of command and any knives out were returned to their place. The point of the sword was slightly withdrawn and the Qarmatian slithered sideways so that he could rise awkwardly to his feet. He glowered at Ethelwulf and spat into the dust to show his contempt for his conqueror. Then he nervously circled the armed Christian, followed by his followers;

quickly they hurried on their way, not choosing to look back at the Benedictines. Soon they'd disappeared into the distance.

A puzzled, if relieved Brother Theobald, stepped forward as Ethelwulf replaced his sword into its scabbard. "What did you say to that man to make him turn away from violence?"

Ethelwulf grinned. "I told him we were Varangian warriors under vow to dress as monks until we'd reached Jerusalem."

Brother Theobald had to smile as he looked at their six companions; two certainly were pushing their physical strength to its utmost simply by making the journey and two would certainly never see the age of fifty again. They were no warriors, but Benedictine habits could conceal the truth so easily.

*

At Nazareth Brother Samuel fell sick and, despite all efforts, died. He was an old man, nearly seventy, and he couldn't have died in a finer place than the village where Christ had spent His childhood. A few prayers were said for the departed soul, confident that dying on pilgrimage would erase whatever sins had drifted into Brother Samuel's mind during his sixty years enshrouded by the Order. A plain wooden cross was placed over the cairn, warmed by the certainty God would know a true believer in a land of unbelief.

So the seven figures passed on, along the Jericho road, mindful of the Samaritan. Near Shiloh the company was broken up by the haunted dreams of Ethelwulf. Brother Wilfred had retold the story of how a traveller had been dragged from his ass by robbers and left for dead, in the end preserved only by a hated Samaritan. Then the company retired to rest.

However, for Ethelwulf sleep brought no comfort. At first, urgent whisperings awoke first Brother Edwin and then Brother Alcuin. Then the whisperings became more frantic. Brother Alcuin went to awake the tormented man but was stopped by Brother Wilfred.

"His soul battles with Satan," hissed the Benedictine. "Better for him to fight and triumph in such a struggle here than face such torment in the next life." By now names were beginning to tumble out of the lips of their companion. At first the names meant nothing - "Lydia.....Morkere......George..." Then they became all-too full of meaning, "Edward........Elfrida Ordgarsdotter.......Skaathi....." No Englishman could escape the allusions to the murder of King Edward at Corfe over twenty years before. Should they wake their companion? Brother Wilfred agreed; nobody could stand by and listen to treachery for they recognised their companion as the long-lost Ethelwulf, whom many said had murdered his king.

*

"So we can no longer travel with you," stated Brother Wilfred, with what surprisingly sounded like regret. Ethelwulf had been roused from his nightmares and confronted with the evidence of his own tongue. Not only was he a wanted man in their homeland, which might provoke questions when they returned to Canterbury, but he was also a refugee from the power of the Autokrator, which might cause problems if the Benedictines were forced to travel back through Anatolia or indeed set foot in any imperial possession. Of course, to all that must be added the offence of lying to the Brothers, thereby placing them all in considerable danger with the authorities. Some of the Brothers were prepared to accept him as a fellow-pilgrim to the Holy City, and so a worthy companion as far as the gates of Jerusalem; others, however, argued that with the truth no longer hid, at some time they'd have to identify themselves and with that surrender Ethelwulf.

The Wanderer accepted the judgement that their ways should part; the Benedictines would travel towards Bethany and so enter Jerusalem from the east; Ethelwulf would make his way to Ramah and travel on to the Holy City from the north. At the parting there were downcast looks from some of the Brothers who feared by this act they were condemning a fellow-Saxon to destruction, some insisted on giving him silver for the journey. Brother Wilfred stayed apart, uncertain how to act when the final separation took place. As it was Ethelwulf simply marched up to him, grasped his hand and asked for prayers to be said for his soul in the Church of the Holy Sepulchre.

"Perhaps we'll see you there," muttered the Benedictine, "seeking the forgiveness of Our Lord for a life given over to violence - "

"No, brother," interrupted Ethelwulf, "I'd rather ask God's forgiveness for sins of omission." There was a slight pause, and then with a smile, he added, "one of which is not listening more to your views on the end of the world."

"Certainly, my son," was the answering smile, "if we see you we'll not betray you, rather we shall offer prayers that, purged of your sins, you might go home again to your family in peace."

Brother Theobald had a small personal gift for Ethelwulf, a small wooden cross on which rested a silver form of Christ.

"When Satan tempts you into the ways of darkness, hold on to this cross firmly and pray for the strength that only God can give," he said as he delicately placed it around the neck of the Ethelwulf. "This cross was given to me by the Blessed Dunstan himself when he was my teacher." There was a lingering caress for the cross as he added, "Part of the silverwork he did himself[403] so I know it has great power to resist the Evil One."

Ethelwulf thanked the gentle leader of the Brothers and touched the cross himself. As he did he could smell the scent of honeysuckle drifting on a soft English breeze. He'd seen the Archbishop once when taken by his father to see the anointing of King Edgar at Bath.[404] The tall, grey-haired primate seemed to grow in height as, at the conclusion of the ceremony, he raised on high the crown of Alfred for all to see that God Himself, acting through His Church, had given authority to that master of the British Isles.[405] Who could have guessed that within three years such a noble prince would have been dead and the kingdom threatened with civil war,[406] and within another three years his successor would be murdered and the unity of the realm undermined?[407] Suddenly Ethelwulf's attention was drawn back to the present. The Benedictine lightly touched his arm in farewell and, without any further sound or gesture, turned to follow his companions.

Alone once again and, this time, all too aware of how his tongue could betray him, Ethelwulf turned his face towards Jerusalem. Perhaps he'd been unlucky in the Benedictines being able to unravel ravings in their common tongue, and piece it together with the scandals and tragedies of their homeland. Yet he knew babblings in such an alien tongue could only arouse suspicion in a land mastered by intrigue, where deceit too often was the ladder to riches and betrayal an inevitable consequence of trust. With luck he should reach Jerusalem within three days, certainly less if he could risk sharing the rear of a cart taking vegetables to the city.

*

In fact, it took him all of four days to reach the Bab al Zabra[408] in Jerusalem. Ethelwulf found weariness increasing as he neared the Holy City. Part of him insisted it was all in the mind but, however much he'd try to push his muscles so his legs ate up the dusty miles, the effort dissipated after an hour or so, only to leave him more exhausted than before. This state was not improved by his frequent need to conceal himself in ditches or behind bushes as horsemen galloped past, heading for Jerusalem itself. After an initial couple of feverish forays, Ethelwulf abandoned concealment at any approach from the south. He told himself, with remarkably faulty logic, that no danger could come from ahead, from territory beyond the reach of the Autokrator. On the third day, he realised such ideas were crazy as whoever had passed by from the north, sending him scurrying into a ditch, might easily return by the same route. Besides, they could well carry tales northwards of a lone, foot-sore traveller which might reach unfriendly ears. He couldn't rely on the wretchedness of his appearance or of the environment - the dust, heat and the ever-present danger of robbery – to keep travellers from investigating the unusual or macabre.

Only once did he almost blunder into one of the robber-bands which haunted the road. Fortunately, it had been when dusk was rapidly thrusting its mantle over the world so that, alerted by the cries of victims, Ethelwulf had plenty of time to conceal himself from danger. The next morning he came across one dead body feeding flies by the roadside and another battered frame lying, ensnared by blood and moans, close by. Without hesitation Ethelwulf took on the life-style of the Levite[409] and marched on, inwardly praising the wisdom of not getting involved.

So the journey took him slightly longer than he'd anticipated but he reached the Holy City in the dying months of the old millennium, confident Christ Himself would NOT be in a rush to relieve the world of its misery, but cunning enough to keep such opinions to himself!

*

Slumped against a wall the Saxon looked no different to any of the other pilgrims from all over the known world who, having reached their heart's desire, had no idea what to do next. Ethelwulf had taken over a doorway in one of the alleys to the south of the Suq al Qattanin.[410] It had the double benefit of being hidden away in one of the less frequented parts of the city and of being in the Moslem Quarter. Naturally a Frank stood out in such an area, but his neighbours were used to eccentric pilgrims and by the second night he didn't even provoke a glance. Any Frank showing respect for the practices of Islam deserved toleration as one of the People of the Book. From his doorway he could sleep facing westwards into the Christian Quarter, risking recognition for the chance of getting answers to the half-formed questions which tormented his mind.

Despite his hunger, Ethelwulf found himself readily slipping into a routine. He was too proud to beg but found many passers-by would still slip a small coin in his direction, confident the eye of God would detect such charity in His Holy City. After a morning spent half-drowsing against the wall, Ethelwulf would slip into the Church of the Holy Sepulchre where he was guaranteed a bowl of gruel from Nestorian or Jacobite Brothers, if only to irritate the few Western priests who'd intruded themselves into the building. He would pray at Golgotha, with growing confidence that someday, very soon, his Saviour would return and, in a blaze of forgiveness, Ethelwulf would take up a place in the ranks of followers. For there would be much work to be done in smiting the servants of the Great Beast to bring about the Eternal Kingdom. Here, his talents as a warrior might find a home, as long as his heart could gain the purity required from any soldier in the service of the Lord. Very soon, he was beginning to feel, his sins would be washed away and he'd achieve what he was sent for into this world, before a lifetime of wandering.

Such were his dreams. Ethelwulf noticed another westerner lying half-asleep about five yards[411] to his left but decided against making himself known. He was taking a risk being so close to the church of St. Mary the Minor[412] and the associated hospice for pilgrims to the Holy Sites. He knew the hospice had been entrusted to the Black Monks for many years. Perhaps the Benedictines led by Brother Theobald might re-appear and help him come to a decision – either to rejoin them or slink away into the shadows. However, in two days he recognised nobody and remained unsure what to do next: perhaps worship at the Church of the Holy Sepulchre and, by sharing in the worship of the Sacrifice at Calvary, go some way towards securing Divine forgiveness. Then it would be time to return to the West; but not back to the land of his birth where still Ethelred[413] ruled a realm increasingly threatened by Viking enemies.[414] However, Ethelwulf had heard that in Italy Pope and Emperor[415] were already working together to prepare for the return of their Saviour. Surely he could gain passage on an Italian vessel and so find employment for his sword. Yet first he had to get the means of serving penance for his many sins.

As he looked up he noticed a stranger staring at him from across the other side of the street. For a brief second their eyes met and Ethelred detected the glint of recognition in the other. The cloaked figure hurried away before Ethelred could even react. Jerusalem was filled with imperial spies, testing out any opportunities offered by the Fatimid regime.[416]Certainly, Ethelwulf was sure many surrounding the Autokrator would welcome celebrating the Millennium by recapturing the Holy City, lost to Christendom centuries before.[417]His service within the Varangian Guard had made his face well-known to those who were paid to remember such details. Ethelwulf knew he'd have little time to find refuge.

Somehow resisting the urge to run, Ethelwulf shuffled along to the Church of the Holy Sepulchre. He entered the building and turned right. His mind rejected the area to his left, universally recognised as the Centre of the World,[418] which was just what he didn't want; what he needed was obscurity, but that was an impossible treasure in the Holy City. Immediately he rejected the lure of Adam's skull,[419] hidden away beneath Golgotha itself. The small chapel there might be largely concealed, but it was too well-known, and, more importantly, there was no easy exit. Likewise the crack provoked by Christ's last moments of suffering[420] wouldn't serve as a hideaway. Although Ethelwulf might resort to the plea of sanctuary, he'd seen all too often the politically disgraced dragged from the most sacred spots to endure punishment authorised by their persecutors. Sanctity would not provide sanctuary.

So the fugitive passed on to where the mother of Constantine had found miraculously the True Cross,[421] again spurning any idea of going there because of its very popularity. He then turned towards the confusing maze of cells which made up the possessions of the Ethiopian Community. The area was obscure, and also confusing, with the distinct possibility of escape.

As Ethelwulf entered the first chapel he was challenged by an ascetic figure. "Why does a Frank enter the precincts entrusted to the heirs of St. Philip?"[422] asked the monk in simple but clear Greek, as he barred the armed figure intruding into his world.

"A sinner who seeks time to purge his soul but whose body is demanded by the enemies of God!" replied Ethelwulf in the same tongue, sure any servant of the Autokrator must already be in the grip of Satan.

"Why would an enemy of God seek to destroy a self-confessed sinner?" came the second question, but there was a twinkle in the eye which met Ethelwulf's steady gaze.

"Because they'd wish to deny the birthright of a child of Adam," answered the Saxon, detecting a flicker of sympathy in the countenance of his challenger. "Every child of sin has the chance of salvation through the Suffering undergone on this holiest of spots."

"Well answered, stranger," replied the monk. "I see you're in a hurry but, before you're given sanctuary, you must show trust by surrendering your sword." There was a pause as he noticed the hesitation in the Frankish face. "Remember, we serve the Prince of Peace here, and so would never sanction the shedding of blood." There followed a smile that demanded trust or nothing.

Ethelwulf handed over his weapon with a willingness which surprised himself and was hustled further into the depths of the Ethiopian Empire.

*

The Wanderer found the simple meal of lamb, pita-bread and water satisfying, if uninspiring. The solitude gave him plenty of time to think and the unadorned white-washed walls no distraction. The cell, in which he'd been ushered, belonged to the monk who'd introduced himself as Anastasius. No sooner had he seen the Saxon settled than he'd hurried off, leaving Ethelwulf alone in a light which rapidly disappeared as the sunlight sneaking through the small window began to fade. Just as there was still enough light to distinguish features the door was pushed open and a diminutive monk scurried in, gently placed the meal next to Ethelwulf and, with a nervous smile and a respectful jerk of his head, scurried out again. Ethelwulf sniffed nervously at the meat, remembering his imprisonment in Antioch.[423] He then dipped a finger into the bowl of water and sipped it dry. At last he was satisfied and, with an eagerness which surprised himself, gulped down the sparse meal.

He was really at a loss as to what to do. He had to stay in Jerusalem until the events of the Final Days began, certain he'd see the hosts of Gog and Magog.[424] Naturally, Ethelwulf, if taxed, would have been unable to identify their leader – perhaps it would be Caliph al-Hakim or, even better the malicious side of his character demanded, the Autokrator himself. Certainly, it'd have to be a ruler whose oppressions and tyrannies merited that terrible role. Whatever happened, there'd be a need for his weapon-skills and, with a soul purified by penitence in the Centre of the World, he could help defend *'the camp of the people of God and the city He loves.'*[425] However, for all that to happen he'd have to stay safe; locked up in some dungeon he could do nothing to help in this final purge of evil. He might be killed – and then he'd have to stand by and wait for judgment.[426] So, he'd somehow have to elude capture – and, for that, he'd have to convince the monks he merited liberty. As darkness cloaked his cell his mind began to sketch out a plan.

*

Anastasias returned early the next morning with news that held no surprises. Four strangers had been showing excessive interest in chapels in the Church of the Holy Sepulchre. They seemed especially interested in the darker niches. While one had tried to squeeze his way into the crack created during the crucifixion,[427] the others had been full of questions about any Franks in the church that day. It was a foolish question because such visitors could be numbered in tens, if not hundreds on special days. Yet, the interrogators, especially the two whose accents betrayed a Greek origin, persisted, describing a Frank so clearly a warrior he'd stand out from the crowd. Apparently there'd been reports of a stranger who'd slipped into Adam's Chapel and then passed on. Despite vigorous questions the trail had gone cold; it was clear the Greeks regretted the lack of official authority to prise open whatever secrets were being kept from them. In the end they'd given up and passed on towards the Jewish Quarter. For a moment Ethelwulf was to be left undisturbed, although he was certain that all too soon the men would return. To disappear completely was one thing, but to be seen and lost could never be forgiven among the Secret Agency of the Autokrator.

"So why do the Greeks persist in chasing a Frank - almost one of their own?" asked Anastasius, with a quiet smile breaking over his dusky features.

"I was a soldier," answered the Saxon. "one with no stomach to do certain things and to whom God showed the sinfulness of so much of this world - "

"And they pursue so fiercely for that?" queried the monk, searching the face of his guest. Whatever he saw there worried him, but not enough to accuse the Saxon of lying.

"No," answered Ethelwulf. "For some reason, the authorities decided my company were expendable - foreigners on whom blame could rest and punishment welcomed by the populace." He paused as he remembered the last battle in the Cilician Gates. "For that they handed us over to the heathen!"

"So, why are you here?" asked the monk. "Why, when you were betrayed, did you manage to escape?"

"Because the infinite, and unknowable, mercy of Our Lord spared me from the slaughter of friends, family and followers, " snapped Ethelwulf and then, seeing the shock his vehemence had caused. "Who knows why God allowed me punish those who betrayed my men and yet allowed me to survive?"

"God knows, stranger," replied the monk. "Even now He is looking into your heart, weighing your words and balancing past and future in His judgement of your soul -"

"Which terrifies me, brother," interrupted Ethelwulf. "For I've been a wanderer, cast out into the world like Cain, but without such cause. For years I've wandered through this dying world, searching for peace which could never come. Until Satan - "

"Who is ever-ready to catch a burdened soul such as yours, stranger," responded Anastasius. "But remember the Dark One can only steal into where the foolish or wicked allow him entry - "

"As the Autokrator's service did permit," replied the Saxon. "You cannot imagine what I've seen done - and myself performed, to my eternal shame - in the name of the Beast that sits in Miklagard - "

"So you see the Autokrator as the creature foretold by St John,"[428] whispered the monk, almost to himself. "Then, indeed, it's no surprise his agents pursue you with such energy!"

"Not that I'm an instrument of the Lord," answered Ethelwulf. "At least, not yet! For I desire to purge my soul of the sins of serving such a regime and to serve the Lord when he comes again!"

"Which so many, rightly or wrongly, see happening within a year," added the monk to himself. Forgetting the Saxon his face was seized by signs of personal pain, a strange blend of longing and fear which alarmed Ethelwulf. Although he believed he could trust the monk, and already had surrendered his safety to him, Ethelwulf had come to fear men whose souls were in torment. Never could one be certain of their actions because not even they knew how their souls commanded their decisions. He waited for the monk to bring his face under control and change the mood of their dialogue.

"Still, we, the community, have concealed you and risked punishment." He noticed the protest about to be voiced by the stranger. "Although this city is imprisoned within the grip of Satan's followers, the Autokrator's influence can easily travel as far as Cairo. Favours can be exchanged and communities blotted out, almost at the whim of those who enjoy earthly power."

"So I must thank you for your hospitality," conceded the Saxon, "and pass on before I put your community in further danger - "

"Did I say you should leave these walls?" answered the monk roughly. "Would our Lord want us to cast out the persecuted to the terrors of the world?" He paused as Ethelwulf hesitated to protest. "No, you've given us your trust and we'll not betray it. The Millenium is fast approaching when whatever will be will come into existence. Wait here, in safety, until the New Year ushers in such changes -

then you may leave when mankind is so filled with the consequences that no eye or ear will have time for the movements of one refugee."

"So, I may stay here, praying for the release of my soul from sin?" asked Ethelwulf, thankful the monk seemed to lack the fanaticism of so many as the Millenium approached.

"Yes, stranger," confirmed the monk. "We'll shelter you so that, if the Lord requires, your sword can help in the final overthrow of the Enemy of mankind."

With that, he made a quick sign of the cross and retreated before Ethelwulf could say a word. As the door closed the Saxon waited for the turning of the key which would show that once again he was a prisoner. It never came.

*

Two days later Anastasius returned - and this time with no smile on lips. A frown of concern dominated his brow as he explained the problem to Ethelwulf.

"Whoever you are seems to be of great concern to somebody." He paused, awaiting some trickle of information to be released from the fugitive. Ethelwulf glared fixedly at the scratching he'd made in the dust; he was trying to remember the outline of his home at Arne but found that twenty years of wandering had almost erased the design from his memory. It was a nasty reminder that either he was getting old or he'd become so alienated from the scenes of his youth he could no longer recall them. He could still see his mother's face, long before she'd been butchered by Haakon Skaathi as he'd abandoned England.

"Have you heard what I just said, my son," persisted the monk, likely touching the shoulder of Ethelwulf to bring him back to reality. The Saxon looked up and there was a weariness bordering on despair in his eyes which alarmed Anastasius. This was further cause for concern. To be shielding a refugee from such powerful forces within Jerusalem was one thing, should that fugitive then commit the most terrible act of self-murder was another. He decided to repeat his words.

"I was saying that someone very powerful is clearly hunting for you." This time there was a slight frown on the handsome features, caused by puzzlement not quite falling into bewilderment.

"Are you telling me you are a fugitive ONLY from the Autokrator?"

Ethelwulf almost smiled at the use of the word 'ONLY'. Certainly in his own estimation, and probably in that of most men, the Autokrator was the most powerful man on earth. To be hunted by imperial forces would be enough to occupy any man. However, he could see no reason why the hunt should be so intense in a city outside the immediate grip of the Autokrator. Given he was still alive (and that shouldn't have been assumed) he must either have gone east, into the realm of Al Qadir,[429] master of Baghdad, or else travelled south into the territories controlled by Al Hakim. He was certain both logic and reported sightings had directed the Imperial gaze towards the south. Even so he found it hard to understand the interest being taken in him.

"Yes, Father," mumbled the Saxon. "I escaped from his clutches and slipped over the border." His voice became stronger as he added, "I can assure you I might easily have sought a vessel to carry me westwards, back to the land of my people." Here he moistened his lips - and his hearer was unsure as to whether this was due to nervousness. "However, overcome - burdened - by the realization that I was filled with sin, and the End of the World was almost upon us, I decided instead to travel to the Holy City so that I might be here to welcome Our Saviour on His return and gain forgiveness." Here he dropped his head.

Brother Anastasius felt moved to place his hand lightly on the bowed head of the fugitive, impelled by the desire to give some small taste of the forgiveness to come. Beneath his hand Ethelwulf questioned what he'd just said. Did he really believe in the imminent Second Coming? He was not sure. The ravings of Epaphroditus, with his certainty that the Autokrator, the living image of the Beast, should by dying herald the End of the World, had made him turn against the belief he'd encountered in so many different places during his travels. However, since wandering in the Holy Land, perhaps affected by the death of his wife, he wasn't so sure the final hours were not almost upon them. Perhaps it was a bottomless will to end it all, rid himself of a life meaningless with the deaths of so many and the loss of whatever he'd come to value. So why had he not simply killed himself? Pride? Fear of the Final Judgement preached in his youth against self-destruction? He was sure, however, his offences had been committed against the imperial regime and none other.

"All we know, my son, is that, even though the four searchers have been withdrawn from our precincts, at least half-a-dozen remain on the outside, watching, waiting for someone or something that remains inside - and that can only be you!"

Anastasius withdrew his hand and Ethelwulf raised his eyes and stared into the face of the monk.

"Can you be sure, Father, that such men are indeed waiting for - "

"Believe me, stranger, we who spend our entire lives in the service of Our Lord in this holiest of places know when our surroundings have changed." He paused, as if a sudden thought had struck him. "Of course, we know the hopes and fears of many have changed the pattern of behaviour outside in the streets and alleys of the city itself. We've counted the hundreds of new faces - pilgrims and old sinners - who shuffle intro these chapels every day, perhaps half-hoping Christ will return at the very moment they kneel in here at prayer, perhaps merely praying that somehow God will recognise them more clearly as His own." Anastasius half-turned away from the fugitive, as if unwilling to force him to open up his soul. "We know these men are different. They make no attempt to cross into our precincts - indeed we're certain they're among those who spurn Our Lord as the Son of God - but they search the faces of all who come out of our church, never the faces of those who go in!"

"You're most observant of the ways of men, Father."

"No, my son. Even a blind man would smell them as different!"

Ethelwulf started to ease himself to his feet, certain that, without saying anything, the monk was really asking him to leave.

"So, my Father, I must leave the sanctuary of your church - "

"And how can you expect to slip past such vigilance?"

"At night, when tired eyes sleep and men grow careless."

"Perhaps, if those eyes stay the same!" snapped the monk, but then instantly regretted the vehemence of his reply. "I failed to tell you these six men are replaced by four more when the last muezzin calls into the sky." He smiled as he noted the defeated look which flickered across the face of the fugitive.

"Could I be concealed in - "

"Everything capable of concealing a man is examined by these men."

"For what purpose?"

"Because they say they fear the growing tensions within the city among us believers," and here Anastasius had to smile in spite of the serious nature of the charge, "and they think some troublemakers have duped us into concealing weapons among our chapels - "

"But - "

"Yes, I know it's ridiculous," countered the monk. "But when you have power you've no need to fear the mockery of those who feel that power. You do not - "

"Yes, I well know how power gives stupidity armour and vicious blindness a terrifying edge!" declared Ethelwulf, remembering especially the dictates of the ministers surrounding the Autokrator, prepared to waste treasure and lives in pursuit of what had become already a sated passion.

"I can see that, as a sharer in the sins of the world, you know all too well how wickedness can march alongside ignorance, smashing down the doors of Love and Truth -"

"Which, as a man of God, you hold are what is vital for the preservation of the human soul?"

"Indeed, my son," smiled the monk. "I don't see how we can let you run out again among such wolves."

"But I can't stay here hidden away from the world," protested Ethelwulf, but immediately recognised that was his only option. Anastasius sensed the fugitive's resignation and said nothing. For a moment there was silence as both men realised there could be no change in conditions, at least for the foreseeable future.

"May Our Lord watch over you, my son," said the monk at last. "I'll see food is brought to you on the condition you keep yourself hidden from any strangers to our church. I myself will visit you when I can because I can see you're a soul in turmoil and it is my spiritual duty to offer comfort and reconciliation to Our Lord in what may be the last days of this world. In the meantime is there anything else I can send you?"

Ethelwulf thought for a long moment and then suddenly asked for reading and writing materials, although adding such materials must be in the Latin script. Anastasius promised he'd receive whatever materials he could, as long as he could obtain them without arousing outside suspicion (which, in his heart, he thought would be more than likely). He knew at least two monks who were entirely trustworthy and they'd become Ethelwulf's link to the outside world. Once again he described exactly where Ethelwulf could roam and where he should stay away from. All the Wanderer could do was humbly accept the conditions and mumble his thanks.

The weeks of Ethelwulf's exclusion from the world had begun.

*

It was amazing how few texts in the script of the Franks the Ethiopian monks could get their hands on. A copy of *'De Divisione Naturae'* by John Scotus Eriguena[430] proved to be the first to arrive - and the first to go because Ethelwulf was unable to get past the first two hundred lines because of a complete inability to master any of the basic principles outlined in the work. The next offering, the *'Bechbretha'*,[431] got almost as short a shift as, firstly, its Irish origins awakened unwelcome memories and, secondly, its rather restricted subject-matter soon made him realise how much he needed sleep.

The next text delivered by the patient monks proved far more acceptable. It was the "*De corpore et sanguine Domini*" by Gerbert and, at the first reading, Ethelwulf's mind was transported back to Dorset and his meeting with the author itself. After reading it once the fugitive had started on a second reading when he was interrupted by the delivery of Einhard's *'Vita Caroli'*.[432]

The life-story of the greatest man produced in Western Europe in the last three centuries - and Ethelwulf had to put England's own Alfred in second place - marked the eclipse of dear old Gerbert.[433] The ease with which the Franks had worsted the attack by the Danes made Ethelwulf consider how much had changed. Now the subjects of Hugh Capet,[434] and even those of Emperor Otto,[435] trembled when they heard Vikings had landed in their country. Ethelwulf felt disappointed the Franks hadn't marched then against the regimes installed at Miklagard and so prevented the Autokrator ever getting his hands on power. He had to laugh aloud as he realised how much the writings of a long-dead monk were able to get under his skin and awake unwelcome memories. So when Nicephorus scurried in with a copy of *'De Bello Civili'* [436]Ethelwulf abandoned Einhard halfway through the fourth reading.

Julius Caesar[437] completely won over the Saxon and almost immediately he was requesting, rather demanding, a copy of *'De Bello Galliico'*, but without success. Soon he accepted his hosts were supplying him with everything they could. Then he turned to his own shortcomings and decided he should take up the study of the Greek script. In the service of the Autokrator he'd shunned such alien text, being content to surrender any such documents to his cousin, Morkere, for translation. With that he burst into tears.

Anastasius suddenly appeared out of the darkness and sat down next to the fugitive to comfort him.

"If you wish, my son," he said gently, "you could tell me whatever shadows obscure the depths of your soul, shutting out the light that, especially in this holiest of places, Our Lord would wish to bring."

Ethelwulf looked into the dark brown eyes of the monk and saw a compassion so long absent from his life. Again the tears threatened to flow but he gulped them back.

"Yes, Father," he whispered, "I think it's time I released whatever is holding me back from Our Lord."

"Indeed, my son," answered Anastasius. "I'll become to you a Soul-Father as is the practice of our Church - hearing all, bearing all and saying nothing."

All Ethelwulf could do was hang his head, not knowing where to start and yet feeling an urge inside to release the flood which had been poisoning him for so long.

"Before we start, my son," continued the monk, " I should tell you that to us there are five commandments which have greater authority than any others." He paused and stretched out his legs, being aware that whatever he was about to start would take a very long time. "Perhaps they might serve as a key to whatever locks are shutting away your soul from Our Lord." Ethelwulf merely nodded, letting the words wash over him. Anastasius felt that, if he wasn't careful, whatever he said might well simply pass through the system of the warrior without having any effect. "So, my son," he said, " I'll tell you each commandment and you can tell me which is the one which most affects your soul."

Ethelwulf closed his eyes, resting his head against the wall. For the first time in several years he felt comfortable, almost at peace, as the monk began.

*

It was the fourth commandment which really opened up Ethelwulf. "Love your enemies, do good to those who hate you, bless those who curse you."

"No!" snapped Ethelwulf. "That I can never do!" His eyes sprang open and some muscles tried to raise his body but were overcome by a general inertia. "I was an innocent youth, dreaming of a life of peace when butchers who'd killed my King went on to slaughter my mother."

"For which they'll doubtlessly be burning in the fires of hell, even before the Final Judgement when Our Lord returns," stated the monk, placing his fingers lightly on the muscles of Ethelwulf's left arm, aware he lacked any ability to still the passion but confident that forces within the fugitive would do all that. "It is God who judges, not us." He paused. "Did you seek peace with the killers?"

"Never!" growled Ethelwulf. "That would have betrayed all I believed. To even approach such creatures would be like making peace with the wolf - "

"As is the destiny of us men," smiled the monk. "In these Last Days Our Lord would lead us into companionship with the fiercest of creatures so that all can inherit the riches of this earth."

"But I was young - "

"And foolish, as God well knows," said the monk. "Had you but turned to him then, in prayer, he'd have showed you the way - "

"Into a cloister, perhaps," sneered Ethelwulf. He faced Anastasius and there was almost a fury in eyes. "Far away from my home, shutting out the tears of deserted mother and wails of abandoned peasants!"

"You couldn't be expected to fight the whole world, my son," answered the monk. "Our Lord would have given you strength - "

"So that evil would triumph, gloating - "

"For but a little while, my son," answered Anastasius, "until death ushered them down into eternal pain."

"Ordered by a loving God?" queried the Saxon.

"Yes, my son," countered the monk," but by One who is Just!"

*

So the debate continued well into the night. The next day Anastasius returned both intrigued and alarmed at the memories pouring out from the tormented soul. As he listened the monk was transported into a completely alien world. Almost all his life he'd spent in either the Egypt of the Fatimids or the Holy Land itself. He'd believed he knew whatever wickedness could stalk this world, dragging down men and ruining both innocent and sinful alike. However, as he listened to the tales of Irish carnage, Icelandic witchery or the savagery of the Wendish forests he realised that what he'd taken to be the blackest of evils was merely of a greyish hue. Naturally, he attempted to shrug off such horrors by telling himself that the northern world was one governed by pagans, where monsters bred in the minds of man became gods, or perhaps they really were the creation of the Evil One. Yet even as he tried to shrug off the inhumanity of the men haunting the memories of his charge, he had to admit that indeed they were men - or women - no different from those with whom he had dealings every day, or even himself. That was possibly the ultimate horror, the twisted image of himself in any of the monsters described by Ethelwulf.

By the third day, the fugitive had passed on to the realm of the Autokrator. Here, Anastasius admitted, whatever evil had been done, had been committed by those claiming be followers of the Lamb of God. There might be the excuse of ignorance for the soul of Bluetooth but there was none for the evil of the Eparchos.

As the debate continued, not so much between the monk and the fugitive, but between the ensnared soul of the stranger and the small light for guidance implanted by the Lord in that same man's mind, Anastasius noted how calmer the fugitive became. Not a calmness of resignation or despair, but the peace which came with the surety of forgiveness even for himself. Smiles and laughter might still be absent but tears were also vanishing. The poison was gradually being lanced out of a wounded soul.

At last it was finished and both men faced with the problem with what to do with a re-invigorated warrior, no longer filled with hatred but inspired by the determination to play his part for God in the Last Days which were fast approaching.

*

Ethelwulf had taken to skulking about on the edges of the territory controlled by his hosts. Partly this came from the restless urge to participate in whatever was going to happen in the coming months, partly because even the writings of Julius Caesar start to pale after a time. Anastasius had at first been unenthusiastic about this change of habits because the watchers outside had shown no sign of tiring. Ethelwulf hoped some other Frankish stranger, perhaps in one of the Mediterranean ports, would have been mistaken for him and so taken off the pressure. He'd considered disguise but rejected it immediately because both height and build ruled out any such conceit - except for the more obvious types such as a monk which would immediately invite suspicion.

So he'd settled into the routine of patrolling the boundaries of what he'd come to see as (partly) his domain, peering out at the pilgrims, vendors and the general comers and goers in the Holy Sepulchre complex. Obscured by shadow, and the discouraging surroundings of decay, Ethelwulf could look out at a humanity completely unaware of his existence. He was pleased the watchers exercised the good grace of staying at some distance from the precincts of the Ethiopian quarters. But then he remembered they couldn't know he was concealed among the cloisters, chapels and corridors which made up this section. Indeed, they couldn't be certain he was anywhere near the Holy Sepulchre itself; it was just there'd been no sighting of any Frank matching his description anywhere else. Again the persistence of the watchers caused him concern. How had the long arm of the Autokrator managed to reach so far? Also he was perplexed as to why the Autokrator hadn't turned his gaze elsewhere, unless it was simply hurt pride when such a prominent prisoner had escaped after murdering two officials of the regime.

One day while gazing out at the stream of strangers drifting into the chapels of the Holy Sepulchre he suddenly opened his mouth in surprise, just in time smothering a cry. He was certain among the crowd was his cousin, Morkere. Furiously his eyes searched the crowd a second time, frantically looking for the black hair and tall build of the man he believed to have been killed at the Cilician gates. There he was again, the man in the dark blue cloak. Ethelwulf screwed up his eyes, willing the stranger to turn around and reveal his features but the stranger appeared immersed in a statuette over in the Coptic area. Without removing his stare, Ethelwulf's mind frantically searched for a place from which he could secure a better view of the stranger. Of course, he could always slip out through one of the tiny openings cut into the fabric of the walls and approach the man - but that would be far too dangerous. So he had to resort to willing the man to turn around, exchanging the blue-cloaked shoulders for a clearer view of his features. At last the stranger obliged and he turned to stare almost straight back at Ethelwulf. Had he been aware of such concentrated interest on his person? Certainly anyone could have moments when they felt themselves under scrutiny, but Ethelwulf doubted the stranger could so pinpoint the source of that interest. For, alas, stranger indeed the man appeared to be. His features were adorned by a grey-streaked beard which would never have been assumed by Morkere. Ethelwulf recalled the teasing his cousin had suffered over the previous twenty years because of his reluctance to grow a beard. Poor Edwine, killed by Pechenegs years before, had almost eagerly taken to a beard, perhaps the more easily to mark him off from his twin. Morkere, however, alone had persisted in shaving his face regularly, despite the occasional problems of cuts and soreness; one day he'd confessed it was mainly for fear of losing his youth. This had produced such a hail of laughter from those overhearing this confession - which had danced up and down the gunwales as they rowed in the Gulf of Bothnia - that he'd never again been so revealing.

So Ethelwulf was certain this man was not his dead-cousin brought back to life, but he was also sure the man was not a total stranger. Furiously his memory went through the hundreds, thousands of images of men he'd had known over the previous twenty years; and all the time the man continued to stare in his direction, as if to give Ethelwulf's memory the best chance of making a match.

At last it came. Ethelwulf was sure the man was Sweyn Haraldsson, a distant cousin, last seen in Aldeigjuborg. As he and the man seemed to exchange stares, with a strange abandon of any feeling of immediacy, Ethelwulf's memory traced out the exact connection between them. He remembered Sweyn's father's cousin had married the cousin of Ethelwulf's (and Morkere's) grandfather! Quite an obscure link but one substantiated on the shores of Lake Ladoga when their physical resemblance had caused Morkere and Sweyn to exchange family histories.

Ethelwulf heard a slight sound behind him and turning quickly, saw Brother Thomas giving him a strange look.

"I speak you, " he said, in his limited Greek "but you not here."

"I'm sorry, Brother Thomas," apologized Ethelwulf. "I see my cousin - out there!"

He summoned the wizened monk to the chink in the wall which acted as a window on to the wider world and, in whispers, pointed out Sweyn Haraldsson.

"Please, bring cousin to me!" he urged. "But, quietly!"

There was hesitation in the eyes of Brother Thomas. He wasn't sure whether he should let this Frank have any contact with the outside world, but then he hadn't been barred from bringing any member of that outside world into the precincts of the Ethiopian community. Everyone knew every hour the Frank spent huddled up within their boundaries was an hour of danger for the community. No one knew why the Frank was being so remorselessly hunted, but all were sure he'd made some powerful enemies in the outside world, men who could mark down their community and destroy it. Should he allow any contact with the outside world which might endanger his community? Should he try to bring about an end to this state of tension which had existed for weeks?

Brother Thomas decided to help the Frank meet the stranger whose attention had now reverted to the icons of the Copts to their own community. Reluctantly the monk agreed to signal there was someone who wished to meet with the Frank in less public circumstances. Ethelwulf wondered how Brother Thomas, with his limited Greek, would ever manage to convey such an idea - and then smiled inwardly at the thought that Sweyn Haraldsson had acquired ANY knowledge of Greek.

*

Ethelwulf waited anxiously in the shadows next to the triptych showing the ascent of Christ into heaven, the conversion of Saul on the road to Damascus, and the meeting of Philip the Deacon with the Ethiopian eunuch.[438] At last Brother Thomas scurried in, closely followed by the stranger, his hand firmly fixed on his sword and alert to any sign of danger.

"Sweyn Haraldsson, why are you so alarmed?"

Sweyn turned towards the shadows from where the question had come but his eyes failed to penetrate the gloom. He took one step towards that area of darkness, his grip still on the hilt of his sword. There was a chuckle from the gloom and the voice spoke again.

"I note, Sweyn, you've lost none of that wariness with which you approached the Finns when they attacked by Lake Ladoga."

Sweyn's grip loosened from his sword and he took another step towards the shadows.

"Is that Ethelwulf hiding himself away in the shadows?" He laughed but the sound that emerged was too tense to possess any degree of pleasure. "Have you taken to skulking away in churches now?"

Ethelwulf stepped out from he shadows, his hands stretched out in welcome.

"Unfortunately, my cousin, events have driven me to these most desperate measures." As Sweyn advanced to meet him Ethelwulf gestured to the shadows. "I'm afraid I'm forced to shelter within darkness because of the enmity of man." He paused, extending his arm even further. "Come join me, cousin, so we can talk without fear of interruption."

With that he turned his back on the Varangian and stepped back into the shadows. Without hesitation Sweyn slipped after him, immediately being forced to duck in order to penetrate a small hole which existed to the left of the triptych.

*

Sweyn knew little of the adventures of Ethelwulf since they'd parted on the shores of Lake Ladoga, with Sweyn leading a party of traders to the west as Ethelwulf was preparing to set out on the slave-hunting expedition.[439] Ethelwulf had heard Sweyn had migrated to the easier life-style of Bornholm, but there the knowledge had dried up. For his part Sweyn had heard how Ethelwulf had found service with the Prince of Kenugard but then even that rumour had become so distorted he'd dismissed any such tale from the east as a mere travesty of whatever was going on. It was Ethelwulf who first, with an excitement that surprised him, described all that had happened since. Sweyn frowned at the death of Edwine among the marshes of the Kuban, horrified at the barbarities of the Pechenegs, of whom he'd heard very little. However, the frown was transformed into anger as the tale had moved on to the adventures in the land of the Greeks. Even when Ethelwulf described successful campaigns on behalf of the Autokrator, Sweyn was disgusted by the meagreness of official rewards handed out to the Varangians. The riches boasted by those Varangians who'd managed to come westwards must have been gained privately, if not illegally. Although the Varangians were valued by the Greeks they weren't yet prized sufficiently to fill their helmets with silver! When Ethelwulf came to the final treachery of the Eparchos and the destruction of so many good fighters at the Cilician Gates Sweyn cried out in horror, and had to be reminded by his cousin that sound carried too easily in these buildings and voices should be kept to a minimum. Above all, Sweyn mourned the death of Morkere, remembering how their physical likeness had first established their connection. He was pleased to hear of the survival of Gunnar, although sure the Gall-Gael would be unable to stay long in Greek service due both to his ignorance of their language and his wild temper. Finally, he was sympathetic with Ethelwulf's loss of wife and child - as well as being intrigued as to why he was still being pursued in the Centre of the World.

However, Sweyn's tale also had much to recommend it. After leaving Finland he'd passed on to Bornholm but found it little recovered from the depredations of Olaf Trygvasson two years before. So he continued westwards but found King Sven so bound up with the Jomsvikings, after old King Harald's death, that he'd little use for new swords. So Sweyn turned eastwards, joining up with Jarl Haakon[440] from Norway in a gigantic attack on Gotland.[441]

"But in the midst of plenty I wasn't happy for I could see the Jarl had the air of a doomed man about him, even though it appeared his schemes triumphed," commented Sweyn, using the tool of hindsight to justify desertion from the forces of the Norwegian ruler.

He'd then heard the young Viking, Olaf Trygvasson[442] was collecting forces to amass treasure. Rumour said it was to be used to seize his ancestral throne back from the usurper, Jarl Harald.[443]

"I didn't know whether the tale was true or not. All I knew was that Jarl Harald looked as if Urd[444] herself had cast the runes and found his fortunes wanting," explained the Viking. "However, when I saw Olaf Trygvasson I knew the Norns themselves had combined in this man to lead him to victory."

So Sweyn had followed the young Olaf when he'd joined the forces of Jostein and Guthmund in a violent attack on Folkestone.[445] Here Sweyn judged it best to pause before he embarked on the story of the depredations suffered by the native land of Ethelwulf. However, there was no reaction. Even a dozen years before there'd been surprisingly no interest above what any Viking adored, to hear of brave deeds and great rewards. Prolonged stay in the Empire had sapped any feeling Ethelwulf might have had for a land controlled by an enemy whose harassment was responsible for his exile.[446] After a check Sweyn continued with his tale.

"We found the land very rich, fattened by years of peace beyond any deserving, for its rulers had grown soft." He paused, holding up his hand to check himself before he could be accused of misjudgement. "No, there was one leader worthy of the halls of Valhalla and his men with him -"

"Byrhtnoth?" suggested Ethelwulf, having heard of the gallant fight of the earl of Essex at Maldon[447] which had been carried even as far as Miklagard.

"Yes," smiled Sweyn. "If England had been defended by more warriors like him we'd never have gained so much plunder." He paused and the smile broadened. "If honour hadn't forced the earl to allow our men safely across the waters so that we could fight on equal terms, we'd never have won - "

"But I heard," interposed Ethelwulf, "it was the desertion of the sons of Odda, leading away men who could still have worsted the raiders, which caused the defeat - "

"Not so, cousin," stated Sweyn. "Before that took place Byrhtnoth himself had been killed and the battle lost. - "

"But his men fought on - "

"Yes, they fought until they'd joined their lord in death,"[448] said Sweyn in a quiet voice. "It was a gallant gesture, and one which will keep their fight alive in the memory of man for ever, but it was without value."

"It showed what Saxons could do," protested Ethelwulf.

"So more the pity their king didn't learn from it," sneered Sweyn, "because he paid us much silver to go away and leave his land in peace."[449] He laughed. "But next year we were back again, for where you've found silver once you look for it again." The laughter died as he remembered how they'd been almost trapped in the Thames estuary but only escaped with the connivance of the earl Aelfric.[450] "But that time the king tried to trap us we slipped away in the fog, not happy for being cheated of our silver." There was a pause and then Sweyn continued, "Next year, we weren't so easily caught for we destroyed the English fleet under Frythegyst in the river you call the Humber."[451]

Sweyn looked askance at the fugitive. He was surprised there seemed so little feeling for the sufferings of the English. Now, looking back on the raids of his youth he regretted the misery inflicted on the English people. Their king didn't appear to have suffered; certainly his court, as he'd witnessed at his baptism, was filled with riches. He knew the king's agent had simply introduced a new tax on the people to pay off Viking attacks, not caring that one payment must encourage further demands.

"In the next year[452] again I joined Olaf Trygvasson, with over ninety ships, and we attacked London itself because the English king's capital couldn't be reached. We'd hoped the citizens of such a rich town would pay us to go away directly we appeared but, much to our surprise, they fought so hard we couldn't break into their town. But the king sent envoys, offering us money if we went away; this time they promised us yet more silver if we suffered drenching in water in the name of the Christ-god.[453] We found this amusing and willingly accepted for we believed that in the next year we could return and be drenched again and get even more silver."

Ethelwulf remembered how among the Rus he'd seen similar practices. Men would be baptised and receive gifts welcoming their entry into the Christian communion; the next year they'd return demanding both a second baptism and more gifts. Some considered baptism a good luck charm; if, of course, bad luck followed they'd probably not survive but would be taken to Valhalla.

"Olaf seemed to change from that point, taking more seriously the prayers of the priests.[454] He started to force more of his men to assume the practices of the Christians, even though it was obvious their God didn't protect them from our axes."

"Because it's not His purpose," interrupted Ethelwulf.

"So I've come to believe," conceded Sweyn. "I took the water at the same time as Olaf at what you call Andover. But to me it was just a means of getting more silver so, at first, I was amused at Olaf's attempts to win more converts to his faith. After all, I was a 'Christian' already - and had nothing to fear from his bullying. Then, however, I grew irritated at seeing good warriors drift away rather than put up with the whining of those priests."

Sweyn frowned as he recalled how he too had chosen to drift away rather than face the fury of Olaf Trygvasson when he wished to continue the raids on England.

"Anyway I left and only once again troubled your native land, in the far west." He paused and a strange sadness came over his face as he remembered going further westwards to fight for King Sihtric of Dublin. "Then we journeyed into Ireland but were beaten there by both their High kings - "

"Both their High Kings?"[455] interrupted Ethelwulf who had a too vivid memory of Irish politics. "The Irish cannot have two High Kings!"

"Well, my doubtful cousin," answered Sweyn. "let me tell you that Brian Boru of Munster and Mael Sechlainn met together and agreed each should be High King in whichever part of that land they ruled." He paused before adding, "At the same time Mael Sechlainn got rid of that harridan, Gormflath, he'd taken to wife - "

He saw Ethelwulf stiffen,[456] not realizing his cousin had enjoyed fifteen years before a relationship with that Queen which had caused him to be forced out of Ireland. Then seeing Ethelwulf relax, Sweyn continued, "but she rushed off to her son, Sihtric of Dublin, and persuaded him into rebellion.[457] Like a fool I was one of his followers when we were destroyed and I learned the Christ-god can give power to the arms of his followers." Ethelwulf smiled at that, recalling how priests surrounding the Autokrator had prayed for the triumph of his arms, confident that imperial might rested on the support of the Almighty. "Perhaps the king of the English is no true follower of the Christ-god, however many priests he has, - "

"Or perhaps he doesn't truly place his trust in the strength of Our Lord?" suggested Ethelwulf.

"Anyway," shrugged off Sweyn, "that day I learned of the power of the Christ-god and I was pleased I'd been baptised." He smiled, "But then I remembered all the sins I'd committed since that rite and so I was sprinkled with water again - this time by an Irish priest in whom I had more trust. I came to believe in Christ and lessened my worship of Thor."

He looked down at his feet as he carried on. "Filled with remorse at my desertion I hurried to find Olaf Trygvasson, now king of Norway, begging him to take me back because now I'd come to believe in the power of his god." His eyes moistened as he said quietly, "And he wasn't quite the fierce warrior he had been, forcing men to yield to his beliefs or die. Instead he received me back and I became part of his army. For he'd great need of warriors, even if he believed his god would protect him. Together we sailed down towards Wendland where we made a treaty with its king. However, on our return we were ambushed at Hjorungavang[458] by King Sven of Denmark, Jarl Eirek (the son of Jarl Haakon) and the King of the Swedes. Worst of all, however, was Sigvald, chief of the Jomsvikings,[459] for he pretended to be our friend and led us like lambs to the slaughter."

He placed his hand lightly on that of Ethelwulf as if to convey the misery of the climax of his tale.

"My king was in the greatest longship in the world, the 'Long Serpent', while I was in the 'Crane'. Even before we knew the enemy were there, they were upon us. We fought like heroes but were outnumbered. I've been told my king fought like two men but, seeing that not even his might could prevail, he preferred death to capture and leapt overboard."

"What?" whispered Ethelwulf, unable to believe any great Viking would risk eternal damnation in both Christian and pagan hereafter by committing suicide.

"Certainly he still wore his coat of mail and had been wounded," confessed Sweyn. "But he was a strong swimmer so who knows." He paused before giving the final epitaph. "He's never been seen again although there are many in his land who wait for him."

"So what happened to you?" asked Ethelwulf, wondering how Sweyn Haraldsson had survived defeat by King Sweyn. He recalled the coldness of the eyes at Hedeby fifteen years before.

"Seeing the 'Crane' was about to be taken I stripped off my mail-shirt and plunged over the side." He tried a morose smile as he added, "You see, unlike my king, I didn't have such trust in the Christ-god but relied on the strength of my arms." He paused. "Somehow I made it to the shore and soon reached my home. However, I felt the Christ-god had shown me the depths of the sins which would drag me down to hell - and I saw no hope for me in the new Norway of Jarl Eirek - so I determined to come south to the Centre of the World before the End should come." He took a confident look around the Church of the Holy Sepulchre. "As you can see I've just made it in time!"

"You've certainly made it in time to help me," stated Ethelwulf instantly realizing this could be his one chance of getting away from the Ethiopian community. He needed the cooperation of Anastasius, if only for the return of his sword. Sweyn could play his part by creating a suitable diversion. Furiously he started to explain his plans to his cousin and was delighted at how Sweyn fell into line. It didn't take long to cobble together a scheme which appeared to offer a chance of success.

*

Ahmed almost jumped when he heard the raucous singing from his left. He'd been so intently watching the exits from the infidel church he'd almost gone asleep to anything else in his surroundings. He looked across at Feisal and saw the little man was already scurrying in his direction, under his arm the small basket of figs and flask of water which was all the bankrupt trader from Aleppo seemed to require during the day. They'd become friends right from the first day two moons ago; both of them were failed businessmen who welcomed the chance to find such easy employment while relatives back home tried to sort out the financial mess which had undermined their income. It had seemed simple at the time; they received a fairly good description of a Frank and were sent south. Once there they were told the man had been spotted slinking around by the infidel church. They'd been positioned carefully, given strict instructions and told to report if such a man ever came out of the complex of buildings. If he did they were to report to the Muhtasib[460] and follow the infidel wherever he went. However, nobody answering such a description had ever showed his face and Ahmed was now certain the information delivered by the ghilmān[461] Omar had been wrong. He'd never liked the man whose very effeminacy made him suspect Omar had not been given authority over them on account of his intelligence. It was even more suspicious the original information had come from a discharged member of the infidel army of al Rūm.[462] He wasn't sure why the man was being hunted. He only knew Amir Haroun ibn Nasr, master of Aleppo, was paying.

"What's happening?" asked the little tailor from Aleppo, as usual expecting Ahmed to exercise some kind of sixth sense and tell him things beyond human comprehension. Without answering Ahmed turned his head and noted the arrogant Mustafa ibn Mahmud with his hanger-on, Suleiman, were also hurrying in his direction. He realised that, given any encouragement, Mustafa would start giving orders as if he had the responsibility instead of himself. The young man was too greedy for power, forgetting he was but a mutaṭawwi ah[463] and it was Ahmed who'd been given the honorary position of Arif.[464] So he was determined to make a decision before the arrival of Mustafa brought a challenge to his authority.

"Why are you here, Feisal, and not at your post?" he snapped, once again looking over the little man's shoulder for the source of the disturbance.

Feisal shrugged his shoulders and simply pointed. "Look, Ahmed! Look!" he craned his neck as if giving instructions in the art of observation. "See people are running, knocking over the tables of traders and pushing old men out of their way!"

"Yes, I can see that, Feisal," snarled Ahmed. Really Feisal was a silly little man and he wondered why he was being used. "But why are they running this way?"

"I can hear infidels singing, Ahmed," replied Feisal, again stating the obvious. "Perhaps they've drunk too much wine and are looking for some peasants to terrify!" The little man shook in anticipation and Ahmed knew such fears weren't groundless. Sometimes the infidels grouped together, drinking so much wine they could scarcely stand. Then they'd link arms and charge through the narrow streets of Jerusalem, shouting what he was sure were obscenities or singing raucously in their infidel babble.

Ahmed made a decision. With so many people scurrying about it'd be impossible to continue in their position. They should retire down a nearby alley, wait for both the crowd and the drunken infidels to pass by and then return to their watch. He'd worked this out before Mustafa and Suleiman arrived, out of breath and clearly alarmed. Ahmed issued his orders and was pleased to note Mustafa, although actually opening his mouth to protest, rapidly shut it again when Ahmed raised a questioning eye-brow in his direction. All four agents quickly made their way into an alley, pushing aside a couple of infidel pilgrims already sheltering there.

*

From the shadows inside a narrow exit Ethelwulf watched the four watchers assemble and retire to the greater safety of the alley. He smiled broadly; the plan was working. Sweyn had taken a small bag of silver pennies along to a tavern where Franks were known to hang out. There he'd been most generous with his silver in buying them cup after cup of wine. Although he may have longed for the good ale of the northern realms, wine had far greater impact on the sensibilities, at least for some of the Franks.

The next stage was to introduce into the thinking patterns of some of the more drunken elements that now was the time to celebrate the building of Vanaheim, even though, in this miserable land where the nip of frost seemed reluctant to remind man of the gifts of the Vanir, the pleasures of alcohol were ignored. Some immediately took up the chant of "Vanaheim! Vanaheim!" to the terror of the locals. Now Sweyn stopped his recruits slumping down into drunken stupor but rather launched them on the world as a clutch of missionaries, anxious to introduce the locals to the joys of alcohol.

One red-haired youth tripped and cracked open his skull, producing so much amusement among his fellows that they lurched out of the tavern, determined to introduce the locals to alcohol, if not to that master of the senses, ale.

One or two locals who didn't run fast enough were forcibly introduced to alcohol before, being abandoned by the alcohol missionaries, they were left to try and vomit what to some was a gross infringement of their faith. As the word spread locals ran in all directions, but the Franks seemed fired with even greater zeal to spread the word of their new religion - wine! As more joined them so they were manoeuvred by Sweyn in the direction of the Church of the Holy Sepulchre. Their shouting grew louder and their behaviour more violent. Nowhere did authority try to restrain them, deciding there was more urgent business in another part of the city.

By the time Sweyn's charges reached Ethelwulf they were driving ahead of them a mass of terrified citizens, anxious to avoid being forced to drink alcohol. As the flood of men, women and children came past Ethelwulf slipped out of the shadows, maintaining a close watch on the four spies who'd retreated even deeper into the alley to avoid their fellows. Immediately the worshippers of the Vanir were upon him and he found it very difficult to fight his way across their impetus. At one point he was buffeted by one Swede who urged him to swig, "What passes for good mead in this wretched country!" To avoid a confrontation Ethelwulf obliged and at once felt light-headed due to his enforced abstention in recent weeks. However, he found himself flanked by Sweyn and an immense Swede who, as they swept their way across the stream of revellers, sang lustily about the war of the Vanir and the Aesir.

At last all three were across and gratefully slipped into a small alley. Ethelwulf wanted to stay to check the four spies had indeed been fooled but Sweyn urged him on. "My good friend, Godfred, has met you before, cousin, but so far away and so long ago his brain cannot recall the occasion," shouted Sweyn in his ear, while Godfred simply nodded stupidly. "Go with Godfred to his lodgings - if he can still find the way," added Sweyn with quiet intensity. "I'll stay to set your mind at rest when I report to you."

Ethelwulf grinned his thanks as he lurched with his new companion away from the Church of the Holy Sepulchre, each with their arms fixed around the other's shoulder.

Meanwhile Sweyn moved back to spy on the spies and was pleased to note that, once the tumult had disappeared into the distance, the four men quickly returned to their former posts, their eyes intent on the buildings which no longer contained their quarry.

*

For several weeks Ethelwulf stayed in hiding; finding the hours only slightly less tedious than the time with the Ethiopian community. What made the difference were his companions, coming as they did from all parts of northern Europe, with a smattering from France, Spain and Italy. They'd all drifted there with the common purpose of being at the Centre of the World when it was supposed the End would come. Most of them had their doubts, whether expressed or not, including Ethelwulf. All agreed no day within the year to come would be THE day. Many believed it'd be New Year's Day - but then most people accepted that to be in March but some did not[465].

As the festivities linked to the birth of Christ faded into the background excitement grew as impatience meant most came to see the End as coming at Easter. On occasional forays into the crowded streets of the Holy City Ethelwulf realised how tension within the streets was about to erupt as the longed-for year arrived.

He stepped out into the street, dressed not as a Frank but in a jubbbah and loose sarāwīl which enabled him to merge more easily with his surroundings; underneath the jubbah the broadsword would certainly have stood him apart if he'd been searched. Yet Ethelwulf scouted along close to the wall, pausing at every alley in case approaching danger might demand rapid retreat. At first such progress had been almost too disturbing to endure, but gradually he became used to such a crab-like pace, after all he had plenty of time and no particular place to go!

Ethelwulf was just passing a small alcove when he heard the sound of loud, angry voices ahead of him. Instantly he stopped, pressing himself against the wall while trying not to display any signs of alarm. He noticed others also paused, unwilling to progress on to what was sounding like the beginning of a brawl.

Even though he couldn't translate any of the angry words he recognised the style of the owner of the loudest voice. The man was clearly a Jew, or at least so the peculiarities of his dress proclaimed, but his language was making him the object of attention. His neighbours started shouting at him in some form of Aramaic and then a bastard type of Greek. Now Ethelwulf could understand vaguely what was wrong. The big man had laughed at some Christians, probably Jacobites, making their way back from the Church of the Holy Sepulchre. However, he hadn't stopped there, but had gone on to deny "Jeshu" could ever be able to return from the dead. When he added that he'd possessed no right to take on himself the style of 'Son of God' there were loud murmurs of approval from the Moslems close-by. By now, two smaller men, dressed in the rough brown burnous costume favoured by Egyptians screamed abuse at the man, declaring him to be, in Greek, "a pig and the son of a pig". The Jew answered in kind but suddenly found himself attacked by one of the two men. At first a couple of young Moslems went to interfere, perhaps to support someone who upheld the unity of Allah, but they were dragged away by their women.

The result was two more of the Jacobites leaping on the Jew from behind. None of them held knives but something flashed in the sun, provoking yet more fury from bystanders. Now the Jew lost his balance and tumbled to the ground, seemingly felled by the weight of his two assailants. At that point their supporters decided to join in and the Jew was now at the supreme disadvantage of trying to fight back from a prone position. His struggles were undermined by a savage kick to the head and then somebody, from somewhere, acquired a slab of stone which was smashed down at his skull. There was a scream and the crowd, now curried by excitement into a mob, all set about the downed Jew. Feet and fists rained down on the helpless man; some in the crowd turned to find sticks or stones to be used to express their hatred of this abuser of their Saviour, others, mainly Moslem, tried to push themselves away from what was becoming carnage in the middle of the street.

This brought about stage two in the episode, for the inert form of the Jew revealed stage one had definitely come to an end. The Jacobites saw the Moslems as a threat and, grouping themselves together, shouted out passages from the Nicene Creed at the top of their voices.

".We believe in one Lord, Jesus Christ, ,the only Son of God, eternally begotten of the Father, God from God, Light from Light, true God from true God, begotten, not made, of one Being with the Father......"

The chant made them ever angrier as they saw themselves surrounded by a hostile mob of unbelievers; so grouping together they charged towards the Moslems cowering in front of Ethelwulf. Everyone, including the Saxon, turned and ran. Heartened by their speedy triumph, the group of Jacobites tightened as they chanted again and again the words of their creed. With each repetition the anger, and perhaps the fear, growing with the long wait for the End, seemed to expand within them. From nowhere they produced sticks and began beating them against any object which could make a sound - walls, the ground, metal. One or two smashed windows as their voices rose to the heavens. Then they turned and marched back the way they'd come. When they reached the body of the Jew they continued to march straight over it as if it didn't exist, trampling it underfoot as, with the lust for triumph in their hearts they headed back towards the Church of the Holy Sepulchre. With their noisy departure normality returned - except nobody was willing to go near to the mangled remains of what once had been a Jew.

Ethelwulf returned to his lodgings. He'd had quite enough of Jerusalem street life for one day.

*

Later Sweyn arrived with tales of violence elsewhere in the city. To the north, by what the Christians called the Gate of St. Stephen, there'd been a major clash between Jacobite Christians and the Fatimid authorities. Again the cause was uncertain, although the centuries of what Jacobites considered restrictions under Moslem rulers couldn't be ignored. Three people had been killed in the fighting, including a Seljuk mercenary[466] employed by the city rulers. This made certain all four Jacobites who'd been seized when reinforcements had arrived would be executed.

Sweyn was surprised there hadn't been any real trouble among the Frankish visitors to Jerusalem. The 'riot' which he'd engineered weeks ago was almost the sole example of unrest from that section of the population. In a way that might prove unwelcome as the authorities, if they chose, might look more closely at its origin and observe a possible link with a fugitive hiding in the Church of the Holy Sepulchre. Sweyn was pleased to report the authorities still believed Ethelwulf was in hiding, even though the expense had forced them to cut back the watchers by half. He still couldn't guess the reason for the great interest in his cousin. All he could suggest was it probably stemmed from the desire of Amir Haroun ibn Nasr to gain favour with the Autokrator; his keenness must be linked to a weakening in Fatimid control over the whole area which had been noticed since the accession of Al Hakim. Ethelwulf was certain the Autokrator himself had long forgotten him; the continued effort must originate in the frustrated friends of the Eparchos - and even they'd lose patience in time.

*

The Wanderer 9:3

*"Everyday I look for that time
When the cross of Our Lord,
Once but seen in a dream on earth
Will snatch me from this short life
And carry me off to a home
Of joy and happiness....."*
('The Dream of the Rood')

Journey's End

The New Millenium had come to Jerusalem with an awe which seemed to fill every crack in the battered walls of the Holy City. As a New Year's sun arose over the fields to the east the muezzin called out his prayers as usual to the Moslems but even they, although it was neither a New Millenium nor a New Year to them, could feel the tension throughout the city.

Many among the diverse Christian communities in Jerusalem had believed that with midnight the heavens would have opened and Christ returned to bring about the End. Nothing had happened and some of those whose belief had ruled their lives for month after month felt cheated and disappointed. A few might have lost that faith, feeling God had abandoned his children due to the weight of sins of the world stifling their prayers. More would have had their hearts hardened into the growing doctrine that human action would open the gates of the world for the Lord to re-enter and preside over the Last Judgement. Finally there were others who believed the Last Days wouldn't start until this last year had run its course. These were prepared to wait in patience for whatever might happen - but they were in a minority.

Also there was a fourth group, made up of those unsure what to believe. Perhaps they formed a majority but their voices weren't to be heard in a city expecting the Last Days to come about and they'd been disappointed - as yet. It must be confessed both Ethelwulf and Sweyn were in this last group. Although Ethelwulf's soul seemed largely purged by the efforts of Anastasius he still lacked the resolution to commit himself in any direction. Conscious of his own past heaped up with sin, and also doubtful regarding the nature of vocation, he couldn't slip away from the world into the security of a religious order. An alternative might be to travel down to the coast and make his way westwards, perhaps to Italy or Spain. He'd heard the efforts of the Emperor in Rome had plunged the whole region into uproar[467] producing fine opportunities for what had become his major talent, that of war. The Spanish kingdoms were in a continuous state of warfare with their Moslem neighbours, even more so since the successful raids of Al Mansur.[468] Sweyn himself was at a loss, knowing that return to Norway might prove most unwelcome, and yet unwilling to embark on a career in the softer climate of the Mediterranean.

However, Ethelwulf felt compelled to stay within the walls of Jerusalem until the year of the Millenium had passed - just in case those believers who argued the End would come were right. As it was he found time drag as the year trudged its weary way through days, then weeks, and finally months, of waiting for what never came. The reaction varied among the believers; the headstrong abandoned whatever belief they'd had of the imminent return of Christ, some even discarding their faith altogether, throwing themselves into bouts of sin and depravity as if to make up for the months of spiritual preparation; others quietly left the city and ships which had feared but a one-way transit of pilgrims to the Holy Land found their holds filled by those anxious to return to their lives in the West, prepared to face perhaps mockery for the sake of once again finding their niche in THIS world, content to leave the next one till after their death.

There remained another group, mainly made up of the dreamers and fanatics who believed human action would precipitate the Final Coming. With Epaphroditus Ethelwulf had experienced the full force of such fanaticism several years before, so he was moved to hide himself even further away from the public view. He found he could earn some silver as a translator of documents, for his enforced idleness had driven him into setting about mastering the Cyrillic script and he was pleasantly surprised at how easily the Latin of his youth returned. He couldn't believe the number of travellers from the northern lands who'd found their way to Jerusalem either through Italy, or Miklagard. Obviously he assumed once again the name of "Osbert of Middlebere" which had served well in England over twenty years before, and on several occasions since. Age, and particularly the sufferings of the last eighteen months, had altered his appearance. His fair hair had turned grey and, unlike his usual practice, he'd assumed a full beard, one of grizzled red, and his frame had become more gaunt. Even so, he did maintain a strict regime of exercise to maintain fitness and the strength of his muscles; he also, where opportunity offered, practised with his broadsword, often against his cousin.

For Sweyn found himself in much the same condition, although with less reason to hide and more access to funds. He scoured the market-places, or employed an army of youthful deputies, to sniff out strangers who might need assistance. On several occasions he was recognised and the reaction was an outbreak of drinking, boasting and trying to dredge up memories of ice and snow amid the heat of a Palestinian summer. Sweyn was pleased the one or two northerners Ethelwulf later admitted recognizing failed to penetrate the changes in Ethelwulf's appearance. On reflection the cousins considered perhaps this wasn't so surprising as for last ten years Ethelwulf had either been in Gadarike or the Empire. Even so, Ethelwulf became accustomed to doing most of his business at night, when flickering light might make identification more difficult; the actual translation of documents being performed during the day.

The cousins recruited into their business a young Syrian, Yussuf ibn Ibrahim, who'd been captured during the siege of Antioch and, before his ransom two years later, had acquired a good grasp of Greek. So Yussuf would examine documents issued by the Muhtasib as part of the regulation of markets and trade worrying the pilgrims, translate the Arabic into Greek and Ethelwulf would render that in turn into Latin, or possibly Norse or English. Of course, the accuracy of translation could not be guaranteed, and some jargon remained unintelligible when transliterated, but both men tried to give an honest service, comforting themselves that their clients were in a far better position than before. The major cause of concern were documents issued by the 'master of taxes', for here both men had to admit, to themselves, almost total ignorance of much of what they were reading. On extreme occasions they might, in as indirect method as possible, ply a local shopkeeper with questions about some of the terminology defeating them. Whatever their efforts their income remained pitifully small and their frames took on an even greater degree of gauntness.

Naturally, this made none of the three happy and sometimes rising irritation would force them to abandon business for up to a week. This didn't help their finances, or their diet, but did, at least, maintain some degree of cooperation. Despite considerable reluctance Ethelwulf found himself resorting to borrowing small sums from trusted money-lenders. The best of these was Aziz ben Toghrul, whose origins in Damascus, also made him feel somewhat exposed to critical comment from the locals. His cooperation was enhanced by the timely intervention by Ethelwulf one evening when Aziz had felt threatened by a pair of Armenians unwilling to continue payment at an agreed rate. Their manner had become increasingly threatening until the arrival of a tall Frank, with a long sword threateningly placed across his shoulders, had caused them to make their excuses and depart. Ethelwulf had merely wanted to ask a couple of questions about the customs duties established by the Fatimids in the area and had been unaware of the terror his sudden intrusion into the meeting evoked. Only when a relieved Aziz blubbered out his gratitude did he realise how opportune his arrival had been. Obviously, any straight-surrender of dinars was impossible but the Damascene proved remarkably patient when it came to repayment. If Ethelwulf had thought more deeply he might have realised the two Armenians hadn't been alone in being terrified by his broadsword and his manner!

Even so, as weeks turned into months, both Sweyn and Ethelwulf grew increasingly restless. Their mood was shared, if not magnified, throughout the entire city. Not a week went by without a squabble, seemingly deliberately produced, breaking out between one or other rival groups of Christians or Moslems, or else involving the Jews. Whether the perpetrators believed that suddenly the heavens would open and the End would come about is probably unlikely, but Ethelwulf became convinced some of the more extreme elements haunting the streets half-believed any onslaught of their peculiar version of the Truth would provoke some form of Divine intervention. Yet he was certain that in most cases the squabbles resulted from a combination of heat, boredom and the frustration of seeing the Millenium pass by without a miracle.

*

Frustration was clearly present in the single room making up the business centre and living quarters of Ethelwulf. He lay slumped on a pile of rags and straw which had come to form his bed. His head was resting against the wall while he savoured the coolness of the shade as the afternoon sunlight plunged through the single window. His air of tranquillity infuriated his cousin who felt moved to comment on what seemed to be an endless drift downwards.

"You may have become accustomed, cousin, to the softer clothes, the richer food and the wines of this culture, but I have not," Sweyn declared as he brought down his palm on the table as a signal that argument wasn't expected.

"And what about the dark-eyed beauties?" laughed Ethelwulf, half-yawningly content to keep his eyes closed.

Sweyn coloured, fully aware Ethelwulf had tucked him up in bed but two nights before with one such maiden when he'd returned, much the worst for the effects of wine. "I accept, cousin, the women in these parts have been starved of true men for so long they become irresistible -"

"Shouldn't that be the other way round, Sweyn?" smiled Ethelwulf. "Shouldn't it be YOU they can't resist?"

"That goes without saying, Ethelwulf!" snapped his cousin. "What I mean is their plight makes it hard - very, very hard - for a young man to resist their charms."

"So you still consider yourself to be a young man?" teased Ethelwulf, well aware Sweyn Haraldsson was fast approaching his thirtieth birthday.

"Which is just my point," laughed Sweyn, joining in the jibe at himself. "In this climate a man ages too fast - and that, unfortunately, is also true of women." He paused. "Perhaps it's the miserable diet on offer or just this interminable round of sun!"

"So you'd prefer to be lost in some dismal fog or drizzle on the western seas, would you?" laughed the Wanderer.

"Perhaps," smiled his cousin, and then added with a shrewd glance in Ethelwulf's direction. "And, of course, that is one direction we've never considered -"

"Oh, sail off the edge of the world," laughed Ethelwulf, ""out of boredom with sun, wine and sex?"

"Don't talk rubbish, Ethelwulf," answered Sweyn. "I meant Skrælingaland[469] offers new opportunities to anyone and - "

"They must all be crazy to go that far west," stated Ethelwulf. "Iceland was far enough for me - and it would be for you, if you ever got there!"

Sweyn swung himself to his feet, with all the pretence of being put out by the last taunt. In fact, as they both knew, he'd had every intention of marching off to the nearest tavern for some time now. He never asked Ethelwulf to join him, certain his cousin would decline. Sometimes the Wanderer would turn up, perhaps in that outlandish outfit he often wore those days, filled with a need for company and a zest for life. Unfortunately, such behaviour was not very common, and becoming less so as the Wanderer realised opportunities seemed to be running out. Sometimes these moods became blacker as he remembered the many men, especially Edwine and Morkere, he could never hope to see again in this world. Of course, there was scant possibility of his ever seeing friends such as Gunnar Thorgeirsson again, now they appeared to have settled into a permanent life under the command of the Autokrator. Even so, a vague inkling that chance COULD throw them together put off the gloom when such names were mentioned. Sweyn was well-aware that, in many ways, he was some kind of replacement for the dead Morkere - but he knew he lacked many of the skills of the dead man, as well as the ability to read the mood of their cousin.

"I'm off!" he grunted. "I'll be back when you're prepared to take my ideas more seriously!"

"Have you taken silver enough to last - "

But this last taunt was cut off by the slamming door as Sweyn disappeared and Ethelwulf was left to himself - and his memories.

*

Three hours later Sweyn returned - visibly excited. In fact, he could scarcely shut the door, before he turned to Ethelwulf with a grin on his face such as his cousin had never seen before.

"I was seated in the corner of 'The Horn' when guess whom I saw coming in?" he challenged.

Ethelwulf was tempted to respond with suggestions like the Archangel Gabriel or the Autokrator but decided that such wouldn't be worthy of the sincerity of his cousin.

Seeing Ethelwulf was unable to even supply a single name, Sweyn decided to relieve his curiosity. "Olaf Trygvasson," he remarked in tones which, despite whatever restraint he might have tried, were clearly overwhelmed by excitement. He obviously expected some kind of reaction - astonishment, disbelief, ridicule or alarm.

"Who?" Somehow Ethelwulf managed to give that single word an edge of all four emotions. He was astonished to hear the holder of such a famous name could be here, in Jerusalem, especially as it was hard to believe the King of Norway was alive, as, but a few weeks before, Sweyn himself had recounted his death. He found it ridiculous that such a famous Viking, after losing but one battle, should abandon his country to the tender mercies of Sven Forkbeard.. Finally, if, indeed, the impossible had happened, might not the fugitive King be pursued by agents of his enemies and Ethelwulf couldn't imagine they'd leave another old enemy such as himself in peace, if they discovered him?

"I can see, my cousin, you find it hard to believe - and, to tell you the truth, I found it hard to believe my eyes when I first saw him - "

"It must have been someone who resembled the dead king," asserted Ethelwulf, starting to recover the use of his rational powers and remembering how, initially, he believed, when first seeing Sweyn, the dead Morkere. was alive again.

"No, cousin," answered Sweyn," for I made sure by speaking to the man!" He paused before he revealed what words had been exchanged, part of him willing to punish his cousin for his doubts. "Of course, I noticed how much the King had changed." Again there was a pause. "Not only had he grown a beard but that beard was streaked with grey, even though he's not much older than me!" He saw Ethelwulf was trying to conjure up a memory of Olaf Trygvasson, undermined by Olaf being then only eighteen years old, and yet already a fierce warrior. "That fair hair, inherited from his royal grand-father, can mask grey, but his beard has developed a more reddish hue, revealing signs of age or care more easily."

"So what did you say to this phenomenon?" demanded Ethelwulf, but his question was shrugged off by his cousin.

"Also, the King has aged somewhat in his bearing," he continued. "His shoulders have a slight stoop not there when I fought alongside him less than a year ago." Again he paused, whether from sadness or tiredness, or merely a malicious intent to spin out Ethelwulf's patience, was uncertain. "He's suffered - as we all have - and I'm not sure how devoted he was to the people of his realm - "

"But he was their King!"

"Indeed he was," muttered Sweyn, quietly and almost to himself, as if unwilling to challenge the reputation of his hero. "Yet he was a Viking by chance stumbling on a kingdom and, almost as a whim, taking on the task of government, just to see if he could!"

"But you described all his efforts to convert his people to the faith of Christ!" protested Ethelwulf. "He must have only done that out of care for their souls!"

"Perhaps," yielded Sweyn, "but I really believe he did it because of the challenge itself." He smiled. "Look what happened to old Bluetooth when he tried a similar trick in - "

"King Harald never attempted the conversion of his people," protested Ethelwulf. "He merely entered into the faith for himself, trying to get members of his family and household to follow his example - "

"For which he was expelled by his own son, spending months as a miserable fugitive among the Wends!"[470] spat out Sweyn as if such a fate outweighed a dozen deaths under torture.

"But what did he say?" asked Ethelwulf, blatantly revealing the triumph of his cousin's strategy.

There was a cackle from Sweyn before he answered, "You mean to my tactful question whether he was the dead King of Norway?"

Ethelwulf smiled. Games were one thing, and Sweyn enjoyed his little victory, but if he wanted to carry on the charade he could talk to himself or the wall. He went to leave and was restrained by his cousin.

"No, Ethelwulf," protested Sweyn, with a quiet vehemence adding credibility to his words. "I sat down beside him, lightly touching his forearm so that he turned to face my scrutiny. Then staring into his eyes I asked if he knew me from the battle of Hjorungavang; he never blinked but scrutinized my face in turn, and then revealed all by repeating my name!"

Sweyn noted how this convinced his cousin of the truth of his tale. The conviction grew as he asserted both men had realised that revealing their past in a public place might place them in danger. "So, cousin, we agreed he should come here this evening - for we've grown more settled in our ways whereas, being a stranger among these streets, a visit from the likes of us would certainly raise interest."

"So you mentioned me?" asked Ethelwulf, not realising the full import of his words.

"No, Ethelwulf," said Sweyn quietly, "not by name for interested ears to pick up! I said I lodged with an old mutual friend - "

"I was never that," protested Ethelwulf, remembering how his relations with Olaf had been only slightly better than those with the homicidal Blood-Harald.[471] He vaguely remembered the tall Varangian, flaunting hair of the colour which had given his royal grandfather his name, with already a fine reputation and anxiety to scorch his name throughout the entire world. He'd reminded Ethelwulf of Styrbjorn whose death he'd so recently witnessed. Styrbjorn had been terrifying in the urgency with which he pursued fame; at the time Ethelwulf couldn't recall the similar cases of

Achilles, Alcibiades and Alexander, but enforced idleness at odd times since then had let him explore such comparisons and come to a better assessment. Even so, without those parallels, Ethelwulf feared such heroes, certain that death followed in their wakes. Even Olaf's conversion to Christianity seemed to have been stage-managed, an incident to fill out the lines of sagas.[472] His passion for spreading Christianity was no different - but that opinion had been based on what he heard from others. He wondered if they'd recognise each other.

*

Ethelwulf and Sweyn filled the next few hours exchanging memories and opinions of the exiled King of Norway. The Saxon had the more hostile approach, perhaps not helped by Olaf's depredations in England over the previous decade. Only the missionary activities of his hero, especially in Iceland, held any qualms for Sweyn; otherwise Olaf was simply the greatest Viking produced, worthy to march alongside Inar of the Broad-Embrace or Ragnar Lodbrog. Ethelwulf held back his judgement, realising his personal knowledge of the man had been very limited.

At last came a knock, and, with a speed rivalling that of a young girl for her lover, Sweyn opened the door. In stepped a figure which certainly wouldn't have awoken any memories in Ethelwulf. It was gaunt and stooped shoulders so contrasted with the haughty swing he remembered from Olaf Trygvasson that Ethelwulf would have denied Sweyn's identification. The grey hair and heavily-lined features pointed to the suffering endured by Olaf. Only the blue eyes burned with an intensity matching those in Ethelwulf's memory. The stranger spoke also in a voice unfamiliar to the Saxon.

"I too have no recollection of you!" smiled the stranger as he slid down to a sitting posture just inside the door. Months of uncertainty had nourished a mistrust which denied his back to even supposed friends.

"You've changed, Olaf, since we last discussed the profit to be gained from Gotland - "

"No, that's not so, my friend," smiled the stranger, and this time some of the strain melted away from his features. "If anything, Ethelwulf, we talked about the LACK of profit from Gotland - "

"And you preferred the pleasures of visiting the citizens of Bornholm," grinned Ethelwulf, pleased Olaf had so speedily corrected his deliberate error. Unwilling to place himself in a superior position, he swung himself off his bed and on to the floor, always retaining a clear view of their guest's face.

"Certainly, I found the visit profitable," muttered Olaf almost to himself. Olaf's stare seemed to penetrate Ethelwulf's soul. "But your wanderings, Saxon, have proved no more fortunate than my own - at least, according to your appearance."

"Which is why," interrupted Sweyn, joining the other two on the floor, " we three are here, in this infernal heat and among heathen."

Ethelwulf laughed. "I think we'd find more heathen in northern lands than in the Holy Land!"

"True," conceded the Norwegian. "If you're willing to give the deluded followers of Mohammed a status above that of those poor heathen of the - "

"But we're not here to discuss religion!" protested Sweyn, anxious to find out the story of how his king had managed to escape from that last battle.

Over the next hour or so they exchanged tales of their recent lives. Olaf showed great interest in Ethelwulf's account of the Varangian role in Miklagard, possibly employment there had crossed his mind. He smiled at Ethelwulf's confession of how he'd upset the powerful of Gadarike. Olaf was sure most of such mistakes came from the Saxon's limited familiarity with the culture of the region.

At last it came to Olaf to describe his recent history and, fortified by a strong draught of wine Sweyn had summoned up from somewhere, the exiled-King of Norway made a start.

"You've doubtless heard how, finding the 'Long Serpent' couldn't resist the enemy onslaught, I leaped overboard," said Olaf Trygvasson and was rewarded by nods from his audience. " Let me assure you," he smiled, "I had no intention of self-murder!" Sweyn's glance at his cousin was not lost on their guest. Neither had been willing to consider suicide as a motive for the king's leap, but they'd been puzzled by his subsequent disappearance.

"Among the vessels following me into that disastrous fight were three sent by King Boleslav," explained Olaf Trygvasson. "These had played little part in the battle because they'd been in the rear, not through cowardice but because more experienced crews, anxious for glory, had manoeuvred their vessels into the better places in our battle-line." Olaf glanced at Sweyn to see if his words might be questioned but there was no reaction. "It was my plan to swim to those ships and slip away, confident my brother-in-law[473] would help me recover my fortunes." Olaf paused, remembering how Christ had intervened to thwart his bloody ambitions. "However, in the confusion of picking me out of the water one of their oars smashed against my skull and I sank beneath the waves. It was only the prompt actions of two the crew which saved me from drowning because they leaped in, heedless of their own safety, and somehow dragged me to safety."

Ethelwulf was tempted to ask why he hadn't led the vessel in an attempt to recapture the 'Long Serpent' but a warning glare from his cousin caused the question to freeze on my lips.

"I was completely unconscious as I was dragged aboard their ship, unable to urge them to stay in the fight, and so the Wends turned tail and fled from the battle." He closed his head in despair as he recalled the sickening wrench of disgrace as, on recovering consciousness, he realised what had been done. By then they were nearing the shores of Wendland and an inner voice kept telling him his warring days were over. He realised that all he'd achieved in the north would need hands other than his if it was to be planted firmly. Perhaps for the first time he had doubts about the wisdom of his methods in Iceland and elsewhere, where the Ministry of God's Love had been spread by violence. Vaguely he even remembered wishing they might come ashore in a Christian land, where he might find an immediate way of serving God and setting aside the burden of sin oppressing him. But it was not to be, for they landed in a heathen region where only a demand for vengeance would stir any understanding. However, vengeance was not what he wanted, rather a passion to perform a pilgrimage to the land of his Lord became dominant. Somewhere an inner voice swore that, once in Jerusalem itself, he'd receive a sign on how he could serve Christ.

Of course, his natural desire had been to go to Boleslav, reveal his identity and see where fate would place him. However, this dream was suppressed as he saw the Wends had no wish to fight the King of Danes, the natural consequence if Sven Forkbeard had any idea his enemy was being sheltered by the Wends. He knew that, if he appeared before Boleslav, the Wendish king would have to acknowledge him and bring about a war not to his liking. Olaf observed the sceptical frown on Ethelwulf's face.

"Oh, yes, Saxon, " he conceded. " I can guess your opinion of me for when we met, a long time ago, I was a warrior caring only for fame, coming from the battlefield so beloved by my ancestors." There was a slight nod as Ethelwulf accepted the accuracy of the analysis. "But I've changed, far more than even Sweyn here can realise!" Sweyn started to protest but was silenced by his former king. "You knew me, Sweyn, as a man taken over by a mission - no, an ambition to spread belief in Our Lord by any means possible."

"While I knew you, sire, there were certain changes - not entirely - "

"-acceptable to you, and others like you," completed Olaf. "I certainly was aware of a resistance not only from my enemies but from many of my friends." Any protest was stilled by a gesture. "However, I'm no longer that man, Sweyn. I've become emptied of all ambition save waiting here in all patience for the imminent return of Our Saviour."

"So you believe the Second Coming is almost upon us?" asked Ethelwulf, whose doubts had grown with every day not seeing any sign of the miracles predicted by St. John the Divine.

"How else can I interpret the destruction of my ambitions by that child of Satan, Sven Forkbeard, and his lackeys dragged up from the Swedes and my own countrymen?" Olaf paused as he recognised the surprise these words registered. "For the Holy Word says the Beast shall seem to triumph in the Last Days, his legions stalking the world in supposed victory." He looked from Ethelwulf to Sweyn and back again, as if challenging them to deny Scripture. "So my land now endures the attentions of Sven's followers - and I'm sure Satan's ambitions won't stop there - but that is enough of my own spiritual journey through faith, let me continue with my physical voyage through this world."

His hearers nodded and the exiled king continued to describe how he'd travelled from the wastes of the Swedish Sea to the plains of the Holy Land. At Lebus he'd found himself presented with an unexpected supply of silver - but not so surprising seeing he was an embarrassment to the Wendish King anxious to establish good relations with his neighbours in the West -

"But surely," interrupted Ethelwulf. "there's no love between the King of the Danes and the Empire!"

"Certainly both the grandfather and father of the German Emperor had more trouble with the Danes than they desired," allowed Olaf. "Yet, the Emperor has his eyes fixed on the Eternal City and would certainly be angered if any excuse for Sven to stretch his power southward was offered."

"But why should Sven not attack the Germans anyway when their Emperor had wandered off into the South," persisted Ethelwulf. He'd been well-versed in how the Emperor Otto, backing his protégé, Gerbert, as Pope was being sucked deeper into the intrigues of Roman politics. He knew that, just before his visit to Hedeby, Sven had driven occupying German forces out of his father's kingdom - before seizing it for himself!

"Because his ambitions are turning towards the land of your fathers, Saxon," snapped Olaf. "The land of Ethelred has grown weaker and weaker as its king has proved incapable of driving off the brigands attracted by such a rich, and undefended, land." He paused, pleased to demonstrate his grasp of the political strategies of lands so far away. "Sven sees a land for the taking, with even some of its people willing to welcome his army as liberators!"

"Never!" grunted Ethelwulf, recalling the tales of the glorious defeat at Maldon but the even more impressive resistance of London to Viking attack. Then he remembered Olaf himself had played a key part in both events and so was much better qualified to comment on English morale.

"Indeed Saxon," smiled the exiled king, "there are still many fearless Saxons, bred in the image of the great Alfred; but there also are the offspring of my ancestors settled in your country who, perhaps, don't share such loyalties." He raised his hand as Ethelwulf opened his mouth to protest, anxious to continue with his saga. "Anyway, I realised King Boleslav wanted me safely out of the country, while at the same time, fulfilling his duties as host, so I accepted the silver and made for Meissen on the Elbe."

He made his way to Bamberg and then on to Regensburg. He found the road through Salzburg almost as difficult as travelling among the Wends. On all sides were suspicious eyes, perhaps his fair hair making him too conspicuous among the darker-haired inhabitants there. Several times questions almost made him throw off his obscurity and announce they had among them the exiled King of Norway. However, doubts as to the effect caused him to put aside such gestures and continue with the mask of humble pilgrim which had served him since leaving behind the land of the Wends.

At last he reached the land - or rather the islands and lagoons - of the Venetians.[474] Here he found the citizens filled with excitement at their conquest of the land of Dalmatia.[475] For generations their commerce had been plagued by pirates until the successes of their present ruler and his father.[476] He was amazed by that city, especially when told that, within his lifetime, much of Venice had been destroyed when they'd driven out a hated ruler.[477] He was impressed by the toughness of the citizens, not only in warfare but in the transactions which made up commerce. All this existed against a background of hundreds of small boats, many making even Varangian longships look enormous, within the maze of waterways making up this strangest of cities. For a few days Olaf toyed with the idea of settling among these people, exploiting his seamanship to find work and perhaps even managing to grasp a little of the singsong which made up their language.

However, although he found most people friendly, eager (if only by signs) to offer help to a stranger, a few had heard tales of Hasting, crossing themselves at his approach or shuffling away as if he were a half-tamed wolf. At first he laughed at such fears but then one evening, wandering into the half-completed restoration of the Basilica[478] he saw himself once again as such people saw him - a half-pagan, half-civilised refugee - and felt the shame of so nearly having abandoned his ambition to travel to the Holy City. So he found his way on to one of the many ships plying a fine trade shipping pilgrims eastwards to celebrate the Millenium.

He was shocked by the stiff price demanded but saw it as but a reflection of the Venetian lust for profit; for if they excelled as traders, then their success rested on the sacrifices of others. He was disgusted by the too-apparent scorn for the fervour of some of his fellow pilgrims, perhaps acquired by a too-intimate relationship with the Levant. Anyway, he kept his mouth shut and his sword out of sight until the passengers had been disembarked at Ascelon - at an extra charge - instead of the usual trading partner, Antioch. At last, he arrived in the land of his Saviour, and the Millenium had not yet been completed.

*

With Lent came a growth in tension. The groups looking for the Second Coming this year had first named Easter as the anniversary of Christ's Resurrection. When that passed they awaited the remembrance of the Ascension, assured that, just as the Lord had departed on that day, he'd return during the Year of the Millenium. That passed and many gave up their hopes, preparing for the long and difficult journey back to their homeland - but some were persuaded that, because Whitsun had seen the descent of the Holy Spirit as guardian of human souls, so after a thousand years the return of Christ would bring this period to an end. However, Whitsun came and went - and so did even more pilgrims disappointed the End had not arrived. For a brief period Ethelwulf, like others of his countrymen in the Holy Land, was convinced great events would take place in September,[479] but nothing of consequence happened. Then the faithful fixed their minds on Advent, for, after all, they told each other what better way for God to indicate the time of the Second Coming.

It was during this period Olaf Trygvasson had arrived in Jerusalem and within days became the inseparable companion of Ethelwulf and Sweyn. As much as possible they kept away from the crowds, alarmed by the increasing vigilance of the Dīwān al-Shurṭah[480] provoked by the violence in the streets and alleys of the Holy City. As the festival of Christmas approached rival interpretations of the Second Coming came to the fore. Some insisted the Holy Host would first descend on the forces of Anti-Christ to be found in Baghdad and Cairo,[481] others preferred to point in the direction of the Autokrator as the Servant of the Beast. As December 25th was passed so the Western pilgrims became disillusioned, not encouraged by their Eastern rivals that the true commemoration of the Birth of the Lord was the sixth day of January.[482] Yet, that day passed without the anticipated opening of the heavens to reveal the Majesty of the Second Coming.

Several of the sects became desperate, convinced the End would never come without the direct intervention of mankind. God was waiting for humans to commit themselves to the Second Coming by rising up against the tyranny of the servants of Satan. Even so, there was disagreement as to where this tyranny lay, and many believers rushed to denounce the followers of rival sects as the followers of either the Beast from the Sea,[483] the Beast from the Earth[484] or even of the Scarlet Whore of Babylon.[485] Preachers daily appeared in the streets, calling upon the Almighty to bring about the destruction of their rivals and usher in the promised Rule of the Just.[486] Some would tear their clothes and cut themselves, declaring they were those who'd suffer in the Last Days as foretold by St John.[487] When the authorities moved to seize them and so stem the flow of hatred and discord pouring from their mouths, their followers took up weapons, sometimes driving off the squads of police but more often finishing up in houses serving as temporary prisons by the increasingly frustrated Muhtasib. Then, naturally, their companions would try to free them, promoting fresh violence. By February Jerusalem had become one of the most dangerous cities in the realms of Al Hakim, Al Qadir or the Autokrator himself.[488] And still the violence grew.

*

Anastasius, one of the leaders of the Ethiopian Community clinging to a share of the Church of the Holy Sepulchre, had been unable to rest at nights for some time. Since the disappearance of Ethelwulf from his control he'd felt relieved. He'd liked the stranger from the north but had been horrified by his history, believing that somehow the man was set upon a spiritual journey to purge his sins. He became convinced that, shut away in the obscure recesses of the Church of the Holy Sepulchre the man would have little opportunity to carry out the sacrifice ordained for him by God; only by such sacrifice could the weight of sin be lifted and, perhaps, time was running out for such contrition. Once Ethelwulf had come to see where his path lay he was disappointed that Anastasius appeared to wait for the Lord to show the Saxon a way to slip out into the world outside and work out, somehow, his own salvation, before it was too late. How the man eluded the watchers outside remained a mystery. Brother Thomas spoke of another stranger from the north ushered close to their guest; then he left them to their own barbaric tongue, hoping they'd come to a mutual realisation of how much in the mire of sin they had become. Soon afterwards Ethelwulf was nowhere to be found, although the continued presence of the watchers outside the confines of their community convinced Anastasius Ethelwulf had eluded capture. Anastasius was pleased the watchers continued for so long with their thankless task but even they, in the end, became convinced their prey had slipped away. One day they just weren't there and the relief of Anastasius turned to a deep sense of calm.

However, that feeling didn't last long as he became more aware of the growing violence in the streets beyond the confines of his oasis of peace. Gradually a trickle of believers in the Ethiopian version of the Will of God began to drift into the precincts of the Community. At first they were welcomed as refugees and somehow sustenance and shelter provided. However, the unrest outside produced an unwillingness to leave their sanctuary, and the trickle steadily grew in volume. On the feast day of St. Dionysius the Great all the refugees were gathered together and urged to return to their homes; Brother Euthanasia preached a sermon on how St. Dionysius had not hidden away in the shadows, even during the great persecution,[489] but had gone out into the streets, helping his fellow Christians and trusting in the power of Our Lord to watch over him. A few of the congregation took the hint and left the Church of the Holy Sepulchre, to varying fortunes outside. By the feast of St. Daniel the Stylite[490] the Ethiopian Community reluctantly placed sentries at the entries to their precinct to prevent their charity being overwhelmed. On the whole it worked; one or two of the more vigorous, and persistent, dodged the attentions of the sentries, suddenly appearing in their midst as if ghosts taken material form. They were accepted, after under-going a penance meant to discourage any from smuggling out invitations to relatives or friends outside.

However, after Christmas the situation outside the quiet retreat of the Church of the Holy Sepulchre worsened. Anastasius had nights disturbed by a series of most unwelcome dreams.

Sometimes he was presented with a series of images from the Apocalyptic writings of St. John the Divine. Perhaps the worst involved the seven angels and their bowls filled with the wrath of God;[491] here the tormented monk saw in the faces of God's instruments not the features of good men but of the workers of evil he'd known. He was distressed to recognise in the face of the fifth angel Ethelwulf, largely because of the wicked delight convulsing the features as the worshippers of the Beast writhed in torment in the pit of their own making. He awoke from what he hoped must have been a dreadful dream in a fierce sweat, amazed he hadn't unleashed a cry of horror. Anastasius now wondered what horror had been released on to the world with his disappeared guest and determined to discover the whereabouts of the Saxon. However, three days of enquiries failed to produce any sign of the existence of the Wanderer in Jerusalem so he was forced to admit he'd no chance of turning the man from whatever dreadful vengeance he was about to wreak, for Anastasius was convinced that with that particular vision God had allowed him a glimpse of the future.

The next night he dreamed he was one of the two witnesses[492] foretold by St John who'd been seized and put to death. Try as he would he couldn't glimpse the face of his companion in this martyrdom until they were finally under the earth, battered, with their cuts oozing worms and rotting despite the dryness of the sand over their heads. Then, somehow, he managed to turn his head and saw the face of his companion, but the features were those of an unknown northerner. The stranger opened his mouth and, instead of swallowing the sand of their grave, his words passed through that barrier. "I've fulfilled what God meant me to do. I am content." With that he closed his eyes and turned away, slowly merging with the sand and Anastasius was left horribly alone in that torment of death. Although wanting confirmation that, as promised, in three days he'd rise from the dead and, confronting his enemies, be summoned to join the Almighty in heaven, he remained ensnared by the bounds of death until he awoke, once more consumed by sweat.

A third night he dreamed and perhaps this was the most disturbing of all his nightmares. He was confronted by a woman clothed in purple and scarlet, again foretold as part of the Second Coming by

St. John,[493] whom he recognised as his sister, Anastasia. Across her features was a name but, as he leaned forward to read it, the letters faded causing his sister to laugh. But her laugh was not like that of his sister, nor of any other earthly creature; perhaps it resembled the howl of the jackal long ago heard in the sands of Egypt, then it became the screech of something trapped in a snare of its own contriving, Then, looking into her eyes in a desperate attempt to find the measure of this infernal creature, he saw his sister's pupils had simply turned into flat, lifeless globes; gradually their opaque nature evaporated and he saw two shrunken visions of himself, in one he was tied to a stake and burning fiercely and in the other nailed to a cross. He felt alone and woke up with a start.

This time he was determined to do something about the nightmare. His sister was a member of the small Order of the Annunciation in a nearby chapel. They'd been apart now for over twenty years and he'd only occasionally met her, making sure others were present to avoid scandal. With a start he reminded himself he hadn't seen her for nearly three years, before all the madness of the Millenium had convulsed the world. Now he'd make his way to her, revealing his nightmares and asking her advice. Despite being younger than himself she'd always had a greater touch with the mystical elements of their faith. If there was anyone who could interpret these messages from God then it would be his sister.

*

Anastasius sensed his sister had changed considerably since they'd last met. Her face had become more drawn, presumably she'd undertaken an extensive period of fasting along with others during that year, and her eyes appeared somewhat glazed - with a strange air of looking into the future rather than contemplating the present. However, as soon as she spoke he recognised the sister he'd known for over thirty years and felt easily able to unburden himself of the nightmares so troubling him.

Anastasia listened carefully to all her brother said. She was aware, from gossip among those frequenting the Church of the Holy Sepulchre, that her brother hadn't been completely won over by the Millenialist enthusiasms convulsing the Holy City. She, for her part, had become convinced of the arrival of the Last Days foretold by St John *"when a thousand years have passed Satan will be set loose from his bondage and come out to deceive the peoples of the world"*.[494] She'd heard tales of the new ruler in Cairo,[495] how he was defying his vizier and taking a harsher look at the faiths of his subjects. Anastasia was convinced that this child was the Beast who'd try to lead astray the believers in the Last Days. After all, St.

John had said the Beast would be given freedom for forty-two months to spread pollution[496] and she knew the blasphemer had been installed just over three years ago. She was seeking further signs that the Second Coming was imminent. She could make no sense of her brother's dream of the angels with their bowls of destruction, dismissing them as manifestations of her brother's dreadful past acquaintances and his reading of the prophecies of the Last Days. She was intrigued by Anastasius's identification with one of the two witnesses sacrificed for the truth. If only that could be true! For years she'd been disappointed in the liberal ideas of her brother, his dealings with strangers from across the seas and his too-ready forgiveness for the lapses among his flock. Now could be the time when he'd atone for such shortcomings by bearing witness to the Truth. She was puzzled as to the identity of his companion in the grave but dismissed it as merely his mind needing to make up the required second witness with a half-recalled portrait of one of the strangers he'd welcomed.

Only the third nightmare alarmed her, for she was horrified by the identification of the scarlet woman with herself. She'd lived a life of chastity, of purity of thought. She'd shunned the defilement growing up around her, avoiding the polluting touch of sinners, shutting herself away in her Community where only the like-minded could approach her consciousness. Naturally, she'd heard of the evils stalking the world, but had made sure they remained distinct and separate from herself. Hours in prayer had convinced Anastasia that God had chosen her for some special purpose and she longed to sacrifice herself, anything or anybody, to achieve the will of the Almighty. With the Millenium here she was certain His purpose would be revealed.

So how could she explain this horrible blending of herself with the servant of the Beast in the dream of her brother? Clearly it stemmed from the mind of Anastasius, and she doubted his fitness to be a servant of the Lord. Somehow she was sure Satan had entered his mind to lead him astray, to prevent him finding salvation through revealing such dreams to his sister. She was flattered he'd come to her for help, but put aside such guilty thoughts by assuming he'd recognised her greater devotion to the service of their Lord. However, she frowned as she wondered how to interpret such a dream to her brother; then she decided the truth was the only vehicle for such advice.

"I can see why Satan should choose to mask the features of the Scarlet Woman with those of my own," she stated with the authority of certainty. Anastasius couldn't hide his surprise. How could his sister accept such monstrous identification? Anastasia could see the doubt and smiled. "The Dark One intended you to run from me rather than bring your dreams, and your tormented mind, to me for comfort." She saw him relax as he started to absorb such an idea. "For these dreams tell you, my brother, we're very close to the Second Coming and perhaps, I say 'perhaps' because I hesitate to assume the ability to see the Will of God, we're meant to play a key part in the salvation of the world."

"But the world won't be saved, my sister!" protested the monk.

"Whatever is worth saving will be saved, my brother," she replied with the complacency of a missionary. "In the new world [497]created after the destruction of the Beast and all his minions there'll be places for all worth saving in this miserable world of ours!"

Anastasius nodded, only half-understanding her words but assured of the greater devotion of his sister to the workings of the Almighty. He recognised his own sinful nature but was convinced the greater seclusion exercised by his sister had preserved the purity of her baptism. Perhaps he'd been too open to strangers, too willing to help the half-pagans and unbelievers flooding into the Church of the Holy Sepulchre. For a moment he doubted his own generosity of spirit but then acceptance of the Will of the Lord pushed aside such doubts. He'd acted with prayer, always questioning his motives, prepared to subsume whatever he desired to the voice which spoke in his heart. He was sure God intended him to mingle among such barbarians, while his sister had been intended for a life of greater purity. This must mean she was closer to their Lord in thought and deed. With that thought he decided to return to the Church of the Holy Sepulchre and devote himself through prayer to discovering the Will of God. With almost rude haste he left his sister to wonder how they might both help bring about the Second Coming.

*

On his way back Brother Anastasius came across a typical incident in the factional strife of the city. A Moslem trader became embroiled with two Christian passers-by because of the too-persistent opportunism of the trader which had provoked the Christians to question his very existence in the Holy City. Soon, however, their shouts attracted the attention of some Maronites[498]who, immediately condemning the trader to hellfire as an unbeliever, turned their wrath on the pilgrims from the West. Just as the Westerners had denounced the trader so they identified as intruders into the Holy City, the Maronites insisting God had entrusted the Holy Land to generations of their own faith. Shouting turned into violence as one of the pilgrims tried to push his way through the growing crowd. Somebody thumped his shoulder as he passed, causing the man to stumble into the crowd. Someone struck out and the man fell. His companion leaped forward to his aid but, in turn, became the victim of assault. The screams of the two Westerners was quickly lost in the cries of hatred as, in a flurry of violence, their bodies were ground into the dust. Meanwhile, the Moslem trader, blessing Allah for giving him the cloak of invisibility, slipped away. Soon the Maronites stepped back from the battered bodies of their victims.

Brother Anastasius was horrified and rushed forward, too late to offer protection to the inert forms but launching into an impromptu sermon.

"I've witnessed what was promised by St. John. In such violence the Pale Rider has laid hands on yet another victim. The Fourth Horseman[499] will bring with him the power of destruction and you animals are but the instruments of Death! For without the murderous hands of the offspring of Adam Satan cannot hope to bring about the desolation which is his ambition. Without the hatred in your hearts the Beast can never obtain the mastery of the world, for that short-space of time allotted to him. Without the venom in your eyes the Dragon, expelled from heaven by the angelic host, will have no hiding place. But you have granted him sanctuary within your hate-filled hearts. Beware your souls teetering on the brink of that pit into which the angel will pour the wrath of God. Beware your eternal life about to be condemned to an existence in the Kingdom of the Damned."

At this point there were shrieks of hatred from the crowd which moved to surround the intrepid preacher. Fortunately for Anastasius his words had attracted the attention of passers-by and several large men thrust themselves between the Maronites and their intended victim. As both sides threw themselves at each other with fists, sticks and knives, others seized Anastasius and started to hustle him away. He protested, reluctant to abandon the field to violence, perhaps anxious to sacrifice himself in the cause of peace. The monk tried to plunge himself into the midst of the fight provoked by his own words of denunciation. However, as he moved one of the more ruthless of the monk's would-be saviours struck him a sharp blow on his head so that Anastasius slumped into unconsciousness. Even before his body hit the ground it was seized by two men and carried away from the conflict which was spreading as more rushed to let loose the tensions of recent weeks.

*

Arif[500]Mahmud bin Harpoon had expected to be given the responsibility of quelling a dangerous riot. However, with two men incapacitated with broken arms and another man nursing a stab wound (which had narrowly missed his jugular vein), he wasn't in the best of moods. He'd never really volunteered for service in the Dīwān al-Shurṭah, only for a chance to escape from the slums of Alexandria. A short spell serving as assistant gang-master on board one of the caliph's galleys had made him vow never to go to sea again. It wasn't that they'd been forced into action - that was unlikely on the Red Sea, despite the pirates pouring out of Aden - it was simply the motion of the vessel making him empty his stomach at too frequent intervals over the side. Unfortunately his fellow-seamen hadn't been sympathetic; shame rather than physical discomfort had driven Mahmud to ask for a transfer out of the Fatimid navy and into - anything.

So seven years ago he'd found himself in the Dīwān al-Shurṭah unit responsible for Gaza. Under the old caliph[501] there'd been little fear of trouble; the government, with its mass of spies throughout its possessions, was quite capable of smelling out trouble before it became too nasty, and dealing with it. Mahmud worked hard, was attentive to his superiors and fair but ruthless with the native population; so it wasn't long before he obtained promotion as Arif. And there he had stuck. The next step up - to be in charge of a district - was rather a large one and Mahmud was unfortunately subordinate to a younger man who'd largely gained his position through connections with 'those in the know'. With the new caliph, a child, these people became even more important. Consequently, Mahmud made a fatal mistake of revealing ambition to excel in a tougher environment.

Three years ago he arrived in Jerusalem and, at first, the job was reasonable. He always prided himself on maintaining a tight administration, with duties and personnel clearly defined, so his superiors smiled on him. This started to change with new policies fed through from Cairo, as if the government was growing unsure of itself. Mahmud at first linked this to the growing use of Turkish mercenaries from the north. From the beginning he had little time for these rather dour troops, who preferred to keep themselves largely shut away from their fellows. However, it wasn't so much changes emanating from Cairo as growing tensions within the city itself that alarmed Mahmud. He'd been promised success here would ensure him promotion - elsewhere, but no longer could he trust in such promises. Jerusalem, largely thanks to the hundreds, if not thousands, of pilgrims pouring in from everywhere, was a morass which could engulf all efforts to maintain security.

Now his patrol had suffered casualties and he'd been merely offered Turkish replacements. He was uncertain how the new men, when they arrived, would fit in; furthermore he doubted their loyalty to Cairo. He'd heard Turkish recruits from the north were too inclined to give first obedience to Aleppo. Meanwhile, he had to identify the cause of this latest outbreak and deal with it, even if he had to do so without the three Turks!

Gradually Mahmud pieced together the story of the origin of the trouble. A Christian monk had taken it into his head to savage members of another Christian sect and they'd attacked him. He cursed every Christian sect he could think of - and they were many - for making his life more miserable than necessary. Further enquiries revealed the lunatic starting the riot had managed to slip away when some of his supporters rescued him. Mahmud, sure this monk, if free, would start another riot, redoubled his efforts and at last secured the name of Anastasius, apparently settled within the Ethiopian Community at the Church of he Holy Sepulchre. Yet, a unit of the Dīwān al-Shurṭah couldn't just march in and arrest one of these infidel troublemakers. If only the place was demolished[502] it would make an arrest far easier; he'd heard the building was a warren of chambers and corridors in which the guilty could easily scurry away to some hiding place. He had to lure the infidel troublemaker out of this maze. Mahmud set his mind to the problem.

*

Anastasia had also been thinking. She'd heard of the trouble her brother had provoked and that the authorities were looking for him urgently. She also knew elements within the population would be blaming her brother and anxious for vengeance. Sister Anastasia tried to fit all this in with what she considered to be his destiny as a witness for the faith. She knew the bodies of the witnesses would, according to St. John, "*lie in the street of the great city*" but how would that be enough to bring about the Second Coming, if he was merely the victim of an obscure fracas? No, somehow the agents of the Beast himself would have to be drawn in, making her brother the required victim of the Beast's oppression. She was prepared to hand her brother over to the authorities, certain that a public arrest would provoke such an outbreak from the Christians that the Almighty would dispatch His angels to their aid.

Realising no such public arrest could take place within the confines of the Church of the Holy Sepulchre, Anastasia decided to make sure the arrest took place in full public view. She summoned Sister Lydia, who could always be trusted to keep secrets because she never really understood what was going on. Anastasia entrusted the innocent child with a short, sealed note addressed to Rahman Aziz, the Muhtasib, and which she neglected to sign. After the emissary had departed she summoned a second sister, Theodosia, for a second letter. In this she begged her brother to come to her at midday because she'd heard the Chapel of the Annunciation was in danger of being invaded by Fatimid officials, entrusted with seizing non-existent proof of treasonable correspondence with the Autokrator. She stressed the importance of the message to Theodosia, confident this sister possessed sufficient acumen to persuade her brother to obey her summons.

*

Mahmud read the note which the Muhtasib handed to him. It was very brief and to the point: "Brother Anastasius will come to the Chapel of the Annunciation at midday." It wasn't signed. He looked up but before he could ask the question it was answered.

"The messenger said the note came from Anastasia, the ruler of the infidel community," snapped the Muhtasib. He glared at his Arif. "Surely you didn't think I'd react to an anonymous note?"

The subordinate tried to assure Rahman Aziz he'd never doubted the shrewdness of his superior but his protests were shrugged off.

"I need you and your patrol to seize this dangerous fanatic before he can cause any more trouble." The Muhtasib reached up, silently demanding the return of the note. Mahmud handed it over. Both were well aware why it was unsigned; the writer believed, with every justification, the note would be filed as evidence, and didn't want to be identified in any resulting legal process.

Mahmud decided to stay silent. There was little affection between the Muhtasib and himself; respect between them as both being dedicated to their jobs but differing personalities meant they could never be close. Even so the Arif knew Rahman Aziz was almost as furious as he was at the violence inflicted on his patrol; the Muhtasib obviously didn't know the victims as individuals but he felt Fatimid authority had been challenged. Mahmud, however, was irate at losing the services of Yussuf and Abdul with broken arms - especially as they'd been replaced by Toghrul and Mehmet whose Turkish origins didn't mix easily in his unit.

"I hope I can rely on you to seize the infidel with the minimum of fuss!" Again there was the glare as Mahmud understood his superior was terrified of any further losses to his force. He knew reports would have gone to Cairo and the Vizier been angered by a challenge to authority. Besides, loss of experienced personnel could damage the effectiveness of a force already under pressure by the squabbles between infidel ruffians in Jerusalem.

Mahmud nodded and then added, "I assume you want to discover any connections the man might have with foreign elements wishing to undermine our control - "

"You can assume what you like, Arif!" snapped the Muhtasib. "I'll make up my mind when I visit the fanatic in his cell." He paused to make sure his subordinate fully understood. "I don't want Cairo to ask awkward questions AFTER we've settled the matter."

Mahmud understood perfectly. A dead fanatic wouldn't be of any use in the diplomatic manoeuvring he knew to be the constant occupation of his masters and the regimes of Constantinople and Aleppo. A live fanatic could be induced to say whatever would be most useful to Cairo, reveal contacts which might be genuine or not. However, for this to happen there must first be a record the Muhtasib had personally interviewed the fanatic and ordered a more detailed interrogation.

Rahman Aziz dismissed the Arif and turned back to the note in his hand. He gently caressed his dyed beard as he wondered about the connection between the writer and the fanatic. Their names were remarkably similar but why would an infidel devoting her life to a perversion of the True Faith be willing to sacrifice another infidel to what they'd consider unbelievers. His fingers tightened as they reached the end of the beard. He wasn't happy. He almost smelt a trap but couldn't see how it could be sprung.

Suddenly the Muhtasib released his beard and placed both his palms flat on his desk. He'd have to consult Nicephorus Eupator. The old man might be an infidel but he knew the value of silver having been an agent for the authorities for fifteen years. All that Nicephorus required was discretion and regular payments, and his information had proved valuable over the years. He'd warned the Muhtasib of the potential dangers of this accursed year two years ago but Cairo had shrugged off all his requests for more men to deal with the anticipated disturbances. Well, now they were paying for it. Rahman Aziz bent his fingers so that his nails bit into his desk, screwing up his eyes and tightening his lips. No, HE was paying for it while they sat back, sending out impossible orders and giving all sorts of lying excuses when he asked for reinforcements. He trusted the Arif to act with efficiency in seizing the fanatic; on reflection, Rahman Aziz was praying the Arif would succeed.

*

Mahmud had placed his patrol well. Two men were hidden right next to the entrance of the Chapel of the Annunciation in case the main body of the patrol failed to seize the fanatic. Ahmed had done a brief circuit of the building and assured the Arif there was no other entrance. The Arif was certain about the way the fanatic would be coming, confident the man would have no idea he was walking into a trap. The fanatic wouldn't even consider he was in ANY danger, such was the arrogance the infidels often had in the workings of their god. Now, with four other men, he was concealed in the doorway of a small bakery on the corner of the street. Even though the baker was a Moslem the Arif had detailed another man to wait in the backroom with the family, just in case anybody should consider warning the fanatic. That left the two Turks. Mahmud had been reluctant to use them. He could trust his men to obey his commands to the letter but not the newcomers. So he placed the two men in a small alleyway further along the street, as back-up he'd said when he noticed the suspicious gleam appearing in the eyes of Toghrul. Did the man believe he was being swindled out of some bounty? Mahmud knew Turks were greedy but they should have known this was simply an everyday arrest - no bounties, just punishment if they fouled things up!

*

Anastasius had been puzzled by the letter from his sister, mainly because it was the first she'd sent him in over twenty years. He doubted very much he could do anything to resist intrusion by Fatimid agents; in fact, he'd advise his sister to cooperate with the authorities while lodging a formal protest. Even so, he was sure he could provide some form of moral support, if only as a potential witness, by preventing any excesses by soldiery faced with a collection of females! Overall, Anastasius was prepared to answer the summons because he couldn't see why he could fail to!

Accordingly, the Ethiopian brother scurried out of the Church of the Holy Sepulchre shortly before midday, all too aware he might find himself too late to help his sister. As he passed close by a beggar who daily propped up a crumbling wall next to the church he felt compelled to offer a small prayer for the wretch as his remorseless adherence to the vow of poverty meant he'd little more to give. He was rewarded by a knowledgeable smile from the fragile frame as both knew the other had little to offer in this world, except that spiritual comfort and sympathy in short supply in the Holy City for the last few months. He knew it would take but a short time to reach the Chapel of the Annunciation and yet, because he was terrified of being late, the monk almost trotted in his haste to help his sister.

As he entered the street leading to the chapel he could see the figures of two of the Dīwān al-Shurṭah. Although they might be better than ordinary soldiers, Anastasius was terrified he was already too late. His swift walk became a strange mixture of jog and brisk pace as he approached the two men. Behind him he sensed movement and then some kind of blanket was thrown over his head, blotting out the sun and throwing him into isolation. At the same time he felt several hands reach to grasp whatever part of his body could be seized.

A rough voice grunted, "Silence, fanatic, you've caused us enough trouble already!"

Anastasius started to protest, certain this was a matter of mistaken identity. He certainly wouldn't describe himself as a fanatic and, as for being a troublemaker, well, he spent most of his life trying to STAY OUT of trouble. However, as he opened his mouth a fist crunched into his left ear and whatever he was about to say became a scream of pain.

*

Ethelwulf, Olaf and Sweyn had decided to explore the possibilities of finding passage on any vessel heading west, With February coming to an end, the year of the Millenium had only weeks to run and no miracle seemed about to happen. Even the strange optimism of the fugitive King of Norway had been blunted by mere tales of petty squabbles and nastiness, not a magnificent parting of the clouds as the promises of the Apocalypse were fulfilled. Only that morning he'd been persuaded by the cousins to head for the quarter where traders would know what was coming and going between the Holy Land and, perhaps, Italy. So, dutifully muffled up in long cloaks which, while betraying their western origin, gave them adequate hiding place for their swords and the semi-anonymity of modestly-successful traders, all three set off on the short walk required.

Ethelwulf suddenly spotted Brother Anastasius crossing the junction ahead of them. He'd promised to introduce Sweyn to his mentor on several occasions but promises had come to nothing as lack of real motivation changed 'tomorrow' into 'next week' and then into a vague time in the future. Sweyn would have liked meeting the monk who'd offered his cousin such comfort (and shelter!) but appreciated the security needs which made Ethelwulf think twice before venturing near such a public place as the Church of the Holy Sepulchre. Olaf, of course, had never met Brother Anastasius and, as he pointed out, one Ethiopian monk was just like another, persisting in wrong interpretations and odd practices instead of bowing to the will of the Holy Father; so he'd shown no enthusiasm to meet any one particular monk.

"That's Anastasius," half-shouted Ethelwulf to his companions, and then suddenly realised how easy it would be to draw unwelcome attention to themselves. He dropped his voice as he hoarsely added, "Come on! I'll introduce you," before extending the length of stride to increase speed while still trying to resemble a walk.

Olaf was about to protest but, seeing Sweyn match his cousin's pace, felt he'd no choice but to fall in line. As they reached the corner they heard the sounds of a scuffle and then a cry from the monk as he was set upon by four members of the Dīwān al-Shurṭah. Ethelwulf didn't hesitate; he knew Brother Anastasius would never intentionally act against authority. What was more, the monk had come to his aid when he'd been close to sliding into that chasm which produced self-murder. Finally here was a fellow-Christian beset by infidels. On all three counts there could be no question. With never a second thought the Saxon reached under the folds of his cloak for his sword and, with a loud shout, rushed towards the struggling figures.

*

Ali heard a loud cry and turned from his frantic attempts to grab the left arm of the monk. He saw a tall infidel brandishing a broadsword rapidly approaching him. He frantically reached for the knife in his belt to parry the blow but was far too late. Even as his blade left his belt the broadsword cut into his face, severing his jaw-bone as it hacked into his brain. With a scream Ali fell but Mustapha and Al-Mansur had been better warned. Just as Al-Mansur, whose blow had provoked the monk's scream, drew his scimitar, Sweyn's sword jabbed into his arm causing him to drop the weapon. However, Al-Mansur was a big man, priding himself on years of violence in back-alleys, and he reached to grapple with Sweyn. The Viking foot struck out, smacking so smartly into the Cairene's testicles that, without even the strength to yelp, Al-Mansur belied his name[503] by crunching into the dust. Having felled one opponent Sweyn cut at Mustapha who screamed and fell backwards as he half-parried and half-dodged the blow.

By now other members of the Police were hurrying to help their comrades. However, they hadn't come fully equipped, expecting only to seize a solitary monk; Aziz and Ibrahim had long knives; weapons too feeble to resist the onslaught of the Varangians. Aziz took a slash in his leg and, almost thankfully out of the fight, slumped into a doorway. Ethelwulf lunged at Ibrahim, piercing his heart with one well-aimed thrust. Adil the Far-Travelled, a Kurd from the shores of the Caspian, attempted to circle behind the two strangers but found himself lifted into the air and thrown against the baked walls of a house, on impact consciousness and Adil parted company.

Haroun, was better equipped and advanced with a determination bolstered by the scimitar in his hand. However, he was unwilling to charge the two armed Varangians, having seen the effect of the broadswords. For their part Ethelwulf and Sweyn stepped forward so that the form of Anastasius, groaning and struggling to escape from the folds of the blanket thrown over his head, was behind them. Haroun felt his courage needed the support of the rest of the patrol to press home any counter-attack. Behind him he could hear shouting and the sound of running feet.

Aziz and Ahmed positioned by the entrance to the chapel had seen the attack on their comrades and, drawing their only weapons (a pair of clubs), rushed to their aid. They expected to be joined by the Turkish recruits but neither Toghrul nor Mehmet moved. The Arif stepped out from his position of command across the street and started bawling at the two men, advancing as he shouted. He drew his sword but Aziz and Ahmed, noticing the Arif's attention seemed confined to their comrades, slowed down and came to a halt so that both Turks and Arif were placed between themselves and the strangers.

Neither Ethelwulf nor Sweyn took any step forward. Ethelwulf urged Olaf to help the victim of the ambush and was pleased to hear sounds indicating Olaf was helping the monk to his feet. However, Anastasius wasn't recovered enough even to extricate himself fully from the blanket.

"Pick him up, Olaf, and carry him back to our rooms!" ordered Ethelwulf. Then noticing the Turks were dredging up the courage to advance, drawing their rather wider scimitars, he added, "Hurry!"

Sounds told Ethelwulf Olaf had seized the groaning monk still muffled in the blanket. He assumed the Norwegian had retired to the corner and turned it. There were no sounds behind them; even though the fight must have seized the attention of anybody neither dead nor asleep in that street, nobody emerged from the shelter of their homes. It would appear the Fatimid authorities in no way could call upon assistance from the locals. Ethelwulf had long known Fatimid control wasn't popular in Jerusalem but he hadn't reckoned on it being so unpopular that, after several members of the Police had been either wounded or killed, nobody seemed anxious to help.

"I think, cousin," suggested Sweyn, almost out of the side of his mouth as if their opponents were skilled in the Norse tongue, " it's time we joined Olaf." However, both realised that to do so would mean either simply turning to run or else walking slowly backwards, daring their opponents to restart the fight. Both knew running would destroy that strange air of superiority which they enjoyed, keeping them from attack by the remaining members of the Dīwān al-Shurṭah. So they had to retire slowly, watching for any move threatening their retreat. Of course, this meant their refuge would become known; they could only hope night would allow them to escape from the trap.

Without a word the cousins took one step back and were pleased to see this even had the effect of halting the reluctant advance of the Turks. Now the survivors of the patrol just stood and watched the steady retreat of the infidels. Apart from the groans of Al-Mansur there was an eerie silence in that street; even the Arif couldn't muster the will to continue the mixture of pleas and threats to bring his force into action. However, after the infidels had covered six paces and were approaching the corner, the Police came to life, splitting up across the street and slowly, with a care generated by fear, making sure they stayed well out of the reach of the broadswords. As he reached the corner Ethelwulf stepped forward, as if to renew the fight, and was pleased to see two of their opponents immediately stepped back. But he noticed neither of the men positioned on the extreme edges of the streets retired so he was in danger of being out-flanked; the tall man, who, by his shouting, appeared to be in command, continued to advance. Ethelwulf made as if to attack and smiled as he saw the other flinch and stop. Having re-asserted superiority Ethelwulf retired quickly to rejoin Sweyn so that both turned the corner together. As they did so Sweyn glanced over his shoulder and saw Olaf, still carrying the monk sprawled over his shoulder, enter their lodgings. Otherwise the street remained silent and empty.

Quickly the cousins retired to the entrance of their lodgings, followed at a suitable distance by the survivors of the Dīwān al-Shurṭah. As they reached the doorway, Sweyn leaped inside, closely followed by Ethelwulf. No sooner were they in than the door was slammed and they found Olaf ramming a bench against its handle to force it shut. Sweyn and Ethelwulf together carried across a table and rammed it against the door to provide extra defence. The siege had begun.

*

The Arif sent to the Muhtasib for reinforcements. The message was quite simple: your patrol has been attacked, four members have been wounded and one killed so send me more men. Rahman Aziz responded immediately with the dispatch of two more patrols under Abdullah ibn Yussuf and Selim the Beautiful who, much to the irritation of Mahmud, was placed in charge. Selim had acquired a name for efficiency and cruelty which made him outstanding among the Police based in Jerusalem. Naturally his Turkish origins were held against him, but he'd been born in Egypt thirty years before. So to many of the regime's forces Selim could be counted a native. His reputation had been enhanced by his successful crushing of an uprising at Damascus, despite the attempt by the rebels to burn down half of the city. Selim had simply charged through the flames, straight at the men who were trying, with little success, to burn down the Accounts Office.[504] Two comrades who charged with him were overcome by the flames and perished, screaming to be carried off by death. Selim, with another two comrades, had breached the flames and killing the rebels, prevented an inferno. During the charge somehow Selim's long hair had caught fire and the flames had seared the left half of his face; he was scarred for life and gained the nickname 'the Beautiful' - but also a reputation.

Now Selim quickly positioned five of his men so there was little chance the Varangians could simply charge out; he placed two archers to shoot any Varangian foolish enough to appear at the upper window. However, he soon found the peculiar geometry of the building structure meant that was a natural barrier against arrows. Toghrul was sent to scout the rear of the building, very close to the wall and the gate which led to Antioch. Adil was sent to inspect the area and quickly reported back there was no rear entrance to the building

Mahmud suggested they should try to negotiate the surrender of the monk. "After all," he concluded, "there's no way the monk can be of any real interest to the northern devils!"

"Perhaps," muttered Selim and then added, mainly to himself, "perhaps not."

"It was an obvious case, " persisted Mahmud, "of two or three drunken infidels getting involved - "

"So were there two or were there three?" snapped Selim. He'd little time for Mahmud - efficient enough at the administrative side of the job, certainly sufficient to flatter himself he was promotion material. However, when it came to risking your neck when dealing with armed ruffians, Mahmud wasn't the first to come forward. The man was not a coward, just over-cautious.

"There were three infidels," answered Mahmud, barely managing to keep insubordination out of his voice. " But only two of them actually attacked my patrol."

"And worsted ten police!"

"Surprise can upset the balance of forces," answered Mahmud with a steely calm in his voice. " Once we'd overcome that factor the infidels had to retire."

"With a prisoner responsible for another riot, I hear," answered Selim, deliberately turning his back on Mahmud as if to stress his lack of respect for how the police action had been conducted. Mahmud made no attempt to flatter the Turkish Arif by trying to respond to that jibe. Instead he merely walked off and started directing his men as if Selim were invisible.

*

Meanwhile inside the building everyone had retreated to the upper floor where Anastasius had been discarded in a corner. Then without a word Olaf began hacking at the plastered ceiling with his sword. Within minutes his grey hair had become even greyer, matching the unnatural pallor of his face and the grubby hue of his clothes. However, a small hole had appeared in the roof.

"I have learned, Ethelwulf," he smiled grimly, "that it's always best to have a way out the enemy may not suspect."

"Over the roofs?" questioned Sweyn, grinning at Ethelwulf.

"At night, darkness will hide our retreat," answered the former king. "We have only to hold out five hours!"

"Only five hours!" laughed Ethelwulf. "I think, Olaf, it's time for you to compose your death-song."

"And what about you, my Saxon friend?" smiled Olaf Trygvasson.

"I made up mine many years ago," replied the Wanderer, " and have been adding to it ever since." He crept to the side of the window to peer out in the street. "I'm sure you'll hear it by-and-by."

He could see the disposition of the Dīwān al-Shurṭah and was glad that, not by design, they'd taken up lodging in such an easily defensible building. It would be very difficult to approach the entrance, except directly, and that would expose the attackers to fierce resistance. The structure of the building meant that, with care, they could avoid arrows and javelins; on the other hand, they could pour down death on any who approached the sole doorway. Their building was linked to others which ran up in a continuous strip until it almost reached the road for Antioch and the north. He knew Olaf was planning an escape across the flat roofs under the cover of darkness; it was a good strategy, especially as anybody would expect the forces of the Dīwān al-Shurṭah to rely on the twin dragons of heat and thirst to secure the surrender of the besieged.

Ethelwulf looked at Anastasius, wondering why he should have been seized by the police. The monk was recovering from the combination of shock and violence which had removed him from reality for some time. He obviously recognised Ethelwulf as an attempt at a strange smile altered his features but the smile vanished as he gazed up at Olaf, still hacking away at the ceiling.

"What's wrong, Brother?" asked Ethelwulf as he eased himself down next to the prostrate monk.

"That man," began Anastasius in a voice that was both high-pitched and hoarse as if he had a problem framing his words. "That man, Saxon, who is he?"

"His name is Olaf," snatching a glance at the Norwegian busying himself at securing a way of escape. "And he's a friend, a stranger in this land and to your ways but one that can be trusted."

"But I've seen him before!" gasped Anastasius, remembering the face of his companion in the nightmare when he'd been condemned under the ground. He clearly recalled the features of the stranger who'd slipped away from him with his declaration of completing a task. Brother Anastasius knew Olaf Trygvasson was the man in that dream and he was afraid.

"You're mistaken," replied the Wanderer, perhaps a little roughly. "He's been in this land scarcely six weeks and has travelled from the far north."

"And yet I've seen him in my dreams," protested Anastasius and proceeded to describe to Ethelwulf the series of nightmares he'd experienced. Ethelwulf was disturbed to see he featured in one, but whether because he was somehow linked with evil-doers or simply part of a catalogue of disaster he was unsure.

"So it would appear, Brother, we're all doomed men," Ethelwulf concluded after he'd absorbed the recitation. He glanced at Olaf, still beavering away at the weakened ceiling, and at Sweyn, calmly keeping an eye on whatever was going on outside. His lips formed an enigmatic line as he added, "But we've all been doomed from the beginning of time." Then softly he murmured to himself:

> "The Wand'rer voyaged to distant shores
> Seeking out Fate in Death and Pain;
> Slashing aside whatever dreams
> He had of peace and hope and love."

Sweyn turned at the murmuring he heard behind him. "Is that the Death Song you promised, cousin?" he asked.

Ethelwulf nodded, dragging himself to his feet. "Man must do what man has been given to do," he remarked. "No more, no less." After a pause he added. "For over twenty years I've been making my slow way to this place."

"Which was how I thought of Hjorungavang,"[505] interrupted Olaf, resting from his task. "But God had chosen otherwise." He glanced up at the hole in the ceiling, now wide enough for a man to climb through and started to shake off the plaster which had settled all over his frame. "How else would I have found myself with such delightful company?"

Ethelwulf laughed. Perhaps Olaf was right; whatever might seem the end didn't have to be so. After all, he'd been in some very awkward situations before and managed to survive. His mind went back to the destruction of all his hopes at the Cilician Gates. Perhaps the difference now was he no longer wanted to survive.

> "Left far behind the lands of snow,
> And farther still the family home
> By way of sea and rushing stream
> He came to lands where warring faiths
> Besmirched the will of God and man
> And there he found strange peace at last
> Beneath the sand, interred by stone
> To wait for what he knew must come

The Judgement of his God and Lord."

His murmuring stopped as, all too aware of the alarmed looks at his comrades he realised he was enshrouding them all in a web of gloom. Only Anastasius, with his ignorance of the Norse tongue, hadn't understood the meaning of Ethelwulf's verse; but he could detect the apprehension the words aroused in his comrades.

Ethelwulf stepped up to a small stove constructed in the middle of the room and started a small fire. Then he raced downstairs and immediately returned with some of the supply of olive oil which formed part of their business. The ibn Abdullah family, their landlords, had left early that morning to visit their relatives in nearby Bethlehem, little knowing they'd have no chance of returning to their home. The Saxon began slowly to heat the oil in one of the pans so kindly left by the ibn Abdullah family; when it had reached a fairly high temperature he carefully removed it from the flame, covering it with another pan to preserve the heat as long as possible. Sweyn meanwhile calmly made sure the only bow they possessed between them was in good order, carefully marshalling the fifteen arrows (their sole supply) so he could quickly lay hands on them. Olaf, satisfied the escape route was sufficiently widened carried, with the help of Sweyn, a solid table, placing it gingerly under the hole, taking care they didn't disturb Ethelwulf's 'cooking' operations.

Suddenly the business-like silent preparations were interrupted by what an impartial observer might have styled the sanest person in the room.

"But why am I here?" the monk asked, bewildered by what had happened since he'd left his church but hours before. He could almost smell the fatalism in the room, but it was not the welcome scent of submission to the will of God but rather a last defiant shout at the jaws of destruction. He had no part in this! His faith had schooled him, perhaps, in the will of the Lord culminating in the End of the Old Order in this year; certainly his life had taught him God fashioned all things to a purpose, that humans were set upon a way designed by God even though they might choose which path to take. Now he recalled how vehement had been his sister when they'd met years ago about how the destiny of the world was stretching towards this year, and no further. Then he'd rejected her confidence in the Divine intervention which would lay aside Fatimid and Byzantine with equal ease while it battled with the Forces of Evil, knowing that being directed by the Almighty there could be but one outcome. He'd found it hard to believe that God, having created all the myriad wonders of the world, would contemplate bringing it all to naught, and yet he knew that evil, like weeds in a garden, had swarmed into every niche in this world, spreading corruption and arrogance and sin. In his own little world of the Holy Sepulchre he'd tried to shut it out, even though every day the growing tumult of pilgrim and fanatic brought into stronger focus the ambitions and desires of mankind. He'd slowly come to realise that perhaps this year hadn't been set aside by God to bring about the Second Coming but rather structured by Satan himself to ensnare mankind into false hopes and dreams. He recalled how the Scriptures denounced the false prophets who'd lead astray the faithful, and realised that somehow he'd fallen into that very trap. He too had come to believe this year would bring about the final end to the battle between God and Evil. And that was why he was here now, with these doomed men.

Ethelwulf turned and the smile on his lips was both condescending and grim. "Why is any man condemned to this short time on earth?"

"Because we're the playthings of the Norns!" laughed Sweyn. "Each of us has his path marked out for a certain distance and then - "

"We seek the loving mercy of Our Lord," interposed the Olaf. He came over and slumped down next to the monk. "I used to be like Sweyn, believing the Fates determined our existence. For years I wandered the northern seas, not knowing where I was going, lost!" He lightly laid his hand on the thigh of the monk." Then I found the Christian God and for a time, when I look back, it made little difference. Naturally, I felt I should be an active fighter for Our Lord and so I harried any who dared defy His Name and my sword carved a wide path for Christian missionaries throughout the Northern world. But I was wrong!"

Anastasius, despite bewilderment at the unintelligible gabble of the warrior's language, looked with horror at his companion, for whom he already felt such dread from his nightmare; was this man about to confess his apostasy? Olaf sensed the tension stiffening the monk's limbs and, loosening his grip, gently massaged the thigh.

"God himself revealed the truth with my final defeat, when I saw the mightiest longship could not withstand attack while it wasn't on the right course!" He half-laughed to himself. "But even then I didn't really see a king could not serve the Prince of Peace by slaughtering his subjects for refusing to admit the Truth. Better for me to have been content to leave them to Divine Judgement. But in that moment of defeat I threw myself overboard in despair. Whether I really did intend self-murder I can't say but I certainly looked into the face of Hell itself and saw it wasn't an old crone as pagans would tell you but a vibrant and powerful monster." Olaf felt the monk relax as he realised he'd also been aware of the nature of Hell, and its Satanic master, for some time. "So I knew I had to escape from the battle and determine how I should deal with what seemed defeat for the Gospel in the North. Unfortunately or not, chance played a hand and I only became fully aware of my surroundings when I was being taken far to the south, too late to revive my followers or collect any force to prevent the rape of my country which followed." The fingers tightened and the monk winced. Suddenly Olaf was aware of his companion's discomfort and, without any apology, withdrew his hand.

"Anyway, I determined to travel to Jerusalem and, whatever the outcome of the prophecies filling the Northern world, offer my sword to the Prince of Peace." Olaf smiled. "Perhaps I should have become a monk like yourself, serving Our Lord in a humble fashion." He paused to look around the room at their two companions preparing for a fight. "However, it looks as if God's determined differently and I'm content."

With that he eased himself back to his feet. Anastasius wanted to tell him about his dream, beg for some interpretation that could tell him what he, Anastasius, the life-term servant of Christ, should do. However, he'd no way to communicate the words and the monk slumped back against the wall, praying for the end of whatever had been fixed as their fate.

*

Selim was growing impatient. He'd shrugged off the suggestion by Abdullah ibn Yussuf that they should simply besiege the building and wait for heat, thirst or hunger to do the work for them. He put it down to the softness he claimed to see in the Sudanese. Anyway he knew Rahman Aziz couldn't afford to have agents of the Dīwān al-Shurṭah sitting around waiting for nature to overcome resistance. From what he knew that monk was dangerous - and he didn't want the Muhtasib asking why he hadn't been able to recapture the infidel quickly; every hour spent outside here was an extra hour for troublemakers to get to work. So Selim determined to act quickly and efficiently.

The attack came very suddenly and from two directions at once - eight men had encircled the street so they could attack from the Chapel of the Annunciation. Two men carried large axes with which to batter down the shutters barring entry to the ground floor, a further four men carried a makeshift battering ram, consisting of two benches lashed together, very solid but unfortunately very heavy. He'd toyed with the idea of adding two more to this battering party but a rapid practice in a nearby alley had shown only four men could hold the weapon and swing it effectively. Both advance and swing would be slowed down by the weight but Selim reckoned it would be effective. Finally eight men would rush in from the unexpected quarter and charge through the useless barrier.

The two men alerted the defenders who'd almost slipped into that inertia which comes with a hot afternoon and insufficient activity. The first thud against the shutters caused Ethelwulf frantically to pile fresh fuel on the stove so that the pan's contents could reach boiling pitch. Meanwhile Sweyn rushed to a window from where he launched an arrow at the attackers. His first arrow missed, harmlessly clattering against the stone walls. However, a second arrow sank deep into the back of Khalid as his axe half-carried him through the window.

Now came the attack by the battering ram and Sweyn spotted the advance. Even as the four men swung the ram to smash into the door Ethelwulf struck, pouring the contents of the pan over the attackers. As the boiling oil smashed over the shoulders of the leading two police their screams sent a shudder through the monk whose attention became riveted on the window. Ethelwulf rushed over to the stove and, seizing a fiery brand, returned to the window, pitching it out on to the men below. If the screams before had been horrible the sounds which now arose to the defenders were twice as hideous. The flames appeared to sweep on to the oil-smattered shoulders of the two leading attackers and from there snatch at the robes of the remaining two police. Immediately all four police were on fire, and with them the improvised ram. Anastasius was horrified as he recognised the angel of his nightmare in the singing, taunting and dancing form of the Saxon. It was one of the demons rejoicing in the horrors of death which had replaced the Wanderer. But only for a moment; an arrow from one of the police outside struck the window-frame causing Ethelwulf to return to reality. With almost an apologetic glance at the monk he returned to the stove where he furiously stoked up the fire for the next pan of oil. Sweyn crossed over and began filling the first pan with fresh oil, eagerly waiting his turn to create a hideous weapon. The monk wondered what monsters had been let loose by God in these Last Days.

*

Selim stood and watched in horror as four of his men burned to death before his eyes. Omar, having smashed in one window's shutter had been about to return in safety when the tragedy had occurred. Instantly he'd turned in a frantic attempt to drag one of the burning victims to safety. He yelled out for help but none of his comrades moved, petrified by what had suddenly erupted before their eyes. Omar realised his efforts were useless, and at the same time how exposed he was to a similar attack. With a last yell he released his hold on Haroun and rushed back to safety.

Even after the screams of the men had died away their bodies continued to burn, watched by their comrades. Selim became insane with rage as he recalled the dreadful time when he'd been scarred by fire, gaining the title of 'the Beautiful'. With that insanity came a passion to lay blame on anyone but himself. At first he cursed Mahmud but then realised the Arif wasn't within earshot so all his curses were wasted. Then somewhere in the back of his mind sprang the memory of what he'd been told by the Muhtasib and with it a horrible idea. The monk had been betrayed by his sister but neither he nor the Muhtasib could understand what could have provoked such treachery. He wondered how the Varangians just happened to be there to rescue the brother and almost start a riot. Yes, that was the reason. The whole plan had been to start a riot; he'd heard some fanatics dreamed of bringing about the End of the World by sacrifice. Now he knew why the monk had been betrayed but, owing to the incompetence of Mahmud's patrol and the cowardice of the local population, the plot had failed. As a result he'd lost good men and the bitch would pay, and in a way which her brother would appreciate! Quickly he ordered two men to force their way into the Chapel of the Annunciation, seize the sister of the infidel who'd started all this trouble and bring her here. Finally he added he expected them to return with all possible speed - or their heads would be hewed from their bodies.

*

By now Brother Anastasius was in a state of acute panic. He'd seen the vision in one of his nightmares and he dreaded the fulfilment of the other two. Olaf tried to calm the Ethiopian as he screamed Ethelwulf would burn in hell for what he'd done to the men outside. He hadn't witnessed the actual burning of the agents of the Dīwān al-Shurṭah but their screams would haunt his dreams for ever.

Ethelwulf simply turned his back on the hysterical monk. Part of him regretted what he'd done but his brain told him the method made no difference; this was war and that meant men must die. Perhaps he had to face his Maker soon but he could declare his actions were provoked by the need to protect the innocent. Was that an excuse? He almost laughed at the futility of his own words. Would he dare stand before his Saviour and say he'd done that to human beings in the name of humanity? He looked across at Sweyn and his cousin gave him a quick smile. What did Sweyn think? Would he condemn him as he was sure most Christians would, or would the Norse pagan be strong enough to shake off such scruples.

At last Olaf calmed the monk down, mainly by forcibly holding him against the wall and whispering that whatever was happening must be the will of the Almighty for certainly no other power could exist in the Holy City at this time. Brother Anastasius believed he understood what the stranger said and wanted to believe him but could not, and yet he was over-awed by the dreadful silence which followed the deaths of the four police agents.

Gradually the silence seeped away with sounds of activity, but none near enough to be identified by the watchers. Both Ethelwulf and Sweyn, sheltered by shadow, watched from the windows to see if any further attack was coming.

Suddenly there was a lone voice, high-pitched as if under strain, which called out. "See, fanatic, the one who betrayed you! See, the child of Judas who schemed to bring you into our hands!"

Brother Anastasius, no longer caring for his safety, rushed over to the window and, shrugging off the restraining hands of Ethelwulf, placed himself in clear view of the street. By the doorway opposite stood his sister, her veil had been torn and she'd been cruelly bound. Even as Anastasius looked upon this unexpected image of misery, the tall man shouted again.

"See the woman who betrayed her own brother into our hands!" He looked up into the horrified face of the monk and laughed. "And what should be done with such a bitch? Surely her soul has been abandoned to the Evil One!"

Anastasia started to protest and Toghrul viciously slapped her face so her shouts turned into a scream.

"Yes, infidel, if she were my sister and she'd acted thus, I wouldn't want her to live!" He paused briefly and quickly made some gesture to Toghrul who grabbed hold of Anastasia and swung her easily into his arms. The tall man looked carefully at the two windows, one filled by the monk and the other in darkness, and almost smacked his lips. "But I'll leave that decision to you!"

With that Selim clapped his hands and Toghrul rushed across the street and with a single action pitched his fragile burden through the smashed-in window. Immediately he turned and scurried back across the street - but he wasn't quick enough. A spear buried itself in his back, thrown by Olaf who'd quietly made his way to stand slightly back from the window so that he couldn't easily be seen from the street.

Now all feeling except anger left Selim but before any police agent could throw a missile at the monk Ethelwulf dragged him back into the safety of shadow. Foiled of immediate vengeance Selim had recourse to his main purpose. Mehmet and Samir tore across the street; Mehmet threw a bottle of oil through the window after Anastasia and Samir followed it with a fiery brand. Then both turned sharply and scurried away using the shelter of the building itself.

Immediately screams from below revealed Selim had reacted to Ethelwulf's stratagem in kind. Anastasius rushed to help his sister and had to be tripped by Sweyn to prevent him scurrying down. He fell heavily and was lifted to his feet by Olaf who didn't relax his hold while the screams continued. Finally there was silence and Sweyn moved quickly to the door. Below were flames but it didn't look as if Selim's aim of burning them out would be achieved. In fact, Sweyn reported that perhaps by dusk whatever fire was below would have died out.

Brother Anastasius went limp in Olaf's arms as he realised not only had his sister died but the fate meted out to the Scarlet Woman as described by St. John[506] had been carried out. Indeed the nature of her death transfixed the monk. For if God had allowed her to perish in the way foretold by his dream then she must have been guilty of the treason declared by the voice. Even in his state of physical collapse the mind of Anastasius sought an answer and it came. He understood his sister had been one of those believing the Second Coming would only take place if the faithful by their actions forced it to happen. He remembered how interested she'd been when he had described himself as one of the two witnesses promised in the Scriptures. That strange gleam in her eye he'd dismissed as interest he now saw that even then she'd plotted his death. In his misery the monk forgave his sister, certain she'd only acted in accordance with the will of God, as she saw it.

By now the light was rapidly fading and Olaf reminded his three companions they'd have to make their way over the rooftops to safety once darkness had come. He looked closely at the monk, wondering if Anastasius would be recovered enough from the trauma of the afternoon to face the prospect of clambering over the roof. If he couldn't force himself to go then one of them would have to drag him up on to the roof and then, perhaps, carry him across the neighbouring roofs to safety. His only fear was the monk might fall and give away their escape route.

*

In the doorway opposite Selim also waited for darkness. He'd been frustrated in his attempt to burn out the defenders. How appropriate it would have been to let fire do the work for him after one of the infidel devils had used that very weapon to defeat his main attack. Still he was pleased they'd been able to get rid of that screeching fanatic from the chapel. From the moment she'd admitted she'd started the train of events which would destroy his world he had hated her, recognizing in her eyes the mark of the insane.

So now he'd have to rely on a second attempt at a rush to the main door. However, this time he'd wait till darkness when it would be more difficult for the defenders to target his men carrying the battering ram. Also, immediately after the earlier fiasco, he'd sent away for a proper ram from the garrison in the south of the city. It had arrived soon after he'd seen the infidel bitch hurled through the windows. Then, however, he'd hoped fire would do the work for him; now he trusted darkness would shield his men from harm.

From a position further along the street Mahmud watched the Turk and was already framing in his mind the report to be given to the Muhtasib. He'd seen valuable lives thrown away because of the impetuosity of Selim the Beautiful. He certainly wouldn't have tried a frontal assault with an improvised ram. Guile might have been a better tactic, try to get the infidels to open discussions while getting close enough to strike. Yes, he was certain the Muhtasib wouldn't like the report he'd receive tomorrow on this incident. Mahmud was sure Abdullah ibn Yussuf hadn't been pleased to see his suggestions so brusquely dismissed; the Sudanese would certainly put in a complaint that lives had been thrown away, probably underplaying the delay his own plan would have risked. Even if Selim's attack after darkness was successful it would still be wise to put in some form of complaint; Mahmud was convinced the earlier fiasco would count against Selim. However, he knew his own bravery would need to be shown to secure a favourable eye for his own report. He was determined to play a key role in the attack - but without the ridiculous bravery the late Toghrul had exhibited.

*

At last darkness swept visibility behind its shutters, and the quietness which followed the last call to prayer of the muezzin seemed almost too profound. Inside the upstairs room the light from the stove still threw a strange blend of light and shadow to different areas. It was almost time to go. The three Vikings listened to the street outside, straining to hear sounds of movement with suspicion growing as they heard nothing.

Ethelwulf felt that was nothing to fear from guile or trickery. He'd become convinced a fool who'd tried a frontal assault once would try it a second time. Olaf agreed but pointed out the commander might have been replaced but Sweyn thought that might happen the next day.

"Which means I think another attack will come tonight," insisted Ethelwulf, imagining he could hear footsteps in the street. He paused, making sure what he'd just heard had really been his imagination.

"So that means," said Olaf, "if the attack is coming tonight we should be going now - "

"When it's scarcely dark?" queried Sweyn.

"Quite," countered Olaf. "Now's the time they'll not be expecting us to do anything. Indeed," he added, with a smile which the shadows concealed from his companions. "I wouldn't be surprised if they're themselves waiting for more time to make surprise doubly sure."

Further discussion was interrupted by a groan from Anastasius. Olaf looked in his direction, conscious the monk was on the point of collapse. Given an hour and he doubted if Anastasius would be capable of doing anything beyond sitting in a corner and emptying the misery from his soul in tears. He looked at Ethelwulf but the flickering shadows masked any reaction from the man who'd assumed the role of leader. After all, thought Olaf, with surprising bitterness creeping into his heart, he was the one who attacked the police and so got us all into this mess. Then he was reminded of what he'd said to the monk but hours before, that God would only allow to happen in Jerusalem what he intended. With that he relaxed. It was strange comfort in a darkened room besieged by an unknown number of enemies.

As if reading Olaf's thoughts Ethelwulf spoke. "I think it's time to slip out on to the roof." He sensed Sweyn was about to remonstrate so he added. "Once out there we can wait, if we prefer, until it's even darker before moving over the roofs. It may take us some time to get out there - and we don't want to do it under attack." Ethelwulf smiled and then realised that whatever his companions saw would certainly not be a smile, more like a grimace.

By then Olaf had moved over to the monk and gently coaxed him towards the table. He appealed to Sweyn for help, asking him to climb up through the hole and then drag the monk up after him. Anastasius looked from one barbarian to the other, not understanding a word of the whispered Norse. Sweyn nodded, jumped up on to the table, then, reaching down, took the bow and several arrows from Ethelwulf and passed that up through the hole. The next thing to follow was his sword and then he reached up and gently heaved himself up through the hole. One or two bits of plaster broke away but the hole remained sound. There was a pause while Sweyn repositioned his weapons away from the hole and did a rapid reconnaissance of the way they were to travel. Finally he returned and thrusting his head and right arm through the hole whispered for Olaf to pass up the monk.

When Olaf placed Anastasius upon the table the monk started to whimper. It looked for a moment as if he was going to resist and Ethelwulf wondered what chance they'd have if they had to pass an unconscious form up through the hole. Then the monk calmed down and Olaf was able to persuade him to stand upright on the table and stretch his arm up towards the hole. Sweyn's arm snaked down and grasped the monk, starting to haul him upward. Anastasius gibbered and his legs began to thresh about as they lost firm contact with the table. Amazingly, however, he remained fairly quiet and his head and shoulders safely passed through the hole.

It was then they heard a crash from below. Sweyn would have dropped the monk back through the hole if Anastasius hadn't already been over to one side so he was able to grasp the roof for support.

"No!" shouted Olaf as he saw Sweyn was about to jump back down the hole. "It appears our enemies are almost as impatient as ourselves! Ethelwulf and myself will hold them off and while they're busy with us you can slip away with the monk."

Before Sweyn could make any response they could hear the sound of men entering the room below as a loud crash revealed the door was about to give way.

"Do as Olaf says," shouted Ethelwulf. "If God means us to live then we 'll survive, if not, well you've heard my death song!"

At that moment the head of Anastasius appeared beside that of Sweyn. Olaf looked up and his eyes locked on to those of the monk. "I've fulfilled what God meant me to do. I am content," was all he said before Anastasius screamed as he 'heard' the very words of his nightmare were repeated.

Now Sweyn took charge and dragged the monk back from the edge. "Farewell, Olaf and my cousin! May we meet in Valhalla or in heaven - whichever awaits us!" he cried as he turned away from the sight of two Vikings heading for the door.

*

Selim had seen three of his men climb through the unprotected window without any challenge. As ordered they moved silently and he heard no sound of fighting. He decided to send in the ram, this time carried by six men, and the weapon was advanced with a shuffle, awkwardly performed by police agents little used to such a weapon. It crashed into the door of the building. At the same time two more members of the Dīwān al-Shurṭah were sent scurrying across the street to climb in through the windows. As the ram smashed into the door a second time Selim felt there was less need for silence and grouped another ten men ready to rush in when the door was finally smashed down.

Following the third attack on the door by the ram which splintered the door close to the hinge, there was a loud scream from within the building. Mahmud, still sheltering in the shadows with the other nine men prepared to follow the ram in, heard the sound. For a moment he thought fighting had begun, but the absence of any subsequent screams dismissed that idea. Remembering he had a special account to settle with the infidels in the house, he found himself edging towards the front of the group as if anxious to get at the enemy, but then, with the second thoughts which come with age and command, eased himself more to the rear of the patrol. He was pleased to note none of the group were members of his own patrol; as Arif they might have expected him to take the lead but he'd no intention of offering himself as sacrifice.

Mehmet, who'd placed himself in charge of the ram, started shouting encouragement to the rest of the gang. That last charge had almost got rid of the door. It seemed as if the infidels had retired to the upper floor to make their stand; or, perhaps, he thought, almost with a hope which surprised him, they'd decided to kill themselves rather than risk capture. Immediately he pushed aside the hope; no, he wanted to kill the infidel who'd murdered his friend, Toghrul; he didn't know who it was, so any infidel would do, any except the monk - that fanatic had to be handed over to Selim. Now the gang had taken a few short breaths Mehmet felt they were ready for the final assault on the door. With a loud shout to Allah for support the gang charged.

The ram smashed into the door and jerked it of its hinges. As the shattered remains caved in the impetus of the charge drove the ram into the room. The leading pair, the brothers Hashem and Abdullah, knew they couldn't drop the ram immediately; the whole unit had to be into the room before they could disperse. They were overwhelmed by the darkness of an area denied the benefit of the pale moonlight illuminating the street outside. For a brief second their eyes needed to adjust to the changed conditions, at the same time being aware of movement of men to their left.

Suddenly directly ahead of them the door at the top of the steps leading to the upper floor opened. As it did there was a sudden burst of light and they saw, lit by the brilliance of a glowing ball, the shadowy figure of a man. However, it was the light which flew towards them which terrified Hashem and Abdullah. Both dropped their burden to throw themselves out of its path but they were too late. The container filled with burning oil smashed into the ram and disintegrated, throwing its contents over both men. At the same time the second pair of ram carriers stumbled as the front of the ram was thrown to the ground. Ahmed pitched forward straight into the centre of the fire, flames tearing at his face provoked screams which could be heard on all sides; Mustapha was more fortunate because he tumbled to the side, bundling into Abdullah who was frantically trying to douse his enflamed shirt. The final pair, Ali and Mehmet, were much luckier. As the ram collapsed in front of them they were forced to let go; at the same time, partly due to the bodies in front of them and partly due to a desire to escape the fiery attack, they blundered into the door's uprights. Mehmet felt the pain travel from his shoulder into his chest as he dropped his scimitar. Somehow he managed to stay on his feet and for some reason look behind him for support. Reinforcements were rushing across the street.

*

As the monk had disappeared from view Ethelwulf seized an empty pot and furiously poured in the contents of the pan heating on the stove. Some of the hot contents splattered over his fingers causing him to flinch but not to drop the pot. Then he called on Olaf to throw open the door, seizing a torch which he thrust into the pot. Immediately a flame soared out of the mouth of the pot and, at the same time, Ethelwulf yelled with pain as the heat transmitted from its interior to the pot's handle burned his hand. By now the door had swung open and Ethelwulf charged through the door, hurling his missile at the front door. By sheer luck, or unconscious calculation, the pot was thrown just as the ram smashed its way through the door; so the impact of the missile had maximum effect.

No sooner had Ethelwulf thrown the improvised version of Greek fire than, ignoring the pain incapacitating his left hand, he drew his sword and rushed down the steps, closely followed by Olaf. At the foot of the steps he heard a sound and, turning instinctively to his left, parried a swing from a scimitar before thrusting into the darkness where he presumed the assailant stood. However, the temporary night-blindness caused by the flaming pot disappeared almost immediately and he was able to see his surroundings. To his right he noticed Olaf had downed one opponent. In the eerie light provided by burning men and ram he could see the turmoil which the flaming pot had caused. The screams of Ahmed had died away and he lay still with flames gradually dying as the food provided by his clothing came to an end. Hashem and Abdullah were busy extinguishing the last remnants of fire from their clothing while Mustapha was just recovering his feet, still in a daze from the effects of the opening attack by Ethelwulf. So it was Mustapha who first felt the blade of Ethelwulf as it sliced into his dorsal muscles.

> "See, how the Hawk sets its keen claws
> On flesh placed as gifts to Odin
> A Christian blade can still cut deep
> On what is offered to the gods."

He laughed as the first two agents of the Dīwān al-Shurṭah burst through the door over the muddle surrounding the burning ram. For now Ethelwulf had that battle madness upon him experienced in the past when the fight seemed impossible. Just as then it served him well because behind the passion with its awesome fearlessness came a cold calculation giving his moves a precision and speed beyond what was normal. He was unaware of Olaf fighting beside him, as if only enemy weapons could penetrate his consciousness. One scimitar bit into his shoulder but merely provided another spur to the frenzy which had seized his whole frame, matching the fury generated by the painful burn on his left hand and wrist. Even as he was wounded Ethelwulf killed one opponent and then with an ease which would have been surprising even in full daylight cut down the second opponent who'd wounded him.

Olaf Trygvasson had emerged from the shell encasing him since he'd left the Swedish Sea. During his travels across Europe he'd come to believe that firstly killing in the name of Christ was wrong and then that killing itself should be avoided. Although he'd retained his broadsword it had been only for self-defence. The change had begun with the sight of police agents hurling a sister of a Christian order into the fire, ignoring her screams; it was then he'd killed Toghrul with a single throw and no more thought than putting down a mad dog. He hadn't chosen to become a protector of the Ethiopian monk but now accepted that as the role for which Christ had preserved him. He'd rejected the chance to join the monk and Sweyn in a dash over the roofs which would have meant abandoning Ethelwulf. Certainly he was increasingly irked by the imperious style the Saxon had assumed and angered by the hasty intervention which had provoked this confrontation with the police.

Now, however, he was again the Viking who'd terrorized the English waters ten years previously. After cutting down the first opponent he trod viciously on Abdullah's face while lunging at the leading agent following the ram. The man ducked and swung his scimitar so Olaf had to give ground, feeling the inert form of Abdullah almost too late. Instead of falling backwards he checked the momentum of his body and cut at his opponent. The police agent yelped as the broadsword cut into his arm and he had to drop his weapon; he turned to run but a second swing from Olaf cut deeply into his leg.

From across the street Selim could see the doorway was becoming cluttered with bodies, some alive and wriggling, others dead. He was wondering what was happening to the other agents who'd earlier climbed through the window. One of these now struck at Ethelwulf from the rear and the Saxon felt a sharp pain in his thigh; his cry of pain caused Olaf to turn and cut down this new assailant. However, both were now aware of enemies already within the house, sheltered by the darkness. So Olaf placed his back against that of Ethelwulf, narrowing his eyes in an effort to penetrate the gloom, for the flames consuming the first victims had almost sunk to mere embers. Meanwhile Ethelwulf scoured the street because the deaths of the first men to enter through the doorway had caused the others to scatter. He waited silently in the shadows between the crowded doorway and the defenceless window, knowing any attempt to clamber in by the window would prove too awkward to have any hope of success.

Suddenly Ethelwulf noticed a movement from outside as Mehmet tried to squeeze in past the turmoil in the doorway. He let the man come far enough in to handicap any bowman outside and then thrust his broadsword into the man's stomach. At the same moment, however, he felt Olaf slump against his body as out of the darkness a knife had been hurled into his chest. Somehow the

Viking stayed on his feet and his free hand tore at the weapon, casting it down to the floor. In his weakened state Olaf was not able to properly deal with the attack which came simultaneously from two men who had, up till then, skulked in the darkness, too afraid to attack either barbarian. One man was cut down before he could reach Olaf by a vicious swing of the Viking's sword; the other, however, struck once and struck deep. Olaf felt his death wound as the Fatimid blade stabbed into the exposed flesh below his throat. He felt a tearful mist come into his eyes and just had the strength to swing his broadsword back in a reverse arc to slice off the opponent's head. The effort proved too much for him and he slumped on to his knees, managing to prevent a complete collapse by burying his sword in the floor.

"This is no time for prayer, Olaf!" shouted Ethelwulf as he felt the movement behind him and was shocked when he heard the reply.

"Indeed it is, Saxon, for I am about to meet our Maker!"

With that Olaf careered forward into the dust and Ethelwulf knew he was alone.

*

Selim recognised the operation so far had been a disaster. Again the use of fire had ruined his initial charge and cost valuable lives. At first there'd been sounds from within the building but now there was silence; as none of his men had come to the doorway to signal success he concluded they were all dead or, at least, incapacitated. Of course, EVERYONE could be dead but somehow he doubted that; these infidels seemed most difficult to kill. He decided to wait before sending for more men, because he knew doing that would signal a major setback. He wondered if he could try and talk to the infidels, perhaps ask to get his wounded. But would they listen ?

Then Selim heard a voice chanting in an unknown tongue:

"In this world nothing is simple,
All under heaven fate commands.
Here goods may pass and friends as well,
Here life is short for man and kin;
Everything lacks shape and order.
So spoke the wise man inwardly
Sitting apart in thought's own world.
Brave is the man who keeps his faith,
Nor shall he reveal his heart's sorrow

> *Till hope gives him its mastery.*
> *Better for man to seek mercy*
> *And comfort from our heaven's Lord*
> *Where safety stands for everyone.*"[507]

Selim knew the infidels had survived and was certain he needed even more men if he hoped to break through that doorway and carry out the orders of the Muhtasib. Whatever fate awaited him he was determined the infidels should not triumph over the forces of justice. Wearily he summoned Mahmud and issued instructions, not noticing the smirk Mahmud concealed behind an apparent cough before departing for the Muhtasib.

*

Somehow Ethelwulf had gained comfort from a verse mastered during his childhood. Even as he chanted the words his memory was able to summon scenes from far-off Dorset. In the corner of the darkness smothering the carnage that had taken over one house in Jerusalem he could see again his mother, with a quiet smile on her lips, listening to him proudly reciting some of the greatest poetry of his race. There by her side, but strangely aged, were his cousins, Edwine and Morkere. He realised he was confusing time and place, piling one memory on top of another, trying to ensure images too sorrowful to recall were twisted into more acceptable counterparts. He could never see again the body of Edwine slaughtered by Pechenegs in the fens of Gadarike nor the bloody corpse of his black-haired cousin lying amid so many friends and followers in the Cilician Gates. That thought reminded him of Gunnar and he smiled as he knew how difficult the giant must find dealing with the intricacies of the Greek language and the perversities of imperial practices without the light-hearted commentary of Morkere or his own guidance. Had he really helped the Gall-Gael? Perhaps, in so far as anyone could control a natural force likely to erupt at any time. Sadly he reckoned Gunnar by now had probably perished in the land of the Greeks; he hoped death had come in battle and not after the hideous tortures inflicted on those challenging the Autokrator's will.

What had his life meant? Was the world any better for his passing? He leaned on his sword as he answered his own question. Probably not! It had all been a gigantic error, a diversion away from the path his ancestors would have set out for him - guiding his people in Dorset, backing the King to bring order to the land and resist foreign intruders. And what of the other lands he'd seen? Perhaps some people had gained by his meddling, but most certainly others had not. He had to admit not only evil men, such as the Eparchos, had suffered but many good men had reason to regret his existence.

Ethelwulf found himself breathing a silent prayer to the Almighty as he recognised his state of sin. Last week he'd been sure that, thanks to Brother Anastasius, he'd confronted his own sinful self for what it was and then seen it off; certain he'd mastered his darker nature and his sword would be of service to Our Lord when the Second Coming took place. Now all that had gone, and the violence permeating every corner of his existence had returned and he was back as his old sinful self.

Suddenly he doubted that. After all Brother Anastasius, who'd been threatened with almost certain death at the hands of the heathen, should be safe by now, along with his cousin. Perhaps there'd be no Second Coming but was it all a question of renewal of energy in the service of God? Perhaps he'd been preserved just to ensure the survival of one good man. He could try and tell himself that as he breathed heavily in the darkness awaiting another attack from the outside but -

"You don't believe that, little man, do you?" mocked the voice of Gunnar Thorgeirsson so close to his ear that Ethelwulf turned expecting to see the giant Gall-Gael in the darkness. Then he dismissed the idea, for how could the dark-haired brute move with the silence necessary to sneak past the unbelievers outside.

"It might be, Ethelwulf. Remember God's purpose can never be known to us," comforted the voice of Ulf Ethwoldsson and he remembered the reeve who'd trained him to fight so long ago at Arne. He made no move to see the arms-master who'd perished over twenty years before. He knew it was just the pain from his wounds giving his mind full rein to wander and search for any comfort it could find.

"And you always have been true, darling," whispered the soft tones of Lydia, his wife, and he was amazed how these characters inside his head all spoke with a single tongue. He smiled, wondering what his mother would have ever made of the Syrian girl who'd borne her grandchild. Then he remembered the baby had been born dead, in the process killing its mother, and shut out such memories.

*

Mahmud had returned surprisingly quickly with another twenty men. Selim hadn't been too pleased to find himself still in charge of the operation, convinced that, if the Muhtasib had asked Mahmud to take over, that snake would have declined. Well, let him think he could pick up the pieces after it was all over. He still had the weapon of command and was determined to use it. Selim decided to order Mahmud to lead the next attack on the infidels in person.

All was ready. Still sheltered by the cover of darkness for it hadn't yet reached midnight, twenty of the police should position themselves alongside the walls of the house occupied by the infidels and, at a signal charge along those walls; the first three from the right would climb in through the windows, the remainder enter by the main doorway. Abdullah ibn Yussuf suggested they distract the infidels by passing along the tops of adjacent property and cutting their way in through the roof of the house. He admitted that probably they'd have little chance of playing any real part in the fight but the noise of their attempted entry would mask the advance of the real attack. Selim considered it a sound plan and placed the Sudanese Arif in charge of four men to carry it out. Two men were armed with axes to cut their way through the roof. A single whistle from himself would start the attack.

Selim glared across the street. He could clearly make out Mahmud nervously fingering his scimitar as he waited to charge the doorway. Selim smiled as he thought of the tension clawing at the Arif's guts. He looked up and saw shapes up on the roof of the building next to where the infidels were in possession. Here you go, my lads, he thought as he placed his fingers in his mouth and gave a single shrill whistle.

*

The whistle awoke Ethelwulf from the doze into which he'd retreated rather than face any more harrowing memories. He heard something over his head and then the sound as something struck the roof. He was about to turn when a sound from his left betrayed a tall officer in the opening. Ethelwulf had taken the precaution of standing slightly back from the doorway to cover, as far as possible, both doorway and window.

Before the man even knew he was there Ethelwulf's blade had slashed across his throat and the officer fell, impeding a second man who only just managed to parry the thrust of Ethelwulf's sword. However, to his right the Saxon was aware of somebody scrabbling through the window and was faced with the need to prevent an attack from the rear by retreating and so allow his enemies freer entry into the building. Suddenly he heard a cry from above and realised whoever was on the roof had discovered the escape hole cut by Olaf. Ethelwulf smiled at the thought of how far away Sweyn and Anastasius must be. Now was the time to bring this farce of human existence to an end.

His left hand, having passed through the initial pains of scalding, was able to hold Olaf's sword. He retired towards the side wall from where he could see the approach of enemies through window, doorway or steps. Even as he took up his new position two men slipped through the doorway and a third gave way to a fourth entering by the window. At first all four men paused, unable to penetrate the greater darkness within the room; Ethelwulf considered attacking them as they hesitated but abandoned the idea because the gap between the two parties was too great. Now the doorway at the top of the steps was filled by another vague shape and there were cries of recognition. Suddenly there was another yell as someone detected him waiting in the corner. One of the men by the window charged at him. Ethelwulf parried the cut of the scimitar with the sword in his right hand and then cut down the man with his left. The man at the top of the steps chose to jump down and took the Saxon off-guard. Before Ethelwulf was able to turn the man's scimitar sliced into his thigh. However, Ethelwulf turned and cut the agent almost in half with a mighty swing of his sword.

At least four more men had entered through the doorway, another two by the window and two more men were descending the steps. For a moment they paused and Ethelwulf wondered if they'd been ordered to take him alive. He certainly had no intention of facing the torture chambers of the Dīwān al-Shurṭah for he knew no mere dungeon would satisfy his enemies. Yet he was wrong in thinking the police agents had been told to take any of the infidels alive; only the monk would have been given that privilege and by now the police knew the monk was nowhere to be found. Anticipating the rage of the Muhtasib they'd no intention of taking the infidel alive.

Suddenly four of them charged. Ethelwulf swept both swords outwards and one cut into the side of one opponent while the other was parried. However, that action exposed his body to the stab of one of the police blades and it dug deep into his stomach. As blood spurted out, the world for the Saxon went a deep shade of red and he stepped forward slashing blindly at his enemies. One to the left was cut down and another to the right felt a sharp pain as the Saxon blade cut into his shoulder. A scimitar cut at Ethelwulf's throat but missed, slashing across his chest. The Saxon staggered as another blow, this time from the rear, plunged deep into his kidneys. Ethelwulf slumped to his knees, one hand dropping Olaf's sword while the other retained possession of his beloved blade, and the scimitar of Abdullah ibn Yussuf cut off his head with a single stroke.

*

The Muhtasib had been most displeased. The whole city had heard how the infidels had defied the Dīwān al-Shurṭah for the best part of a day. What was more, eighteen agents had been killed and ten more wounded in this operation and all there was to show for this carnage were two infidel corpses. What had become of the troublemaker who'd started it all? The police had discovered a hole cut in the roof which had allowed the escape of the man, accompanied, it was believed, by another of the infidels. They'd not been captured so they were well on their to Antioch or Acre or any town beyond his jurisdiction.

Of course, he'd take his revenge on that idiot, Selim who, stripped of whatever authority he'd once possessed, was even now waiting in his dungeons. Perhaps he'd send the wretch to Cairo in the hope his master would punish the Turk as an example - but he doubted it; Turks were finding their way into every position of importance and it wouldn't be long before they took over the state. By then he hoped to be with Allah!

*

Anastasius found shelter with fellow-believers but never recovered his complete sanity from the shock of his sister's betrayal and her horrible death. His friends told Sweyn the monk was grateful for his rescue but the Viking doubted it. Rumour told him of the deaths of Olaf and Ethelwulf, and that convinced him there'd be no Second Coming, because God wouldn't have thrown away the swords of two such warriors. So there was no place for him in the Holy Land.

It was with the resignation of a sleep-walker that Sweyn set off to serve in the guard of the Autokrator, largely moved by the desire to tell the Varangians how one of their number had ended his wanderings in the City of Our Lord by giving his life for a monk.

*

Palestine Afterword

All the characters, apart from Olaf Trygvasson, in this part are fictional, as is most of the atmosphere. There was some apprehension as the Millenium approached but most Christians would have little knowledge of the year as chronology was normally linked to contemporary rulers and not a universally recognised event.

Fatimid control was about to undergo dramatic tensions with the extremism of Caliph Al Hakim (996-1021) which undermined their power. They proved unable to resist the First Crusade (1096-1100) sent to 'rescue' the Holy Land from Moslem control.

Islamic society was then far more advanced than that of the West – but probably not as finely organised as this novel suggests. Tax collecting, security and the like did have special units and by 1000 they were being infiltrated by Turks.

Within a century a crusading army had captured Jerusalem, Antioch and Edessa. However, they soon became 'corrupted' by Islamic culture, provoking further influxes from the West. The temporary unification of Islamic effort achieved by the Kurdish leader, Saladin, recovered Jerusalem for Islam in 1187 and the rest of the crusading states had been conquered by 1291.

The various sects and groups of the three major monotheistic religions continue their struggles to the present day, especially in the divided city of Jerusalem.

*

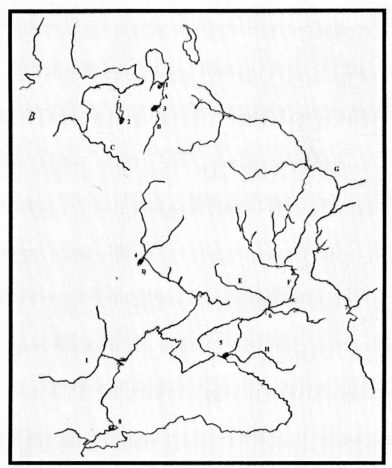

Places mentioned in 'The Wanderer' 7: Gadarike

Towns
1. Aldeigjuborg
2. Pskov
3. Holmgard (Novgorod)

Rivers
A. Volkhov
B. Lovat
C. Dvina
D. Dneiper

4. Kenugard (Kiev)
5. Tmutorokan
6. Sarkel

E. Donetz
F. Don
G. Volga
H. Kuban

7. Itil
8. Miklagard
   (Byzantium)

I. Danube

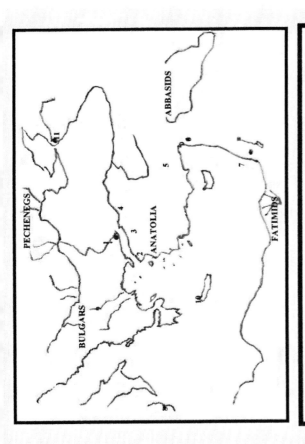

Sketch-Map of Byzantine Empire c.1000 to indicate featured places.

Key:
1. Constantinople / Miklagard
2. Opsician Theme
3. Bucellarian Theme
4. Optimatian Theme
5. Cilician Gates
6. Antioch
7. Jerusalem
8. Taormina
9. River Strymon
10. Crete
11. Tmutorokan

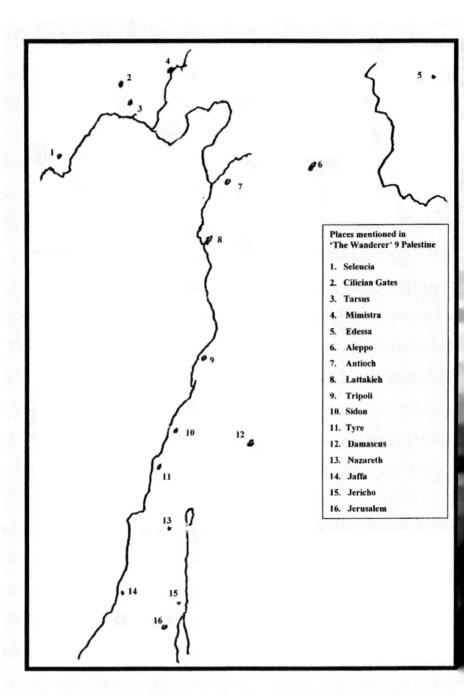

The House of Edwy (840-1135) (see 'The Wanderer')

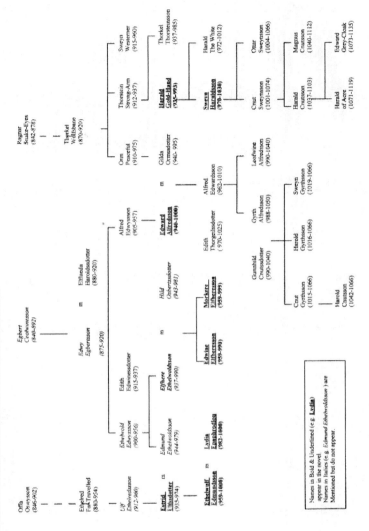

1   A type of native beer mentioned by Ibn Fadhlan, one of the chief contemporary sources for Russian life, as being used among the Swedish Rus along the Volga c.922.

2   Medieval church walls were covered by drawings illustrating Bible stories or human destiny for the benefits of the illiterate. Edwine & Morkere had followed their cousin, Ethelwulf, into exile from Dorset in 979 (nine years before)(see 'The Wanderer' 1:4).

3   Aidan of Wimborne was the gentle priest responsible for much of the earliest spiritual development of Ethelwulf, Edwine and Morkere (see 'The Wanderer' 1:1)

4   The home of Edwine and Morkere in Dorset (see 'The Wanderer' 1:1)

5   Gunnar Thorgeirsson, a Gall-Gael (half-Irish, half-Norse), had joined Ethelwulf in 983 (see 'The Wanderer' 3:3)

6   Erik Barelegs had been killed by Gunnar after Ethelwulf had freed war-captives in return for the curing of a pestilence which had threatened the Varangian base. He had acted in the absence of Oleg, lord of Aldeigjuborg and Erik had been killed during their escape. ('The Wanderer' 6:6)

7   The main base for the Varangians on Lake Ladoga which was the scene for the latter part of 'The Wanderer' 6. Ethelwulf had released war-captives from slavery.

8   Or 'Island-Fort" was the name given to Novgorod by the Vikings.

9   Holmgard (Novgorod) was subordinate to Kenugard (Kiev) but exerted some form of authority over the original Varangian settlements on Ladoga.

10   Svyatoslav of Holmgard and Kenugard (945-72) had smashed Khazar power in 965 and had bequeathed Kenugard to his elder son, Jaropolk.

11   Vladimir (978-1015) from his power base at Holmgard had killed his brother and united Kenugard and Holmgard. Later he unsuccessfully attacked   Constantinople, was converted to Christianity and was given a Byzantine princess.

12   Possibly = "Boat-Fort" was the Viking name for the city of Kenugard.

13   = "Kingdom of the forts" was a name given by the Vikings to Russia & the Ukraine; another one was 'Sweden the Great' reflecting the role of the Swedes in developing the area.

14   Odin, chief of the gods of the north, had given an eye to drink from the stream of Mimir which gave wisdom. So such a term might be used for a blind entry.

15   'Alsvid' means 'All-Swift' & had been the name given by Ethelwulf to a series of vessels he had commanded since leaving Jersey ('The Wanderer' 2)

16   Miklagard = the Viking name for Constantinople or Byzantium, the capital of the Eastern Roman Empire which forms the background to 'The Wanderer' 8.

17   It is significant that Pekka uses the terms associated with Hel; 'Helmets of Secrets refers to Clouds and 'Whirling Wheel' describes the moon.

18   = 'Distress-Bringer', the name of Gunnar's axe

19   See 'The Wanderer'4:3 where the Vikings had killed the witch Thorkalata because she had brought about the death of Eyjolf.

20   Skoll was the wolf pursuing the sun until Ragnarok when she would devour it.

21   Gjall and Greip were giant sisters who tried to murder Thor. Gjall employed her menstrual flow without success and Greip's throttling proved ineffective.

22   One of the names given to the Shape-Changer, Loki, whose evil was to bring about the destruction of the world at Ragnarok.

23   Grobin in Latvia was most noted in the West for its export of amber; with its neighbour Apoula it was typical of the cooperation between Swedes and Gotlanders for the general exploitation of the eastern Baltic.

24   The name which the Finns give themselves; Finn is, in fact, a Swedish term.

25   'Dreki' or 'Karfi' were common names for smaller warships employed by Vikings.

26   'Despicable girl' (Old English); of course, other languages would have been used in such a polyglot troop!

27   Styrbjorn was one of the great heroes of the sagas who was killed at Fyrisvold while trying to seize the throne of his uncle, Eric Sjersal of Sweden (See 'The Wanderer' 5:4).

28   As Fate she was one of the Norns which governed human affairs.

29   Yaroslav the Wise (c.977 – 1054) succeeded to the throne of Kenugard in 1019.

30   Perun was the chief god & at his shrine at Holmgard a fire was kept constantly alight. The actual statue had disappeared some time before.

31   Chroniclers allege that the pagan Vladimir had 300 concubines at Vychegorod, 3000 at Bielgorod & 200 at Berestov

32   In 988 Vladimir had lent troops to Basil II when the emperor had been attacked by Bardas Sclerus & Bardas Phocas

33   In 971 Svyatoslav had failed in his siege of Constantinople

34   The supposed founder of the Kenugardan state c.860 is really a legendary figure

35   Vladimir had seized this Byzantine possession in 988 and almost demanded a Byzantine princess as bride with the threat that more conquests could follow. Instead the tables had been turned and the lord of Kenugard had been persuaded to adopt Christianity as the price of acquiring such an asset.

36   See 'The Wanderer' 6:5 where such an expedition provoked violence between Ethelwulf and the Finns.

37   Varangians in April 989 at Abydos destroyed the forces of Sclerus (who appears in 'The Wanderer' 9:1).

38   In actual fact Vladimir was to undertake a complete transformation of life-style, including the forcible conversion of many of his subjects. The result was that he was made a saint with his feast-day on 11 July. In this he was following the example of his grandmother, Olga.

39   'Sin' is an Arabic form of China. The Khazars might have called the country ''Qitay' while the Byzantines referred to China as 'Taugats'. All 3 names might have been used in this area at this time. Limited contact had been made with China for a thousand years.

40   Such a funeral is described by Ibn Rustah who travelled among the Rus at Holmgard in the early 10th century.

41   Control of the Rus or Varangians depended on control of the rivers.

42   The Pechenegs were at their height c. 1000. They dominated the lower reaches of the R. Dneiper & the lands to the north of the sea of Azov..

43   The Khazars had been at their most powerful c.750 when they had been converted to Judaism. They dominated the lower reaches of the Don.

44   In 972 Svyatoslav had been ambushed & killed by Pechenegs on his way back from reaching agreement with the Byzantine emperor, John Tzimisces. His skull was used as drinking cup.

45   In 969 Svyatoslav had been forced to break off a successful campaign against the Bulgars by having to drive off a Pecheneg attack on his capital.

46   Constantine Porphyrogenitus, writing c. 950, describes an extensive cattle trade between Rus & the Pechenegs who controlled many trade routes.

47   The Norns were Urd (Fate), Skuld (Being) & Verdandi (Necessity) who were constantly weaving the destinies of men.

48   Here Ethelwulf was wrong as there is no reference in Einhard's biography of Charlemagne. Yet, the Emperor Nicephorus of Byzantium was defeated by Krum, the Bulgar Khan on 24 July 811 in the Pass of Verbitza and killed. His skull was mounted in silver and used as a drinking cup by the victor.

49   In fact these people occupied the territory around the Vistula.

50   Julius Caesar (100-44 B.C) wrote on his 'Gallic War' and 'Civil War'

51   Sextus Julius Frontinus produced his 'Stratagems' c. 90.

52   Flaviius Vegetius Renatus wrote 'On Military Affairs' c.385 examining how the Romans could adapt to the changing demands of warfare after the disastrous battle of Adrianople in 378

53   This distinction has been noted by archaeologists

54   The Khazars in the 8th century had dominated a large Empire & had been converted to Judaism. Their power had declined and almost destroyed by war with Svyatoslav. The resulting power vacuum attracted the Pechenegs for another century.

55   The modern town of Gomel

56   The Pechenegs incorporated 8 clans & this was the closest to the lands of Prince Vladimir.

57   An area under Yggdrasill dominated by freezing mist and darkness & holding Hel.

58   'Necessity' who with her two sisters formed the Norns controlling human destiny.

59   A cruel death in which the victim's back was cut open and his entrails withdrawn while he was still alive.

60   The Hall where fallen warriors, as guests of Odin, spent days in fighting and nights in feasting, until they were needed to join he forces of the gods in the last battle with those of Darkness known as Ragnarok.

61   A poem appearing in 9th century Mercia soon to be devastated by Viking assault. It recounts the crucifixion with its origins and effects.

62   Also known by the Slavic name of Byelaya Vyezha or 'White Fortress' because of the bricks used in its construction. It was seized by Svyatoslav in 964 and later redeveloped as a trading centre.

63   Literally 'peace' it was the name given to a commune governed by a vetche.

64   A union of the councils of the individual communes controlled by the elders, one of whom had superiority.

65   Literally 'town' but really an enclosed community.

66   The pagan deities of the flocks and the labourers respectively.

67   For possibly 2000 years amber had been a key export from the Baltic regions to the Mediterranean and the Near East.

68   A title adopted by the rulers of Kenugard from the Khazars.

69   Goddess of Fate & with Skuld (Being) & Verdandi (Necessity) member of the Norns.

70   Basil II (976-1025) was one of the greatest emperors of the Eastern Roman Empire. Officially he shared his throne with his brother, Constantine VIII (1025-28), and both had been controlled by expansionist predecessors such as Nicephorus II Phocas (963-9) and John Tzimisces (969-76).

71   Basil acquired the title of Bugaroctonus ("Bulgar-Slayer") because of his triumphs over the Bulgars who dominated the are between the Byzantine and Rus realms.

72   He missed out the subjection of the Khazars originally to the Kok Turks c.600 but the territories of the Khazars stretched from the Dneister in the west to Uzbekistan in the east and the Caucasus Mountains in the south.

73   The Caspian Sea which even today in Turkish is styled the 'Hazar Denizi'

74   Some were driven westwards to form the modern people of Bulgaria, initially acquiring an Empire of their own which was destroyed by the early 11th century. To the east others settled along the banks of the Volga where they grew wealthy on trade.

75   ólpa is an old Norse word for a caftan, usually made of wool & an over garment, with the right arm free.

76   Matthew 27:25

77   The area south of the Aral Sea around Khiva which played a key part in the trade between Rus and the East.

78   sable, ermine, otter, mink, marten and fox were a major export through intermediaries such as the Volga Bulgars to the East where they highly valued as luxury items.

79   Probably the ivory obtained from the narwhal or walrus which was highly prized as material for hilts of weapons and other ornaments. It could fetch up to 200 times its original value.

80   Practice of prayer to be performed 5 times daily facing Mecca.

81   Once capital of the Khazar empire, this had fallen into decline during the 10th century with the collapse of that power.

82   A group of Turkish tribes originally from eastern Siberia which included the Seljuk Turks. By the early 11th century they had become dominated by the successors of Seljuk and established a strong Empire.

83   Caspian Sea. Samandar had been the capital of Khazaria c 720-50 & was famous for its gardens and vineyards.

84   A genuine Anglo-Saxon riddle, originally set in verse with two answers - 'penis' or 'onion'.

85   A kyrtill was a long tunic, usually knee-length, with sleeves & belted. In battle it might be covered by a hauberk of leather or mail.

86   'Distress-Bringer'. The name of the giantess on whom Loki fathered the Fenris Wolf, the Jormungand Serpent and Hel.

87   The Pechenegs were divided into 8 clans who distinguished their battle-standards by the chief colour of the horses they rode. The most easterly were the Boulatzoupon & the Borotalmat.

88   Cumans or Polovtisans were a Turkish people who by the mid-11th century had replaced the Pechenegs as the dominating force in the grasslands. They were beaten by the Russians in the early 12th century and absorbed by the Golden Horde after the Mongol invasion (1237-42).

89   Koran Sudra 20

90   She married Ali and the Fatimid caliphs of Egypt (909-1171) claimed descent from her. Ali was the fourth caliph but was assassinated in 661. Only his descendants are accepted by the Shiah as legitimate leaders of Islam.

91   Fatima's son, Al-Husayn was killed in 680 on the orders of Yazid, the second Umayyad caliph, and is held to be a martyr by the Shiah to this day.

92   Samako in Finnish means 'frog'.

93   Finnish woodland god who protected wild cattle with the aid of woodland spirits.

94   See 'The Wanderer' 6:6, Ethelwulf & Thorgrim had exchanged alliance for hostility in Finland. Ethelwulf was wanted by Eric Sjersal for his actions at Uppsala (see' The Wanderer '5:4)

95   See 'The Wanderer' 3:2

96   The Pechenegs are credited with introducing the cavalry sabre into Europe.

97   Tmutarakan on the Taman peninsula was ideally situated for trade between the rivers of Russia and the cultures south of the Black Sea. It was first developed by the Rus c. 800 but subject to Khazar intrusions for over 50 years.

98   Burial mounds are not uncommon along the banks of the river Kuban. Most are associated with the Scyths who dominated the region c. 500 B.C.

99   Virgil's 'Aeneid' Book VI

100   See J.G.Frazer 'The Golden Bough' Chapter 71 for examples.

101   Such a contest features in 'The Wanderer' 4:1 & produced a catalogue of violence which led to the expulsion of Ethelwulf from Iceland.

102   The Vanir were the older fertility gods of the Norse world. They included Freyr, Njord and Freyja. One story was of a primeval war between the Vanir and the Aesir (another group of gods including Odin & Thor) which ended in a truce and them all living together. Obviously this reflects the merging of two mythologies.

103   The one-eyed king of the gods, closely associated with the spear, hanged men, wisdom and poetry. He was linked with the Taman peninsula.

104   High King. c.1000 the title was contested between Brian Boru & Mael Sechlainn (see 'The Wanderer' 3)

105   See 'The Wanderer' 3:4

106   A common belief, supposedly & so used in this novel, as the year 1000 approached (and this part of the 'Wanderer' saga is set in 990) was that Christ would return as prophesied in 'Revelations' and the End of the World would come. See 'Wanderer' 8:4 and 'Wanderer' 9:3 for sequences in which this idea is prominent. However, most chronology rested on the reigns of local rulers & such ideas were limited in reality.

107   See 'The Wanderer' 1:3

108   Such vessels were constructed by the Krivichians and other Slav tribes as a flat-bottomed vessel. It was then transformed into a longship by the Rus and sailed down such rivers as the Dneiper, Don and Volga.

109   The son of Baldur and Nanna. He was the god of Justice.

110   The pseudonym adopted by Ethelwulf in his escape from England ('The Wanderer' 1:4)

111   Procopius in the early 6th Century mentions this in his 'Gothic War'.

112   Now called the Black Sea, the Pontic Sea occurs in the 12th century Kyiv Chronicle from the Ukraine. The name came from Pontos Axeinos ('Hospitable Sea') which was the name the Greeks used. Arabs called it the 'Rus Sea'.

113   'Sea Bird'

114   A reference to Thor's achievement during his trip to the giant's realm of Utgard of nearly drinking the ocean dry.

115   Niflheim was a region of mist and darkness which Norse mythology said occupied the area under one of the roots of Yggdrasil (the world-tree) and enveloped Hel, the home of the dead.

116   or 'kerling' (keelson) a large block of oak contained a socket to take the boot of the mast. Above it another block of wood, the mast partner, was designed to really take the strain of raising or lowering the mast.

117   A tacking boom used for adjusting the position of the sail.

118   Aristotle (384-322 B.C.E.) in ،Nicomachean Ethics ˏ8:10 called democracy the least bad of perverted system because it could do the least evil.

119   Ran was the wife of Aegir, the sea god, and delighted in dragging men into the sea with a net and so drowning them.

120   The Quaestor had general supervision of foreigners throughout Constantinople. He was also head of the court of appeal and dealt with questions of wills and guardianship.

121   Autokrator was one of the titles employed by the Byzantine emperors. The ruler during this story was one of the strongest, Basil II (976-1025) who ruled with his younger brother, Constantine.

122   Vladimir I of Kenugard (980-1015) married the sister of the emperor of Constantinople or Byzantium in 988 after receiving baptism. He introduced the Byzantine rite into both Kenugard and Holmgard. Also he is featured in 'The Wanderer' 7

123   Bardas Phocas, a successful general, was proclaimed emperor in 987 and, agreeing to divide the Empire with the rebel, Sclerus, then imprisoned Sclerus and besieged Constantinople. Basil was saved by the intervention of Vladimir of Kenugard. Phocas was struck down in battle, possibly by the young prince, Constantine.

124   The Grand Chamberlain, Basil the Parakoimomenos, was deposed in 985 and died in exile almost immediately. He was the son of the emperor Romanus Lecapenas and, as a eunuch, barred from imperial ambitions. He had been the dominating figure in Byzantine intrigues for twenty years and his greed and wealth were notorious.

125   The City Prefect or Eparchos was addressed as "the Father of the city". He was responsible for the guilds, trade and commerce, the police and the fire-brigade, foreigners engaged in trade and observance of Sundays. He ranked 18th in the 60 officials of the Empire. In this novel the fictional holder of the office dominates the imperial system.

126   Technically both Basil II and Constantine VIII had been co-emperors since the death of their father (Romanus II) in 963. However, the throne had also been occupied by the powerful generals, Nicephorus Phocas (963-69) and John Tzimisces (969-76). Constantine VIII for most of his life was content to let others exercise power in his name.

127   see 'The Wanderer' 7:4 The successes of Svyatoslav of Kenugard (962-72) against the relatively peaceful Khazars opened up the grasslands to the depredations of the wild Pechenegs.

128   On the Crimea. Bosporus was part of the Byzantine province of Cherson. It should not be consumed with the Bosphorus near Constantinople near itself. Cherson had been briefly seized by Vladimir as a means of coercing Byzantium to surrender a bride in 989. This would have a discouraged Ethelwulf from touching land there even though it had by then been restored to imperial control.

129   See 'The Wanderer' 3:4. They had tried to rescue Gunnar's betrothed, Deirdre, from Brian of Clonmel. Gunnar killed Brian but Deirdre had already killed herself.

130   Brimfugol means "Sea-Bird" and had been acquired on the Sea of Azov. Alsvid ("All-Swift") was Ethelwulf's ship between Ireland ('The Wanderer' 3:1) and Finland ('The Wanderer' 6:5) but had been abandoned to the north of Holmgard ('The Wanderer' 7:1)

131   Ethelwulf had freed hundreds of Karelian slaves & so provoked Oleg's anger. But Oleg never made any serious attempt to seize him. (see 'The Wanderer' 6:6)

132   Thorgrim had hated Ethelwulf since events at Uppsala & sold his head to Eric the Victorious (see 'The Wanderer' 5:4). In Khazaria Ethelwulf had disobeyed the orders of the governor of Sarkel & destroyed some Turkish troops . (see 'The Wanderer' 7:4)

133   The origin of the word was the old Norse "Vaeringi" and was adopted by the followers of Rurik or the Rus as they were called in the 9th century. It was taken over by the Byzantines as a general word for such northerners and especially those who chose to act as mercenaries. Svyatoslav had been bribed to help the Byzantines fight the Bulgars but soon the alliance collapsed and war broke out in 969. The Rus were forced to retire & in 972 Svyatoslav was ambushed & killed by Pechenegs at Byzantine instigation.

134   Rus (or Rus) was the Slavic name for the Viking immigrants into the river systems of Dneiper and Volga. Most of these immigrants were Swedish, but not all.

135   An ortug was the basic weight for silver among the Vikings and was roughly 8 grams. Hack-silver was made up of crude strips of silver which could be cut up and used in barter.

136   Gall-Gaels were the half-Irish offspring of Viking and Irish.

137   The tagmata were the imperial units split into 4 divisions the Scholae, Excubiti, Arithmos & Hikanatoi. They often held privileged positions in the capital.

138   Eparchos = City Prefect & in this novel it is used for Alexius Euergetes

139   The Postmaster General (Logothete tou dromou) had assumed control of foreign affairs and for this purpose employed a staff of interpreters. He had a daily audience with the Emperor.

140   This knowledge of languages had been gained in the course of the wanderings described in other parts of this work. Variations of Norse could be heard wherever Vikings had made their way. Waterford is in Ireland (see 'The Wanderer' 3:1), Breidavik is in western Iceland (see ibid 4:2), Jelling was the capital of Harald Bluetooth in Denmark (see ibid 5:1), Ladoga was near the chief route north into the lands of the Lapps (see ibid '6:2) and Kenugard was the chief base in Russia (see ibid 7:1). Other

languages included Norman-French in Jersey (see ibid "2:1), Wendish in northern Germany (see ibid '5:3) and Rus (see ibid '7:3)

141   The Byzantine army's basic fighting unit was the bandon (or regiment) which was subdivided into five Pentekontarchies (each of 40 men). The Banda were then grouped into Morai (brigades) and Turmae (divisions).

142   Anna, the sister of the emperors Basil II and Constantine VIII, had been married off to Vladimir of Kenugard as part of the price for his saving of their thrones. Vladimir had been baptised in 987, but he was re-baptized before his marriage to the reluctant imperial princess in 989.

143   Aithmos were the palace guard, never having the independence or power of the old Praetorian Guard.

144   Basileus (Greek for king) had been adopted by Heraclius in 629 after his crushing defeat of the Persians. Within a generation much of the Empire in the east had been lost to the Moslems.

145   A Chartularius (or actuary) was a lower-ranking financial official, or member of the Secreteci. The higher level of officials were called Logothetes (accountants).

146   Ibn Fadhlan in the 10th century described how a band of twenty such traders would all use the same bowl of washing water, regardless of hygiene or decency.

147   Bardas Sclerus had revolted against the emperor and then joined the more dangerous uprising of Bardas Phocas. After defeat he had been forgiven but revolted again and, with difficulty, had been crushed. He had advised Basil not to allow his nobles to become too-powerful and had willingly gone into exile on a country-estate.

148   Modern Ankara

149   apelatai means "cattle-thieves" but the word was used to describe brigands in general.

150   the stade was about 200 metres and Ankara is about 450 km. from Constantinople.

151   Constantine, after accepting Christianity, moved his capital to Byzantium away from Rome – supposedly away from pagan influences but rather nearer the real centre of power. In 325 he held a grand council at Nicaea to settle doctrine. Its decisions survive in the Nicene Creed. Note Constantine was not baptised till his deathbed in 337.

152   Ever since the quarrel between Pope Nicholas I and the Patriarch Photius c. 860 there had been little love between the two traditional rivals for Christian headship. These quarrels were to lead to the final schism in 1054.

153   The Sacellarius was the head of the imperial financial administration. However, the land tax was the responsibility of the Logothete tou genikou.

154   The Macedonian house had been established by Basil I (867-86) and lasted till 1056.

155   Despite frequent government purges prostitution remained rife in the capital, largely being based on inns and bath-houses.

156   Theophana, a Greek inn-keeper's daughter, married the emperor Romanus II in 958. She was alleged to have murdered this husband to marry the general Nicephorus Phocas in 963. Her new husband in theory ruled in conjunction with her infant sons Basil and Constantine. Then, when Nicephorus proved unattractively austere, she conspired with John Tzimisces to murder Nicephorus in 969. The new emperor, however, soon banished this dangerous woman. Theophano's liaisons were to be somewhat copied by her granddaughters, Theodora and Zoe, in the dying years of the dynasty.

157 see 'The Wanderer' 3:3 for the violent betrothal of Gunnar himself and 'The Wanderer' 3:4 for the rape of Deirdre Dark-eyes which had provoked the battle in Clonmel.

158 Constantine I (306-337),the first emperor to formally tolerate Christianity, had called the Council of Nicaea in 325 to denounce Arian heresies and establish a creed to form the basis of unity. In 330 he built a new capital to replace Rome on the Bosphorus named after himself, Constantinople.

159 On his defeat Sclerus had a personal interview with Basil II before going into exile. At the interview the historian Psellus describes how he advised the emperor to beware of over-mighty subjects and limit their power. Basil carried out the advice by cutting down on the power of Asiatic nobility.

160 Heavily-armoured cavalry or cataphracts were the flower of Byzantine armies. Often they combined with Trapezitae, or lightly-armoured mounted bowmen.

161 Anthemius of Tralles and Isidore of Miletus were the architects employed by Justinian to construct Sancta Sophia in 548. The dome collapsed in 559 and had to be repaired.

162 Pankrator means "Ruler of all" and was a common term used by the Byzantines for God.

163 A silver coin introduced by Constantine V (720-41) & worth 1/12 of a solidus. In 800 it was worth about 2 silver pennies of Offa of Mercia.

164 Crete had been re-captured from the Saracens, who had held it since 845, by Nicephorus Phocas in 961. Its capital was Chandex or Candia (now Heraklion). It was an outpost of the Empire.

165 Niflheim was a region of mist and darkness which Norse mythology said occupied the area under a root of Yggdrasil (the world-tree) and enveloped Hel, the home of the dead. Gunnar had acquired the vessel during the flight from Gadarike see 'The Wanderer' 7:5.

166 The main Byzantine naval bases had been in the Cibyrrhaeots theme (south-west Anatolia)

167 The eastern part of Anatolia containing the ancient city of Ephesus.

168 The port for Cairo constructed by the Fatimid caliph, el-Mo'izz (953-75) and 600 ships were built there. Cairo itself had been established by the caliph's general G'awhar.

169 The Fatimid caliphate of Egypt reached its height under the ambitious abu-Mansur Nizar al-Aziz (975-96). However, he began the practice of importing Turkish mercenaries who were eventually to snatch Egypt from their masters.

170 The rapid expansion of Islam around the eastern Mediterranean in the 7th century was greatly helped by local Christian groups (e.g. the Copts in Egypt with their Monophysite faith) not resisting Moslem advance, preferring it to the 'heretical' dictates of Byzantium. The situation had not improved over the next 400 years.

171 Caliph abu-Mansur Nizar al-Aziz had blue eyes and red hair.

172 Spirit forms, usually evil and very powerful, found in the "Thousand and One Tales of the Arabian Nights" etc. Their name is usually westernised as "genie"

173 Household troops formed an essential part of the invasion force of Nicephorus Phocas in 960. He was not warned of the landing of 40,000 Saracen troops but, by forced marches, managed to ambush and destroy them. The display of their severed heads in a ghastly circle around the Rabd al Chandak (the defences of Chandax or Heraklion) helped produce the Saracen surrender in March 961.

174 The Norse god of lies and trickery whose evil scheming eventually bring about the destruction of the Ragnarok.

175 In 'The Wanderer' 5:3 Hallbjorn had, with the help of a dog, guided the Vikings to a scene of pagan sacrifice and acted as one of the leaders on the retreat.

176   To the south of Heraklion are the remains of the palace of Knossos. It remained unknown until 1878 and was excavated by Sir Arthur Evans in the early 20th century.

177   In fact, the Labyrinth (or Maze) constructed by Daedalus was probably the complicated passage design at the royal palace which was destroyed by earthquake c. 1300 B.C.E. The Minotaur was said to be the offspring of Pasiphae, the wife of Minos, & a bull!

178   The princess was Ariadne whom Theseus chose to desert on the island of Naxos.

179   The Cretan (or Minoan) sport of 'bull-leaping' might have been the origin of the whole Minotaur myth. Certainly such images can be seen in the remains of the palace today.

180   Persephone (or Proserpine) was the daughter of Demeter (Ceres) kidnapped by her uncle, Hades (Pluto) to be his Queen of the Underworld. The mother only partially recovered her daughter which was how the Greeks explained the difference between summer and winter.

181   In 990 Sweyn Forkbeard of Denmark and the Jomsvikings invaded Norway but were defeated by Earl Haakon at Hjorungavang. There was no love lost between Ethelwulf and either Sven, the son of Harald Bluetooth, or the Jomsvikings (see 'TheWanderer' 5:1 and 5:4)

182   The name given to Ethelwulf's sword because of his nickname of Hafoc (Hawk). The first such sword earned its name during the flight from Dorset (see 'The Wanderer' 1:4). However, it was later broken although its successors enjoyed the name.

183   The emperor personally paid out salaries to the leading officials in the week preceding Palm Sunday to stress the personal relationship between master and servants. The Protovestiarius (head of the private wardrobe) regularly paid out imperial alms.

184   Original senatorial ranks of (downwards) illustres, spectabiles & clarissimi became downgraded with time.

185   Kractae was a special choir of lay court officials, who joined with the Psaltae (clergy) to salute the emperor with hymns and anthems.

186   The Praepositus was the eunuch in charge of ceremonial at court.

187   Allusions to Luke 2:32 and Matthew 4:16 respectively.

188   Samuel, Tsar of the Bulgarians (976-1014) had restored the former Bulgarian Empire of Symeon (892-927). He threatened the northern frontiers of the Empire until crushed in a bloody series of campaigns (see 'The Wanderer' 9:3).

189   Constantine was an effete who delighted in gluttony, lechery and the theatre. During his short reign (1025-28) he re-introduced the gymnopodia, a form of gladiatorial duel. He delighted in fighting in the arena himself, like the earlier emperor Commodus (180-192).

190   By tradition imperial dinner-parties were restricted to twelve guests.

191   The younger two of the three daughters of Constantine played a key, if not entirely beneficial role, in Byzantine history. The eldest, Eudocia, retired to a nunnery after suffering a scarring attack of small-pox. The youngest, Theodora, was plain and easily dominated by the middle daughter. Zoe had a succession of husbands who frittered away the resources of the Empire after the death of Constantine VIII in 1028. For a brief period (1042) the elderly sisters ruled jointly and Theodora later ruled alone (1055-56).

192   A Drungarius was an admiral.

193   Orthanotrophus was in charge of the state orphanage at Constantinople. He was a cleric.

194   Psellus in his Chronographia, written in the eleventh century, describes the rapid speech of Constantine VIII, which some mistakenly took to be intelligence. He also describes the appearance and personality of Zoe and Theodora whom he had seen in old age.

195   Greek fire had been developed in the 7th century to a secret formula. It was catapulted against enemy vessels and burst into flame on impact. Greek fire was even used in a 'hand-grenade'.

196   The author of the work now usually called 'De Imperio Administrando' was Constantine VII Porphyrogenitus (913-59) which was a collection of data, probably actually written by various authors, produced as guidance for his son, Romanus II (959-63), The Autokrator was Basil II (976-1025). The work is now chiefly used as a source for information about peoples living on the edges of the Byzantine Empire, especially Croatians, Serbs and Bulgars in the Balkans and Pechenegs & Rus in modern Russia.

Please note that great liberties have been taken with the contents of this work as known to the modern world from the first copy (by John Doukas in the late 11th century).

197   For example in 475 the library held 120.000 volumes but was destroyed by fire. The size shrank considerably during the early Middle Ages – note the expansion of libraries in the Islamic world at the same time.

198   Secretary

199   Emperors bearing either name included Theodosius III (408-50), Phocas (602-10), Theodosius III (715-17) and Nicephorus II Phocas (963-69). One should also remember Sclerus Phocas who had almost toppled the Autokrator himself and appears in 'TheWanderer' 8:1

200   Founded in 717 by Leo III (717-741) and ending with the death of Leo V (813-20). The great achievement of the dynasty was to withstand the full impact of Islamic attacks.

201   The Byzantines had been losing a war of attrition vs. the Saracens since 827. The final defeat was off Messina and the last resistance at Rometta ended in 965

202   The Eparchos (or City Prefect) controlled the capital's police force and fire brigade. Foreign mercenaries often performed the unpopular police duties.

203   Keeper of Imperial Archives and so responsible for the Library

204   Generally responsible for the security of the Palace & its environment

205   See 'The Wanderer' 8:2

206   This meant that shipping tended to stay within sight of land wherever possible, maximising the use of winds sweeping down from the hills to the north.

207   But had clearly forgotten that fraternisation could lead to trouble (see 'The Wanderer' 8:2)

208   A trade agreement between Venice & Byzantium had been signed in 992 although the Byzantines were angered by Venetian breaches of their embargoes on trade (e.g. wood) with potential enemies. Eventually the Venetians dominated the rump of the Byzantine Empire in the 13th century.

209   The Fatimids controlled Sicily through the 10th century but entrusted the rule of the island to the al Kalbi dynasty. Three years later Basil II was to move against Fatimid control in Syria but in 993 he was still trying to subdue the Bulgars.

210   It surrendered in 902, transferring control of Sicily from the Byzantines to the Moslems. Etna has been an active volcano throughout human occupation of the area.

211   An ousiakon was a two-banked galley operated by 100 men of whom the lower bank rowed while the rest fought. The pamphylos was slightly larger while the Dromon had over 200 men plus about 50 marines on board.

212   The Emperor (527-65) who restored Byzantine control over most of Italy, Sicily & North Africa. However, the effort weakened Byzantium, as did subsequent internal rivalries, & the control had been mostly swept away by Moslems & Lombards within two centuries.

213   The weapon was the mysterious, but highly effective, Greek Fire invented in 673 and used soon afterwards to destroy a Saracen attempt against Constantinople. Its production at Galata was a closely guarded secret. Siphonarioi were like gunners, discharging the weapon.

214   An organisation of raw silk merchants in Byzantium. The whole silk industry was heavily controlled and the associated trade was 'forbidden' and subject to close scrutiny & high taxation.

215   The basic Byzantine coin (= 1/72 of the Roman pound) became known in the West as the bezant. It was steadily debased by the Imperial members of the Macedonian House. In 970 the annual military service of a cavalryman cost 85 numismata

216   Palermo (as Bal'harm)became the capital of Sicily after the Moslem conquest, becoming one of the finest cities in the Moslem world. Syracuse had been the capital under the Byzantines until its fall in 878 when Taormina had been made capital until its fall in 902.

217   Doge Pietro Candiale IV (959-76) married the sister of the Marquis of Tuscany but failed to secure the Republic's support for his brother-in-law. He also squandered state revenues. During a coup his Palace was burnt down and he was hacked to death.

218   Pietro Orseolo II (991-1009) was one of the great Venetian Doges. He established commercial links throughout the Mediterranean, had good relations with both the Holy Roman Empire & Byzantium (into whose royal family he married his son). However, his son & family died of plague & the Doge retired in misery.

219   The repeated use of amphorae on trips both ways is described in an article by van Doomink the Project Director of the excavation of Serce Limani ship in1977-9.

220   Thomas Magistros, a 14th century traveller, described the use of 'mixed Greek' among the crew. Clearly when sailors came from all over the Eastern Mediterranean a form of lingua franca was used, especially in emergencies.

221   Ruins still there near Castelmola are perched above Taormina itself.

222   A qadi was a judge and a diwan a council in Fatimid administration which operated through a multiplicity of councils organisation aspects of political life.

223   Saracen cavalry of the period

224   The active craters of Etna when churning out a stream of lava produce a powerful and acrid smell of sulphur. The gasping sound was the release of the lava from the crater.

225   The birthplace of Venetian power saw the foundation in 639 of the cathedral of Santa Maria dell' Assumpta containing the remains of the 3rd century St. Heliodorus. Some of the present church dates from before 1000 but much was completed before Torcello fell into decay in the 14th century.

226   This island is now called Castello and the grandest stone building there was the cathedral of San Pietro di Castello until replaced in 1807 by the Basilica di San Marco..

227 Magistrates holding judicial & civil power who, with the Pregadi (prominent citizens) advised the Doge, They were replaced (1272) by the Maggior Consiglio (480 citizens) from which came the smaller Signoria to advise the Doge. From this organisation emerged the Senate.

228 First mentioned in 982

229 Thee had already caused clashes between Venice and Byzantium – which the 992 treaty was partly aimed to remove. In 1002 Basil II tried to bind Venice more into the Byzantine system by yielding authority over the Dalmatian coastline to the Republic. By 1204 Venice was able to dominate the Empire itself.

230 Gusty northerlies which can make passage in the Aegean Sea difficult.

231 A high-ranking officer. By the 10th century the Domestikos of the Scholarii was, in effect, the commander-in-chief of the Byzantine army.

232 Recycled parchment invented in the 6th century.

233 Treasury official

234 Byrhtnoth was the ealdorman of Essex who was defeated and killed by Viking raiders led by Olaf Trygvasson at the battle of Maldon in 991.

235 The murder of Edward the Martyr by his step-mother's agents at Corfe castle in 978. As a witness Ethelwulf had been forced to flee England (see 'The Wanderer' 1:2).

236 After a successful career as a Viking, Olaf Trygvasson seized the throne of Norway in 995 and proceeded to introduce Christianity. He quarrelled with Sweyn Forkbeard and was defeated and killed at Svolder – or was he? This novel supposes he survived!

237 Nicephorus Phocas (963-69) and John Tzimisces (969-76) both ruled officially in conjunction with the infants, Basil II and Constantine VIII. Both were great soldiers who expanded the frontiers of the Byzantine Empire helped by the collapse of Abbasid power based at Baghdad.

238 Faced with a revival of Egyptian power under the Fatimids, the Emir of Aleppo, an imperial protectorate, appealed for help. The governor of Antioch, Michael Bourtzes, was defeated by the Fatimid commander, Manjutekin, on the Orontes (15 September 994). Basil had been trying to cut down the growing power of Samuel, Tsar of Bulgaria, when he received a second summons from Aleppo.

239 40,000 is the figure given by Arab historians. Basil certainly did supply each man with two mules, one to ride and one to carry equipment, to help rapid deployment of his forces.

240 Elfgivu was the maid at Ethelwulf's birthplace at Arne. His mother was Estrid Ulfsdotter. Both were murdered by Haakon ('The Wanderer "1:4)

241 In the seventh century Constantine of Cibossa developed the concept of duality of forces which is linked to Manichaeism - the struggle between Flesh & Spirit, Law & Grace which he noted in the Epistles of Paul (hence the group became known as Paulicians). Such ideas are also seen in the Docetist heresy which rejects the earthly aspect of Christ's Ministry. The Paulicians were Monophysites (seeing no separation between the physical and spiritual natures of Christ). Their ideas included the following: the world was not created by God; they rejected the Eucharist, marriage & Infant Baptism; they had no place for either the sign of the cross or the hierarchy of the Church; they believed the Old Testament was produced by the Demiurge, not God; icons etc. were rejected. Their preferred name was the "Holy, Universal and Apostolic Church" and they often assumed the names of companions of

the Apostle Paul. They were virtually wiped out in the 11th century by the empress Theodora, although their ideas spread westwards to influence the Cathars and early Protestants.

242   It was a common belief that Christ would return at the end of the millennium.

243   Jeremiah 4:6. The evil predicted was, in fact, the destruction of Jerusalem by Nebuchadrezzar in 586 B.C. The Paulicians rejected the entire Old Testament as divinely inspired and only accepted some of the New

244   The Key of Truth was produced in the 9th century and summarises Paulician ideas while they were still of importance throughout the Empire.

245   In 726 the emperor Leo III launched the iconoclastic attack on images throughout the Empire which lasted for almost a century. It was inspired by the ideas of Islam, Judaism and such Christian sects as the Paulicians.

246   Romans 6:13

247   Basil I (867-86) the founder of the Macedonian house which ruled Byzantium till 1056.

248   1 Thessalonians 2:16. Even so later transfer of Paulicians to Thrace brought their ideas to Europe. These ideas, adapted by the Bogomils, became a leading component of medieval heresy.

249   2 Thessalonians 2:10

250   1 John 4:3 Epaphroditus differed from the normal Paulicians in having a working knowledge of the Old Testament and, even more, a liberal reference to the Epistles of St. John and the Apocalypse. These last books in the Bible have been a source for Messianism throughout the ages.

251   Revelations 13:11 Basil II and Constantine VIII were not the first co-rulers of the Empire.

252   1 John 2:22 This refers to the orthodox rejection of the Monophysite heresy associated with the Paulicians.

253   2 Thessalonians 2:3-4 The Byzantine emperor played a key part in defining doctrine and liturgical practice.

254   The Paulicians argued that the earthly form of Christ was but a shell wrapped around His Divinity. So Christ was never truly human - this was the Monophysite heresy.

255   Paulicians developed the Manichaean ideas of duality of forces in the universe, also seen in the Docetist heresy. They rejected the world as being created by a spirit called the Demiurge.

256   2 Thessalonians 2:11-12

257   Hebrews 4:3

258   Philippians 3:20. This is the common cry of Messianic preachers throughout history.

259   See 'The Wanderer ' 3:1 set in Waterford, Ireland where the Vikings crossed the lake haunted by a sea-serpent.

260   Corfe is the setting for 'The Wanderer '1:2 where the murder of the king forces Ethelwulf to leave home. The Wends appear in 'The Wanderer 5:2 where the Vikings set out to destroy the forces of the Sons of Hel. The Kuban appears in 'The Wanderer '7:5 where Edwine meets his end.

261   Revelations 2:7

262   1 John 5:1. Paulicians, with their Manichaean origins, stressed the contrast between light and darkness.

263   Ephesians 6:12

264   Until the schism in 1054 the Byzantine emperor retained respect within Western Christendom. The Pope in 995 was John XV (985-96) who was dominated by the local Crescentius family; the emperor of Germany was Otto II (983-1002) whose mother, a Byzantine princess, had exercised a regency until 991 and who would seek a bride at Constantinople for himself.

265   1 Thessalonians 4:16-17.

266   Romans 1:18

267   Ezekiel 30:6 Epaphroditus is an unusual Paulician in his familiarity with the Prophets, although this is connected with his Messianic streak. The Fatimid forces had just been forced into retreat by the imperial army.

268   Zephaniah 2:13. By Assyria Epaphroditus means the Abbasid caliphate which had entered its decline and would be finally destroyed in the 13th century by the Mongols.

269   Revelations 20:1

270   Ezekiel 29:19 Byzantine armies were steadily advancing through Syria towards Jerusalem.

271   See 'The Wanderer '1:2 (the murder at Corfe)'The Wanderer '3:3 (Gunnar's wedding) and 'The Wanderer '5:3 (the Wendish sacrifices of the Sons of Hel).

272   2 Timothy 2:3

273   Revelations 2:11

274   Psalms 58:10

275   Revelations 7:3

276   Revelations 21:11

277   Revelations 6:8

278   Revelations 19:11

279   Revelations 20:7. This verse formed the basis for Milleniarism.

280   Vladimir of Kenugard and his bride, Anna, were accompanied home by clergy from Cherson who spread the Byzantine form of Christianity and so started the conversion of Russia.

281   Akritai were frontier troops who normally operated independently of central command.

282   Traditionally translated as a shilling. The Nomisma was worth one pound and the more common Follis a half-penny.

283   A light-cavalryman usually armed with a bow.

284   One such tune was noticed by Guido of Arezzo (c.995-1050) and entitled UT-RE-MI as it passed from one note of the major scale to another. From this is derived the Do-Re-Mi of music.

285   Confidential secretary

286   In 962 Otto of Saxony had been crowned Holy Roman Emperor by Pope John X11. His son had married a Byzantine princess, Theophano, in 972. However, the bride, as the niece of John Tzimisces, lacked the aura of a genuine member of the ruling Macedonian house.

287   Charlemagne, ruler of western Europe, had been crowned Holy Roman Emperor by Pope Leo III in 800 when the Byzantium throne was held, with questionable legitimacy, by Irene (797-802). His position had never been recognised by Byzantium.

288   Liudprand of Cremona had led an embassy to the court of Nicephorus Phocas in 967 to secure an imperial bride for his master's son, Otto. However, the embassy had been completely

unsuccessful and Liudprand had five bales of purple cloth, intended for his cathedral of Cremona, confiscated in October 967 before being hustled out of the capital.

289   A surviving document quotes the Patrician Christopher referring to Liudprand's pallor and generally sick appearance.

290   Pope John XIII had sent a letter to support Liudprand's embassy in which he referred to Otto as "august Emperor of the Romans" and Nicephorus as "Emperor of the Greeks".

291   In 996 an embassy was sent by the half-Byzantine Otto III to secure as a bride one of Constantine's daughters. The embassy was headed by Bernwald of Wurzburg and John Philagathus, bishop of Piacenza.

292   In 981 Otto II having spent years trying to seize imperial lands in Italy, attacked the Saracens in Calabria, who were backed by Basil. His army was destroyed near Stilo and he died soon afterwards.

293.   See 'The Wanderer' 3:4. It had been a brief and tempestuous relationship with this famous beauty, the wife of Viking and Irish leaders of the time. Her final treachery drove Ethelwulf from Ireland.

294   See 'The Wanderer' 5:4. Her father Mistivoj tried to murder Ethelwulf who was saved by Skuna, thus repaying her rescue from the Sons of Hel.

295   In January 996 Basil II ordered that land-holding in Anatolia must rest on grants made before the decree of Romanus Lecapenus (920-44) in 935 banning the seizure of peasant lands by the powerful. He thus ruined some of the more dangerous elements in the state.

296   Syncellus was the liaison officer between the emperor and the Patriarch. The Comneni were becoming one of the more important families in Byzantium. Within a century Alexius Comnenus had seized the throne (1081-1118), which his family was to hold for most of the twelfth century.

297   The Logothete of the Praetorium and Sympanos was the chief assistant of the Eparchos in the area of city administration.

298   Theophilus (829-42), the most successful of the Amorian House emperors (820-67).

299   In 867 Basil, an illiterate protégé of Michael III the Drunkard (842-67), with whom he had been co-emperor since 866, hacked to death his benefactor and seized the throne. He founded the Macedonian House and ruled (867-86)

300   Michael III (841-67), known as the Drunkard, had shut out his own family from power (including his wife, Eudocia) & adopted as his heir a penniless stranger, Basil. Within a year Michael was murdered & replaced by Basil I(867-86) who established the Macedonian House.

301   Eudocia, the eldest of the princesses, had suffered a childhood attack of smallpox which removed her from the intrigues which were to fill the lives of her younger sisters.

302   Warden of the Gate of the palace.

303   A company of 40 men. There were five such companies, each under a Pentkontarchos, forming a Bandon.

304   Ares, the god of War, and Aphrodite, the goddess of love, had been caught making love by a net especially constructed by Aphrodite's husband, Hephaestus.

305   The remains of Minoan civilisation, with its complex palaces at Knossos and Phaistos, have revealed the origins of the legends of the Minotaur living in the maze-structure called a labyrinth. The double-axe symbol, common in Crete, was called a labrys.

306   The Hypsipylae of Euripides dealt with the Lemnian women's plot through jealousy to murder their menfolk. A fragment of the play was discovered in 1908.

307   Domestic of the Scholae was the commander-in-chief of the cavalry. There were also (Great) Domestics for both West & East.

308   A Kleisurarch was in charge of Kleisurai or mountain passes. He had under his control detachments of mountain troops.

309   See 'The Wanderer' 3:2 where the natives secured a tight grip on Vikings based in Waterford.

310   Brigands who specialised in rustling tactics.

311   Specialist frontier troops, commanded by a Strategos, who tended to operate independently of imperial control. The Empire employed a system of bounty as an incentive for such forces.

312   See 'The Wanderer' 9:1. Sclerus had been an old rebel escorted to the capital by the Vikings. However, a hit-and-run attack had been induced by the Eparchos.

313   John I Tzimisces (969-76) had shared the throne with the more legitimate rulers, Basil and Constantine, through marriage with their mother. He led several expeditions against the Saracens.

314   Leo III the Isaurian (717-741) saved Constantinople from capture by Arabs and recovered much of Anatolia.

315   Constantine V 'Copronymus' (741-775)

316   Heraclius (610-641) had survived the near destruction of the Empire by the Persians under Chosroes, recovering Jerusalem which had been sacked in 619. However, in 638 Jerusalem was seized by the emerging Moslem forces and never recovered by the Byzantines.

317   Constantine V (741 & 743) & Constantine VI (780-797) throughout whose reign he was merely a figurehead for his powerful mother. In the end he was deposed, blinded and subsequently murdered on the orders of his mother,.

318   Irene (797-802) for long the power behind the throne, ruled solely despite her unpopularity for a few years. She schemed to marry Charlemagne but was overthrown and exiled.

319   Constans II Pogonatus 641-668 attempted to restore imperial power in Italy. He was killed while bathing.

320   Abd-al-Malik (685-705) ruled the enormous Islamic Empire from his capital at Damascus. For a time he paid tribute to the Byzantine emperor, Justinian II Rhinotmetus (685-695), until he felt secure enough to attack the infidel.

321   Abd-al-Malik was succeeded by his four sons who together occupied the years 705-720.

322   abu-Jafar (754-775), better known as al-Mansur (the Victorious), firmly established the usurping Abbasid dynasty. At this time the caliph in Baghdad was still an Abbasid, al-Qadir(991-1031), although with little authority. The Abbasids persisted until destroyed by the Mongols in 1258.

323   Pepin II (751-768) pushed aside the last Merovingian to seize control of the Franks. In 754 he rescued the Pope threatened by Lombard attacks in Italy. He was surpassed by his son, Charlemagne (768-814), and so his family is called the Carolingians.

324   Nicephorus Phocas (802-11) had replaced Irene but had quickly become unpopular, largely due to spasmodic efforts against the Bulgars.

325   Krum later defeated the emperor Michael I (811-813) and besieged Constantinople in 813. However, Krum died of a stroke in 814 and the Bulgars retired.

326   See 'The Wanderer': 6:5 when a slave-hunting expedition had been part-successfully mounted in southern Finland.

327   Although Vikings believed that some warriors might be fortunate enough to enter the feasting-fighting paradise of Valhalla, the majority of men would be taken to the dark cold world of the monster, Hel.

328   Ketil lacked the violent temper of his namesake Ketil Club-foot that had provoked the blood-bath accompanying the Egilsskard horse-fight ('The Wanderer' 4:1).

329   From Thessalonica via the Rhodope mountains the river Vardar passed through the Demir Kaja pass & on to Stoboi & on to Skopia & Naissos.

330   The Althing was the regular meeting-place for settling disputes in Iceland. It is featured in 'The Wanderer' 4:5 where a fight breaks out.

331   See 'The Wanderer' 8:1. Sclerus had been a defeated pretender and confidant of the Eparchos. Ethelwulf had first antagonised the Eparchos by ruining the attack on Sclerus.

332   See 'The Wanderer' 8:4 where Psellus had led Thorgeis Green-Eye to Zoe's bedroom in an attempt to murder Ethelwulf.

333   See 'The Wanderer' 8:2. Morkere was seized by the governor of Crete furious at the seduction of his daughter.

334   See 'The Wanderer' 8:4. Ethelwulf was kidnapped by the fanatical heretic, Epaphroditus.

335   See 'The Wanderer' 8:1 where Ethelwulf had first met the Imperial Family.

336   Otto III 983-1002 was the Holy Roman Emperor. His mother was a Byzantine princess, Theophano, and he had sought a marriage alliance in 996 (See 'The Wanderer' 8:4)

337   See 'The Wanderer' 8:1 where the Varangians had defended Sclerus against the intrigues of the Eparchos.

338   See 'The Wanderer' 8:4. The Varangians had been despatched to rescue Antioch under attack from the Moslems. On arrival in Antioch Ethelwulf had been abducted.

339   In 996 El-Aziz was succeeded by his young son, Al-Hakim (996-1021) and control over the young prince became disputed between Ibn-Ammar (from north Africa) and the emir Bargawan, backed by Turkish mercenaries. The latter won, and until the assassination of Bargawan (1000)by the young Caliph, dominated Fatimid Egypt.

340   There were 14 levels of officials headed by the Magister, with gold-lined tunic and a variety of Patrician grades. Seleucia being a medium-sized province and not a frontier area had little prospect of advancement.

341   Pentekontarchos was literally a leader of 50 men. Cappadocians were key elements in the armies of the Byzantine Empire until the loss of the Anatolian interior to the Turks a century later.

342   Literally a patrol of ten men.

343   In Norse mythology Odin, Vili and Ve made the first man from a fallen ash tree. He was called Ask.

344   Harold had joined Ethelwulf when they had both been outlaws in Dorset twenty years before

345   See 'The Wanderer' 8: 2 Brimfugol was the vessel commanded by Ethelwulf.

346   Among the Vikings, nicknames were often sarcastic in origin. Thus Olaf the White was likely to possess a sallow complexion and Snorri the Short could be very tall. Of course, sometimes such names can be taken literally.

347   The district in northern Iraq, east of the Euphrates.

348   Samsam-al_Dawlah engaged in constant warfare with his brother, Baha-al-Dawlah (989-1012) who had deposed the Caliph of Baghdad in 991. Such wars made the later establishment of the Seljuk Turk Empire much easier.

349   Thor, one of the most powerful Norse gods, was revered by warriors everywhere. Urd (Fate) was one of the Norns.

350   Verdandi (Necessity), another of the Norns, was one of the rulers of destiny of men.

351   Eljudnir was the hall of Hel who ruled the kingdom of the dead (Niflheim). Hermod rode there to recover from the dead Baldur, the most popular of the gods. Baldur had been killed by the trickery of Loki and Hel demanded that only if every creature mourned for the dead god could he return to Asgard. In disguise Loki made sure that this was not achieved.

352   Magnus had first served the regent Theophano in Germany, through her ally, Willegis of Mainz. Then the emperor's grandmother, Adelaide, in Pavia. Theophano had died in 991.

353   A theme was an administrative district of the Empire. In order going north from the coast the themes on the eastern frontier were Seleucian, Cappadocian, Charsinian and Armeniac.

354   Nicephorus Phocas, governor of the Anatolikan theme and conqueror of the Saracens in the area. In 960 he had seized Crete for the Empire and in 963 the Empire for himself. Despite continued military success this unattractive man grew increasingly unpopular and was assassinated in 969.

355   Alfred Bat-Ears owned Middlebere the farm next to Ethelwulf's home at Arne. He hated the family of Arne and conspired to destroy them. See 'The Wanderer' 1:3.

356   Edwine had loved the daughter of the owner of Wytch farm and had rescued them from attack. However, Cynegils had been ruined because of his support of the family of Arne and had migrated north. See 'The Wanderer' 1:3

357   Ethelwulf's mother, Estrid Ulfsdotter, had been murdered by Haakon, the murderer of King Edward at Corfe in 978. Her head had been brandished in Haakon's attempt to stop Ethelwulf's escape from England. See 'The Wanderer' 1:4

358   Harald Bluetooth (died 986) who had despatched Ethelwulf against the Sons of Hel. See 'The Wanderer' 5:1

359   William of St. Ouen controlled Jersey - & imprisoned Ethelwulf.. See 'The Wanderer' 2:5

360   See 'The Wanderer' 6:2. Aslak came to believe that Ethelwulf had seduced his wife.

361   The monstrous children of the evil god Loki were the wolf Fenrir, the Midgard Serpent, and Hel, the ruler of Niflheim. They were to help in the destruction of the gods in the final fight of Ragnarok.

362   See 'The Wanderer' 5:1. Willibrord was a missionary to Harald Bluetooth of Denmark.

363   See 'The Wanderer' 8:4. Epaphroditus was a fanatical Paulician who linked the Empire with the kingdom of Antichrist.

364   The runes were carved signs used to foretell the future throughout the north.

365   Theophrastus Eumenides was the owner of the Virgin's Well in Byzantium.

366 See "Revelation" 'The Wanderer' 8:4 where Ethelwulf was kidnapped by the Paulician Epaphroditus who tried to induce him into assassinating the Autokrator. Ethelwulf had escaped with the help of the fanatic's daughter, Lydia.

367 The murder of Edward the Martyr in 978 at Corfe Castle on the orders of his step-mother, Elfrida, had been witnessed by the young Ethelwulf (See 'The Wanderer' 1:2). The young son of the murderess had become king as Ethelred II and begun a most unsuccessful reign.

368 Lamentations 1:10 - although the reference is to Jerusalem

369 II Peter 3:3

370 A Greek measurement approximately = 1 furlong or 1/8 mile

371 Isaiah 30:21

372 Malachi 3:9

373 Malachi 2:17

374 Revelations 7:4

375 Revelations 7:16

376 Ruth 1:16

377 Nicephorus Comnenus : see 8:4

378 Gormflath, widow of Olaf Cuaran, lord of Dublin, and later wife of both Mael Sechlainn, High King and Brian Boru. One of the most dramatic women in the history of Ireland. See "The Wanderer" 3:2 'Winter's Pleasures' for the account of the affair of Ethelwulf and Gormflath.

379 Olaf Cuaran, Norse king of Dublin (944-980), who conquered Meath in 977 but was driven out by Mael Sechlainn in 980.

380 At first Ethelwulf had spoken in Gaelic, or at least the version used among the Gall-Gael in 10th century Ireland. Now he switched to Wendish. Both languages, however, would be completely unknown to Lydia.

381 Idun was the custodian of the Apples of Youth so vital to the Norse Gods. She was secreted away by Loki and handed over to the Giant Thiazi. Loki was forced by the gods to recover her, which he did by changing her into a nut and flying off with it as a falcon.

382 These words were addressed to Skuna, Wendish princess, who was rescued from the nightmarish Sons of Hel and returned to her father. She then saved Ethelwulf from the treachery of her father. See "The Wanderer" 5:3

383 Song of Solomon 4:16

384 Genesis 3:6

385 Sihtric Silkenbeard , king of Dublin (994-1040?), whose supporters lost the battle of Clontarf in 1014. See 'The Wanderer' 3:2 where Ethelwulf's affair with Sihtric's mother caused conflict.

386 See "The Wanderer" 5:3 where Skuna, having been rescued from the Sons of Hel, helped foil the treachery of her father.

387 Daughter (d. 1045) of the emperor Constantine VIII (976-1028) whose intrigues nearly led to Ethelwulf's assassination (see 'The Wanderer' 8:5)

388 Responsible for her step-son's murder at Corfe in 979 (see 'The Wanderer' 1:3)

389 St Cyricus was the young child of St. Julitta, and was martyred under Diocletian on 16 June.

Although his name is the origin of St. Cyr, the tale of his being murdered by being thrown down steps was rejected in the West before 700 A.D.

390   See 'The Wanderer' 2:2 for the disputed election at St. Helier.

391   Ezekiel 39:10

392   Literally 'bone-biter'. It was common practice to name weapons. Ethelwulf's weapons had been called 'Claw'.

393   1 John 5:18

394   Exodus 3,7-8

395   See Daniel 7

396   See "The Wanderer" 8:1. The fire had been started by agents of the Eparchos and had proved another reason for that enmity which caused the destruction of the Varangians. Later Simeon had secured the release of Morkere from captivity (8:4)

397   For the tortures of the Sons of Hel and others by the pagans see 'The Wanderer' 5:3

398   This was the name adopted by Ethelwulf when he bought the 'Hilde-Gicel' for his escape from England in 979. He had been driven into outlawry after witnessing the murder of Edward the Martyr at Corfe Castle the previous autumn.

399   Revelations 21:2

400   Revelations 13:4

401   The Byzantine emperor, Basil II (976-1025), who officially shared power with his brother Constantine VIII, had been Ethelwulf's employer for several years (see 'The Wanderer' 8) but had finally ordered his arrest.

402   Formed by Hamdan Qarmat c. 875, and expanded by al-Jannabi into an independent state c. 899, this Moslem sect advocated communal holding of wives and property, were based in Iraq, and practised violence against any opposition. By 1000 they were in decline.

403   St. Dunstan of Canterbury (909-988) reorganised English monasticism through his 'Regularis Concordia' (970), patronised a revival of English learning, and guided a series of English kings. He also had considerable skill as a metalworker and his emblem is a pair of tongs.

404   At Bath in 973 St. Dunstan added a sacred element to English coronations by introducing the anointing of the king.as already practised in France. Naturally this magnified the role of the Church in the whole process.

405   In 973 Edgar (959-75), according to tradition, celebrated his thirtieth birthday by being rowed on the river Dee by six kings as a sign of his overlordship of Britain.

406   Edgar died suddenly and a struggle was threatened between his son by a former marriage, Edward and his son, Ethelred, by his second wife. However, largely due to the intervention of St. Dunstan of Canterbury, the throne was given to Edward.

407   The murder at Corfe in 979 of King Edward by his step-mother is the incident which starts 'The Wanderer' trilogy. Ethelred (979-1013) was styled 'the Unready' because of the clear lack of unity in government policy, especially after the restarting of Viking raids in the 980's.

408   Or Gate of Flowers, from the rosette over the gate's arch. It is now called Herod's Gate.

409   Luke 10:34

410   Market of the Cotton Merchants

411   1 ell = 45 inches

412   Endowed by Charlemagne (772-814) for the use of pilgrims & served by Benedictines. It was destroyed by Caliph Hakim in 1009. Its site is in the Muristan.

413   Ethelred the Unready (979-1013) had secured the throne by the murder of his half-brother, Edward, by his mother at Corfe Castle. This incident had been witnessed by Ethelwulf & brought about his flight from England and wanderings throughout Europe.

414   In 1002 a desperate Ethelred struck against the friends & relatives of his enemies & so provoked a full-scale attack on England by Sven Forkbeard of Denmark (who appears in 'The Wanderer, 4:1). Ethelred was driven from the country in 1013 & his realm eventually became part of the Empire of Sven's son, Canute (1016-35).

415   Pope Sylvester II (999-1003) or Gerbert of Aurillac was a close friend of the Emperor Otto III (983-1002). However, the emperor was driven out of Rome in 1001 by popular revolt.

416   Al Hakim (996-1021) throughout his reign showed increasing signs of mental instability.

417   Jerusalem was captured by Caliph Omar in Feb 638 during the reign of Heraclius (610-41) who survived a Persian onslaught only to go down before the onslaught of Islam.

418   Medieval maps centred the world on this spot in Jerusalem, confident that only here would Christ have sacrificed Himself for mankind. Of course, as they believed that the earth was the centre of the universe, around which (according to Ptolemy) stars, sun & planets revolved, this made this spot the centre of the cosmos!

419   Origen (185-245) records that beneath Golgotha (or Cavalry) had been buried the skull of the first man. Today this is the site of the Chapel of Adam.

420   Medieval tradition held that the crack in Golgotha had been caused by the earthquake described by St. Matthew (27:51)

421   St. Helena discovered the True Cross during a pilgrimage in 327 according to a 4th century account. Certainly the sacred object was transferred to the new capital of Constantinople where it proved of immense propaganda value.

422   See 'Acts' 8:26-40 where Philip baptised the Ethiopian eunuch.. This led to the legend that the chamberlain returned to Ethiopia and spread the gospel. However, in reality, it was only after the conversion of Constantine in the early 4th century that the conversion of the country began.

423   Ethelwulf had been held by the Paulician fanatic Epaphroditus who had planned that the Saxon should assassinate the Autokrator and so usher in the Second Coming.

424   Revelations 20:7

425   Revelations 20:9

426   Revelations 20:13

427   Matthew 27:51

428   Revelations 13:11

429   Al Qadir was Abbasid Caliph (991-1031), nominally head of the Islamic world (Sunni versions). However, in practice he was dominated by the (Shi'ite) Buwayhid emirs. During this period Iraq was seized by the Ghaznawid ruler, Mahmud, who controlled the Caliphate at Baghdad.

430   John Scotus Eriguena(?-?), an Irish scholar flourishing c. 850, was a key member of the Carolingian Renaissance. His work 'De Divisione Naturae' deals with a 4-fold division of 'nature' or

reality in a Neo-Platonist way. It was a distinct influence on much of the philosophy of the period - although some of his ideas on Predestination & the Eucharist were later condemned, as well as the Pantheism in 'De Divisione Naturae'...

431   An old Irish Law Tract on bee-keeping.

432   Einhard (?-740) was a monk & official of Charlemagne (772-814) whose biographer he became. Charlemagne expanded the realm of the Franks into Germany, Italy & northern Spain. In 800 he was crowned Holy Roman Emperor. He encouraged the revival of learning known as the Carolingian Renaissance. The last of his descendants was replaced in 987 by Hugh Capet.

433   Gerbert had a brilliant academic career, being tutor to both Otto II & Otto III. Although he was appointed Archbishop of Rheims (991-7),he lost his position due to the political manoeuvring surrounding Hugh Capet. He was appointed Pope (Sylvester II) (999-1003) but failed to retain control of Rome after the sudden death of his patron, Otto III in 1002. Many believed Gerbert was a magician & he had a great reputation as a mathematician. He is supposed to have introduced the use of Arabic numerals. In' The Wanderer 'I:3 Gerbert had been rescued by Edwine from robbers & had spent some time with the outlaws in Wareham Forest. Of course, Ethelwulf would not have heard that his old friend had become Pope in 999.

434   Hugh Capet was Count of Paris when in 987 he became legally what he had been in fact for several years - king of France, pushing aside the last Carolingian. He was a patron of Gerbert and encouraged monasticism. He died in 996 although his descendants ruled France until the Revolution in 1789. Ethelwulf may not have heard that he had been succeeded by Robert II (996-1031)

435   Otto III (983-1002) after an extensive minority was crowned Holy Roman Emperor in 996. He patronised Gerbert & made him Pope in 999. However, they were driven from Rome & Otto died.

436   The Civil War may not be entirely the work of Julius Caesar, describing his struggle for power 48-45 B.C. It is generally considered markedly inferior to the Gallic War.

437   Gaius Julius Caesar (100-44 B.C.), as a relative of Marius Caesar spent his youth in danger but survived to divide power with Pompey & Crassus in 61. He showed his military genius in Gaul (59-49 B.C.) & then seized complete power from Pompey & his followers (48-45 B.C.). He was assassinated by opponents believing he was aiming at kingship, but his heir became the first Emperor, Augustus. Caesar was also noted as a great writer.

438   The subject matter of the Triptych are intimately linked. In the centre Christ leaves the world (Acts 1:9), on the right the greatest of the early missionaries (St Paul) is recruited on the road to Damascus (Acts 9:5) and then possibly the first contact between Christianity and Ethiopia (Acts 8:27-39)

439   See 'The Wanderer' 6:5. The failure of the expedition permanently caused friction between Ethelwulf and certain traders.

440   Jarl Haakon Sigurdsson of Hladir ruled Norway 974-94 having displaced Harald Greycloak. However, he was dependent on the power of the Danes. and was plagued by Harald's sons.

441   Described in 'Olaf Trygvasson's Saga' (Chap 28)

442   Olaf Trygvasson was the great-grandson of Harald Fair-Hair , first king of Norway (858-928). He was considered one of the most famous Vikings of his day.

443   Jarl Haakon had seized the throne from the grandson of Harald Fair-Hair in 974, largely with Danish help.

444	Urd (Fate) together with her sisters Skuld (Existence) and Verdandi (Need) were known as the Norns. They looked after the giant tree, Yggdrasil, which maintained life even though itself was in decay. In fact, the sisters controlled the destinies of men.

445	The Anglo-Saxon Chronicle says Olaf attacked with 93 ships in 991, attacking Folkestone & Sandwich. The raiders crossed the Thames estuary to Suffolk where they were caught at Maldon.

446	See 'The Wanderer' :1 - 2-4

447	Subject of one of the greatest poems in Old English

448	Such is the main point of the poem, the code of loyalty by huscarles to their lord

449	The first instance of Danegeld which went on being collected till 1154!

450	Under 992 the Anglo-Saxon Chronicle records the treachery of Aelfric

451	The other English commanders were Frena & Godwine who, according to the Anglo-Saxon Chronicle, were the first to flee. The Vikings had already sacked Bamburgh.

452	In 994 according to the Anglo-Saxon Chronicle. The attack on London was a disaster.

453	Baptism was a common ploy to remove troublemakers - with mixed success

454	Note Iceland where the king was responsible for its FORCIBLE conversion in 1000

455	The title of High King (Ard Ri) was merely one of prestige (Like the Saxon Bretwalda). In 998 Mael Sechlainn & Brian Boru met at Clonfert & basically divided the honour between them on a geographical basis. However, in 1002 Mael Sechlainn was forced to grant the sole title to Brian although on Brian's death (1014) he recovered the High Kingship until his own death in 1022.

456	See 'The Wanderer '3:3 & 5 for Ethelwulf's affair with one of the most dangerous women of the time.

457	After his marriage to Gormflath Mael Sechlainn had installed her son (by Olaf Cuaran), Sihtric Silkenbeard, as king of Dublin in 994. However, when he abandoned Gormflath she encouraged her cousin, Mael Morda, to claim Leinster & her son, Sihtric, to assert independence. Their rebellion was crushed at Glen Mama. When he married Gormflath in 1002 Brian restored Dublin to Sihtric & Mael Morda to Leinster.

458	The actual battle site is unknown but is near the island of Svold off Rügen. Whether Olaf was sailing back from Wendland or south from Norway is also unknown. The account of the battle in the Heimskringla is generally rejected.

459	Sigvald's role as traitor is highly suspect. The Jomsvikings were a semi-legendary fighting society. They appear in The Wanderer ''5:4

460	Chief of the town police

461	A young man given special responsibilities, but often linked to homosexuality.

462	Rome or Rhum was the name given by the Moslems to the Byzantine Empire.

463	A soldier or agent on a temporary contract, for a specific purpose.

**464	Commander of 10 men**

**465	Calendars are both confusing and fascinating. Dionysius Exiguus (c.470 – c.544) developed the system of dating from the birth of Christ and (possibly) began the year on the Feast if the Annunciation (25 March). This rivalled 1 January as New Year's Day until the Gregorian Calendar replaced the Julian Calendar at various dates in different countries after**

1582. So in Britain before 1752 dates are given as Julian/Gregorian e.g. the murder of King Edward at Corfe took place on 18 March 978/9.

466   From the early 10th century Seljuk Turks were employed as mercenaries with the Abbasid Caliphate. Gradually they acquired independence so that by the late 11th century they had set up a series of states throughout the Middle East.

467   Holy Roman Emperor, Otto III, proved unable to hold on to Rome and died in 1002.

468   During this period Christians were inspired by leaders such as El Cid (1044-99) but still could not resist the successes of Mohammed-ibn-abi-Amir,, who assumed the title of Al Mansur ('The Victorious') & dominated Cordova (977-1002)

469   Skræling were the native inhabitants in areas discovered in America (e.g. Hellulamd, Vinland & Markland) after the discovery of Greenland by Eric the Red in 1985. The areas are not positively identified but probably are Baffin Island, Newfoundland and Labrador respectively.

470   Sweyn is confused here. Harald was expelled by his son briefly & hid among the Wends. He recovered his power but died soon afterwards (See 'The Wanderer' 5:4)

471   See 'The Wanderer' 6:1 for their meeting on Gotland.

472   In the 'Heimskringla' (Chap. 32) Olaf's conversion is bound up with a prophecy about his surviving wounds in a battle etc.

473   According to the 'Heimskringla'(King Olaf Trygvasson's Saga 106) Olaf's sister, Ingeborg, had married King Boleslav.

474   Ethelwulf had made a brief visit there & been equally impressed (See 'The Wanderer' 8:3)

475   Doge Pietro Orseolo II (991-1009) had completed the conquest of this neighbouring region in Sep 1000. His triumph is still recorded in the Venetian practice of wedding with the sea. Pietro Orseolo himself was content with the title of Dux Dalmatiae, recognised by Emperor Henry II

476   Pietro Orseolo I (976-78), later canonised, had started the recovery of Venetian fortunes, continued under his son, Pietro Orseolo II (991-1009) The elder Orseolo had suddenly abandoned his family in 978, retiring to a monastery in the Pyrenees and then becoming a hermit; he died in 987.

477   In 976 Venice revolted against the ambitions of Doge Pietro Candiano IV (959-76) who had married the sister of the Marquis of Tuscany and schemed to install a son as the Bishop of Torcello. Much of the city was destroyed by fire and the hated ruler was butchered.

478   The Basilica of St. Marks was restored by the efforts of the Orseolo family, importing Byzantine artists, although the church had not acquired the magnificence achieved during Venice's period of greatness.

479   September to the Saxons was Halig Monath or Holy Month

480   The Abbasid police department headed by the Muhtasib

481   The bases respectively of the Abbasid and Fatimid Islamic powers.

482   Pope Julius I (337-52) had transferred the date of Christmas from 6 January to 25 December, but (like his continued support for Athanasius) it had been ignored in the East. Here it was pointed out that the appearance of the star, linked to 6 January, which guided the Magi to Bethlehem would have risen with the Holy Birth

483   Revelations 11:1

484   Revelations 11:11